WILD IRISH BOXSET

VI CARTER

ALSO BY

NEWSLETTER

JOIN MY NEWSLETTER AND NEVER MISS A NEW RELEASE OR GIVEAWAY.
HERE

VICIOUS

TITLE: VICIOUS
SERIES NUMBER: BOOK ONE

BLURB:
Killing for me is easy. Loving is an entirely different thing.
Una is the only person I ever gave a damn about, but she's off limits. I'm grateful she only spends the summer with us. I can't risk her getting involved in my life of crime. But now she's here, all grown up, and this time, I don't think I can stay away from her. When Una starts partying with Darragh, who's as wild and unpredictable as they come, I can't afford keeping my distance any longer. Bodies seem to stack up wherever he goes. Cleaning up his messes used to be annoying. Now I have Una to consider, Una to protect. My family is belly deep in the criminal underworld, and she's a distraction I can't afford. The closer she gets to me, the more I'm spiraling out of control. I can't let her see who I really am, but I can't seem to let her go.

CHAPTER ONE

SHANE

"**P**ASS ME THE SHOVEL." I gesture to Finn as I stare into the shallow grave. The smell of decay rises up to greet us. Recent rainfall has caused the grave to sink in further. Coming here tonight was the right thing to do. If we left it any longer, the body would be exposed.

"I can't do this."

"You will do this." I glare at Finn to drive my words home, and he's shaking his head like he has options.

Sinking to his hunkers, he runs both hands down his face, like he can erase what he's seeing. "That's Siobhan's aunt."

His eyes are glued to the grave. Regret at bringing him here is starting to slowly raise its head. Finn and Darragh, who are the youngest of us brothers, have it way too easy. They were born with silver spoons in their mouths. So right now, I just want to dirty Finn's hands a little bit. The idea is giving me far too much joy.

"I don't really care who it is. Now pass me the shovel."

Finn gets up and takes both shovels that lean against the boot of my Mercedes. His steps are careful across the bog. The land we purchased was deliberate. A bog is ideal for what we're currently doing.

The lights from my car shine on the ground and stop just at the grave. The sun is nearly gone, and soon, the car will be our only source of light, so I want this done before that happens. Once the shovel is in my hand, I start to dig. Finn stands still, leaning against his shovel, watching me.

"Finn," I warn, and he starts to dig. It doesn't take us long before all the clay is off the body. Wildlife have gotten to her. We wrapped her in plastic, but her head hangs out, her neck twisted at an awkward angle. Finn turns away and gags repeatedly. His early dinner splashes on the mud and on his shoes.

"You'll take off your shoes before you get back into my car," I warn him. Holding my breath, I pull the body fully out of the grave. We need to dig deeper. We buried her in a panic in a shallow grave.

"You're heartless." Finn wipes his mouth with the back of his hand.

"Who was the one who bashed her head in?" I question, and his eyes shift away from me. "You had one job, Finn—to keep an eye on Darragh. But you couldn't do that could you?"

His head snaps up, his eyes bulging. "I'm not his fucking babysitter."

"That's exactly what you are," I remind him. "If you hadn't been lying with that girl, none of this would have happened."

"Shane, don't bring her into this." He's taking a step toward me. I'm not threatened by him. My shovel sinks into the wet ground easily, and I start digging, ending our pointless conversation.

We work in silence and once the grave is deep enough, I dump the body in. Finn looks away in horror, and I suppress a smile.

"Jesus. We should say a prayer."

Prayer? Like that will bring her back. I leave Finn to say his prayers. The heavy plastic that I pull off the dead animal releases a smell and a swarm of flies. I turn my head to the left to avoid a mouthful of them.

"Finn," I call. His low words cease, and he tuts before he joins me. I've already tied ropes around the front of the cow's legs. It's an odd-colored cow. Black, white, and red—a mixed breed. Not that it matters. I pick one of the ropes up and hand the other to Finn. He's gawking at me, and I exhale loudly.

"We use the cow to cover the body, so if anyone digs, they hit the cow first and don't bother digging any further," I tell him and start pulling. He doesn't say anything but pulls too. It's heavier than I expected, but we manage to get the cow into the grave. We push it in on top of the body, and the impact is loud.

"Did you hear something break?" I ask Finn, and his eyes narrow.

"Are you fucking joking?" He has no sense of humor.

We finish off by covering the body with clay just as the sun sets. I close the boot once everything is cleaned up and stop Finn from climbing into my car.

"Remove your shoes." I didn't forget him retching on them. He shakes his head but kicks them off. They join the rest of the stuff in the boot.

"I need my bed," Finn says, closing his eyes and leaning back against the headrest. The first pitter-patter of rain hits the windshield as I start the car.

Leaving the bog, I then drive home to the Whitewood house.

CHAPTER TWO

SHANE

MY FATHER GLANCES UP from his desk as I close the double doors behind me. Dark circles under his eyes, along with his disheveled appearance, make me want to tell him to go to bed. He's loosened his tie and opened the top button of his shirt.

After his declaration that he knew where Connor was, I had to talk to him. I don't like finding things out along with the others; I thought I was more privileged than them. He asked me to get Connor, his request taking the sting out of it, but not enough for me to let it go.

"How long have you known where Connor is?" I ask. His rising hand, holding the letter opener, cuts me off. A half-opened white envelope is the only thing on his desk.

"I don't." He shakes his head while he speaks, then puts down the letter opener. "I had eyes on him until last week."

The bookcase that fills the wall behind his desk is a display of colors—mostly browns, reds, and greens. I've always hated the smell and general appearance of the books. As I sit down, I try to make sense of what my father is saying.

"So why only send me now? Why not a week ago when he went missing?" Irritation pours over my words, and I don't try to lessen it.

Connor is a valuable source to our family. He isn't exactly family, but we need him. He maintains a balance that we can't seem to find without him. We try, but things never sit right when he's gone.

"I thought maybe he was having an off day. But a day turned into a few. I've recently gotten word that he's crossed the border." Father rubs between his eyes, and I find myself picking up his letter opener and standing it up on the desk.

This isn't good. Crossing into the north isn't allowed; it's declared by a different group. One we don't interfere with. They claim to be the real Republican Army. So, we keep far away.

"Why would he do that?" I ask while sitting back and taking the letter opener with me. It's not sharp; I stick it against my thumb and spin it.

"I'm not sure. But I want you to find out why, and I want you to bring him back." Father holds out his hand, and I tap the letter opener against my palm.

I want him to answer another question before he dismisses me. "Did you ring Tom and have it confirmed?"

His eyes narrow at my question, and his jaw clenches. He holds out his hand again, and I give him what he wants. Once he has it, he finishes opening the letter.

"Of course I did. He's seen and heard nothing." My father won't meet my eye, and I question what he's holding back.

I sit back in the chair and twist the silver band on my thumb in circles. "And you believe him?" I quiz.

I don't get an answer. Loud commotion in the hall has both of us standing up and leaving the study. Finn, Darragh, and our stepsister, Una, are in the hall. My eyes snap to Liam. He stands to the side, still wearing a full suit as he observes Darragh, who is drunk, and Finn, who is the only one trying to control the situation.

My attention is drawn back to Una. She's always had an ability to capture my attention. Her fiery red hair hangs dark and limp down her back. She looks like she just stepped out of the ocean. A pool of water is gathering around her, but she doesn't seem aware of it. Her cream top is see-through, and a bright pink bra is visible and full.

"Get me some towels," Finn barks at Darragh. Darragh doesn't move. He stands still and laughs at Una. He's pointing at her like he's five. I turn as I hear receding footsteps behind me to find Father leaving.

"Finn, take care of this," he calls over his shoulder. Finn's head snaps up, and he looks ready to lose it.

I don't try to defuse the situation. Instead, I stand and observe to see what will happen. Finn doesn't ask me or Liam to help. Maybe he knows we won't.

Once again, Una captures my attention as she pulls a plump lip between her teeth and bites it. A laugh leaves her mouth, and she opens her eyes. They still manage to hold me in awe—one blue, the other green.

I've never seen anyone like Una. Her eyes suit her. She is two very different people. She's unpredictable, and I often think that's why I'm drawn to her. Right now, she holds out her arms and starts to twirl.

"Una, stop it." Finn tries to pull her hands down, but she keeps spinning, and Darragh joins her. That's when I decide I've seen enough. I cast a quick glance over to the spot where Liam stood, but it's empty.

As I enter the garage, I don't have to flick on the lights; they're already on. Liam waits for me by my car. "We need to take a drive."

I don't question him and slide into my Audi as he gets into the passenger seat. The garage door opens as I back out.

"You look at Father differently," he says.

"What are you talking about?" I take a left out onto the road.

"Just an observation," he says, and when I peek at Liam, he's staring at me with brown eyes that are almost black. They're the same eyes I see in the mirror.

"Don't try to analyze me. Stick with analyzing Finn and Darragh," I tell him.

"Is this topic making you uncomfortable, brother?" Liam is enjoying himself. He likes to torture me in the smallest ways. The ways I don't like.

"Of course not, *brother*," I answer as my hands grip the steering wheel.

"Take a left at the next crossroads," Liam informs me, no teasing in his voice now.

"He's different," I say, and at once, I hate that I said it. Liam is watching me again.

"How so?" To anyone else, his voice doesn't rise and fall. It's almost monotone. But listening to him for so long, I can hear that tilt in his words. It happens when he's truly curious.

"I'm not sure. I think he's hiding something." I take a left at the crossroads as he instructed.

"What were you talking about in the study?"

I laugh. I can't help it. This level of curiosity is unusual for Liam.

"Indulge me." His lips lift slightly as he speaks. "Take a right at the next crossroads," he adds.

"If you told me where we were going, it would make this easier. Is it Kells?" I question.

"It doesn't matter. Now tell me what you were talking about."

I grip the steering wheel again at his demand. "It was about Connor. He doesn't really know where he is." This conversation is annoying me. I glance at Liam, and he sits back, not facing me any longer. He stares out the window.

"To the land."

I stop at the crossroads and take a right back toward Nobber. "You've just taken us in a full circle," I say, but Liam has gone quiet. I turn up the music as I put my foot down and drive at a hundred and twenty kilometers an hour the rest of the way. We reach the land fifteen minutes later. I pull up along the lane and lower the music.

"She's been declared missing," Liam says, looking out onto the land.

My stomach tightens, but I knew this would happen. "But nothing is pointing at us?" I question, and Liam gives me a quick glance before he starts fixing his cuffs, then his collar—things that don't need to be fixed.

"No, but I have a bad feeling. I want to dig her up."

"Liam, it's been weeks," I remind him. An old moldy body after a few days isn't something I want to dig up.

"We didn't go deep enough." We buried her late at night, and he was right, we hadn't gone deep enough. It was something that had bothered me too.

"I went back a while later. I buried her deeper." Surprise is visible on Liam's face. It's small, but his eyebrows lift slightly. To anyone else, he would seem emotionless.

"I covered her with the carcass of a cow," I add.

"You did it all by yourself?"

I smile at his question and pull out away from the land. "No, I had help." It wasn't the nicest thing I've ever done, getting Finn to help me move his girlfriend's aunt's body, but it was fun.

"I got Finn to help me." I can see the wheels turning in Liam's head.

"You should have left him alone," he says, and I glance at him.

"Why? Because him being upset just might upset poor little Darragh?" I hate how soft Liam is when it comes to Darragh. I don't have a clue why. If I had a choice, I would have both Darragh and Finn out of the family business. They're both weak and cause more problems than we need.

"No, Shane. You did it with emotion, and that is stupid."

"He's a little spoilt prick. He never has to do anything. He has it easy. I just wanted to get his hands a little dirty." I'm smiling again. I can't help it. It was satisfying to see him squirm and panic.

"His hands are dirty now," Liam says, and I hate how he sounds. It's like he's telling me it will come back and bite me in the ass. I don't care.

I drop Liam off at home. He says no more about Finn or the body, and I pull away from the house before anyone else comes out. This time, I blare the music and let it pound into my head. It's senseless music, the type you can get lost in. I lose myself for the next twenty minutes as I make my way to the last place Connor was seen.

I park in a gravel car park that holds two cars and make my way into the stone building. A few men are drinking while watching a show about darts. They study me as I enter, and I let them.

My clothes speak of wealth and good taste. I know how I look. Everything is tailor-made. The barman is wiping the same spot he has been since I entered. I don't sit, but I stop at the bar.

"I'm looking for my brother," I say, and he snaps his head up at me and then at the picture I have of Connor. It's a few years old, but I can't imagine he's changed too much in the last two years.

Recognition lights up in the barman's eyes. "Connor is your brother?" He sounds unsure, and I don't blame him.

"Half brother. I'm the good-looking one." I flash a quick smile to add to my joke, and it puts him at ease. I ask my questions, and he tells me that Connor was a good tenant, and he always paid his rent on time.

"Would it be possible to see where he was staying?" I ask.

"Sure. Just give me a minute." I don't even have to wait the full minute before I'm taken upstairs, and he leads me into a small, poky, and unlivable space. I'm not sure what I thought I would find here. But a single bed with a double-doored wardrobe is all that greets me. I leave with no leads as to where Connor is.

***

It's getting late, so I call it a night. The house is quiet when I return home. A drink is what I need. The hallway is lit by lights that hang over large paintings. Rugs under my feet make my footsteps silent. Dark wood gives the large hallway a warmth it shouldn't hold for its sheer size. I enter the bar and find my father smoking a cigar, sitting on a Queen Ann chair with his eyes closed.

"Any luck?" he asks, not opening his eyes, and I'm curious about how he knows it's me. I pour two whiskeys, and he opens his eyes when I place his glass on the table beside him, the one that holds a large crystal ashtray.

"No, none." I take a deep drink before putting the glass on the table beside the couch I sit down on. Air brushes my skin as I roll up my sleeves. I had a tattoo done, and the skin is still fragile.

A large blank band that goes the full way around my arm joins the other eight. The tattoo starts at my elbow and reaches my wrist. Nine bands—one for each life I've taken.

My father's eyes linger on my tattoo. It's something we never speak of, but it's my way of remembering every life I ended. It's never easy to take a life, but sometimes it's a matter of theirs or mine. Or my family's.

"Una is asleep. I couldn't get a coherent word out of her." Father sounds tired again.

"Send her home." Even as I say it, I know it's a lie. I don't want her to leave. But this place has a way of twisting people, and she isn't someone I want to see hurt.

"I'll discuss that with her in the morning. But while she's here, I expect you to keep an eye on her."

I nod into my glass; I knew I would be asked. He might give Finn responsibility, but really, it's me and Liam he trusts, and Liam makes most females uncomfortable.

"Of course," I tell him before emptying my glass.

We say good night as I leave the bar. He's still smoking his cigar, and puffs of smoke swirl above his head.

A part of me says to take the left once I reach the top of the stairs, but I take the right. I should turn back, but I don't. Instead, I stand outside the room that is Una's. She never declared it, but it's a room we all know as hers, even if she doesn't. I open the door and step in.

She's lost in the four-poster bed. Her hair has dried out, and it fans around her head like a burning sun. The covers are to her neck and tucked in around her body. She's afraid of the dark. She thinks if her legs or arms aren't tucked under the quilt, something will grab her.

I smile. That's what she told me when we were kids. But she has always tucked the blanket tightly around her, even as I watched her grow from a girl into a woman. I relax as I focus on her sleeping form. This is something *I've* always done—snuck into her room and watched her sleep. It helps me. I stay for until she stirs. She's never caught me in her room before. I leave, not wanting to make this the first time.

CHAPTER THREE

UNA

I STRETCH OUT MY arms and legs, and still, my legs don't dangle out of the bed like they would at home. A strangled scream is pulled from my mouth as I open my eyes. Darragh is sitting on the side of my bed, dressed and freshly washed. His blond hair is combed back. The red collared T-shirt is pressed and sits perfectly on his lean frame.

"My God, Darragh, you nearly gave me a heart attack." I sit up and clutch the quilt to my chest. His blue eyes disappear as he starts to laugh.

"What are you doing in my room?" I'm still angry, as my heart hasn't returned to its normal rhythm.

"Do you know you talk in your sleep?" Darragh tilts his head, his eyes filled with devilment.

I narrow my eyes at him and loosen my death grip on the quilt. "No, I don't," I reply and his smirk grows.

"How would you know? You were asleep."

An excellent question, just one I wasn't going to give him an answer to. "What are you doing in my room?" I ask again as I lie down. My headache returns with a vengeance. "How much did I drink last night?" I cover my eyes with my arm. His laughter isn't doing my head any good.

"You jumped into the lake."

I sit up again as snippets come back, and I let out a groan. I had; I remember now. Partying down at the lake. Darragh had dared me. "We are so stupid," I tell him, and he grins as he gets off my bed.

"Correction—you are stupid. I didn't jump in. I dared you to jump in, not thinking you would actually do it." He walks around the bed and sits on the other side. "I had to send Fran in to get you."

I cover my burning face. I remember a boy with long blond hair pulling me from the lake. He pulled me on shore. I could have drowned if not for him.

"Why didn't you rescue me?" I ask, observing him through my fingers.

"The jumper I was wearing was brand new. So..."

"Get out of my room." I'm pissed at Darragh again. Not about him not jumping into the lake to rescue me. Two drunken people in the lake wouldn't have been the best idea. Especially Darragh and me. But the fact that he picked a jumper over me—yeah, that stung.

"Are you staying with us?" Darragh asks, backing out of my room. He doesn't sound offended at me asking him to leave the room.

"I'm not sure," I tell him honestly. I need to talk to Michael first.

"Well, if you are, I have a party we can go to." He grins as he closes my door, not waiting for an answer. Darragh knows how to party hard. I'm not sure my head is up to it.

***

After a shower, I get dressed. I came with nothing but had left some clothes here last summer. Jeans and a moss green jumper are the best I can pull out of the bundle.

I find Michael in the kitchen. Something tells me he's been waiting for me.

"It's great to have you home." His arms are outstretched, and I can't stop the smile that spreads across my face as I walk into his arms. His warmth envelops me as his arms circle around me.

Just like that, I'm a little girl again. Michael has always had the ability to make me forget the bad.

"But what's brought you here?" he asks before planting a kiss on my head. I want to stick out my bottom lip and ask him to skip this part, but I know we can't. Michael gets me a coffee as I push my drying curls out of my eyes and sit at the breakfast bar.

"I needed to get away," I answer as he pushes a coffee into my hands.

"You want me to have a chat?"

I smile and pat his hand. "Nope, I already had words with her." I shrug as I take a drink of coffee.

Michael takes a drink of his own coffee before setting down the mug and fixing his tie, which is slightly crooked. "You can stay here as long as you want."

Relief bubbles through me. I never thought he would throw me out, but hearing him say I could stay relaxes me. He stands again and comes around to me. Brushing curls off my forehead, he gives me a kiss. "But there is a condition, my dear."

I raise both eyebrows as I wait for Michael to tell me. I can see a spark of mischief in his eyes.

"You have to work. I will get Shane to give you a job." Michael releases me and puts on his suit jacket.

The thought of working with Shane does funny things to my stomach. I've always crushed on him, but he's always looked at me like I'm repulsive. A part of me kind of gets it. My hair and eyes don't exactly make dating easy. I've been called every variation of red, and not in a pleasant way. And my eyes get me a lot of attention, but I've been called a freak because they are different colors.

"It won't be hard, Una." Michael has taken my internal struggle as a problem with him getting me to work. I shake my head.

"No, that's fine. Sorry, I was miles away." I push a smile forward, and Michael nods.

"Okay, I'm off to work," he tells me as he takes his coffee down to his office.

After the conversation with Michael, my mind moves to my mother. She was angry the last time we spoke. I was studying accountancy, following in her footsteps, and I could do it. But I found myself getting bored. I did it because she wanted me to. I had one final year, and I knew finishing made sense, but I had enough of silence and numbers. Her life wasn't for me.

I leave the kitchen with a granola bar. Mary would fix me breakfast if I wanted, but right now, I want the fresh air. I've spent way too much time indoors, and I hate it.

It's foggy this morning but warm, so I don't need a jacket. I can hear the horses in the stables as I walk along the pass. The boys have no idea just how lucky they are living here.

Stephen, one of the stable masters, comes into view. His navy boiler suit covers him as he shovels out the stables.

"Good morning, Stephen." I nearly give the man a heart attack and laugh.

He smiles. "Una, you're back."

I shrug. "Yeah, I think so." His brown peaky cap covers his balding head. He's been here as long as I can remember.

"How is she?" I ask as I make my way to the third stable.

"She's good. Her form has been off lately," he tells me as he leans the shovel against the stables and walks down to me. I stop outside my mare's door, and there's that sudden rush of sadness and happiness at seeing her. She moves back away from me, dancing slightly.

"I've had a hoof trimmer here. Her shoes are fine." I'm nodding as I open the door. But she's unsteady while moving deeper into her stable.

"How long has she been like this?" I ask as he closes the gate after me.

"A few days."

"Could she be pregnant?" I hold out my hand, and when my fingers meet her hair, she settles, allowing me to rub her side.

When Stephen doesn't answer me, I glance at him, and he's smiling. "You're the first who's been able to touch her." At his words, I lean my face into her and inhale the warm air that rises from her coat.

"We checked, but it could be too early to tell if she's pregnant. But it's possible."

I stay with her for a while, just rubbing her, and she lets me. I never named her. Shane bought the horse for me on my sixteenth birthday. I thought if I referred to her as 'her' or 'the horse' that I would never get attached. I was wrong.

It's a while later that I leave. The cold and hunger drive me back inside, and I smile when I see Mary in the kitchen. She's taking cookies out of the oven. I knock on the door, not wanting to frighten her. She has a weak heart already.

"Hi, Mary," I say. Her eyes widen, and her eyebrows rise. "Una. You are more beautiful each time I see you." She's always been too kind to me. Before she pulls me into a hug, she places the cookie tray on the counter. "Are you staying long?" She asks the same question that everyone has asked, but I'm not sure what I'm doing.

"For a few nights," I tell her as I sit down while focusing on the cookies. "They smell lovely," I say, and she bustles over to the coffee machine first, where she fills me a mug. I sit at the breakfast bar and watch her move around the kitchen.

Mary moves fast, but she's a stout woman with short curly hair that's always wild. Her hair is kind of like mine: unmanageable.

A tray with milk, coffee, sugar, and cookies is placed in front of me as Liam comes into the kitchen. The atmosphere instantly changes. Mary doesn't like him, and she doesn't hide it. Liam, to me, has always been different. But he doesn't scare me off.

"Cookie?" I offer him. His eyes flicker to the cookie, and he actually takes it. Not what I was expecting. Nor do I expect it when he sits down across from me.

He could be a model, waiting to have a photo taken. He isn't exactly fully sitting on the stool; one foot rests on the floor. He unbuttons his suit jacket and rests one hand on his leg. He has no idea how he appears as he eats the cookie. I want to laugh, but I don't. Instead, I pour my coffee and thank Mary as she leaves the room.

"How are you, Una?" He doesn't glance up at me as he speaks, his focus solely on the cookie that he still eats. His words are filled with boredom, like somehow, he's being forced to make small talk.

"Great, and you Liam?" I ask. Some amusement has slipped into my words, and he peers up at me.

"I have no complaints at all, Una." His monotone voice has me hiding a smile behind my coffee mug. He gets up and bids me a good day. Nothing weird or odd about that at all.

I spend the next hour searching the house and grounds for Shane with no luck. I find Darragh and Finn fighting in Darragh's room. My mind takes in the floor, which is covered in clothes. Darragh's room is like a teenager's, and he has banned Mary from cleaning it.

"Okay, okay. Calm down." I step in between them. It hasn't come to blows, but it doesn't seem like that's far off.

"Una, this is private." Finn's sharp words sting, but I fold my arms across my chest.

"And what? Let you kill each other?" I ask.

"Don't fucking speak to her like that," Darragh jumps to my defense, and I snap my gaze to him. His jaw is red, and his fists are clenched. I'm not sure what has him wound up, but seeing Darragh angry is odd.

"It's a private conversation. That's all I said," Finn replies. He's calmer now.

"It's my fucking room. And Una stays."

"You know what..." Finn doesn't finish his sentence but storms out of the room. I watch him leave, silently questioning what has everyone fired up. I turn to Darragh to ask, but he throws himself on his unmade bed.

"Don't ask," he says, and his serious tone has me leaving it alone.

"Your room is disgusting," I tell him, glancing around me. How does he live like this?

"Yeah, it is," he agrees and starts to smile. "Want to go to a party?"

***

The "party" that Darragh takes me to is in a small village. The pub has locked its doors, so we're free to party. Smoking is prohibited in all pubs, but here, I walk through another cloud of smoke. The smoking isn't the worst that's happening here. Most people are high and jump around as a guy with a red long beard beats the shit out of a bodhrán.

Darragh takes my hand and pulls me through the crowd. He looks alive as he smiles at me, and I find myself loosening up.

"Una, this is Brian." I'm introduced to a really good-looking guy. He's tall, with wavy blond hair and sparkling blue eyes I could fall into.

He gives me a quick glance, but his attention is back on Darragh. "You better have brought my money."

I focus on the floor as Darragh smiles and promises his way out of not having the money for Brian. I steal glances at Brian. He knows he's attractive.

All eyes are on me, and it's for the wrong reasons. I wish I had tied my hair up and put on some sunglasses. But the more rebellious side of me sticks out my tongue at them. It's fun, and when Darragh swings around and places a pink pill on my outstretched tongue, I swallow it with a long drink from the bottle that I hold.

Time moves in a funny pattern. I'm dancing. All the colors—I can't catch them. The vehicle under us is moving. Blond hair and blue eyes fill my vision.

"Brian," I manage to say, and everyone laughs. I'm sitting in the pool house. Brian's there again, and his lips move against mine, his tongue forcing its way into my mouth. The weight of a small tablet registers with me as he passes it into my mouth, and I swallow.

The tiles under my feet are cold but shiny. They move like water. I touch them, and they bark at me.

"Una, leave the dog alone," someone shouts. The beast moves toward me, and I run toward the light. I know its safety. I'm in a glass house. Water fills my mouth, and I can't breathe. Someone pulls me back.

A girl laughs. "What are you doing in the shower?"

Shower. A solid cold pane of glass presses against my fingers. I'm in the shower. She puts something into her mouth while offering me a small pink pill. I decline. I'm aware that what's happening is happening, but it seems like it isn't.

She shrugs and puts the second pill in her mouth. I watch her slide slowly to the ground. I reach out to her, but my head collides with glass, and I find myself on the ground with her.

Laughter bubbles from my mouth. Large legs cross my vision. I see blond hair from the back. "Brian," I whisper, and he grins down at me. He's so tall; he's like one hundred feet high.

I try to reach out to him, but my hand is tiny. "My hand!" I panic, but he laughs, and I laugh too. Brian's mouth is huge, stretching and growing, and I blink a few times before the darkness consumes me. I try to fight it, but it's no good.

CHAPTER FOUR

UNA

THREE PEOPLE LIE BESIDE me, their hands behind their heads. I blink and three becomes one. My stomach tightens with the pain that rips through it. I manage to crawl to the shower, where I heave. Every glance I flicker toward the girl on the floor doesn't make her move. I want her to move; my brain is telling me she's too still, too pale. My hands tremble as I wipe wet hair from my forehead. I notice then that I'm soaking wet.

I'm looking around the bathroom, trying to make sense of this. I need someone to tell me what happened. I use the tiles to hoist myself up; standing is a challenge I somehow manage. I'm so cold. *How long have I been lying here?* My attention draws to the girl again. From this angle, I can see her face fully, and she's dead.

Her coloring isn't natural, nor is the stillness of her chest. I've never done CPR, but I know I can't stand here and do nothing. My hand trembles as I reach out to her while kneeling down, covering one hand with my other one as I close my eyes.

You can do this, Una.

Slowly, I open my eyes. I try again, but I can't touch her. She's dead. I know she's dead. I move back away from the body and glance around the room. Once again, no one is here. The floor is rising and falling as I rock back and forth. A single black marble tile becomes my sole focus as I try to calm myself, but it isn't working.

It's wet, and I reach out and touch it. The tips of my fingers turn red. I yank my hand back to my chest. My breaths are bursting from my lungs, and I can't stop blinking as I stare at the body.

"What happened?" Arms pull at me. The dead girl disappears, and Darragh's face fills my vision.

"She's dead." My words are a whisper.

"What happened to you? Da is going to kill me." A burning pain ignites in my head as Darragh's fingers brush across my forehead. Automatically, my own hand joins his. My fingers are red when I glance at them.

Darragh moves out of my line of vision, and the dead girl is back.

"She's dead," I whimper, and this time, Darragh seems to hear me. He's returned with a towel, but he doesn't put it to my head. Instead, he joins me in staring at the dead girl.

"She's dead?" he questions.

"Yes." I can't process this. *What will happen to me? Will I go to prison? Was it me who killed her? Was it the drugs? Who will be held responsible? Okay, Michael is going to kill us for bringing this into his home. My mother?* My mind is growing more frantic.

"She's dead." Darragh's shout snaps me out of my own inner turmoil. He paces the floor. A vein bulges in his neck as he roars. "Fuck. We are so fucked."

Tears burn my eyes at his words. "Do something," I tell him as I start to rock again.

"This isn't my mess." His calm accusation knocks me out of my state.

"Darragh, this is your party. There is a dead girl in your bathroom." Now I'm the one shouting.

"Everything okay?" someone asks through the door.

Darragh stares at the door, and I stare at him. We can't let anyone else see this. I get up and make sure the door is locked.

"Yeah, be out in a minute," I say and wait for a few seconds. Darragh is fixated on the body.

"Darragh, give me your phone." I don't have a clue where mine is, so I hold out my hand.

"What do you want my phone for?" Confusion fills his voice. It must be the shock.

"To ring the Gardaí and an ambulance. We need to report this."

He turns his back on me, shaking his head.

"Darragh, we need to report this." I shiver again at the thoughts of what will happen to me. But leaving her lying on a cold tile floor seems wrong.

"Darragh," I shout and get his attention.

"Yeah, I'll ring. You get rid of everyone." He seems together, and I find myself nodding. He comes to me, and I want to roar, crying in his arms, but he moves my hair.

"We need to cover the cut so no one asks questions," he says before stepping away. His coldness is something I've never seen before, but I tell myself it's the shock. A dead body isn't something either of us has seen before.

There are three people left in the pool house, and they are easy to shift. No one seems to search for the dead girl, and I feel relief and guilt that no one remembers her. I search the room for a bag or jacket—something to give the guards so they can identify her—but there's nothing in the room. When I return to the bathroom, I find Darragh sitting beside her, having a fag.

"How long will they be?" I ask, and he gapes at me with that confused stare again. "You go on to bed. I'll sort this."

I laugh. "Go to bed?" My chest is tight, and I'm struggling to breathe. I don't need him to go into shock on me. I need him to be strong until the Gardaí get here.

"Fuck's sake, Una." He's up quicker than I expect. Throwing the half-smoked cigarette into the sink, he marches toward me and yanks me by the arm.

"What are you doing?" I ask, trying to get free, but Darragh is stronger than he looks.

"Go to bed," he says before leading me out of the pool house. I'm left standing outside, freezing and confused. Darragh glances back at me over his shoulder. He looks focused and angry, but he doesn't appear to be in any kind of shock.

SHANE

I check my phone. It's four in the morning. I'm not sure what woke me. I lie back down as I hear another loud noise coming from down the hall. I climb out of bed, pull on jeans, and grab the bat from behind my door.

The hall is dark, and I keep it that way while moving along the wall slowly. My bare feet help keep me soundless. I start to realize it isn't an intruder as light shines under the door from the fourth bedroom down from mine. Also, an intruder wouldn't be as noisy. Another bang sounds before a female voice curses.

What is Una doing? I lower the bat but still keep it in my hands as I open the door. She's wet again. This girl has a thing for water. She's searching for something in the wardrobe. In the process, she's knocking boxes and clothes onto the ground.

"What are you doing?" I ask.

She spins around, her wet long hair flicking water with the speed of her movements. The wildness in her eyes has my stomach tightening. I'm beside her, searching her face. Her gaze lowers, and she shakes her head.

"Una, what's wrong?" I ask the crown of her head, and when she peeks up at me, her eyes are watery. She stares at me, unblinking. A tremble has entered her body, and my heart starts to pound.

"Una, what's wrong?" I ask again. I want to grab her and shake her, but touching her has never been a luxury I've allowed myself. Right now, I seem unable to move.

"I can't find dry clothes." She blinks and tears fall. I loosen my grip on the bat.

"Because this isn't your room," I tell her, taking a step out of the wardrobe, but she doesn't follow.

She moves around the wardrobe like it's her first time seeing it. She's shaking as she slowly skims her fingers across a pile of blankets. There's blood on her hands. I take her wrist as I step back into the wardrobe, and she flinches at the contact as her eyes widen. I've dealt with blood before, but her blood is doing something entirely different to me.

I'm searching her face, her arms, but I can't see anything.

"It's my head. I don't... I don't know..."

I find it quickly. It's a deep gash. "We need to get you to the hospital."

She's shaking her head. "I didn't know."

I don't have a clue what she's babbling about. Her standing here, bleeding and cold, isn't doing any good for my heart. "It's fine. Let's get you sorted first." I smile when she nods. Finally, I can take care of her.

When I release her wrist, her eyes widen, and she shakes her head again. "We need to go to the pool house." She moves past me, and I'm trying to catch up with her.

"Una, why?" I'm whisper-shouting, not wanting to wake up anyone else.

"Shit." It's not until I'm out in the courtyard that I remember I have no shoes and no shirt on. The cold air has me moving faster after Una. All I want to do is get her head looked at and out of those wet clothes.

The pool house is a mess, the embers of a party dying slowly.

"Una." I call her again as she makes her way to the bathroom. Her blue lips and pale skin have me itching to get her to a doctor, and whatever she wants to show me, I'll check out so we can go. I curse Darragh because I know this is his doing. He's a heavy hitter when it comes to partying, and I question now if Una is on something. I'm going to kill him.

Una steps inside the bathroom, and I follow her. What I find isn't what I was expecting. Darragh is sitting beside a girl—a girl whose lips are blue. Her body lies limply on the floor.

Darragh's eyes snap up to mine as I step into the bathroom. I try to control my anger as I take in the mess before me.

"She's dead." Una's crying beside me, but all I take in is Darragh. What a screwup.

"Get the fuck up," I tell him, and he jumps up quickly. I check the girl for a pulse and don't find one at first, but there's a flicker of life there.

"What has she taken?" I ask Darragh, and he shrugs.

"You are so fucking useless." He lowers his head. Una is still shaking, her eyes shooting everywhere. She's in shock.

"Una. I need you to focus, sweetheart." Her eyes snap to me, and she blinks, allowing more tears to fall. "She isn't dead. But what has she taken?"

She moves quickly to get beside me. Her bare arm brushes mine, and I hold my breath at the contact.

"She isn't?" She's smiling, her fingers moving up my arm, and I'm staring into her eyes, not sure how to sort through everything. I need her to stop touching me. Her eyes search the floor as if she can see the past play out before her. "She took pills." Her head snaps up, and she's almost excited with this information.

Darragh takes out a pack of fags, getting ready to light one up. "Darragh, take Una back to the house and get her dry clothes. Then take her to my car where I will meet you. We need to get both girls to the hospital. You think you can manage that?"

"Yeah, yeah, of course," he answers like a fucking victim. He makes me sick. Turning to Una as she clings to my arm, I force a smile.

"Go with Darragh. Everything will be okay."

She's nodding, but it's like she's boneless. The adrenaline is leaving her body. I snap my head to Darragh, and he helps Una stand.

I wait until they've left the room before I hoist the girl off the ground. I'm trying to wake her, but shaking her and even slapping her across the face doesn't have any impact. She's getting cold. *Did I imagine the flicker of a heartbeat?* I check again, and it's still there.

I bend her over before opening her mouth and sticking my fingers down her throat. Nothing happens at first, but she starts gagging before sick pours over my hand and out onto the floor. I hold her up as liquid continues to pour from her. I repeat the action until there's nothing left for her to bring up.

When she pushes my arms away, I lift her up onto the counter and get her a glass of water; she brings back up the first sip but manages to keep the second mouthful down.

I leave the girl there as I return to the house and get dressed.

She's still in the same place when I return. I carry her to the garage. Una sits in the front of the car. Her eyes are wide, and I can see the quick rise and fall of her chest as she stares at the girl. She's in dry clothes, and that relaxes me until my gaze settles on Darragh sitting in the back of my car. I open the door.

"Get out," I tell him, and he does as I place the girl in the back. Once I have the door closed, I turn to Darragh and grab him by the neck.

"You're such a fucking waste. Go tell Liam the mess you made while I take these two to the hospital." I let him go, pushing him away from me, and he rubs his neck. His anger, I can see, and I almost want him to put his hands on me so I can hurt him. But he turns away and goes back into the house.

Una wrings her hands as I start to drive to Navan. It's the closest hospital to us.

"How's your head?" I ask, and she shoots me a sideways glance. She pulls her lip between her teeth and chews on it.

I need to focus on the road and not Una.

"It's sore now. I didn't really notice it earlier."

I nod. "It was the adrenaline that was keeping it at bay. We're nearly there, so you'll be seen soon." She isn't sitting as straight anymore. "Una, don't fall asleep." I flicker a glance at her, and she rubs her eyes.

"I'm so sleepy all of a sudden." Her words are slurred.

"Yeah, it's the cut on your head. You've lost a lot of blood. It's important that you don't sleep, okay?"

"Okay." I don't like her one-word response.

"Stephen told me you saw the horse I got you," I say, and straight away, I regret it. It's not her reaction—she sits a bit straighter—but it's how it makes me feel. It was the first time I tried to show her I cared.

She had been so excited that day, and getting her the horse was the best decision I had ever made. But as she had sat proudly on top of the horse, Dad had squeezed my shoulder. His words had my stomach tightening. "You're a good brother to her."

The way I looked at her wasn't how a brother looked at a sister. I had shrugged his arm off. "She's not my sister." My angry words were heard by all, even Una, as I stormed off.

"Yeah, she's the best." Her words are still slurred, but she's happy and she's talking. "I'm not sure if I ever thanked you." She reaches for my arm, but her hand flops down halfway across. I glance at her, and she's smiling at me with lids half-closed.

"You're welcome, Una," I tell her before focusing on the road. I remember the day I saw the horse. She was wild. The handler wasn't able to control her, and all I saw was Una. I knew they would be a perfect match, and I was right. "We're nearly there."

She shifts, pulling herself up more. The sign for Navan has me lifting my foot off the pedal, but I still move quickly through the empty town. It takes five more minutes before I pull up outside the Emergency Room. Department.

I open Una's door and help her out. The fresh air has her eyes opening a bit wider. I close the door and lock the car, leaving the other girl in the back. She's asleep, and my number one priority is Una. For now, she seems to have forgotten about the girl. She allows me to lead her into ER, where a few people wait. I smile at the receptionist. She doesn't return the smile as I give Una's details.

"Fill out this form and take a seat." She slides the form to me.

"I'd like to be seen now," I tell her, glaring over her shoulder in search of a doctor.

"And so would the man behind you with only three fingers. We're moving as fast as we can." I don't look at the man in question. This place makes my skin crawl. I hate being so close to other sick people. I direct Una to a seat and kneel down in front of her.

"I'm going to step out for a moment, but I'll be back," I tell her.

She's far more alert. Her eyes focus on my face, and my stomach tightens. My thumb brushes her thigh, and she jerks. I quickly get up and go outside.

I carry in the girl, and the receptionist raises an eyebrow. I give her another smile, and yet again, she doesn't return it. "I found her on the sidewalk. I think she's taken something," I tell the receptionist.

"Her name?" she asks with fingers hovering over the keyboard.

The girl is heavy, and I move her to the closest seat and sit her up, but she slumps over. The receptionist continues to observe me.

"I don't know," I answer and return to Una. I've done my part. Now I need to figure out what the hell we're going to do with Darragh.

CHAPTER FIVE

UNA

MY HEAD HURTS. I get four stitches and strict orders to stay awake for the next twelve hours as a precaution. I'm waiting to be discharged, and Shane is sitting in a plastic chair while he scrolls through his phone. I still can't believe all he's done for me tonight. When he peers up at me, my pulse spikes. I want to ask him why he's being kind to me, but the doctor returns.

"Okay. You're all set to go." He hands me a prescription. "If the pain persists, take one every four hours." I'm nodding as Shane rises and tucks his phone into his pocket.

He reaches out his hand to the doctor. "Thank you," he tells him, and the doctor takes his hand. The silver band on his thumb reflects the light, grabbing my attention. My eyes roam up his arm, where a small band of black is visible, but it quickly disappears under the sleeve of his jumper. When my eyes meet his, my heart leaps in my chest.

"Ready to go?" he asks, and I give a quick smile and get down off the bed. "I'll take that." Shane reaches out his hand for the prescription, and I give it to him.

He's always careful not to touch me. But earlier, I could have sworn his thumb stroked my thigh. Maybe I imagined it. My head wasn't exactly in a good place.

Back in the car is the first time my mind wanders to the girl. "The girl, is she okay?"

Shane starts the car and pulls out of the hospital parking lot. The sun is up. It's nine in the morning, and I'm sleepy, exhausted from everything.

"Yeah. They pumped her stomach, but she's going to be fine." Shane focuses on the road as he drives, and I steal glances at him. This is the longest I've ever been in his company, and my opinion of him has changed. I always fancied him but never got close to him. He wasn't an easy person to get close to.

We don't go home. Instead, Shane pulls up at Whitewood Lake. There's a fog sitting on the water. I don't move as Shane climbs out of the car and walks around to my side. I unbuckle my seat belt as he opens the door.

"I thought the fresh air might help keep you awake." I step out of the car, and he places a large jacket around my shoulders.

Now all I smell is Shane, his cologne along with the scent of leather and trees. It's a weird combination, but it's uniquely Shane. My stomach trembles as he leans around me and closes the door.

Shane walks with his hands behind his back, but there's a bounce in his step. He doesn't seem like someone who has been up half the night. I can only imagine my appearance, but instead of focusing on that, I give all my attention to Shane.

"Do you know that Whitewood Lake has its very own monster?" I love the lilt that enters Shane's words. It makes me glance at him, and I see his small grin. I find myself smiling at him.

"I've been around these parts for a long time, and I've never heard anything about a monster," I say. His grin expands into a smile, and my heart skips a beat. But I don't lose eye contact. His beauty entrances me.

"In 1981, it was spotted and sounded similar to the Loch Ness monster."

"May be a relative," I answer, and Shane gives a small laugh that has my stomach erupting in butterflies.

We're silent for a moment, and I find myself staring into the water, questioning if things like monsters really are under the murky surface. Shane walks on the inside; he's closer to the rippling waves. He seems at peace, his face relaxed and a constant smile visible. My mind goes back to what happened, and most of all, Darragh.

"Can I ask you something?" We stop near two large trees, and I'm nervous now that Shane is facing me. His brown eyes are like orbs of chocolate; they could really pull a girl in. I'm so sleep-deprived that I can't focus for a second.

"Of course." Shane folds his arms across his broad chest as he stares out at the water. A chest I saw bare a few hours ago. To see him standing in only a pair of jeans in the closet had nearly undone me. He's waiting patiently, and I pull my mind from the gutter.

"When I thought the girl was dead, Darragh was supposed to ring the Gardaí, but he didn't." I chew my bottom lip, pondering if I had said the right thing. Shane is his brother, after all, and I don't know what I'm even trying to say.

"Maybe he was in shock," Shane tells the lake.

"Yeah, maybe," I respond, but I don't believe it. I don't know what I believe, but he wasn't in shock. It doesn't really matter, I suppose, since it turned out all right. I pull Shane's jacket tighter around me, trying to smell it without making it noticeable. Shane takes my movements for me being cold, and he shoos me back to the car.

I don't argue and I don't remove the jacket, but Shane doesn't ask for it. His phone rings, and he struggles to get it out of his pocket.

"Need a hand?" I ask, and his no is resounding and quick. I sit back, a sting of embarrassment snapping my head away. He manages to get the phone out and answers it. I want to tell him that driving and talking on a phone is illegal, but I do it all the time.

It's Liam on the other end of the phone. "I can't talk," Shane says. "Yeah, we'll talk when I get home." There's more of Liam's voice, but I can't understand what's being said. But Shane laughs, and it's not a sweet laugh. "Like I said, we'll talk later." He hangs up without saying goodbye, and the car moves faster under us.

"Everything okay?" I ask after a moment, and he slows down slightly.

"Yeah. Just Liam being Liam." We pull into the drive, and I feel disappointed that my time with Shane will end. I don't speak as we make our way up the drive.

I expect Shane to pull into the garage, but he doesn't. Instead, he drives out back and through the courtyard, and we pull up outside the stables. I glance at him, but his fingers drum on the steering wheel as he faces forward. He doesn't speak as he climbs out, and once again, he opens my door for me.

"I thought you might like to check in on your horse." He's holding open my door, but he isn't looking at me, and now I question what Liam said to him. He seems far away. As I get out, he's still holding the door, my face flush with his chest.

"Shane," I whisper, and my stomach twists as he looks down at me. My heart starts to pound as he stares at me.

"Good morning, Mr. O'Reagan." Shane gapes at Stephen like he materialized from thin air. Shane steps out of my way and gives me a quick nod. He greets Stephen stiffly. This is the Shane I've become accustomed to, the one who treats the staff like tools and not people.

"Morning, Stephen. How is she today?" I ask as I make my way down to the stables. Stephen walks beside me.

"She's a lot better. Still can't touch her, but I'm confident you can." He's grinning at me as he veers off to do his jobs. I stop at my horse's stable, and Shane stands a few feet away. He doesn't join me. I'm not sure what he's doing, but I open the door and step into the stall. She moves back as I slowly approach but settles as I place my hand on her before leaning into her coat. My face heats up against her skin.

"She was kicking and bucking the day I saw her. She was uncontrollable, and the handlers couldn't break her."

I lean out as Shane steps into the stable with his hands behind his back. He doesn't make any attempt to rub her or come closer as he tells me about the horse.

"She had reared back, and her mane caught the sun, and I don't know..." He frowns. "I thought of you."

My heart flutters at his words.

"She was unpredictable." He looks at me for the first time. "Untamable."

My pulse spikes with how he looks at me, and it might be the lack of sleep, but I feel like I've stepped into a twilight zone with Shane. It's like that feeling when you're lying under the stars knowing the world is asleep. It's magical, but it has to end.

"I remember that day also Shane. When you told everyone how I wasn't your sister." It was childish of me, but it had hurt. He said it with such disgust that it's stayed with me through the years. I never looked at him as a brother, but it was the disgust in his voice that had shattered me. I remember thinking that I couldn't blame him with how odd I was, and odd isn't always good.

The moment I flicker my gaze at Shane, I regret my words. His jaw is clenched, his shoulders tense. At least I know he remembers. I didn't really expect that.

"Sorry, that was childish," I say quickly. "It was a long time ago."

He shakes his head. "No, I hurt you."

My throat burns as he speaks, because he really had hurt me. "It's fine," I say as I continue to run my hands along my horse. When Shane's hand rubs close to mine, I freeze along with the animal under us.

"I'm sorry." His words are low and precise, like he's trying out a new language. I glance at him, causing our shoulders to brush, and this time, it looks like he's the one who freezes. He takes a step away from the horse and me. "You need to eat." The declaration is like a light bulb going off over his head, and I can't help the smile that grows on my face.

"I do?" I question, and he smiles, sending butterflies scattering to the corners of my stomach.

"Yes, you do," he says before leaving.

I shake my head while I give my horse a final rub. I glance around me, making sure that Shane is gone and Stephen can't see me before I bury my face in Shane's coat and inhale.

A giggle erupts from me. I'm acting crazy. It was the bang to the head that's causing me to act odd, I decide as I lock the stables and make my way to the house.

The kitchen is warm, and Mary smiles at me the moment I enter. "Una, I'm making your favorite."

The smell of pancakes has me drooling. I didn't expect to see Shane sitting at the table. It's set for two people. He's on his phone, fingers moving rapidly across the screen. He has such a serious expression on his face.

"Orders from Master Shane," Mary adds and that grabs my attention and Shane's.

"Master Shane?" I question, not wanting to mention the fact that he knows pancakes are my favorite.

"Sit down, Una." The demand is sharp and comes from Shane.

I don't like it. I shed his jacket and place it on the chair, but I don't sit. He flashes a glance toward Mary as she prepares pancakes and coffee before they snap back to me.

"Please." He says it through gritted teeth, but I take it and sit down. I'm sitting across from him, and the setting is almost intimate except for the bustle of Mary. Shane focuses on his phone, and I take in the circles under his eyes.

"You should go to bed," I tell him.

"I'm fine." He doesn't glance up from his phone as he answers me. Mary places a coffee in front of me, but she pauses as she hovers over me. "What happened to your head, sweetheart?" I had almost forgotten about it.

"Oh—" I start to explain, but Shane cuts me off.

He stands up and takes the paper from his pocket before handing it to Mary. It's my prescription. "I'll finish up here. You go and get the prescription."

Mary glances at me and hesitates, and it's like I can see the wheels turning in her head as she looks from me to Shane. The way she glances from me to Shane makes it appear like she thinks Shane did this to my head.

"I fell," I tell her. As she moves back slightly, her eyes widen, then they narrow in disbelief.

"Why are you still here?" Shane's words are quiet, but they would move a stone. She leaves quickly, and Shane is up, making pancakes. I've lost my appetite.

This is how I remember him with the staff—an actual asshole. I don't speak even as he puts a plate of steaming pancakes in front of me. They aren't as perfectly circular as I've become used to, but he buttered and sugared them just as I like. A jug of maple syrup is on the table, and I don't hold back in coating them in the sticky substance.

"I really shouldn't eat your pancakes since you were so rude to Mary," I say as Shane sits down.

He's rolled up his sleeves, his tattoo on display. It's an odd one; large, thick black bands circle his arm. I often wondered what it meant but never asked. "No, you should starve yourself. That way, I'll be kinder to Mary."

He takes a forkful of the pancakes, and I'm transfixed on his mouth as he chews. He doesn't show any remorse as he pauses and raises an eyebrow.

"Eat, Una," he tells me once his mouth is empty, and I gaze at him as he refills his mouth.

Before I lose all self-control, I start to eat the best pancakes in the world. "Okay, these are delicious," I tell him. Shane has finished his, and he watches me eat mine. I can't stop smiling in between mouthfuls. "Why are you watching me?" I ask, but I don't mind that he is.

"Why are you smiling?" he fires back.

"Because you're watching me."

He smiles, and I shake my head. He's gorgeous. "I've been thinking about your job."

I don't like the change in topic, but I try to hold the smile. I want to talk about why he's watching me, eat not some stupid job. I sugar and milk my coffee. "Let's hear it," I say, and he sits back.

"I need a bookkeeper." He waves his hand in my direction, like he made me, the bookkeeper, appear.

I'm shaking my head, and he sits back, his recent confidence leaving. "What you've done for me tonight is more than anyone ever has," I answer honestly. When he leans in, his eyes crinkle at the corners, but I hold my hand up, knowing I need to finish.

"Seriously, I can't thank you enough. But working with numbers... I can't." I clean a spot on the table that isn't dirty. I swallow, surprised by the level of emotion that's coming with my words. "I'm not her. I don't want to be her. I'm not my mother, Shane."

His eyes light up with understanding. "You don't want to be an accountant?" he asks, and I nod my head, trying to keep the tears back. "So what do you want to do?" Shane takes a drink of his own coffee, and his brown eyes have softened.

"That's it? You're not going to try to convince me that I'm throwing my whole future away?" I'm not sure if that's what I want to hear, but it's what I'm used to hearing. So having someone accept what I'm saying is a shock.

"When dad asked me to get you a job, I don't recall him telling me to make you miserable." His small smile has my heart beating faster.

"I know what I want to do." My heart is racing. The idea that I could do what I truly love is rushing the blood through my body. "I want to work with Stephen. Help out with the horses." It was Shane buying me the horse that made my love for horses grow.

It's because of him, in a way, that I no longer want to be an accountant. That I want to be free. Be me. I should be thanking him for more than tonight.

"Okay, we can organize that."

I'm beaming with joy. "Seriously?" I ask, and Shane's eyes are soft as he smiles at me. It sends butterflies erupting in my stomach.

"Yes. It's so nice to see you happy."

I'm a little speechless right now. I'm ready to burst with so many emotions as I take a drink of coffee. Glancing at Shane over my cup, my pulse spikes as our eyes clash.

"Thank you." It's nearly a whisper, but it's the most heartfelt thank you I've ever given.

"You're welcome," Shane says with a slight nod. We sit and sip coffee while staring at each other. It's perfect until Liam walks in, and I know our time together is up.

CHAPTER SIX

SHANE

THERE'S THE SMALLEST SMUDGE of blood near her hairline; I notice it when she tilts her head. Otherwise, her face is flawless. Her skin has a shine to it. It's like the beauty inside her is trying to shine through. I love watching her mouth when she smiles. It's as fascinating as her different-colored eyes.

I take another sip of coffee and continue to take her in. She's sleepy, her lids dropping every few seconds, but we both sit up as Liam enters the kitchen. He's rang a few times, and we need to talk.

"How are you feeling, Una?" His words are precise as he speaks to her, and I want him to stop. I'm not entirely sure why. Maybe because he makes her uncomfortable. Maybe because he normally doesn't interact, so why with Una?

"I've had the best nurse take care of me," she tells him as she smiles at me, but there's a sadness in her eyes that I don't understand.

"I see. We need to speak." His attention is on me, and that sits better on my shoulders. I get up and ring Finn.

"Una's in the kitchen. I can't stay with her, so I need you to watch over her for the next few hours." Una tries to object, but I keep my back to her. Finn agrees. I don't glance back at Una as I follow Liam out the door.

We go to my bedroom. I'm exhausted, and this day hasn't ended yet. I sit on my bed and start pulling off my top. Liam stands along the wall. He never sits. He never appears comfortable.

Now I question what my brother's relationships with women must be like. I've never really thought about it before—I never cared—but spending the day with Una makes me question if he's ever felt like that. I put on a clean T-shirt and sit back down on my bed.

"Did you talk to Darragh?" I ask, pulling off my boots and socks.

"Yes, and Darragh is the least of your worries." Liam's controlled words make me want to lose control. I snort.

"Darragh is a huge problem, Liam. You'll have to see it sooner rather than later. He's going to get one of us killed. One of us," I state, pointing at myself.

"You can't punish him for something that hasn't happened."

I grit my teeth. "You can't ignore the signs that something *will* happen, Liam. Give him time."

"I'll have a word with Finn."

I'm shaking my head even as Liam says it. Finn has always been Darragh's babysitter, but he isn't going to solve this. Finn hasn't been himself since Connor disappeared. To me, the solution to this is to find Connor.

"A new supplier has moved into the area. He's trying to take over three of our areas. Dad wants it stopped and cleaned up straight away."

I rest my elbows on my knees. This isn't good. "A name?" I ask, but Liam is already shaking his head.

"Nothing. But Dad's informant said Dublin will be the first hit."

I snort again while glaring up at the ceiling. "Dad's famous informant. I don't suppose he told you who it was?" I ask, already knowing the answer. But Liam is moving to the door; this conversation is over.

"You need to sleep." I don't wait until he's gone before I climb into bed. I dream of Whitewood Lake and monsters.

I wake up and immediately check my phone. It's six in the evening. I've slept for roughly four or five hours. I can't even remember what time I went to bed. My mind is still circling back to the monster in the lake with a mix of my conversation with Liam.

I'm out of bed, making my way down the hall, and once I push open the door, something twists in my stomach as I take in all her curly red hair fanned out around her head like a burning halo.

Her cheeks are pink, and I can relax at the rise and fall of her chest. She's wearing a white top, the straps only strings, allowing me to see a lot of milky skin. I should wake her and make sure she's okay. A concussion was a very high risk with someone in her case. I gently and carefully shake her arm that's covered by the blanket.

"Una," I say gently as I shake her, but she doesn't stir. While standing back, I stare at her. Nothing. I try again, shaking her with more force.

"Una, wake up." It's a little too loud, and she sits up quickly, nearly colliding into me, but I'm quick and jump back. I don't get the smiling girl I had in the kitchen. Una's eyes are narrowed as she glares at me, her chest rising and falling quickly.

"What is with this family? You guys like waking me up."

"Who else wakes you up?" I fire back dryly, not liking that idea at all.

She shakes her head. "What do you want, Shane?" She's almost barking, and I drop the whole subject of someone waking her up. But I will ask her another time, when she's not ready to kill me.

"Go back to sleep, Una," I tell her, and her eyes grow in size. I want to smile. She's beautiful in the morning, but I know better.

"*Go back to sleep, Una!* Well, what did you wake me up for?" She's shouting, and I can't help but smile as I make my way to the door

"To make sure you were alive," I say as a shoe hits the wall an inch from me.

"Can a dead person throw shoes?" She's red in the cheeks with temper.

"They say redheads have foul tempers. Now I have proof that it's true." I make it out the door in one piece as something else hits the wall. I assume the other shoe.

I shower and change before getting into my car and making my way to a meeting in Dublin with one of our main customers.

It takes me forty minutes to reach The Marker hotel, where I set up the meeting. I park in the underground parking before making my way up to the veranda. As the doors open, I'm greeted by a member of the staff. "Mr. O' Reagan."

I nod in greeting as I'm taken outside to my seat. Overhead heaters keep the area warm, but the night's not cold. The large couch is comfortable, and I sit down, peering out over the city. Lights sparkle from the hundreds of windows, and it makes me think that Una would like it here. I've never appreciated the view, but I would love to see it from her eyes.

"The usual, Mr. O'Reagan? Should I bring it now or wait for your guest to arrive?" The waiter stands next to the table, one hand behind his back.

"You can bring it now and double the usual," I tell him, and he leaves as Gary arrives. Gary is a bull in a suit. That's what comes to mind when I take in his huge frame. The gray suit he wears could tear at the wrong movement. The white collar is open; he couldn't close it even if he wanted to. His neck is as thick as three men's.

He takes off his sunglasses as he sits down and puts them on the table. It's dark outside, so the sunglasses aren't necessary.

"Got to say, I was surprised when I heard you wanted to meet me. I'm not in trouble, am I?" Gary smiles. Meeting me isn't necessary very often, unless prices go up or we've run into a problem.

The waiter arrives back and places a brandy in front of us. "You're not in trouble. Relax," I reply to Gary, and he rubs his hands together while sitting back with his drink.

Gary reminded me of a Ken doll, but no matter his appearance, he wasn't stupid. He didn't supply nearly all of Dublin with drugs by being stupid.

"I wanted to check on business," I say and take a drink, relaxing back into the orange couch. Gary hasn't the same level of comfort that I have. The wicker chair is larger than most, but it wouldn't have the same space or comfort as the couch.

"Yeah, it's good." His eyes slightly narrow. "It's about the new supplier."

I clap for a moment. "Right to it. I like that, Gary. So what can you tell me?" I take a drink. He shifts in his seat before leaning forward. The joking Gary is gone now, and I'm eye to eye with the businessman.

"Look, his product is clean. I don't know where he's making it or how. But it's cheap, and it's huge in London."

"What's his name?" I ask, and Gary leans back, opening his arms.

"Come on, Shane. You know I can't do that. You're not losing me as a customer. It's just that this guy has a new product."

A product I'm sure we could replicate. "Do you have a sample?"

"On me? No man. Gardaí everywhere."

I don't fully believe Gary. I don't trust any of my customers. A man who can take a life isn't an easy man to figure out, and Gary has taken a lot of lives.

"I need a name, Gary."

He tilts his head at my request, as if to say he doesn't know.

"Have you ever met my brother, Liam?" I ask, and he sits back again.

"Bernard," he finally coughs up.

***

"I didn't do anything." Neill has his hands in the air. He's four foot nothing, an easy target, but I'm not here to hurt him. After leaving Gary, I decided to drop in on an old 'family' friend.

"Is that how you answer your door?" I ask, and he quickly drops his arms and lets me in. I double-check that my Audi is locked. It's a council estate, and black wood from a recent burning still sits in the center of the play area outside Neill's house.

The sitting room holds battered couches. Neill scoots around me and turns off the television, but I catch what he was watching. When I return my gaze to him, he shrugs.

"I might be small in height, but I'm big in other ways," he tells me as he sits down on the couch.

I'm not here to talk about his dick, so I don't. I sit down in the armchair across from him. "Any new fighters or people moving through your circle recently?" I ask. Connor was his number one fighter, and he made a lot of money off my brother.

His feet dangle. They don't reach the floor as he sits back in the couch. His white tracksuit is cheap and a copy of a popular brand.

"A few new ones. None like Connor." He's smiling with genuine affection for Connor. Connor isn't exactly the friendly type. I often see him as a mix of us all. At times, he reminds me of Liam, but he can be a mess like

Darragh—only, Darragh is women and drugs, where Connor is fighting and drink.

"Have you heard the name Bernard going around?" The moment I ask, I can see he's heard of him. His eyebrows lift at the same time.

"Yeah, I have. He's been supplying some new drug. Some of his men were giving out samples at one of my fights, but I ran them off."

"You personally?" I know he didn't, but I can't let this conversation go by without him understanding that I could crush him.

"No, my bouncers. Shane, I respect you and your family. You have my word that I'm not holding back." So he knew what I was doing.

"Good." I stand now, not wanting to spend any more time here than necessary. "If you hear anything, I expect you to call me," I tell Neill as he shuffles off the couch.

"There's one more thing." He stands. "He had a Northern Ireland accent."

That's the last thing I wanted to hear. "You're positive?" I ask, and he nods. *This isn't good at all.*

***

I arrive home close to eleven. The house is quiet, but that doesn't mean that everyone is asleep. I find myself upstairs, knocking on Una's door. When I don't get an answer, I enter, but the room is in darkness. The bed is made, and Una isn't here.

I find her in the library, sitting barefoot on a Queen Ann chair. She's twirling a curl around her finger while holding an old paperback in her other hand. I can't read the title, but I can tell she's enjoying it. I'm about to leave when she peeks up from behind the book. Surprise filters through her eyes.

"Don't throw the book at me," I tell her, and she sticks her tongue out, making me smile. Her tongue is really pink, and I'm glad when she puts it back in her pretty mouth. It's tantalizing and distracting.

"I think I will have to start locking my door." Her tone is playful, but I freeze. Does she know that I watch her sleep? I'm not sure what she sees on my face, but she laughs.

"I'm joking. It's just, I'm not a morning person. I had Darragh the other morning, and you this morning."

I relax and enter the room. So the other person was Darragh. He has no respect. "I apologize about Darragh," I tell her as I sit down.

"And who will apologize for you, Shane?" Once again, her tone is playful, but I sense she knows that I watch her.

"I have nothing to apologize for." Her smile slips at my serious words. I don't like sitting here and being questioned, but I don't want to leave her either. Standing, I focus on her, and each step I take closer to her causes a strain on her shoulders.

"I'm going to check your head," I say, and she bends her head for me.

With all her hair, it takes a few seconds to find the cut. The stitches are neatly done. And honestly, there isn't really a reason for me to check it. I rub her hair between my thumb and forefinger. It's extremely soft.

"What are you doing?" Suspicion coats her words.

"I told you, I'm checking your head, so hold still," I tell her. She hadn't moved, but she shifts under my hands. She doesn't like being told what to do.

"It feels like you're touching my hair."

I grin. "I am touching your hair; I have to move it to see the cut."

"It's taking a pretty long time," she huffs, and I can't stop the smile.

"There's a lot of hair to move."

"I'd move a dead body quicker." Her dry comment has me laughing. I don't think she has any idea how ironic it is that she would say that.

"What's so funny?" Darragh comes into the library, and I quickly step away from Una. His smile slips as I stare at him.

"What do you want?"

"I just want to talk to my sister," he says, jutting out his chin. I want to scream at him that she's not his fucking sister. If she was, then she would be my sister, and that was too messed up.

"I want a word," I tell him, leaving the library. I don't turn to see if he follows. I know he will.

He has the sense to close the library door as he leaves. I stop two doors down from it, not able to contain myself.

"She's off-limits from now on," I say. Darragh opens his mouth to speak, but I click my fingers in warning. "I don't care what Liam said. I don't care what you feel or think. She is off-limits."

He's shaking his head. "Why do you even care?" he asks, but he takes a step back while he speaks.

"Because father has left her in my hands, and I'm not a fuckup like you." I can see I've hurt him. Darragh takes another step back.

"Don't forget, Shane, you're not Liam in his eyes either." I hide all emotion at his words, but it stings. It's always been there. I know Liam is the next in line to take father's place, not me.

But when I was younger, it never bothered me to support my brother. I knew he was more vicious than me. He was more controlled when he needed to be, and he could lose control when he needed to as well. My emotions played too heavily into my actions.

Darragh hasn't taken two more steps when the door opens and Una steps out. I can tell from her red cheeks that she's all fired up. Darragh doesn't even stop when she speaks.

"How dare you," Una says. "I can talk to whomever I want. You or your father can't make decisions like that for me."

I glance at Darragh's receding back, his words about Liam still stinging me.

"I'm speaking to you, Shane."

I snap my gaze to Una. I can't do this. "Go back in and read your book," I tell her, expecting her to do as I say, but her dry laugh reminds me she isn't like other people.

"If I had the book, I'd throw it at you right now." Her words are said with hands on her hips. "That was a horrible thing to say to Darragh."

Now I'm starting to question her anger. "Which part?" I offer through clenched teeth.

"You're a piece of work." She shakes her head and storms back into the library. But I can't let it go. It's starting to sound like she has feelings for Darragh.

I'm right behind her. "Why are you getting so mad over Darragh?" I question, and she swings around.

"What are you trying to imply?" Her hands have returned to her hips, but I can see the strain in her face as I keep stepping closer to her.

"You're hell-bent on defending Darragh. Now that I think about it, you spend a lot of time together."

Her face blazes at my accusation, but she takes a step closer to me and pokes me in the chest. "He's my brother." She pokes me a second time. "He treats me with more kindness than you could ever muster up, Shane." She pokes me again while saying my name.

I move closer, stopping her from poking me. Her hand smashes against my chest.

"He is *not* your brother. I'm not your brother." The moment I say it, I regret it. The hurt that crosses her features has me leaving before I explain to her why I said that.

CHAPTER SEVEN

UNA

Hᴉs ʙʀᴏᴀᴅ ʙᴀᴄᴋ ꜰɪʟʟs my vision, and I want to pull all the books from the shelves. I'm angry with myself more than him. I allowed myself to feel for him, when all along, I was a job. His father told him to take care of me. That's the whole reason he went above and beyond to help me.

Tears burn my eyes at how stupid I've been. It was like I had spent my whole childhood and into my twenties craving attention from someone I saw as untouchable. Then he gives me a few hours, and I'm falling at his feet like he's some kind of god. The burn that travels up my neck has me covering my cheeks.

It's the burn of shame. I've been such a fool. He must be laughing at me. I don't allow the tears to fall. I'm stronger than this. I leave the library, and with each step, I want to defy him. No one has any right to tell me what to do or who I can hang out with. I go to the bar, knowing that's where I'll find Darragh. He's smiling when he sees me.

"I knew you couldn't resist the dark side." He pours me out a shot of vodka, and I stamp to the bar.

"I'm so fucking angry," I tell him and take the shot. It burns my throat, but it does nothing to quench the fire that's burning in my veins.

"Wow," Darragh yelps while he slaps the bar. "I knew redheads were fiery." He refills the shot glasses, and we both take them at the same time. "Let it out," he tells me, refilling the shot glass again.

"I don't think I could ever let out all the anger I'm feeling right now." Darragh refills his shot glass and downs it.

"He's a dick. Don't let him get to you." Darragh comes around from behind the bar and puts his arm around me. "Fuck him, Una. It's Shane. Just like it's Liam. They aren't like us. We're free," he tells me with a smile before pouring himself out another shot and placing the one I haven't drank in mine. "To freedom," he says, holding up his glass, but I can't drink to that.

"We aren't free, Darragh," I say quietly, because it's true. I'm caught up in what my mother wants me to be. And Darragh is being pushed into a box he refuses to stay in, yet no one is listening to us.

"I don't think I like it when you're acting like a Debbie downer." Darragh drinks his shot, then takes mine out of my hand and drinks it. And just like that, because I'm not partying, I'm not wanted.

My temper flares, and I swing around in the chair, grabbing the bottle of vodka. When I hold it up, Darragh smiles, placing the two shot glasses on the bar. I fill them but don't let him take his. "You answer a question, and then you take a drink," I tell him.

"And what, I ask you a question and then you drink?" He's smirking.

"Yeah," I agree, and he rubs his hands together.

I go first. "Why don't you stand up to Shane?"

"What the fuck kind of question is that?" Darragh is as volatile as me. I smile to ease the tension.

"Do you want a drink or not?" I say, and that does it. He settles.

"I'm only here as long as he allows it," he answers, and I don't even get that, but he knocks back the shot, and I remember that it's his turn to ask me a question.

"Do you have a boyfriend?" His question surprises me.

"No." I drink my shot. "What do you mean you're only here as long as he allows it?"

Darragh refills both shot glasses. "He doesn't like me, and if he had his way, I would be gone." He drinks his shot.

"You don't really believe that?" I question, and he grins.

"That's a second question, and it's my turn."

I reel in my irritation.

"When was the last time you slept with someone?"

"You get to ask me anything, and that's what you ask me?"

Darragh grins. "That's my question."

I roll my eyes. "About three months," I answer honestly, and he hoots while slapping the bar.

"Three months," he roars like I said three years. I knock the shot back.

"What do Shane's tattoos mean?" I ask. The moment it's out of mouth, I can see the wheels turning in Darragh's head.

"This is starting to sound like it's all about Shane."

My heart starts to pound, and I force a laugh while refilling the shot glasses. "It doesn't matter, then. It was a stupid question." I take a shot and Darragh rises.

"He's a prick, Una." The way he says it has me nodding at him. His fists are clenched.

"I know," I answer weakly.

"You're such a fucking liar." He storms from the room, and I feel terrible.

I shouldn't have started this stupid game. It was selfish of me. I take a swig from the bottle and chase after Darragh. My feet aren't as steady as I expect, but I catch myself before I stumble.

"Darragh." It doesn't seem to matter how many times I call him. He won't stop. It's not until he goes into the and sits down that I can see his face.

"I'm sorry," I tell him, knowing quizzing him about Shane wasn't right. "I was curious..."

"Liar." He's shouting again, and I'm questioning if following Darragh was the right thing to do. I want to tell him to calm down, but something is stopping me. "It's always: get close to Darragh to get close to Shane or Liam. Keep Darragh quiet. People can hear him. Hide him away, so no one can see him. I'm fucking sick of it."

I'm frozen as he takes his anger out on a wooden chair, smashing it to pieces. Violence isn't something I've ever been around. Darragh's anger has me rooted to the spot. "I see how you look at him. You have since we were small. You look at him like he's a fucking god." He's too close for comfort, and I step away from Darragh. He throws his head back and really laughs.

"Go on, sweetheart, run back to your prince. You have no idea who he is."

I want to shout at him to tell me, but speaking doesn't seem like the best idea. He's staring at me, and it's like someone snaps their fingers, and he's Darragh again.

"Jesus, Una, I'm sorry."

I'm shaking my head, trying to tell him it's fine.

"You're as white as a ghost. I've really fucking scared you." My heart is still pounding, but my muscles relax slightly as Darragh steps away from me and sits on the couch.

"It's obviously something you need to talk about," I say from the same spot.

Darragh is sitting down and pours white powder onto the small coffee table. He uses a card and cuts the cocaine up. "Nah, it is what it is."

Clearly not, I think, but I don't voice this as he rolls up a fifty and uses it to snort the powder up his nose. As he sits back, he inhales deeply before lying back into the couch.

"Want to go to a party?" He's up now, rubbing his nose. "Have some," he says, pointing at the two white lines that are still on the table.

"No, I'm fine," I tell him, and he shrugs before snorting up the other two lines. Watching him, I see how far he's gone. Does his family see how damaged he is?

"Your nose is bleeding, Darragh." My heart is heavy for him, but he grins and goes to the bathroom. While he's gone, I start to tidy up the smashed chair. He's going to get himself in trouble with that temper, or God forbid, hurt someone or himself.

"Do you want me to get Finn for you?" I know they're close, and I don't want to be around Darragh, but leaving him alone isn't a good idea either.

"He's off duty tonight. Don't worry, Una, you can go. You don't have to stay." He lights up a fag, and there's so much wrong with that sentence, but I wouldn't know where to start.

I don't move, and I can see the irritation in his shoulders. "What are you still doing here?" As he blows smoke into the air, he focuses on the floor to the left of my foot. *This is Darragh*, I tell myself. *I have nothing to fear. We all lose our cool now and again.*

"Where's the party?" I ask. He grins, and now, so do I.

"Let's party," he tells me, throwing the fag into the pool. We leave, and I don't allow myself to think. I get into his car with him.

***

I'm not sure how we make it safely, but we do. I'm still pumped from the speed the car was going and from the near misses. I'm not an adrenaline junkie, but the vodka and rush has me alive as Darragh and I get out of the car.

The party is a rave, and it's being held in an exhibition center in Navan. Its beat can be heard from where we parked, which is like the size of three soccer fields away. From the moment we step out of the vehicle, the party has started. There are people everywhere. Laughing, drinking, making out, getting sick, and even having sex. Yeah, there seem to be no boundaries.

"Darragh." Brian moves toward us, saying Darragh's name in a deep voice. They embrace, and when Brian notices me, he winks.

"Red. You came back for seconds," he says. He reeks of cologne and alcohol, but those blue eyes are a vortex.

"I didn't realize I had firsts, blondie," I tell him, and he grins, handing me a bottle of something. I take it, and it burns. Whiskey, I think. When I cough, the two girls behind him giggle. They both wear bikini tops and short denim skirts. I'm overdressed in jeans and a jumper, but I'm not here to get laid. Brian hasn't taken his eyes off me, and I start to question what exactly happened between us.

"What was the stuff you gave me the other night?" I ask, and he throws his arm around my neck as we walk toward the rave. I glance back to see Darragh with an arm around each girl.

"You want some more, red?"

I glare sideways at Brian and shrug his arm off me. He's hot and all, but something about him isn't right. "No, I'll pass. And stop calling me red," I tell him, and he laughs at me like I'm a little child having a cute tantrum.

"Find me later when you mellow out." He walks on into a crowd and greets some guy with a shaved head. I give his back the fingers.

"Come on, play nice." Darragh's beside me with a blonde under each arm. They smile in unison at me.

I give Darragh a fake smile. "This is me playing nice."

We get split up the moment we enter the rave. The heat has started a coat of sweat over my body. My skin is itchy and tight as I push through and make my way to the bar. Drink is slopped everywhere, and my top soaks up some from the counter.

"A large vodka," I roar at the barman. He has one of those really big ear piercings that must be painful.

"Mixer?" he shouts back, and I shake my head. He pushes a pint of pure vodka toward me, and I pay a twenty for it. I don't mind. I stand at the bar and drink the whole lot while holding my nose the whole time. When it's gone, I'm not yet out of it enough to join everyone around me as they move to the music.

Whatever pumps through their bodies has them in their own little world. I want to be in mine. The heat has the air hot, and I pull off my jumper. My pink bra blends in with all the multitude of colored bras that flash around me. Wrapping my jumper around my waist, I move through the crowd. Warm flesh pushes against mine, most of it wet with sweat, and there's something freeing about it. Closing my eyes, I let the beat take over, and the vodka fully enters my blood stream.

When I open my eyes, Brian is there, and I smile as he wraps his strong arms around me. His mouth goes to my neck, and I wrap my arms around it, pulling him closer.

"I was searching for you," he whispers in my ear, and my smile widens.

"Yeah?" My word slurs, dragging out at the end. I try to make myself more alert, but I'm cocooned in heat and bodies, and now Brian. I don't want the world to come back into focus.

When his tongue finds its way into my mouth, I don't stop him, not even when the sizzle of something on my tongue reminds me of the last time I kissed him. I swallow the tablet, and when Brian moves away, I allow the music and drugs to take me.

Lights burn my eyes, and I move away. "Get up, Una." Brian is there. Why does my face sting? Grass is under my hands. The music pounds behind me. I must be outside. Lights are still shining, burning me.

"Knock off the headlights." Brian is shouting, and the light vanishes.

My body bounces up and down. "Put her top on." I'm sure that's Darragh's voice. The vehicle moves under me. I can smell smoke. Trying to sit up has me falling over, and someone laughs. I join in their laughter.

The car stops, and a door slams. "Hurry the fuck up." It's Darragh's voice again.

"Brian, put her top on. How many more times do I have to fucking say it?" I'm dragged roughly off the floor of the car, and my stomach hurls.

"Open the door quick." I'm pushed out onto gravel as my stomach empties all over my hands.

"I'm so fucking dead." I'm not sure who's speaking. Darkness moves in along the edges of my vision.

CHAPTER EIGHT

SHANE

I T'S ONE IN THE morning when I leave Dad and Liam. I've informed them of everything I found out about the new supplier. Dad wants me to take a step back from it until we find out exactly who this person is. Anyone crossing over the border isn't someone we want to get tangled up in.

I understand what he's saying, but to me, this is a different time. We should attack first, not sit back and wait to be attacked. This is our turf, and I'm not letting it go. I don't care about the cost.

But we have more problems. It seems to be coming from all sides. Liam met with all the brothels in the area, and there's a huge demand for virgins, which we can't seem to meet. It isn't my problem, and I'm pretty confident that Liam is capable of handling it.

I find myself outside Una's door again, and a part of me knows I should stop this. I hurt her so much today, and maybe that's all I will ever do to her. I rest my head against her door as I try to talk myself into going to bed. She's asleep, and if I keep sneaking into her room, I'll get caught.

No matter the thoughts that go through my head, I find myself opening the bedroom door. I'm not sure how I feel when I see her bed made. She isn't here. Maybe she returned to reading her book. I need to give her some space. I return to my own room and climb into bed.

I wake up and check my phone. It's four in the morning. I'll kill Darragh. I climb out of bed and peer out the window. My room overlooks the courtyard. I see Darragh's car parked out back. Another one has arrived, the noise and rattles of a hole in the exhaust bangs away until they park. The people in the car climb out, and I get back into bed. Once they are all in the pool house, the noise disappears.

I'm out of bed again as my stomach tightens, and I find myself at Una's door, pushing it open. I curse. Her bed is empty. I return to my room and get on a T-shirt, jeans, and this time, I put on shoes and socks and make my way to the pool house. The closer I get, the clearer the noise of music and laughter is.

I open the door and am surprised to see Brian here with Darragh. Both of them cheer when they see me, like they've been awaiting my arrival. My eyes skim the two half-naked girls as I search for Una. Fear tightens like a fist in my stomach.

"Where is she?" I'm in front of Darragh, and it's taking everything not to kill him.

"Shane?" The bathroom door has opened, and Una is standing in the doorway. She tilts her head and furrows her brows in complete confusion at seeing me. My heart pounds in my chest as I take her in.

"I told you to put her top back on."

My head snaps to Darragh, and with narrowed eyes, I give him his last warning. If I don't leave now, I will kill him.

Everyone is silent.

"Put your clothes on," I tell Una quietly and stop staring at her chest. It takes a lot of my willpower. Her eyes are dilating rapidly; whatever she took is still in her system. I'm not sure if she heard me. Her mouth moves like she's trying to form a word, and I cross the room and pick her up. She gives a little squeal as I carry her out of the pool house. The air is cold on her bare skin, which I'm trying not to stare at.

But Una is lying back in my arms, her head thrown back, a smile on her face. But I don't feel like smiling. I don't know what's happening to her. She never used to be like this. She was outgoing, wild in a way, but not going out and doing drugs. I won't allow myself to think about why she is half-dressed. I can't.

"Brian." I tighten my grip on her as she calls his name, and instead of thinking about her calling another man, I keep moving forward. My sole focus is on each step I take as I climb the stairs.

Una stirs, pulling herself closer to my chest as she tightens her arms around my neck. I wish I could take the steps two at a time. Her breath on my neck and the soft flesh against any available skin I have on display is driving me mad. I make it to the landing when she speaks again after inhaling deeply.

"Shane." My pulse speeds up as she says my name, and I shush her. Her chest vibrates with laughter. "Still telling me what to do."

She leans out so she can stare at me, and I'm surprised at how alert she is. Small marks are on her cheek, like she was scraped. I want to run my fingers along the area and remove the marks from her skin. I'm close to my room, and I carry her into it.

"You won't listen, Una," I say back, and she smiles at me, her eyes staring at my lips.

"You're gorgeous, Shane."

I stop walking and stare at her. For a moment, she's sober and knows what she is saying, and that's how she really sees me. But reality kicks in, and I snap my gaze away from her smiling face and carry her into my bathroom. She has her own in her room, but I haven't a clue where anything is.

I slowly lower her down onto the closed toilet, and she becomes intrigued with her surroundings. "Will you stay here for a second?" I ask her, and her eyes rest on me. She nods but doesn't speak. I quickly grab a T-shirt, and she is still sitting on the toilet when I come back in. She doesn't object as I carefully put it on her.

Her eyes never leave my face. No one can make me as unsettled as Una does. A smile grows on her face, and she reaches out and embraces my face. I'm frozen.

"I've crushed on you for so long." The confession is said with a small laugh, and I want to hear this, but the drugs are making her talk crazy.

"Let me check your face," I say to her, leaning away from her hand so I can get some disinfectant wipes. She doesn't move. Her eyes flutter closed as I return.

I dab the area, and her eyes shoot open. "I'm sorry," I tell her as she bites her lip.

"You were untouchable to me. So out of my league." Once again, I focus on cleaning her face. She's distracting, and it's taking all my willpower not to listen to her words. She laughs softly again, and when I flicker my gaze to hers, her eyes are glistening.

"You'll just keep hurting me, and I'll keep letting you." I don't have a clue what she's talking about, but her eyes are filling up, and I'm not sure what to do.

"You need to wash your arms, Una," I tell her, and she nods. She seems more together, and I leave the bathroom and sit on my bed. I don't leave the bedroom in case she needs me.

Taking out my phone, I ring Finn. It's close to five in the morning, but he answers. "You need to get home and sort Darragh out," I tell him, expecting him to do as I say. What I don't expect is for Finn to say no. Now isn't the time for him to grow a pair of balls.

"How would you like for me to reunite Siobhan with her aunt?" I stand. I don't need his back talk. "I don't care about her. I'll make it so fucking slow. Now get your ass over here and sort Darragh out, and I want Brian off my property too." I hang up and sit back down. I need to calm down before I go down and sort it out myself.

The bathroom door opens, and my head snaps up. Una is standing there, one arm behind the door. She looks so good in my green T-shirt. That's all she's wearing. I swallow as my eyes drink in the sight of her. She's in my room—how many times have I fantasized about her? She takes a step toward me, and I grip the blanket under my hands. She isn't thinking straight, but I can't find the words to stop her as she advances toward me.

She reaches me, and I settle my hands on her hips, stopping her from moving any closer. "Una, you don't want to do this," I tell her quietly. Her skin burns under my hands, and I'm losing the ability to stop this as she easily moves forward. I release her as she straddles me. I keep my eyes closed at the contact and breathe her in.

"Una." I say her name as I grip the quilts. This is wrong, but her body this close to mine feels so right. When her hands grip my shoulders, I allow my eyes to reach hers.

"I want this, Shane," she tells me.

My heart pounds, and I release the quilt and flip her around until she's under me. Her eyes are wide, her chest moving quickly, and I'm waiting for her to say no. I'm searching her face for a sign that I need to stop this, but she reaches up and caresses my face, her body pushing against mine. I can't stop the moan that escapes my lips.

Her hands direct my face closer to hers. I can't stop staring at her. I can't stop this. I'm falling too deep, and I don't think I can climb back out. Her breath brushes against my lips, and everything in my body jerks. She will undo me, and I want her to, but not like this. When my forehead touches hers, I try to calm my pounding heart.

"Una," I say her name, and it's what gives me the strength to pull back. I remove her hands from my face, and already, I can see the damage my actions are causing. I'm shaking my head, searching for the right words.

Her eyes grow wider, her nostrils flare, and she's wriggling under me. "Let me up." Her voice is rising, and I don't release her. She's too angry, and when she's angry, she seems to do stupid things.

"Let me up, Shane. I'm going back to the party. Brian will give me what I want."

I push her hands above her head, my anger at her words barely containable. The air is sucked out of the room. I'm searching her face, but she's grinning at me like this is one big fucking joke.

"What do you want?" I shout, and her grin slips, but I can't figure her out. She wriggles, and I push my body harder against hers.

"You will answer me," I demand, and her eyes flare to life. I know I've pushed too hard; now she'll push back.

"Not this," she tells me, and I'm off her in a second, imagining what she must think of me.

"I'm sorry," I tell her. I want to pull down my T-shirt so it covers her legs, but I don't dare move as she sits up on my bed.

She wraps her arms around her waist as if she has a pain in her stomach, and I take a step closer to her. Her head whips up at my movement, and she raises a hand.

"I'm going to bed. Don't you dare follow me." She rises, holds her head high, and walks out of my room. I count to ten before I follow her. I check to make sure she does go into her bedroom. She slams the door. She has some temper. I don't know what to do. I can't stand in the hall all day and night and guard her. It's been a long time since I felt this close to snapping. I leave my room and make my way to the gym, which is located in the basement. I need some sort of release, and violence will have to do.

CHAPTER NINE

UNA

I WAKE WITH A sore head. My cheek stings as I brush it off the pillow while turning. As I slowly sit up, I try to remember how I got to bed last night. My clothes send alarm bells ringing in my head. It's not that they're nonexistent. Instead, I'm in a man's T-shirt. I quickly snap my gaze to the left side of the bed, but no one is there. While hanging out over the bed, I scan the floor for anything to suggest what happened last night, but there are no clues.

Dancing at a rave—I remember that. Brian. I groan as I slowly begin to remember the rave and the car drive home. It's all foggy like a dream, but I know it happened. A squeal leaves me as I start to also remember Shane. "Nooooo," I cover my mouth, trying to push last night's words back down my throat.

The burn of humiliation has me burying my head in my quilt. "Noooo," I growl into the quilt. I told him that I liked him. I said he was a god. I tried to seduce him. Right now, I want my brain to short-circuit. He turned me down. Oh, God. This is humiliating. I can never face him again. I try to calm myself by taking deep breaths.

It's okay. He'll avoid me like the plague. He won't want to be around a desperado. Oh, God. I told him I wanted to sleep with him. I bury my head deeper in my blanket. The burn on my face isn't lessening. It's spreading to my whole body. I want to die. I think dying from humiliation is possible.

"Good morning."

I freeze, holding my breath, and I hope I'm still remembering. I'm praying that Shane isn't the one saying good morning to me. I can't cope. I slowly raise my head and yelp when I my gaze lands on him, standing in my bedroom. Shane is fresh and clean and gorgeous in tan trousers and a black fleece jumper. I'm on fire with embarrassment.

"Can't you knock?" I shout while pointing at my door. I want him to disappear. I can't deal with this.

"I did. Several times," he answers dryly. My hands grip the end of the T-shirt that I'm twisting in knots under the quilt. Then I remember it's Shane's top, and I release it quickly as a new burn erupts across my face, traveling all the way up to the tips of my ears.

"Fine, what do you want?" I want this to be quick. Like pulling off a bandage. I imagine an apology is in order for throwing myself at him. I hope not, but if it ends this torture, I'm willing to consider it.

"You have work in thirty minutes. You've been slacking off since you arrived here. So you either meet me in the kitchen in fifteen, or you can pack your belongings and go home."

I'm stunned momentarily. What the hell is his game? He can't kick me out. But then I see that he wants me to run home with my tail between my legs. He might not like me, but I swallow the humiliation that burns through me. I keep eye contact as I throw the covers back and am glad when his jaw clenches. A reaction.

"I'll be down in fifteen," I tell him as I stroll past him. I'm not sure how the hell my legs are carrying me as I go into my wardrobe. It's there I tell myself to breathe as I gather fresh clothes with trembling hands. When I return, Shane is gone, and I let out a shaky breath.

***

As I enter the kitchen, I'm repeating a mantra in my head that Shane isn't there. But everything is working against me. He's there on his phone. My attention snaps to Mary, who smiles at me, but it fades as her eyes roam my face. "What happened now, Una?"

Shane clears his throat, and I keep my back to him. "Me being drunk and stupid last night. I fell on the gravel."

Mary inspects me closer, and I want to tell her to leave it, but she's always been a mammy to us when we're here. Well, to some of us.

"You cleaned it out?" she asks. Shane clears his throat again, and I'm tempted to offer him a glass of water.

"Yes," is all I say before sitting down the furthest away from Shane as I can. I don't glance up to see if he's watching me, but I sense his eyes on me. His hands were gentle while cleaning my face last night. If I keep this up, I'll be permanently red. I remind myself that I am stronger than this. So he turned me down. I need to get over it already.

"Two fried eggs and one piece of bacon?" Mary asks once I'm seated.

"Yes, that's perfect. Thanks, Mary." She turns back to the pan, and I focus on the fixture and fittings of the kitchen.

It has every mod con a kitchen can have. An island that can seat six dominates the large space. A breakfast bar runs half the length of the kitchen, separating the cooking area from the dining area, where I'm sitting. I'm a bit overenthusiastic when Finn arrives in, but sitting in silence with Shane is painful.

"Good morning, Finn. I haven't seen much of you," I say, and he grabs a banana and starts peeling it as he makes his way over to the table and sits beside me.

"Yeah, I've been busy." Shane clears his throat again, and Finn and I are on the same page as we both ignore him.

"What happened to your face?" He takes a huge bite of the banana as he speaks.

"What happened your face?" I throw back. *Lord, it's a scratch.*

He holds his hands up. "Hungover, are we?"

"Sorry. Yeah, a bit. But don't tell anyone," I say with a grin, and he smirks. "Where's your other half?"

Now Finn isn't smiling. "In bed sleeping off the mother of all hangovers."

"Are you not going to greet me, brother?" Shane asks as Mary places my breakfast in front of me. Everyone's attention falls on Shane, and the tension in the room seems to grow. Mary shuffles back to the stove, and I start to eat. I'm not hungry, but I don't know what else to do.

"Why should I? You threatened Siobhan." Siobhan is Finn's new girlfriend, and from the sounds of it, their relationship is serious. But to hear that Shane threatened her has me raising an eyebrow at him. His jaw is clenched, and he flickers a glance at Finn and away from my questioning stare.

"Don't be so petty. It was a few words."

A vein is flickering like a heartbeat in Finn's neck. "No, it wasn't. You know what you said, and I'm not having it." Mary puts a fry in front of Finn, and he quickly thanks her.

"What are you going to do?" Shane is leaning forward, and there's something in his stance that tells me this is far more serious than it appears to be.

Finn has a death grip on his knife and fork. They appear as deadly weapons now. His nostrils flare as he stares down at Shane, and he looks like he wants to hurt him. But Shane's eyes are shining with violence. It's like he's excited at the idea of hurting Finn.

I want to defuse the situation, so I do the one thing I can think of. I knock my coffee over with a little more force than intended. I wanted to send the coffee pouring over the side, but the mug goes too, smashing into pieces on the floor. All eyes are on me.

"Sorry, my hand slipped," I say, getting up. Shane stares at me, and I'm not sure if he's mad or what he's thinking.

"I'll get it. Una, finish your breakfast." Mary is there with a cloth, but I start picking up pieces of the mug.

"Una, leave it alone before you cut yourself." Shane's words are barked at me, and I'm close to losing it with him.

I take the cloth off Mary. "Please, Mary, I'll clean it up." She gives me a nod before leaving me.

"Mary, clean it up." Shane stops her in her tracks, and I grind my teeth. He's controlling. I gather up the rest of the mug and stand.

"Mary, it's done. Seriously, it's fine." She's waiting for Shane's word, and he nods at her to go back to the kitchen. I'm shaking my head in disgust at him. I really want to throw the broken mug at him, but I can't. Michael picks that moment to enter the kitchen, and he smiles when he sees us all.

"Ah, I was wondering where everyone was." He stops me as I make my way to the bin and kisses the top of my head. When he sees the broken mug in my hand, he leans out. "Be careful not to cut yourself."

"That's what I said," Shane chimes in from the corner like I'm some fragile little flower.

"It's a mug. Not a sword." Michael doesn't appreciate my smart mouth, but lets me pass as he sits down.

I'm ready to return to the table and eat my breakfast when Shane stands up all cheery. "Are you ready to start work, Una?" he asks me like we're best pals. I narrow my focus at my breakfast, and Shane flashes a glance at his watch. "If you need more time?"

I wave his comment away. I'm hungry, but I'll be dammed if I ask for more time. "No. I'm good to go."

"I'm very proud of you." Michael's words cause a swell to rise in my chest and deflate, leaving a sense of tightness behind. My father always told me he was proud of me. Whether I made a daisy chain or passed exams, he was there raising me up. Swallowing the lump, I tighten my lips before nodding.

"Thanks," I tell him and quickly leave the warmth of the kitchen. My mother never told me she was proud of me. If I really think about it, I was always a disappointment. I never stuck to anything, and she hated it.

She enrolled me in Irish dancing, which lasted a week. Drama class lasted a day. Football ended up being the longest, lasting three months, but she pulled me from the team saying it was too boyish. I hated piano. The violin—someone shoot me. I tried many things but hated them all. The first time I fell in love with something was on my sixteenth birthday, when Shane bought me the horse. The happy memory dissolves as Shane walks ahead of me in wellies.

"What are you doing?" I try to catch up with him. Panic is making me stand in his path.

"I'm going to work?" He walks around me, and I'm standing there stumped but soon catch up with him. Working with Shane isn't a good idea. "I'm fine with Stephen, Shane. I seriusly don't need you babysitting me."

"You needed me last night." His smartass words have me storming ahead of him.

"No, I didn't. You needed me to need you last night. That's why you arrived like some avenging angel." I'm talking through my ass, but I haven't a clue what to do. When I look back at Shane, his jaw is clenched like I've really hit a nerve, and I think, *Good*.

I check the area but can't see Stephen. I start to call him but get no answer.

"I told him he could have the day off," Shane informs me. When I flicker a gaze at him, he's leaning against the wall, staring at me as I run around like a headless chicken.

"So, what, you're working with me today?"

Now he smirks, and it isn't a nice one. "No, you're working. I'm overseeing."

I could walk away, as this is just a game to him, but I have my pride, and I'm not afraid of work. I get my gloves on and start at the first stable. Wheeling up the barrow, I then leave it outside the stable as I shovel it out. Once I have that done, I fill it with fresh straw and remove any strands of loose straw from the drinking sink in the corner.

Shane does as he promises. He watches me—or oversees things, as he put it. I remove my jacket as I get to the fifth stall and start again.

"What is your job?" I ask him. May as well have someone to talk to. The farm brings in most of their income, but when I really think about it, I never see any of the boys working around the farm.

"The family business." Shane's answer captures my attention, and I stop working and rest on the shovel. I push hair out of my face. I tied it up earlier, but some curls have managed to burst free and find their way into my eyes.

"Which is what? The farm? I never see you do any work."

Shane stares at me. It's unsettling, but I hold my ground firmly. "We have other businesses," he answers, and I can see this will be like trying to get blood from a stone. I return to work.

"It isn't exactly above board," he adds. I narrow my eyes at Shane. His look of innocence causes a smile of surprise to spread rapidly across my face.

"An upstanding citizen like you, Shane? Never," I joke, and his lips tug up, sending my stomach erupting with butterflies. Butterflies that I want to crush under my wellies. They have no business being here anymore. That ship has sailed.

"I don't think you would approve, Una, if you knew." He lowers his lashes as he speaks, but his smile is gone, and I'm taking a step closer to him. Now I want to know.

"Maybe I will," I tell him seriously, and his lashes rise. He's studying me carefully, making an assessment to find out how serious I am.

"Let's just say it isn't legal."

His answer has me rolling my eyes. "That's just like saying it isn't above board. It means the same thing. So all of you work in the unsavory business section?" I say unsavory with air quotes, and Shane smiles at me.

"You could say that."

"I could say a lot of things," I mumble under my breath and return to work, but from his soft laugh, I know he heard me.

"We need to talk about last night."

That's the last thing I want to talk about. "No, we don't," I tell him. I glance up as the straw crunches behind me.

"We do," he says, way too close to me, and I need to save face.

I take a deep breath and turn around. My pulse spikes at his closeness. "I had too much drink on me. I have needs, and you where there." Heat rushes across my face, but I hold eye contact.

"That's all it was?" he questions, and I can hear the control in his words. I'm searching his face. My heart is ready to leave my chest.

"I don't know why you came down there and got me. I can't make sense of it." I turn the whole thing on him, hoping to deflect from my embarrassing behavior.

"You had no idea where you were. You were half-naked, Una. Hanging out with a bunch of lowlifes." He stuffs his hands into his fleece pockets roughly, like if he doesn't, he might strangle me.

"I'm sorry you don't approve of who I hang out with. But let me remind you that one of those lowlifes is your brother, and Brian is nice." Okay, that last part is a lie, but I can see it's winding him up.

"Brian is nice? He's a scumbag. You should be thanking me for coming down there and getting you."

I laugh with anger. "Or what, Shane? God forbid I enjoyed myself."

"With Brian? You were mumbling his name."

I want to wipe the smirk off his face. "I was mumbling lots of stupid things." I'm breathing heavy, and I don't want this conversation anymore. I go to leave, but Shane stands in my way. His hands are lost at his side. When I raise my lashes and gaze up at him, I can see he's working a muscle in his jaw. He's no longer smiling.

"Did you mean anything you said?" His brows are furrowed; there's something vulnerable in how he's looking at me. My heart kicks up a notch, and I'm confused.

I'm not sure if I want to hurt him or be honest. But being honest seems to lead to one road, and that's hurt. "I was just looking for some fun."

He lowers his lashes and gives a quick nod before he peers back up. His brown eyes appear almost black as he stares at me.

"It's lunchtime," he tells me, and I stare after him as he walks back toward the house. Something is sitting on my chest, and I can't breathe. Drops land on my cheek. I'm crying. I stay in the stall and cry. I'm not sure why, exactly. It isn't like he cares. *So why did he look so hurt?* But goddamn it, he hurt me.

CHAPTER TEN

UNA

I'M NOT A GIRL who cries over boys. This isn't me. But deep down, I know this is more than a crush. This has been years in the making. I didn't think it would end like this. Tears keep falling without my permission, and I wipe them away angrily. I leave the stables and make my way to the ones that the livestock are being held in. There, I find my horse. She's not as jumpy, and she lets me rub her straight away.

"Una."

I inwardly scream leave me alone, but it's Finn, and Finn is sweet. I pop my head out of the stall. "I'm here," I tell him with a smile.

His eyebrows dip. "Are you okay?"

Ah, shit. He can see I've been crying. "Yeah, I got some dung in my eye," I tell him with a wave of my hand. But the O'Reagans are always hands-on, and Finn is holding my face. He's taller than me—all the boys are—so he's looking into my eye.

"Don't blink," he tells me while stretching my eye slightly, and I can't stop blinking.

"I don't see anything," he says, but he still hasn't released me.

"Must be gone," I tell him, and he steps back.

I rub my eye to add to my story. "Yeah, it's a bit sore, but I think I'm good."

He smiles. "I thought, for a second, that Shane had upset you. He has a habit of upsetting people."

"I see that. He sure upset you," I say, closing the stall. "When am I going to get to meet Siobhan?" I add before looking at him. I don't want to talk about Shane and me. Our names being uttered in the same sentence does something funny to my heart.

"Soon, I hope. We'll organize something."

I smile genuinely. "I'd really like that."

"I've been sent out to get you for dinner."

"I'm not hungry."

Finn shrugs apologetically. "Dad's orders."

Well, I can't say no to Michael. When we arrive inside, I wash up before going to the main dining room where everyone is sitting. A seat is vacant between Shane and Liam, and the seat is pulled out for me already. I sit down with dread as I face Darragh, who winks at me. Michael nods in approval, and Mary starts to bring in steaming plates of dinner.

"How's your eye?" Finn asks, and I want to kick him for directing all attention on me.

"What happened?" Shane, the caveman, is sitting forward, looking ready to start a war.

"My eye is fine, Finn. Thanks so much for asking." He gives me an apologetic smile at my sarcastic tone.

"I leave you for ten minutes and something happens?" I turn to Shane, because I can't believe his attitude.

"Yes, you're right, Shane. Where would I be without my knight in shining armor? I suppose you would have deflected the lump of dung and stopped it from hitting my eye."

Darragh snorts, and Liam shifts beside me. I turn to him, and I swear Liam's eyebrow rises slightly, but I could be wrong. Shane, on the other hand, is angry. His face is tight, and he gives me a quick nod.

"There's no need for such hostility," Michael says, and I remember my manners and that I'm in someone else's home, and fighting with his son isn't nice. Michael isn't looking at me. He looks at everyone as he speaks. But his words are for me. I am being hostile.

"I'm sorry, Michael. I'm tired and cranky," I say against every fiber in my body, and Michael seems pleased. Mary has set a plate in front of everyone, and when I stare forward, Darragh is still smiling and mouths, "Woman things" to me. I give him a glare of pure disgust.

Michael says a short prayer to God over the food before we start eating. I'm starving, and the roast dinner is divine. I pour more gravy over my spuds, and when I glance up, Michael is smiling. "Nothing as nice as seeing a girl *really* eat."

I smile at him, not sure if that was really a compliment. I dig back in to my food when he returns to his. Shane's arm keeps brushing mine, and I flicker a quick glance at him. His face is serious, but his movements seem intentional.

"Your mother rang," Michael kicks off, and I freeze, my fork held in midair. My eyes shoot to Darragh, then to Finn as they glance at me and then at Michael. I put the fork in my mouth and chew the food that has turned to lead.

"She's worried about you," Michael continues. Now I'm questioning if that's what this dinner is about. And she isn't worried about me; she's worried about what the neighbors will think when I'm not around. Or what my work must be saying since I never arrived in. Or what college is saying. That's what she cares about, not me.

I pour more gravy over my food. "Anyone want some?" I offer. Darragh and Finn are shaking their heads, trying not to make eye contact with me. Like I might freak out any second.

I offer some to Liam, and he meets my eye. "Please. Just on the carrots." Odd, but okay. I pour until he tells me to stop. I don't want to turn to Shane and Michael, but I have to.

"Gravy?" I ask Shane, and his eyes have softened for the first time since he left me in the stables. I don't need his pity. He nods his head, and I pour nearly half the jug over Shane's food.

Michael is peering up at me, and I hate it. I don't offer him gravy. I hate that he brought her up. He was married to her. He divorced her because he knew how she was.

No one speaks to me again as I finish my dinner. But a nice flow of conversation takes over the table. It's about cars, but it's really soothing to hear the boys getting on. Even Liam chimes in, and I try not to stare at him when he laughs. It's not a huge laugh, but it's not a sound I've heard before.

Shane eats his dinner that's soaked in gravy. It must be stomach turning, but he never complains, and I start to shift in my seat at every forkful that enters his mouth. I'm angry because he turned me down, but he doesn't deserve my anger. I try to cheer up as the dessert arrives. It's pavlova and strawberries with cream, and this meal is looking like my favorite food. The lump in my throat is back.

"I bought a bike over the summer," I offer up, trying to join in the conversation.

"Like, with pedals?" Finn says, and I laugh at him. Darragh snorts too, and Shane shakes a little beside me.

"You are so funny. No, with an engine." The room grows serious. I don't need a lecture about safety.

"I have a helmet," I add, and laughter erupts around the table.

"I bet it's a moped," Darragh offers up, and he laughs harder.

"No, it's a scooter," Finn teases.

When I glance up at Michael, he's really smiling. I join the laughter. I love seeing him happy.

"Is it running?" The serious question comes from Liam, and I turn to him.

"No, I was saving up to restore it. But I will get it running," I tell him, and he gives me a nod of what looks like approval.

"What make is it?" Liam is being quite the conversationalist. I'm surprised.

Mary arrives in with teas and coffees, and I thank her before answering. "It's a Honda. Really sweet. It needs a few parts and a bit of a paint job, but then it should be good to go."

"Shane's really good with engines." Darragh gives up this information, and when I glance at Shane from under my lashes, my stomach tightens.

"If you want, I can check it out," he says. My pulse spikes at how he's looking at me.

"Yeah. That would be great," I tell him. This could be a peace offering on both ends.

"I might get a bike too," Darragh says. "We can ride together."

"You'd be dead in a day," Finn tells him. "How many cars have you gone through?"

"A few." Darragh shrugs like it's no big deal.

"Try six. I know because I pay for them." Michael's words have my mouth dropping open.

"Six! You are so spoiled."

"You bought Finn a house. No one's shouting about that," Darragh fires back.

There's an odd silence around the table, but my mind is finding this conversation crazy. He bought Finn a house. What dad does that?

"I bought you one, too," Michael says before taking a forkful of dessert.

I follow suit, taking a bite of my dessert. Darragh's face turns slightly red. Now I question why they live here, if they both have houses. And if they do, there's no doubt that Liam and Shane have their own homes too. But this house is enchanting. I would live here, too.

"You are all spoiled," I say, then shovel a forkful of the most delicious pavlova into my mouth.

"I'm glad someone said it." I grin at Michael, and we finish our desserts. I don't want to leave. Michael chats about his first car, and I love listening to old times. Liam excuses himself and then Finn. Darragh isn't far after, leaving me with Shane and Michael.

"Do you still have the car?" I ask, wanting to see it. It sounds like something from the movies.

"I do. I'll show it to you some day."

I'm smiling. I have a love for old things. I don't know why exactly, but I do.

Shane hasn't said much beside me, and I glance at him to find him watching me with a soft smile on his handsome face. "I wasn't aware you had a love for old cars."

"Yeah, I've always loved Cadillacs and Pontiacs—cars like that."

"You're so like your mother." The softness in Michael's voice surprises me, but I don't like the comparison. I also don't want to spoil the evening.

"She likes cars?" I ask, and Michael laughs.

"No, she wouldn't be able to tell one car from the other. But you have her passion for life. When she talks about something she loves, she lights up, and so do you."

The compliment has me blushing.

"She's a good woman," he adds.

I can now see where this is going. "Is that why you divorced? Because she's such a good woman?" I can't help the scratchy tone to my voice.

Michael lowers his spoon, and already, I want to apologize. "No, your mother and I weren't compatible. That doesn't make her a bad woman, Una." Michael dabs his face with a cloth napkin before excusing himself.

"Sometimes I don't know what's wrong with me," I say to the almost-empty table. I'm waiting for Shane to leave, but he doesn't.

"I think you're hurting."

I glance at him sideways, and he's staring me. "I think so, too." I whisper the truth, and a lump forms in my throat.

"Do you want to talk about it?" There's a gentleness in his tone that nearly undoes me.

"No. Yes." I laugh. "I'm not sure."

CHAPTER ELEVEN

SHANE

I WAIT, NOT SPEAKING, allowing her to make up her own mind. I want her to tell me. I want to know every part of Una, but I won't rush her. She's staring down at her coffee cup, and I take in the beauty of her face. Her lashes lift, and I'm looking into her eyes. My stomach squeezes.

"My looks come from my dad," she says with a sadness tugging at her voice and eyes. She pulls a curl and lets it bounce back. I'm picturing a male version of Una, and I try to imagine her with him. "He got it, you know. He got how it felt to look different." She angles her hand at her eyes.

"He must have been very handsome," I say, and she smiles sweetly. Her head dips, and she rests her face on her hand. She smiles. "I think he was," she tells me. The sadness is still there, but she's smiling.

She glances away and licks her lips, and her brows pull down. She's so close to crying. "I miss him," she tells the floral wallpaper. I want to reach for her, comfort her, but I wait until she looks at me again.

"What happened?" I asked. I know her dad died when she was young, but I never knew how.

"It was a freak accident. A tree fell, blocking the road. My dad being my dad, tried to clear it." One free tear falls, but she doesn't stop talking as it drops off her chin and onto the table. "Another fell and killed him."

"I'm sorry." I whisper the words, knowing they are meaningless, but she takes my hand in hers.

"It was a long time ago, and I know you lost too. With your mum." I'm nodding, but all the blood has rushed to my hand where she touches me, and I allow myself to touch her back. I rotate my hand until our fingers line up, and I entwine them. Una sits back, slightly startled, but she doesn't pull away.

"Yeah, that should have never happened," I tell our entwined fingers. My mother was far too young to die.

"Did they ever find out who it was?"

I glance up at Una, my focus on her lush lips. She licks them, and my attention is taken with her pink tongue. When it disappears back into her mouth, I speak.

"No, but we will." I stare at her. "I will," I add. My mother was murdered in a drive-by shooting. She was in the wrong place at the wrong time. But even so, I still want to find whoever did it and kill them myself.

Una's focus is on our hands, and when I glance down, I find myself smiling. "My mother bought me that ring," I tell her. "She said that when she saw it, she thought it was very Shane." My smile widens as I gaze up to see Una smiling at me. "I've never taken it off. I never will."

Una's head lowers, and my body stills as her lips graze the band on my thumb. Her lips make contact my flesh, and I wait for her to sit back up. "I wish I had met her," she says, but my mind is reeling from the kiss to my thumb.

"She would have loved you." I'm searching her face, knowing I speak the truth.

"Sorry, I was just..." Darragh's voice breaks through my thoughts. "I thought you were on your own." He's entered the room, but he pauses and goes to leave and then turns back around.

I release Una's hand, and she stands quickly like we've been caught doing something wrong.

"I better get back to work," she says, not meeting my eye. She squeezes Darragh's shoulder as she leaves. It's a simple touch, but I don't like her touching anyone else.

"You have my attention," I tell Darragh. He hesitates at the door. "You're wasting my time, Darragh. Come in." Even looking at him makes me want to hurt him.

"It's okay," he tells me, turning back toward the door.

"Close the door and sit down." I push the mug and plate away from me as Darragh closes the door. I don't need any temptations. I even move my chair away from the table and pull up one of my legs onto the other to create some kind of barrier.

"I'm having a—"

I cut him off as he goes to sit on Una's chair. "Don't sit there."

"Where would you like me to sit?" He shakes his head as he speaks, and I point at the chair opposite me. He sits down with a huff.

"You kill people, and you don't seem to care," he says, anger lacing every word.

"Is that a question?" I ask. I'm not sure what he's doing here.

"No." He grits his teeth and shifts on the chair. "I can't sleep."

I release my leg. I'm done with this conversation. "Go to a doctor."

"I can't sleep because I keep seeing her face." He swallows, and his brows pull down.

"Whose face? What have you done?" I sit forward, questioning what kind of mess I have to clean up now.

"Siobhan's aunt. I keep seeing her face. It doesn't seem to matter how much drink I consume. She's still there. Her head is all smashed in. Blood bubbles from her mouth."

The sad part is, I understand how he feels. I have to live with the nine lives I took or helped take. At night, they come for me. Darragh rubs his neck. It's now that I notice the strain on his face, the bloodshot eyes from lack of sleep. He's thinner than before.

"You need to find your peace with her."

His head snaps up. "How?" The way he asks is like I have some secret ingredient that will make all this go away. But it's not that simple. I think about what I do to survive. If it becomes a question of me or them, it's an easy one to pick.

"Think about why you killed her. You need to remind yourself that she attacked." I wanted to say it was a life-or-death situation, but with Darragh, I didn't think it was. I was pretty sure he lost control.

"She didn't attack me." The confession pours from him quickly. "I wanted to know how it felt. I wanted to be like you and Liam. I wanted..."

I stand up, closing my eyes and cutting him off. I can't believe what I'm hearing. "You wanted to know how taking someone's life felt?" Oh, God. This was much worse than I could have imagined. I always knew it hadn't been self-defense, and that was disturbing enough. But to think he did it so he knew how it felt...

"Yes, and I wanted to be accepted by Dad." He's shouting, and I can't stop the laughter that bubbles from my mouth.

"How did it feel, baby brother? Did you enjoy taking her life?" I ask when the laughter dies down.

"Fuck off," he tells me, getting up to leave.

"You're a coward. I'm ashamed to call you my brother." My words have him pausing, but he rips the door open and storms from the room. I should stay and let him go, but I can't.

"You couldn't even finish her, Darragh," I shout. He pauses, the rise and fall of his shoulders noticeable. "Once again, me and Liam had to clean up your mess. You couldn't even kill an old woman." I was jagging him. I wanted him to face what he had done. He turns with clenched fists.

"Shut up. I'm glad I'm not a killer like you. How many lives have you taken?" He starts walking back to me, screaming at me. "Who tattoos themselves every time they take a life?" He's reached me, and we're toe to toe. "You wear your kills like a fucking badge."

"Darragh." It's Liam. Darragh deflates straight away. He doesn't step away from me, and he's huffing and puffing.

"Darragh. Leave." Liam's raised voice has Darragh stepping away and racing down the hall. Liam takes a few steps toward me. "What has he done?"

"He killed that woman just to kill her." Even as I speak, I'm struggling to accept that he really did it. Taking a life comes down to a final decision—it's either you or them. That's how I always say it. There are no half measures, and in our line of business, people die. But each one has a reason. To have none... I can't imagine it.

"You have to leave this alone, Shane." I snap my gaze up to Liam, and I don't expect him to start shouting, but his easy words have me shaking my head.

"What do you do when he kills someone else, and then the bodies are stacking up?"

"He won't." Liam sounds sure.

"He killed, Liam, just to know how it felt." When Liam looks at me, there's something in him that I don't recognize, and now I ponder if that's what he and Darragh have in common. Does Liam recognize the darkness in Darragh that I see in Liam? I could never tell what it is, but what if it's this?

"Have you ever killed for no reason?" I ask, not backing away from this. I need to know who I'm sleeping under the same roof with.

"No. But I've been curious."

"I've been curious when I heard older men talk about it. I wondered what it would be like. I didn't go out and actually do it. I'm curious about a lot of things, Liam. It doesn't mean I act on them." I can't believe he would try to dismiss this.

"It's our fault that he's like this."

"I feel like you've put two and two together and got fifty," I tell Liam, not accepting what I'm hearing.

"We've always pushed him away, and this is our price." I glance down the hall that Darragh disappeared down.

"We treat Finn worse, and he hasn't killed anyone for the fun of it."

"We don't know that." Liam blinks as Mary makes her way down the hall.

"Leave it with me. Let me deal with it," he asks as we stand shoulder to shoulder, facing each other. I always place my trust in Liam, but I'm not sure I can let this one lie. I nod at Liam, and he nods back before leaving.

I go outside and the smell of fresh air is nice. I still can't shake off what Darragh has done. Flaming red hair comes into view. I need to check on Una. I hate it more now that she hung out with Darragh. What if he gets an impulse again, only this time it's Una he hurts? Something sits on my chest, and I breathe in through my nose and out through my mouth.

"Hi." Una is waving at me while she leans on a pitchfork, and her voice settles me, the weight lifting off my chest.

"Hi," I say and walk toward her while stuffing my hands into my pockets. It gets them out of the cold, but it's also something to do as Una smirks while she studies me.

"Just wanted to check on you," I say when I reach her, and her smirk turns into a full smile.

"Make sure I'm doing my work?" she teases.

"No. I wanted to make sure you were okay after our conversation."

Her smile slips, but her eyes still hold it. "That's really sweet of you."

I give a short laugh. "Sweet? I don't think anyone has ever called me sweet before."

Una is trying to suppress a smile, but she fails. We're smiling at each other when my phone rings.

"Just give me a second," I say as I pull it out of my pocket and see Neill's name on the screen.

"Go ahead," I tell him as I take a few steps away from Una, not wanting her to hear the conversation.

"At a fight last night, one of the guys dropped dead. I knew he was off his head, but I thought it was cocaine or something. It's that new stuff from Bernard, and I managed to get some for you," Neill says proudly, and he should be.

"I'll be around soon to pick it up," I tell him before hanging up. Una is still observing me and wears a smile on her face. "My mind is still reeling with you calling me sweet," I say because I want her to continue to smile.

This time she laughs. "I regret saying it already. I think your ego is big enough, Shane."

"*Tá tú go hálainn*," I say in Irish. I'm too much of a chicken to say it in English. But I realize my mistake when Una turns red and repeats my words to me in English.

"You think I'm beautiful?" Why does she sound like she doesn't believe me?

"Now I think our egos are the same," I tell her and something crosses her face.

She doesn't focus on me as she speaks. "You said that for my ego."

I can hear the hurt in her words, and I question why everything I say comes across as an insult. I take a step toward her, and she tilts her head up. Her eyes shift left and then to the right. I keep my focus on Una. "I said that because I do think you are very beautiful."

She smiles but covers her mouth with a gloved hand. My heart pounds as I remove the shovel from her hands and place it against the wall. Una's hands fall to her side, but I take up the right one and remove her work glove. I raise her hand to my mouth. Her eyes are wide, and her mouth has formed a small *o* as I place a kiss to the inside of her wrist.

Her pulse beats quickly against my lips, and it satisfies me that I've evoked that emotion in her. I want to linger longer; kissing her flesh is sending waves through my body. But I tell myself not yet. I stand up straight and put her glove back on. She's still focused on me with pure awe on her face, and I want to kiss her lips. I find myself leaning in, and she swallows hard before wetting her lips.

A horse neighs a few stalls down, and Una clears her throat.

"I have to go. I might see you later," I tell her, and she nods. She doesn't smile but watches me leave. I glance back at her, and she's still staring at me, and now I smile.

***

I wish I didn't have to go. I ring Neill back as I make my way to my car. He answers on the second ring.

"I need a job done. Are you up for it?" I smile when he repeatedly says yes. I remember now why I like him. "I need that stuff sent up to Dublin. I've a friend, Rachel, who works in the Dublin lab. She'll expect you in one hour. Can you do that?"

"Yeah, of course, man. No problem. Consider it done." Neill's answer is quick, but I won't consider anything done until it's done.

"I'll text you the address," I tell him and hang up. I need to see what's in this new drug and if we can replicate it—hopefully cheaper than what Bernard is selling it for.

Once I text him, I get into my car and visit some old friends to see if they've heard anything about Bernard or Connor. But all avenues turn out to be dead ends. No one seems to know anything. To me, that's worse than someone knowing something. They're being careful, and careful people are dangerous people in my eyes. It means they have something to hide.

***

I return home to a dark house. It's two in the morning when I get inside and make my way to Una's room. She's asleep, and I can't stop the smile when I see she's wearing my T-shirt. I don't stay long tonight. Instead, I go to my room and take a quick shower before getting into bed.

I get up around nine and get dressed. Pushing open Una's door, I'm surprised to see her bed made and her window open. Mary comes out of the bathroom, and surprise lights up her face.

"Shane." She says my name like she expects an explanation.

"Mary," I say back, and she quickly looks away.

"Are you looking for Una?" Her question is said as she polishes the windowsills.

"Why, is this Una's room?"

She narrows her eyes at me over her shoulder. "Yes."

"Since you're keeping records of Una's whereabouts, where is she?" I can see the further annoyance in her eyes, but she shields them, letting her lids close. When she opens her eyes again, she's better composed.

"She's at work, Master Shane."

I'm done talking to her; I leave and make my way downstairs. The smell of freshly baked scones in the kitchen makes me pause, but I don't linger. Instead, I grab my wellies and jacket and go in search of Una.

I don't have to search very hard. She's in the yard with Stephen. I dare him to look at me funny. Today, he decides to ignore me, and that suits me fine.

"I got quite the shock when your room was empty this morning," I tell her, and she looks up from brushing one of the horses. It's cold this morning, and the tip of her nose is red. Our breaths come out in small white puffs, but Una is alive. The outdoors really suits her.

"You know, I'm thinking of getting a lock put on my door," she tells me, but her words are soft.

I lean across the stall door. "Why? You already have a perfectly working lock on your door," I tell her.

"Yeah, but it's funny there isn't a key? I can't find it anywhere." That's because I took it. But I don't tell her that.

"That is funny," I say, and she smirks.

"So why are you looking for me this morning?" She rubs the horse while she speaks. I'm not even sure she knows what she's doing.

"I was thinking after dinner, we could take a look at that bike of yours?"

She stops rubbing the horse. "Yeah. Yeah, that would be great." She's smiling, and I love that I put it on her face.

"It's a date," I say, and a laugh falls from her lips as she quirks an eyebrow.

"A date?" she questions.

"You know what I mean. I'll mark it in my diary," I tell her with a serious tone.

"Nope, that's not what you said. You said a date." She's unsure if I'm joking or not. "Oh…" she says suddenly. She lets out a heavy breath. "I'd need you to help me get it."

She sounds miserable, and I'm not sure why. "It's at my parents' house," she volunteers, and now I get it.

"I'll be there with you." I hope my words comfort her as she focuses on the horse and then the ground before looking back at me. She's chewing her lip. I don't push and wait for her answer.

CHAPTER TWELVE

UNA

I AGREED TO LET Shane come with me. I've braided my hair to the side. My eyes rise in the mirror, and I hate what I see. Pulling out the restricting neckline of the black polo jumper doesn't help. I appear professional—presentable, as my mother would put it.

I'm wearing black trousers and a pair of small-heeled boots. I'm ready to walk into an office. After grabbing my long black coat, I go downstairs to find Shane in the kitchen. The moment I enter, he raises both eyebrows.

"You look…" he starts, but I roll my eyes.

"Stuck up? Stiff?" I could think of a few more names.

"Older," Shane offers.

"Oh," I say as he stands up and stuffs his phone into his pocket. After getting into his car, I put on my seat belt and open the glove compartment to have a look. Shane glances at me but doesn't say anything. Instead, he backs out of the garage as I continue to have a nosy.

He has chewing gum, tissues, and a pack of wipes in his glove compartment. The middle pocket holds two phones. I glance at him, and he's focused on driving out into the courtyard. There's nothing really in his car, but it's only a few months old.

I wait as he gets out and has Stephen help him attach an Ivor Williams trailer to the back of the Audi. Placing my hand on my leg, I stop it from jumping. When Shane gets back in, I don't look at him but stare out the window.

"You should know you're not walking into a friendly environment," I quickly tell him, already thinking of how wrong this could go. Shane shifts gears.

"I'm used to hostile environments."

I know he is, but still. "My mother can have a wicked tongue." I look at him.

He glances at me with a smirk. "I remember."

I laugh at that. Of course he remembers. How could he forget my mother? "I don't know why she disliked you so much," I say more to myself.

"Most women dislike me." He sounds sure.

"I don't," I say honestly. His gaze flickers to mine, and I hold his stare until he looks back at the road.

"I knew you fancied me," he says, and I laugh—like proper laugh—and it's nice.

"You don't fancy me?" he questions while trying to appear wounded, but he isn't, and I know this is my chance.

"I told you before that I did."

His eyes dart from the road to me. "I wasn't sure if that was the drink."

"It was all me," I tell him. My heart is pounding.

He nods his head. "That's good to know," he says, and I smile at the window.

My smile is short lived as we arrive at my house. My mother's red car is parked in the driveway, and all my hopes of her not being home are dashed. Shane hasn't even turned off the engine when she's out the door, and I can see in her eyes that she's livid.

My mother is still attractive in her late fifties. High cheekbones and full lips are still her best features. Her hazel eyes also show her emotions easily, and I know I'm in a lot of trouble.

"Stay in the car," I quickly tell Shane as I jump out. My mother stares at Shane before her head snaps to me.

"How could you? Do you know how worried I was?" She folds her arms over her white shirt.

"I needed to get away," I tell her. My voice is small.

Her hands rise in the air, and she shakes her head while jutting out her chin. "Una does what Una wants, be damned everyone else."

"No. I'm just sick of doing what everyone wants," I say.

My mother glares at Shane again before turning back to me. "Get in the house." She's pointing at the front door, then she folds her arms again, and I deflate. Sadness has me stepping closer to her. I don't want to fight, but I want her to see me as I am. I want my mother to see *me,* not an extension of her.

"I'm not staying," I whisper with a pleading in my voice that she ignores. She moves around me and is banging on Shane's window.

He's staring at her. Her banging isn't necessary.

"Mum, what are you doing?" I'm beside her.

"Get in the house, Una," she says again as Shane rolls down the window.

"I don't know what she told you, but you can go on home. My daughter is staying here with me."

My cheeks and neck burn, and anger replaces my sadness as Shane addresses my mother in a tight tone.

"It's up to Una what she wants to do, Niamh. She's a woman now." My mother moves back from the window like he slapped her. Her eyes widen with some realization, and she lets out a bitter laugh.

"A woman? Is that what you have been filling my daughter's head with?"

I am a woman, but I can read between the lines and understand what my mother is implying. Mortified takes on a whole new meaning for me. Before either Shane or me can respond, my mother swings around toward me.

"I pray that you haven't been near Liam. Tell me you haven't." Why does she look stricken?

"Mum, what are you talking about? God, you sound crazy." My anger snaps, and Mum takes a step back.

"I can't stop you, Una. But that family isn't right." She's pointing at Shane, but he doesn't as much as flinch.

"They're good to me," I tell her, pleading again and not wanting us to part on such bad terms. "You belonged to it once. You raised me with them. I don't understand," I tell her, and I have no understanding why my words deflate her.

"You've come to get your stuff." She sounds resigned to that fact, but when I tell her I'm here for my bike, hope blossoms in her eyes.

"I need some space," I tell her, but she shakes her head in disgust.

Folding her arms again, she shrugs. "I'm here when you come to your senses." She doesn't look at me as she walks back into the house.

***

I undo my hair, letting the curls free; they bounce around my face and shoulders like they rejoice in their freedom. Shane loaded my bike onto the trailer. I'm not sure where we're going, and honestly, I don't care. My mother's coldness is cutting me deeper than I expected.

I glance at Shane, but he grips the steering wheel, his face tight. Yeah, he's pissed. Maybe even at me for having him sit there as my mother scolded him like he's a child. I want to apologize, but I don't. I sit back and stare out the window at all the passing trees.

When Shane pulls up at the biggest store in Monalty, I'm tempted to tell him to leave it, but he has taken time out of his day to help me. I unbuckle my belt.

Shane's hand covers mine, stilling me, and I gaze up at him. "Are you okay?"

I'm looking into soft brown eyes. Flecks of gold seem to move, and I swallow. Am I okay? I'm not sure. "I will be."

I'm still staring into his eyes, and my body moves closer toward his. The heat of his hand on mine is sending warmth up my arm.

It's Shane who breaks away, his eyes snapping forward.

"You better get started," he says, trying to sound happy, but the strain in his voice is the opposite of happy. I'm still looking at him, confused at his change again. I'm beginning to think that Shane O'Reagan has lost his mind for a minute or is playing games with me.

Either way, it won't end well for me. I climb out and close the door with more force than necessary. I don't turn to check if he follows. Instead, I walk right into the store. The bell behind me rings, and I know Shane is in. He's beside me in a second.

"You want to tell me what's wrong?" he whispers close to my ear, his shoulder brushing mine.

I'm not doing this here. "Why would anything be wrong?" I ask him sweetly.

"Can I help you with anything?" A tall man—he must be over seven feet tall—approaches us. His voice is droll, and his name tag reads John.

"Yes," I say the same time Shane barks, "No." John departs like a sensible human being, but I'm pissed that he listened to Shane and not me.

"There is clearly something wrong," Shane offers through gritted teeth, and I smile sweetly again while blinking several times.

"You are mistaken." I walk off again with no idea where I'm going, and Shane clicks his fingers while calling John over. It's disgusting.

He rhymes off everything I need, and John makes a joke that a new bike would make more sense.

"Una, can I purchase you a new bike?" Shane asks, but he isn't looking at me.

"Of course not," I bite back.

"See," he says to John, as if to say I'm awkward.

"I'll get my parts another time," I tell John and leave the store. I can't do this with Shane. I'm at the car when I realize it's locked. Glaring back at the store changes nothing. I can't see in, but the Audi unlocks with a click. I climb in and wait for Shane. He comes out, and John is behind him with a trolley of all the parts. After loading up the car, Shane gets in, and I'm shaking my head.

"I told you I would get them another time." I was never going to get them all at once.

"We're here now," he says while buckling his belt.

I want to scream. "Why don't you listen to me?" When I narrow my eyes at Shane, I'm surprised to see him smiling. "You're very sexy when you're mad."

My mouth opens and closes like a bloody goldfish. I have no words. Secretly, I'm smiling, but I stare out the window and don't show it to him.

***

When we arrive home, Shane drops me off at the front door. I don't argue. I want to get out of these clothes. I enter the house and pause on the third step.

The sound of laughter and a strange voice has me walking toward the kitchen, where I find Finn and a girl who is fabulous looking.

She has big brown eyes, long hair, and her complexion is something any girl would envy. Mary is smiling, her cheeks red. Darragh winks as I enter—even he looks happy. There's a nervousness with Finn as I walk in, but he seems to relax when he sees I'm alone.

"Una, this is Siobhan," Finn says.

I take Siobhan's outstretched petite hand. Her skin's so freaking soft.

"Hi. I've heard tons about you," I say, and she smiles.

"All good, I hope." She's still smiling. Her teeth are sparkling white, and when she looks back at Finn, who smiles at her, I can see that they love each other.

"Of course all good," Finn says with a hand over his heart. She slaps him playfully.

"It was all good," I agree, sitting down. Darragh is having a bottle of Miller, but he isn't drunk; he's only started.

We chat a while. When I learn that she's a caregiver at the hospital in Cavan, I have a million questions. What's the worst injury she's ever seen? What's it like to see a baby born? Has any patient ever hit on her, and are there any hot doctors? This gets a laugh out of Mary and Siobhan, but not out of Finn.

Darragh stays a while. He doesn't say much, and at times, I think I see guilt or sadness in his eyes. He leaves, but I stay. I like Siobhan. She's easy to chat to. Of course, she asks me about myself, and I tell her I dropped out of college, and right now, I'm not sure what to do.

Shane arrives in the kitchen, and I think that both Finn and I stiffen together, for two completely different reasons. I tell myself to relax, and when I peek up, Shane is staring at me, not hiding the fact that he's doing so. I drop his gaze, and he comes and sits beside me, so close that his thigh is brushing mine.

"Did you meet Siobhan?" I glance at him. Our shoulders brush at the movement, and all of a sudden, I need space.

"No," he tells me, and I narrow my eyes. She's sitting three feet away, surely watching this. When he looks away from me to Siobhan, he's the perfect gentleman and takes her hand in his.

"Pleasure to meet you. Finn has spoken very highly of you," he says, and Finn's mouth opens slightly. I don't like the fact that he's still holding her hand.

"Siobhan's a nurse," I say, and everyone turns to me. Shane releases Siobhan's hand.

"I'm a carer," Siobhan corrects me, and I roll my eyes playfully.

"Potato, patato. You practically do the same," I say, and she grins.

"That is true. Just don't tell the nurses."

We all relax fully, and Shane soon excuses himself. I'm tempted to follow him but don't. The conversation flows easily, and when Finn keeps throwing glances at the door, I question if he's waiting for his dad to meet Siobhan.

I excuse myself, saying I'm going to the bathroom, but instead, I make my way to Michael's study. I hope he's there. It would make Finn's day to have everyone meet Siobhan. I can see the nervousness in him, but he's proud of her and delighted with how well it went with Darragh and Shane.

I reach the study, and Michael and Shane's voices have me pausing. I don't want to walk in with *him* there, but getting Michael is more important to me. I freeze, as the conversation taking place behind the door is hard to process.

"I have Rachel looking into duplicating the drug," Shane says.

"We can't have someone else coming in supplying what we can't," Michael reinforces, and Shane agrees.

"There's a new shipment arriving in the docks on Tuesday. I have Gary picking it up." There's movement, and I'm not sure what's happening.

"It better be cleaner stuff than the last," Michael says sternly.

"It's seventy percent cocaine. After it's mixed, it will be thirty percent, but that's still high."

I'm moving away from the door, and I'm struggling to breathe. They are drug dealers. *Big* drug dealers. As I pass through the hall, I notice that all the paintings, furniture, and even the rugs are too rich for a farmer. I wasn't aware of this before, but now everything is in my face.

I can't go back into that kitchen. I head toward the front door. I need air.

I find my way to the stables as the first drop of rain falls. The sky is low—gray like my mind. It's a jumping jumble of too much. I'm overwhelmed with what I heard. I question if they could have been code words, but I know what I heard. My heart picks up speed when I think of this family with their secrets.

My mother's warning comes to me now, and I ponder if she knows. She can't; she would never have let me leave. But she must have seen the wealth and known it didn't come from farming. I move into the stable that holds my horse and out of the rain that's coming down in sheets.

Shane is a drug dealer. It's hard to picture, but not. Michael is a drug lord. I laugh, hysteria taking over. Darragh and Finn can't be involved—they're nice. Liam? I rub my forehead. My head hurts, and I know I need to get away before I start to really freak out.

When I climb onto my horse bareback, she doesn't protest. Neither does she protest as I direct her out of the stable. I duck my head under the door, and once outside, rain pelts down on top of us. I move her through the yard slowly.

I want to race, but I wait until we're in the open fields. It's not until then that I open her up. Holding her mane, I allow it all to go and focus on riding her. It's freeing, and I'm shaking but smiling a few minutes later. The rain has soaked me, but that doesn't bother me. The lighting that crosses the sky is what I don't like. I'm in the middle of the field, wet, on horseback. There's an old outbuilding near here; I remember it from when I was young. I gallop there quickly as the storm grows closer.

I can't bring the horse into the outbuilding, but she seems to stay close to the stone structure. I'm lucky the roof is still on it, but the two small windows and door are gone. I'm really cold and pace the small space, waiting for the storm to pass. But time seems to tick by slowly, and the storm grows more frantic.

My horse races away at the roar of thunder. I don't chase after her; instead, I stay and wait. The roar of an engine doesn't give me the relief that it should. I'm being rescued. Dry clothes, maybe hot food. My stomach rumbles. But the idea of seeing them has my heart pounding.

I'm peering out the door and can see the land cruiser tear up the ground as Shane drives like a lunatic . He jumps out and runs straight toward me. I question what he's going to do.

CHAPTER THIRTEEN

SHANE

"WHAT IS IT WITH you and water?" I ask her while taking off my jacket. She's soaking through, and a shiver has taken over her small frame. There's a strangeness in her eyes that I don't like. As I take a step toward her, she takes one back and holds out a shaky hand.

I recognize the fear. She swallows while frowning at the ground before looking back up at me.

"You told me that what you do is illegal," she says, and I nod.

"Una, you're soaking. We can talk in the Jeep." I take a step toward her again. Her hand collides with my chest, and she shakes her head.

"No, I'm not going anywhere with you." I have no clue what's gotten into her, but she's upset, and I want to take it away.

"I heard you and Michael speaking," she tells me. Her hand flutters away from my chest and falls limply to her side, yet she still stands tall, holding my stare.

"About what?" I ask, knowing what father and I have just spoken of. I can't hold her eye, because I don't want to see that look in it. The one of disgust and fear.

"You know what?" she shouts, her hand slamming into my chest. My eyes snap to her face. My chest tightens, not from the impact of her hand but the way she looks at me. Like I'm a despicable human being.

"Say something." She hits me with both hands. I shift back slightly from the impact.

"What do you want me to say?" I growl. "You want me to paint you a pretty picture? You want me to tell you that you heard wrong?"

She curls her hands into a fist and hits my chest again, and I let her, hoping the disgust will seep out of her with each hit she places to my chest.

"No, goddamn it, Shane. I want you to be honest." She wheels away from me, her back rising and falling quickly.

"Yes, what you heard is true. We make our money by doing illegal... things."

She spins around, a fire in her eyes, and she laughs, but it's full of anger. "You can't even say it," she spits out.

"We supply drugs to most of the Northeast. We earn our money from brothels. We hurt people. We launder money. We're criminals." The more I say, the paler she becomes. But for me, there is something satisfying about telling someone the truth for once in my life.

She stands taller. "Okay. Okay." That's all she says before she walks past me. I turn and watch her climb into the passenger side of the Jeep. I have no clue what that means, but I follow her and get into the vehicle.

Her shivers are worse now. I don't know if it's a mixture of the cold and shock. I turn up the heat.

"Take off your top," I tell her while I pull my own jumper off and fix my T-shirt. When I glance at her, she hasn't moved. "Don't make me take it off you, Una."

She stares at me for a moment before she pulls her top off over her head. I focus my gaze out the window as the rain continues to beat down on us.

The storm is overhead. The lightning is coming quicker. Once she has her top off, I hand her my jumper. She pulls it on, and my shoulders relax a bit more. My eyes move to her trousers, and she shakes her head, but still, she sits up and pulls them down. I drink in her long, creamy legs.

"Stop staring at me," she barks, and I snap my attention forward. I flicker a glance at her as she removes her boots before pulling off her trousers. I don't want to drive back to the house, not with so much hanging between us.

"Did my mother know?" she asks once she has her trousers off and is sitting back up.

"No, of course not," I answer her.

Her lips twist in a snarl. "So, what, you have a secret life?"

To me, it isn't a secret. It's all I've ever known. I can't meet her eyes, not when they hold so much hate.

"What about Finn? Darragh?" Her voice takes on a shriek, the panic rising. I turn to her as she pulls her legs up to her chest. I'm not even sure she's aware of what she's doing. But all my eyes see is her skin, and I pull my focus to her face.

"Yes, it's a family business."

Her mouth opens slightly, and silence fills the Jeep for a moment.

"I'm sorry," I tell her, because I am. I'm sorry that she's seeing this side of us. It's a relief for me but a burden for her.

"Sorry that you didn't tell me, or sorry that you got caught?"

I blink at her. "Both," I tell her honestly.

Her hands are still shaking as she wraps them around her legs. "Jesus, Shane. This is crazy. I just... I know it's true, yet I don't," she says.

When I glance at her, I hate the fear I see. When I reach for her hand, she pulls back, and it's like a slap in the face. I turn to her fully. "I would never hurt you, Una."

She searches my face. For the truth in my words? I'm not sure. But I reach for her again, slower this time, and when I take her hand, she doesn't pull away, and it's like a balm to a burn. The tips of my fingers line up with hers, and I slowly take her hand fully in mine. Once I have twined our fingers, I gaze at her. Her eyes appear huge in her pale face.

"You know that, right? I would never hurt you."

She swallows and then she nods. "I know," she admits. It's a baby step, but it's good.

"I don't want to lose you." When I glance up at her from under my lashes, I can see the rise and fall of her chest. I want her to tell me what she's thinking as a tear falls from her one blue eye.

"You won't."

I smile even though I can still see the uncertainty in her face. She doesn't return it. "Can I take you back to the house to get you dry clothes?" I ask her softly, and she swipes away another falling tear but nods. When she takes her hand from mine, I miss her warmth. I drive slowly back across the fields while ringing Stephen.

"Una's horse got loose. I'm sure I've seen her in the field that runs along the river where the old stonehouse is," I tell him, and he says he will get her once the storm passes. I glance at Una when I'm done with the call, but she still has her knees up to her chest, and her faraway gaze is focused out the window.

***

Una's in the shower, and I'm sitting on her bed with no idea of what to do. She will have questions, and I'm prepared to answer some of them. I look out again into the hall for the hundredth time, making sure no one is nearby before I close her door over again. This time when I sit down, she comes out of the bathroom.

She's wearing a gray-colored cotton dress with emerald green sleeves and a band of emerald green around the waist. She's beautiful. She pads across the room barefoot while towel-drying her long hair. Her eyes seem to bounce around me, like I'm not here, and I can't sit still. I stand and move toward her. She pauses drying her hair and peers up as I take the towel from her hands and drop it on the floor.

I take both her hands and direct her toward the bed, where I make her sit before sitting beside her. She looks like someone who just woke up, like she's not entirely sure what's going on.

"Are you okay?" I ask, releasing her hands. She immediately folds them across her chest, and I try not to focus on the *V* of the dress where her plump flesh is rising and falling quickly.

"I don't know. I'm just..." She doesn't finish, and when she settles her gaze on me, I glance away. She's hurt. Her lips have tugged down into a frown, and it looks like she might start crying.

"I..." She can't seem to find words, and she stands up, moving away from the bed. When she turns around to face me, my stomach tightens at the intensity of her stare.

"I don't want to get hurt." Her words are whispered, and before I can respond, she does a bizarre thing. Una kneels in front of me and takes one of my hands in hers.

"I know you would never physically hurt me." She speaks to my chest. I'm holding my breath as I stare at the crown of her head. "But it's emotionally that I'm worried about." Now she peers up at me, her eyes wide and softer.

"I will never hurt you in any manner," I tell her while embracing her face. She leans into my hands, and the motion makes me feel powerful.

We stay like that for a few moments before she slowly stands and sits down beside me. Once again, we're silent, but it's a different kind of silence now.

"Do you sell the drugs yourself?" she asks, but straight away, she retracts it. "Don't tell me. I don't think I want to know." She's standing again, her emotions raging. Something crosses her face as she tilts her head. "Does Brian work for you?"

I don't want to lie to her, but she must know that the more knowledge she has, the worse this will be. "Why do you ask?"

"Don't answer my question with a question," she fires back.

"Yes. Now why do you ask?"

She nods at my answer and wrings her hands before she loosens them and shrugs. "Do you try to get people addicted and you charge them, or how does it work?"

I don't like the light she shines on this. "You're a million miles off. I have never touched or sold a drug. I supply. There's a difference."

She snorts, and I clench my fists. "You want to explain to me what this has to do with Brian?" I ask her. Did she see him push drugs on someone to get them hooked? It doesn't make sense.

"Just... it's nothing." She shrugs again, and I'm standing as her eyes shoot around the room, refusing to stop on me.

I stand in front of her, and she has no choice but to look at me. "It's nothing, Shane," she tells me with too much false bravado.

"I'll decide that."

"When I was with him—"

"With him in what way?" I cut her off with a growl.

She throws her hands in the air. "I can't talk to you," she tells me, and I reel in my frustration.

"I'm sorry," I say softly.

She eyes me. I'm ready to lose my cool, but thankfully, she speaks. "Twice, while we were kissing"—I clench my fists but stay still—"he slipped a tablet into my mouth. I was pretty drunk, but I was out of it after that. So whatever he gave me was really strong."

I'm struggling to breathe. A tightness has banded itself around me. Her voice is still there. I hear her words, but it's like she's further away. She takes my silence as permission to go on.

"It was weird. He gave me the creeps, but I don't know. I don't think I'm the only girl he did that to."

"Did he touch you?" I manage to ask, and my voice has her standing a little straighter, like she was confessing to the room, and now she remembers I'm standing in it.

"No. No..." Her brows draw closer as she bores holes into the floor with her gaze. She takes a slight step back.

My hands clench and unclench as I see the growing doubt on her face. There's a pounding in my ears, and my pulse elevates as I walk away from her.

"Where are you going?" She grabs my arm, the panic in her voice rising.

"I'm going to kill him," I tell her and try to walk away, but she doesn't let me go. She's in front of me, her eyes wild as her fingers run across my clenched jaw.

"No, he didn't touch me."

It doesn't matter. He drugged her, and that, for me, is enough. The desire in me to get to him far outweighs anything now.

I remove her hand from my face and take a step, but she's blocking me. I try to calm the rage in me, promising myself that it's only for a moment.

Taking her face in my hands, I want to remove the worry and strain that tightens her eyes.

"Shane, please leave it alone." Her pleas are said through a trembling lip, and I know if she cries, I won't be able to leave.

Quickly, I pick her up. The action elicits a squeal from her. Dumping her on the bed, I leave her room with an order not to follow me slung over my shoulder.

If she does follow, I don't hear her. All I can hear is the pounding of blood in my ears, and the want for violence courses through my veins.

CHAPTER FOURTEEN

SHANE

S MYTH'S PUB HAS A few lads hanging out in front, all smoking and huddled together. I'm sitting across from it, ignoring my ringing phone. I don't check to see who's calling. I won't allow myself to picture Una upset. I unload the gun regretfully and stick it in the waistband of my trousers before climbing out of my car.

I enter through the lounge where I hope I'll find Patrick. He takes a quick glance up as I enter and goes to return to his conversation with three other men at a small round table, but he does a double take. His brows rise in surprise.

"It's closing time," I tell him, and he rubs his hands down the front of his yellow T-shirt, but he doesn't hesitate as he makes his way behind the bar. As I leave the lounge area and step into the bar, he rings the bell, alerting the younger and louder crowd that closing time is upon them. The ringing bell elicits groans and curses, but the loudest of them all is Brian.

"Nah, Patrick, this ship is still sailing," he tells him. Patrick turns a bit paler as he looks to me. Brian slowly follows his gaze, and it takes everything in me not to attack him. I wait as the bar slowly empties. Patrick rings the bell more urgently, and soon, it's Brian and one of his friends. I don't so much as glance at or acknowledge them as I walk toward him.

"Shane. What's up, man?" he asks, trying to sound calm, but I delight in the hiccup of fear in his words. I shove him into the booth and slide in beside him, trapping him. It's then that I give his friend a moment of my attention—a tall, thin boy with freckles. His eyes shine with too much drink.

"I'll talk to you later," Brian tells him.

"Sit down," I tell the boy, and his eyes bounce from Brian to Patrick, then back to me before sitting down. I nod at Patrick, and he leaves, taking his dismissal. The pub is silent, and when Brian goes to speak, I snap. My fingers grip his neck, and I smash his face into the table, causing all the glasses to rattle. One falls off and smashes on the ground. His friend makes a move to leave, but I snap my gaze to him, and he stays still.

"Jesus Christ, Shane," Brian cries out. I slam his face into the table again, knocking over a pint on his friend, who has learned fast and sits still. Brian's nose pumps blood all down his white shirt as I yank him back up. His blood feeds my rage.

"What's wrong?" He's crying. His hands move to his broken and smashed nose.

"You drugged Una," I say.

"Who?" His response is unsatisfactory. I slam his face into the table again, then I decide he doesn't need all his teeth. I put a lot of force behind it this time.

Blood is everywhere—his blond hair is growing damp with it.

"You drugged Una," I repeat, and his cries come out in whines.

"Shane, I'll do anything," he starts, and I move to smash his face again, but he starts pleading, pushing against my hand. I release his sweaty neck.

"Get me a cloth," I tell his friend, whose skin has turned an ugly gray. When he stands, I see his trousers are stained with all the drink that spilled, but he gets me a cloth. I use it to clean my hands. Brian continues to cry and plead beside me. But I don't feel satisfied. I take the gun out of the band of my trousers, and he slams his back into the wall.

"Ah, no. Jesus. please, Shane." His hands are trembling and raised.

"Una was with Darragh a few nights, and you where there as well. Did you feed her drugs while she was drunk?" I ask while pointing the gun at his head. I know Una told the truth. I need to hear him say it.

"Yes, and I'm so, so sorry."

I slam the gun into his jaw, and my reward is his teeth on the table. "Did you touch her?" I ask.

The no he gives me is hard to understand, but I make it out. I push the gun against his forehead and ask again.

"No, I swear. I'm begging you. Please..."

"Shut up," I roar while I push the gun harder into his head. His eyes are closed tightly like a fucking coward.

"Open your eyes."

He does straight away.

"Did you touch her?" I ask again, and he cries a pathetic no. He's telling the truth, and that gives me some relief. But I want more from him. I use my fists and the gun to pound his face. He tries to cover it with his arms, but I still make an impact. When blood spits back at my face and neck, I stop.

The minute I do, he slumps onto the table. I'm not sure if he's passed out or not. I stare at his friend for a second, breathing heavily before getting up and leaving the pub.

I'm driving home with red hands covered in so much fucking blood. I take a quick glance in the rearview mirror, questioning whether Brian is dead or alive, but something is pushing me back to the house. Una.

I need her now more than ever. I need to touch her and tell the rage that she's fine and that she's mine. I'm not satisfied with just beating Brian. I wanted to pull the trigger.

When I enter the garage, I don't get out of the car immediately. The harsh lights wake me up, and seeing myself in the mirror has me trying to wipe some blood from my face. All I'm doing is smearing it, so I stop. I need a shower.

I don't meet anyone as I make my way to my room. It's something I'll have to deal with later, but right now, I want to wash the blood from my body. I step into my room and pause as Una's head snaps up. She's been sitting on the end of my bed, her eyes downcast, but now her eyes shoot all over my face as she stands. She's shaking her head, and her chin and lip tremble as she races across the floor.

She's wearing the same dress from earlier. Her hair is now dry, and her beauty is all I see. I close my eyes as her hands flutter to my face. She moves my head to the left and right.

"Where are you hurt?" There's a touch of hysteria in her voice, and when her hands run down my arms, I know I should tell her it's not me, but I'm a bastard for enjoying this moment.

"Shane." She's pulling at my top, and I open my eyes. The tremble in her lip has intensified, so I speak up.

"It's not my blood," I tell her as tears slip from her wide eyes. Her eyes slowly move down me, and she covers her mouth with her hand. It trembles, and I take her by the shoulders. She's shaking her head while looking at me.

"I'm fine," I reassure her. She searches my face and then steps into me, her arms hugging me tightly. She's not asking whose blood is all over me. She seems content to know it's not mine. But I want her right now like I've never wanted anything before. Her smell is everywhere, and the thoughts of anyone hurting her, of Brian putting his hands on her, drives a new need.

"I want you," I tell her, and she slowly releases me and leans out. She doesn't say anything but stares at me, and when I pick her up and carry her to the bed, she doesn't protest. One arm hooks under her cream legs, the other at the back of her head. I can't take my eyes off her. I know I need to claim her, brand her, make her mine. Adrenaline still pumps through my body, and focusing on anything tender is hard.

"I need you." I lay her down, and the rise and fall of her chest is the only movement from her. I kneel on the bed and wait for her to protest, but she doesn't. I move over her, positioning my body on top of hers.

She nods, but her eyes are wide with fear and awe. I don't look away from her as I open my belt and pull down my jeans and boxers; I keep eye contact as I reach under her dress and move her underwear aside. I sit myself at her opening, and when she doesn't object, I enter her.

My hands move to her hair, where I bury them. I thrust inside her again, and Una is perfect around me. She moans quietly, her hands clutching the quilt. She's everything I imagined she would be and more. I grip her hair tighter as I fasten my pace. Una releases the quilts, her hands reaching for my shoulders, pulling me closer to her, but we can't get any closer.

I lay my head against hers and inhale her moans. Each thrust I take makes her more and more mine. The ecstasy that crosses her face has me quickening my pace until I fill her. We are both breathless, and we haven't looked away from each other. A tear slides from her green eye.

CHAPTER FIFTEEN

UNA

MY BODY IS TREMBLING from the rush of release and also because Shane is still inside me. His hands are still buried in my hair—his hands that are covered in blood. There's a savagery in his eyes that is dying down now as he continues to breathe deeply.

My own breaths are still fast as I continue to take his perfect face in. The blood that flecks his face makes him appear wild. I should be afraid, but a sort of excitement at seeing him feral courses through me. I slide my thumb across his lips, and it's then that he closes his eyes.

I can't look away from him. I can't believe this is Shane. My mind is overwhelmed with what happened. When he opens his eyes, I move my hands away from him. Butterflies erupt in my stomach with the intensity of his stare.

"Are you okay?" he asks. His eyes flicker over the tears that are leaking from my eyes.

I don't know why I'm crying. There's so much—too much. I nod and swallow. Shane slowly extracts himself from me, and the loss is immediate. He goes to the bathroom, and I don't move. But for the first time, I can breathe. The noise of the tap running reaches my ears, and when Shane reappears still covered in blood, I inhale a quick breath.

He doesn't speak, and his stare has rendered me speechless as he slowly parts my legs and lifts up my dress. The lights are on, and there are no barriers. It's like I'm baring my soul to him. The warm cloth he presses between my legs and cleans me with is enough to almost break me.

The gentle strokes. The awe in his eyes. The thoughtfulness of the gesture. I stay still, and when he's finished, he asks me again if I'm okay.

"Yes," is all I manage.

He's standing at the foot of the bed. "Will you stay with me tonight?"

The question has my heart pounding, and I still can't manage words so I nod, and it's enough for him. He goes back into the bathroom, and this time the shower is turned on.

I pull my legs closed. My hand flutters to my chest, telling my heart to settle down. As I lie there, I question so much, like why I still can't find it in me to ask him whose blood is on him. I have a good idea it's Brian's, but it's not the asking; it's that I don't care as long as it isn't Shane's. What kind of person does that make me?

My thoughts are cut off and shut down as Shane comes out of the bathroom wearing only a towel. I suck in a deep breath. His sculpted chest and wide shoulders are enough to make me want to reach for him, but I show some self-control.

I don't know what to call what we just did, but I have never felt more intimate with someone. And yet now, as I stare at his plump lips, I question what it must be like to kiss him. My stomach flutters. His lip tugs up slightly into a half smile, showing some teeth, and I'm like a drowning sailor. I need to pull myself together. I sit up and pull my knees to my chest.

"Are you okay?" This is the third time he's asked me this. I'm not sure what he sees, but I want to put his mind to rest.

"I am. I'm just..." Emotions lodge in my throat. "I'm fine." When Shane drops the towel, I turn into a twelve-year-old schoolgirl, and I actually cover my eyes. A small quick laugh leaves my lips. It's Shane's soft laughter that has me opening my eyes.

"Una, you're blushing," he teases as he pulls on black jogging pants and moves toward the bed.

I'm on fire, so blushing is a nice way to put it.

"It was just unexpected," I tell him as he climbs onto the bed. My emotions jump again, a giddiness taking over.

"You can't just do that," I add before I laugh, and Shane captures my face, my laughter dying in my throat.

"Thank you for tonight," he tells me, and my stomach hollows out at the words. You thank someone who buys you a drink or someone who holds a fucking door open for you. You don't thank someone who lets you see a part of their soul. My breath catches in my throat, and I try to tell myself to calm down. His lip lifts up.

"You look angry, so I must be saying this all wrong," he says, and my heart slows, my temper calming. I don't speak but allow him to.

He smiles and kisses me on the nose. I savor the pressure of his lips on me and think again what it would be like to have them on my lips.

"You were all I could think about. Your face consumed me. So I'm saying thank you for being mine tonight."

"You're welcome." I want to kiss him, but as I move in toward him, his lips move and I get a kiss on the forehead.

What the fuck?

You kiss your grandmother on the forehead. Or I don't know, old people, even someone dying. I close my eyes. I'm overreacting. I need to calm myself.

Shane doesn't seem to be aware of the turmoil that barrels through me as he pulls me down in the bed and spoons me. He pulls the blankets up over us, and I'm still not fully accepting that I'm in his bed, in his arms. But there is a blissfulness that fills me again, and I snuggle closer to him.

He claps his hands, and the lights go out. I start to laugh. "That is the laziest thing I have ever seen. And why don't I have that in my room?" I can't see him in the dark. I clap, and the lights come back on.

His smile is wide. "I can get it installed in your room," he tells me and claps, plunging us into darkness, and like the child that I am, I clap again.

"Will I have to tie your hands together?" The question is asked with a serious face, but there is laughter in his tone.

I clap before he can, and the room goes dark. He pulls me closer against his body, and I let the temptation die away and focus on the sensation of his body against mine. It doesn't take me long to fall asleep.

***

I wake to someone turning on the lights. "What time is it?" Shane asks as he sits up.

"What have you done?"

I don't sit up at the sound of Liam's voice. It's like it rattles in his throat. It's an odd sound.

"What time is it?" Shane asks again and reaches for the black clock that sits on his bedside table. "It's four in the morning, Liam," he barks and climbs out of bed. I pretend to be asleep. I'm not ready to face this.

"Do you know the mess you've made?" Liam speaks again; he's barely controlling his voice. Not seeing his face, I can picture a snarl.

"We can talk somewhere else." Shane lowers his voice, but the threat in his words is clear.

"You did this for her?" He sounds almost disgusted, and it's odd to hear so much in his voice. I move under the blanket before sitting up. Liam's eyes snap to me, and I regret coming up.

"Father is beyond words," Liam tells Shane, his voice more controlled now that he sees I'm awake. Shane ignores him and pulls on a top before coming back to the bed.

"You need to sleep. I'll be back later." His voice is soft, and I'm not sure how he manages to keep it that way as he speaks to me. Liam is boring holes into his back, and I want to warn him, but he smiles at me. "Go to sleep," he tells me again before turning to Liam.

"I'm not talking here," Shane growls, the contrast between the softness seconds ago to the anger now tells me so much. He cares about me. A lot.

When they leave the room, I debate with myself whether to go and search for them, but I don't, knowing that would be stupid.

Yet I toss and turn, clapping the lights on and off. I'm curious—will it break if I keep this up? I do keep it up for a while as my mind keeps conjuring up images easily of Shane covered in blood again. What if Liam hurts him? I fling the covers back but don't get out. Liam would never hurt Shane. I clap, turning the lights off, knowing I need to stay put. But what if they lose their cool?

Clap! Lights are on.

What if Shane hurts Liam? *Clap. Lights off.* For some reason, that doesn't bother me in the slightest. I lie down and count sheep. At some stage, I manage to fall asleep.

The moment I stir, all I smell is Shane. The night comes rushing back—Shane covered in blood, Shane inside me. I open my eyes and glance over at his side. It's cold. He never returned. I sit up and gnaw on my lip. I should search for him, yet I know that will make this worse. Maybe he did come back, and I didn't hear him.

I get out of Shane's bed and slip into my room to shower and change. I don't have a clue what to do. Going to work with the horses seems the safest bet.

Making my way to the kitchen is odd now that I'm aware of how everything in this house is paid for. It all seems strange. My skin stretches with anxiety across my face. Entering the kitchen, my pulse jumps, and I pause briefly. Liam is sitting at the table, a paper in front of him. He doesn't glance up, and I question if slipping from the room would be a good idea.

"Good morning, Una," he says, and his controlled voice and suit give me a cold impression. Before, I thought Liam was odd but cute. Now I don't know. A small shiver snakes its way through me. Now, I see someone dangerous.

"Liam," I say, getting a coffee. Mary isn't here, and that's typical. I put bread in the toaster and wait for it to pop, hoping Liam will be gone by the time I sit down.

No luck. I'm ready to butter my toast when he starts.

"We need to talk."

"Fire away," I tell him with as much cheeriness as I can manage.

"What Shane did was reckless and stupid. You know he did it in your honor." His foreign way of speaking seems sinister. "You implied that you had been drugged and raped."

I can't breathe at his words. Is that what Shane thought? Had I said that? No. But when he asked me if Brian had touched me, I couldn't answer him, because I wasn't one hundred percent sure.

"Words can be very powerful, Una. Even more so when they aren't true."

I'm sitting silently, not sure what to say to Liam. My throat burns at what he is saying. "You think I would have lied?" My lip trembles, and I bite it.

Liam shows no emotion as he speaks, and that hurts more. "Did you?"

The chair legs scraping along the floor is the only noise that fills the kitchen as I get up. I'm disgusted with Liam. He knows me better than that. I lean in, supporting myself with knuckles clenched on the table. "You can go to hell," I tell him.

His eyes burn into my back as I leave the warm kitchen and make my way out in the farmyard. I swallow the lump in my throat and try to focus on walking, but my mind won't allow me to.

Fire burns inside me at the idea that Liam thinks I would make something up. I don't know what happened with Brian. I don't think he raped me, but I never said he did. That fact keeps rotating around in my head.

"Morning, Una." Stephen is carrying two buckets of nuts. He places them on the back of a quad. "I'm going to feed the cows. I'll be back shortly," he tells me, and for Stephen, I force a smile as he gets on the quad and kicks it into gear. I give a wave as he drives off toward the cattle sheds that are close to the bottom of the landline.

I find my horse in her stable. She's getting more and more relaxed around me. "Hi, girl," I tell her as I rub her down. Tears burn my eyes, and I stare up at the beams on the ceiling to try to settle myself down.

"It's not bats, is it?"

My heart trips over itself at the sound of Shane's voice. I don't turn immediately as I try to settle the weakness in my knees. When I do, his smile is all dimples and teeth. My stomach squeezes, and I inhale a deep breath.

"I hope not," I say on an exhale that carries a short laugh. My gaze takes him in, and every part of me tightens. His dark denim jeans fit him snugly, and the green wool jumper he is wearing today gives his brown eyes a softness.

I love him.

When I look at him, I fill up with love. I think I've loved him since I was sixteen. The summer he gave me the horse—the summer I secretly stalked him. I take a step toward his smiling face, and it slowly grows serious.

My throat is still burning. I'm an emotional wreck, but I have this need to give him something back.

"I've decided on a name for my horse," I tell him, and he closes the distance between us. His focus is on my hands as he takes them in his before they flick back up to me, causing my pulse to pound.

I want to tell him about Liam. I want to tell him I love him. I want to tell him I think I've always loved him. I need to explain how afraid I am of the rug being pulled out from under me. But I say none of that.

"Summer. I'm going to call her Summer," I say slowly, my own focus going to his perfect moist lips before flickering back to those brown eyes that smile at me, the corners crinkling.

"It's beautiful. I'm glad you finally named her," he tells me as he raises my hands to his mouth. Butterflies dance and swirl in my stomach as his lips press against my flesh, and it burns everywhere. What would it be like to have those lips on mine?

"You noticed I hadn't?" I ask with a breathiness that has Shane staring down at me.

"I notice everything about you," he tells me, and my knees weaken further.

I search his face. I'm not sure what for, but his words are overwhelming me. I hope he never gets used to me. I hope he never stops looking at me the way he is now.

"Why did you not come back last night?" I ask. Shane releases my hands, and the loss is instant. I observe him as he stuffs his hands into his jeans pockets.

"I'm sorry. I had something to take care of. But I'm here now." His words kind of sound like an apology.

"Yeah, you're here now," I repeat back as a smile crosses my face.

His lips twitch, and he lets out a breath on the word, "So…"

"Do you want to work on your bike today?" he finishes.

The idea of spending more time with Shane is perfect, and I agree.

"I've some other work to take care of but after dinner." He takes a step backward out of the stable, his hands still shoved in his pockets.

"It's a date," I tell him, and both his eyebrows rise, making me laugh.

"A date?" he questions playfully, and I shrug at his words.

"Only if you want it to be a date?" I'm still smiling at him, and when he laughs with his head tilted to the side, it takes everything in me not to run to him and crash my lips against his.

"It's a date, Una *álainn*." Beautiful Una. Hearing it from his lips has my heart pounding. The Irish language makes it more. So much more.

CHAPTER SIXTEEN

UNA

I WORK IN A blissful daze after Shane leaves. I want to tell my own heart to slow down, that it's moving too fast on this, but I can't.

Dinnertime arrives, and I enter the wet room and peel off my coat and boots. The cream wool jumper is three sizes too big for me, but it's warm. I enter the kitchen to find Michael at the table. The moment I come in, he smiles. It's odd. I see him, I do. But knowing the truth makes it hard to hold his stare.

"Una, you don't belong on a farm," Mary says with a smile as she moves past me holding two steaming plates of food. The smell of roast has my stomach gurgling. After skipping breakfast, I'm not surprised. In my wooly socks, I pad to the table and try not to act nervous with Michael.

"Why not?" I ask Mary as she winks at me.

"You're too pretty. You belong on the front of a romance novel."

I laugh. "I don't know what romance novels you're reading Mary. But this"—I point at myself—"isn't it."

I take in the plate of dinner. Marofat peas, carrots, stuffing, roast spuds, and the roast makes this a mouthwatering dinner.

Mary scoffs before getting two more plates.

"Mary is right. You should think of modeling," Darragh says as he arrives into the kitchen with Finn behind him. Finn sits across from me, and Darragh, beside his dad. Now I'm facing all three. When Mary doesn't come with more plates, I'm relieved that Liam isn't joining us but disappointed that Shane isn't here. There's such a weirdness to be around them now.

I give Darragh a tight smile at his compliment, and he narrows his eyes at me.

"Are you enjoying the work?" This comes from Michael, and I finally meet his eye.

He reminds me of the Godfather. My toes curl in my socks as I push them against the floor, reminding myself that this is Michael. The reminder doesn't exactly help. "Yes. Thank you, for the job." Oh lord, I sound so formal.

Darragh continues to assess me, and even Finn seems confused at my tone.

"Good to hear it," Michael says with a tight smile. Wrinkles appear around his eyes, which are sharp, almost predatory.

I focus on my food, shoveling it into my mouth. Darragh's laughter has me pausing.

"Calm down, Una. No one is going to take it from you. Maybe you want to join the cattle outside."

Heat rises in my cheeks, and my whole face burns. I'm staring at a laughing Darragh, thinking he's part of this criminal world. He always appears so carefree, and I struggle to meet his eye.

"Are you okay?" Finn asks, his baby blue eyes focused on me.

Michael is studying me too, and it's all too much. I quickly excuse myself from the table and race up the stairs and back to my room. I make it the toilet before I empty the small amount of food that I ate. Tears stream down my face as my body rejects the idea of what Shane has confirmed.

I can't find the strength to get up. I sit against the wall as I tell myself that this will pass. But it's a bigger shock than I thought.

"Una."

I would roll my eyes at the intrusion from Darragh, but right now, I don't want to see him. Privacy is really nonexistent in this house. Darragh pushes open my bathroom door with his foot. His permanent grin is on his face as he raises both eyebrows.

"I'm not much for a chin wag, but I think you need to talk," he tells me, sitting down on the tile floor with his back against the wall. My focus goes to the gold band he wears on his pinky finger, a red ruby in the center. It's new and isn't cheap.

"Nice ring," I tell him, and he gives it a quick appreciative glance before flicking his hand like a rapper would.

"Yeah, it's alright," he says with a nod of his head.

"Looks expensive." I pull my knees closer to my chest. The black jodhpurs are allowing the cold of the tiles to pass through them easily.

"A few quid. So are you going to tell me what's wrong?" He nods his head again.

I'm not sure if it's for him or me.

"What's a few quid?" My throat is burning now. Sitting here with him, the sense of betrayal is almost stifling. How many times have we partied together, and yet he never told me about his family's true nature? Now I'm giving him every opportunity to tell me.

"Do you want the ring?" he asks while taking it off. I stand, and he frowns at my actions.

"No, keep your stupid ring." I retrieve mouthwash from the cabinet and rinse the taste of sick from my mouth.

"Are you pregnant?" The easy way Darragh asks has me glaring at him in the bathroom mirror. He stands, his grin gone. When he's serious, he looks so much like Finn. Both are extremely good-looking, and the saying that looks can be deceiving springs to mind.

I need to get a grip. After refilling my mouth with more wash, I gurgle it before spitting out the mouthwash into the sink as I turn around to Darragh.

"No," I answer, holding on to the sink with my hands as I try to calm my racing heart.

"On the rag?" he questions, folding his arms over his chest.

"I know what you are," I whisper-shout at him, and he drops his hands. A smile starts to grow on his face.

"Ah, is that the movie where the ugly guy is a vampire?"

I stare at Darragh, thinking he must be fucking with me. He can't be that stupid. But the smile on his face has me storming from the bathroom and into my bedroom.

"How much was the ring? How did you pay for it, Darragh?"

I can slowly see the realization of what I'm asking sink in. He's across the room in a second, closing my bedroom door, and now I remember the angry Darragh. The one who smashed the chair.

I back away from him and move toward my bed. I don't stop until my legs hit the frame.

"Say whatever you need to say," he says to my silence. I swallow as I search his face. He isn't angry, but there's a strain visible around his eyes and a tightness in his jaw. "Una, I'm the safest person for you to talk to."

"I know you're a criminal," I say quietly, afraid of what my words will erupt.

He snorts but doesn't laugh. "'Criminal' is a nice way of putting it. But how do you know? Was it Brian? Is that why Shane beat the shit out of him?"

"So you're one too?" I find myself saying as I sit down on the bed. I knew he was, but seeing the answer clearly on his face makes me question my judgment on so much. How the hell had I not noticed? First and foremost, the wealth, yet no one actually worked.

Darragh sits beside me. "Yeah and no." His answer sounds sad, and I glance at him. I can't see his eyes. He's focused on his ring.

"I'm not like Shane or Liam." He speaks to his fingers. "I'm me." He shrugs. "But yeah, I do what they do." We fall into silence.

"So are you going to tell me who told you?" he asks.

I opt for the easy way out. "No one told me. I figured it out."

Darragh's eyes fill with doubt, and one brow rises in question.

"The wealth, but no one works..." I say, and his doubt melts away before he bumps shoulders with me.

"This has got to be our little secret. You can't tell the others," he tells me. I don't meet Darragh's eyes as I agree, but he isn't satisfied. "Una, I'm serious. They aren't like me. Don't ever say it."

"Why? What would they do?" Shane would never hurt me, but the seriousness on Darragh's face has me curious.

Running his hand through his short hair, he stands. "I don't know."

"Would they hurt me?" I ask on a whim.

"Yes." His answer actually surprises me. I don't know what he sees on my face, but he's beside me again. "No, no, I didn't mean that. Look, you can't tell anyone, okay?"

I can sense his panic, and I nod again.

"I promise," I tell him, and he lets out a shaky breath. "I better get back to work." I stand back up, and Darragh nods several times while rubbing the back of his head.

"Right. Glad we had this chat. Good chat." He's rambling as he leaves my room.

I find myself smiling even as dark as this situation is. That tells me I'm going to be fine.

After Darragh leaves, I brush my teeth and make my way back downstairs. I'm on the first step when Shane is there, stealing my rational thoughts away.

"I was looking for you." His eyes search behind me like he's waiting for someone else to materialize. His brows are drawn together; his fingers tighten around the banister. "Finn said you left the table in a rush."

I move down the steps quickly until I'm on the one above his. This puts us at the same height, and my eyes flicker to his lips before I reach up and touch his drawn brows. He relaxes under my fingers.

"It's a bit weird looking at everyone now," I whisper while focusing on his brow. His hand captures mine, snapping my attention to his eyes. My stomach squeezes.

"It's all new. I know that, but you can talk to me." His words are low, and I find myself moving closer when it's not necessary.

But I want to be closer to him. I close my eyes against all the irrational thoughts that are bouncing around. He's making me lose any sense of myself. His hand still holds mine, and I try to focus on the touch, but I can't. It's Shane's touch, Shane's hand that has my pulse racing.

"Una." My name is whispered, and I open my eyes to stare up at him. "You have nothing to fear." His brows are drawn together as he speaks furiously.

I'm looking at this man, and fear of him isn't possible. I'm afraid of losing myself with him—in him. I'm afraid that he might not feel the same way about me that I feel about him. I'm afraid of the rest of his family. Once upon a time, they were mine, but I didn't know them.

"I know," I find myself saying. A door banging downstairs has Shane returning to normal.

"Are you ready to work on your bike?" The excitement in his voice has my mournful thoughts fleeing.

"Yeah, I would like that."

Shane doesn't move. "First, I want you to eat. You left your dinner behind."

I can't stop the smile that crosses my face. "Finn sure gave you a rundown," I tell him, and one side of his lip lifts slightly, like he's fighting off a smile.

"He was concerned."

"About little old me?" I tease, but my words seem to sober up the mood.

"You're safe with us, Una. We all care for you." His eyes roam my face as he speaks.

I bite my lip, chewing on it as I think of his words. Conflicting thoughts rattle around in my head. On one hand, I always thought they cared for me in some way, but now I'm not sure. Their intentions seem different now that I know what they are. As Shane continues to study me, I tell myself that I need to respond.

"Thanks, Shane," I answer, and from the tightness around his eyes, I gather that it's not what he wanted me to say. I'm not sure what he wanted to hear, though. Maybe that I know I'm safe? But I'm not safe.

"Come on. We'll get you food." As he speaks, he turns around and walks down the stairs, and I follow.

***

When Shane flicks on the lights in the second garage, I roll my eyes, and he actually laughs. The sound scatters my nerves.

The garage would easily hold six cars or more, but right now, the center has a beige tarp, and standing on it is my bike, all the parts laid out around it. I walk toward it with my hands behind my back. "You know, the size of this place is scandalous," I tell him.

Shane still wears a smile and places his hand behind his own back as he walks in the opposite direction as me. Both of us circle the bike, staring at each other. It's like a dance. "It's for our bikes," he says with a shrug.

"I only see mine," I tell him, still moving, still smiling.

"I had the rest cleared out," he answers easily, like emptying the garage for me wasn't anything. The garage is virtually empty except for ten large stainless-steel drawers that line the back wall. I'm assuming that's where all the tools are.

I stop walking and so does Shane. My heart is pounding while I gaze up at him. "So where do we start?" I ask while being careful about how I breathe. I want to inhale quickly as my heart demands more oxygen, but I take slow, controlled breaths. When I look at Shane, I don't think I have any impact on him. He kneels down on his hunkers and stares at the bike. He's relaxed, and when I kneel down on my knees, he glances at me.

"We clean it," he says with a wink that nearly topples me over.

CHAPTER SEVENTEEN

SHANE

As I get buckets and sponges, I leave Una to check out her bike, which she seems pretty taken with. The cleaning isn't really necessary. It can wait until after, but the simple task with Una is all that matters.

When I return, she's sitting cross-legged on the tarp, chewing her lip, and my heart stills. Her fiery red hair is like a halo, and I think again of what this place will do to her. Since arriving, she's lost weight, and dark circles have grown under her eyes.

She's been strong for all she has found out, but I'm not sure she's strong enough. I don't want her to have to strengthen herself to our way. This is why I never got close to her, why I never touched her, and now I'm terrified that I can't let her go, even if it damages her.

She looks up, and a smile lightens her eyes. She takes in the two buckets and sponges that I carry. Once I set them down, I take two pairs of rubber gloves from my back pocket—one is yellow, and the other is pink. I hold the pink pair out to her, but she shakes her head while biting her lip.

"Nope, I want the yellow," she tells me, taking them from my hands. She's trying not to laugh as she puts on her yellow gloves.

"Put on your gloves, Shane," she tells me as she snaps the rubber band at the wrist before grinning up at me.

"You think I'm afraid of a bit of pink?" I ask her, and she laughs. I want to keep her laughing, so I put on the stupid gloves.

"I need to take a picture." She's still laughing as I kneel down and pass her a bucket and sponge.

I open out my arms. "By all means, snap away," I tell her, and she sticks out her pink tongue at me. I'm transfixed and don't look away from it until she pulls it back into her mouth. My focus is on her moist lips. My heart gives a heavy thump, and I glance away.

After dipping my sponge into the water, I start cleaning the frame. Una does the same. I follow her sponge, hitting it with mine and causing her to laugh and tell me to stay on my own side.

There's something amazing about being this close to someone but having a separation between us. I can see everything clearly, but I can't touch her, and that makes me observe her and take every tiny detail of Una in. The freckles that coat the bridge of her nose. The beauty spot under her left ear. Her lashes rise as she pins me with those eyes. Her beauty undoes me all the time, and I snap out of it when she flicks me with water.

"Oh, it's like that, is it?" I say while wiping my face with my sleeve. I'm quick to act and scoop up a handful of water before soaking her jumper. She jumps back with a squeal.

"No, no," I tell her as she picks up the bucket. I hold my hands out, trying to make her put it down. The cold of the water pulls a screech from me, along with a few curse words. She's upended the full bucket on me.

When I blink water from my eyes, her face is flushed with excitement. We both move for my bucket, and I get it first. She runs, but I use one arm to grab her around the waist and pull her back.

"Okay, hold on. Hold on. Let's talk about this," she says, straining to see me, and I entertain her pleas, moving her slowly toward the wall.

"Talk," I tell her once I have her back against the wall. I keep one arm close to her waist as I hold the bucket with the other—the bucket that she keeps looking at.

"I have a cold, and if you pour that water over me, I'll get really sick, and it will be your fault." She says it with a quick jerk of her head, like she's stating a fact.

Water is still dripping from my hair, but I don't wipe it from my face. I keep my hands firmly where they are. "Not good enough," I tell her, lifting the bucket, and she holds out her hands, touching my chest.

"If you do that, I will run up to your room in my wet clothes and roll around in your bed."

I snort. "Mary will have more work. This is your last chance," I say with a shrug and lift the bucket a little higher. I love the way her eyes dart from the bucket to me. I'm not going to pour it on her, but seeing her trying to worm her way out of this is fun.

Instead, this time, she leans in closer to me, her hands still on my chest, her focus is on my lips, and my heart beats faster under her hands. Her lashes rise, and there's something different in her eyes.

"I love you." Her lips tug down as she whispers it, like she might cry.

My heart is ready to come out of my chest, and I know she feels it. I'm frozen, unsure of what to do. I jump away from Una with a curse as water pours over our feet; I forgot it was in my hand. When I glance back up, Una isn't facing the door.

I want to tell her that it all starts and ends with her. Seal it with a kiss. My mother's voice comes to me, her stupid saying that, for some reason, really sank in, took hold, and has never left me.

The door opens, and it's like a bubble burst. Liam sizes up the situation. Una stiffens at Liam's arrival, and I don't like it at all.

When he turns back to me, his words carry more weight than normal. "I need to have a word with you." I stare at Una, but she's still focused on the door. "Now," Liam adds, and I grit my teeth at his words.

"Una." When I say her name, she peeks at me.

The hurt that shines is quickly covered up with a smile. "Yeah, go. We can do the bike later."

Like a coward, I nod and leave her. I'm afraid she said it as a joke, but it didn't seem like one. Once we leave the garage, I tell Liam that I'll meet him in the library once I change my clothes.

When I enter the library, Liam stands with his back to me. "Your actions have consequences."

My mind hasn't left Una's words. Her face is there in front of me, her lips tugged down as she tells me she loves me. The longer I'm away from her, the more I question if she was messing with me. The part of me that wants to believe she meant what she said is taking over.

"Are you listening to me, brother?" Liam faces me, one hand in his navy suit trousers pocket. He's talking about Father's source telling him that Brian is out looking for vengeance. I don't want to be here, but I'll do this back and forth with Liam.

"I'm beginning to see the funny side of all this," I tell him, and Liam doesn't so much as shift. "So Father has a source who gives him information." I take a step closer to Liam. "Yet"—I hold up a finger—"Father has never mentioned this source to me, only you."

Liam exhales. "Your point?"

My point... I'm not entirely sure I have one, but I know something is off. Or maybe I'm being paranoid.

"I don't know, but why does he not tell me?" Now I sound jealous.

"Because I'm the next in line. You know this. You know you will be my right-hand man. You are already."

Sometimes I feel like a puppet. I've never really cared; I just care about my family. But Una? She's changing me.

"Either of you see Darragh?" I turn to Finn, who hasn't entered the room. The disdain in his voice drips into his words.

"Did you let him off his leash again?" I bark my anger at him, and Finn steps into the room.

"Actually, I wanted to talk to both of you about that."

Liam moves and steps up beside me like we're a united front. With both of us standing in front of him, Finn shrinks back.

"I'm moving in with Siobhan, so you'll have to hire someone else to babysit him."

"So you no longer want to be part of the family business?" Liam asks, and Finn folds his arms over his white T-shirt.

"I didn't say that..."

"You didn't have to. If you leave this house, you leave this family."

I glance at Liam, questioning when that became a rule, but he holds Finn's steady eye.

"What, you want me to let Siobhan live here with you two?" His smirk is joined with a shake of his head. I have no interest in Siobhan, so I step away and sit down.

"He threatened to kill her." Finn points at me, anger growing around him.

"You're still hampering on about that," I say with as much boredom as I can muster.

"How would you like it if I threatened Una?" Finn asks.

I sit a bit straighter, and Liam takes in my reaction. They're aware of Una and me.

"Make the threat," I demand, standing and trying to clamp down my temper. He won't, but even the thought has me wanting to reach him.

"You know he wouldn't." It's Liam who speaks, and Finn shrugs as if to say he might. "Also, Shane would never harm Siobhan. You have my word."

Finn glances from me to Liam, but his eyes settle on me. "I want to hear him say it," he says to Liam, but he's staring at me.

"Remember that story Dad told you about him and his brother killing the boy?" I ask. Finn's fists clench, but he nods and says a quick yes.

"He lied to you," I tell him and can see color growing in his cheeks. "When the police came, he told them that it was his brother who killed the boy. His brother, Tom, who spent ten years in prison for it."

"He said the father went down for it. That he was an alcoholic..."

I wave off the fairy tale Dad told Finn. "He told you that so you would always protect your brother."

Liam is staring at me, but I hold Finn's gaze.

"So why are you telling me the truth now?" Finn asks.

I don't blame the suspicion that fills his voice. "Because father lying to you didn't keep you here, so maybe the truth will. Maybe working with us more would make you stay."

Finn walks closer to us and I can see the want there. The want that we can never truly fill.

"But Darragh's safety is important," Liam says. "And you are the closest to him." I glance at him as he touches Finn on his right shoulder. "Also, Shane will give his word that he will never threaten Siobhan again."

"You have my word," I say, knowing if she ever needed to be removed, it would be done, but Finn relaxes at my words.

"What else would I be doing?" he asks, and his blue eyes are shining eagerly. I never thought Finn wanted in. I never really thought about Finn at all, only for him to keep Darragh in check.

"I have a few jobs in mind," Liam answers. "But for now, pick one of the outbuildings on the property. Do it up, and you and Siobhan can live there. You don't have to live in the house."

I've never considered leaving our home, but the thought of all of us on the same property doesn't entice me.

"Yeah. Yeah. Okay." Finn smile is wide, and I can't help the smile that tugs at my lips too.

"What about a drink later to celebrate?" I tell him, and once again, he seems uncertain.

"Okay," he finally says.

"We will speak to you later." Liam's gentle dismissal is a reminder of his place in the family. Finn's eyes dim, but he nods and leaves us alone.

"Well played," Liam says, opening his suit jacket and sitting on the couch across from me.

"I wasn't playing," I tell him. My gaze follows the pattern of gold and red swirls on the large rug under our feet.

"You were. You're that used to it; you were doing it without thinking." Liam's heavy brown eyes take note of my every move and reaction. "You need to repair the damage you did with Brian."

I know I do, and I will. But right now, all I can think about is Una.

"I will." I rise but sit back down as Liam speaks.

"You're too distracted, brother. That will cost you."

"I'll fix it, Liam," I tell him with a warning. I don't regret beating Brian. My only regret is not killing him. I have to fix it for the family's sake.

Liam stands and slowly buttons his suit jacket before pinning me with a stare. "Good," he says, and when he walks away, I find myself smiling. He's like Father.

After checking the garage, stables, and my room, I find Una in hers. She's lying on her bed. She changed her clothes to jeans and my green T-shirt. That pleases me. She glances up at me, and color enters her face.

"I'm sorry about leaving," I tell her, walking around her bed so I can see her face.

She glances up again, but her mouth is buried in her crossed arms as she lies on her belly. "It's fine," she mumbles.

I don't want to sit on her bed. I can sense her upset, so I lean against the wall right across from her. "It's just Liam..."

She gets up on her knees, her eyes alive and on fire. "I said it's fine. I don't really care what you and Liam spoke about." Her lips form a thin straight line.

"You're angry." I state the obvious, and she drops my gaze while shaking her head.

"No, it's not your fault," she says, sliding off the bed and sitting on the edge facing the door, her back to me. I move around to her and can see her shoulders tense as I stand before her. "I know your family business, so it's no big deal. We can do the bike another time."

I kneel down, and when she glances at me, I try to keep my focus on her words and not my desire to have her right now. "I know, but my time with you is just as important," I tell her and she quickly drops my gaze before she returns my stare.

"Okay." She doesn't believe me.

I lean in and put my forehead against hers. "I mean it, Una. You are important to me."

She leans away from me, and I give her some space but stay on my hunkers. "Summer is important to me."

"You're comparing yourself to a horse?" I ask, not liking that.

"Should I?" Her words are loud, and her anger is building to a point that I don't know how to contain.

"I don't know what you want from me?" I'm fucking confused. I'm telling her she's important, but I don't think she knows what that means. Saying anything else has me shrinking like a coward. I stand up and let her cool down. I tell her this, and she starts laughing.

"I told Darragh." She's standing, her anger moving her lips. "He knows that I know about your family. About you all being drug lords."

I can't stop the words that bubble up her throat.

"Do you want to know what he said to me?" she asks, but I clench my fists, not answering her. She doesn't want an answer. "To not tell any of you. That I would get hurt."

"You think I'd hurt you?" I ask through clenched teeth.

"You already have," she shouts, and it's like a slap to my face.

"Is this about what you said in the garage?" I ask and her eyes blur.

"God, I'm not doing this with you." She storms into the bathroom.

"Una, open the door."

"Go away," she screams back, but I can't leave.

"I'm sorry," I tell the door, only to be answered with silence.

"Una, please."

"Please leave me alone." Her whispered words sound tired, and when she says please again, I give in and leave her.

CHAPTER EIGHTEEN

UNA

TEARS FALL QUICKLY DOWN my face as my heart threatens to come out of my chest. He has no idea how hurt I am. I told him I loved him, and he didn't say it back. I know it's not his fault, but it doesn't stop it from hurting. I need him to leave before I say something I regret. Like begging him to tell me he loves me. *God, no one tells you how much this hurts.*

I hear the door close, and the fact that he actually left hurts even more. I can't stop crying. When did I fall so deep? I knew this would turn out badly. If Liam hadn't arrived, would he have said it? I don't think so. Even coming into my room, I really thought he might, but instead, he acted like I was mad that we didn't finish the stupid bike. I'm half laughing, half crying at how stupid I am. Getting up, I don't meet my eyes in the mirror. If I do, I will understand why he doesn't look at me the way I look at him. He's out of my league.

"You're so stupid, Una," I tell myself and leave the bathroom, taking my phone with me. I have one destination—the bar. After snagging a bottle of Jack Daniels, I make my way out to the pool house. Thankfully, Stephen is finished for the day; I don't bump into anyone in the yard.

As I suspected, the pool house is empty. I don't turn on any lights. Instead, I sit down on the couch that's against the wall and stare out at the pool. I sit until the night settles in, the bottle of JD still tucked under my arm. I want to drink it, but another part of me doesn't. In my other hand, I hold my phone. It's sad; I have no one to ring. Acquaintances, I have in the dozens. Friends—zero. I often think I was born into the wrong era.

I set the phone down and unscrew the cap of the bottle of Jack Daniels. The first sip burns, and I let it dull my pain for a second before the pain returns. It seems worse, if that's even possible. Pulling my legs up to my chest, I take another drink of JD as my phone starts to ring.

I laugh when I see Darragh's name flash across the screen. I turn the phone facedown. I lie back and slowly drink from the bottle. The conversation with me and Shane keeps going around in my head, and no matter what way I view it, I can't seem to find the good in it. I say I love you. He doesn't. When he comes back to me, he tells me I'm important. Not losing my ID is important, or something as equally shitty as that. My phone rings again.

"Why are you being so persistent?" I answer.

"I need your help," Darragh responds.

I sit up and drink from the bottle again, but I roll my eyes at Darragh's words. "With what?" I ask, ready to end this phone call.

"Please, Una."

"Are you crying?" I question, thinking he can't be. But he doesn't sound good.

"Can you come and get me?"

I lie back and take another swallow from the bottle. "Can you not ring someone else?" I ask back. The JD burns a path of fire down my throat. It's nice; it's starting to numb me.

"If I could, I wouldn't be fucking ringing you."

"Keep your knickers on. Fine, give me the address." I laugh at my little joke, and Darragh rattles off the address of where he is. He's in Kells and not far at all.

"Give me twenty minutes," I tell him, and he hangs up without even a thank you. I take a final drink before I pocket my phone and creep out into the dark night. An idea starts to form in my head—a bad idea, but it's making me giddy with excitement.

I make my way into the garage and open the box that holds spare keys for all the cars. I get the Audi unlocked with the second key. Sliding into the driver's side, my heart squeezes. Shane's car purrs when I press the button. The rational part of me says he's going to be pissed, but the reckless side of me thinks it's a bit of justice.

When I start to reverse, the garage door lifts up, and I back out without crashing the car. I floor it as I race up the drive, sending dust and stones against the side of the car. I smirk as I hit the main road. There's a sense of freedom as I keep changing gears. Once I shift into sixth gear, I let out a yell. Yeah, this is fun.

The estate I pull into is run down. Gray two-story houses are lined until I can't see them. They don't end but keep going in some infinite line. There is a good chance if I leave the Audi and go and get Darragh, it won't be here when I get back. Darragh had said number three, and I pull up outside the house. No lights are on, and all the curtains are pulled. Several car tires are sitting on the lawn, which is dead and bleeding out onto the cracked asphalt.

I pull the phone from my pocket, then ring Darragh. He doesn't answer. I peer around the estate. It's quiet around, but still, I don't want to chance losing Shane's car.

"Where are you?" Darragh asks when I ring for the third time.

"Outside. Why wouldn't you answer your phone?"

He doesn't answer me. "I need you to come in."

When I start to protest, the asshole hangs up on me.

"Shit," I say as I turn off the car and get out. Locking it doesn't make me feel any better as I walk up the driveway to the front door. I don't have to knock, as Darragh opens the door and yanks me in.

"Does anyone know you're here?" he asks. "Is that Shane's car?" He spins around on me.

I shrug. "I'm alone. And yeah, it's his car."

He closes the door and scratches his neck. "This was a bad idea."

"Yeah, it was. Why couldn't you come outside?" I say, peering around the hall. It isn't dirty, but the simple beige linoleum on the hall floor has lots of cracks and holes in it. The door to the right of Darragh is pine and light enough that if you punched it, your fist would go through. A small lamp that's shining from under the stairs is the sole light in the hall, but I can still make out the paleness of Darragh's face.

"I've fucked up."

His words have dread dripping down my spine. The alcohol burns out of my system as he pushes open the sitting room door. Three dark, stained couches fill the room. A TV that's showing static lights up the room. The light bounces off the face of the girl in the silver disk dress. Her purple lips and still chest have me frozen in the doorway.

"Oh my God, is she dead?" I ask, not taking my eyes off her.

"Yes, she's dead."

I glance at Darragh. "And you ring me?" I can't for a second understand this. My eyes go back to the dead girl. This isn't like the bathroom with the other girl. This girl is dead, dead. Like really dead. My stomach heaves, and I turn, but nothing comes out.

"If I ring my family, they'll kill me this time." The fear in Darragh's words isn't enough for me to not miss the 'this time.'

"You've rung them about a dead body before?" I ask. "Don't answer that," I say quickly as he sits down beside her. "Oh my God, Darragh. She's dead."

When I shout at him, he gets up. "Calm the fuck down, Una. I need you to stay calm and help me, not fucking lose your shit over a prostitute." I stare at the girl again, and my pity for her increases.

"She's a person," I tell him.

But he doesn't hear me. Instead, he lights a fag. "First time, it's hard, but you're part of the family now, and family comes first." He's rattling off words while staring at the girl.

"First time for what?"

"We need to get rid of her."

I can accept a lot of things, but murder isn't one of them. I take out my phone to ring the Gardaí, but the carpet scrapes against my face as my phone hits the skirting board. I didn't even see Darragh move.

"Who are you ringing?" He sounds calm, but it doesn't match his actions. His hand is on my head, keeping my face pressed into the carpet. A terrified part of me questions if he'll kill me, too.

"No one." I try to peer at him, but he forces my face harder into the floor. "Please, Darragh." I whimper now. I was stupid for coming here. He releases me, and I sit up but don't stand. I don't think my legs could carry me.

Darragh is still on the floor. "They will kill me," he says as he peers at me.

"Who? Shane? Liam? They wouldn't," I tell him, and he starts to laugh.

"You have no idea."

A shiver snakes its way around my spine. "Tell me," I say, but I don't want to know. My brain has short-circuited on the fact that there's a dead body not ten feet from me. My ringing phone has both of us jumping, and I don't go for it. Feralness has entered Darragh eyes, and I'm afraid.

"Darragh, please. Let me ring for help."

His eyes snap to mine. "Are you fucking thick?" he barks, and there's a huge part of me that shrinks back and shrivels up at his words. But the survival instinct kicks in, and I stand.

"What do you want me to do?" I ask, but I can't stop the tremble that's entered my voice and lips.

"We need to find something to wrap her in and then get rid of her."

My phone rings again, and Darragh marches across the room and picks it up. His back is to me. I could make a dash for the door, but he's too close. My eyes dart to the dead girl, and my stomach rises and falls. This isn't happening.

"Fuck!" his roar has me frozen as his eyes snap to me. "Did you ring him?" he asks, marching back to me.

"You need to calm down." I push as much authority into my voice as I can. My phone is being waved around in his hand.

"Did you ring Shane?"

"No, Darragh." The fear and upset is in my words, and Darragh pauses his raving and exhales a breath.

"I'm sorry," he tells me, pulling me into a hug, and every part of my skin crawls. I want him away from me, but I force myself to wrap my arms around him. I hope he can't feel the dampness on his neck as my tears trickle down my face. I squeeze my eyes as his phone starts to ring. When he peers down at it, he pulls his hair, but I'm surprised when he answers.

CHAPTER NINETEEN

SHANE

"DO YOU HAVE SHANE'S car?" Liam asks as I sit back on the couch. My head is pounding. An hour ago, I found my car missing, and also Una and Darragh. It's a bad combination. Liam insisted he would ring Darragh before I jumped to any conclusions.

"Have you seen Una?" I stare at Liam as my heart starts to pick up its pace. I'm checking his features for any change, and when he turns his back on me, he's hiding something. I'm standing now, and when I reach him, the call ends.

"Our brother needs us," Liam says as he turns to me. "He needs us to be calm."

We take Liam's Range Rover. "Are you sure Una isn't there?" I ask him again as I glance out the window. He's withholding something from me.

"I told you, Darragh wasn't very clear. Just said he needed us."

I hate being the passenger. Liam is a careful driver, and I'm trying not to tell him to stop the Jeep so I can drive.

"Our brother needs us," Liam speaks again when I don't.

"That's the problem. He always needs us," I mumble.

"Family comes first." Liam says our family motto with a ferocity I understand.

"If she's here, I'm going to kill him." This time, I stare at Liam, but he doesn't flinch.

"She may have decided to go with him. You don't know the facts."

"She's with him, isn't she?" I clench my fists. I should never have left her. She must have gone drinking with Darragh, and he wouldn't take care of her.

"Family comes first, Shane."

I snap my attention to Liam. "She is family," I tell him, and he glances at me.

"She's not blood," he reminds me.

But she's more than that to me. Fuck, she takes place over Darragh any day.

We pull into a run-down estate, and my car is parked outside the third house. I'm surprised it's still sitting there. My focus goes to the house.

"I'll go in first." Liam speaks as he pulls up behind my car. I jump out but wait for him to go first. Darragh opens the door, and Liam steps through. He goes to close it, but I push it open. There's a change in his face—he pales. He wasn't expecting me.

Liam enters a room, and Darragh skips ahead of him. I tell my heart to slow down as a horrible thought comes to me. What if he hurt Una? I step into the room as Liam speaks. "Everyone needs to remain calm," he says, but my sole focus is sitting on the couch.

My heart gives a heavy thud as I skim over the dead girl and take in Una. She's sitting on the couch with tears streaming down her face. She's staring at her hands, which are folded in her lap. Her face is obscured from her hair. I can't take my eyes off her. I can't breathe. Air gushes from my nose.

"Shane, calm down." Liam speaks again. Una's head snaps up, her lip trembles, and all I can do is uncurl my fist and stretch out my hand for her to take. She steals a glance at Darragh and Liam but stands quickly, ducking her head as she comes to me.

Pulling her into my side, I glance up at Liam. I can't speak. If I do, I'll kill Darragh. I'm not sure what Liam sees on my face, but he turns to Darragh. The contact isn't enough for me, but the slap has Una tightening herself closer to me. I wrap my hand more securely around her frame.

"Out of all the stupid and reckless things you have done, this is the worst." Darragh holds his face. His coloring darkens to a gray. Liam has never put his hands on any of us, so this tells me he's angry.

"I didn't mean for her to die." Another slap is delivered to Darragh's face, cutting off his words.

"I'm talking about Una. You had no right involving her in this." Liam's raised words are feeding into the need to hurt Darragh myself, but I'm unable to move. I can't let Una see that side of me, and I can't let her go right now.

"I knew if I rang you, Liam, that you'd kill me." Darragh throws his hands in the air, a shiver in his tone. He's avoiding eye contact with me.

"It's not me you should be worried about," Liam informs him as he glances at me.

"I know." Darragh still doesn't meet my eye, but I can't stand here any longer and not kill him.

I turn and take Una with me out of the sitting room and enter a clean but scarcely furnished kitchen. A large table takes up most the room, and I pull out one of two chairs that remain tucked under it. Once I have her seated, I kneel down in front of her.

"I'm sorry." She swallows her tears as she speaks. My fingers cup her chin and gently tilt her head up. She meets my eyes.

"You have nothing to be sorry for," I tell her, holding her face as gently as I can.

"I stole your car." Her lips are in a frown as she speaks, and my thumb strokes her lips gently. They turn up slightly.

"It's only a car," I tell her, and she shakes her head.

"I was stupid to come here, there's a dead girl in there, and I don't think he cares." Her words hitch at the end, and her eyes blur before tears start to fall again. Pulling her into my arms, I hold her, and she shakes with large sobs.

I'm going to fucking kill him.

"I tried to ring the Gardaí, but he wouldn't let me." Her words have me closing my eyes briefly. She sounds stunned that we wouldn't ring the Gardaí. Her innocence is refreshing and also a reminder of what our life will do to her. She sits back and sniffles, her face flushed.

"You'll ring?" she asks, but she's nodding as if to say of course I will. I don't want to lie to her, but I'm also not going for the truth.

"Let's find out what happened first. Okay?" I tell her, and she nods.

"He rang me. I thought it was to pick him up. I didn't think it would be this." She flicks her head in the direction of the door.

"It's okay now," I tell her, brushing back some red curls from her face.

"I'm going to go in and see what's happened. I want you to stay here," I tell her, wanting nothing more than to scoop her up and take her from this place. But she gives me a little nod, and I press my lips to her forehead before I rise.

I enter the sitting room, and Liam takes a step toward me. The girl is in the same position, and Darragh is sitting on the couch smoking.

"It wasn't his fault. She overdosed. He had sex with her, so he was worried about his DNA." Liam is explaining the stupidity that is our brother.

"Shane," Darragh pleads, and I manage to raise one finger.

"Not a word," I tell him, and he gives Liam a final glance before his eyes settle on the floor.

"I'll get him to ring it in and report it," Liam tells me, stuffing a hand in his pocket. Darragh's head snaps up to Liam, but he has the sense not to speak. Liam's handprints are still on Darragh's face, but it's nothing compared to what I want to do to him.

"Darragh, go wait in my Jeep." Liam speaks to Darragh, but he's focused at me. Darragh gets up and gives me as wide a birth as the room will allow.

Once he leaves, Liam opens the top button of his shirt. "I've never asked for anything from you. I beg you, leave him alone. You have my word he will never go near Una again."

It means so much coming from Liam. If this were for anyone else, I would agree. But right now, at this given moment, I can't.

"No," I tell him and leave the room to go get Una. When I walk into the kitchen, her head snaps up to me. She's stopped crying, but the circles under her eyes have grown darker.

"Liam is ringing the police now, so we better go." I've never seen Una appear fragile. When I reach out my hand, she takes it easily and twines our fingers together. Her face is still tense.

I remind myself I'm doing this for her as I speak. "She overdosed. Darragh didn't hurt her. He panicked because he was intimate with her." My words don't come out as soft as I hoped, but when Una glances up at me, I see a spark there, like everything is going to be okay.

"He didn't hurt her," she says like she's waking up from a dream. I squeeze her hand.

"Of course not. He just panicked." I open the passenger door for her and don't glance back at Liam or Darragh. Liam has started the Jeep but hasn't pulled away.

Once Una is safely inside, I move around to the driver's-side door. It's then I peer up to find both of them watching me. Once I climb into the car, I turn on the heat. She's shivering. It's not from the cold, but I'm unsure what to do, so I just start driving.

"God, I'm so, so sorry for everything," she begins. "I acted like such a child earlier." The car has been moving for a few silent minutes. I thought she fell asleep.

"Una, everything is fine. You did nothing wrong," I tell her, and she falls silent again.

My hands hurt by the time I pull into the garage. I unclench my fists from the steering wheel, and once I knock off the car, I turn to Una.

"He scared me," she tells the window. "I tried to leave, but he wouldn't let me. Only for Liam ringing, I don't know what would have happened." Her lips tug downward as she blinks back tears. She doesn't cry, but her gaze becomes more focused on me.

"He's your brother. I'm sorry." She frowns and shakes her head, like she's trying to stop herself from talking. My silence probably isn't helping, but the idea of him not letting her go is killing me. "I'm just tired," she says and reaches for the door handle.

"I wish you didn't have to see that tonight," I manage to say, and she glances back at me over her shoulder, her eyes blinking with exhaustion.

"Me too."

Una changes her clothes, and I wait as she gets organized before she slips into the bed. After tucking the surrounding covers, I trace the darkness under her eyes. "You need to sleep. Everything will be better in the morning," I tell her.

She manages a weak smile. "Liar," she says, but I'm smiling because so is she.

The relief has me almost thinking of getting in beside her. But I don't. I can't.

I kiss her on the forehead and leave on the lamp as I make my way to the library, where I know Liam and Darragh will be.

The door is closed, but I can hear them behind it. Once I enter, they stop talking, and Darragh moves behind Liam. That sets me off.

I charge him, grab him by the shirt, and drag him out.

Liam doesn't move a muscle, but his sharp words cut through the air. "Shane, don't."

I don't pay any attention to his warning.

"Jesus. Please..." Darragh, the coward, covers his face, but I put as much force as possible into the punch. Holding him with my other hand, I don't let him fall. Liam drags me off him after three punches, but I'm only getting started.

"Family comes first." Liam holds me around the chest. His words are spoken harshly and close to my ear. Darragh is lying against the bookcase, his face a bloody mess.

I breath fast with adrenaline. I'm not satisfied, but Liam repeats his words again, and I try to bring some calm back to me.

"Let me go," I tell him, but he doesn't immediately. "Liam, let me go. I won't touch him." He releases me, but I don't release Darragh from my stare. A shaky hand rises, and he wipes blood from his mouth and nose. Liam walks over to him and drops a white handkerchief into his lap. Darragh picks it up and starts wiping at his face.

"Are you done?" Liam asks me, and I flex my fist, my knuckles burning. I don't answer his stupid question.

"Have you wondered why he rang Una?" Liam asks while he glances back at Darragh, who's still trying to clean his face.

"Because he's a spoiled little prick who thinks he can do whatever he wants," I say, but my stomach tightens at the question.

"Someone told her about us."

"Is there something you want to ask me?" I shoot back to Liam.

"Is there something you want to tell us?" Liam sounds righteous.

"Yeah, that he's always high. Maybe he told her and forgot."

"No, I didn't."

I take a threatening step toward Darragh, and he shuts up, but Liam moves closer to me. "Liam won't always be here to protect you, Darragh. You're such a fucking disappointment to us. To Dad."

"Shane, stop." Liam, the peacekeeper, speaks again, but I don't so much as give him a glance. I keep Darragh pinned to the floor with my stare as I speak.

"It's only a matter time before we're pulling you out of a ditch as you rot away like a sheep." My words have him standing, fire in his eyes, and I grin at him.

"Look, I know I fucked up..."

I have to walk away from his pathetic words. But as he keeps speaking, I turn back around. "I never put a hand on her," he says. His words have Liam closing his eyes, but my whole body tenses.

"I never said you did, so why would you say that?" I take a step back toward him.

"I'm just saying. I don't know why you're so angry." He's still dabbing his nose with his little white handkerchief.

"Shut up, Darragh," Liam tells him, and his eyes widen.

"No, it's fine, Liam." I hold up a hand toward Liam to let him know to say silent as I educate my dimwit brother. "You rang an innocent girl who, number one, is a girl. Number two, she has no dealings with our world. And you don't just ring her to pick you up from a junkie's house, but you what, expect her to help you get rid of a body?" I laugh again. "Are you that fucking stupid?"

"I panicked." He's acting like a victim.

I move quickly and slam him against the bookshelf. "You're a self-centered little prick." My hands go to his neck, and I squeeze. He's trying to claw my hands away from his neck. His eyes widen as he stares at me.

"Shane, let him go." Liam is there now, but I don't let go. His words have me squeezing tighter, Darragh's eyes growing wider. Liam grabs my face. "You're going to kill him. Let him go."

His calm words in a moment of chaos have me releasing him. Darragh falls to the floor, gasping and retching for air. But once again, I'm not satisfied. I can no longer stay in the room with them.

CHAPTER TWENTY

UNA

I WAKE UP WITH a racing heart. All I see are silver disks that belong to the dress of a dead girl. Tears leave the corners of my eyes, and I blink quickly, wanting them to stop. As I sit up slowly, I'm faced with Shane's back. He's sitting on the bed, his head bowed. I can't see his face.

"Shane?" I whisper, and his head shoots up. The strain on his face disappears, and his eyes grow lighter.

"I didn't mean to wake you," he tells me as he gets up and makes his way around the bed.

"You didn't." I don't tell him what did. "Are you okay?" I ask. Dark circles under his eyes are worrying me. A frown appears on his face as he sits down on the bed.

His eyes roam my face, and my stomach squeezes.

"You're too kind, Una," he says. I'm not sure why, but I don't object as he moves closer and pulls me slowly into his arms. I come out from under the covers and wrap myself around him while inhaling his scent, and it relaxes me. In his arms, I feel safer.

"I keep seeing her face when I close my eyes," I tell him like a confession, and his arms tighten around me. "What happened with her?" I ask him.

"Her family has been notified. She's in good hands now. Poor girl was an addict." Shane doesn't sound like he thinks she's a poor girl. His words are robotic, and I try to see his face, but he holds me closer. "Just let me hold you for a while longer." His request scares me.

Every few seconds, Shane plants a kiss on my head, and I'm sure his hold grows tighter to the point of being almost crushing.

"Shane." When I speak his name, he loosens his hold on me but doesn't release me, and the longer he keeps me in his arms, the bigger my fear grows. It almost seems like a long goodbye.

"When I saw you sitting on that couch..." He stops speaking and releases me, allowing me to sit back.

I'm on my hunkers in front of him. He won't look at me, and I swallow the ball of fear that has lodged itself in my throat.

"You don't belong here. I've been so selfish holding on to you." His eyes hold such conviction, and my heart slams against my ribcage. "If you want to leave, you can." I'm gaping at him and struggling to breathe. He's trying to get rid of me. Telling him I love him seemed to have messed everything up. I want to take it back, but looking at him, it hurts too much to speak.

"Una, don't look at me like that." He reaches for my hand, and I pull it back.

Tears fall quietly. "I've been forward with you." My nose, throat, and eyes burn, and I have to stop speaking before I bawl. "Too forward," I whisper and wish my stupid emotions would stop until I get the words out.

"I can take a step back," I tell him with a shrug. I sound pathetic. The pity in his eyes has heat traveling up my neck. Oh, God. Has everyone been laughing at the lovesick fool pining after Shane?

"It's not you, Una."

I laugh at his words, but it dies down and ends on an angry sob. I climb off the bed, needing to get away from him.

"This is coming out all wrong. You're picking me up the wrong way." His words are barked at me as he gets up too.

"Tell me, Shane. Do you and Liam laugh about how stupid I am?" I question, and Shane tilts his head with narrowed eyes.

"What has Liam got to do with this?" He takes a step toward me, and I ignore the tightness that enters my stomach.

"He warned me away from you. Did you ask him to do that because you're not man enough?"

Shane's eyes widen, nose flared, and I'm surprised at the frozen stature of his frame. He clenches his fist. I see the red and swollen knuckles. I'm there beside him, taking his damaged hand in mine.

"What happened?" I ask him quietly. He didn't have this before I went to bed. "What did you do?"

His chest rises and falls quickly, and when I put my hand over his thundering heart, wild eyes meet mine. I want to know what the hell is going on inside his head.

"What I had to," he answers through clenched teeth. I'm shaking my head.

"Shane," I start. He tries to move past me, but I race to the door. I don't have a clue what I'm doing, but the violence in his eyes is scaring me. "You hurt Darragh?"

His eyes snap to me. "Move, Una."

"You can't go around hurting people," I tell him and force as much authority as possible into my words.

"They can't go around threatening and terrorizing you," he shouts back, and I jump slightly.

"It wasn't like that. He was concerned for you."

Now Shane is shaking his head. He's in front of me, a head taller as he stares straight ahead. "Move, Una," he tells me again.

He glances at me as I place a hand on his chest. "I'm begging you, for me. Don't leave this room. Not tonight." His eyes roam my face, jaw clenched. He doesn't answer me, but he doesn't ask me to move again either. I'll take it as a small victory.

God, my love for him is affecting my judgment. With anyone else, I would be long gone. I can't figure him out. I tell myself I'm doing it to calm him down, but I can't manage to keep away from him. My hands leave his chest and roam to his shoulders. I want to pull him into a kiss, but something stops me. Slowly, moving him back toward the bed, he lets me. My heart picks up. Every part of my body squeezes at the thought of having him again.

The weight of his stare nearly undoes me, but I keep some form of control as he sits on the bed. Pulling his jumper off, I inhale the scent of him as my eyes devour his flesh. His muscular torso has me squeezing my legs together.

I kneel in front of him and spread his legs. Shane doesn't stop me as I move close to him. When my lips press against his stomach, the muscles flex and tense under each kiss I plant there. I trail kisses up his chest and along his neck; I have never been so taken or consumed with someone before.

Holding his face, staring into the darkest brown eyes ever, I flicker a glance at his lips. He tenses when I move close, so I place the kiss on his shoulder instead. His hands move now and pull off my top. My cream bra is unhooked quickly, and it finds itself on the floor.

I don't cover myself but allow Shane the same access as he gave me. My fingers sink into his hair as he starts a trail of kisses down my neck. My stomach twisting and yearning building inside me, I'm not sure I can hold on. The intensity grows on Shane, too, as I find myself on my back on the bed. His strong hands and damaged knuckles graze my thigh as he pulls off my trousers. His eyes devour me, and I arch my pelvis up.

It seems forever as he removes his trousers and boxers. His erection springs out, and I'm spreading my legs for him as he moves on top of me. Pulling my underwear aside, Shane places his erection at the opening. His focus is back on my face. Biting my lip is the thing that stops me from shouting out that I need him now.

When he enters me, I let out a long moan. His thrusts are slow and deep, but I want it quick. I want all of him in me. Pulling him down closer by the shoulders, I widen my legs even further, and Shane plunges deeper, faster. I close my eyes as each roll of ecstasy courses through my body. The final one ends when Shane slams into me and pauses as he releases before moving out slowly and back in two more times.

After slipping out of me, he moves down until his head rests on my stomach while he still lies between my throbbing legs. We stay like that as we catch our breath. A kiss to my stomach has my heart picking up speed again. Watching Shane now as he hoists himself off me, my stomach twists and dances. It's there, that stupid three-word phrase that I want to tell him. I drop his gaze.

I don't know what to do as he arrives back from the bathroom with a face cloth and cleans me up. I bite hard on the inside of my jaw so I don't cry. How can I let him go? Once he has me cleaned, he goes into the bathroom and turns on the shower. It's then I get up and put on his green T-shirt and a clean pair of underwear before climbing back into the bed.

When Shane climbs in beside me, my breasts swell in his T-shirt with a want to have him again. The need has me almost turning around, but I don't. He's beside me, and the heat of his body sends me into a slumber. I'm nearly asleep when his arm drapes over my stomach, and a kiss is left on my cheek.

***

I wake. My body tells me I had sex last night. I still throb. Opening my eyes, my stomach sinks. Shane isn't here. While sitting up, I stare at his side and find a small note sitting on his pillow. I'm smiling like a fool as I open it.

The sun is shining, so get dressed. I'm taking you out.

One line has me racing from the bed like a kid on Christmas morning. I jump in the shower and then spend time picking out a nice cream lace summer dress. It's really pretty, and this is the perfect occasion for it. The buttons start at my belly button and go the whole way to my neck. I leave the top two open and grin at myself in the mirror.

My hair is wild today, and no matter how I try to tame it, curls stick out and spring wherever they want. Today is going to be warm—my hair is telling me that. It never behaves in good weather. Oh, well.

After grabbing a pair of green runners, I slip them on. A bit odd with the dress, but I want to be comfortable.

When I enter the kitchen, Mary gives me a smile. "He's waiting out front for you." Her words have my chest swelling, and I can't stop the ridiculous smile that's plastered across my face.

A squeal tears from my throat when I make it outside, and Shane's lips lift, his dimples appearing. I would be consumed by him, but the Cadillac that he stands beside gets most of my attention. But not all.

"Where have you been hiding this beauty?" I run my hand along the leather roof that's rolled back. I can see my reflection in the black Cadillac—my eyes are huge, and I'm still smiling.

"She's new," he tells me, removing his hand from his trousers pockets. The short-sleeved navy T-shirt is allowing me to see his tattoo in the light of day. The thick black bands are such a statement.

"You like her?" he asks, and I snap my attention back to him.

"It's a 1941 Convertible Cadillac. I mean, what's not to like?"

His smile turns into laughter at my enthusiasm. Moving around to the passenger door, Shane opens it, and I climb in. I don't say anything about the wooden weaved picnic basket in the back seat.

Shane starts the engine, and I close my eyes in bliss as the engine rumbles under us. "Should I give you a moment?" Shane teases, and when I glance at him, I want to tell him how much I love him. How he undoes me every time I set eyes on him.

"No," I answer, and he takes in a deep breath through his nose like he heard my three words on that one answer.

The wind whips my hair around my face. It's not a pretty picture. It's most certainly not like the movies. It's like a sheep slammed into my face, and Shane has been proper laughing for the last few moments as I battle with the red curls.

"I'm cutting it off," I threaten as it settles. Shane knocks off the engine as we pull in at Dun Na Ri Park.

"Don't you dare," he warns.

"You laugh at me again, and I will," I reply. A yelp jumps from my lips as he pulls me close. My heart slams into my chest. When Shane presses his forehead against mine, I'm disappointed, but also, I'm beginning to think this is how he kisses. Like penguins use their noses, Shane uses his forehead. A quick abrupt laugh leaves my lips. I don't answer Shane's raised eyebrow. Instead, I jump out of the Cadillac.

The grass under my feet has recently been cut, the ends of the grass sending small shock waves up my legs. I glance at Shane as he sits on the rug and eats grapes out of the basket. He packed our breakfast, and it's perfect.

With my stomach full and my soul light, yesterday seemed like a distant dream. "I don't know how you're doing that," Shane says, and I lift a leg before slowly lowering my bare feet into the grass. He visibly shivers.

"Come on, try it," I tell him, but he's shaking his head.

"No, grass and sand are two things I don't like touching my skin."

I roll my eyes. Bending at the waist, I pull out a handful of grass.

"Oh, Shane O'Reagan is afraid of a bit of grass." I throw it at him, and one piece manages to float into his mouth, which he spits out, and I laugh. Laughter turns to a yelp as he gets off the grass and chases after me. My destination is a large oak that stands in the middle of the park. My feet leave the ground as Shane grabs me and spins me around. The world halts as he drags me down onto the grass.

I laugh as he pokes my stomach, and when he stops, all I see is the blue sky and brown eyes, and it squeezes my heart. Shane is above me, resting on his tattooed arm, and I don't move. There is such a seriousness in his eyes that I hold still.

"When you first came to our house, I hated you," he says. Not what I was expecting to hear. His confession has me wanting to rise, but he continues speaking. "I hated you because I wanted you. I wanted you like I'd never wanted anything." His brows pull down as he speaks. His focus is on my shoulder. "I didn't want to ruin you," he says and glances at me.

My heart gallops as he reaches out and moves a curl off my cheek. "I know the right thing to do is to convince you to leave…"

I try to sit up, but his free hand on my shoulder stops me. "Not this again," I tell him as my heart thunders in my chest. He's going to tell me to leave again. My heart can't take this.

"Please, let me finish." He closes his eyes on the word please. I try to remain quiet. "The right thing would be to tell you to leave, but I'm too selfish to give you up, Una." Heat rises in my cheeks at his words.

Reaching up, I hold his face, and he leans into me. "I won't leave, anyway. I'm like a bad infection."

He snorts a laugh at my words before turning my hand around and kissing my palm. Electricity zings down my arm and goes straight to my heart. "My mother, she had this funny saying. 'Seal it with a kiss.'" At the mention of a kiss, my heart grows almost frantic in my chest.

"At night, when she tucked us all in, she would tell us how much she loved us. A kiss to the lips was the final part. She said it sealed in her love, and that when we truly love someone, it's so important to seal it with a kiss."

I nearly can't breathe at what he's saying. His eyes flicker to my lips, which I must have wet a million times since he started talking about kissing.

"I'm going to kiss you now," he tells me.

I'm shaking my head. "Wait." My one word is breathless, but I can't stop the panic that races through me.

"What if it's not good?" I ask, my insecurities rising like a tidal wave to the top. "What if I'm too sloppy or too dry?"

"Una," Shane says, but I cut him off.

"There's too much pressure, I don't know if I can live up to such…"

"*Cunas*, Una." The softness and the Irish word for quiet has my words silenced as Shane moves closer to me. A sense of sinking into the grass and going deeper down the rabbit hole has me holding my breath. His breath brushes my lips, and my hands sink into the grass.

"You look terrified," he says, and I blink, wondering why the hell he's talking and why his lips aren't on mine.

Our breaths mingle together, and I flick out my tongue one last time as his lips brush mine. My whole body seems to sigh before a drum beats within my veins, pushing the blood around my body way too quickly. A sense of swaying as Shane parts my lips with his tongue makes this all seem unreal.

His kiss is full but not urgent. It's slow and perfect, and I can't get oxygen into my lungs. Shane's smell, taste, and mouth are taking over every part of me, and I give myself up to him.

CHAPTER TWENTY-ONE

SHANE

U NA UNDER ME IS as I had imagined. Kissing her is a high I've never felt before. I deepen the kiss, forcing my tongue deeper inside her mouth, and she gives me entry easily. Her hands grip my shoulders as she pulls me closer. I have to pull back. My body is demanding more, but I remember we're in the middle of a park.

"Wow." Una's swollen lips move. I smile down at her.

"Yeah, wow," I repeat, and her lips tug up into a smile that shows me a set of perfect white teeth.

"Can we do it again?" Her wide eyes and eagerness have me giving her a soft kiss on the lips. "Anytime"—I kiss her again—"you want." Another kiss, and this time, she forces her tongue into my mouth, and I pull back again.

"There could be children around," I tell her, and she nods, fixing her dress.

"Yeah, you're right." Color coats her cheeks as I sit up and take her hand, helping her sit up too. Pressing a kiss to her shoulder, I glance up at her from under my lashes, and there is pure awe in her eyes.

"Tell me about your mum?" she asks.

The question surprises me. "She was really great." Great doesn't even cut it. "She was fun." I smile at the memory of her once waking us up at six in the morning. She had spent hours filling water balloons—she must have filled hundreds of them. She took us outside, and we had the biggest water fight ever.

We were all red and marked when we came inside later that morning, but we were all smiling. Even Liam used to smile then. My smile must falter as Una squeezes my shoulder.

"Are you okay? I'm sorry if I pried."

I cover her hand with mine. "I was thinking about how Liam used to smile more when Mum was alive."

"Liam and smiling in one sentence? Never." Her wide eyes and exaggerated surprise have me smiling again. My lips find hers, and my fingers sink into her hair. Her lips are warm and moist and fit perfectly against mine. She was created for me. My heart thuds as I think of what she means to me.

"I don't think I could ever get used to this." She speaks in between kisses.

"Stay with me," I ask, and she leans out.

"Like in your room?" She seems confused.

Holding her face, I swallow before speaking. "No, stay with me forever."

Her chest rises and falls quickly. "Forever is a long time." Her whispered words are accompanied with blurred eyes.

"Not long enough with you." I wipe away a falling tear. Turning her face, she kisses my hand.

"Forever," she says, and my heart swells.

My phone ringing can't be ignored. I kiss Una on the nose before getting up to take the call. It's Neill. I've been waiting on any word from him about the new supplier.

"What news do you have?" I ask after taking a few steps away from Una. Glancing back at her now, she has her hand covering her swollen lips, but I can see the smile in her eyes as she gazes up at me.

"Brian is out of the hospital and meeting with the new supplier today." The little prick. Liam warned me about this happening. Brian had to know that word would get back to me.

"Where?"

"Smyth's in the next hour."

"Thanks, Neill," I say and hang up. Each step toward Una makes guilt churn in my stomach. I hate that I have to cut our first proper date short, but we have forever to make up for it. I sit back down and kiss her on the shoulder again. Her eyes roam my face.

"What's wrong?" she asks as I kiss her on the shoulder.

"I have to go to work," I tell her. "But I'll make it up to you." A spark of desire flares to life in her eyes.

"I can think of a lot of ways that you can make it up to me," she says, and I kiss her softly on the lips.

"Care to share?"

She bites her lip. "I'd rather show you later."

My trousers tighten at her words. "You're killing me," I tell her.

She gets up while wiping grass off the back of her dress. "Good." She winks before strolling back to our picnic basket. She throws a smile over her shoulder, making all her red curls bounce. Everything about Una takes my breath away.

I hadn't told Una that I bought the car for her. I know she won't accept it, but it's in her name. I put the roof up this time but leave the windows down. Watching Una glance around the car while she touches it like it's a pet lets me know I made the right decision buying it.

Once we get home, I switch cars and give Una one final kiss. "I'll try not to be late," I tell her as I climb into the Audi but roll down the window.

"I'll wait for you." She sways like an innocent girl would, but her words and eyes are full of devilment.

I leave before I change my mind. Twenty minutes later, I pull into Kells. It's two in the day. The pub won't be opening for another two hours. I take my handgun out of the glove compartment. After checking to make sure it's loaded, and the safety is on, I push it into the waistband of my trousers.

I knock three times before Michael opens the door. He quickly steps aside before closing the door behind me. "Shane, this is my livelihood. Please don't wreck it." His words have me pausing, and I give him a curt nod that seems to relax him.

I'm not sure what exactly I'm walking into. I go into the lounge, knowing it will be empty, and then jump the counter. I move down the bar and ring the bell as I enter the bar area. Two men sit at a corner table. Both face me, and I force a smile.

"A drink?" I ask. Brian's face is covered in a white cast that covers the top part of his face, showing his eyes.

"A whiskey," a Northern Ireland accent says. I pour out three whiskeys. Bernard gets up from the table and sits at the bar before picking up a whiskey. He holds it up to me. "To family," he says, and I knock my glass against his.

"To family," I repeat.

"You know each other?" Brian speaks now for the first time, getting up, and I slide the glass down to him. He's too slow, and it slides off the end of the bar and smashes on the floor.

"How's your face?" I ask him, and I'm not sure, but I think his eyes narrow. Hard to tell with all the bandages.

"Michael's not impressed with you crossing the line," I tell Bernard as he finishes his drink.

"Michael? That's what you call him now? I call mine Da."

I smirk, but it's stretched across my tense face. "You've no right to be here," I tell him.

"You think your family is better than mine." It's not a question but a statement.

My heart thumps wildly in my chest. "At least my Da isn't a rat."

"You know each other?" Brian parrots again.

"He's my cousin," I say, not looking away from Bernard.

"They were kids, and name-calling isn't very smart of you," I say through gritted teeth.

"What are you going to do, Shane? You touch me, and the RA will be down here tearing this place apart."

I force a laugh before refilling my drink slowly. "Trust me Bernard," I say and take a drink, "you're not important."

His annoyance grows. "I've every right to be here. You treat your men like animals, so I'm taking over."

I finish my drink, tired with this conversation.

"I'm not looking to get employer of the year. But you taking over? Let's see," I say and decide that he's no real threat. Gary in Dublin would never bend to Bernard's terms; he's too cocky. The real problem is Brian. I need to get him on my side. I refill two glasses, and this time, I walk down to Brian and place a drink in front of him.

"Water under the bridge." I hold up my glass, and I one hundred percent expect him to do the same. Relief swims through me as he picks it up and clicks glasses with me.

Bernard is standing now. "You can't do that. We made a deal."

"The deal is off," I tell him, and his face grows red.

"You can't do that."

"I just did."

"Do you know who I am?" His arrogance is pissing me off.

I move back toward him and lean across the bar. "No, Bernard. Do you know who I am?"

"Yeah, I do. You're a whore's son."

I look away before snapping back and slamming my fist into his face. He falls back onto the ground as I hop the bar. Spitting out blood, he laughs as he stands and wipes his mouth.

"You know she was giving my Da head." He chuckles. My head connects with his nose, and he hits the counter before the ground. I'm down on my knees, my fist hitting his face.

"Stop! Shane!" Brian doesn't touch me, but he pulls me back from the edge of darkness that's threatening to consume me. A pool of blood is growing under Bernard's head. His still chest has me sitting back. I hit him a few times, and his head had collided with the counter, obviously harder than I thought.

"He's dead," Brian says as he places his hands on his head and walks away from me before returning.

"Help me get him out back," I say, getting up and pulling Bernard with me. "Just open the door," I tell Brian as he stares at the pool of blood. I take Bernard out back to where the smoking shed is.

"Get me a towel." When he returns, I tell him to keep the towel to Bernard's head to stop more blood from leaking everywhere. After leaning him against the tin structure, I go back into the pub and start to clean up the blood. I don't think about what happened; instead, I just clean. After scrubbing the floor twice with bleach, I gather all the glasses and take them with me.

"Are you still there?" Brian shouts in from the back like a moron.

I take a final look around. It smells funny, but nothing appears out of the ordinary. Going out back, I give Brian the glasses to hold and take the towel and Bernard from him. I need to get my car around back. I'm about to tell Brian when the back door opens.

"Who's been pouring bleach ov—" I don't turn as the girl speaks, but her words are cut off.

"Ava. Yeah, our friend here pissed himself," Brian says. "We're taking him home."

"Is he bleeding?"

This is too risky, letting her see so much. I shift, and Brian must sense my urgency.

"Yeah, he fell over," he continues. "But you better to go inside and do your job." She must be able to see half of Bernard's face, and that's making me nervous. But when the door slams, I glance at Brian.

I leave him with Bernard's body and make my way out the back of the building. The girl is annoying me. She saw Bernard and me. She needs to be eliminated. After getting the car, I drive around back. My eyes scan the area for cameras, but I know there are none. That's why I picked this small pub. There is no surveillance in this area.

Opening the double green doors that have No Parking painted in white across them, I reverse the Audi in as close as I can and pop the trunk. Once I have Bernard, the towel, and the glasses in the boot, I tell Brian to get in. He hesitates but jumps into the front seat. Closing the gates, I pull away from Kells and drive toward home.

"Who was the girl?" I ask Brian, who hasn't spoken a word.

"Shane, she can't be touched."

I glance at him. "What, is she your sister?" She didn't resemble him, but I could tell they knew each other.

"No, it's complicated. But she thought he was drunk. There's no need to go near her." Panic is rising in his voice, so he must be intimate with her.

"She's a loose end," I tell him while making sure I'm keeping within the speed limit. I don't need to attract any unwanted attention.

"Shane, you have my word that she'll never tell a soul." His word means nothing to me. We reach the bog land fifteen minutes later, and I back up my car into the mud.

"It's too risky, Brian," I say, opening the trunk.

"Leave her alone, and you have me, I will never look at anyone again. You will always come first. If I break my word, you can kill her."

I mull over his words. It would be something to have that power over him. "I'll think about it." My words seem to satisfy him as I start to pull the body out of the car. I should have waited until nightfall, but we don't have that luxury.

Brian follows my steps as we make our way carefully across the land. I send him back for the shovels as we start to dig. I don't bury the towel or glasses with him. Once he's covered over, I take a breather.

"I'm going to drop you back at the bar. You make sure Ava saw a very drunk guy." He's nodding like a fucking dog, and I don't like how overeager he is. But if he betrays me, I'll kill her first and make him watch. "Clean the bar—every single place he could have touched. If I go down for this, so do you," I tell him as I start back to the car. "Burn your clothes."

He nods. "Okay, I got it. Don't worry."

Worry is exactly what I'll end up doing.

CHAPTER TWENTY-TWO

UNA

I T'S THREE IN THE morning when the bedroom door opens, and I question for the hundredth time tonight if this is going to be my life. I don't want to be all "Where were you?" but I'm curious about where the hell he was until three in the morning. I can see his outline as he creeps to the bathroom. Clapping my hands, the room floods with light, blinding me momentarily. Once I open them, I wish I hadn't.

"What the hell?" There's blood on Shane's clothes and arms. My eyes travel to his feet. "Is that mud?" Muck coats the side of his black boots. *Did he trek through a muddy field?*

"It's okay. My car got stuck." His explanation has me folding my arms across my chest. The small silk nightdress doesn't cover much, and right now Shane is taking me in. For once, I won't be distracted.

"Was the car bleeding?"

Hanging his head, Shane takes a deep breath. When he peers back up at me, he seems more composed. "I don't want to lie to you," he says, pulling his top off, and he's all flesh and muscles.

My eyes roam his body. There isn't a mark on him, and I'm grateful that he isn't hurt.

"Then don't," I tell him as he opens the belt of his trousers. Pulling them off, he turns to me in his boxers, and it's not fair.

"Una, I do things in my line of work that aren't easy to do."

I tighten my arms at his half explanation. "The other person? Are they okay?" I can't look at him now. What would my dad think of me? I know he's hurt people. I've seen the blood, the anger, yet I love him. What kind of person does that make me? There's a lull, and that's what makes me glance at Shane.

"No." It's stupid of me, but I'm shocked. I take a step away from Shane; I need to think. I also need more answers, but I'm not sure I can take them in right now.

"No, as in he's in the hospital? Or not, as in he's..." I can't finish my sentence.

Shane glances away from me. A muscle twitches in his jaw as he debates what to say. I want the truth, but that terrified part of me hopes he lies.

He settles on "I don't know what you want me to say," and my stomach twists.

"I don't know either." I swallow the lump in my throat, but I have my answer. Whoever's blood is on him is dead. As I sit down on the bed, I try to process this.

"I thought it was just drugs?" I ask the stupid question, and I can almost see Shane grin at my naïve question. He runs his hands through his hair before coming to me. His muscles seem to flex and roll as he walks, and I think it's a nicer thing to focus on. Kneeling in front of me, Shane takes my hands in his bloodied one. We both stare at the blood for a moment.

"Una, I know this is difficult for you, but I would never harm someone for no reason." His brown eyes hold mine, and I nod.

"But sometimes, in this job, there are losses."

"I can't bear to think that one day it will be you." I swallow the tidal wave of emotion that wants to consume me. He pulls me closer to him and lays his forehead against mine before kissing me softly on the lips. I melt into his arms and kiss him like its oxygen for my screaming lungs.

"It won't be," Shane tries to reassure me as his hands roam into my hair.

"You can't promise me that," I say, and he holds my stare.

"If you keep dressing like this, I will always come back to you."

I give half a laugh and half a sob at his stupid statement. He can't actually promise me his safety. All I can do is hope and pray that God keeps him safe. As I flicker my gaze to his lips, I stroke his face, my thumb moving back and over his cheek.

I give a quick glance up at Shane. He hasn't taken his eyes off me before I close the distance and kiss him. My tongue gains entry easily into his mouth, and I give him the same access into mine. My skin burns as his hands leave my hair and roam my body. His touch isn't gentle, and the kiss has grown in intensity to an almost frantic rhythm. We break the kiss as Shane yanks my dressing gown over my head. Our lips smash back together as I move further back on the bed.

My hands roam his wide back as a pool forms between my legs. When Shane enters me, he lets out a moan. His thrusts are as frantic as his kisses. It doesn't take long before I release, and Shane follows shortly after. His head is on my chest now as he breathes fast, and I kiss his hair, running my hands through it, fighting for air too.

"I love you," I tell him as my heart thunders in my chest. It's the type of beat that almost hurts as it slams against my chest.

Shane raises his head and removes himself from me. He climbs up to me. He doesn't say anything, but he kisses me, and I can feel the seal.

***

The next morning, I wake up to an empty bed. Things always seem better in the morning, but honestly, I'm questioning if going to bed alone and waking up alone is something I can get used to. Do I really have a choice? The idea of not having Shane at all causes me to pull my knees up to my stomach. I can accept having a small bit of him rather than none of him. With that thought, I get out of bed and shower and get ready for work.

After putting on my work clothes, I go downstairs and smile when I can smell the pancakes wafting from the kitchen.

"They smell—" My words fall silent.

"Delicious," Liam finishes for me, and I don't smile at him as he cuts up a pancake. Mary isn't here, but I know Liam didn't make the pancakes. A plate is sitting across from him.

"Sit, Una," he tells me, and I reluctantly sit down. The pancakes aren't as enticing now as I glance up at Liam. The hairs stand on my arms as he assesses me.

"How are you?" The question has me narrowing my eyes, but Liam doesn't react to that. Instead, he waits with his knife and fork poised.

"Fine," I answer, and he continues cutting up his pancake in tiny, little pieces that he chews like fifty times before swallowing.

"How was Shane this morning?" he asks, and I try not to let him see how much he bothers me as I place a piece of pancake in my mouth. "I don't know. He wasn't there when I woke up," I bite out.

"I'm worried about him." I'm not sure if Liam is being sincere or not, but this is about Shane.

"Why?"

"Because, Una, he's acting out against anyone who looks at you funny. I fear you've cast a spell over my brother."

I drop my knife and fork at his words. "No one looked at me funny. Darragh wouldn't let me go; that's not a look. And Brian was an asshole. I don't want Shane go around beating anyone up, but don't make it out like I'm whispering lies to him."

Liam continues to chew slowly, not reacting to my words.

"Screw you, Liam," I bark when he doesn't respond. I take half the pancake and jam it into my mouth, unable to press my lips together, but I chew and swallow the lump before washing it down with a glass of OJ that had also been left out on the table for me.

"I wasn't insulting you. I was stating a fact." The want to stick my tongue out at his righteous tone is squashed as he stands.

"That's not a fact, Liam. You know what? I used to think your weirdness was cute. Now I see you for what you are."

He places his knife and fork on the plate. "And what's that?" I'm honestly surprised he asks, and I have no problem delivering my answer.

"An asshole," I tell him, standing too. I leave my plate in the sink before going into the wet room. It's there that I slip into my wellies and take my coat off the hook. Leaving the house, I slide my phone out of my pocket and ring Shane. No answer. I honestly don't know what he has a phone for.

I don't see Stephen around the stables. He could be over at the cattle sheds; I feed and bed all the horses. I leave Summer until last so I can spend some time with her. The noise of a quad has me smiling. Stephen must be back. I close Summer's stable and make my way to the front yard. But it's not Stephen.

Darragh falls off the quad, his face black and blue. As his eyes snap to me, he glowers. I'm not surprised, but it still hurts. He gets off the ground and makes his way to the shed. I know what's in it, and against my better judgment, I follow him in.

"Darragh." I speak his name gently as he removes a gun from the wall. The double barrel is empty. I know because I checked them yesterday.

"Go away, troublemaker." He's not just drunk. I'm pretty sure Darragh is high too. The way his eyes grow and shrink rapidly tells me it hasn't been that long since he got high.

"You're in no fit state to take a gun." I'm not rushing toward him, as he doesn't have any bullets.

"You sound like your mother—a broken fucking record. That's why my da had to get rid of her just like Shane will get rid of you." I force a smile even as Darragh's words sting. He isn't himself, and Shane did a number on his face. I have to remember that he has a right to be angry with me.

"Okay. I'm not fighting with you, Darragh," I tell him as he starts opening the cabinet close to the gun rack. He rattles the locked doors.

"Give me the key," he says, and I fold my arms across my chest, satisfied that he can't get the bullets.

"Nope. And I'm doing this because I care," I tell him, and he snorts.

"You're trying to control me like everyone else." The gun is making me uncomfortable as Darragh waves it around, and I have to keep reminding myself that it isn't loaded.

Something my father used to say plays around in my head. "The devil puts a bullet in a gun every ten years." Not a clue where the saying came from, but I'm moving every time the gun is pointed in my direction.

"Give me the key now, Una." Once he doesn't have ammunition, not much can go wrong. I leave the shed, as I'm too uncomfortable with him waving it around. The sound of shattering glass causes a shiver to skitter up my back, and I run back inside.

"There's more than one way to get in," Darragh says, taking a handful of bullets and shoving them into his pockets.

"You're being stupid," I tell him, trying to get him to put the bullets back. But that's not happening.

"I'm going to shoot the pheasant who keeps stealing my boots." He's on the quad, the gun in his hand.

"Darragh, seriously…"

My words fall on deaf ears as he kicks the quad into gear and races from the farmyard. "Shit."

***

"And you let him leave?" The question Liam asks me has me tightening my fists. His back is to me as he checks the cabinet for the missing gun and bullets.

"I couldn't stop him. You're wasting time. I told you the gun he took," I say, but he isn't listening to me. Once he finishes searching, Liam leaves the shed and starts in the direction of Darragh. I'm on his heels.

"Should you not ring Shane?" I ask, and Liam glances at me sideways. He's walking fast, and I have to walk/jog to keep up.

"I assume I wasn't your first choice. So I can also assume you've already rung him and he hasn't answered."

Liam and his know-it-all ways. I don't answer. He's right, I did ring Shane first, but once again, his phone is going straight to voicemail.

"Go back. I don't need you," he says, and I jump over a log that was hidden in the long grass.

"I don't feel comfortable leaving you alone with Darragh," I tell Liam, and it's weird when his lip twitches.

As we approach the tree line, Liam pauses, and it takes a lot of control not to take a step back from him when he levels me with a stare. "I want to make it clear that I've advised you to go back."

I roll my eyes at his words and move past him. Fingers that are long and cold circle my upper arm, and my eyes snap up to their owner.

"I'm not joking, Una. You're responsible for you." I swallow and nod, and Liam releases me. As we enter the forest, I sound like an ogre moving through the debris. I have to keep checking behind me to make sure Liam is still there. He doesn't make a sound. Lucky for us, Darragh is nearby, and he's making plenty of noise.

"Here, here, little pheasant." He's calling it like you might call a dog.

"The gun isn't loaded," I tell Liam as the world shatters. I'm on the ground, covering my head as everything explodes for the second time. My heart pounds in my ears, and when something touches my leg, I scream. I look down to see a black shoe, and my eyes move up the trouser leg until I stare at Liam, who stands over me.

"Are you okay?"

Am I okay? Two rounds were fired. I'm thinking about how they could have hit us. I'm not sure where Darragh was pointing, but my hands are patting my body down, looking for holes. Thankfully, I find none. I can see the amusement in Liam's eyes. I'm about to tell him that I'm glad I amuse him when a third shot is fired. This one is too close to home. Liam throws himself beside me as wood from a nearby tree sprays us.

"Darragh," Liam's raised voice makes me still.

"That little bitch get you?" Darragh asks while repumping the gun. He's lost his mind.

"Stay down," Liam says.

He doesn't have to. I have no intentions of standing up.

"Darragh, I'm going to stand up. So don't shoot me." Liam rises slowly. I can't see his face.

"I'm so sick of being the last one." Darragh's voice carries such a note of despair that as I lie here on the floor of the forest, something inside me twists for him.

Liam ducks again as Darragh fires, and that has my sympathy fleeing. Is he trying to kill Liam?

Liam's eyes clash with mine. "How many bullets did he take?"

My mind races back to the moment in the shed. "I don't know. Four... five, maybe."

Liam rises quickly as Darragh repumps the gun. I'm moving, reaching for Liam's leg to pull him back down. Four rounds have been fired. There could be one more. The tips of my fingers skim Liam's trousers as he charges toward Darragh. The noise of their struggle has me sitting up. Liam has wrestled the gun out of Darragh's hands.

"Did you just shoot at me?" Liam says. Darragh is pinned under Liam, shaking his head, but it's Liam's fury that seems to be multiplying and growing around us. My lungs squeeze.

"I'm the only one who cares." Each word that Liam shouts is like a punch in the stomach. His pain, I don't understand, but it's etched like a name would be into wood.

"I'm the only one." He's breathing heavy, still holding Darragh down, and I stand up now, but I try to make myself as quiet as possible. Tears run out of the side of Darragh's eyes as he battles with the war that rages inside him. I have no idea what passes between them, but seeing Liam lose control is unsettling. As if my thoughts summon him, his head snaps toward me.

CHAPTER TWENTY-THREE

UNA

"Y OU LET HIM BEAT me." Darragh recaptures Liam's attention.

"I stopped him." Liam's voice is calm, but he hasn't let Darragh up.

"You stood there." Darragh's words quiver he shouts at Liam.

"What do you think would have happened if I wasn't there? I pulled him off you."

Darragh shakes his head and turns it away from Liam. Now his focus is on me. "Since you arrived, everything has gone to shit."

Liam releases him as he starts at me. My gaze flickers to Liam, wondering what the fuck he's doing as Darragh walks toward me.

"Liam!" I shout his name, and he doesn't even blink. The bastard. I return my focus to Darragh. "That's not true," I tell Darragh, hating how my voice trembles. I turn and start to leave with a thundering heart. I hold my shoulders high, like they might protect me as Darragh follows me.

"Yeah, you fucked everything up for me. With Brian, Shane, and now even Liam."

I spin around, my temper taking over. "No, you did that. That's all on you and your drug habit. I have nothing to do with any of this," I tell him, and there's some part of Darragh that I can sense peeking out at me behind the madness.

"You're like my brother," I tell him trying to restore some sense to this.

"What, like the way Shane is?" His sneer has heat rushing to my face. "You fuck all your brothers?"

My throat burns. Liam stands behind Darragh, not intervening. My temper flares again. "Just the good-looking ones," I tell him as I force a smile.

"Keep away from me." Those are Darragh's departing words as he walks out into the field.

"Gladly," I shout after him.

Liam stands beside me, the gun in his hand, and now it seems more dangerous than it ever has before.

"Burning the candle at both ends will soon leave you without a light."

My attention snaps up to Liam. "What?" I question.

"Go home, Una." Liam steps out into the field, and I stare at him as he departs. I don't think he means *his* home. He wants me to leave. I march across the field, so done with today.

***

After a shower and pulling bits of twigs out of my hair, I go to the sitting room to try to do something normal like watch TV. The blue suite of furniture is velvet and has been brushed recently. The marks are visible.

I love the smell of this room. It's like lavender mixed with freshly cut wood. The wood smell is coming from the logs that are stacked either side of the fire all the way up the wall. To get to the top of the pile would require a ladder. But that wood is never used. A wicker basket holds the wood for the fire that isn't lit. I could call Mary. I could light it myself, but I don't. Opening a large beige trunk that's behind the couch, I take out a floral throw and take it with me to the couch.

I haven't been in this room since I was a child. I spent so many hours in here with Connor. He was such a movie buff and easy to be around. He was always kind to me. I put on one of his favorites, Rambo. Not one I particularly like, but one that gives me happy memories.

The credits roll, and I end up putting on Taken, another favorite of Connor's. This one, I actually love.

I'm at the part where the hero is on the boat, and I love when his daughter finally sees him. A knock at the door has me pausing the movie. I'm hopeful that when I turn around, it'll be Shane, but no, it's Liam, dressed in a suit and looking perfect again. I turn back around to my movie.

"Una, someone is here to see you."

I glance over my shoulder, and my stomach twists. My mother's here. My eyes snap from her to Liam, and the soft smile she wears worries me.

"What's going on?" I question, standing up. "What are you doing here, Mum?" She walks to me before pulling me into a hug. I stare at Liam over her shoulder.

"I saw the signs but ignored them," she says. I lean out at her words.

"What are you talking about?" I ask as Liam closes the door and moves toward us. "What is going on?" I untangle myself from my mother. I don't like Liam being here. It's making me nervous.

"I told her about your drug problem," he says.

The color drains from my face.

"I'm going to get you help." My mother nods as she reaches for my hand, but I pull it away. I can't stop staring at Liam.

"Don't be mad at Liam, sweetheart. I'm aware that Darragh got you into it."

I'm shaking my head, trying to make sense of this. "I don't have a drug problem." My words fall on deaf ears. I knew they would.

"You did this to get rid of me?" I take a step toward Liam. He puts his hand in his pockets.

"Darragh is on his way to rehab. He's getting the help he needs."

"Darragh is here, after his little episode in the forest?"

"What episode, sweetheart?" my mother asks. Liam is acting like a normal person would to reassure my mother that the drugs have warped my mind. He's convincing. I'm actually pondering if I am losing my mind.

I have to step away from both of them as I try to gather my thoughts. "This is ridiculous. I'm not on drugs. I'm fine," I tell my mother, but when she reaches out her hand to me like I'm a child, I know she is listening to Liam's lies.

"Come home, sweetheart."

"No." I shake my head while folding my arms over my chest. "You need to go home." I hate the hurt that flickers in her blue eyes.

"You need help," she protests, and I throw my hands in the air.

"He's lying to you. I don't have a drug problem."

"So you're telling me you've never taken drugs?"

The lie is on my tongue. I know how the truth will sound. "I have..."

"Oh, dear God." My mother's acting like I'm the addict that Liam is trying to paint me to be.

"Am I that much of a threat to you?" I grin at Liam, but my temper is flaring. "Are you that insecure about me and Shane that, what, you lie to my mother, thinking she will take me home and your problem is solved?" I'm hitting a nerve as Liam remains silent.

"Oh, you're not with that boy."

I rub my forehead. "Mum, not now. I'm not doing this with you," I tell her as I turn and knock off the TV.

"He is no good for you. He's a thug."

I clench my fists. "So was Michael, but you married him," I tell her, and she pulls at her ear—a tic I'm used to seeing when she's uncomfortable. She's here because she's been lied to.

"Mum, I love him, and I'm not leaving him," I tell her gently, hoping she can understand.

Tears brim in her eyes, and I hate seeing how upset she is. "Your father," she starts, and my heart slams against my chest, "would be so ashamed of you."

My nose burns, and my lips tug downward. "Don't bring Dad into this." It's whispered.

"Shane is no good for you. You can do so much better. An accountant or a doctor."

"My brother is as good as any other man." Liam's words annoy me.

"We all know what Shane O'Reagan is."

My stomach twists at the viciousness of her words. "What is he?" I'm looking from her to Liam, and they're having a stare off.

"Not good enough for my daughter." Her words seem final. "Come on," she tells me, and I can't understand why she won't listen.

"I'm not leaving him," I tell her, more firmly this time. Her lips twist into a snarl.

"If you don't come with me now, you can stay here for good."

I stand my ground even as my heart pounds.

"You stupid girl" are my mother's departing words. I'm still standing in the same place after she leaves, and my mind is caught on one thing.

Your father would be ashamed of you. She voiced a fear of mine. My lip trembles, and I bite it. I exhale a deep breath as my vision blurs.

"I know you don't understand, but I love him, Liam." Tears fall as I face him. "I know I should leave—I know that—but I can't leave him." The thought twists my stomach painfully. Tears continue to trickle down my face. Liam doesn't react or say anything. I didn't think he would.

"I hope, one day, you find love too." I leave the room feeling crushed.

Flickering on the lights in the garage, I focus on my bike. I bought this because of my dad's love for bikes. Right now, I want to be as close to him as possible. I want him to tell me that he isn't ashamed of me. Kneeling on the tarp, I run my fingers along the frame of the bike.

It's clean from the last time Shane and I worked on it. I think my dad would have loved Shane, but if he knew what he did, he would have been more afraid for me. I shake my head as the bridge of my nose aches and sit back on my bum; I bury my head in my knees and cry.

I want my dad back, even if it's only for a moment. I want him to hold me and call me his girl like he always did. Dreaming of him used to ease my yearning. Now I hate how his face is fading.

"I miss you," I tell the empty garage. My tears come heavier. I hate this place. I hate everything right now. It all seems unfair. I want to scream or smash something, but I don't do either. I get up and leave the garage. Right now, I need him.

***

He's the fifth headstone down, under the weeping willow. Wiping some falling leaves off his grave, I sit down. I haven't been here in a while. The white pot that holds dead flowers tells me no one has. I remove the flowers and sit back down, staring at the headstone. At the start, it was nearly a daily journey for me, and I'd tell him all about my day, but these days, it's getting less and less.

"I'm sorry I haven't been around much." I sit on the curb now, my back to the headstone, and stare up at the tree. "Everything is a mess, and I'm worried that it's my fault." A shiver assaults my body.

"I met someone," I tell him with a smile, opting for a happy story. He doesn't need to hear my woes. "His name is Shane. You'd really like him. The man that Mum married after you, it's his son. But that's neither here nor there. Anyway, his brother Liam is being a pain. He wants to get rid of me. Darragh, who's Shane's other brother, is mad at me too. Oh"—I give a little laugh—"so is Mum, no surprise there."

I focus on my fingers, my ramblings not over. "I left my job, got the courage to walk away. I'm working with horses now." I start crying again. I'm not entirely sure why this time. "I named my horse Summer. You would love her. She's real feisty, a bit like me." I snort a laugh again. "I think she's pregnant, but we'll find out soon." Wiping away tears, I stop beating around the bush. I know why I'm here.

"I'm so afraid, Daddy." I snivel a cry. "I don't want you to be disappointed in me." I hiccup and bury my head in my knees as I bleed my soul on my father's grave. He doesn't answer me, but being here and telling him my fears gives me some comfort.

CHAPTER TWENTY-FOUR

SHANE

THE WATER IS SILENT as I sit on the bank of the lake. I used to come here with Liam and Connor as a child. That was before we found out he was our half brother. Back then, you couldn't separate us. A smile tugs at my lips now as I picture the three skinny kids in white vests jumping into the lake. We were happy until we had to leave and go home.

The walk back was filled with skitting and laughing. Back then, Connor was the comedian. Back then, Liam smiled. Back then, life had more meaning. The clay on my shoes mocks me. The man I have become isn't what I wanted.

I exhale and stare out at the lake, trying to find a peaceful place in my mind. I've always had to be ten steps ahead of everyone else, and it's exhausting. After leaving last night, I dug up Bernard's body and reburied him on land we own near the Loch Leigh Mountains. It isn't far from us, but after digging up Bernard's rancid body and reburying him, I was exhausted, and not just my body but my mind. I couldn't trust Brian with the knowledge of where the body was. That was my only reason for moving it. I know I'll have to move Siobhan's auntie, too, and the girl from the house that Darragh killed.

I think that's what hurt the most. They lied to me. They told me they were ringing the Gardaí. I laugh now at my own stupidity. Since when do we hand over bodies? We bury them.

Rubbing my forehead doesn't ease the ache there. The whole ordeal makes me question what other secrets Darragh and Liam carry. Why Liam protects him continuously. They share something that strengthened that bond, and now they have another secret that they've kept from me. But soon, they will know that I know. Once the body is moved, they'll figure it out.

Standing, I move around the lake. I want to go home to Una, but I also don't. I don't want to see those same questioning eyes from when I came in late. Worry was gnawing at her, and it killed me. If I'm going to keep her, I need her away from the house.

She'll end up too damaged with all of them. Even with me. But I can't let it go. Tomorrow, I have an appointment to view Deerpark Stud Farm, and the idea of owning it is exciting. That's where I will place Una. She will have a home, a job. She will be safe from my family. It's still close to our home, because no matter what, family comes first. That's inside me, and no matter what, I can't let it go. No matter what my brothers do, I will be there to help them. When you bury a body with a person, you're tied to them for life.

Returning to the car, I take my phone out of the glove compartment. I have two missed calls from Una, one from Liam.

My stomach twists as I dial Una's number, and it goes to voice mail. The engine starts as I turn the key. That's another thing I need to do, burn this car, and I actually like it. I ring Una again, and she still doesn't pick up. I don't ring Liam back. I'm too pissed at him right now after lying to me. Instead, I ring Neill. He answers on the first ring.

"Any word?" I ask while leaving the lake.

"All quiet. Brian is back to business as usual."

I nod at Neill's words. I can breathe for the moment. "Anything on Connor?" This is something that shouldn't have taken so long, but it's like he's gone.

"Not a thing, but I'll keep my ear to the ground."

"Thanks," I say before hanging up. When the car settles in the garage, I want to find Una straight away, but I don't want her to see me covered in mud. Showering in my room isn't an option. There's a shower room off the garage that holds fresh clothes in case of emergencies. I make it quick. Once showered and dressed in a fresh pair of jeans and a red T-shirt, I go look for Una. I ring her three more times as I search the house. I get no answer, and my stomach tightens.

The intensity of her stare as she focuses on the bike has me pausing in the doorway. Red curls are piled on top of her head as she sits barefoot on the tarp. An oversized brown jumper and cream leggings make her look a picture. I'm not sure what's she's trying to do, but I could stand here all day watching her. Her eyes grow wide, and a smile shows a set of perfect white teeth.

"Hi." She's beautiful.

"Hi," I say back, stepping into the room. "I've been ringing you," I tell her, waving my phone at her, and she tilts her head.

"Funny, that is. I've been ringing you too."

Sitting down beside her, my fingers find her hand, and I entwine them. "Yeah, I left the phone in the car," I tell her.

Her smile widens as she looks at our hands before her gaze travels up to my eyes. "You showered."

My heart gives a heavy thud as I see that uncertainty in her eyes again. "I did." I look at the bike now as I clench my jaw. I hate this. I hate how she's looking at me.

Her small, pale hand takes my face, making me look at her. "You smell lovely," she says, her eyes lighter as she dips her head toward me and places a soft, precise kiss on my lips.

"I love you, Shane O' Reagan, in every shape and form." Her eyes shine as she tells me this, her hand clutching my face, like it's by sheer force that I will hear what she is saying, and I do.

She's telling me that she knows what I do and that she still loves me regardless.

"This life that I live is dangerous, but I love it. I love my family, and I know I could never walk away."

Una's eyes are wide as she takes in my words. There's such a look of fear on her face that I pause and press my fingers to her cheek. I'm smiling now at a warning that Liam always gave me.

"Liam used to say that love makes a man weak." At the mention of Liam's name, her eyes close slightly, and that makes me smile more. She isn't a fan, but who could blame her?

"Your love makes me stronger," I admit, and her lips form a small *o*, and her chest starts to rise and fall wildly. "You're intoxicating, Una, and I want to share all of this with you. The moments I hold on to the most are the ones with you in them. I love you."

A tear trickles down her face. "Wow," she says through a half sob, half laugh. "Seal with a kiss," she tells me.

My chest tightens, but I don't hesitate. I seal our love with a kiss that reaches inside me and heals some dark part of me that had me keeping Una away. Now she's in fully.

The clearing of a throat is what breaks the kiss. Finn is wearing a goofy smile, and I can't hide my own.

"Dad has surprised us all with a family meal."

I raise my eyebrows, hoping Finn can shed some light on this family meal. Dad doesn't do anything for nothing, but Finn shrugs.

"Siobhan's coming." Finn sounds nervous as he tells Una, who still clutches my hand.

"She's so sweet, Finn. This is going to be fun." Her words have Finn relaxing, and when she rests her head on my shoulder, I can't help but relax even further.

Liam and Dad are the only two in the dining room when Una and I arrive. Liam looks up, and there's something in the way he looks at Una that I don't like.

"Liam," she greets him sharply with a raised chin.

"Una," he responds, but he adds a nod of his head. Like approval or something.

Dad has been looking at my and Una's joined hands, and when I meet his eye, he doesn't show what he feels. Releasing my hand, Una sits down beside

Dad, but first kisses him softly on the cheek. His face melts, and a smile is there just for Una. I don't mind. As long as he's kind to her, that's all that matters. I sit beside Una and across from Liam, who stares at me.

"Hi." A shy voice at the dining room door has us all looking to Siobhan.

Una gives a seriously enthusiastic wave beside me, and I can't stop smiling. Siobhan slides in beside Liam without hesitation, and sitting opposite him, seeing him sitting beside a girl, is almost amusing. Has he ever pictured himself settling down? He was too used to the whores he managed.

"Siobhan, I'm glad you could come." Dad sounds like he means it, but I'm still nervous about why we're all gathered around this time. It's like the last supper. Finn nods at everyone, hands jammed into his pockets, before he sits down beside Siobhan.

"Thank you so much for the invite. You have a beautiful home, Mr. O'Reagan."

"Please, it's Michael."

We're all waiting for Darragh, but when Mary enters and places plates in front of us, I look to Liam. I don't know why.

"Where is Darragh?"

"Darragh has gone away for a while," Liam says, looking at Finn before facing me and finally Father. Una seems to be frozen beside me.

"Gone where?" I ask, and from the look on Finn's face, this is news to him as well. My attention goes to Liam.

"What happened?"

"Please, we have two ladies at the table. Can we just have this meal?"

No, we fucking can't. Now all I can think of is the dead girl. Does this have something to do with Darragh's disappearance? Liam is eating his dinner, and Finn is too, along with Siobhan.

"I'll tell you later," Una whispers to me, and I steal a glance at her. She knows? So it couldn't be about the dead girl. That makes me breathe a little easier, and I give her a nod. She squeezes my leg under the table, and I suppress a smile.

"So you two are a thing?"

My attention snaps to Finn who is smiling at me, delighted at how uncomfortable things at the table just became. "Yes, we are."

Siobhan gives a big smile, and I nod at her in response before turning to Una, who has an eyebrow raised.

"We are?" I ask.

Una tilts her head while smiling. "Yes, we are." I want to kiss her, but everyone is staring at us.

Dad is waiting for me to explain, but I cut into my chicken. I ignore a kick under the table from Una and grin as I continue to eat. Her heavy sigh has my lips tugging.

"Michael, I hope you're okay with this." Una's voice is so sweet, and I take a quick glance at Father.

"Are you happy?" he asks her, and she doesn't hesitate, much to my delight. "Very."

"Well, then it's okay."

His blessing does mean a lot, and when I glance to Una and see the happiness on her face, I know it means a lot to her too.

I surprise her when I place a gentle kiss on her lips. Her cheeks turn pink, but she's still smiling. A snigger from Finn has me returning to my food, but I can't get rid of the stupid grin I'm wearing.

The conversation flows easily around the table as the two girls chat about movies. I knew Una loved watching movies with Connor, but I didn't know she was still into them.

Her biggest love seems to be Denzel Washington. "I cry every time," Una tells Siobhan, who's nodding.

"Me too," Siobhan responds. It looks like a friendship is blossoming.

"But if you saw it already, why would you cry?" I ask once Mary has set out the dessert, tea, and coffees.

"He dies for her," Una says like I'm stupid. I love her feistiness.

"Yeah, but you already know that." I seriously can't understand this.

"It's just Denzel's acting," Siobhan interjects and Una agrees. It's fun at the table. It's different. The only person not taking part is Liam, but that's not unusual. What is unusual is how distant he's being. His mind isn't here, and that makes me think of Darragh.

"I think the girls make a great point." This is the first time Father has spoken through the meal. He's nodded and smiled, but he hasn't spoken.

"The kidnappers didn't do their homework. If they did, they would have never taken that girl. Denzel does a superb job. There are people in life that you shouldn't hurt." I glance toward Liam, but he's focused on Dad.

"It's like the most recent news," Dad says, putting down his spoon. "A young Northern Ireland boy, I think connected to the IRA, is missing, presumed dead. Whoever made the mistake of hurting him has messed with the wrong people." Silence fills the dining table, and I remind myself that he doesn't know.

"Oh, that would make a great film." Una's words are like water on flames, and she jumps right into a film about the IRA she saw and was disappointed in. I'm not sure if she's aware of what she's doing, but Father isn't finished, not by a long shot.

"Does the IRA kill the man's family for hurting one of their own?" he asks. I clench my jaw.

"I don't think so." Una shakes her head. She's really thinking about it. "No. No, they don't," she answers with more certainty.

"In real life, they would." Dad smiles after that before returning to his food.

"I didn't hear about that," I say, then I take a drink of tea. Liam and Dad are observing me way too closely, but I make my mind go blank.

"I did hear about the house that burned down in Kells," Liam says. That causes a flicker of fear to ignite in me.

"What happened? I hope no one was hurt," Una says, her voice kind.

"My friend, who works with me in Cavan, lives there in Black Water Heights," Liam explains. "She said no one was hurt, but the house burned right to the ground. The houses on either side didn't survive either. But thankfully, no one was hurt."

Una is frozen beside me, and my eyes snap to Liam, who doesn't seem to give a shit.

"I wonder what caused the fire?" I ask Liam.

"A cigarette not put out, faulty wiring, cooker left on... The list is truly endless."

I'm trying not to snap at him. Glancing at Una, I see she's as white as a fucking ghost. She's putting two and two together.

"Are you alright, Una?" Dad's hand covers hers, and I want to rip it off her. His patronizing words grate on me.

"Why wouldn't she be?" I snap, and silence fills the room.

"Shane." Una's surprise at me raising my voice has me reeling in my irritation. "I think I need some fresh air," she tells Father, and he smiles at her.

"How about a swim?" This suggestion comes from Finn, and Siobhan nods beside him.

"I don't have a swimsuit," Siobhan says with disappointment.

"I don't mind," Finn says, and she nudges him with her elbow.

"I can give you one," Una says. "And a swim actually sounds good." I'm surprised she spoke, and she looks up at me with such an innocent look on her face. "Are you coming?"

"You go ahead with Finn and Siobhan. I'll catch up," I tell her.

She hides her disappointment well before giving me a kiss on the cheek.

Once Finn, Siobhan, and Una leave, I ask about Darragh.

"He's in rehab," Liam explains. "Where he should have been a long time ago."

I agree with that assessment, if it's true.

"I have work to do." Dad stands now, his focus on Liam. He ignores me as he leaves. Angry, I suppose, that I raised my voice.

"You burnt the house down?" I ask the moment Father is gone. Liam pushes his chair out slightly from the table.

"Darragh left a cigarette lit."

I'm not buying it. He didn't know that I found the body, but I don't say anything about it. It's small compared to the other topic that Father brought up.

"Any idea who this boy is that Father was talking about?" I place my elbows on the table. I'm observing Liam for any signs that he knows.

"No, but it sounded like he was asking us."

I nod. That's exactly what it sounded like.

"Do you know who the boy is?" The question is delivered with a slight raised eyebrow. He thinks I'm involved, but he's grasping at straws.

"No, not a clue," I lie.

CHAPTER TWENTY-FIVE

UNA

I'M GLAD WHEN FINN suggests swimming. Really, I would have grabbed any excuse to get out of that room. After coming back from my dad's grave and having a shower, telling Shane about Liam and my mother wouldn't help anyone.

It would cause more rows and more hate. I hope that Liam took my silence as a peace offering. I 'll find out in time if he accepted it or not.

Siobhan comes out of the bathroom of the pool house in the red bikini I gave her, and she looks like a sun-kissed goddess.

Her tanned skin seems to glow. Brown eyes smile at Finn as he appreciates each step she takes toward the pool. She's beautiful. Finn's very handsome. All the O'Reagans are. Too much, at times. Growing up around such stunning men had my expectations for the real world set too high. I think that's why I spent far too much time alone. Coming here in the summer was spent swooning over Shane. To think we're together now is crazy.

"What are you smiling at?" Siobhan asks me as she swims over to the side where I relax.

"Shane," I admit, and it's nice to say it out loud to another girl.

"I'm not going to lie. He scares me." Siobhan's voice is still light as she confesses how she feels.

"Liam scares me, but I get why Shane would."

"Liam is strange," Siobhan adds with narrowed eyes, and I laugh.

"Finn's a great guy."

"I can hear you," Finn says as he comes out of the changing room in a pair of white long shorts that ride low on his hips. He's all abs and wide shoulders, and Siobhan drinks him up.

I'd roll my eyes, but I can imagine that's how I view Shane too. Ducking under the water is nice. The water temperature is warm, but still, the initial sensation of being covered sends a shiver through me. After breaking the surface, I push my wet hair out of my face. Siobhan is swimming while Finn relaxes along the edge. I swim over to him.

"Did you know about Darragh?" I ask, treading water.

"No. I can't believe he's gone to rehab." Finn's face grows serious, and he scratches his brow. "It was sudden, because I'm sure I saw him this morning."

"Well, he's in the best place, I suppose." I move to the side of the pool and face out toward the large windows.

"When was the last time you saw him?" Finn asks, and I pretend to consider his question.

"Yesterday, I think," I tell him with a nod. "What do you think about your dad saying that about the Northern Ireland boy?" My question, I think, sounded simple, but Finn looks at me differently now as he moves around to face the window too. Glancing over my shoulder, I see the red bikini down the far end of the pool.

"I don't think anything about it. Why do you ask? You know something?" The suspicion is growing in his voice and the way he stares at me.

"I thought it weird, that's all," I answer while giving him a nudge, and he grins.

"You're starting to sound like one of us."

Flicking water at him, I laugh. "Shane is rubbing off on me," I say, and even as Finn laughs at me, I can see the question in his eyes. He's wondering what I really know.

For me, I can't help but think Michael was asking his sons, and it was last night that Shane had killed someone. Instead of letting the fear fester, I dive under the water.

Swimming relieves some tension that had been building inside me. Today was crazy, but chatting with Siobhan makes me feel normal. I'm not sure she could ever understand what her presence does for me. This big house with so much time on my hands can drive me a little crazy.

"Anyone want a drink?" Finn asks, climbing out of the pool. Siobhan takes the moment to admire him as water streams off his body, and he pulls his white shorts a bit lower.

"Yeah," I answer, and she looks at me over her shoulder and grins.

"Me too," she tells Finn.

We both get into the Jacuzzi. The water, at first, is almost too hot, but as I close my eyes, my whole body relaxes. "I so need this," I say.

"Me too. Finn's been so stressed lately." I open my eyes and look at Siobhan. "Over what?" I ask.

She pushes the water away from her with a delicate arm. "His brother."

I can't stop the snort that leaves my mouth. "Which one?" I ask, and she laughs.

"Yeah, I know. It's normally Darragh, but lately it's Connor. Who I have never met. I assume you have."

A fist tightens inside my belly. "Yeah, Connor's cool. He comes across a bit dark, but he's cool." Connor always reminded me of the Incredible Hulk.

He was bigger than the other boys, and he was a force to be reckoned with. Anyone who stood in his way fell, and they fell hard.

"He misses him so much," she adds, and all I can do is nod.

The day I left my job, I drove to the cross guns for a few quiet drinks. It was there that I met Connor after three years of not seeing each other. We laughed a lot, and it was like old times. He made me promise that I wouldn't tell anyone, and I haven't. It hasn't crossed my mind, but right now, I question if telling Finn where Connor is would ease his mind. Finn arrives back with the drinks.

"I turn my back, and you girls are lapping it up," he says, handing me a bottle of Budweiser. Siobhan gets hers delivered with a kiss.

I look away even as I smile. It's nice to see Finn happy and see him with something that's his alone and not his and Darragh's.

When I finish my drink, I leave Siobhan and Finn alone. He's sitting closer to her, and I can see it in their eyes that they need some alone time.

I pull on a dressing gown and flip-flops as I make my way across the courtyard. It's cold outside, but after the heat of the pool house, I'm not surprised.

I pause at the door when I find Shane lying on the bed, his arm covering his eyes. Moving to him slowly, I notice the soft rise and fall of his chest. He's asleep. I need to get into dry clothes. The strap of my dressing gown is pulled, and I can't stop my heart from tripping as I turn to Shane. His eyes are open and focused on me.

"Did you have a nice swim?" he asks, pulling me closer while he sits up.

"I did," I tell him with a smile.

"Finn got to see you in a swimsuit before me?"

Finn's eyes were focused on Siobhan, and she was beach ready. My emerald green one-piece, along with my pale skin and red hair, isn't on the most desired list.

"You had your chance," I tease as he opens the belt of my dressing gown. I don't know why it's odd, but a nervous energy zings up my spine with the idea of him seeing me, yet I don't stop him. When he has it open, his warm hands go to my hips, and I shiver at the contact.

"A good job I didn't go swimming."

Holding my breath, I fear the worst.

"I don't think we would have done much swimming."

And like that, all my worries and insecurities fly away.

My body fits perfectly onto his lap. He doesn't complain about the cold water against his skin, and the contrast of his hot body has me pushing myself closer to him. Being this close to Shane allows me to see the strain around his eyes. Dark circles ring them. My lips press against each eyelid before I kiss his nose.

"As nice as this is, I need to have a shower and warm up," I tell him, leaving one final kiss on his lips. It's hard to walk away, but I need to warm up. The shower looks nice, but the bath is what calls to me.

I strip off as I pour in a bubble bath and run the taps. It doesn't take long for the room to fill with steam. Stepping into the bath, I lie back and close my eyes.

"I've changed my mind," I call out to Shane, in case he's waiting for me. "I'm taking a bath." Colors move from behind my eyes.

"I can see that." Water sloshes over the tub and onto the floor. I open my eyes and then narrow them at Shane.

"You nearly gave me a heart attack."

He's kneeling down along the side, his arm resting on the lip of the tub. He must have gotten wet, but he doesn't seem to care.

"I want to tell you a secret." I settle down as Shane speaks and rest my head against the back of the tub again. "You're not scary when you're mad. You're sexy as hell." I want to be offended, but his words send a thrill through my body.

"I can be scary," I tell him.

"Never," he tells me. His fingers dip into the water. He grazes my arm with his fingertips, and the sensation has a heartbeat thrilling in between my legs. I focus on his arm, his tattoo that always captures my attention.

"What does it mean?" I ask before gathering a pile of bubbles in my palm and blowing them toward Shane. He swipes them away quickly with a grin.

"My tattoo?" he asks, and there's uncertainty there. He isn't looking at me now.

"If it's private, you don't have to tell me."

"It's not that it's private. I just don't think it would do you much good knowing."

Now I want to know. I try to pull myself up in the bath, but Shane's fingers hold on to my arm. "I want to know who I'm lying beside," I say.

He laughs at my words, but his laugh is so tired and drained that my stomach churns with guilt at pushing him. But I hate not knowing every part of him.

"Okay, I'm going to tell you. But—and I mean it—no questions. No names. I'll tell you what it represents."

Why is my heart pounding? I nod my head. Shane holds my eye, and that gives me confidence that what the tattoos mean can't be so bad.

"For every death that I experience, I get a band added." My eyes are counting the bands rapidly, and Shane moves his arms.

"Una," he warns.

"I'm only counting them," I tell him, but I know that's not enough. Who died? Is one for his mum? The man who isn't okay from the other night? But no new ink covers his arm. The atmosphere becomes somber as I think of the man, the one who has been spinning around in my head.

"The missing boy from the North. Is he the same person as the man from the other night?"

There's a wild look of panic in Shane's eyes, but when he closes them and looks back at me, it's gone. "No, and don't ever let anyone hear you say that." He's taken my face in his hands, his words soft, and I nod.

"I won't," I tell him.

He relaxes back down along the side of the bath. We're both silent. I'm studying him as he stares at the water, and there's such a sadness there that my heart hurts. It's funny to feel such pain for someone else.

"What's bothering you?" I ask him, thinking there's no way he'll actually tell me. But I can ask. His gaze flickers up to me, and he reminds me of a cute puppy with his big brown eyes.

He exhales heavily before speaking. "Connor. I can't find him, and we need him home." I look away from Shane. I promised Connor I wouldn't say anything, but that was before.

"If you knew where he was, what would you do?"

Shane tilts his head and sits up a bit straighter. "I'd ask him to come home. We need him."

"Did he run away?" I ask.

"No. Una, do you know something?"

"I know where Connor is," I tell him, and his eyes widen like it's a miracle. Laughter bubbles up from his throat, confusing me, but when he looks at me, the light in his eyes has me smiling.

"I've been searching for him for a while. Is he far away?" Now that Shane is looking happier, I can use this to my advantage.

"The information will come at a price," I tell him with a smirk. I squeal as Shane jumps into the bath fully clothed. I think most of the water is now on the floor, but I can't stop the laughter.

"What the hell, Shane," I say, but he's moving over me, his lips getting closer.

"Name your price," he tells me, not an inch from my lips.

"You," I tell him, and he pays in full.

CHAPTER TWENTY-SIX

SHANE

I 'M LYING, GAZING AT her as she sleeps, and it's more beautiful now being this close. How many years have I watched her from the shadows? Her long stretches are pulling the quilt down slightly, showcasing the curve of her breast through her silky cream-colored, nightdress.

The desire to see her eyes has me running my fingers along her jawline. She stirs under my touch. Her lids half-open, and a goofy smile coats her face. "Good morning," she tells me, becoming more alert.

"*Is breá liom tú.*" I tell her I love her before kissing her puffy pink lips.

"*Tá mé i ngrá leat freisin.*" Her words have me smiling.

"I didn't know you spoke Irish so well."

She leans in and kisses my arm. "It's a phrase I know well, along with *póg mo thóin.*" Now she's giggling, and I can't help pulling back the covers and doing what she asked—kissing her perfect arse.

She's still giggling when I come back up and kiss her. "I have a surprise for you today," I tell her, but I'm nervous. Today, I want her to see Deerpark Stud Farm with me. I hope she loves it as much as I do.

"What should I wear?" Always such a dilemma for a woman. But with Una, she could wear anything.

"Be comfortable and wear whatever you want," I tell her with a final kiss before getting out of bed. She's still smiling as she gets dressed, and I can't stop myself from stealing kisses as we make our way down to breakfast. Mary has pancakes ready as I had requested the night before.

"Thank you, Mary," I say, and she looks at me twice. I hear "You're welcome" as we sit down.

"I'm going to get fat with all these pancakes," Una warns. The navy-and-cream sleeveless swing dress she's wearing makes her look sexy yet innocent.

"Even fat, you would be adorable," I tell her as Mary places the pancakes in front of us.

***

I've taken the Cadillac again today, knowing that it's Una's favorite. She's rubbing it and making small noises as she checks it out, and I'm afraid at how perfect everything is with her. I'm waiting for the other shoe to fall, always pessimistic. I push the darkness aside and steal glances of Una. Her smile is infectious, and I find myself grinning now and then.

"So where are we going?"

She's asked several times, and we're almost there. "Patience," I tell her, and she sticks out her tongue. If I wasn't driving, I know what I would do with it.

Pulling up at the large steel gates, I ring the bell, and a voice speaks out from the intercom. "Welcome to Deerpark Stud. Do you have an appointment?"

I flicker a quick look at Una, and her eyes dart to the large gates with the horse heads on them and then back to the monitor.

"Shane O'Reagan. I have an appointment." It takes a moment before the gates start to open.

"Please, come on in." I wait until the gates have fully opened before I drive up slowly. I let the roof down, giving Una a panoramic view.

I want her to love it.

"Why do you have an appointment here?" she asks, but her eyes are roaming the well-groomed fields. The old outbuildings come into view; they've been restored. But the most stunning part is the house.

A two-story white house that's over 12,000 square feet. Not as big as home, but still decent. The grounds, buildings, and house are in perfect condition—move-in ready.

When I stop the car, the auctioneer greets me. "Mr. O'Reagan." Then he takes Una's hand and shakes it. Afterward, she places her hands behind her back, looking unsure. Taking her hand, I twine our fingers together.

"There have been two more views for this place. Take a look around, but I wouldn't take long making a bid."

I nod, not wanting to talk money in front of Una.

"What kind of money are we talking?" Una asks sweetly.

The auctioneer looks at me, and I give him a nod that I hope Una doesn't see.

"One point five million. But I would say bid two million, and the place will be yours."

Una stumbles, and I hold on to her hand tighter.

"I'll leave you both to it. You can find me in the foyer after." He leaves, and he's not even out of earshot before Una starts.

"Two million euro! Why are you looking at this place?"

"*We* are looking at this place," I tell her, making my intentions clear.

"We," she repeats, color rising in her cheeks, and I can't help but kiss her lightly.

"We will need our own place, and Summer would be happy here," I say. She looks unsure again, so I take both her hands. "It's an investment."

"A huge one that I can't help with."

"I know that. But you would help run the place. It's a profitable business," I tell her, and I can see her softening.

"Just two million, Shane." Her exhale ends on a laugh like she can't believe it.

"Look at the place and tell me what you think."

We walk, and I observe Una as she takes it all in. "It's perfect Shane. But I mean, it's your decision."

I squeeze her hand. "There is no more me. Only us," I tell her, and she looks so perplexed that I find myself kissing her again.

"Can you see yourself living here?" I ask her as we make our way around to the house.

"Yes." She sounds almost breathless as we stop and admire it.

"Can you see yourself having a family here?" As I say it, my heart beats a little faster. It's something I've never thought about—something I never thought I would have. My own family. Una turns to me, her eyes searching my face.

"Yes." I kiss her deeply this time. "I love you," I tell her before we make our way into the house.

The auctioneer, as promised, is waiting in the foyer. The moment he sees us, he stands up. I let Una wander off as I speak to him. "I'll take it," I tell him.

"There will be other bidders," he starts.

Una looks happy here. That's all I need to know.

"Two million, and I want the deal closed by the end of the week," I tell him, and he's already getting his phone out to make the call.

***

After leaving Deerpark Stud, I take Una out for food in Cabra Castle. It's close to home and serves decent food. It's the first day in a long time that I can breathe. I know I still have a lot of problems, but they all seem easy to solve. Knowing where Connor is has made it all so much easier. Later tonight, I'll go get him, and his first job will be finding out what that girl Ava knows and keeping an eye on her. Brian will keep his mouth shut. If he doesn't, I won't touch him. I can get Connor to do that as well.

Moving the bodies is vital now. We need to clear out the bog. Leaving any form of evidence around isn't wise.

"You have to taste this pavlova. It's delicious." Una holds up a spoon to my lips filled with dessert. I take it and smile at her before breaking off a piece of my sticky toffee pudding and feeding it to her. She moans, and I think I'll keep doing this for a while.

"So you like the house?" I ask her in between spoonfuls. She nods and smiles. The auctioneer got back to me not long after leaving. The offer was accepted. The place is ours.

"Well, it's our new home." She stills for a moment, a piece of chocolate falling onto her chin. I reach across and clean it.

"Are you serious?"

I can't stop the smile. "Yes, I am," I tell her, and she squeals, getting the attention of an elderly couple beside us. She's around the table and in my arms quickly.

"I don't know what to say," she says with a look of awe on her face.

"You don't have to say anything. Just be my forever," I tell her and mean it. As long as I have Una, I'm stronger and better. Without her... I don't let that thought form.

"I've always been your forever." Her words send a thrill through me, and I kiss her lips softly.

Seal it with a kiss, I can almost hear my mother whisper. I do. I seal it all in, knowing it will always be there.

***

RECKLESS

TITLE: RECKLESS
SERIES NUMBER: BOOK TWO

BLURB:
She owns the land that I need... to hide bodies.

Siobhan.

A city girl with no ties to the land. It was supposed to be an easy buy. No complications. And definitely no conflicts.

But her soft eyes have me hooked. Having her is all can I think about.

But she isn't the reason why I'm here. The task at hand is crucial. There can be no room for mistakes.

Family comes first. It's what the O'Reagans have always lived by. Returning home without this land isn't an option.

Is losing my family worth gambling with my heart?

CHAPTER ONE

FINN

"W HERE IS YOUR BROTHER?" My father bends over a map that takes up the top of the table. His index finger stops moving as I enter, but he doesn't look up at me. Shane stands firmly beside him, arms folded across his wide chest. I scratch my eyebrow in annoyance.

There is so much I want to say, like, 'Just because we're twins doesn't mean we keep tabs on each other.' Or 'Do I look like a fucking slave?' But our motto is carved into the wood that hangs over the dining table that is mostly used for meetings.

The Irish word *chlann* was carved into that piece of wood by our father's father, and it is carved into all of us. The family comes first, no matter what. My eyes flicker back to Shane, who still stares at me, a shadow of a grin on his face.

"Probably in bed with a whore," I rattle off, and that gets my father's attention. His finger slightly curls.

"Watch your mouth, Finn." He speaks but doesn't look at me. Is he fucking kidding? His mouth spews poison half the time.

I flicker a glance at Shane, expecting the grin to be visible, but it isn't. Instead, his head tilts slightly toward our father, his way of telling me to shut the fuck up and go get our brother.

"I'll get him now." With a sigh, I close the door behind me and take the stairs two at a time, slowing down once I reach the landing. I can hear the undercurrent of a beat. Darragh never switches his music off. In his life, the party never seems to stop. I can smell the cigarette smoke before I even open his door, and once I do, a lot of other smells follow.

Disgusting.

"Darragh, get up." I kick the base of the bed, where three sets of legs hang out. The alcohol fumes in the room have me wanting to open a window. My steel-toe boot connects with the bed frame again. A blonde pops up like a blow-up doll, mumbling as she looks around the room. Her eyes settle on me, and she slowly grins.

"Good morning." A polish accent or maybe Russian—I can't tell the difference—coats her words.

"Get out," I tell her. Her brows furrow as she looks down at sleeping beauty, who I'm tempted to kick the shit out of if he doesn't wake up soon. "Darragh, get the fuck up."

This time he does, and the second blow-up doll inflates. Topless. She does a double take at me and then Darragh. "Twins."

"You're a genius. Now get out," I say slowly for her. They both get out of the bed, and the second one yelps as Darragh lands a slap to her arse. I wonder sometimes how we're related. The idea that we shared the same womb is baffling.

"Da is waiting, Darragh, and he's pissed." I don't blatantly watch the girls as they get dressed, but I can't help the occasional glance; they are fit, a little too thin for my liking, but still nice. I light a fag as Darragh finally gets off the bed and pulls on a white T-shirt.

"Pick a different color," I tell him. I'm wearing a white T-shirt, and I'll be fucked if we are dressing the same.

"You know who you are like?" Darragh asks while pulling the T-shirt off. I don't acknowledge him but smoke my fag, hoping by the time I'm finished, Darragh will be ready. "You're like Da."

I snort because I'm the furthest from our father, and Darragh knows it. I don't respond as each girl moves past me and out the door. Darragh promises to ring them later, and they believe him. Our front door has become a rotating one with all of Darragh's women. None are ever brought back for seconds. He pulls on jeans, and I want to tell him to change them. I'm wearing jeans, but I don't want to sound whiny.

"What does he want?" Darragh slaps his face twice, and I'm glad that he shaves daily. I'm growing a beard just so we look different. Being identical twins is a pain in the ass.

"I don't know. Shane's with him," I say as I make our way downstairs and return to the dining room with my brother, like a good little doggy.

"Close the door," Dad barks, and Darragh does. Once we all stand around the map on the table, he finally looks up, blue eyes snapping from me to Darragh.

My father is a man that many admire.

For me, I hate him and love him. I hate how he sees me as someone to take care of Darragh. I hate how he treats Connor, my brother. I hate the control.

My mind moves back to the meeting as Shane kicks it off. "Land close by has come up for sale."

Normally, Shane doesn't speak unless father has asked him too, but I can see the irritation in our father's stance.

The smell of alcohol from Darragh is wafting through the room, and he looks like he smells. Bloodshot eyes blink several times as he slaps himself across the face again. If he keeps it up, he won't have to slap himself anymore; Dad is ready to flitter him.

Shane jabs a finger at a patch of green fields circled with a red marker on the map. "Over eleven acres has come up. Seven of it is bog land." We all stare at the green patch that Shane points at.

"Darragh, I want you to convince the new landowner to sell it to you," Father cuts in, and Darragh folds his arms across his chest while nodding.

"She's only just moved back here. She has no family or attachment to the land, so it should be an easy sell." Shane sits down at the table, his black shirt and slacks making him look like he's going to a funeral. Maybe he is.

"You go with him," my father says, cutting me with his sharp eye. Once again, I try to hide my irritation at being Darragh's babysitter.

"How much?" Darragh widens his eyes, and I wonder if he's high. I want to kick him and tell him to get his shit together.

"Offer her a hundred thousand."

Darragh nods.

"For *bog* land? That's worth like, what, two or three an acre? The good land no more than ten." I can't for a second understand why he's over paying.

"I didn't realize you were my financial adviser."

Darragh shifts beside me, and I clench my jaw. If Shane gave his opinion, it wouldn't be shot down, but the moment I do, I get a smart fucking answer.

"You both tidy yourselves up. You leave in an hour." My father dismisses us with a wave of his hand. I'm out of there and taking the stairs two at a time. My mind, for some reason, begins conjuring up images of Connor. It's weird how much you can miss a person. I hate him for abandoning me, but he has always been there for me. Now I feel so out of place in our dysfunctional family.

Slamming my door feels pretty juvenile, but I need to release some of my anger. I also need to get showered and ready to go purchase bog land.

Land that's only good for one thing.

Dumping bodies.

CHAPTER TWO

SIOBHAN

"*D*EATH. *IT COMES TO us all.*" That line is from Gladiator, one of my all-time favorite films, and it rings true to me. Right now, it's on a loop as I look down at my father. All the wasted time. All the what-ifs and whys. They no longer matter. All that matters is saying goodbye and hoping that the next time I meet him, we might spend some time together. I might actually get to know my father.

"Ah, Siobhan, I'm so sorry for your loss." Another farmer I don't know takes my hand in his. His other holds a hat that he takes from his balding head. His tweed jacket is worn and looks like if you'd slap it, dust mites would fill the air. But these are their Sunday clothes, their funeral clothes. Irish Farmers have their own unique style.

"Thank you…" I don't know his name, and there is a pause, like he's waiting for me to say it. His hand tightens on mine. "Michael." Another part of me wants to say Patrick, but I'm wrong either way.

"Peter."

I exhale a breath. "Ah, yeah, Peter."

"Peter, you're holding up the line." Olive, bless her heart, leans in across my shoulder. Peter is a big man, nearly seven feet tall, so being told off by a woman who is small and round is funny. But he moves along the line that just isn't stopping. The room is filled with men, mostly farmers, all chatting about how great my dad was.

My eyes flicker once again to his corpse. Each story I hear makes me wish I had known him. I don't feel sad or upset like any normal daughter would. No tears come. I even try to force them by thinking back to burying my mother when I was only fifteen. But I have nada.

The wake is to last three nights. Three long nights. Honestly, I don't understand why we have to wait so long, but it's a tradition, in case he wakes up. But my father isn't waking up. He's dead. For sure.

"Olive, I'm going to take a break." I need to get out of this room of strangers.

Olive nods sharply. "Don't you worry, Siobhan. I'll keep this show on the road." I suppress a smile that threatens to appear. She pats me three times on the arm. "You take a wee break. Come back when you're ready."

I don't delay. Instead, I move through the house quickly and out into the small backyard, which is walled in. I open the gate and move out into the farmyard. The large slatted shed that housed eighty cattle is now silent. It's an odd sound. Spending most of my childhood listening to the wails of the cattle, the silence is another reminder that everyone here is gone.

Swallowing the first sign of tears, I tighten my arms across my chest. It's freezing outside—my breaths form small white puffs in front of me. The light black dress isn't doing anything to fight off the cold. The wind prickles my skin, making me feel, and I allow it. Standing still with my eyes closed brings back so many memories.

My mother wasn't a conventional mother by any means. She would roll up her sleeves and come out to help Dad with the cattle. She would shovel dung, feed them silage. A pair of overalls was something she owned.

A small laugh bubbles from my lips, accompanied by my first cry. Dad loved her so much. I remember watching him watch her, hoping someone would look at me like that one day. But that was the before. Before she got cancer. Before everything changed and then he changed. Our home changed.

"Siobhan?" My name is spoken softly and like a question, which has me wiping my eyes quickly. Two young men—brothers—are standing in the yard. Neither are farmers, and they look out of place in my yard. Like when city slickers arrive and stumble upon our house, either looking to buy it or looking for directions.

The one who's closer has a soft smile on his face. His black suit fits him snuggly. His freshly shaven face gives him that city slick feel. Blond hair brushed to the side finishes off the look.

My eyes move to the brother who stands a few paces back. He doesn't wear black. His jeans and white T-shirt are finished off with a black suit jacket. His wild beard and wild blue eyes do funny things to my stomach. They're both attractive. *What an odd thing to think when my father is lying out a few feet away.*

"Yes, I'm Siobhan," I finally answer on an exhale.

"Darragh O'Reagan," the closest one says. "Knew your father. He was mighty." I take his large, and surprisingly soft, outstretched hand.

"Thank you." He's smiling too hard, and the smell of alcohol emitting off him has my eyes flickering to his brother.

"Sorry for your loss." His voice is deep, and I find myself nodding at him.

Darragh still holds my hand, and my eyes snap back to him. "We wanted to know if you had a minute for a chat."

It's my father's wake. But sure, why not?

"What about?" I remove my hand from his and take a step sideways just to put a bit of space between us. Folding my arms across my chest doesn't do anything to fight off the cold biting into me.

"We want to buy your land."

Anger I wasn't expecting ripples through me. I unfold my arms and refold them while shifting on my feet. I look at both brothers. Waiting for what?

I'm unsure. Darragh is still smiling while the other is looking around him, like he wants to find somewhere to hide. The fact that he reacts like that makes me like him a small bit more, yet these two brothers have arrived to my father's funeral to buy stupid land. I push down my anger, not wanting to create a stir.

"I'm not sure what I'm doing with it." There is a time and place for everything, and this isn't either. "Thank you for coming," I add while moving past both men before the second one with the beard stops me with his words.

"Your father was a good man." I look at him now. Really look at him, because he sounds so sincere, so honest.

"Was he?" I find myself questioning. I am sick of hearing what a good man he was. I want to scream that I don't know the man that was left after my mother died and took him with her, leaving behind a shell. Well, not a shell, apparently. Everyone else seems to think he was great.

His brows pull down, and I don't blame him. He's a stranger, and he doesn't need to know about our family problems.

"Sorry. Yeah, he was." I leave quickly and go back into the house. I don't go to the sitting room that my father is lying out in. Instead, I make my way into the kitchen that also holds a group of farmers eating sandwiches and drinking tea. A big pot of stew sits on the stove. The kitchen is warm and cozy after the cold outside. I settle into an armchair that faces the window and let the room warm me up.

"Siobhan, sweetheart, will you have a bowl of stew?" I smile at Teresa. She's a neighbor. Our home is down what is known as The Black Lane. It sits at the end by itself. Teresa is the closest, and her house is across the road from the lane. I don't know her, but when I got back, she was there taking over, and I didn't mind.

Everyone in the area is here to help, united in their love for my father. Teresa wears a woolly cream Aran jumper and has red rosy cheeks. Sleeves rolled up to her elbows couldn't cool her down. That wool is thick; I used to own a few of them. Once I moved to Dublin, I left it all behind. Just like the life I knew before.

Sandie settles at my feet—another thing I'm trying to adjust to. She is my father's sheepdog, one he got after I left. She follows me around like she knows I'm her owner's daughter. I'm not exactly an animal lover, and I don't want to get attached. I can't take a sheepdog back to my apartment in Dublin.

"I'm fine, Teresa," I tell her. My stomach grumbles, but the thought of eating makes my mouth water.

"Just a small bowl." She has kind gray eyes that smile, even when her lips don't.

"A small one then," I tell her, and her smile spreads fast across her face.

"A bowl over here wouldn't go astray," Peter speaks up from the group of farmers, and a few of them follow suit. Teresa is quick to dish out bowls of stew and smiles as they start to dig in. Compliments on the stew are passed around the kitchen, making Teresa's face redden and her laughter deepen, and it's in that moment I find this sense of peace. In my family's kitchen, surrounded by strangers, with a dog I don't own at my feet. The heat of the bowl is warming my hands, but the love of these people is going deeper.

Then silence descends on the room, and the shift is immediate. I look up to find the brothers standing in my doorway.

CHAPTER THREE

FINN

"HER FATHER'S *WAKE*?" I lean in toward Darragh the moment Siobhan is out of earshot. I feel shitty now. One thing I don't like is messing with the dead.

"Dad said she'd be vulnerable, make it an easy job." He stuffs his hands into his trouser pockets as we both watch Siobhan disappear inside.

"Clearly, Dad isn't always right," I say, and Darragh looks at me with a grin on his face.

"It ain't over yet, brother." He moves toward the house, and I follow quickly on his heels.

"You're not going in?" I ask, waiting for him to turn away from the house and toward the car, but no, instead, I follow him under the arch of the front door. This isn't right, but it'll be worse if I'm not there, just in case it gets out of hand. Darragh, on a good day, can't control his mouth. This morning, with so much alcohol still fueling his body, anything is liable to come out of his mouth.

I've been to lots of wakes, for lots of ages, and most daughters would be devastated about the death of a parent. Siobhan seemed lost in a way that I wanted to help her find whatever it was she was searching for. I scratch my eyebrow, not meeting the eye of the men who line the hall. Silence already fills the house, but a new silence follows us all the way into the kitchen, where we find Siobhan.

She's sitting in an armchair, a sheepdog at her feet. Its head lifts slightly as it takes me and Darragh in before settling back down between its paws. Siobhan holds a bowl of steaming food, and the look on her face appears to be contentment, which is unexpected compared to the girl I saw outside. The guilt that was gnawing at me lifts. The silence in the kitchen has her looking at us. Big brown eyes meet mine, and her nostrils flare slightly.

"Ah, Teresa, I'll have a bowl of stew there." I didn't think my brother would be able to stoop any lower, but yet, he does.

Teresa, who we all know as the area's gossip mill, takes a bowl and fills it for Darragh, who accepts it and manages to squeeze in on a bench with the other men. The only noise is of him eating, and I don't know whether to admire his brazenness or kick him.

"Would you like a bowl, Finn?" My attention is drawn to Teresa, and I shake my head.

"No, thank you." Scanning the room, I meet Siobhan's eye again. She has been watching me. Now that she has my attention, she lets the silky curtain of long black hair cover her face. My lips twitch but stop as Darragh starts talking.

"Teresa, you have a mighty pair of hands on you. Another bowl would be nice." He holds his bowl in the air, and Teresa looks like she might pour the stew on his head. That, I wouldn't stop. I move toward Siobhan, noticing the way her hands tighten on the bowl and spoon that she holds. It's the only tell that she knows I'm approaching. She looks so slight in the armchair. But outside, when she was standing in the yard, she was curvy and womanly.

The women Darragh brings home have that look in their eyes, like they've seen too much of the world. The bad part. But with Siobhan, there's an innocence I find myself drawn to.

I sit beside her and immediately rub the dog behind the ears. "What's her name?"

She turns her head while tucking her hair behind her ear, and up this close, I can see that she is indeed beautiful. Her lips are slightly red from the hot food—they're distracting—but what's captured me since I saw her in the yard are her eyes. Brown eyes that are deep and rich. Her eyes hold her emotions, and now, she's nervous.

"Sandie." Her pink tongue flicks out to lick her lips. I follow her movements.

"Beautiful," I find myself saying, mesmerized.

"Excuse me?" She seems surprised, and I stop looking at her lips and focus on her eyes instead. "Sandie. She's a beautiful sheepdog." She looks down at the dog as if it's her first time seeing it. My hand still rubs behind the dog's ears.

"Yeah, I suppose she is." From her face and tone, I can see she has no attachment to the dog. A part of her has no attachment to this moment.

"Jesus, Teresa, that is a mighty stew." I clench my jaw at how loud Darragh is being. He's normally a little more discreet. He must be still pretty hungover to not give a shit at a wake. I look cross at him, but Teresa is filling his bowl for the third time. At least that will keep him quiet.

"I'm sorry about him," I say to Siobhan.

She shakes her head slightly. "You are twins; not the same person."

"Yeah. Identical twins." I rhyme it off like I have a million times.

"Oh no, you are so different."

I'm smiling at her. "We are identical—same blond hair and blue eyes, same facial structure. It's the beard, isn't it?" I say in a joking manner. But she's shaking her head.

"You might both have blue eyes, but yours are different from his." Her words trail off like she might have said too much.

"How so?" I ask, wanting to know, like really know. Hearing someone see me and Darragh as different people makes my stomach tighten. It's all I've ever wanted to hear. With my family, they see us as one, and I hate it.

She frowns. "I don't know. You're different but the same." Her cheeks color, making her even more beautiful. "Now I sound silly." She sits up straighter, and I can see the strain on her face.

"No, you don't."

The conversation has picked back up in the room, but as Darragh stands, dragging his chair with such fucking disrespect that even I want to hit him, the room grows silent again.

"Teresa, you're a gem," he tells her, handing her his bowl like she's here to pick up after him. I can see the tightness around her eyes, but she just nods, taking the bowl from him. Each step Darragh takes toward Siobhan, I find myself leaning closer to her, wanting to protect her from him. He pulls up a small stool sitting in front of her.

"Me and Teresa go way back." He smiles at Siobhan—the smile that breaks so many hearts. I remove my hand from Sandie and sit straighter.

"I won't keep you, Siobhan, I can see you have your hands full." He waves around the room like she's having a fucking party. I can't stare at him any harder, yet his focus is solely on Siobhan. "I just want to make one final offer." He hands her a piece of paper from his pocket, something he must have prepared before we came here. Something I wasn't informed about. Siobhan reluctantly takes the piece of paper and opens it. I can see what's scrawled across it.

Darragh is smiling like he just won. "Now that's a mighty number, Siobhan."

I can see the side of her face, and it looks like she's holding her breath. Her delicate fingers move swiftly as she tears the piece of paper in two.

"No," she says, and I don't know why, but I'm so fucking proud.

CHAPTER FOUR

SIOBHAN

M Y HEART IS RACING in my chest for more than one reason. My emotions were already a jumble before Finn and Darragh arrived, but now I feel like instead of walking, I'm crawling.

"I want you to leave," I find myself saying.

The room is deadly silent. Finn is the first to move. "Darragh, now," he says, his voice deeper. His words are quick, quiet—words his brother obeys.

Darragh gets up. He's no longer smiling, and a shiver snakes its way down my spine at how he looks at me. His eyes are hard and narrowed. He doesn't like being told no or what to do; that's obvious. But I'm not afraid of him, so I don't look away from his hard eyes.

"I'm sorry, Siobhan." I don't look at Finn as he speaks. I don't take my eyes from Darragh until he turns away. Finn walks behind him and leaves my kitchen. I can nearly tell once they've vacated the house as the noise level around us starts to rise again to normal conversation.

"Are you okay?" Teresa sits down where Finn had been sitting, and I find myself rubbing Sandie where he had.

"I'm not sure," I tell her honestly.

"They are bad news. Darragh is a pup." *Yeah, I can tell that already.* But she doesn't mention Finn. She's silent. I'm silent. I hate silence.

"What about Finn?" I ask stupidly, and Teresa is smiling.

"He's not the worst." I'm not sure how I feel about that. It's good because she says it softly, but 'not the worst' isn't the best.

"Yeah, well, they're gone," I say, wanting to wipe the smile from Teresa's face. I didn't want her getting any ideas.

"They'll be back. The O'Reagans don't give up that easy."

My pulse spikes, and I bite my lip to stop the smile which threatens to spread across my face. There's something seriously wrong with me that I'm happy about seeing Finn O'Reagan again. I get out of the chair feeling silly.

"I better go back in." Teresa is no longer smiling but squeezes my hand as I leave and take my place beside my father's coffin. Olive hasn't moved from where I left her, like she had promised, and I resume the senseless motion of shaking hands and making small talk while I listen to a room full of strangers talking about my dad.

My room is the same as it always was. Posters of Boyzone and Westlife are still on the wall. I'm shaking my head as I scan the room. The pine shelf over my bed holds a dozen books and a Mickey Mouse alarm clock I refused to get rid of. The bed is freshly made. The cream floral quilt cover isn't mine; it's from my parents' bed. Someone had pressed it, and the smell of the fabric softener has taken over my room. Sandie jumps up on the bed as I admire it.

"Just one night," I tell her firmly, and she lies down with her head between her paws.

But that's not what happens. One night turns into four. Sandie stays with me through the three nights that Dad is waked in the house and the night after I bury him. I still haven't cried, and each moment here in this place makes me feel more lost than I have ever felt before. Lost in a sense that I know this is where I came from, but I feel like I don't belong. I want to. The more I'm around these people, the more I want to fit in. In Dublin, it's a fight for yourself. It's a city and busy, and everyone is rushing with their heads down. But here, they look out for each other. They know each other. It's nice.

I wake up to an empty house and make myself a tea before sitting at the table. I miss the noise of the people. The tile floor is freezing, but the fluffy socks I put on help keep some of the cold away. I've switched my phone off since arriving here and know I have to turn it on soon and let my life come back in. I have so many decisions to make and a small amount of time to make them. Darragh's crazy offer plays around in my mind, but I did the right thing. He was being disrespectful, but on the other hand, that kind of money is life-changing.

I need a distraction, so I decide to finally turn on my phone. Immediately, it starts to bleep, and it doesn't stop as I top up my tea. Sitting back down, I scroll through messages from friends and work. I have only four more days of leave before I have to go back. My stomach tightens at the idea of returning to Dublin. A part of me doesn't want to, but I push the feeling aside.

Sandie's bark lifts me out of the chair as the house phone rings loudly. It feels out of place after the intense, empty silence in the house. I pick up the phone quickly.

"Hello."

"I'm looking for Siobhan Walsh." The man's voice is very formal, but I recognize it. I try to remember the name of the familiar voice.

"Speaking. How can I help you?"

"It's Brian Harris."

Ah, yes, that's how I knew him. He's my father's solicitor, the one who told me that my father had left everything to me. I was his only child, and with no other family and mother gone, I was the only option.

"Hi, Brian. How can I help you?" Sandie rubs against my bare leg like a cat would, and I shoo her away.

"We've run into a complication," he says, and I stop focusing on Sandie.

"What kind of complication?"

"Your father's sister is contesting the will."

I sigh. Great. Just what I need.

CHAPTER FIVE

FINN

DARRAGH TURNS AROUND IN his seat, looking through the back window. "Are we being chased?"

I lift my foot off the pedal, slowing the car down slightly. My hands sting from the grip I have on the steering wheel, so I loosen them.

"Finn, is there something you aren't telling me?" I glance at Darragh as he lights a fag in my new car.

"Don't smoke in here," I tell him, but he shrugs his shoulders while rolling down the window slightly.

"Oops," he says as he blows smoke out the window.

"You are so fucking disrespectful." I want to take my anger out on the pedal and slam it to the floor, but the winding roads won't allow it, and breaking every two seconds is taking the joy out of speeding. That's one of the downsides to where we live. The roads are only good for one car, and the bends are pretty severe. You can't open the car up here.

"I'll get your car valeted, okay?" Darragh blows smoke through the crack in the window again. It isn't just about the car. It's about Darragh being Darragh, and yeah, I also don't want smoking in my new S-Class Mercedes. She's my baby, and he's polluting her, and not just with his smoke. I've just picked him up from a house party and am taking him home. He had been drinking last night, and he still reeks of whiskey. His crumpled shirt and slacks are the result of falling out of bed.

"So now that we aren't going to crash, can you tell me what's going on?" Darragh flicks the cigarette out the window, and I can't stop my mind from wondering if it has hit the shiny silver exterior. Paying ninety thousand for a car isn't worth it when you have a brother who disrespects everything, including money. "You're not still mad over the chick with the land?"

Now I glance at Darragh, and he smirks.

"You know, her name is *Siobhan*, and yeah, I'm still pissed." He rolls his eyes at me before lowering himself in the seat and putting on sunglasses. The sun is hiding behind the clouds, but his headspace couldn't have been great. He looks like shit.

A moment of silence passes, and I slow down as we enter the small town of Kingscourt. It's dark and depressing—one long strip of shops that sells a little bit of everything, yet nothing at the same time.

"What did Da say?" Darragh sounds serious, but I can't tell for sure with the sunglasses on. I can never really tell with Darragh. He often smiles when he's serious and smiles when he isn't. Most people think that because we're twins, we finish each other's sentences. That makes me fucking laugh. I have no clue of what goes on in his screwed-up mind.

"That we should use scare tactics." My hands clench around the steering wheel again. The thought of doing that to Siobhan seems almost barbaric, and I'm lucky enough that I've talked him into letting me handle it, but once the funeral is over, that's my proposal. He surprised me by giving me a week to obtain the land.

"We should. She thinks she's playing smart, holding out for more money." Darragh slides out his phone and checks it before lifting himself up slightly and stuffing it back into his pocket. Irritation grows on me at Darragh's words.

"She was angry because you did it at her father's wake. Are you that thick, Darragh?"

"Let it all out, Finn."

It was all bottled up inside, ready to pour out of me. After we left Siobhan's house, I drove home and didn't speak to him for a few days. Every time I thought about his behavior at the wake, I wanted to find him and punch him. Each time I did see him, he was drinking, drunk, or with a woman. I told myself it was a sign to stay away from her.

"What you did was a dickhead move," I tell him, putting my foot down. We're on a straight road that leads toward our home.

"Are you going to start rooting and tipping at that?" he asks while lowering his glasses, and I want so very much to punch him in the face.

"I'm going to go like a normal person and make an offer on the land. I waited until today, when the funeral was over." I slow down as we approach our house. Most days, I don't notice it, but sometimes I can see how the house looks like a hotel. With twenty-four bedrooms, a gym, library, and even our own bar, it's a monster of a house, but it's home to us.

The sensor on one of the garage doors kicks in, and the door opens slowly. Four cars already take up most of the large space, but two spots are still available. I don't even have the car turned off when Darragh jumps out.

"Mind my fucking door," I say as he nearly connects with Shane's Audi.

"You need to get laid." Those are his departing words. I sit there, knowing that going inside and seeing if Dad or Shane are looking for me would be wise, but I restart the car and pull out of the garage, leaving Whitewood house in my rearview mirror.

I'm going to see Siobhan and convince her to sell the land.

CHAPTER SIX

SIOBHAN

"**S**ANDIE." I'VE BEEN CALLING her for the last ten minutes. Normally, she appears quickly, but right now, she's a no-show. It's not like her, and the worry I'm feeling makes me realize I'm getting way too attached to a dog I can't keep.

I return to the house and grab a woolly hat and my long black coat. It's freezing outside, and my Aran jumper, which normally fends off the cold, isn't working today. I hate that Sandie is missing, and also, talking to the solicitor and finding out my dad's eighty-year-old sister is contesting the will isn't helping my mood either. My father didn't speak to her, and I'd never met her, but my mother told me she was very wicked to my father and to the world.

"Sandie." I tuck my hands into my jacket pockets as I leave the front yard to check the lane. Turning the bend from my small farmhouse, I see someone bent down, petting Sandie. My stomach flips as Finn looks up. He's too far away to talk to unless we shout, but he gives me a wave, and I can't stop the smile that tugs at my lips or the butterflies that erupt in my stomach.

He rotates from looking at Sandie to me.

"Hi. I've been looking for her," I say as I finally reach them just as Sandie, the traitor, jumps up and starts licking Finn's face. He laughs, and heat rushes to my cheeks at the sound.

"She likes me," he declares, looking at me from under his lashes.

"She likes everyone." I say it without thinking, and Finn rises, still smiling, still causing my heart to pound.

"Does she now? And here I thought I was special."

A small laugh escapes my lips. "Sorry to disappoint you," I tell him. He's wearing jeans again but with a red jumper, and his gray jacket is open but the collar sits up. *He could model,* I tell myself.

"I was wondering if we could chat." The uncertainty in his voice has me agreeing. A part of me is wondering if he felt the pull that I feel toward him, but the more rational part of me is telling me this is about land.

"Let's go back to the house." He smiles with a nod, and Sandie follows us back.

"How have you been?" His question is sincere.

"Honestly, a little lost. I didn't know my dad," I tell him as we step into the house. "He was great when I was a kid, but... then my mum died." I remove the jacket, not looking at Finn. "Everything changed." I pull off the hat and try to compose myself as I turn to him. Finn has a way of making me say what I think. It's odd and refreshing.

"Woah." He moves back out of my personal space as my nose brushes his chest; he was standing that close.

"Sorry, I was just going to hang up my jacket." He holds his gray coat in his hand. The red jumper hugs him, and my stomach tightens again. He definitely works out.

"What happened to your mother?" We haven't moved. I look up at him, and his eyes stare at me intensely.

"Cancer. It was a long time ago. Sometimes it doesn't feel that long ago, though."

"I'm so sorry, Siobhan." His kindness is going to make me cry. I sidestep so he can hang up his coat.

"Thanks." I make my way into the kitchen, where Sandie lies in front of the fire, and put the water on the stove.

"Tea?" I ask as Finn enters behind me, making the room feel tiny with his presence.

He sits down across from me. "Yes, please."

I smile at him. "He has manners," I say jokingly.

"I make up for the lack of Darragh's." I can see the regret the moment he mentions his brother's name, and the relaxed atmosphere disappears.

"So you wanted to chat," I say, getting to it as I place a cup of tea in front of him. Milk and sugar were already set out on the table this morning.

He shifts in his seat while scratching his eyebrow. "About the land. I want you to reconsider the offer."

I take a sip of the tea. "To you, Finn, I would sell it." His blue eyes light up with surprise. I don't want the land. I have no intentions of farming it, so selling it is the only option, and to someone as nice as Finn seems like a good choice.

"Great." He smiles, but I don't.

"But I can't. An aunt has contested the will. Otherwise, it would be yours."

Finn seems quiet as he sips his tea. "Is she from the area?"

I'm shaking my head, but I can't stop the smile. "What are you going to do, send Darragh to talk to her?"

"No, I would talk to her."

"Finn, the charmer," I say, and my cheeks heat. Words jump from my mouth without my approval, but I like the spark they set off in Finn's eyes.

"You think I'm charming?" he asks, leaning in slightly.

I hug my cup closer to give my hands something to do. "I didn't say that. I said, *charmer*. There is a difference."

"There's that word again." He looks intense, and I find my own smile slipping.

"What word?" I'm starting to feel warm and want to take off the Aran jumper.

"Different. You said I was different from Darragh." He's so serious, like me saying it means more to him than he wants me to know, and I want to give him an honest and open answer.

"You have a stillness in you that he doesn't. You're like... a tree." It's coming out all wrong.

"A tree," he repeats, amusement in his voice.

"Yeah," I say on a small laugh. It sounds daft, even to my ears, but that's what he is. Strong and tall and sturdy, like a tree.

"I'll take it as a compliment," he says, and I pray for my cheeks to cool.

"It was." The room grows serious, and I wonder if I'm flirting with him without knowing. Is that possible? To be flirting subconsciously?

"I'm not very romantic, so I don't know what to compare you to."

"You think I'm being romantic by calling you a tree?" I drink my tea, but he can see the smile in my eyes. He's smiling again too, and it's doing crazy things to my stomach.

"I don't get out much," he says on a laugh.

"Me neither," I admit. Even in Dublin, all I did was work. I worked at Connelly's Hospital and took every shift I could, saving for a home. It's not important now, as I inherited one. I'm still not sure what do about the house. Selling it seems wrong, since I was raised here, but moving here isn't an option. I'm not going to commute such a long journey.

"Maybe we should go out sometime." His words pull me out of my thoughts.

"Yes," I answer way too quickly. My heart feels ready to explode. He just asked me out on a date, and I just accepted.

He takes a large drink from his cup before standing. "Perfect. I'll see you tonight, then."

I stumble after him, shocked at his words. *Tonight?* It seems too sudden; I don't feel ready. As he gets his coat on, I stand silent in turmoil, wondering if I should cancel.

"What should I wear?" *Nice, Siobhan. You don't sound desperate or anything.*

"I was thinking dinner," he says. I'm nodding because his jacket is on; there are no more distractions as he faces me. "Is eight okay?"

"Perfect," I tell him, and he grins.

"Perfect," he repeats before leaving.

Sandie appears at my leg, and I bend down to rub behind her ear. "I have a date with Finn O'Reagan," I tell her.

CHAPTER SEVEN

FINN

"H E'S NOT HERE?" I ask as Liam looks up from his laptop.

"He's out with Shane."

I want to get this over and done with. I've hated waiting to hear what his decision will be after finding out that Siobhan's aunt has contested the will. Liam is still looking at me.

He's the next in line once Father steps down. He never says much, but he's a dark horse in our family. His suits and slicked-back hair make people think his appearance means too much to him. But it's a control thing. I've never seen him lose control. His hair always sits perfectly, his skin is always clear, and his hands are always clean—to the naked eye only.

Liam isn't one for words, but he gets things done behind the scenes. He just doesn't like working with any of us.

I make a decision and close the door behind me. "I'm in a bit of a situation."

Liam sits back and joins his hands together on the table. The laptop is still open, a soft glow shining on his face. Sometimes he's like a fucking robot, and I falter, wondering if I should just wait for Shane and Dad to get back. At least they'll say it as it is.

"I have to get land signed over for Dad."

"I'm aware of that," Liam says while I pull out a chair and sit down.

"An aunt is contesting the will; otherwise, I would have bought it today. She's seventy and—"

Liam cuts me off with a quick wave of his hand. "You're giving the situation too much life. When something gets in your way, it's an object that needs to be removed. Not a he or she but an object."

So clinical. "Okay, so this *object*... What do I do?" I ask, hoping he has an answer for me.

"I don't know, but you have to consider the cost of moving the object. Will it disturb what it surrounds? Then you must deal with it at the lowest cost and with the lowest impact."

Great. That's some fucking riddle.

"Anyone know where Da is?" I don't look at Darragh as he enters the room; I focus on my fist resting on the table.

"He's out with Shane." Liam gives Darragh the same answer he's given me.

Darragh eyes me with a smirk. "Did I interrupt something here?"

"What, you've never seen us sit in the same room?" I ask him. His stupid grin and his stupid shirt irritate me. "What are you wearing?"

"This is my new lucky shirt." He's still smiling while he pulls out a chair. His shirt is bright yellow with palm trees on it.

"You look like a moron," I tell him, and he isn't fazed at all. Instead, he turns to Liam.

"So, stony, what have I missed?" He's the only one who can get away with giving Liam a nickname. Right now, Liam isn't smiling or showing any indication that he likes Darragh, but we all know he's the favorite brother.

"Finn has a problem with his most recent job. An aunt has contested the will, and he isn't sure what to do."

"I got this." Darragh cracks his knuckles while Liam looks at me. "Problem solved."

Problem solved? Problem fucking doubled. Send Darragh to do a job, and he creates a problem that I somehow become responsible for.

"No," I tell Darragh and get up.

"He is the lowest price tag," Liam reminds me.

"He's the highest."

"Why do I have a price on me?" Darragh asks.

Now, Liam looks intrigued. "This is personal?"

I want to hit Darragh as he smirks. "Yeah, he's banging the landowner."

"Shut up, Darragh. I just have a conscience." I can hear the half-truth in my answer. Yeah, I don't feel comfortable scaring a woman into stepping away. A man, I wouldn't think twice. But an old lady? That just doesn't feel right.

"And a dick." He's hooting with laughter at his own joke, and even though he's pissing me off, maybe letting him deal with the old woman would be for the best. That way, I would have clean hands.

"Fine, you do it," I tell him with a grin, and he narrows his eyes.

"Is this a trick?"

"Is it?" I ask him back, just to confuse the fuck out of him as I leave the room and start to get ready for my date.

CHAPTER EIGHT

SIOBHAN

S ANDIE BARKS AS A car pulls into the drive, and my stomach tightens. Standing up, I fix my red dress. It's tight fitted and goes to my knee, so I get that sexy-yet-not-too-revealing look. The doorbell makes my pulse spike, and with one deep breath, I open it.

Finn's eyes roam my body, and I feel each place they touch. I shift, unable to hold still, and his gaze snaps to mine. Closing the door behind him, I notice he's holding something.

"Wow, you are stunning," he says with a smile as he takes a bunch of roses from behind his back. He holds the bouquet out to me, and I take it and smell the flowers like they do in the movies. Now I know why women do that. It isn't because they care about the smell of the flowers, but because it gives them a moment to gather themselves.

I lift my head from the roses to find him still watching me.

"Thank you. You look great." His red, black, and gray striped shirt, along with a pair of black jeans, looks so good on him. "People will think we're trying to match," I add out of nerves, and he grins.

"People will think we're a couple." His lip tugs slightly, and I shift on my feet as his eyes darken.

My stomach tightens, and I give myself a moment to think about what it would be like to be a couple. My heart starts to race, so I push the thought away. "Let me just grab my bag and jacket." I bite my lip, trying to keep some of my emotions hidden, but from the smile on his face, I'm not doing a good job.

"We could always just stay here?" The boldness in his eyes has me laughing, but staying here sounds like the perfect idea.

"Finn O'Reagan, what do you take me for?"

His smile is gone. "It's not you. It's me. I'm not sure I'll be able to control myself."

And I'm laughing again. When I look at him, I suck in a large breath. He's looking at me in a way I've always hoped someone would look at me.

"What's wrong?" He's in my personal space now. "I'm sorry if I offended you." Stuffing his hands into his pockets, he ducks his head, looking at me with furrowed brows.

"No, you didn't do anything wrong." There's something that draws me in with Finn. I feel like I know him, like he sees me. I close the distance, and I can see the uncertainty in his eyes. He hasn't a clue what just happened.

"My parents loved each other so much. As a kid, when my father would look at my mother, I always hoped someone would look at me like that someday." My throat tightens from the emotion the memory evocates, surprising me.

Finn takes my face in his large hands. "Whoever gets you, Siobhan, will never stop looking at you." His eyes roam my face, and his thumb strokes away a stray falling tear. "Can I kiss you?" His breath brushes my lips, and my eyes flutter closed as my tongue flicks out and wets my lips in anticipation of the kiss.

"Yes." I whisper the single word, and his lips touch mine, and I'm on my toes, my fingers burying themselves into his hair before running along his beard. The bristle of hairs send electricity through my hands. His hands are still holding my face while his tongue flicks out and touches my lips.

Sucking in another deep breath from the sensation, I allow him entry into my mouth. I push my body harder against his, and I can feel the full length of him. He moves me carefully against the wall, one hand on my waist. But it's not enough for me, so I break the kiss. Both of us are breathless. I'm inhaling his cologne and that manly scent that has me squeezing my legs closer together.

"Too fast. I'm sorry." He's apologizing, but if he could see inside my head, he might think me very wicked.

I smile, taking his hand as I lead him to my bedroom. Flicking on the light, all my posters look bigger. I turn to him, and one side of his mouth tugs.

"Didn't take you for a Boyzone fan."

I don't release his hand as we look at the posters. "What kind of fan did you take me for?" I don't care about bands or music; all I want is Finn in my bed.

"Not sure, but not Boyzone. Maybe Steps?" he says. I'm laughing as I pull him to my bed, and his eyes narrow before they darken. "Are you trying to seduce me?"

I bite my lip as I sit him on my bed. "Would Finn O'Reagan like to be seduced?" I reach back and unzip my dress. I feel empowered when he swallows.

"Yes, please," he says as I let the dress slip to the ground.

I step out of it and kick it to the side. He reaches out, touching my bare thighs, and pulls me toward him. I sit on him, my hands around his neck. He's still fully clothed, his eyes roaming my face. I'm not normally this forward, but I know my time here is limited, and if I let this opportunity go, I would never forgive myself.

Finn pulls me into a kiss. I shimmy closer to him, and he moans as his bulge rubs against me. I sink deeper into the kiss, moving my hips, which causes our breathing to increase faster. I'm unsteady, wanting the fabric between us gone.

Sliding off his lap, I pull at his jeans, letting him know what I want. He stands up, stripping them off along with his boxers. His erection makes my heart pound. He doesn't unbutton his shirt but pulls it off over his head. He's perfect. His lean body is toned, but not too much. Gold hairs coat his chest, and I like it.

As we stare at each other, I reach back and remove my bra and then my underwear. I've never been naked like this in front of a guy, especially with the lights on. I'm more of a lights off kind of girl. But since opening the door and seeing how Finn looked at me, it made me feel not just beautiful but also empowered. I want to keep feeding the hunger inside him with each piece of my body.

"Sit down," I tell him, and he does slowly. He looks good naked on my bed. He helps me position himself at my opening, and when I sit down fully, we both gasp. All I can feel is him inside me, and it makes me grip his shoulders as I move up and down.

Staring into Finn's eyes, I see the ecstasy mirrored back at me. But behind it all, I see his vulnerability—the mark this world has left on him. Closing my eyes, I only allow the feel of Finn inside me to consume me as I move faster and faster. His pants and moans make me come fast, and he follows shortly after.

CHAPTER NINE

SIOBHAN

I'M LYING IN FINN'S arms, both of us still naked under the quilt. My fingers play with his chest hair as we chat. "That's a lot of brothers. Who's your favorite?" I ask.

"Connor." There's a sadness to his answer, and I look up at him. His eyes are half-closed, and his lips tug down slightly in the corners. I want to erase the look of sadness from his handsome face.

"You want to talk about it?" I kiss his shoulder.

"Connor gets overwhelmed with our family and likes to take a break every once in a while. I just miss him when he goes." His eyes look haunted, and I wonder why. But a part of me doesn't want to pry too much. I don't want to scare him away.

"Your family sounds intense."

"They can be."

"Any sisters?"

"My dad has been married three times, so we have one half brother and sister, and his second wife had a daughter from a previous marriage. But we don't see any of them." I nod. It sounds so nice to have such a big family.

"I wish I had siblings," I say honestly, and Finn kisses me on the forehead.

"Sometimes I wish I had none." We smile at each other just as Finn's phone rings. "Highway to Hell" blares in my room, and I raise both eyebrows in question.

"I took you for a Nokia ringtone kind of guy."

He scratches his eyebrow. "That's the ringtone I have assigned to my family members only." I'm laughing, and Finn lets the phone ring out. Pulling me against his body causes electricity to spark between us. I move my body over his and feel him come to life.

"I'm thinking we should skip the meal and just hang out here," I suggest seductively, and he laughs. "Our reservation was two hours ago, maybe more. So we have definitely skipped the meal." I kiss him just as "Highway to Hell" blares again.

Finn groans. "I have to get it," he tells me as he gets out of bed, and I admire his backside while he gets his phone out of his jeans pockets. I love how his bum is full and muscly but not too hard to touch.

Taking the phone, he goes out into the hallway, naked. His voice is low, but I can hear what's being said on his side. "What? I'm busy." The irritation in his voice makes me smile. "What has he done now?" Silence follows as the caller speaks. "I'll be there in twenty."

My heart deflates at his words. He's leaving. As he comes back into the bedroom, I try to pretend I wasn't just eavesdropping on his conversation. He picks up his boxers and puts them on. "Siobhan, I'm so sorry, but I have to go." I can hear the regret in his voice, but it doesn't stop my disappointment.

"Is everything okay?" I ask as he buttons his jeans. He pauses briefly and looks at me. I can see the turmoil in his eyes.

"Yeah, it's just Darragh being Darragh," he says. I want to ask why one of his brothers can't take care of it, but I bite my tongue. "I don't want to go." Pulling on his shirt, he sits back on the bed with a soft sigh and kisses me gently on the cheek.

"I don't want you to go either," I say, and he kisses my hand before getting up and putting on his socks and boots.

"I might get back, but give me your number, and I'll let you know." That makes me feel a bit better, so I rhyme my number off. I get one more kiss before Finn leaves.

The house is too quiet, and it's weird that I miss him already. What will I be like when I go back to Dublin? My stomach tightens at the thought. My phone beeps from the kitchen, so I get up and wrap myself in my dressing gown. Sandie opens one eye and looks at me from where she's lying in front of the fire. I refill her water dish before checking my phone.

I miss you already. I'm smiling at the message. The number is new, so I know it's Finn. He's too sweet. I save his number to my phone before I quickly fire a message back. *I miss you too. Hope you get to come back soon.*

CHAPTER TEN

FINN

I ARRIVE AT THE location that Liam gave me and park down a lane. He told me to go the rest of the way on foot. My stomach won't settle; I'm dreading what I'm going to find. Liam was brief, as usual, on the phone. He only said that Darragh's in trouble, and they need me. Darragh's always in trouble, but this feels different. Liam being present was the first thing that tipped me off. Then during the phone call, I could hear Shane in the background, so I knew this situation was serious.

I didn't put on a jacket, and the cold has me stuffing my hands into my pockets. The road is dark. Liam said to walk for five minutes, and on my left-hand side, I'd see a small bungalow. He was right. I stop at a bungalow, but no lights are on. The large black farm gate is half-open.

The gravel under my feet sounds too loud. No lights come on as I move closer to the gray dashed house. I opt to walk on the lawn; it'll be less noise. I take one small jump across the small hedge that acts as curbing around the lawn before I approach the side of the house. Liam materializes out from the wall and nearly gives me a fucking heart attack.

"Watch where you step." He turns, and I follow him into the house. We walk into the utility room that's neat and tidy—nothing out of the ordinary.

"What's going on, Liam?" I wish he would just tell me instead of playing the fucking silent game. But we step into the kitchen, and a small light in the corner allows me to see the scene before me.

My eyes snap from Liam to Shane to Darragh before settling on the body that we all stand around.

"What happened?" I ask, feeling sick. The woman isn't dead. She's like a fish out of water; her body is jerking as she tries to breathe. But it looks like her neck is broken, her face is covered in blood, and a pool of it is growing around her head.

No one answers me. Shane and Liam look down at her like someone spilled milk and they're wondering how to clean it up. On the other hand, Darragh is freaking out. On his haunches, he keeps glancing at the body and then shooting looks at all of us. A fag was burning away in his hand.

"What did you do?"

"She attacked me. I panicked." He stands up, his eyes wild. He's high.

"You fucking bashed her head in. Is this Siobhan's aunt?" I ask, but I know it is. My stomach twists. Oh, God, this was the last thing I wanted. Real fear crawls down my spine at the thought of Siobhan finding out.

"Man, she was crazy, scrapping me, telling me to get out." He babbles as if he's not hearing me, so I look to Liam.

"What do we do?" I ask.

Liam doesn't look away from the body. "Kill her and bury her."

I'm nodding, but inside I'm saying, No, this isn't right. Maybe we can help her.

I run my hands through my hair and step away from this madness. "Or we could ring an ambulance." I know that's not going to happen, but for Siobhan, I feel I should try.

"I'll get the stuff out of my car," Shane says, ignoring my comment, and Liam nods at him.

"Pick up the cigarette butt," Liam tells Darragh, who's lighting up another one.

"Are you fucking stupid? They'll take your DNA off that," I growl. I want to strangle him as I pick up the butt and take the fag out of his mouth. I run it under the tap, then put both into my pocket.

The woman is still twitching, and I want someone to put her out of her misery. Rubbing my face, I turn away from the scene again, hating what my family can do to another human being.

"I'm sorry, Finn." Darragh is beside me. The smell of drink emanating off him has me closing my eyes. "I fucked up."

He's nearly crying, and I hate that. I hate what he's done, but I don't like to see him hurting either. I know behind all this, he's a good person.

"It's fine, Darragh. Just try not to touch anything," I tell him as Shane arrives. I notice that Liam has been watching us with interest, but he says nothing while he helps Shane lay down heavy plastic.

"Grab her legs," Shane tells me, and I do as he asks as he takes the top part of her body. I try not to think about the flesh in my hands. I try not to think about the fact that I'm helping to kill someone.

I try to just do as my brother asks and not think too much about it. We lift her onto the plastic. We've just laid her down when Liam kneels in a suit and covers her mouth with a cloth. I can't take my eyes off her—she twitches and fights, but she has no chance. I wait until her body stops jerking before I look away.

"Is she dead?" Darragh asks, kneeling down again and staring at her. Having him here is pointless.

"Shane and I will bury her and clean up here. You take Darragh home, and in the morning, call the Gardaí and report his car stolen. We'll burn it." I'm nodding, feeling a sense of relief at getting out of here.

"Darragh." Liam says his name harsher then I've ever heard, and we all stop and wait for him to speak again. "You were partying all night." Darragh nods. "Burn your clothes too."

"We will," I tell Liam. I just want to get away from here.

"I'm sorry," Darragh pleads with Liam, but he's already rolling up the body. I take Darragh by the arm and out of the house.

I'm staring into the fire as the last fibers of our clothes go up. Darragh's asleep in bed. Tomorrow, this will all feel like a bad dream to him. For me, it's a waking nightmare. My phone sits on the mantelpiece as I poke the fire while drinking straight from a bottle of whiskey.

I want to ring Siobhan, and I want to ring Connor, but I don't for two different reasons. With Siobhan, it's the guilt of knowing what I know. Knowing that my family is responsible for her aunt's death. With Connor, I feel that hearing his voice will push me over the edge. He's the one who beat up the bullies in school. He's the one who dusted off my clothes when I fell.

He told me I was a good person, worthy of a happily ever after. He told me I would always have him, but as we grew up, he disappeared more and more.

"Finn." I turn as my father enters the empty room. Once, it was a ballroom, but now it's empty. I chose this room so no one would come near me.

My father stands near the fireplace, his head held high. He isn't looking at me.

"What you did today for your brother... He will always be grateful." *Well, that's a load of horse shit*, but I nod my head like I agree. "You don't believe me?" The question surprises me. He never asks my opinion or thoughts on things.

"No. I don't," I tell him honestly. "He will do it again because, like all things with Darragh, there are no consequences. You taught us that sometimes blood has to be taken, but never from an innocent or a woman."

Father nods his acknowledgment at that statement, and lines appear on his forehead like he's really thinking. "But how many times has he broken that rule? How much more blood will he spill before he's caught? Or worse, someone else gets to him first."

My father nods again before he starts to speak. I fold my arms across my chest, trying to push down the anger that's growing inside me.

"When I was a kid, my brother and I were playing in a farm shed along with the farmer's son."

I'm glued to each word. Him talking about his childhood rarely happens, but hearing about his past makes my father seem more human. Maybe that's why he never speaks of it. I unfold my arms now and stuff my hands into my pockets.

"The farmer had left a double barrel shotgun lying around. He went out that day to shoot crows that had been picking holes in his cover for the silage, but by tea time, none had arrived. So he left the gun in the shed. Loaded."

Father unbuttons his suit jacket, like a man who's getting ready to sit down, yet he stays standing.

The door opens, and Shane looks in. Once again, Shane is dressed in all black. His dark brown eyes remind me of trying to see the bottom of a well, and you're just not sure you're seeing the end.

"Come in, Shane. I'm just telling Finn a story." Shane doesn't blink. He comes in and stands around the dwindling fire, looking from me to Father, but he doesn't speak. Father waits until the room settles again. I want to ask Shane if it's done—is the body gone? But I know better than to interrupt our father.

"The farmer's son, Patrick, was my and Tom's best friend. Anyway, Tom found the gun and was playing with it. We didn't know it was loaded, but Patrick told him to stop waving the gun around. When Tom went to lower it, he hit the trigger by accident and blew a hole in Patrick. It was a mess; we were only sixteen. He was dead within minutes. He was innocent. It was an accident. But I knew no one would believe us. Everyone saw my brother as someone evil. He liked to torture small animals, but that didn't make him a serial killer."

My father's gaze falls on the bottle of whiskey. "Give me that," he says, and it takes me a second to realize he's talking about the bottle.

I hand it over, and he takes a deep swallow. I want to ask what happened, but Father hands me the bottle. I take a quick drink, letting some of it drip down my chin before handing it to Shane, who declines and places it back on the fireplace.

"So we dragged him over to the silage pit and placed him slightly under the cover. We washed away the blood and spread fresh straw, burned the bloodied ones, and wiped down the gun before placing it where we had found it."

I feel sick at his story. But covering up a crime at the age of sixteen does explain how my father can now do it so easily, and like with everything this family does, he justifies it.

Father indicates to Shane to pass him the whiskey again, and Shane does. The bottle goes around again. Shane drinks this time, and from the look on his face, this is his first time hearing this story too.

"When all was said and done, the farmer had a drinking problem, so he thought he had done it. That bit of information we actually hadn't known. It was pure luck. But me and Tom walked away from it all. The farmer, however, went down for ten years. Wasn't really that long of a sentence."

This time, I take the whiskey. That wasn't the end I was expecting. The man served time for a crime he didn't commit. But it wasn't that part that messed me up; it was living with the knowledge that he had killed his son when he hadn't. There might be a wife or other siblings that would think their dad took their brother's life.

"The reason, Finn, I am telling you this is because Tom is like Darragh, and just like I stood beside Tom, you stood beside Darragh. Right now, he might not appreciate it, but one day he will." He squeezes my shoulder as he goes to leave the room.

"Did Tom appreciate what you did?" I ask.

"Yes." Father sounds distant, and I want to see his face, but his back is still to me.

"Why have I never heard of Tom?"

When my father turns around, his eyes have hardened. "That's a story for another day."

I'm left with Shane now, and I honestly don't want to be alone in his presence. He unsettles me in a way I can't explain, but I want to ask about Siobhan's aunt.

"So you and Liam finished that," I say and he nods. "Where?" I ask, and he folds his arms across his chest.

His tattooed arm is a reminder of why I don't like being around him. He has twelve black bands now that are thickly inked. Each time I see a new one, my stomach heaves, and I find it hard to hold eye contact with him. Each band is for a life that he took.

"Do you really want to know?" he asks.

"I'm off to bed," I tell him. I don't want to know. He's staring into the glow of the fire. I take my phone off the mantelpiece and leave the room that will forever remind me of a woman we killed, and Patrick. This house is filling with ghosts, fast.

CHAPTER ELEVEN

SIOBHAN

I T'S ODD. THE SMELL of the farmyard is giving me peace. Whereas before, If I ever got a hint of farmland in Dublin, it used to remind me of home, and that would put me in a foul humor. But now it smells like freedom. Hope. It's filled with memories.

I wish I had known my father. I wish I had grown up here and known Finn. I know I'm only twenty-six, but already, I feel as though I wasted years not knowing him. How can I feel this way about someone who I've just met? I'm smiling as Sandie follows me around the yard.

I'm wearing my Da's size ten wellies, so I'm swimming in them. But I don't care. I want this to become a memory—a little girl who wore her daddy's wellies out into the farmyard.

"You look good." Finn's voice sends butterflies erupting in my stomach. It takes all my will not to look at him. After not coming back to me last night, I do feel a bit of punishment is due. So I keep walking slowly, but I can't not look and find myself taking quick glances at him, sending my heart pounding.

"So this is what you country boys are into?" I tease, and Finn smiles, walking with me but not beside me.

"I like the boots and all, but it depends on who's standing in them."

I stop walking and smile at him. "Is that so?" He's freshly showered. His blond hair is still damp. The red T-shirt and jeans hug his slim body, and I let myself admire it for a moment.

"You can leave them on if you want to," he says, taking a step toward me.

"They're my dad's," I say honestly, and the horror on his face has me laughing.

"I'm so sorry, Siobhan." I can hear him, but the laughter isn't easing up, and soon he joins me. Sandie starts to whine, and I pull myself together.

"Not exactly sure why that was so funny," I tell him, and he nudges me.

"I'm sorry for not coming back last night. Did you get my text?"

I did. He apologized, saying Darragh had gotten sick everywhere, and he was covered in it. He had to shower, and it was way too late to come back.

But still, I felt disappointed and hurt. The idea of Darragh always coming first didn't sit well with me.

"I did." I kick a pebble with my huge boots and watch it roll toward a slurry pit.

"I got you something." Finn sounds nervous, and that's what makes me look at him more than the box he holds out to me.

I take it slowly, looking from the box to him. "You didn't have to," I tell him.

"Open it." He's smiling, and I open it to see a gorgeous slim bracelet. Finn removes it from the box and puts it on my wrist. "Do you like it?"

My throat closes as I move my wrist, the light catching it.

"It's beautiful, Finn." I'm looking from him to the bracelet. It's perfect and he's perfect. This moment is perfect, and it's making my throat tighten.

"Why do you look so sad?" He lifts my chin, making me look at him.

"I'm not staying, Finn." I whisper the words that have lodged themselves in my throat, not wanting to come out.

"Staying here?" he questions, and I nod.

"I have to go back to Dublin tomorrow—to my job, to my life." *What life?* An empty apartment. Twelve hour shifts at the hospital. For the first time, I feel like I'm living. But I can't run away again. I did it once and swore I would never run again.

I want to remove the bracelet because now it doesn't feel right, but he stops me. I've never seen his face so serious.

"I got it with you in mind. It's yours, no matter what."

My throat burns, and I have to look away. I hate the silence.

"Maybe a cup of tea would be nice?" I ask, and when I look at him, he finally smiles again. It's not one of his full-on smiles, but I'll take it.

"Is that code for something else?" he asks, and just like that, the tension is lifted, and I laugh and try to look sexy as I shuffle in my dad's wellies back into the house.

I'm through the back door when his arms wrap around me, stopping me in the tracks. Sandie zooms past us and goes to her usual spot beside the fire. I'm lifted slowly out of the wellies, and Finn doesn't put me down until we're standing in the kitchen. His breath is hot on my neck, and I close my eyes and inhale him.

As he spins me around, I wrap my arms around his neck. I look into his heavy blue eyes, and I feel so much is said between us. This isn't love; it's not there yet. But it's so close that it's scary when I think of it. Once again, I don't want to go back to Dublin, not when I have so much standing in front of me.

"I'm taking the lead," Finn informs me, and I don't disagree.

CHAPTER TWELVE

SIOBHAN

THIS TIME, IT'S *MY* phone that keeps ringing. I'm so cozy in bed with Finn, and I don't want to come back to the real world. He pulls the blankets off my head; I've been hiding out down here, lying on his chest of manly hair as I just enjoy the feel of him under me. The smell of him surrounds me, and I'm pretending that this is normal. That this is mine forever.

"Your phone is ringing," he says with a smirk, and I know I should answer it.

"Fine," I mumble and reluctantly get out of bed. Throwing on my dressing gown, I make my way to the kitchen, where I left my phone. Each step away from Finn makes me want to run back to bed and curl up with him. I need to get a grip on myself. I'm leaving tomorrow. That thought fills me with dread. I reach for the phone, wanting to stop my thoughts. "Hello."

"Siobhan, it's Brian Harris."

I sit down, waiting for what could only be more bad news. "Hi, Brian. I hope you have some good news for me."

"Actually, I do."

I sit up straighter and rub Sandie behind the ears as she lays her head on my lap.

"Your aunt is no longer contesting the will. Everything is yours." His news should give me a sense of relief, but it makes me feel unsettled.

"Just like that?" I ask, and Brian clears his throat before answering.

"Yes. Her reasoning was false, and after being advised by another solicitor, she withdrew."

"What reasoning?" I want to be happy, but I don't know what I'm really asking. I think to the man in my bed—the one who wants this land. The one who was going to talk with my auntie. He must have, and that's the real reason she withdrew. I wonder now if he paid her off. I wonder if he was sleeping with me to get the land. I tell myself no. I told him the land was his already, only for my aunt who contested the will.

"That, I am unsure of, Siobhan. It could be for a lot of reasons. But it's good news, right?" I don't blame Brian for sounding so unsure. I sound very ungrateful.

"Of course it is. Thanks for letting me know."

"No problem at all. Have you decided what you're doing with the land?" Once again, my mind wanders to the man in my bed. I hope him being here isn't just about the land.

"Not yet," I lie. I don't want a hundred phone calls about land. I just want to digest this bit of information.

After hanging up, I give Sandie a final rub before returning to the bedroom, where I find Finn dressed. He's pulling on a boot when I walk in, and he pauses, looking up at me. My stomach twists, as my thoughts won't slow down and stop with the idea that I'm being used.

"Everything okay?"

It must be written on my face, so I just jump in with both feet. "Did you talk to my aunt?"

He pauses again before he pulls on his boot. Then he answers me. "No, I didn't. Why?" As he looks at me, I can't see any deceit in his eyes, and I relax slightly. I don't know what I was thinking, and even if he had spoken to her, that wasn't such a bad thing. But I can tell he isn't lying.

"She's no longer contesting the will." I still watch him for signs.

"You don't look happy about that."

"I am, I am. It's just... odd. But Brian did say she spoke to a solicitor, and he had advised her against proceeding."

Finn stands up and walks to me. "You should be happy, Siobhan." He takes my arms and gives me a kiss on the cheek, relaxing me further.

"Yeah, I am." I let my stupid worry float away.

"So what are you doing for the rest of the day?" Finn's hands linger on my hips, and I entwine my arms around his neck. I step into the smell of him, and it's so good. My bracelet shines and sparkles as the lights hit it, and it captures my attention. It's really beautiful.

"Thank you so much for my bracelet. It's beautiful," I tell him, looking from the bracelet and then back to his smiling eyes.

"A beautiful bracelet for a beautiful woman."

"You're such a charmer, Finn O'Reagan." I'm smiling—really smiling.

"You're calling me charming again," he says before capturing my lips with his and cutting off the short laugh that threatens to spill from my mouth. His kiss is soft and tender, like he's savoring our final time together. My stomach twists again. I'm not ready to leave him. Maybe he's ready to leave me, though.

When we break the kiss and look at each other, I wonder if I will ever be ready to leave him. It surprises me how quickly I feel so much for him. But there's also the voice in the back of my head that's telling me this is all about land, and once I sell it to him, he'll be gone. Wham, bam, thank you, ma'am.

He hasn't mentioned the land since our last discussion; not since he said he would speak to my aunt. I can't hold his gaze as mixed feelings rush through me, so I focus on my bracelet again.

"What's going through your mind?" he questions, and for the first time with him, I don't want to share my insecurities, because they're about him. So I remove my arms from around his neck and step out of his hold.

"That I have so much to pack before tomorrow," I say instead, giving him a quick glance. His lashes flutter down, not allowing me to see what he's feeling, but I notice a muscle twitch in his jaw.

"Do you want me to give you some space?" He sounds unsure, and his brows furrow.

I wonder if he wants to leave. I'm nodding as I start to gather my clothes off the floor. I don't want to look at him. My heart is pounding out a tune, and my head is screaming at me to tell him not to leave.

CHAPTER THIRTEEN

FINN

M Y HEART'S READY TO come out of my chest. I want to leave so badly. Standing in this room with her and knowing what we did to her aunt is torture, but leaving her feels worse. So I stand still as she gathers her clothes. I have so much I want to say, but I can't seem to find the right words.

"Don't leave," I settle on, and she snaps around to face me, her eyes wide.

"What?" She sounds breathless, and I haven't a fucking clue what's going through her mind. Maybe I was a bit of amusement while she was here, but I can't help how I feel about her. I know I can't just walk away and not try to make this work. But what we did to her aunt is eating away at me. I know I should walk away—that secret is huge—but I love her.

"Maybe you could stay longer." I stuff my hands into my pockets to give them something to do. I'm not normally nervous, and I've never asked a girl to stay before, so I'm feeling out of my depth here.

She's clutching her clothes tightly to her chest; the look on her face is conflicted. I want to know what's going through her head. I want to know what she's thinking. "You want me to stay?"

Why does she sound so unsure? Each step I take toward her has her clutching her clothes tighter, and I loosen her hands and remove them, letting the clothing fall to the floor.

"I know we haven't known each other that long, but I'm going to put all my cards on the table, even though my dad told me never to do that." I smile briefly because he would think I was a fool right now. Actually, so would all my brothers. I push my family out of my mind and focus on Siobhan. "I don't want you to go. I want you to stay here with me."

"Here? With you?" The way she says it has me smiling.

"Yes. *Here* with *me*. I think we have something strong here. And I know you feel it too." My heart is pounding, being this honest.

She's in my arms and her lips touch mine. I kiss her back. "I don't want to go either. I want to stay here with you."

My pulse spikes at her words, and my body wants her. The adrenaline from her words has my blood pumping all to one place. I push my body against hers and deepen the kiss, moving us back toward the bed. I have her nightgown off within seconds, and it falls to the floor. My hand goes to the warmth between her legs, and she moans as I easily slip a finger inside. She's as pumped as I am. She makes me feel powerful.

I trail kisses slowly down her jawline, and she throws her head back, offering me her neck, which I kiss. Her moans are growing, and I want nothing more than for her to come in my hand. I move faster as I bend and take one of her nipples in my mouth, sucking it slowly before releasing it. "Oh, God, Finn. I'm going to come!"

I increase my movements as I suck harder on her nipple, and then she releases. Her warm fluid coats my fingers, and it nearly makes *me* come. My jeans have shrunk several sizes, to the point of being painful.

"You're so beautiful," I tell Siobhan as she opens her brown eyes and smiles at me. The bliss on her face makes me feel ten feet tall. Her fingers move to the band of my jeans, and my erection jumps. I need to release.

She opens them and pulls them down, along with my boxers. Looking down at Siobhan on her knees is the best sight I have ever seen in my fucking life, and when she takes me into her mouth, I nearly lose it, but instead, I hold back. I want to savor *every second* of this. Her tongue flicks out, hitting the head, and it jumps again in her mouth, telling me this might actually only be seconds long.

"I can't hold it much longer," I say honestly, and she starts a quick rhythm that has me sinking my hands into her hair as she releases me into her mouth. "Wow." I'm breathless as Siobhan releases me, and when she looks up at me, my heart beats faster. She's everything I could want.

"Give me a moment," she says, leaving the room with her dressing gown. I sit down on the bed until I hear the shower running and decide I could do with a shower too.

The bathroom I walk into is small and made to look even smaller, as it's covered in wooden pine from floor to ceiling. Even the toilet seat is pine; the bathroom hasn't been updated in a long time. My eyes snap to the white shower curtain, and I smile as I pull it back and step in.

"Finn, what are you doing?" With a gasp, Siobhan runs her hand over her face, pushing water away so she can see me.

"I need a wash," I tell her, and she smiles.

"Since you're here, you can wash my back." She hands me a bar of soap, and I grin.

"Let's hope I don't let it drop." She laughs, and it's music to my ears.

"If you drop it, *you* are picking it up," she says once I start to wash her back.

"Oh, you'd like that, would you?"

She glances at me over her shoulder; the grin on her face has my body coming alive again. She turns back around, and I take a moment to admire her perfect backside. She turns around again and speaks. "My back is clean." She has a look in her eyes, one I recognize, and one I would never ignore.

Lathering up the soap, I start with her breasts before making my way down to her sensitive area. "You're a very bad girl, Siobhan," I tell her.

"Then punish me." The answer is unexpected, and I give her what she wants.

CHAPTER FOURTEEN

SIOBHAN

"Sᴏ ᴀʀᴇ ʏᴏᴜ sᴛɪʟʟ interested in buying my land?" I ask Finn as we take Sandie for a walk. It's cold outside, but it always is. The cream jacket I'm wearing has fur on the inside and is waterproof on the outside—perfect for walking in.

Leaves fall from the trees. The orange, green, and yellows are so beautiful. I'm so used to inhaling car fumes in Dublin that the crisp fresh air is nice. It's really nice. It's another reminder of why I don't want to go back to Dublin.

"Are you still willing to sell it?" He kicks a falling twig. The lane is scattered with them. Any kind of wind that blows causes the pass to be coated in leaves and twigs.

"Yes, if the price is right." I glance at him, trying not to smile.

"I feel like you're using me for money." He's teasing; the smirk on his face has my stomach tightening.

"So what am I worth to you, Finn O'Reagan?" We stop walking and stare at each other. His smile slowly fades.

"You are priceless. But the offer of a hundred thousand for the land still stands."

Priceless. I smile at the word. He thinks I'm priceless. He watches me closely.

"That's a crazy amount of money. We should get it valued correctly. I know you're overpaying." And the money sounds nice, but I really don't want to have Finn overpay for it. It just doesn't seem fair.

He removes the few feet between us and pulls me into his arms, surprising me with a kiss to the nose. "You're so moral, and I love that."

The word love has my stomach flipping. I know we aren't fully there yet, but we're so close. Before I can answer, he places a kiss on my lips.

"But take it. It's my father's money, not mine. So take it." He's serious, and I can hear resentment in his voice. I nod as he takes my hand, and we continue walking down the pass. I hope one day he'll tell me his story. I can see he has one to tell.

"Okay. I'll take your father's money," I tell him, and he snorts a laugh. The recent tension leaves, and I'm glad. I hate seeing him upset. It's crazy to care this much for a person in such a short time. But I do.

"How did work take you not going back yet?"

The change in topic has my stomach tightening, and I chew on my lip. I worked so hard to get that job. After taking night courses as I worked in a clothes shop, just to get into a nursing home where I wasn't happy, I continued to take courses and waited until a job came up in the HSE. Then factoring in the time it took to get my Gardaí vetting form—to lose this job wasn't a nice feeling. But leaving Finn was even worse.

"Yeah, they're fine, but I hate not going back. I mean, it's a state job so, you know, it comes with perks that a private nursing home wouldn't provide." We're silent for a few more minutes when we reach the end of the pass. I can see Teresa's house. She lives across the road, her bungalow standing proudly by itself.

"I can put in a word so you can be transferred to Cavan."

I stop walking and pull my jacket tighter around me.

"Are you serious? You could really do that?"

Finn is smiling again. "It would come at a price."

I'm smiling too, my mind going to one place only. "Name your price."

"We could do it in IOUs." Finn takes my hand as we walk back down the pass, and Sandie follows close.

"What kind of IOUs?" I don't actually care; I just love when Finn teases. His blue eyes become so alive, and that cheeky grin does funny things to my stomach.

"Breakfast in bed."

"That's easy," I say.

"Massage my feet."

I laugh a little. "Okay, I could do that."

His lips tug on one side. "You would have to tell me that I'm very well endowed."

I snort a laugh. "You want me to tell you that you're well hung?" I ask incredulously, trying not to giggle.

Now Finn laughs. "You have a way with words, but yes, basically that."

"That's it?" I ask, and his eyes darken.

"Not even close."

"You want to cash in on your IOUs?" I ask as everything starts to tingle, and I wonder how I could do it again, but I can. With Finn, I can.

"I would like that very much." His serious tone has me walking faster to the house.

"You better live up to your word, Finn," I tell him, and he tugs on my hand.

"Consider the job in Cavan yours."

I haven't a clue if he's serious or not, but the idea that it might be remotely possible marks today as the best day of my life, and as we enter my house, I know this will be the cherry on top.

CHAPTER FIFTEEN

FINN

I DON'T KNOW WHY I'm hesitating outside the dining room. My dad is in there alone, so this is the perfect opportunity to talk to him.

After leaving Siobhan's, I got Shane to call in a favor at the hospital, making sure Siobhan has a job to start in the next few weeks. When I rang her, she was on cloud nine, and my heart squeezed with pride that I had done that. Shane didn't ask any questions; he did it for me without hesitation. Him doing it so easily had me wanting to back away, but it was worth it. No doubt I would owe him in the future, but for Siobhan, I didn't mind. I suppose our family could be useful at times, though I didn't know what Shane had to do to call in the favor.

I knew Liam was the one who had spoken to Brian Harris; he took care of any official business like that. A stuffed envelope was never passed up, and as much as I hated the bullshit of politics, I was glad for it now.

I have one last thing to do, and that's to tell my dad that the land is ours. I wanted him to be proud of me, but now... I don't know. It's Siobhan's land, and I just don't feel that way anymore.

"If you want to speak with him alone, I'll wait five more minutes." Liam speaks from behind me, and I turn to see him in a new suit, his eyes skimming over me like he doesn't actually see me. His brown eyes are almost black, and I wonder about the saying that the eyes are the door to the soul. If it's true, his soul is a very dark place.

"Yeah, thanks," I tell him and go into the dining room. My father doesn't look up from a file in front of him. He keeps flicking until I'm close enough to see. It's then that he closes it.

"Finn, your week is almost up," he tells me with a gleam in his eyes, one that warns me not to disappoint him.

"We have the land."

He doesn't smile just nods. "Good. Now don't forget we're all having dinner here tonight."

I groan internally. I completely forgot. We celebrate the anniversary of our mother's death every year by all coming together and having a meal. It's painful, and I hate it.

"Of course. I can't wait," I tell him, and he gives me a second nod. He's not one to show too much emotion, but his nods are a really good sign and would normally have me feeling ten feet tall, but now the only person who seems to have that power over me is Siobhan. Maybe I should be grateful to my father—if only for him wanting the land. Otherwise, I never would have met Siobhan.

I leave as he returns to his file, and I pass Liam as he goes in. I used to wonder what they got up to, but as I grew older, the thoughts of being involved in their meetings made me uncomfortable. The depth of criminal activity they're involved in is far too deep for me. I often think that me and Darragh only ever see the surface.

"What's the jazz?" Darragh arrives at the front door, and he doesn't look hungover. This is a surprise.

"We have the family meal tonight." That gets a string of curses from Darragh, and I smile at how inventive he is.

I go into the kitchen to get a bowl of cereal; Mary isn't in today. I'm not sure why, but I want one of her turkey and cranberry sandwiches that she makes with the most perfect stuffing. But cornflakes will have to do. Darragh follows me in and pours himself a bowl. He's like a pig at a trough as he eats. Milk drips down his chin, and his noises are loud and disgusting.

"You're turning my fucking stomach," I tell him while shifting in my seat so I don't have to look at his slobbering face.

"What's wrong with you?" he asks. His mouth is full of cereal, so I don't answer. "Ah, you got blue balls."

Now I glance at him. "Why is everything about sex with you?" I shake my head. I know he's prodding me to see if I'll spill, but I won't.

"There are four things that are everything to me." Darragh holds up his spoon. "One is sex." He grins, and I continue to eat my cereal, not really caring what the other three are, but he wants to share. "The second is money, third partying, and last family."

I snort. "In that order?"

He actually thinks about it. "Yes, but hold up. So the four Ps—partying, pounds, pussy, and papa."

Sometimes I want to deck him. He starts rhyming it off again, trying to sing when Shane walks in.

"You're a jackass," I tell him as I place my bowl in the sink.

"I'm with Finn on this," Shane says, but he's grinning at Darragh. It's odd to see Shane smiling, and I don't ruin the moment with morbid thoughts.

"Okay, fine, what about the four Fs?" Darragh continues. I'm a glutton for punishment and actually wait to hear how he will rhyme this off. "Family, fun times, the fifties and fannies." I'm laughing when I shouldn't, but it's so bad that it's funny.

"Don't start singing that at the table today," Shane says, sobering up the room. He goes to the fridge with no idea of the change in atmosphere. He's like Liam in ways—they don't seem to understand human emotion or the impact their words have. I can only hope the meal is quick and quiet.

Dad sits at the head of the table with Shane to his left and Liam to his right. I sit beside Liam and across from Darragh, who's playing with his peas. One bounces across the table, and we all focus on it. I gulp my wine. It isn't always like this. Once, this table was filled with laughter, but we've lost too much.

Father raises his glass. "To family. *An clann*." He says the English and the Irish of it, and we all repeat his words as we drink. I look at Darragh; his glass is empty, so he's sucking in air. He looks across at me and winks before his foot connects with my leg. I don't shout out like I want to, as Dad isn't finished speaking.

"I have allowed Connor his vacations many times." He says this with a wave of his hand, but my heart races. "This one has been the longest and I'm ready for him to return home."

I want to see Connor so bad, and I'm angry at him for leaving, but the thoughts of him being dragged back here isn't fair. He deserves to find his happiness, and I know he will never find it in this place.

"You know where he is?" I ask. The stillness around the table tells me I'm not the only one who's been impacted by my father's words.

"He has a job, a place to stay. A friend of mine is keeping an eye on him. But I want him home." Father's words are said as he looks at each of us. When he looks at me, I speak up.

"I'll go," I say. I'm angry at Connor for leaving, but to have him back would complete me. Especially after finding Siobhan. God, he would really like her. I know wanting him back is selfish, but I'm no angel.

"No." My father turns to Shane. "I want *you* to bring Connor home." Shane nods and raises his glass. We all follow suit.

I look at Darragh, and he's no longer messing around. I hate that Shane is the one to get picked again. He always gets picked. He doesn't even get on with Connor, but Shane will bring him home.

If I went, my heart might overrule my head, and I might tell Connor he doesn't have to come. Maybe Father sees that weakness in me. Does it matter who brings Connor home? The fact he's coming home is the important part.

"To Connor," Darragh says, and I find myself smiling. I'm about to get my brother back.

"To Connor," we all repeat, except for Father. He does raise his glass, but he never toasts to Connor.

RUTHLESS

**TITLE: RUTHLESS
SERIES NUMBER: BOOK THREE**

BLURB:

She was only supposed to be a job, but now I can't seem to walk away.
Connor
Fighting is all I've ever done. I've fought for my father, my brothers. I've fought
for money or just for the thrill of it but now I have a new reason to fight. I must
fight to keep Ava safe only this time it's not with my fists.
Ava
I'm broke, working a dead end job while hiding from my abusive ex. So yeah
life isn't great right now, that is until Connor. He arrives at the bar I'm working
at, strikes up a conversation and I'm hooked.
I'm hooked because he's awkward and there's darkness in him that I'm drawn
to. Yet it's also the reason that I know I should stay away.

CHAPTER ONE

CONNOR

F EAR. I CAN TASTE it on my tongue. My heavy limbs move from side to side, shuffling. My body tells my brain that I need to stay warm against the harsh cold. My hammering heart wants me to leave. My feet glide back slightly, and a weakness has me blinking rapidly. A voice inside my head warns me away from this fight as my eyes take in the crowd that pulsates around me.

Men wearing woolly hats, their hands shoved into pockets, huddle in a large circle around me. Their heavy jackets and warm clothing are not enough to keep the sharp cold out.

I want to feel the pain that accompanies the bitter cold, but I don't. I only feel fear. My opponent moves around the circle, arms outstretched as his fingers flex, enticing the crowd to feed off his energy. His bare back is covered in acne, the steroids pushing his body to places it shouldn't be pushed.

A young boy, maybe sixteen, holds up his phone in my opponent's face as he roars into the screen. Muscles straining, veins bulging. I remember that feeling myself. That sense of power. That sense of invisibility. Now I just do it to feel something.

We both wear only tracksuit bottoms. My feet continue to shuffle back and forth on their own accord. The field we stand in is already moist from last night's downpour, and my small and consistent movements are making the ground under my feet slippery. I move with lead feet, my mind once again roaring for me to leave this circle of men.

Rick enters the circle. He glances at me and gives me a quick nod. His red tracksuit is stark in the sea of black clothing. The crowd seems quieter now. My heart pounds in my ears. I'm aware now of all the eyes on me, aware of cold air. It's starting to bite my skin. I enjoy the moment of pain. Rick rubs his hands together, his eyes glowing with excitement. He enjoys the fights, but he loves the money more.

"Okay, lads, let's get started." My opponent and Rick move closer to me. I keep my eyes focused on the ground. I'm sure if I look up and into his eyes, I won't fight him.

"No biting. We aren't animals." A roar goes up as Rick lists out the rules. "No hanging on to each other. You want someone to hang on to, go to your mother's tit."

I nod mechanically. Rick's hand circles my closed fist; the contact of his warmth on my freezing skin makes me glance up at him.

"The balls are off-limits and an immediate disqualification."

I nod to Rick, and my eyes flicker to the pumped-up guy I'm fighting. He smashes his fists together and bounces on his feet. He's on something. His pupils are dilated, and that gives me some peace. The fear in me dilutes. Maybe he won't feel what I'm about to unleash on him.

"Fight!" Rick shouts as he disappears into the roaring crowd. We're far enough away from the main road to go unheard. There's nothing but cows in the near fields and a tire center at our backs. Rick owns the tire center, and I work there for him.

My opponent charges me, and I move quickly to the left. It's that movement that has everything slamming back into me. The time, the noise, the feeling—my whole body feels like it's on fire with the cold.

I turn as he charges me again, and I clothesline him. He's on his back, and his whole body tenses as he tries to catch his breath. Rick moves to the front of the crowd, ready to step in, but he knows I won't attack a man when he's down. Instead, I walk the circle as I wait. I keep my eyes trained on the ground and ignore the roars of the surrounding men. When I do look up, my father's face is there in all the men who roar at me, demanding blood. Demanding that I attack. I blink rapidly as my eyes leave the men and return to the boy on the ground.

He gets up swiftly. He roars again, pumping up the crowd. He's bouncing on his feet like a real boxer and craning his neck from side to side before he rushes me. I clench my fists and wait until he's there. There's a satisfaction when the skin on my knuckles splits with the impact of the first punch I land to his jaw. My aching hands want me to stop, but if I stop now, it will make the second and third punch more painful on me, so I keep hitting him in succession until he topples to the ground again.

As I wait, I push the image of my father out of my mind and focus on my brother, Shane. He hates bare-knuckle fighting, said we should leave it to the travelers and low-lifes. "We are the low-lifes," I would tell him, and his laugh would be filled with hate and a want to hurt me. But in a fight, I would win. Shane always thought of other ways to hurt me. Having money didn't make someone a better person. Shane thought it did. He acted like he was above everyone else. Even the law.

The boy gets up, his face a bloody mess. He bounces again on his feet, but the energy he showed earlier is nearly gone. He doesn't roar into the crowd either. He's a little smarter now when he waits for me to come to him, and one thing about me is I won't keep him waiting. Yet I'm not ready to end this fight. So I move too closely; my foot looks like it falters, causing me to push my hands out and away from my face. It's the opening I offer him. Our eyes meet, and he knows. But he's smart, so he takes it.

Pain races down the side of my face. I push it away and don't focus on it, not allowing him to get two in. I turn, and my fist rises faster than his, connecting with his chin. My skin tears further from the impact as he stumbles away from me. I don't want to stop, so I quickly move to him. His outstretched hands and the way his body twists away from me, like it's trying to protect itself, stops me from hitting him further.

"I'm done," he says along with a dribble of red spit. Rick is there, his red tracksuit filling my vision. He dyed his hair again, this time a dark black. I want to tell him it looks fake. He takes my wounded fist in his. The bite of pain has me closing my eyes as he declares me the winner. I don't look at the men who start to disperse. The cold and the lack of entertainment will drive them all home.

I take the few steps away from everyone as I grab my bag. I take out a T-shirt and hoodie and pull them over my damp skin.

"You free next Saturday night?"

I glance at Rick. He's bouncing now. My eyes are drawn to his white runners before shooting up to his gaze. "Not if you're going to keep giving me jumped-up kids." I slug the bag across my back, then take the money Rick holds out to me and stash it in my pocket.

"He was in his thirties," he says, stuffing his hands into his pockets. The air puffs around our words now. The noise of engines starting up has me glancing at the patch of grass the boy had sat down on after the fight. The same spot is now empty.

"Cocaine and steroids aren't a good mix, Rick."

"What do you want, Connor? You want me to test everyone who wants to fight you? You got your money, so what's the problem?" Rick narrows his eyes while running a hand through his hair.

I want to tell him it's not about the money, that it's about the thrill. But I don't. "Just try to have someone who isn't off their face next time." I pull my bag tighter against my back and Rick nods.

"Fine, I'll try. But it's getting harder to find people who will fight you."

I snort as I walk away. "Someone always wants to fight me, Rick."

"See you next Saturday," he roars as I make my way onto the main road. I take a left at Cassidy's cross. I'm staying only a few miles away from our fight spot, in a restaurant that has some outbuildings for B&Bs. It's clean, and no one knows me. Just the way I like it. I've been staying at the Cross Guns. It's the longest I've ever dared to stay in one spot.

I remember watching a wildlife documentary and the phrase "moving is life" stuck with me, and it's a code I try to live by. But recently, I've tired of running. I've gotten a job at the tire center, helping out with fixing cars.

Money is shit, but what I get from fighting keeps me afloat. That's how I met Rick. He is a decent enough guy, if you minus the secondhand parts we charge full price for.

Lights move past me, and I move in toward the ditch until darkness consumes the road again. I walk with aching and bleeding hands stuffed in my pockets. The fight has released some tension that was bubbling up inside me. Seeing Una, my stepsister, walking into the Cross Guns a few weeks ago had terrified me, but once I discovered she was alone, I relaxed with her.

We always got on, and she hadn't seen the family in months and promised she wouldn't tell. But I knew I would have to move on soon. Secrets never stay buried for long with our family. Eventually, they will find out where I am.

It takes me thirty minutes before the lights of the Cross Guns come into view. I jog out back and go straight to my room. My single bed faces the door, freshly made. The room looks bare; I don't have anything, only clothes that are stacked neatly in the wardrobe.

I switch on the TV and mute it but let the light flicker across the room as I enter the adjoining bathroom. I don't linger in the shower but let the hot water warm me up before I patch up my fists. I tape them up mechanically as I watch the news reporter deliver some news about war in a foreign country. Buildings stand partially erect, rubble and crying people roam around the news reporter. After switching the TV off, I get dressed.

Stuffing some fifty euro notes into my jeans pocket, I put on a clean shirt before looking at myself in the mirror for the first time. I've a small red mark on my jaw—it's nothing much. I normally would never allow someone to get a hit on me, but I needed something to release the energy that was bouncing around inside me.

Leaving the room, I make my way across the gravelled parking lot I enter the small cozy pub, which holds a few patrons. They all turn as I enter but dismiss me. We're all here every night. On the first night, they tried to strike up a conversation, and I kept it to a yes-no answer. Since then, they've left me alone. I sit at the end of the bar.

"A beer," I tell Simon, the barman. He wears a black T-shirt with a Guns N' Roses symbol on the front. His wrinkled and over-tanned skin hangs slightly. Long hair that should be shaved is thinning; his glory days are fading away quicker than he can grasp them.

Simon places the beer in front of me with a nod, and I slide him a fifty. Long manicured fingers stop Simon from taking my fifty.

"Allow me."

I know Simon is waiting for me to agree, so I look up stiffly and nod as my brother sits down beside me.

CHAPTER TWO

CONNOR

"I'll have a Jameson." Shane speaks clearly, and I can hear the smile in his voice. It's a polished smile, one that's forced and controlled.

I sip my pint, trying to calm my erratic heartbeat as my mind races through different scenarios. How is this going to work? He's here to take me home, or worse.

"How did you find me?" I ask after Simon places the drink in front of Shane. He shifts, and I look at him. My brother looks the exact same as he did two years ago. Only now, maybe there is a harder edge to his brown eyes. His face is clean shaven, and the black shirt and slacks makes him look ready to enter a business meeting. He wears the same silver band on his thumb that our mother bought him.

"Nice to see you too, brother," he says before taking a slow sip of his drink. His eyes never leave mine. He's angry, which doesn't surprise me, but the pretend smile that he keeps on his face does. He isn't one for hiding his emotions from me.

His eyes flicker to my knuckles, and the urge to hide them has me sitting still. "How did I find you? The notorious Connor O'Reagan fighting again. You made it too easy. I could have tracked you down months ago."

Yeah, I knew that fighting would draw them out. Maybe subconsciously I wanted this. That idea had me gripping my pint. I didn't want them. I didn't want this life. I never did.

"What do you want?"

Shane's smile slips, and he moves his stool closer to me.

"I want my brother to come home."

I'm shaking my head at his manipulative words.

"Did he send you?" I can't keep the bitterness from my voice, and Shane leans away from me, picking up his glass. He empties it before setting it back down on the bar. "No, Finn misses you."

Hearing my brother's name has my stomach twisting with guilt, and I stare at Shane again. "You didn't come here for Finn. You're a selfish bastard." I empty my pint as he laughs before standing. He follows me from the pub as I knew he would. Once the door is closed to my room, I turn to Shane.

"Look, just this once, can't you say you didn't find me?"

He isn't listening to me; his eyes are roaming my room. "You live here?" The horror in his voice gives me satisfaction, and when I don't answer him, he looks at me.

"Orders are to bring you home, brother, and I always complete my jobs."

I don't have to ask who sent the orders. I don't have to ask what will happen if I don't come.

Bastards.

I'm stuffing clothes into a bag when Shane stops me.

"I'll be outside." His pampered ass leaves my room. I don't linger. I don't tidy over before I follow my brother out into his blacked-out Jeep with my only bag of possessions.

Shane grins as I opt to sit in the back seat. The tinted windows dim the interior.

"I see that you're letting your guard down while fighting." Shane still wears the grin as he watches me in the rearview mirror.

"Is that how you found me?"

He glances at the road as he takes a right, but there's a tension in his shoulders at my question.

"Yeah," he finally lies, and I glare out the window, watching a dark version of the world go by. It doesn't take long for us to reach the house. Shane slows down at the front door, and I jump out, slugging my bag across my back. My eyes travel upward, the sheer size of the large white house something I could never get used to. Entering the house, I get the smell of beeswax and polish, and my stomach twists.

I kick the door closed behind me and head for the kitchen. Mary might be there, and she's worth seeing. The closer I get to the kitchen, the more I relax. I can smell pancakes. It's familiar. I inch the door open and both my brows rise.

"Una."

She screams and drops the spoon she was licking; it's covered in what looks like syrup.

"Connor." After picking up the spoon from the floor, she throws it onto the counter, grinning, and she closes the space between us. I hug her back as the back door opens. Shane's face stiffens. He wasn't expecting Una to be here. He never really liked her. She turns in my arms and smiles at him. It's not the grin she just gave me. She walks to him, and he's taking every inch of her in. My shock expands when she stands on her tippy toes and plants a kiss on his lips.

"You told them where I was," I say, and she faces me, heat scorching her cheeks.

"I'm sorry, Connor, but we all missed you."

I nod at her. That's the story they were selling her. I flicker a quick glance toward Shane, who's watching me.

"It's okay," I tell Una. She's sweet. She was always nice to me. What she's doing with Shane is beyond me.

Una untangles herself from Shane and bounces toward me, but she stops a foot away and leans against the counter. "So are you staying for long?" She's smiling, and I place my bag on the counter.

"I'm not sure," I tell her, and her smile widens.

"I was the same when I came here, and now they can't get rid of me." She says the last part while looking at Shane, who still hasn't stepped away from the back door. He's observing us, like he doesn't know what to make of this conversation. Because he's so uncomfortable, I decide to put on the kettle.

"Maybe you won't be able to get rid of me either," I tell her, and Una narrows her eyes slightly at me, but the smile is still visible. "Maybe we could watch all the movies we never got to," I tell her, and her gaze flickers to Shane. He's clenching his fists.

"I'd like that. I did actually watch *Rambo* and *Taken* recently."

Two of my favorites. "Without me?" I ask.

"You've been gone for a while," Shane says, and I snort a laugh at him.

"Shane," Una pleads, but I can't stop the smirk that grows slowly on my face.

"I can leave again," I tell him, pointing at the kitchen door, and he takes a few steps until he's close to Una.

"Unfortunately, that's not an option," he tells me, and Una's eyes widen.

"Shane, please."

It's funny to watch him squirm. His eyes shift around the kitchen as he plays with the band on his thumb.

"I need to have a word with Connor alone," he tells Una, his tone softer.

I make myself a cup of tea as Una defends me, and Shane gets wound up. It's funny to watch, and I enjoy it, until he promises her it's just a chat and we'll be back shortly. I raise both eyebrows while taking a sip of the tea and walking past Una.

"We'll catch up later," she tells me.

Shane takes us to the room where jobs were always delved out in. The bar is polished, and I sit at it with my cup of tea. When Shane joins me, I want to move, but I don't.

"So you and Una?" I question before taking another noisy drink of my tea. It always pissed Shane off, and I want to maximize that.

"I have a job for you." Shane rubs the bar counter as he speaks.

"Yeah?" I knew I was dragged home for a reason.

"A girl might have witnessed me hurting someone, and I want you to find out what she saw." Shane pulls a piece of paper from his pocket.

Another noisy gulp of my tea. "That's it?"

I take the piece of paper from Shane. *Ava Smith, Apartment Four, John Street Kells* is scrawled across it. I rise and stuff it into my back pocket before sitting back down.

"Yeah, but it's important, so don't fuck it up."

"I see you haven't lost your charm," I tell him, and he gets up.

"Report back to me."

"Not Michael?" I question, and he stares at me before answering.

"Me, Connor. Not Liam, not Michael. Me."

I don't respond, continuing to drink my tea. He thinks I'm the same boy he left here three years ago.

I'm not that boy anymore.

CHAPTER THREE

AVA

*T*HUMP, *THUMP, THUMP.*

I keep my eyes closed as my landlord continues to bang on my door. I keep still, hiding in my bedroom, my hand over my heart as he calls my name.

"Ava, I know you're in there."

Thump, thump, thump.

Oh God, just go away.

This is humiliating, and I want to slide down the wall to the floor, but I don't dare make a sound. I didn't think he saw me come in. I used the back door and was so quiet climbing the stairs to the second floor. The bottom one is occupied by a hairdresser and bookies. The rest of the building has four apartments. I made sure no one saw me, so how did he know I was here? I didn't turn on the TV, and my bare feet didn't make much noise on the floor.

"I'll be back, Ava!" he shouts before his steps descend the stairs. It's only now that I allow myself to slump down the wall until I sit on the coral-colored carpet. I sit and allow my heart to slow down and return to a normal beat.

The front door slams, and my eyes burn, but I don't let the tears run. I hate hiding. I hate being late with my rent, but lately, I've had no luck. The image of my nan with her small blue eyes and large nose makes me smile. If I told her what happened, she would either pay my bill or insist I come back to live with her. But that's not an option. Trouble has a habit of following me around, and that is something I refuse to bring to her door. She doesn't deserve that.

I get ready for work and pray to God, if he really exists, to let me just make it to work without meeting my landlord. I slip from my one-bed apartment and put the key into my gray jacket before taking a sprint down the stairs and out the back door.

The wind has picked up. It's only four in the afternoon and, already, the sky grows dark. I work two doors away from where I live, but I don't want to use the front door, so this way is a bit longer. It's a walk around the block. I hate it, as it's not lit up. Getting to work is fine. It's coming back that always has me walking with hunched shoulders.

I take out my phone to ring Nan, and she picks up on the third ring. "Birdy, I was wondering when you were going to ring me."

I smile into the phone as I duck my head down to avoid the wind in my eyes.

"I know, Nan. I was at the gym." I roll my eyes at the stupid lie, and her soft giggle makes me feel worse.

"I don't know what for. You know an empty bag won't stand."

I grin now. She says this all the time.

"And too full of a one won't bend," I counteract, and I can almost hear the smile.

"Will you be calling later?"

"I'm just heading into work, but I'll give you a call tomorrow. We can talk longer," I tell her, and her disappointment is evident in her tone.

"Okay, birdy. You take care of yourself."

"I love you, Nan." The doorway is littered with cigarette butts I will have to sweep up later. But right now, I just want to get out of the cold.

"Love you, too, birdy."

I say my goodbye as I enter the lounge, ready to stuff my jacket and phone behind the counter, but the room isn't empty like it normally is. My landlord, Sean, is waiting for me. He gives me the creeps. He drinks way too much, and his eyes have a habit of wandering. The apartment is a shit hole, but it's cheap. Even being so cheap, I'm still struggling.

"Ava, I was at your flat earlier." He grins as his eyes rake over me. The tight jeans and top are revealing, but I stand taller, not allowing him to think for one second that he's making me uncomfortable.

"You'll get your money, Sean." My sharp words have him glaring at me.

"I know I will, but..." He moves closer, the smell of alcohol nearly choking me. He looks like a hundred-year-old fisherman, his face weather-beaten. "I could think of other ways." He's so close to my face that I want to gag, but I don't flinch.

"You can keep *thinking*, but that's all it will ever be: a thought." I move around him and remove my jacket while trying to hide my trembling hands and stuff it under the counter. I turn around as his seven-foot frame approaches the counter. I'm glad the counter is between us. I pick up a cloth just to give myself something to do. I don't want to piss him off completely. I don't want to lose my job, but I don't want to appear weak either.

"I promise I'll have your money soon," I say, trying to remove some of the anger from his features. I wipe the clean counter. "What can I get you?"

"A whiskey that *you* will pay for."

I nod, hating that I have to do this, but if it buys me time, I'll consider it interest. I ring it up and stick the receipt into my pocket so I don't forget to pay for it later.

When I started working here at Smyth's pub, friends used to come in, always expecting a free drink, but they soon realized that wasn't going to happen. I pay for every drink I take myself or give away. There are no freebies, and the owner, Patrick, is such a decent guy that I would never do anything to jeopardize his business. It's already slow.

I give Sean his drink and don't even get a thank you, but I'm glad to get away from him. I enter the main bar. A few lads play pool, and pints of lager sit on the edge of the pool table. Paul, a nice guy and a local, grins up at me and gives me a nod.

"Pints off the table, lads," I say, and they remove them with mumbles of sorry. There isn't an ounce of harm in any of them. We live in a town with high unemployment and too many pubs. It causes young people like Paul and his friends to flock to the local pubs.

The door into the back is slightly open, and I push it open further to see Patrick tallying up receipts.

"Ava, you're in." A large smile accompanies his words.

My stomach flutters with what I want to ask, but I keep it calm. "Yep. Just Paul and the lads in, that's all."

He nods. "Yeah, if I didn't need the customers, I'd run them."

"They'd just go to another pub. You'd do no good."

"Maybe they'd decide to do something with their lives."

Not a chance, but I don't say that. "Maybe. I was wondering if there are any extra shifts going?"

Patrick looks guilty, and I want to take my words back. He hates saying no.

"I had to let Lindsey go."

"Ah, no. I'm sorry, Patrick. She was lovely. Look, it was just for extras, so no worries."

"Are you sure?" he asks, and I nod.

"I am." I smile wide. "I better get back to work before the boss sees me dossing," I say, and he laughs as I close the door. I don't let my smile slip until I'm back to wiping the counter.

I don't have a clue what I'm going to do. A new patron enters. His height and width have all the lads around the pool table stopping and gawking at him as he sits himself at the end of the bar. That's the thing with small towns; anyone new gets gawked at like a zoo exhibit. His eyes are downcast, and a few days' stubble coats his face. When he just waits and doesn't order, the lads go back to playing pool.

I make my way down to him with a smile. Smiling in this job is so unappreciated, but it's always important to me.

"What can I get you?" My eyes take in the bracelets on his wrist and the lace necklace that disappears under his checkered shirt.

"Carlsberg." His deep voice is what I expect. His long eyelashes lift, and he flicks me a gaze. It takes me a second to extract myself from his brown eyes.

"Coming right up," I say, more for me than him. He isn't from around here; that, I'm sure of. I would remember a face like that. I place his beer on a beer mat and take the twenty he offers me. His hands are bandaged, and some have small spots of red surfacing through.

I ring it up and return his change as Paul arrives at the counter. He eyes the stranger as he orders three beers and more coins for the pool table.

"You're not from around here?" Paul questions, but he doesn't pay Paul any attention. Instead, he picks up his pint and takes a deep drink. I'm going pretty slow at pouring the pints, but I'm interested to know where he is from.

"No," he answers, not looking at Paul.

"Where are you from?" This time, the stranger doesn't answer, and I know I need to step in. Paul's friends are also watching, and I don't want something stupid to happen. Paul, being the alpha of his group, might not like being ignored in front of his friends.

"Here are your pints," I tell Paul with a smile, getting both his attention and the attention of the stranger.

"Thanks, Ava." Paul automatically relaxes and takes the pints before returning for his change. I start to wipe down the counters, and I want to scream as Sean enters from the lounge area. Why couldn't he just stay where he was? He rattles his glass at me as he takes a seat at the opposite end of the bar.

"What can I get you, Sean?"

"Whiskey that's on you again."

I take the glass and lean into him. "I'll give you a whiskey, but it's not on me. I told you I'd get you your money." I lean out and ring up the whiskey. I don't pour it until he hands over the money, which he does.

Sean drinks the whiskey quickly while staring at me over the glass. He's had a lot to drink, and I have the right mind to cut him off, but I'll keep taking his money since he's such an asshole.

I get him another before I tidy under the counter. I know when I'm being watched, and right now, I am. I clash with a set of brown eyes. My eyes flicker to his half pint, and he follows my gaze before picking up the beer and finishing it.

I make my way down to him. "You want another?" I ask. There's something about his eyes that pulls me in but also make me want to run. It's an odd sensation.

"Yeah, thanks." He speaks with a tilt of his chin.

My eyes flicker to his bandaged knuckles before returning to him. I'm more curious than normal about this guy. I want to know what happened to his hands. Was he in a fight? What would he be like when he's angry? Right now, there's a calm about him, one that wouldn't bring violence to mind. I get his pint and return it, just as Sean howls for me again.

My hand tightens on the twenty that Brown Eyes hands to me, and I pull, but he doesn't release it. I'm surprised when I glance at him to find his intense stare focused on me.

I wait for him to speak, but he releases the money, and me, of his hold. I return to the till and wonder if I just imagined that. Sean howls again, and I've had enough. I'm so close to kicking him out when he squeals.

"Apologize now."

My stomach hollows out as my ex, Brian, grips Sean by the back of the neck. When Sean doesn't speak, he rattles him, and I take a step closer but am glad of the bar counter that separates us.

"Brian, please." It's whispered, but he doesn't hear me. He never has. He pulls Sean from the barstool, and I know everyone is watching. I want to go get Patrick, but I'm rooted to the spot.

"Apologize now, or I'll smash your face in."

Sean looks at me then, his face white and his eyes focused. He doesn't look like the same man who howled at me only a moment ago. Now, he's sober and afraid, and he should be.

"Sorry." He says it through clenched teeth before he yelps as Brian squeezes his neck tighter.

"Say it nicely," he tells Sean, and Paul and the guys giggle. Everyone is watching my landlord's humiliation. Now I'll definitely be kicked out of my apartment.

"Brian." I speak louder this time, and he finally looks at me. "He's just a drunk. It's fine." The towel I grip in my hand does nothing to relieve the stress pouring through my body.

Once again, I'm ignored as Brian leans into Sean. "You will say sorry, and in a very nice tone."

He's enjoying this too much. He always was a bully. I fell for his looks. With bright blue eyes and blond hair, he is attractive. That and muscles that seem to bulge on every part of his body just add to the appeal. And he isn't a good boy. He isn't a boy you get to keep, but I saw the challenge and tried to tame a beast. Only, the beast turned on me.

"I'm sorry, Ava," Sean says, but I take no pleasure in his humiliation.

"It's okay, Sean." I feel terrible. Brian gives him a final shake before he lets him go. My fingers unlock from the cloth, and I flex them as I watch my landlord leave. Now I wish I was going with him. Brian is smiling at me, and I try to keep the disgust from my face.

"You on a break soon?" I flicker a glance around the room. Paul and his friends are playing pool, but I can tell they aren't focused. The stranger is nursing his pint. I can't really tell if he's listening or not.

"Yeah, just let me tell Patrick," I answer. I know saying no to him would be pointless. He'd barge in and demand that Patrick let me go.

I knock on Patrick's door as he's getting up. "Ah, I was just about to come out." I force a smile.

"It's quiet and all, but I was wondering if I could take five," I ask, and he's nodding while shooing me with his hands.

Brian is out back smoking a fag. It's gotten dark, and I shiver for more than one reason. I stay close to the door just in case.

"How have you been keeping?" he asks.

It pisses me off, but I'm not dumb, so I shove that rage down, deep down.

"Yeah, fine. What do you want, Brian?" I ask. A small amount of anger slips through into my words, and he stands a bit straighter making me flinch.

His eyes widen and he looks away, brows furrowed, before returning his glance back at me. The anger in his eyes darkens them.

"Shit, Ava. I'm sorry."

I've heard this song a hundred times. Folding my arms over my chest, I look away. I don't respond, but as he approaches, I'm alert and take a step back.

"Fuck's sake, Ava. You're acting like I'm some sort of fucking animal." His voice rises, and the hairs on my neck stand.

I'm shaking my head at him, but I should be saying he isn't an animal. But he is, and I have some pride left in me. I also don't want him to hit me again.

"I need to go back in," I tell him, but I don't move. There's no point without his approval. I don't get it.

"I want you back."

My eyes burn at his words and the gentle way he looks at me now. That's what I fell in love with, a gentle giant, the side of him that rippled through my heart but wasn't real.

I shake my head as my eyes continue to well up. I want to cry in his arms and tell him how this guy, a monster, put his hands on me. I want to send Brian to beat the living shit out of him. I stand back and push down my tears.

"No," I say, and with all the courage I can muster up, I walk back into the bar. My eyes scan the empty bar and land on Patrick, but his attention is on Brian, who I know stands behind me.

I wait with stiff shoulders until Brian walks past me. His words leave a trail behind him and reach me, strangling the air from my lungs. "We'll chat again."

Like hell we will is my weak ass comeback that I don't even say out loud.

The night drags, with a few regulars coming and going. Patrick stays with me, and a few times, he tells me I can go home if I want. But I have nothing to go home to. It's midnight by the time I leave and make my way up to the Rose Garden's takeaway. There's a few cars around, but the night has really cooled. My breath puffs out as I look left and right before running across the road.

Mae's pub has a few people outside smoking. The smoking ban hurt every pub in Ireland, except the ones who don't stick to the rules after hours. Like where I work. Smyth's turns into a smoking zone when they lock the doors, and the pub doesn't officially close until the last patron leaves. It's that kind of pub.

I look behind me several times, getting the feeling that I'm being watched. But each time I peer over my shoulder, no one is there.

The heat of the Chinese is lovely, and I order a three in one before sitting on the mahogany bench. The Rose Garden is like every Chinese place around. All black shiny exterior with gold writing. On the back wall inside is a gold dragon with lots of floating lanterns around it. The door opens, and I find myself stiffening while looking up, waiting for Brian to appear, but it's not him, just some drunk guy.

The sense of being watched follows me the whole way home and doesn't stop until I close my apartment door.

CHAPTER FOUR

CONNOR

S HE ISN'T WHAT I was expecting. It's been a long time since any woman has really caught my attention. Ava—her name suits her. I had to walk away when Brian arrived into the pub. What she was doing with him was beyond me, and it didn't match the picture that had started to form in my mind until he came in and smashed it. Her emerald green eyes seemed innocent and soft; yet at times, her eyes carried so much weight, like someone who had seen too much. I can tell she's a hard worker. Her boss is fond of her, but the man who kept asking for money isn't.

Now, after seeing her with Brian, I realize I've gotten her wrong. He's a huge cocaine supplier. I've never spoken to him personally, but Shane has. He's bad news. But she's obviously his or one of his client's. Maybe that's how she got tied up in this whole mess.

I'm leaning against an abandoned bakery wall when she finally leaves the pub. It's well past midnight, and I follow her up the street. I stick to the shadows, and I watch her peek back several times. There's something vulnerable about her. There seems to be a fear in her eyes when she peers over her shoulder. I walk slower and hope it will lesson her fear.

She enters a takeaway, and now I know I should leave, but I don't. I feel responsible for scaring her; she looks pale as she keeps looking up at the Chinese door, so I feel like I should make sure she gets home safely. I wait until she gets her food, and once she closes the door to her apartment building, I walk away with an odd sense that she's safe for now.

But Brian springs back to mind. She could be up there now, snorting lots of powder up her nose. The thought disgusts me, and I want to punch something or someone.

Brian. I want to punch Brian.

My ringing phone has me turning away from her apartment and making my way back to my car that I left up near a park. It isn't a long walk, and I stuff the phone back into the pocket. It's Shane, and right now, I don't want to hear what he has to say. The roads are empty as I make my way back to Whitewood

House. It was never home to me; I never felt like I was part of that place. The thoughts of going in has me hitting speed dial.

The phone only rings twice before Neill picks up. "You're alive. Where have you been?" The drum of music pulses in the background, and I know exactly where Neill is. Something in me gravitates toward it.

"Are you looking for a fighter tonight?" I ask, and I can hear him yelp to the crowd. "Connor O'Reagan is coming tonight."

I can hear the roar of the crowd. It's not that anyone likes me; they love money.

"The usual spot?" I ask, coming close to the house, but doing a u-turn on the empty road.

"Don't you fucking know it." His laughter rings through the phone, and I hang up and floor the car. It's not far away. Whitewood Lake is the perfect spot at night for fighting.

A lot of headlights shine in on the makeshift ring. Tomorrow morning, when dog walkers come down here, they will never know what took place. Neill is always very careful about cleaning up after his fights. No litter, no blood stains—gravel covers the blood and litter is collected. He wants to make sure his operation never gets shut down.

I get out of the car, already feeling pumped, and music blasts from speakers in someone's boot while the crowd roars at the two men who fight. Neill is looking around him. When his eyes land on me, he jumps down from the roof of a car that he's using as his stage. He jumps onto the bonnet before he lands on the ground and disappears from sight. At four foot tall and being a punching bag his whole life, it makes you understand how resilient people can be. He made a bargain with his bullies: if they fought others instead of him, he could make them rich.

"Connor, you snake. What grass have you been lying in?"

"I think you've grown an inch," I tell him, and he shows me his runners.

"Nah, I got larger soles put in."

I grin as I remove my coat.

"Got five fights for you. Are you up for it?" he asks while shuffling on butty legs and throwing pretend punches. This is why he's such a great business man. He is always underrated. The underdog.

"Let's go." I didn't come prepared, so I strip down to my jeans, removing everything else. The cold bites at me, but once I move into the crowd, the heat makes me shiver.

The fight ends as I step into the circle. The winner is beaten and bloody; his opponent lies on the ground. Neill has his muscle clear it away quickly so I can begin.

I bounce up and down on my feet. My heart starts to race as darkness closes in. The fear that always overtakes me is here, hovering over my shoulder, and I do everything not to run. Keeping my fists clenched and my focus on the ground, I don't look up as my opponent enters the ring. His feet don't shuffle or bounce, and when I glance up, I can see the fear, and my fear eats it up. I punch quick and hard.

He hits the ground, and the crowd pulses, roars, soars so close to me. I want them to move back. I find Neill and nod. The next guy is placed in front of me, each as easy as the last. When the fifth one falls, I finally leave the ring feeling tired. It's what I need. I want to sleep tonight, and now, I think I just might.

More cars have arrived, and I pull on my clothes as Neill counts out my winnings and hands me a large stash of cash. I shove it into my pocket as a Mercedes pulls up. Spectators from the fight stop to stare at the flashy car. My brother Finn jumps out. I haven't seen him since I returned yesterday. I heard he found himself a woman. Everyone seems to have settled down.

"Thanks," I tell Neill, and then I make my way to Finn.

"Get in the car."

I want to smile. Like he could make me. But he's my favorite brother. I don't mention my car. It can stay here; I'll get it in the morning.

I nod and climb into the car. Finn doesn't wait until I'm fully in before he's pulling out and onto the main road. I buckle my belt as he floors the car; his anger is shown in how he grips the steering wheel. Finn is gentle. For him, violence is a last resort, and I hate seeing the anger that is etched into his face. I know I've caused that. I know he has good reason to hate me. Leaving him behind wasn't easy, but staying was harder.

"I'm sorry for leaving," I tell him, but he doesn't even look at me.

"It's not easy, Finn." I want to punch something again.

"It's not easy on any of us."

I snort at his stupid fucking words. When I glance at him, he's watching me.

"At least you're blood. I'm... not." I shift, hating how uncomfortable this makes me feel, but I don't want Finn to hate me.

"Don't give me that sob story. We all have the same mother." Some anger has left his words, like I had hoped it would. I knew my words would soften him.

"He hates me," I add. I don't really care, yet it's the truth.

"He hates us all."

I snort a laugh at Finn, and when I turn to him, he's grinning. "It's great to see you," I tell him, slapping his arm. "You got bigger."

"I've been taking more care of myself." This could only mean one thing.

"A woman?" I question, and he shifts in his seat, but he has a smile on his face.

"What's her name?" I ask and sit back as he starts to tell me about a girl called Siobhan. Una already filled me in, but I wanted to hear it from my brother. It's nice to hear him happy. I listen the whole way home and even as we sit in the garage.

"I want you to meet her."

I take off my belt. "Of course," I tell him, and Finn does something we don't normally do: he hugs me. It's weird for a moment before I hug my brother back. A knock on the window has us slowly separating. I meet Shane's amused face.

"You boys need a minute?" he asks as he opens Finn's door. Neither of us speak, and he rolls his eyes. "Touchy, I see. You're both wanted." He doesn't close the door, so we climb out.

"When can I meet her?" I ask Finn as we follow Shane. Shane glances at us.

"You get to meet his new prize?" Shane asks, and I clench my fists, stopping myself from punching him.

"Don't start, Shane." Finn's strength surprises me. He wasn't ever weak, but he wasn't brave either.

"Save your strength, little Finn," Shane tells him as he pushes open a set of double doors, and there the king sits.

Along with his most faithful servant by his side, Liam. Michael doesn't acknowledge me; instead, he speaks to Finn. Two years has really aged Michael, and I take in every wrinkle. He is still well groomed and well dressed, but I can see past his expensive suits. Liam is a younger version of Michael but more dangerous.

"Go find Darragh," Michael says to Finn, and I envy Finn for getting the chance to go.

Once the door closes and Shane sits down, I join them at the table. Picking at my plasters that are bloodied and in tatters keeps my anger at bay as Michael dishes out the deeds that need to be done. I flicker him a glance every now and again. Most times, he catches my gaze.

"I want a word with Connor alone." The sheep leave me alone with Michael, and I don't fear him.

"You came back," he says with a smile.

"What do you want?" I'm not in the mood for his mind games.

"I want you by your brothers' sides where you belong."

And there it is—their sides, not his. He makes me know I don't belong but reminds me that I still have to be here.

"I don't belong here, Michael." It's odd saying it out loud. It's the first time I've said this to him.

"You're right, you don't." Michael gets up and brings back a glass canister and two whiskey glasses. I accept the one he slides across to me. His words don't hurt; instead, they give me relief. Maybe I can actually leave and not feel the need to keep returning every time I'm called.

"They say there is nothing as sorrowful as a mother without her children. I say there is nothing as sorrowful as a father with a child that isn't his."

I swallow the drink and let it burn a path down my throat. "Poor you," I tell him, and he laughs before taking a sip of his drink.

"Your brothers need you, so you will be here for my sons. I wish they didn't rely on you so much. But Finn hasn't been himself, and when Finn isn't good, Darragh goes down a very slippery path."

What a bastard. I get half up and grab the bottle and pour myself another drink.

"What about Shane and Liam? Did they miss me?" I wasn't sure why I was doing this to myself, and his eyes light up.

"As much as I." I drink the full glass again before standing.

"I'm going to stay for my brothers, but this job is my last. I want out. This is a family business, and I'm not family," I tell him, and Michael stares at me. I try not to shift under the weight his stare carries.

"We will see."

I release the glass in my hand before I smash it. We won't see. I'm out this time. I can't live like this anymore. Only this time, I'll convince Finn to come with me.

Hope can be a dangerous thing, and right now, it grows inside me. Hope that one day I won't ever have to come back to this house.

"Did you miss us?" Darragh seems to materialize from the wall, a stupid-ass grin on his face. His pupils dilate. He must have taken something.

He falls into step beside me, his shoulder brushing mine. "Want to go to a party?" He's moving to music I can't hear.

"Nah, not in the mood."

"Come on, Connor. One drink." He's walking backward in front of me.

"Just at the bar." Some of his enthusiasm dwindles, but he shrugs.

"Fine, I'll take it."

"You hear about Una and Shane?" he asks as he opens two bottles of Budweiser. I take mine, and he taps his against it before taking a deep drink.

"Yeah, I saw the happy couple when I arrived," I tell him, and he's jerking and nodding.

"She was my party buddy until he fucked it all up for me, whining like a little bitch over her."

I take a drink. "You tell him that?" I ask with a smirk, knowing he didn't.

He grins. "I'm working on it."

"Brothers." Liam arrives, and I find myself sitting a little straighter. Not because I'm afraid of him, but I want to be ready for him.

"What about you, Liam? Did you get yourself a girlfriend?" I ask, and Darragh snorts a laugh. Yeah, it's funny.

"I don't see the need to attach myself to someone like that."

"You could have just said no," I tell him as I get up and arrange the pool table.

"A game?" I ask Darragh, and he's bouncing on his toes.

"Yep, yep, yep." He's hyped, and Liam tilts his head while he observes Darragh. They have a weird bromance. Something ties them together.

I set up the game and break first. I pot none and hand over the cue to Darragh. He takes it. He's high but still steady enough.

"Solids," he tells me as he leans over the table to take the next shot.

When Darragh hands me back the pool cue, I offer it to Liam. I'm not a good player. Surprise filters through me when Liam strips off his suit jacket and unbuttons the cuffs of his shirt. Darragh shakes his head at me. I ignore it and sit at the bar, enjoying my drink. Liam starts hitting balls in and doesn't stop until there's nothing left on the table.

"You take the fun out of everything," Darragh tells him, and I laugh at the perplexed look on Liam's face.

"You want to feel special?" I ask Darragh, and he gives me the middle finger.

"Come on. I'll play you." I set up the table again, and Liam takes my spot at the bar as he watches Darragh clean the table with me.

CHAPTER FIVE

AVA

"**I**T'S ONLY ME," I shout as I wriggle the key out of the door. I deeply inhale the smell of Nan's house as I close the door behind me. The yellow-tinted window lets the light stream into the warm hallway. A large rug covers most of the floor, and three plants dominate the space.

"In here, Birdy," Nan calls from the sitting room. I take the door on the left to find her sitting in her pink-covered armchair. It doesn't fit in with the rest of the room, but it's a bit like Nan—she doesn't fit in with this world. After kissing her softly on the cheek, I sit down on the cream couch that's always clean. Not a speck of dirt would get past Nan's inspection. The room is dust free. All the silverware is sparkling and displayed on her shelving.

"Sorry for not getting around sooner. Work has been crazy."

She's already waving off my explanation. "I know you youngsters do be busy Twittering and Facebooking."

I smile but don't correct her. I don't even have a smartphone. I hate technology and avoid social media at all costs.

"A cup of tea?" I ask, and she's up out of her chair. I tower over Nan. At four foot six, she's such a cute old person. That is until she opens her mouth, and you soon realize that she can take care of herself.

Her navy trousers and cream short-sleeved top sit perfectly on her small frame. Nan has the kettle on and has me sitting at the table as she moves around her small kitchen, cutting brown bread and setting the table.

"I had a visitor recently," she says as she places the tomatoes on the table.

I remove my coat and place it on the counter. "Oh, Father Gerry?" I ask, as he is a regular.

"No, that lovely young man you were dating." Nan places a plate and knife in front of me, but I'm frozen.

"Brian?" I ask while hoping she says no, but I know it's him. He was the only one I let her meet, because I thought he was *the one*.

"Yes, Brian. He came in and had a cup of tea with me."

At each word, my mouth waters and my stomach sours. I force a smile. "What did he want?" Nan is leaning against the table now, her hands pressed into the surface. Her lips are slightly puckered, and I know that face. It's one she uses when she wants me to listen to her.

"He's a nice young man, Ava. And I was very sorry to hear you had broken up with him. Broke that boys heart."

Right now, I would love to tell her that he hit me, but I don't want my nan to know that side of life. When I don't respond, she pours out the tea and places brown bread on my plate.

"You should give him a second chance," Nan adds as I mechanically sugar and milk my tea. A second chance isn't going to happen, but the thought of him visiting my nan doesn't sit right.

"I need you to promise me something," I say, and Nan nods. "If he ever calls here again, ring me, but don't let him in."

Nan's nostrils flare. "What did he do?" She's reaching for my hand, and I love her fierce protectiveness.

"Nothing. I just I don't love him, Nan, and he shouldn't be coming around here telling you his problems." God, he would hurt her too if he thought he could get to me.

I start to butter my brown bread, hoping my statement was said easily enough that she doesn't question me further.

"He's a nice boy."

"He hit me." There, I said it. And I regret it as Nan's face contorts in disbelief before it's replaced with anger.

"And to think I let that toe rag in my house." She stands, looking around the kitchen. I'm not sure what for, but I pat her hand.

"Sit down and have your tea. Just promise me that he won't be in this house again."

Nan pats my face gently. "He hurt you."

I push down the tears that burn the back of my throat. "No, I'm fine, but I don't want to see him again."

"A man puts his hands on a woman once, he'll do it again." She's shaking her head now. "He was so sweet and nice."

"Nan, I know. But promise me you won't let him in."

"I promise, Ava."

I don't feel content. "And don't you dare try to confront him." I can see it in her eyes now, and I nearly bring back up the small bit of tea I've drunk as the image of Brian hurting her comes to mind. When she doesn't reply, I say sternly, "Nan!"

"Fine, I won't. But that boy deserves a piece of my mind." Good Lord, but I need her to understand.

"That boy would hurt you. Do you hear me?"

She tuts but finally agrees not to confront him or let him in. I finish the tea at Nan's, but the moment I'm out the door, I ring Brian.

"Well, hello, beautiful."

I want to spit at my phone. "You were at my nan's," I say harshly.

"Wow, wow, calm down. I only called to see how she was."

"Don't bullshit me. We both know what you were doing."

"And what is that, Ava?" Anger is now filling his words. It doesn't take long to piss him off; I learned that the hard way. I stop walking and watch the cars zoom past as I try to think of a way out of this.

"Can we meet?" I ask with closed eyes.

"Sure. Now?"

My stomach tightens. "Yeah, now. At the café."

He agrees to meet me there in twenty. It will take me about fifteen minutes to reach it on foot. I'm not sure if what I'm doing is right or wrong, but all I know is that I can't have him near my nan ever again.

***

I arrive and grab us an empty booth near the back, hoping we can have a semiprivate conversation. I remove my coat and fidget with the menu as I wait. My blue nail polish, which is the same color as my eyes, is chipped, and I'm tempted to start picking at it, but instead, I file it away as a job to do later.

I know immediately when he arrives. It's like the air shifts. He greets nearly everyone as he makes his way to me. He must be looking into each booth, but he knows where I am. We always sat in this booth.

When he appears, he smiles. "Just like old times." That smile once captured me. He looks good today, but he always does.

I tell myself to stay on track.

He slides in across from me and unzips his red top, only to reveal a red T-shirt—my favorite color on him. Now I wonder if the color choice was intentional. He looks down and swipes a hand across it.

"For you," he tells me, and I want to slap him with the menu. But I manage a smile that doesn't trick him, as his own falls from his face.

"You wanted to meet. So talk." He's all business, and the way he looks at me tells me that I'm already so far out of my depth with him.

"My nan. She's off-limits." I say it sternly, even as he raises one blond eyebrow.

"Is that an order?" His lip tugs slightly as he speaks, as if me giving an order is funny.

"Yes. Yes, it is, Brian. I don't want her dragged into this. I won't have it." I force as much power into my words as I can, but Brian is laughing, and I watch as he throws his head back and really laughs it up.

"Oh, little Ava. You are so cute when you're serious." What an arrogant asshole. My blood boils, and I want nothing more than to get up and walk out of this place.

"Okay, don't get mad." He takes my hands, which I immediately yank out of his.

"Don't touch me." It's out of my mouth before I can think, and his eyes darken, his laughter gone.

"It was once. An accident." He's talking low, gently, and I just... can't, so I look away from him.

"I'm sorry, Ava. It won't ever happen again. Give me a second chance." *That's never going to happen.* "I promise I'll leave your nan alone if you give me a second chance."

Now I glare at him as he sits back, looking smug, and my stomach roils at the idea of ever letting him touch me again, but keeping Nan safe is my number one priority.

"Let me think about it." I hope my words sound real.

Brian tilts his head left and right before agreeing. I can't say I feel relief, because I don't, and I end up having to sit with him for another twenty agonizing minutes as he talks about himself. How could I not see what a self-centered asshole he is?

CHAPTER SIX

AVA

I LEAVE THE CAFÉ and walk another ten minutes to Super Value. I need to buy some food. Shopping hasn't been on the top of my agenda lately, but since Nan mentioned how thin I've gotten, I decided that I needed to get some proper food in and stop eating takeaways.

It's a Thursday, so there aren't many around in the grocery store. I grab a basket and start off in the fruit and veggie section. I get a few bananas and some spuds and turnips. I'm browsing in the bread aisle, looking for non-white, maybe something nutty, when a large frame moves further down the aisle. He reminds me of the stranger from the other night in the bar.

He doesn't turn around, so I take my time watching him and then focus on the bread for a moment. I don't want to look like a stalker. His jeans fit him snuggly, and he's even larger now that I see him standing. He must be six foot or more. His wide shoulders covered in a green-and-navy checked shirt. The sleeves of his shirt are rolled up, and different-colored bands are around his wrist. Large hands pick up a package of Swiss Rolls, strawberry flavored. I grab bread and put it into my basket as I take a step closer to him. He's still looking in the dessert aisle, and maybe I could do with a pack of cookies. I move even closer, and his cologne causes my stomach to squeeze. It's a really rich and musky smell.

I'm close enough that if I reached out, I could touch him. I pick up a pack of Jammie Dodgers and put them into my basket. I've lingered too long and decide to move along, but not without one final glance.

He's watching me from under thick lashes. Lines mar his forehead like he's confused, and it's sexy as hell.

"Hi," I say, and his nostrils flare ever so slightly.

"Ava. Hi." Him knowing my name is like a quick electrical shot to my body. Hearing him say it in his deep voice is more than nice. I don't ask how he knows it, as he must have heard the guys call to me a thousand times in the pub.

He holds out his free hand to me, and I stare at it like it's a foreign object. "Connor," he tells me, and I take his warm hand that still has bandages around the knuckles.

"Nice to meet you, Connor." I'm smiling now. He's a good head taller than me and peering up into his brown eyes could really tangle up a girl.

"Didn't take you for a Jammie Dodger kind of girl."

It takes me a moment to gather my hormones as he smiles, flashing a set of straight white teeth. My laugh is a little too high, and I try to settle down. "Didn't take you for a strawberry Swiss Roll kind of guy," I say, and this time, he looks confused until he glances at his basket.

"I didn't put that in here. It must have fallen in," he says as he places it back on the shelf, and I laugh.

"No, I'm pretty sure you put the Swiss Rolls in there."

He shakes his head, keeping a pretty straight face. "Are you sure?"

I shift my basket from one arm to the other. "Yes. I saw you."

"So you were watching me."

My stomach erupts with butterflies as he dips his head, looking at me once again from under his lashes.

"No... Yes."

He's laughing, and it's like freshly melted chocolate. So good. He puts the Swiss Roll back into his basket, and I can't keep the stupid grin from my face.

"Maybe we could grab a coffee." He says it so offhandedly, but I'm nodding before I can form words.

"I finish work around ten tonight if you want to get one then." I have it said before I realize it sounds silly.

"Sounds great, Ava." My name on his lips again sends my stomach somersaulting.

"Okay, I'll meet you outside my work place, then. At ten," I say, just to clarify as I shift my basket again.

"See you at ten."

I'm smiling, he's smiling. I can't believe I have a date and one that was set up in the dessert aisle of a supermarket.

"Bye," I say to his retreating form, and he smiles over his shoulder and gives me a curt nod. Once he's out of sight, I have the urge to do a little clap, but I don't. Instead, I look around me and wonder if anyone was listening to our conversation.

I only live, like, ten minutes away, but the walk with two heavy bags of groceries is killing me. The only thing keeping me smiling is thinking of Connor. His name suits him. I like it. I have to put the bags on the ground as I get my key out of my pocket. I open the door and reach for my bag, but I want to walk right back out. My landlord is standing in the hall, talking to the owner of the bookies.

They both turn to me as I close the door behind me. The bookie owner—I can't think of his name—has snow-white teeth against an artificial tan. His hair is dyed jet black. The overall appearance is stark. His pink jumper and shirt just make him look ridiculous. I look at Sean as he says goodbye to the bookie. His brown trousers and brown jumper suit his shitty personality. He turns to me with a face, and I try to get around him to go up the stairs to my apartment, but he won't move.

"I don't have your money today," I tell him. I don't tell him that I haven't been paid from work. But he's nodding.

"I don't want your money. I want you out. This is your two weeks' notice." He moves aside to let me go up the stairs, and I climb the steps with my head held high. I wasn't going to argue, but I wasn't sure what I was going to do.

***

For a Thursday night, it's busy. Paul and his friends are back in, taking up the pool table, and a few locals and some students make up the rest. I'm the only one on. Patrick is in the office, so if I need him, he isn't far away. I leave to collect glasses. Arriving back to put them in the washer, I see I have a new customer settling in at the bar.

"A Carlsberg?" I ask as I make my way toward Connor. He looks good in a white polo shirt, the top few buttons opened, letting me see smooth tanned skin.

"A 7UP would be great."

I raise both eyebrows with a smile, and he tilts his head and smiles, making my heart race.

"I have a coffee date tonight. Don't want to be drinking."

I'm smiling from ear to ear as I get him his 7UP. "Who's the lucky girl?" I tease, placing a beer mat in front of him before putting the glass on it.

"She's a barmaid. Really pretty."

His words are making my stomach twist. I wipe down the counter near him before I flicker him a gaze. "I hope you have fun," I tell him, and he nods, his smile gone as he glances at someone in the mirror behind me. My smile goes too as I look up, only to have Harry the absolute asshole in front of me. I'm surrounded by a lot of assholes in my life.

"Ava, have you seen this man?" I don't look at the picture he's holding up.

"No," I answer Harry and try to walk away.

"Ava, look at the picture." Harry has the decency to add please when I stare at him. His small blue eyes shift back and forth; he can't keep eye contact.

"Now you decide to do your job?" I bark, knowing I'm being foolish. Harry leans in, stubble coating his face, making him look dishevelled. Some men look sexy with stubble, but he just looks like he needs a wash.

"Have you something to say?" I can hear the undercurrent of a threat, so I give the picture about a two-second glance, and my stomach curls. I've seen this man, but he wasn't in the best condition. At the time, I thought he was dead until Brian said he was really wasted, and Brian and another guy carried him out of the pub.

"Why, what happened to him?" I ask, and Harry waves the photo.

"Have you seen him?"

"No," I say, lying to a Gardaí for the first time in my life, but Harry shouldn't be allowed on the force. He can be bought by anyone who will give him money.

"Lying to the Gardaí is an offense."

I want to roll my eyes at him, but he just might arrest me to spite me. "It's a good thing I'm not a liar," I tell him and walk away to serve a customer. This time, he doesn't stop me.

It settles down, and Patrick arrives out of the back, letting me finish my shift. I grab my bag and coat, but when I look up, Connor is gone.

My heart deflates, and I find myself standing, staring at his stool longer than what's normal.

"You okay?" It's Patrick's voice that shakes me out of my slumber, and I nod, force a smile, and decide to just head home. Well, what will be home for the next two weeks.

I'm smiling because as I step outside, I see Connor leaning against the wall of an abandoned building across the road. He gives me a salute, and his lip tugs up on the left as he jogs across the road.

"Are you ready for the coffee?" he asks, and I nod while I start walking. Glancing at him, I see he's following.

"You like what you do?" His question is one I have the answer to but hate saying because I like Patrick so much. Stuffing my hands into my pockets keeps them warm against the cold.

Connor has done the same. A heavy navy coat hides that fabulous white polo shirt and smooth skin.

"Not really, no. But it pays the bills, sort of." Now I'm mumbling. It would pay the bills, but I have too many bills.

"Sort of?" Connor questions, and I fire a quick glance at him sideways. He's watching me.

"Yeah, it's nothing. Just in a hobble. But I'll get out of it. I always do." I smile at him now, and he nods, but he doesn't look convinced.

We arrive at the café that I had only met Brian, what was it, a few hours ago? But it was the best in town and stayed open until late.

"Will we sit outside?" I ask, wanting to stay in the cool air. For me, being in a warm place and having to talk about myself made me uncomfortable. But outside, I felt like I could breathe and talk. I'm not entirely sure why, but it worked better for me.

"Perfect. What will I get you?"

I decide then, as I sit down, that Connor is definitely over six foot.

"How tall are you?" My question causes a smirk to grow on his face.

"Six foot four. How tall are you?"

"Five foot six. And I'll have a latte."

Connor nods, still wearing the smirk, and leaves to get our coffees.

I inhale the fresh air while pulling my sleeves down over my fingers. There's a bite in the night air, but I love how fresh it is. The small roads are now empty, and a few people stroll down the streets. Street lamps give a nice orange hue down on the cobbled pavements.

I keep shifting in my seat while glancing at the door. The door and windows are covered in frosted glass, so I can't see in. I cross my legs just as Connor arrives with two lattes and one Danish.

Taking my latte from him, I watch as he bends his large frame into the chair. Being this close to him has my stomach fluttering as his aftershave assaults me.

"Have you lived here long?" This is the part of getting to know each other I hate. So I sip my latte as Connor rips the Danish in half. I take the half he offers me and tear off a small piece.

"No. I moved to Kells a month ago, but my landlord just gave me two weeks' notice, so I'm not sure where to next." I bite my lip, surprised at the emotion the words evoke in me. "What about you?" I ask and sip my latte, which is so divine and frothy.

"Whitewood area. I wouldn't call it home, but it's where I live."

"I know that area. It's nice," I say. My eyes once again get drawn to his hands, still bandaged. When I look back up, he's watching me.

"You should just ask. I've seen you look at my hands a lot."

I bite my lip again, hating how transparent I am. "Okay, what happened to your hands?" I shrug like it's no big deal, and his lip tugs slightly before it settles down.

"I fight for money."

Both my eyebrows rise. I wasn't exactly expecting that. "Like Conor Mc-Gregor?"

His laugh is deep and husky, and I drink it up. "No, not like Conor Mc-Gregor."

I nod like I know what he's talking about, but I don't. "So, illegal?" I spit out and want to kick myself as lines appear on his forehead. "Sorry, never mind," I say quickly.

He sits back. "No, it's illegal. But I'm in between jobs, and right now, it's cash."

"Anything in mind you'd like to do?" I ask him, studying his full lips. They are moist from the latte.

"I want to open my own shop."

That surprises me. He doesn't look like the entrepreneur type; more like the construction type. "What kind of shop?"

I pick at my Danish, and for the first time since we sat down, he looks uncomfortable and moves in his seat. His thumb rubs his upper lip.

"Like art." He's frowning again, the sexy lines distracting me. "I make wooden ornaments." His frown deepens, and I want to tell him to cut it out. I can't even function.

"What about you? What would you like to do?"

I'm back in the spotlight, the awkwardness between us gone. I want to ask more about the wooden ornaments, but I can see we've moved past that.

"Honestly, I don't know. College isn't for me. I don't have any real skills, though I like working with people."

"Yeah, I see that in the bar. You're good with people." His compliment is really nice, and I smile.

"But you didn't seem to like the guard. An ex?"

I nearly spit out my latte at his question. "Harry?" I ask while shaking my head, and I can see that Connor is fighting to hide a smile. "No, no. He's just an asshole."

A small laugh bubbles from his lips, and I'm transfixed.

"Why is he an asshole?" Connor asks before drinking deeply from his latte. I don't know if it's how he asks or the topic, but it's like he's trying to sound casual—but the question isn't. My thought process makes no sense to me.

"Ah, it's stupid history. Not worth talking about."

My answer has him nodding slowly. "I just thought it was deeper between you two."

I shift in my seat, my moral compass kicking in. Maybe lying wasn't the brightest idea. I want to change the subject. This is all making me uncomfortable.

Picking up my latte, I answer him. "Nope, just silly stuff. So tell me about these wooden ornaments." Now he looks awkward, and I know it was a bit of a soft spot. But I really want to know.

Connor takes in a deep breath before leaning both arms on the table. "I carve people from wood." He doesn't look gentle enough to do something like that. But I take his word for it. We talk for a while longer until the café closes. It's near midnight before Connor walks me to my apartment door.

I had a lovely time," I say while stuffing my hands into my pockets. His eyes have shot to my lips several times since we stopped, and I wonder if he is going to kiss me.

"Maybe we can do this again," he says, jutting out his chin, and I smile.

"I'd love that." My words have his lips tugging up.

He takes a step backward. "Good night, Ava," he tells me, and I'm struggling with admiring him for leaving it at that and cursing him for not kissing me.

"Good night, Connor," I tell him as I duck in the door. I smile as I take the steps two at a time. But it dissolves as Brian leans against my door.

CHAPTER SEVEN

CONNOR

I ARRIVE BACK AT Whitewood House near one in the morning. Voices from the main foyer have me pausing.

"She was still alive." It's Finn's, and it's the strain in his voice that has me pushing the door open. The whole family is there.

Darragh and Finn sit on the couch closest to the door, the arch allowing me to see more of Finn than Darragh, while Shane stands near an unlit fireplace. Liam and their father sit on two Queen Anne chairs.

Shane glances at me with raised eyebrows. "Where's your phone?"

Shit. I had turned it on silent when I was with Ava. "I was on a job," I say as I take it out of my pocket and light up the screen to see seven missed calls.

"What's happened?" I ask, and Finn looks from me to Shane, worry etched on his face.

"Nothing. We just all need to stay calm and not get so excited." Liam speaks to where Finn and Darragh are sitting, and I sit down on the couch opposite the fireplace.

"Excited about what?" I ask Liam directly. His suit jacket is open. He sits nearly half off the Queen, his waist coat buttoned, and everything sitting perfectly on him.

"There seems to be a woman missing in the nearby area." His slow words are annoying me, and I'm glad when Finn speaks.

"It's Siobhan's auntie. She's missing." Finn scratches his eyebrow, his gaze flickering to Darragh, who's looking at his hand. His subdued stare tells me something isn't right here. Darragh is always alert and loud, but now he looks unsettled.

"We should tell Connor," Shane says, looking at their father, who is observing me. I keep his stare. He glances away as Shane calls to him. "Father, Connor is family."

I snort a humorless laugh. I wasn't ever sure if all my half brothers could see the distaste that he held for me. This is the first time anyone has ever spoken out for me, and I'm shocked that it's Shane. If I had placed a bet, it would have been on Finn.

"Darragh was attacked and defended himself. In the process, the woman died."

I don't believe a word Liam says. He's really painting a sweet picture, but Darragh has always been his favorite brother. I know he's full of shit as Finn snorts.

"The woman was alive. He broke her fucking neck." Finn's anger surprises me.

My gaze flicks to Darragh, who still stares at his hands, not defending himself. "So the missing woman is dead, and what, the guards have been asking around?" I ask Liam as Michael has decided that the empty fireplace holds his attention better than me.

"They've been here asking questions, but there's nothing for anyone to worry about. We all know where we were the night it happened. Isn't that right, Darragh?" Shane's words rise, and Darragh's head snaps up. He's nodding, and his knee jerks.

"I want a word with Darragh. The rest of you leave." The king speaks, so everyone leaves one by one.

I make sure I'm the last, and he stares at me with all the hate in the world. I get up and leave slowly, not sure what my point is. Maybe to let him know he's not my king.

"You want a drink?"

I smirk at Finn. "Yeah, it would be a start," I tell him. The tension in this house is strangling me.

We go to the bar, and I sit as Finn goes behind the counter and gets a bottle of whiskey and two glasses.

"So, you want to tell me in English what's going on?" I ask, and he's shaking his head.

"It's a mess." Finn sits down and pours out two glasses of whiskey. We lightly touch our glasses and take a deep drink before Finn tells me exactly what happened, and yeah, that does sound like a mess.

"I want you to meet Siobhan this weekend." Finn looks nervous, and it makes me smile.

"Yeah, I'd like that." I squeeze his arm, and he nods. Right now, I know when I leave the next time, I'm not coming back. But leaving him doesn't feel right. I'm glad when Shane asks Finn to give us a moment. It stops the guilt that's swirling around me.

Shane takes the seat Finn vacates. I pour myself another drink. Shane declines when I tilt the bottle toward the empty glass Finn left behind. I wonder if he declined because it's Finn's glass, or if he just doesn't want a drink.

"What did she see?" Shane questions. He doesn't even blink as he waits for me to respond. I take a deep drink before answering.

"Nothing."

Shane's shaking his head, cutting me off from finishing.

"She's lying. I know she saw me." His words are low. He isn't looking at me now, his eyes focused over my shoulder like he's remembering.

"Well, if she did, she isn't saying," I answer while refilling my glass. I have no idea what's going through his head, and that worries me.

"But she will eventually." Shane rises, ready to stand, and I can't let him go. I can't leave Ava in his hands.

"You're wrong." Both eyebrow's raise, and he sits back down.

"The Gardaí arrived into the pub she was working in, and she wouldn't give them any information. They showed a picture of the guy, and she said she never saw him."

"I know she saw me." He's not convinced that she won't say. Yet he's convinced that she saw him.

"Why didn't you have her taken care of straight away?" Saying it out loud feels wrong, like a betrayal to Ava, but I need to know what is driving Shane to make a certain decision.

"I couldn't. Hurting her isn't an option. Until it's an option."

Clear as fucking glass. I let out an irritated breath, and a slow grin grows on Shane's face.

"Don't tell me you care for her." He laughs, and I release the glass in my hand before I smash it.

"I just don't understand what the big secret is." I get up even as my body wants me to sit here and find out what Shane is up to. "But yeah, she's your problem now," I add.

I stop at the door as he speaks.

"Brian is a big client of ours. He's asked for her not to be touched. So unless he says we can, or I risk going to prison, she will be left alone for now. But I want you to still keep an eye on her." I glance at Shane from over my shoulder, his words giving me mixed emotions. Now I want to know why the hell she's under his protection and what happens the moment that protection is lifted.

CHAPTER EIGHT

AVA

IT DOESN'T SEEM TO matter how much makeup I dab on my cheek, the lump and bruising is still visible. I close my eyes, not wanting to look at the girl in the mirror. How did it come to this? How did I end up being hit by a man? If I ever heard of someone hitting a woman, I honestly couldn't understand how it happened the second time. I always thought I'd be out of there and have him in court. Yet, here I am, covering up the marks that Brian left on me again.

He was angrier this time, after seeing me with Connor, and I knew he was going to hurt me. Tears fall silently down my face. I'm disgusted with myself for allowing this to happen. I want to hurt him.

My phone bleeps. I forgot I was holding it. I've rung the Gardaí station several times, only to hang up. No one will listen anyway.

I think of Connor and his admission of being a fighter. I smile as I picture him kicking the shit out of Brian. But he doesn't even know me, so Connor would have no real reason to fight him. Unless I pay him. But I have no money.

I'm thinking crazy. I check my messages to see Connor has sent me one. **I had a lovely time. Hope we can meet again soon.**

My eyes blur with unshed tears at his words.

Are you free? I type out and then erase the message. I don't know what I want—him here, him not here; for him to see me like this or not to see me like this.

I could do with some company. Only if you're free. I hit send before I can change my mind.

My eyes burn again as I realize how lonely I feel. I want my nan so bad, but I don't want to take this to her door. I need to handle this. I return to the mirror, only to see the small cut has opened again, and blood has started to seep out. Wiping off the makeup hurts like hell as I dab at the blood. It isn't deep. Brian wears rings. It's what must have cut me.

I'm back to looking at myself in the mirror, wondering how the hell I got here. Not just with Brian, but being homeless and in a shitty job with nothing to look forward to.

My phone rings, making me jump, and my heart pounds. But I answer it.

"Are you okay?" Connor's voice has me choking down the tears.

"Are you driving while on the phone?" I ask instead, and his short laugh makes me smile, but I hiss in pain.

"No, it's hands free. Are you okay?" he repeats. I can almost picture him frowning.

"Yeah, it's nothing. I hope I didn't disturb you."

"No. I'll be there in a few minutes."

My stomach jumps at that. What am I doing?

"Okay, see you then." I hang up and return to the mirror, not sure if I should try to cover it up, but touching it has it bleeding again. I let my hair fall down my back, pulling it around my face. It shadows the mark, but he'll still see it, and a part of me wants him to. A huge part.

***

The doorbell chimes, and suddenly I question what I'm wearing. I showered after Brian had left and put on gray tracksuit bottoms and a green tank top. I could have tidied up a bit more, though.

Opening the door, my heart rate spikes as Connor stands there. It's so odd to see him at my place.

"Come in." I step out of his way, but he doesn't move, and his stance is almost unnatural. Like someone has hit pause. I notice his fist clench.

"Who did this?" he asks, his eyes flickering from my face to my eyes.

"Will you come in?" I'm not going to discuss this in a hallway. You never knew who's listening. He gives a curt nod and enters.

I sit on the couch and am surprised when he sits beside me and removes his black jacket. A plain clean gray T-shirt fits him snuggly. He doesn't ask any questions, and I try not to flinch when his fingers gently examine my face.

"It's not broken, and the cut's not deep. Where's your freezer?" he asks, getting up, and I point to it.

My throat burns. I don't want to cry, so I sit and try to push the emotions that are clawing up my throat back down. Connor sits beside me and puts a frozen bag of peas to the bruise, once again with such gentleness.

"You want to tell me what happened?" Connor asks, but now I can't meet his eye.

"Just an ex," I say, trying to stop the tremble that enters my hand. It's like the shock is wearing off again. This isn't happening to someone else. It's happening to me.

Connor's silence has me peeking up at him. His clenched jaw and unblinking eyes are unsettling.

"His name."

And there it is—my chance. But I can see the violence in Connor's eyes, and I know this fight would leave him worse off. You don't hit Brian and get away with it. "I don't want to, Connor."

He removes the peas from my face and takes a look. "The swelling is going down," he tells me.

"He's hit me before." I focus on my nails. "The first time was such a shock. I loved him." Now I gather my courage and stare up at Connor. He's just as still as when I opened the door to him. I want to check that he's breathing. He blinks.

"I'm not one of those girls who stays when someone hits them." I hold my head up as I speak. "I walked away." My anger comes out in falling tears. "I left. I moved." I close my eyes to stop the onslaught of not just anger but pain now.

Heat scorches my cheeks and neck. He must think I'm crazy. Dragging him here, crying about my problems. I want to apologize before he runs out the door.

"My stepfather hit my mother," he says. My eyes snap to his. He lifts the peas again, checks my face before turning them and placing them back on my face. "My mother was such a kind and gentle woman. He was an animal to put his hands on her." The tightness around his eyes has him glaring over my shoulder.

"I didn't know at the time. I would have killed him." Connor is looking at me again, and there's something in his voice that makes me believe he really would have killed his stepfather.

"Did your mother get away?" I ask, but I can see that distant look in his eyes.

"No." His one word is monotone, and it squeezes my heart.

"I'm so sorry, Connor." I touch his free hand, and he removes the bag of peas from my face while staring down at my hand. I squeeze his large fingers, and his brown eyes snap up to mine.

"I just wish she had told me. I would have protected her." His brows furrow, and he stands, removing his hand from mine. He's a big guy when he stands, so I don't try to approach him again. There's a darkness in Connor that I want to shine a light on.

The noise of him putting the peas back in the freezer has me relaxing. I thought he might be leaving, and I don't want him to go.

"You need to ring the guards." Connor sits back down while throwing his arm along the back of the couch. I let my hair fall more around my face.

"I can't," I tell him, and the tightness around his eyes has me explaining.

"I went before to complain, and they wouldn't listen to me. Brian has some guards paid off."

"Brian." He repeats his name with flared nostrils. "The blond-haired guy."

I'm taking his hand again, and he holds it still. He doesn't wrap his fingers around mine, but he doesn't pull his hand away either. "He's really dangerous, Connor."

"So am I." Connor might be a fighter, but he's a good guy. Brian came from bad stuff—parents who were into drugs. I suppose I saw a lost boy in him when I first met him. But he's rotten to the core, just like them. But Connor has no idea, and I'm not getting him caught up in the madness of the world that I found myself in.

"Not like him, Connor. Please just leave it," I tell him, and he stares at me without blinking. It's unsettling, but it also sets my stomach erupting with butterflies.

"Move back with your nan. It will be safer." I'm shaking my head again, hating it. I'm still holding his hand, but he isn't holding mine.

"I left to protect her, Connor. She raised me, and I've lived with her my whole life, but when I discovered who Brian really was, I knew I had to leave." I release his hand and stand now. Thinking of Brian hurting her is sending my heart pounding. I don't know what to do. My throat burns again. Leaving her alone isn't an option anymore.

"Where are your parents?" I don't look at Connor as he speaks from the couch. But his voice is controlled. I can feel the tremble enter my bottom lip.

"They live a few towns over with the rest of their kids." A stray tear falls, and I wipe it away quickly. It still hurts, no matter how many times I say it.

At just a few months old, they left me behind to travel, and along the way, they forgot to come back for me. Well, it isn't that simple. I was settled and happy with Nan, so they left me with her. They stopped visiting after I was five, or so Nan told me. I don't remember them.

Large hands rest on my shoulders, and I close my eyes at the contact. His hands are so warm on my bare skin, and I fight off the shiver that moves down my arms. I want to turn, but I don't.

"I'm sorry for dragging you into my drama." I swallow my emotions and clear my throat before turning around. His hands slip from my shoulders, and he towers over me. Lines appear on his forehead as his eyes search my face.

"We have a lot in common," he says. It's whispered, and I'm not sure if he intended to say it out loud.

"Your family left you behind too?" I ask.

"Pretty much, yeah." He doesn't sound pained, and I can't look away from him. I want to know more.

When his tongue flicks out and he wets his lips, I bite my own. His eyes snap to the movement, and he exhales quickly. Large hands slowly return to my shoulders, and I step into him, brushing my lips against him. When I pull away from him, the burn of my cheek after rubbing his beard has me hissing.

"You okay?" he asks while moving back in. This time, he places his lips gently on mine, tilting his head to my unmarked cheek. His kiss is nice; it's warm. His grip leave my shoulders and finds my waist. I'm airborne. My legs wrap around him, and I feel all of him against me. His tongue enters my mouth, and I gasp, pulling him closer to me. My breasts brush against my top, and wetness pools between my legs.

Vibrations attack my hip, and it's not until Connor pulls away and the vibrations continue that I realize it's coming from his pocket. He slowly lets me down with an apologetic shrug before taking his phone out of his pocket. I watch him as he checks the screen to see who's calling. Lines appear on his forehead. He answers it.

"I'm kind of..." He steps away from me and nods. "Okay, give me twenty minutes." He finishes the call and looks at me. "A friend's house was broken into."

I fix my top and try to act as composed as he seems. "Oh my God. Is he okay?"

"I'm not sure," he answers honestly and stuffs the phone into his pocket. Rubbing his forehead with one finger, he fixes me with another apologetic shrug.

"Why don't you come with me?"

"No, I need an early night."

He nods at my answer while fishing out his keys. "When I leave, don't answer the door to anyone," he tells me.

"I won't." I never do. Brian was waiting for me. I wrap my arms around my waist.

"I feel bad leaving you." He's hunched toward me. I can see the conflict in how tense his shoulders are. I unwrap my arms.

"Don't. Thanks so much for coming. But I'm fine now, just tired." The exhaustion isn't a lie. My body feels boneless.

"Okay, if you need me for anything or if he returns, ring me."

"Of course I will," I lie easily. His fingers touch my chin, the contact warm, and I lean into him. His lips brush mine. My body seems to gravitate to him. But the kiss ends sooner than I want it to.

"I'll be in touch."

Closing the door behind Connor leaves me with mixed emotions. My fingers flutter to my lips. He can kiss. I'm smiling as I double-check the locks, but that falters as I remember why I'm doing so. The reminder seems to ignite the pain in my cheek.

CHAPTER NINE

CONNOR

When I arrive at Neill's house, I don't even have to reach the front door to see the place has been trashed. Every window is smashed. The door swings open with a touch of my foot. I try to look around the door.

"Connor, is that you?"

"You alone?" I shout back before entering.

"Yeah, in the kitchen."

I move past the torn-up hall. Pictures crunch under my boots as I push open the kitchen door. Something heavy is behind it.

"Jesus, take it easy."

I duck my head around to see Neill sitting against the door. He's holding his right hand, each finger bent back at odd angles. Blood coats his white hoodie and still runs from his nose.

I squeeze through the door; a towel on the counter is my next move. I hand it to Neill, and he has to release his broken fingers.

"Who did this?" I ask him, kneeling down. Someone took a baseball bat to his kitchen. Everything is torn from the cabinets and smashed on the ground. It seemed personal.

"I don't know. There was a group of them." His nose starts to bleed again, and I push the towel back closer to him.

"You need a doctor." He's shaking his head like a broken nose and fingers will mend themselves.

"Say someone jumped you, which is pretty much the truth." I help him up.

"I can't leave the house like this." He's glancing around him.

"I don't think there's anything left to take. I'll ring a mate to come board it up."

I get him to the hospital quickly, but I don't go inside with him. Instead, I make a call to Russell, a friend who takes care of rental properties around the area. I give him Neill's address, and he promises to do it soon.

I ring Ava, only to get her voice mail. She said she was tired; maybe she's sleeping. I send her a quick message in case she is awake. I wait a few moments but don't get a response. The hospital is quiet, and I find Neill easily. He's loud and has the nurses laughing.

"Here is my friend I was telling you about." The nurses turn to me, and I wonder what he's been saying about me.

"Very brave of you to scare off seven men," one of them says, and I look to Neill, but he shrugs.

"Seven? By the time we leave, it might be ten," I say and get a quick laugh before they leave. Neill has a plaster across his face, and his fingers are in bandages too.

"All broke?" I ask, and he nods.

"Did they say anything?"

"The nurses?" he questions, and I fold my arms across my chest.

"Neill, the guys who smashed up your house."

He glances away, and I know he's withholding.

"Look, it's no skin off my nose. But if you want help, you know I'm here."

"I knew the guys. They lost money at a fight and didn't like it."

"Why wouldn't you just say that?" I ask, leaning against the wall.

"Because it makes me look weak. Word gets out, everyone will be smashing up my house because they didn't win. I may as well quit."

"Retaliate," I tell him, and he hops off the bed.

"How, Connor?" He waves his injured arm in the air and pulls it back.

"Fuck." I glance around, seeing we've attracted the attention of an elderly couple. I apologize to them, but they look away.

"Me. I'll retaliate," I tell him, and he stops petting himself and glances up at me, a slow grin tugging at his lips.

"You'd do that?"

"Why not?" I tell him. I leave before he starts hugging me. I'm in the hall only a few moments when my phone dings with a message from Ava.

In bed. How's your friend? Oh and thanks so much for tonight. X

I smile before firing back a text. **He's fine, nothing serious.** I glance up from the phone as Neill, looking anything but fine, walks toward me.

"You ready to go?"

"Yep, just have a load of pain meds." He yaps on as we head to the car. I finish typing the text. **My pleasure, if you need me just ring. x**

I stuff the phone into my pocket as we climb into my car.

"Have you a place to stay?" I ask. I don't want to bring him back to mine, but if he has nowhere else, I will. He tells me he's staying with his mother, who lives in the next estate. I drop him off.

"Send me the names and address of the guys," I tell him, and he nods.

"I don't have them all, but I'll get them."

I smirk. I know he will.

There aren't any lights on when I arrive at Whitewood House, but that doesn't mean no one's awake. Someone is always hanging around. I enter my room downstairs. It's always been my room. Everyone else stayed upstairs except for Liam, who took over the basement area.

My phone vibrates, and I pull it out of my jeans pocket as I strip off my jacket.

A word in the library.

I could ignore Liam's message, but I don't. He must have heard me arrive. He's sitting on one of the Queen Anne's. It's a rare thing, but he looks thoughtful. His brows are furrowed, two fingers touching his chin thoughtfully.

"You called," I say, and he doesn't startle. He looks up and beckons me to come over with two fingers. So very fucking Michael.

"I'm tired," I tell him.

"It won't take long," is his response. "I'll be blunt. Why did you cross into the north?"

My heart thumps heavily. I blink, knowing I should have some outward reaction. I'm too still, so I lean back into the chair.

"When?" I fire back, and he nods as if to say two can play this game.

"Father's informant was tailing you."

This information doesn't surprise me. But coming from Liam, it does. "Michael knew of my whereabouts at all times?" I clench my jaw. Why wait two years, then? To see what I was doing? If he knew, I would be dead by now.

"I was in Monaghan for work. That's as far into the north as I went. I'm tired, Liam." I rise, and Liam doesn't speak until I'm at the door.

"So you never crossed into Belfast?"

I'm glad my back is to him. "Michael's informant is mistaken," I say.

"I don't really care what you were doing in Belfast. Just don't bring anything to our door."

I stare at him. "This house is filled with secrets already, Liam," I fire back. "What could I possibly do?"

"It's not a secret if it's known by three people."

I reenter the room against my better judgment. Resting a hand on either side of Liam's head, I lean into him.

"I'm not afraid of you," he says. "And I'm not fucking stupid either. Say what you want to say." His unemotional response makes me want to plummet his face in, but I use my better judgment and lean out.

"It is a secret if the three people are you, Shane, and Michael." Because those are the three people in the house that have the darkest secrets.

"You're hiding something," he says calmly, and I smile. He must hate not having a clue, and if he's asking, then he doesn't know.

I am hiding something. I'm here to find out which one of these fuckers killed my mother. I'm not sure which one, but I will find out.

"Good night, Liam," I call over my shoulder.

***

It's four in the morning when my phone wakes me. I'm lying over my blankets, fully clothed. I'm used to sleeping like this in case I have to run and move. Realizing that Michael knew where I was the whole time made every uncomfortable night's sleep for nothing.

I rub my face before looking at the message on my phone. It's from Neill. It's the list I've been waiting for—the names and addresses of five men. I pull on my boots and jacket, knowing this is the release I need.

I'm standing in Darragh's room, not really expecting him to be there, but he is. He's wearing last night's clothes and is strewn across his double bed. The smell of alcohol has me thinking that maybe I should go it alone.

His floor is coated with clothes. Every drawer in his dresser is pulled open; wardrobe doors sit wide open as well. His room is a mess. It's four times the size of mine, but I wouldn't want this luxury. I would feel like I owed Michael something.

"Wake up." I kick his leg. Blue eyes flicker open as he glances up at me, squints, and closes his eyes.

"That really you, Connor?" he asks the gray-striped quilt.

"I need to go hurt some people. You in?"

He's up, and I'm grinning at his eagerness. He grabs a pair of beige boots and notices he already has runners on. Dropping them on the floor, he pats down his white shirt and suit jacket.

"Good to go," he tells me, slapping his face a few times.

It's four thirty in the morning when I reach the first house. They all live in Kells, but I'll do them one night at a time to build up their fear and panic, wondering when they will be next. The first house on the list is a small bungalow. It will be easy to break in to. The garden out front is neatly trimmed, but there isn't a flower or pot in sight. I hope this is a sign that David lives alone. I hate when women or kids are around. They overcomplicate things.

The balaclava I tug over my face feels heavy, but the feeling will settle. I glance at Darragh, and he does the same. We've done this before, and Darragh's presence adds excitement to the job.

Bat in hand, I climb out of the car and creep along the sidewalk. Streetlights cast pockets of light as we move slowly toward our target. Darragh follows suit. His bat has blue eyes with long lashes and large red lips painted on the top of it. He named the bat Rochelle, and now he strokes it.

We reach the back door easily. The back garden is a mirror version of the front. I'm kneeling down, screwdriver in hand as I pop the lock. The door opens easily, and a small dog stares at me.

Fuck.

"Kill it," Darragh whispers behind me.

"I'm not killing a dog," I whisper back while rising and sliding the screwdriver into my pocket. The dog's tail wags, and I'm just glad he isn't barking. I wonder how much time we have left before he starts. It could be seconds. I hold my hands out toward the dog.

"I'll kill it." Darragh moves in front of me, and I sidestep to let him pass. Entering the small kitchen with its green eighties style cabinets and fittings, I turn to Darragh.

"Here, doggy," he says softly, and the dog backs away from him, movings toward the hall door that sits open.

"Don't kill it, Darragh," I warn him. He grabs the dog quickly, its bark lodging in its throat as Darragh holds it by the snout.

"Darragh," I warn, and he tilts his head. I can see the laughter in his eyes, so I pass him and the dog and walk into the hall. No lights are on, and I push open the sitting room door carefully. The room is empty. A small two-seater couch and TV take up most of the area.

The space is smaller than the kitchen. I move back into the hall and flicker a gaze up the stairs. A yelp sounds and then silence falls again around the house. Darragh appears a moment later. The dog isn't in his hands. I'm shaking my head at him, and he shrugs. Stroking his bat has me moving up the stairs. Half of the time, I wonder how stable Darragh really is.

Upstairs has only three bedrooms. I check the front one, which holds a single bed and two lockers. The bed isn't made up. The back bedroom is used as a gym. When Darragh pokes his head around the room, he points at the weights. I don't understand what he's asking. He picks one up, and I shake my head.

"We're only scaring him," I say as quietly as I dare. He rolls his eyes and lowers the weight to the floor. The master bedroom isn't exactly master size, but compared to the rest of the house, the room is large. He's lying on his back, alone. That makes this so much easier. I move around his bed, and a snore rips from his throat. Darragh stands on the other side of him, bat resting on his shoulder.

"David, it's time to wake up." I nudge him with my bat, and he sits up, moving back into the headboard. His head snaps from me to Darragh. Raising both hands, he starts to plea.

"I don't have any money. You guys are hitting the wrong house."

Darragh moves, and David follows his movements as he makes his way to the curtains. I have no idea what Darragh is doing, but I stay focused on the message I need to deliver.

"I don't want money," I inform him and let it sink in. His eyes shoot back to me.

"What do you want?" His breathing is growing heavy now.

"You hurt a friend of mine. Neill."

He's shaking his head. "Nah, man. I swear to God, I don't even know a Neill."

I nod. Denial is always the first step.

The crack of a bat on David's leg has me grabbing for Darrah's arms.

"What are you doing?" I ask Darragh as he tries to take another swing.

David's cries are too loud. I force his head into the pillow.

"I thought we were here to beat the shit out of him." Darragh sounds confused, but I can't deal with him right now.

"David, shut the fuck up," I shout. His cries grow muffled, and I let him up slowly. He whines, drool dripping from the corner of his mouth.

"This will go a lot easier if you admit what you did."

"I swear to God. I don't know a Neill."

I push his face into the pillow before looking back at Darragh, who has Rochelle slung up on his shoulder again.

"Now you can hit him," I tell Darragh. He swings wide, and his bat connects with David's hip. I'm not sure if the crack comes from the bat or the bone, but I'm going with the bone, as he screams into the pillow.

We let him up for air once his cries settle down. I'm surprised with how long he holds out. Five hits later, and he finally admits to knowing Neill.

"Tell all your friends we're coming for them," I tell David as I land the final blow to his face. I use my fist. His eyes close, and I push him over so he's sprawled out on his back.

We leave the room, and I'm taking the stairs two at a time. "Fuck sake, Darragh," I snarl as I pass the small body of the dog.

"The fucker would have barked."

As we make it outside, the fresh air feels nice. I itch to rip off the balaclava, but I wait until I'm in the darkness of my car.

"What did you do to it?" I ask, and he pulls off his own balaclava.

"You really want to know?" He's smirking at me, and I start the car up in answer. "So when's the next job?" His excitement has him sitting forward as he sparks up a fag.

"Let's give it a few nights," I tell him, not sure if I'll bring him the next time.

"Don't you fucking bail on me," he says, and I can't stop the grin.

"Wouldn't dream of it," I tell him as we leave the estate in the rearview mirror.

"Cross my heart, I'll be better behaved the next time."

I take a quick look at him and know he's lying. When I snigger, he just shrugs.

CHAPTER TEN

CONNOR

"WHAT TIME IS IT?" Darragh asks.

I check my phone. "Six." He's not looking like someone who wants to go to bed. His grin has me asking, "What do you have in mind?"

He punches my shoulder as we head for the bar.

"Una, you looking for me?" Darragh teases. Una is staring into an empty fireplace. Her smile is tight. We've intruded on something.

"A drink?" He fires at her.

"Why not?"

I sit down beside her on the couch while Darragh gets the drinks.

"Are you guys just coming home?" She pulls her bare feet under her as she tucks a stray curl behind her ear.

"Yeah. Why are you up?" I ask, shrugging out of my coat.

"Couldn't sleep." She dips her head as she speaks.

"Trouble in paradise?" Darragh teases while handing me a Bud and one for Una, who snaps it from him.

"No, everything is perfect." The bite in her words tells me that it isn't perfect.

Darragh jumps across the arm of the chair, sloshing drink down his ugly brown cords.

He wipes it off with his hand and sucks the excess drink from his fingers. When he looks up to find us watching, he winks at Una.

"I thought you moved out?" he says to her.

"I thought you were in rehab?" she fires back, and that wipes the smirk clean off his face.

"I finished it," Darragh says in his defense, and Una snorts, making me grin.

"You mean you paid them off, because you're not clean."

I don't remember Una being this fiery. The idea that she knows that Darragh takes drugs makes me wonder what else she knows. She doesn't look like the carefree sister I'm used to.

"Don't take your mood out on me just because Shane is being a dick."

She stands, and so do I.

"He's playing with you," I tell Una, and she huffs before sitting back down. Any more than two members of our family in one room always turns into a referee match.

"What's this about you moving out?" I ask Una to divert the conversation to hopefully more mutual ground.

"Shane bought Deerpark Stud." My eyebrows rise, and Una smiles. "Yeah, I know," she says while taking a sip of her drink. Darragh rolls his head back and closes his eyes. He lifts his drink, nearly missing his mouth.

"Congratulations," I tell Una, tipping my bottle against hers. She gives me a shy thank you. I had no idea they even liked each other. To be moving in together is a big step. I hope it works out.

"I missed you," she admits, and a slow smile stretches across my face. "I missed you too," I tell her honestly.

"I thought you would be here sooner." Her declaration confuses me.

"How so?" I take a deep drink. Darragh's foot bounces back and forth, but he still has his eyes closed.

"I told Shane weeks ago about where you were."

The alcohol feels heavy in my stomach. "Maybe he had other stuff on," I offer, but she looks as troubled as I feel.

"Nah, he was pretty worried about you. But you're here now," she says with a chirp in her tone.

"I'm happy you're home too," Darragh says. His voice is drowsy. Una shakes her head, but she can't hide the smile.

"You love him," I tell her, getting up, and she snorts. "Right, kiddos. I'm going to hit the sack."

Darragh mumbles something. The chair will be his bed for the next few hours.

"Night, Connor," Una says sweetly, and I hope Shane treats her right. She's good blood.

***

The idea that Shane knew where I was for weeks isn't sitting right with me. It means he was either watching my movements or he was too busy to care. I'm going with the first scenario. I shower and change into fresh jeans and a shirt before carrying my socks and boots into the kitchen.

The smell of scones wafts into the hall. Mary moves quickly around the kitchen. I bend and kiss her on the cheek. She swings around, her bemused look turning into a smile.

"Connor." I haven't seen her since arriving, and her hug is nice.

"Mary, you're getting younger," I tell her, and she swipes at me playfully. Her round face and black curly hair always makes her look youthful compared to her actual fifty-plus years.

I'm sitting when she swoops in with a cup of tea.

"One sugar and some milk." She tells me with a little pat to my head. I smile up at her.

"You're the best, Mary." I take a sip, and the tea is perfect. Her robust figure moves around the kitchen, and she fills it with warmth. Her stature changes as Shane arrives. Both eyebrows rise as he nods at me. After getting his own coffee, he sits down across from me.

"You still living here?" I ask him innocently.

"This is my home."

"Oh. Just was with Una last night, and she said you bought Deerpark Stud."

He places his coffee carefully on the table. "It's being renovated at present, but we will be moving in soon."

Mary arrives with toast and places it in front of me. It's been buttered for me. "Mary, you're marriage material," I tell her, and she giggles.

Shane's face is stone. He doesn't get toast, and I eat mine slowly.

"Tell me about this guy Brian," I say.

Shane glances over his shoulder.

"She's gone," I tell him.

"No breakfast for me?"

"She doesn't seem to like you," I say back, and he shrugs.

"What about Brian?" he questions, and I'm not sure how much I should say.

"He hits that girl Ava," I admit, the toast feeling heavy in my stomach now.

Shane shrugs again. "And what about it?" He takes a sip of his coffee, and I drop my toast.

"You okay with hitting a woman?" I question, and he sits a bit straighter.

"That's not what I said. She's not our problem." He leans in now. "Look, Connor, you have one fucking job to do. So do it." He rises like it's the end of the conversation.

He pours his coffee down the sink before turning to me. "Don't even think about touching Brian either."

"Why, because of that cop?" I ask, taking a bite of my toast. It doesn't taste nice anymore, and I put the rest of the slice down.

"What cop?" The way Shane asks tells me he really doesn't know.

"The cop who's looking for the missing person. His name's Harry."

Shane's back at the table. "Lying little fucker," he tells the table.

"I take it he kept that one quiet," I say, and Shane's eyes snap up to mine.

"Why hasn't he warned the cop away from the case with the boy ?" Shane stares at me like the answer is within his reach, but then he glances away while twisting the ring on his finger—the ring that our mother bought him.

"I don't know, but I'll find out. Right now, just keep away from Brian." He gets up again, and this time, he leaves the kitchen.

Taking out my phone, I text Ava. **Want to meet up tonight?** I hit send before sliding the phone back into my pocket. After putting on my boots and socks, I grab my keys before heading outside. The fresh morning air doesn't help to clear my head. Shane not knowing about Harry being bought by Brian is bothering me.

I take a walk across the fields. I shouldn't have bothered with clean clothes. My jeans are splashed now with cow dung. I keep walking until I come to the tree line of the forest before I start to relax. I walk deep into the forest, then stop and take out my phone. I have a message from Ava.

Great. Looking forward to it.

I smile at her response before I ring the number I was given to reach my dad.

He picks up on the first ring. His Northern Irish accent makes me stiffen and relax at the same time.

"Son. I'm glad you rang."

"Everything okay ?" I ask. The fact he's glad I rang doesn't make me happy. His gladness is never good.

"We need to meet."

I nod while glancing around the forest. "Where?"

"Monaghan. Today. I'll send you the address. Then delete this number."

"Okay."

He hangs up, and my phone bleeps. Westenra Arms Hotel. 2 pm.

I arrive back at the house and change my jeans and shoes.

CHAPTER ELEVEN

AVA

W ORK IS SLOW, AND I honestly don't mind. I'm keeping my hair down, and it's blocking half my face. I woke up looking worse than when I went to bed. My face has started to bruise. The make-up I applied toned it down but didn't cover it up. Thankfully, my only customers are Paul and his friends, who were playing pool when I arrived.

The glass in my hand gleams. I've been drying the same one for the last few moments. My mind keeps going to the kiss with Connor. I start on another glass as the pub doors open. I turn my back on Harry as he takes a seat at the bar. He isn't in uniform today. I don't know what he wants if he's off duty.

"Anyone serving?" he asks, and I turn with a smile on my face. The sting from my cut has my smile slipping. Harry narrows his eyes on my face, and I push my hair back behind my ear to let him see. His eyes flicker to the bar.

"A Guinness."

I don't speak as I go and get him his Guinness. Once I place it on the mat in front of him, he finally glances up at me.

"I can help you." He sounds so sincere, and I lean in. "If you help me."

His smile is soft and slimy, and I move away from him, letting my hair fall back like a curtain. People always want something in return. Domestic violence isn't enough of a reason to help someone.

I take the twenty off the bar and ring up his drink. Making myself busy down in the lounge area keeps me away from Harry. He doesn't call for me again, and when I return, he's gone, his pint left half-full.

My shift drags by; the pub only starts to pick up when I'm getting ready to leave. My shift is nearly over, and Patrick steps onto the floor at five to six and lets me go.

My bag and jacket are stashed in the lounge. Once I get them, I'm out the door. It's starting to get dark already. I don't have to hide from my landlord anymore, so I use the front door, which is next door to the pub. I still need to find a place. It's something I will have to focus on tomorrow. But right now, I need a shower and get ready for my date with Connor.

I shower and dress, and as I'm finishing up, my phone lights up on the bed.

I'm outside when you're ready. No rush.

I take one final look in the mirror. I've left all my hair down and brushed the left side behind my shoulder and down my back. The right is covering my cheek, and it tumbles down to my waist.

After smearing a bit of Vaseline on my lips, I'm good to go. My denim jacket holds my card, phone, and now keys. I don't need a bag. Locking the door behind me, I question my black trousers that look similar to my work ones, but I'm going for comfort. The flat black boots are my favorite, the sides coated in studs.

Traffic moves fast past me as I search up and down the street for Connor. I didn't ask him what he was driving. He steps out of an Audi, and that surprises me. He gives me a wave, and his lips tug up into a smile. Ducking my head, I run across the road and don't glance up until I'm at the car. Connor still watches me, and I smile while tucking my hair behind my ear. His face hardens immediately, and I let my hair fall back as I climb into the car.

"You look lovely," he says the moment he closes the door. His cologne tantalizes my senses, and I want to lean in and sniff him.

"You too." I'm grinning now as he puts on his seat belt. He does look good, in jeans that hug him and a cream top that molds itself to his wide chest.

"So where are you taking me?" I ask as he pulls out. My excitement drips into my words.

"We're nearly there," he tells me with a quick glance.

"Is our date in the car?" I really don't mind. There's something about Connor that eases me. Just being in his presence is enough.

"No." I sit back as we leave Kells and make our way off of Drumbaragh Road. Connor takes a right up into a local park. I take a peek at him under my lashes, and when he glances at me, he laughs, and it's rough and sexy as hell. Butterflies erupt in my stomach at the sound.

"I think I know what you're thinking, and that's not why we're here." He pulls up to the children's playground, and his words make me relax.

"Come on." He's getting out of the car, and I follow him. The place is deserted, but it's known as a hook-up area. That's what I thought when he pulled up, that he expected me to get dirty in the car. It's well-known for late-night antics.

We walk up the large hill toward the Spire of Llyod. I can't hide the surprise when Connor extracts a key from his pocket and uses it to open the door.

"Are you serious?" The tower is rarely ever open, and I've always wanted to stand at the top.

"A friend of a friend," he says with a smirk, and I smile.

"A friend of a friend. You have friends in high places," I tell him as he holds the door open for me. I start climbing immediately. The stone steps are steep. Lights flicker to life on the wall as Connor closes the door.

The circular stairs are making me dizzy. Rough stone bites into my palm as I run my hand along the wall.

"So do you know why someone built a lighthouse inland?" It always puzzled me.

"Some earl built it in memory of his father. It was used to watch horse racing and the hunt." I want to look at Connor. His tone is serious, and I want to see the lines on his forehead that normally accompany that serious tone. But I also don't want to fall down the stairs, so I focus on each concrete step as we continue to climb.

When we reach the top, my legs burn, and I take a moment.

"You just climbed one hundred sixty-four steps," Connor says.

I glance at him, but my surroundings capture me. I'm standing at the top of world. The only thing separating me and the outside is a pane of glass that runs in a full circle around the top of the tower.

"Wow." It's breathtaking, and I move closer to the glass. Looking at the ground makes me want to take a step back.

"Yeah, I like coming here to think."

"I would too," I answer, not looking away from the scene before us. Green fields stretch out, cut up by trees and small stripes of gray concrete. Car lights flash in the distance. Closing one eye, I cover a moving car with my finger.

"I'm sorry for leaving you last night." Connor's words are close. He's right behind me, and I shiver. My eyes clash with his in the glass.

"Don't be. I was fine," I tell his reflection.

"I hate that he hurt you." When he speaks, the lines appear on his forehead. He looks conflicted now, and I turn around so I can see him properly. His brown eyes flicker to my lips, and I wet them.

His fingers reach out and brush my damaged cheek. Closing my eyes, my skin warms, and I can almost feel it heal with his touch.

"My mother was a strong woman. I could never understand her staying." My eyes snap open at Connor's words. I hate that I'm a reminder of what his mother suffered. I'm not like her. I'm not a victim of domestic abuse. This is different. I'm not staying. I'm not allowing myself to be someone's punch bag. I went to the guards. He just bought them off.

"As I got older, I learned that she stayed for her children. She hid it so well." His smile carries no happiness. There's a weight on his shoulders that I want to lift off.

"She was a good mother," I tell him, and his eyes rest on me.

"She was stupid." His brows furrow as he speaks harshly, and there it is. He thinks I'm stupid too.

"I'm sorry about your mom, Connor, but I'm not her." I don't want to be a ghost of something so painful for him. My words cause him to take a step back while widening his eyes.

"I know you're not. I just... I want to beat the shit out of Brian."

I want him to beat the shit out of Brian too. I allow myself to picture that, and a smile tugs at my lips before reality comes crashing back in.

"I know, but you'd end up hurt worse than him, and I don't want that." My confession surprises me. I don't know Connor, but I don't want to see him hurt.

He takes a step toward me as his lips pull into a smile.

This time, he takes my face with both hands, his eyes searching mine. I don't hesitate to rise on tippy-toes and kiss him. His lips are warm and moist, and I moan into his mouth as he pulls me closer to him. His body is flush against mine. We're moving, and my back touches a cold surface. My tongue slips easily into his mouth and his moves into mine. His moan has me pushing myself harder against him.

His large palm brushes my left breast. Hard nipples push against my black top, and I shift my body so his fingers brush my nipples. Wetness pools between my legs, and I want him so bad. My fingers are digging into his shoulders as I try to move him closer. His bulge brushes my sensitive area, and I'm pushing off his jacket, unbuttoning his shirt, and he isn't stopping me. Opening my eyes, I take in his tanned skin, smooth and muscular. Our kiss is broken, and his deep brown eyes have me holding my breath. The intensity in his eyes nearly undoes me.

I'm shrugging out of my jacket, and when I pull my top over my head, it lands in the pile of growing clothes on the floor. His large hand sinks into my hair as his lips touch mine again. My fingers are greedy and move to the band of his trousers. I want them off. I'm fumbling with his jeans when he pauses, his forehead leaning against mine.

"I don't want to stop, but I'm giving you a fair warning. We're surrounded by glass, and the lights are on so..."

I wish he hadn't reminded me. I'm nodding, trying to gather myself, but I keep my eyes closed as I lick my lips.

He hasn't moved as he waits for me to give the green light. But as much as I want this, I don't want an audience.

"Can you pass me my top?" I ask as my way of saying we're stopping this. Connor lets out a breath that brushes my face, and when he opens his eyes, my stomach jumps. Biting my lip, I force myself to stay still and not close the distance between us. The coldness is instant when Connor steps away and hands me my top. I pull it on quickly and take my jacket. Connor pulls on his shirt, and I watch him button it up. He glances up at me from under thick black lashes. The tug of his lips has me smiling too.

My body is still singing. My blood burns hot, so I go back to staring at the view. I need to bring my temperature and hormone levels down before I change my mind. The room allows you to walk a full circle, and it's just beautiful. Cars have started to arrive at the park, and it's no secret what everyone is doing. Now I envy them. They don't have to stop.

I end up sitting down, my knees brushing the glass. I know this opportunity won't come around again, so I try to take it all in. A new memory. Connor joins me, his leg brushing mine, and I wonder if he sat so close on purpose.

"Someone, somewhere, at this exact moment, is looking at the same sky," I tell Connor's reflection.

"Right now, I'm the only person in the world that's looking at you."

My eyes snap to him. His words burn my throat. It's the way he says it that has my stomach flipping. Like looking at me matters. Like I matter.

His kiss is featherlight. He brushes it gently across my lips before leaning back out and focusing on the view in front of us, like he didn't just say the most amazing thing.

CHAPTER TWELVE

CONNOR

"Wake up." I open one eye and stare up at Darragh. "This better be important," I tell him. My mind is still stuck on Ava. With Darragh sitting on my bed and my mind going to Ava, I sit up and rub my face.

"It's Finn's birthday today."

Rubbing my eyes, I reach for my phone. It's ten in the morning. It feels like the middle of the night with how tired I am.

"I think we should all go to the lake together. Like the old days." There's a pleading in Darragh's voice that's not just for Finn. I'm awake now, the longing on his face obvious.

"Okay, but it's your birthday too," I say and get a punch to the arm for agreeing and mentioning his birthday. Darragh isn't one for celebrating his own birthday. He jumps off the bed before I can say any more.

"Going to wake the dragon," he tells me with a grin.

"Who, Shane or Liam?" I ask, and his laughter lingers in my room after he leaves.

My head dips to my shoulder. I can smell Ava's perfume on me. Last night, we spent time talking in the tower before getting food. She offered for me to come upstairs, but I knew if I did, I wouldn't leave. I wasn't sure if I was stupid or what, but with the cut on her face, I wanted it to heal first, or else I felt I was taking advantage.

I'm dressed when Darragh sticks his head in my room door.

"I got a yes out of Shane," he says, and that clarifies who the dragon is.

"Off to wake sleeping beauty," he updates me before leaving again.

Finn is in the kitchen when I arrive. "Happy Birthday," I wish him while getting a cup of tea. "I hear we're all going to the lake."

"Yeah, can't wait." Finn sounds anything but excited, but his eyes don't lie.

"Everyone is coming," Darragh announces as I sit down. He opts for sitting on the table.

"You're telling me you convinced Liam?" Finn sounds as skeptical as I feel.

"I have a way of convincing people."

"Yeah, hammering on and on until we agree." Shane arrives in the kitchen, and Darragh jumps off the table.

"You out last night?" Finn asks me.

I stare at him through bleary eyes. I feel like I was drinking, but I wasn't. "Work, not pleasure," I tell him. My stomach tightens with guilt at my words.

Darragh arrives back to the table with a bowl of cornflakes. He talks while eating, and it's hard to focus.

"So there are rules about today."

Shane sits across from Darragh with toast and a coffee. "Swallow your food first. I don't need to see what's in your mouth."

"Brothers," Liam greets us, and I flicker him a glance over my shoulder.

"Yep, he's in a suit," I say, and Finn snorts a laugh.

"Are you going to the lake in that?" I ask before taking a sip of my tea.

Liam joins us, and I realize this is the first time in years that we've all sat at a table together.

"Does it bother you?" The question is said as he sits down.

"No," I answer with a shrug.

"It bothers me. I think we should all wear T-shirts and shorts," Darragh shoots out.

"It's freezing outside." Shane's tone is low.

"And I like my suit," Liam finishes off.

I grin at Finn, and he smirks back.

"So we are doing this?" Darragh sits back up on the table. Liam pauses eating his toast to stare at Darragh, but he doesn't notice.

Darragh bobbles his head to music we can't hear, and I wonder for the hundredth time if he's high. I can't blame him if he is.

"I'll ride with Connor," Finn says. I'm fine with Finn riding with me.

"We're going on foot," Darragh says.

Shane's head snaps up from his phone. "I just bought these shoes."

"Change them," I tell him, and he glares at me.

"It's Finn's decision," Liam speaks up, but he's also now focused on his phone.

I shake my head at Finn. Walking to the lake sounds painful.

"Come on, Finn. It will be like old times." Darragh's like a dog with a bone, and I can see when Finn gives in before he even says yes.

"I'm just making a call before we leave." I take my mug of tea with me outside. I glance back into the kitchen as my phone rings; it's odd to see them all still sitting at the table.

When he answers, I say, "Russell, how did you get on with Neill's house?"

"Got it sealed. But they did a number on his house. Haven't seen Neill around. Is he okay?"

"Yeah, they broke his fingers and nose."

"Fuckers. Does he know who did it?"

"He couldn't get a clear look at them."

"Pity," Russell responds. I check over my shoulder to make sure no one is listening.

"You still got that place in Headfort Demesne?" I ask.

"Yeah, you looking to rent?"

"No. It's for a friend." I'm not sure what Ava is, but she's more than a friend.

"Look, Connor, it's a private establishment. I can't have any guys in that party and stuff."

"It's a girl. She's a hard worker and will keep the place clean. No partying." There's a brief pause.

"Okay, it's fifteen hundred a month, and a month's deposit."

I glance in the window to see everyone still sitting around the table. "No deposit and tell her it's four hundred a month. I'll cover the rest."

"She more than a friend?"

"Have we got a deal?" I ask.

"Yeah, we've got a deal."

"Thanks, Russell. I'll be in touch."

I arrive back into a fight between Darragh and Finn. I'm not sure what it's about, but Liam barks a warning and silence falls. Shane glances up at me as I place my cup in the sink.

"What's going on?" I ask, and Darragh jumps off the table.

"I'm always wrong."

"You're always high," Finn fires back.

Shane rises, slipping his phone into his back pocket. "Ladies, really? Is this necessary?"

"Can we go and get this done and over with?" Finn's dry tone is how I feel about this, but for him, I'll go.

"Give me a second." Darragh is out the door, a grin back on his face. His recent anger is gone.

We don't have long to wait before Darragh arrives with a backpack that he slings over his back. No one asks what's in it. I think we all have a fair idea.

Darragh takes the lead, and we follow him. I grin when he steps into the field. We aren't taking the main road. He's taking the shortcut that we all took as kids. We're no longer the young brothers with scrapped knees and ideas about wanting to be gangsters. Now we're all grown, scared, and I'm not sure if we know how to be anything else but gangsters.

Liam looks the most ridiculous out of us all, trekking across a field in a suit.

"Remember that time Liam wore the red T-shirt," Darragh starts.

"Yeah and the bull chased him," Finn finished, laughter in his voice. Shane snorts in front of me, and I can't stop the grin that spreads across my face.

"He was like Forest Gump," I say, and Shane smirks across at me.

"He was slipping and sliding." Darragh's laughing now, and Liam looks across at him.

"Thank you for that, Darragh," Liam says with a smile.

"You are very welcome." Darragh walks backward so he can look at us all. The smile seems permanently on his face. Maybe he's right being so carefree. Maybe the rest of us are way too uptight.

"Oh, I have a good one. Remember when Connor tried to ride the sheep?" I nearly trip at Darragh's words, and he roars with laughter.

"Don't say it like that. I tried to get up on its back," I defend. Finn joins in with Darragh's laughter. Yeah, that didn't sound any better.

Now Shane snorts. "I was small enough to ride it."

"Fuck's sake, you know what I mean. I was young enough, and it was like a little horse." My defenses starts to dwindle, and I join their laughter. It doesn't matter what I say; it's all coming out wrong.

Darragh reminisces about our childhood, and before we know it, we're at the lake. The walk seemed so much quicker than it did when we were kids.

The lake doesn't look as large and overbearing as it once was. As a kid, it was an ocean.

Darragh unzips his bag and takes out two bottles of JD. I take one from him and unscrew the cap. It burns as it makes a path down my throat. I pass it to Liamm who takes a deep swallow.

"I've missed this place," I tell the lake. It reminds me of Mom. She would bring us here and let us swim when we were too young to venture off by ourselves.

Liam moves closer to the lake, hands in his pockets as he peers in.

"Me too," Finn says, and I watch Darragh drop the bag, and he's running toward Liam, each step filled with the excitement of a child. He doesn't just knock Liam into the lake; he goes over the edge with him. Finn, Shane, and myself are peering in, warily looking at each other. I have no intentions of shoving anyone in.

"I just got a new phone," Shane says.

"Me too," I counter.

"I hate water." Finn takes a step back.

Liam surfaces, along with Darragh. Liam doesn't make a sound when he breaks through the water. He swims back toward us, his strokes precise. He looks like a professional swimmer, not someone who was just pegged into a lake while wearing a suit.

Darragh releases a yelp of excitement. "Come in. It's warm," he tells the rest of us as Liam reaches the side and drags himself out of the lake. Darragh's lips rattle together.

"I'll pass," I tell him. I go back to the backpack and retrieve the bottle of JD. Sitting on the ground, I take a deep swallow. Liam's stripping off, placing his suit jacket neatly on a bush.

"You're a moron," Shane barks at Darragh, but his words hold amusement. Shane's phone starts to ring. He takes it out and flickers a glance at Liam.

"It's Dad," he says before answering.

"Don't answer that." Darragh's panicked words have the other shoe falling.

"Why would I not answer it?" Shane surprisingly doesn't answer it straight away, and Darragh pulls himself over the side of the lake.

"Just let me explain first."

"What have you done?" Liam asks, and the way the three boys approach him with such exasperation says that Darragh gets into more trouble than he used to. Shane's phone stops ringing, but Finn's starts right away.

"You've got ten seconds before I answer this." Finn holds up his phone to Darragh. I take another drink and stay where I am. My phone doesn't ring. I've recently changed my number. Liam's phone won't be ringing after going for a swim in the lake, and neither will Darragh's. I wonder now if that's why he threw himself and Liam into the lake.

"I got a tip-off that the guards were going to arrest me today." Darragh drips water around his feet as he glares at his brothers like somehow this is their fault.

"What did you do?" Liam asks again.

"Siobhan's aunt—they found my DNA on a cigarette." Shane shakes his head and steps away from Darragh.

"Did I not tell you to pick them up?" Shane's barking at Finn, who's turned pale.

"Don't start pointing the finger at me," he shouts back. Darragh takes a box of fags out of his shirt pocket. Water pours from the box before he throws them on the ground.

"Who tipped you off?" I ask, and all eyes fall on me.

His eyes shift to Shane before returning to me. "Brian. He has a guard paid off. Heard they were coming for me."

"They can't do anything with just a cigarette butt. Someone could have carried it into her house on their shoe." Shane tells this to Liam like if he can explain it away, it will make all this stop.

"This wasn't even about my birthday," Finn says to Darragh, who rest on his hunkers.

"It was a bit of both." Darragh's voice is low, but I catch his words.

"Oh, so my birthday and the fact you're being arrested for murder. Two birds with one stone. Is that it, Darragh?" Darragh's up, fists clenched, and I'm rising. Darragh sees my movements and takes a step away from Finn.

I'm standing now as Shane's phone rings again. He answers, and the one-sided conversation is hard to follow. His final question has me watching Shane. "What should we do?" he asks Michael. Shane nods into the phone.

"Okay. Yeah." Darragh is holding his breath as Shane turns to him.

"I know he wants you to hand me over to them."

"It wasn't just a fag butt. Your fingerprints were found in her bedroom. What were you doing in her room?"

Finn runs his hands through his hair and turns away from Darragh and Shane. "Oh my fucking God."

"Siobhan's going to know."

"Calm down," Liam tells Finn in a very calming voice, and I find myself taking a step closer to Finn.

"She was asleep, so I woke her up." Darragh shrugs, but the way he won't hold anyone's eyes tells me he's hiding something.

"You didn't rape her?" I ask the question that everyone is thinking.

"Fuck off." The disgust in Darragh's voice gives me the answer. Still, his actions are creepy as fuck.

"What do I do?" he asks Liam.

"You stay calm. You don't say a word. Don't speak. My lawyer will deal with it." Finn glances up at me, the weight of the world on his shoulders. He walks to me and picks up the bottle of JD. He drinks it until he needs air.

"I'm sorry, lad," I tell the side of his face. This is some fucking mess. But I have all the faith in Liam that he will get Darragh out of this.

Shane gives Liam his phone so he can make his call. Sirens blare in the distance, and Darragh pales, moving toward Liam, like he offers some sort of protection.

"I told Dad to tell them where we are. Better here than at the house."

"You're going to let them arrest me?"

"You killed someone, you little fucker, so be a man," I tell him. I shouldn't have said it out loud. But he's pissing me off, running from one brother to another.

"Fuck you. You're not even part of this family."

I laugh at his words, even though they sting. "Get used to the smell of metal bars." My words have him charging me. Two Gardaí cars appear as I take Darragh to the ground.

I'm holding him down when they jump from the cars. I recognize Harry but don't want him to recognize me, so I let Darragh go and try to keep my face hidden.

"Darragh O'Reagan, you're under arrest for the murder of Ruth Walsh. You have the right to remain silent. If you do say anything, what you say can be used against you in a court of law." Harry is the arresting officer and pulls Darragh off the ground while placing cuffs on him. "You have the right to consult with a lawyer and have that lawyer present during any questioning. If you cannot afford a lawyer, one will be appointed to you."

No one speaks as Darragh is placed in the back of the Gardaí car. We watch as the two cars pull out onto the road, and once they leave, I turn to Finn.

"Happy Birthday."

CHAPTER THIRTEEN

AVA

HOW THE HELL DID I gather so much crap? I'm packing a bookshelf. It's small and filled with books and some figurines and picture frames. I feel like I'm packing forever. When I finally wrap the last item, which happens to be a small statue of the Virgin Mary, my bell rings. The statue was previously stashed behind a picture. My nan had given it to me for protection, but I wasn't overly fond of displaying it.

"Hello." I take the receiver away from my face; something sticky is on the side and is now on my cheek.

"Ava, it's Harry."

I want to hang up the phone. "What do you want?" I ask.

"Just a minute." I glance around my apartment. I don't want him here in my personal space, but it won't be mine for much longer. I buzz him in and unlock the front door. My heart hammers as his footsteps echo in the hallway. He appears and gives me a nod as he climbs the last few steps.

I fold my arms across my chest and stay standing in the doorway. "What?" I snap.

Harry glances behind him and even moves a few feet back so he can look up at the stairs to the next floor.

"Just a minute, please."

Against my better judgment, I let him in. I don't like that he's in uniform. He closes the door as we enter the sitting room. He doesn't sit but removes his hat, and now I'm sitting because my mind is going to Nan. Something is wrong. When they remove their hats, it's delivering bad news. I've seen it in every movie. My hand flutters to my throat.

"I just want to talk," Harry says, and my heart flutters before it starts to settle.

Nan is fine, I tell myself.

"I can't help you," he says, "because Brian would target my family."

"Then what are you doing here?"

"I want to help, Ava." Harry's cheeks are tinted with a bright pink.

"Then let me file the complaint against him. He hasn't just hit me once." I'm shouting and remind myself that I have neighbors. Taking a deep, calming breath, I run my hands down the leg of my tracksuit bottoms.

"I can't. But you could do something else." He pauses, his eyes now taking in my living space, and it feels so invasive.

"Which is?" I bark, pulling him back to me.

"You could help us. Brian deals drugs, but we can't pin him down. If you could find something on him, he would be locked up for a long time."

I laugh humorlessly. "You want me to wear a wire?" I ask.

Harry grins, and I want to ask him what's so fucking amusing. "No, just get close to him and maybe let us know if anything arises."

"You want me to get close to someone who's hit me." I stand. I want him out of my apartment.

"Ava, I know he hurt you, but Brian hurts a lot of people who can't do anything about it. He likes you. You can do something."

I can't hold Harry's eye. He's right. Maybe I could get close to Brian, but it feels like a really stupid thing to do. "I'll think about it," I tell Harry and am surprised when he nods.

"Thank you." He places his hat back on his head and leaves.

After Harry leaves, I continue packing, but my mind is a jumbled mess. The missing man niggles at me now. What if something bad happened to him? What if telling the guards that I saw Brian with him could be enough to put him behind bars? I didn't get a good look at the other guy.

Small pieces of glass spray across the floor as the bite to my finger has me putting my finger in my mouth. Crap. A small Galway Crystal holder that my nan got me is in a million pieces on the floor. The tang of metal in my mouth has me removing my finger and assessing it. It's not deep, but it's like a paper cut. The pain is intense.

I clean up and don't return to packing. After sticking a Band-Aid on my finger and grabbing my jacket and bag, I make my way to the Gardaí station.

A *bangharda* is at the counter. They're worse than the men. The glass that divides stays sealed as she glances up but returns to whatever she's doing under the desk. So I take a seat. My stomach won't settle. I withheld information, and now saying that I did so because Harry wouldn't allow me to press charges against Brian just doesn't seem like an option. My phone vibrates in my pocket, and I take it out as the bangharda pulls open the window.

"Next," she barks, but I'm the only one here. She gives me a lazy look, and I answer the phone. She can wait.

"Hi," he says.

"Hi to you too." I smile at his voice. The Bangharda is watching me, so I take my call outside, telling Connor to give me a second. He holds until the fresh air flitters across my face. "Sorry. I'm up here at the guards."

"Is everything okay?" His words are rushed, and I want to ease him immediately.

"Yeah, nothing has happened," I tell him.

"Good. Are you there to press charges against Brian?" he asks.

I want to say yes, but pressing charges against Brian just doesn't seem like an option.

"No. It's about something else. Something I saw." The line is silent. "Connor?" I question, thinking he must have gone.

"Yeah, sorry. I'm here. What do you mean something you saw?"

I chew my lip now. "There's a missing person, and he was in Smyth's with Brian and another man. I think I should tell them what I saw."

"Is this the picture that Harry was showing you?" Connor sounds odd.

"Yeah."

"Ava, I know you think you are doing good, but why didn't you tell the guards before? You'll get into trouble."

I stop chewing my lip when I taste blood. "I thought of that, but I could say that I just remembered." Okay, that sounded lame. I glance back at the door. The Bangharda is out fixing the leaflets.

"I just want it off my conscious," I admit to Connor.

"I know, but they won't care. You withheld information. You will be in trouble for obstructing their investigation. Maybe what you saw was nothing. That guy is probably at some wild party." Connor did have a point, but yet, someone was looking for him, his family. Maybe my information that he was drunk and left with two guys wouldn't do any good.

"Yeah, you're right," I tell Connor, stepping away from the Gardaí station and making my way back down the road.

"I just worry about you," he says, and I pause as the traffic moves past me. Why do his words hold guilt?

"Seriously, don't worry about me. I can take care of myself."

A short relieved laugh from Connor has me smiling.

"Will I be seeing you later?" I ask, and he pauses.

"I'm not sure. We have a bit of a family situation at the moment, but I'll try my best."

I'm slightly disappointed, but I don't say that. "Okay."

"I'll contact you later."

I nod into the phone. "Yeah, that's cool."

"Where are you now?" he asks, and I glance around me.

"I'm at my door. Why?" I ask, expecting him to suddenly appear.

"Just wanted to make sure you got home safe."

He's so sweet. I turn the key in the door. "I'm inside now," I tell him, and he seems content when he says goodbye.

I've got no one waiting for me when I get upstairs. Ringing Nan for the third time has alarm bells going off in my head. Even when Harry was here, she was all I could think about. Her not answering isn't normal, but I have work in ten minutes. Going to the Gardaí station and having Harry here burned through my packing time. I still have so much to do.

***

I'm on the early shift again, so it's quiet.

Patrick appears out of the back. "Just going to do the lodgments."

"No problem," I tell him, and he leaves. The bank is only a few doors down, so he's never long. I take out my phone and ring my nan again. My stomach tightens when she doesn't pick up.

"A pint when you're ready," Paul says.

I stuff my phone in my pocket and give Paul a smile. "Coming right up," I tell him. Placing the pint in front of him, I can see the question in his eyes before he asks me.

"Are you alright?" His eyes linger on my face. I completely forgot about it.

"Oh, this?" I point at my face. "Hit myself with a lamp while packing," I tell him, and he grins.

"Jesus, you gave yourself some smack."

I take the twenty. "I know."

"You need to be a bit more careful," a voice says.

My hand stills over the till, but I quickly remember myself and get Paul his change. I don't look at Brian as he leans across the bar. But he's here, and I hate him for how he's making me feel.

"What the hell do you want?" I can't take much more of him. His smile falls, and my voice carries across the bar. There seems to be a stillness around us, and his blue eyes turn cold.

"How's your nan?"

The question has me locking my knees together, and I'm shaking my head. "No."

"What's wrong, Ava?" The way Brian asks has me moving toward the end of the bar. Patrick arrives in the door, and his eyes flicker from Brian to me.

"Patrick, can I leave early today?" I ask quickly, already grabbing my bag and jacket.

"Yeah, of course. Is everything okay?" His worry is genuine.

"She's fine. I've got it," Brian says, reaching his arm toward me as I come from around the bar. But I'm not pretending.

"Don't touch me. What did you do to her?" I shout, and he steps in closer.

"Shut the fuck up, Ava."

"You promised me you wouldn't touch her." My low words are accompanied by tears. Brian is toe to toe with me now, his breath on my bruised cheek.

"You promised me a second chance."

If I had the courage, I would strike him, but I don't. I move around him and out the door.

"Ava." My name bounces off the cobbled stone pavement, and I don't look back. Instead, I ring Connor, but it goes to voice mail.

"Ava." Brian's voice is more distant now when I wave down a cab and give the driver directions to my nan's house.

CHAPTER FOURTEEN

CONNOR

"WHAT'S TAKING SO LONG?" Finn asks. I can't seem to keep him still. He's pacing the library as we wait for word on Darragh.

"They can hold him for forty-eight hours," I remind Finn. "Liam has someone working on it. Trust me, when the forty-eight hours are up, he will be home."

He rubs his face. "What do I say to Siobhan when she asks?"

I have no clue. "Play dumb," I offer lamely. I wouldn't want to be in his situation.

Shane arrives in the room, his eyes narrowing on Finn, and it's pissing me off how everyone is blaming Finn for Darragh's actions.

"Any word?" I ask Shane, and his head snaps to me. He walks deeper into the room.

"He's staying quiet. The lawyer is with him now. We hope to have him out in a few hours."

"Where were you that night?" he asks Finn, who looks up at him while scratching his eyebrow.

"With you. I helped you."

"You're a moron. If the guards ask, where were you?"

"Shane, just calm down," I tell him, and Finn rises.

"It's fine, Connor. I was with Siobhan, and then I came and picked up Darragh from a party."

Shane nods. "Try to remember that."

"Try not to be such a dick," I tell him as he leaves. He glares at me quickly before turning the corner. Finn needs to start standing up to Shane and Liam. They treat him like they always have, I suppose—their baby brother who they can boss around. I need to return a call to Ava. That's another problem. Her being at the Gardaí station today was too close for comfort.

"I'll be back in a minute," I tell Finn, who is sitting back down. He just nods as I leave the room.

She answers on the first ring. "Ava, sorry I missed your call."

"I can't talk right now." She sounds upset, and all I can think of is that she changed her mind and is making a statement against Shane.

"Where are you?" I ask, boring a hole into the wall.

"At the hospital. I'm okay. It's my nan."

"What hospital?"

"Navan. She's going to be fine, but can I give you a call later?" she asks, and I hate her being alone up there, knowing that she has no family.

"Sure. Chat soon," I tell her, and the call ends. I exhale a breath.

"You okay if I tip out for a while?" I ask Finn, just sticking my head in the door. There isn't much we can do now—only wait for news.

"Yeah, I think I need to get out too."

I nod. He's right to get out. Sitting here will drive him mad.

***

Despite Ava saying not to, I go to the hospital anyway. I go to reception to ask where Ava's nan is, but I don't know her name. Ava's last name is Smith, but I'm sure if it's her nan's is the same.

I sit down on one of the plastic chairs that are designed to break your back and send her a text. **I'm in the hospital at reception.**

While waiting, I send a text to Neill. **Was the message delivered?**

"Connor." I glance up into the emerald green eyes that are filled with worry. "You didn't have to come." She looks pale.

I rise, unsure what to do. I stuff my phone into my pocket and leave my hands in them too. "I wanted to make sure you're okay."

She smiles. "Let's get a coffee."

"Coffee sounds good. That would make this our third date." Her smile grows, and I'm smiling too.

The coffee shop is tiny. Ten tables fill the space, all empty. Ava orders two coffees and tells me to grab a table. I would prefer to be the one getting the coffees, but I think she needs to do something right now.

She lets out a shaky breath, and the tremble in her hands shakes our mugs. When she sets them on the table, I cover her hand with mine, making her look at me.

"No matter what, it's going to be okay," I tell her, and her eyes shine with unshed tears as she sits down.

"It's my fault." She swallows and stares at the ceiling, as if the emotion will somehow slide back down her throat.

"It's okay, Ava." I squeeze her hand, making her look at me. Tears stream down her face.

"I told Brian I would give him a second chance, just to keep him happy. But he knew I was lying. He saw me with you." She swallows again, and I'm holding my breath. I'm going to fucking kill him.

"He hurt her. She's the sweetest woman ever, and he hurt her." Her words turn angry. Her tears continue to roll, and I move my chair so I can pull hers close to mine. She's in my arms, spilling her sorrow on my top, and with each tear that falls, I promise I will take that from Brian.

Her sobs subside, and she leans out. "Sorry, I'm a mess. You shouldn't have come."

I hand her a white napkin that sits on the table. "I want to be here," I tell her, and she takes it and wipes her face. She's beautiful. Her eyes still glisten, but the determination on her face tells me she won't cry anymore.

"Is there any chance I get to meet this famous woman?" When I ask, she barks a short laugh while wiping under her eyes.

"I've told her about you. But be warned, she's fierce."

"I'm sure I can handle her," I tell Ava as I pour milk and one sugar into both our coffees. She's pretty shaken up. Each time she drinks from her coffee, her hands rattle, and something in me keeps stirring and getting larger. I hurt people just to hurt them, but this feels different. I want to hurt Brian so he can never hurt Ava again.

"I hope I didn't pull you away from anything."

"I was just hanging out with my brother," I tell the half-truth.

"You've a brother?" She seems surprised, but I've never spoken of them. I'm not meant to get close. I'm here for a job.

"I've five half brothers and a stepsister," I tell her, and she nearly chokes on her coffee, making me smile.

"Wow, that's a huge family. Do you get on with them all?"

Now I drink my coffee before answering. "I do with three of them. Finn and Darragh are twins, but we've always been close, and my other brother Bernard I get on with," I answer. My stomach twists at the thought of Bernard. I hoped the next time I rang Dad, he would tell me that Bernard was home.

"And the rest?" This really seems to have taken her mind off her nan, but now I feel like I'm dancing around the truth, and it's getting dangerous. But their names won't do any harm.

"Shane and Liam are the older two, so I don't exactly see eye to eye with them."

"And your stepsister?"

"She's great. Maybe you'll meet her someday." The moment the words are out of my mouth, the more unlikely that actual scenario seems. Ava meeting Una would mean her meeting Shane.

"Will we go in?" I ask her. This conversation has veered onto a path I don't want to go down. She nods and leads me to her nan's room.

The little old lady in bed is exactly what I pictured. Ava did her justice. I feel scruffy now as I rub my jaw.

"Nan, this is Connor." Ava's voice shakes slightly, and I try not to lean in too close to her nan. I don't want to scare her after her being attacked. A large white bandage is wrapped around her head, which is the only visible sign that she was hurt.

"Lovely to meet you," I tell her, reaching out my hand, and she takes it. Her grip is firm and warm.

"What are your intentions with my granddaughter?" I'm nodding and trying not to grin at the ferocity in her words and the hold she has on me.

"Nan, please," Ava says while sitting down on the side of the bed.

"I like your granddaughter," I tell her honestly, and she nods.

Blue beady eyes pierce me as she continues to grip my hand. "Don't think you can hang your hat and leave it there."

"Oh my God, Nan." Ava sounds mortified, and I want to smile. I'm not sure what that statement means, but Ava's humiliation is telling me it's sexual.

"I never leave my hat behind." Both her eyebrows rise up to her hairline, and she finally releases my hand.

"So, where are you from?"

I take a moment to glance at Ava, whose face is stark red, and I smile. "Kingscourt area."

"I've relations buried down there. Do you know John McCluskey?"

"I can't say I do," I answer.

Ava's nan asks me lots of questions, much to Ava's embarrassment, but I soon see that her nan is doing it because she knows Ava's embarrassed. She's enjoying it. Ava's right. Her nan is fierce, but I love her strength. Visiting time is almost up when she asks Ava to give us a moment.

"Not a hope." Ava's answer is immediate.

"It's only a minute," I tell Ava, and her eyes widen.

"Why are you encouraging her?" she asks, but she rises.

"Fine, whatever she says is on you," she says to me. I smile as she leaves, but not before she plants a kiss on her grandmother's cheek.

Nan speaks while staring after Ava. "She's a good kid. Had a hard life." It's like the walls fall down, and the pain that I didn't notice before is evident now on her face. The paleness of her skin has me leaning in.

"Shall I get a nurse?"

"No. She can't be left alone. Brian, her previous boyfriend, hit her, and he'll do it again." Her fear for Ava is clouding her eyes.

"I won't leave her alone." I make the promise before she asks, and her body seems to sink deeper into the pillows.

"She has no one in this world. Only me." She speaks to the ceiling before fixing me with a hard gaze. "You will have to mind her until I get out."

"I will," I tell her, and she nods.

"Now, here she comes. Just laugh."

And I do. Some of my laughter is real.

"What's so funny?" Ava folds her arms gently across her chest, but her emerald eyes sparkle.

"Mind your business," Nan tells her. "Now go on. Go home and rest, child." She reaches out an arm to Ava, and Ava steps into her embrace. I put the stool back against the wall and stand, not sure if I should go.

"Don't you renege on your promise," she warns me.

"Oh my God, Nan! What did you make him promise?" Ava sounds seriously worried.

"She's joking," I tell Ava, and she relaxes. Before we leave, I lean in and place a soft kiss on Ava's nan's cheek. "I'll take care of her," I whisper before leaning out, and her eyes fog up.

"Go on," she barks while looking away, not wanting us to see her cry. Ava doesn't want to leave, but when I entwine our fingers, she leaves with me.

She doesn't speak as we make our way out in the parking lot. "I can't go home." Her voice is low, and she looks at me from under her lashes. I would have her stay with me, only the whole Shane thing would be a mess.

"Yeah, I know. I have a friend who is looking for a tenant for his apartment. You could stay there tonight, see if you like the place. If you do, it's yours." Her eyes widen.

"Seriously?" she asks, and I grin.

"Yeah. Just let me ring him."

She tugs my hand, stopping me from walking any further. When I look down at her, I don't expect her to be so close.

"Thank you." She steps into me and rises on her tippy toes. Gently, she plants a soft warm kiss on my lips. The kiss doesn't last long enough.

"You're welcome." I'm staring into emerald eyes that are becoming familiar, and that is dangerous.

***

Russell stays true to his word. A set of keys are left with the security when we check into Headfort Demesne. Ava hasn't said anything since we left her apartment. I brought her back so she could pack some clothes.

The car glides into the driveaway, and I move past the white barrier that is lowered behind us.

"Okay, straight up. I can't afford this place."

I was waiting for that. It's a gorgeous space, with courtyards and private security. You bet you paid through the nose for it.

"You don't even know how much it is yet," I tell Ava as I park, and she snorts.

"I know it's out of my budget."

I don't answer her but get out of the car and grab her two bags. She follows me to number two. The red shutters on the windows are closed. Russell did tell me that they need to be opened.

"You go on in and check the place out. I'll just get the shutters open." I place the keys in Ava's hands, and she stares at them.

"I don't want to go in." Now she has my attention.

"Why?"

"I know I'm going to fall in love with the place, and then I can't keep it." She shuffles the keys from one hand to the other. I snatch them from her open hand and enter the apartment. It's dark with the shutters closed over, but immediately, I can feel the warmth.

Ava still stands outside the door, pouting. "If you don't come in, I'll carry you in," I threaten and laugh when she doesn't move. I take a step toward her, and she holds her hands up.

"Fine, I'm coming in."

I watch her take in each room. The place is spotless. All the furniture is white, and everything looks brand new. The hardwood floors under our feet are polished.

"A four-poster bed," I say when we enter the bedroom. Ava walks to the bed and holds one of the banisters before walking around the other side.

"It's a big bed," she tells me, and I take a step into the room, hoping I'm not mistaking her invitation.

"Shall I get my tape, and we can measure it?" I ask, and she bursts out laughing.

She's so alive when she laughs. The noise that leaves her lips is musical, but it's how it makes her eyes shine and her cheeks glow. Perfection.

I take another step into the room and pretend to be really examining the bed. "I like the floral duvet cover," I tell her, and she's still smiling, still flushed.

"I bet it's comfortable," I say, and she moves closer, kneeling on the bed. She does a half jump.

"It's soft." I use my hands, pushing them deep into the mattress.

"Very soft," I say as I move around the bed toward her. She's still kneeling, but her eyes track me.

I stop when I'm directly behind her, leaning in; I place a kiss on her neck. Her head rolls back, giving me more access to her.

"You smell lovely," I tell her. Her perfume fills the air as I remove her top. The red bra she wears is full, and my jeans tighten. My lips touch her shoulder, and she shivers under me. Her tanned skin is soft and perfect. My hands trail down her front until I brush her breasts. Her moans are a drug that I can't get enough of.

Taking her ear lobe in between my teeth, I suck and bite softly. Her nipples harden in my hands. She's moving under me, growing impatient, so I let her turn and face me. Her arm wraps around my neck as she pulls me to her lips. We move onto the bed, Ava taking the lead now. When her lips brush my neck, the slight pinch of pain mixed with pleasure zooms through my body.

I'm shrugging off my jacket and break the kiss to pull my shirt off over my head. Ava's eyes roam my chest, and she flickers a hungry gaze up at me before she pulls me back down on top of her. Her hands roam across my shoulders and back. My jeans grow tighter, and I reach down and take off Ava's. She lifts easily as I slide them down her legs. She's flushed, the rise and fall of her chest rapid, and all I want is her.

CHAPTER FIFTEEN

AVA

THE AIR HAS LODGED itself in my throat. Connor is staring down at me, and everywhere his eyes touch, I burn. He stands now and removes his jeans and boxers, and my face lights up. I've seen men naked before, just none like Connor. My heart slams against my chest as he moves back up toward me, and I bite my lip as his fingers move under the waistband of my underwear, and he drags them painfully slow down my legs.

I want to close my eyes, but I also don't want to miss a second of this. Connor comes back up, and I spread my legs, but he pushes them together as he maneuvers himself behind me. I glance at him over my shoulder as he lifts my leg and places himself at my opening. I'm wet, I'm ready, and when he enters me, I let out a gasp. I'm slipping and falling, and I need a minute to catch myself but I can't. Brown eyes I cling to as Connor moves deeper and faster inside me. I hold on as long as I can before lying my head back down and closing my eyes. My body wants to let go; glancing at Connor one final time is what pushes me over the edge, and the world shatters around me. His release nearly undoes me again.

I'm breathless when we both lie down in a tangle of legs. I'm not sure I could survive that a second time. Connor twitches inside me, and my body betrays my thoughts. Callous skin brushes my nipples, which have already hardened, and I turn in Connor's arms. I want to watch him this time.

A banging on the front door has both of us freezing. We lie still, but as the knocking continues, Connor pulls out of me gently and places a quick kiss on my lips. Tanned bum cheeks hold my attention until they disappear into a pair of white boxers and then his jeans. That's how Connor answers the door. I lie back down until I can hear voices. After a moment, I get up and get redressed. The front door closes as I arrive into the living and kitchen area, where Connor stands topless. His head snaps up to me, and a slow grin spreads across his face. I try to cover my smile with a fist, but I can't hide it.

"That was Russell. He forgot to leave the keys for the bin area," he tells me, dangling them from his fingers. His phone is sitting on the breakfast bar in front of him, and when he glances at it, something shines in his eyes.

"Everything okay?" I ask, taking a seat at the breakfast bar.

"Yeah. My brother Darragh was at a party, but he's home now. I was just worried."

"Is he younger?" I like the idea of Connor being so protective of his brother.

"Yeah, he's one of the twins. But I'm closer to Finn. Darragh can be a bit of a handful."

"Drinking during the day was a bit of a sign," I tease. His lip tugs up, and I bite my lip. "You've got a lot of tattoos." I'm eyeing them all, and his bare skin too. He's worth looking at.

A serpent is wrapping itself around his chest and shoulders. The artwork is amazing, but there's something unsettling about the tattoo the more I study it.

"You got any?" he asks.

I join my hands and rest them on the counter. "Me and needles aren't a good match. I've always wanted one, but I'm not brave enough."

"I could go with you." Connor now takes my hand in his. "Hold your hand." His smirk has me tightening my legs together.

"I'll keep that in mind."

His eyes roam down to my mouth before flickering back up to my eyes. "We should order food." Connor takes out his phone. "Pizza?" he asks while scrolling.

"Pizza is perfect," I tell him.

He raises his lashes. "What toppings?"

"You pick." I'm hungry, but having Connor here in the kitchen, ordering food, makes me want him again. He orders mushrooms and pepperoni.

"It should be here in twenty minutes," he says as he hangs up and slides his phone into his pocket. I'm nodding as I get off the stool and walk around to Connor. He follows my every move, and my nerves kick in, but I don't stop as I reach up and touch the snake on his shoulder. His muscles clench under my touch.

"Why a snake?" I let my fingers roam across smooth tanned skin, following the serpent to his other shoulder.

"Sometimes life makes it hard to breathe, like something is tightening itself across your chest. You know? So I thought a snake was a perfect representation of that." Lines have appeared on his forehead as he frowns.

"I get that," I tell him, and I do. His hand rises and joins mine, and our fingers entwine perfectly together. Rising on tippy-toes, I kiss him softly first, opening up the invitation. I'm off the floor, and my backside rests on the counter, Connor's strong arms still wrapped around me as he deepens the kiss.

My hands hold his face before roaming down his back. I'm pushing myself closer to him until I can feel all of him against me.

Kisses that he trails down my neck have me gasping when he nips me with his teeth. My nails dig into his back, and he groans before lifting me off the counter and carrying us over to the couch. Our clothes make a neat pile on the floor, my underwear the only barrier between us. Connor's fingers touch the band, and my body grows tighter, wetter at the idea of him inside me. He doesn't remove them. Instead, he slips a finger inside me, and my eyes widen. He's kneeling over me, dark brown eyes looking down at me as I push myself against his fingers. His movements grow faster, and when he dips his head down and takes one of my breasts in his mouth, I release across his fingers. I'm panting when he removes them and puts them in his mouth. His lips touch mine, and I can taste myself. Gripping his rock-hard shaft, I start to pump him.

We rotate positions until he's sitting on the couch and I'm over him, watching his face contort in pleasure. Pleasure that I'm causing, and I want him inside me. I climb onto his lap, and his eyes shoot open as I push my underwear aside and direct him inside me. Connor wraps his arms around my waist and holds me as I move up and down. I can feel that buildup inside me, and I close my eyes as I move faster. Connor's moans are making me go faster.

"Oh, fuck yeah. Faster," he says. I'm staring at him, moving as fast as my legs allow when he pours his seed inside me, his body jerking from the release. I don't come, but collapse onto his chest as we both fight for air.

We have our clothes back on when the doorbell rings. "I'll get it," I tell Connor, going for my bag, but he's already at the door taking in our pizza. The smell of the pizza has me realizing I'm starving.

We sit at the breakfast bar. Connor has put back on his gray jumper, so his skin isn't distracting me from eating. Each bite is heaven, and when I look up at Connor to find him watching me, I can't stop smiling.

"What?" I ask, and he grins. It's dark now, and the thought of him leaving has my stomach twisting. This is the part I hate, where you're not sure where you stand. After sleeping together, it changes everything.

"You're beautiful."

My smile grows until it's almost painful, and I'm covering my mouth now. "Thank you," I tell him, and he picks up a piece of pizza and starts to eat again.

"Will you stay tonight?" There, I said it.

He nods. "That was my plan."

I laugh. "What if I didn't ask you?"

"I would follow you to bed and climb in."

A laugh bursts from my lips at the image of Connor following me to bed.

We sit for a while longer and chat, but after all that happened today, I'm ready for bed. Connor tidies and locks up before we make our way to the bedroom. It feels weird to have him here. But a nice weird. I'm going through my bags, looking for my night clothes while Connor strips down. I forgot he has nothing with him. His leg muscles bunch together as he pulls his jeans down. When his shirt is pulled over his head, I have a full, clear view of his back. A large cross dominates most of the space.

"Didn't take you for a religious kind of guy," I say and realize I've put on bottoms from a different pajama set than my top. Connor is way too distracting. But they'll do. Climbing into bed, I tell my heart to relax. It's more intimate to intentionally go to bed with someone just to sleep than to have sex.

"I like to think that if we don't get punished in this life for our wrongdo-ings, we get punished in the next." He climbs in now and faces me.

"So you think there is more than this?" I ask as he takes my hand in his and twines our fingers together.

"I like to think so."

"So do I. I hope it's the land of milk of honey," I tell him, and he grins.

"I'm not sure about the milk and honey."

I smile into his handsome face. A final warm kiss is brushed across my lips before he turns off the overhead lights. The darkness is nice as I move closer to Connor. His scent surrounds me, along with his arms, as I fall asleep.

CHAPTER SIXTEEN

CONNOR

Waking up this morning to Ava in my arms is torture. She still sleeps as I stare down at her. I'm falling for this girl, and if she finds out why I'm here, it would destroy what we have.

My phone dings, and I know it's Shane or Finn wondering where I am. After getting dressed, I sit on a chair in the corner and wait until Ava wakes up. As antsy as I am to get home, she deserves to sleep. Her arms stretch over her head, and I can't stop the smile that grows on my face. When her eyes land on me, they widen slightly.

"Good morning." Her expression is shock before her cheeks turn a shade of pink. She sits up, running her hands through her hair.

"Morning." I move to the bed, and when I sit down, she gazes up at me with a sleepy look that has me brushing a kiss to her lips.

"I have to go," I tell her, and she nods but kisses me back.

"Will I see you later?"

I brush another kiss against her lips. "I should be able to get back this evening." I hope I can anyway. I don't linger much longer, or I won't leave at all.

***

I'm just in the back door when Shane starts. "Where were you? Why can't you answer your phone?"

I don't answer him. Instead, I give Mary a gentle kiss on the cheek, and I get a smile for it.

"Some toast?" she asks, and I give her another kiss.

"You're the best, Mary," I say. Shane snorts, and I sit down across from him. "I was busy," I tell him and can see a muscle clench in his jaw.

"Doing what, Connor? Your job, I hope."

I lean in close to him. "What do you want?" I'm not in the mood for Shane. His condescending ways aren't going to fly with me.

Mary puts a cup of tea and toast in front of me. Shane's staring at her.

"Thanks, Mary," I tell her. She pats my shoulder and leaves the kitchen.

"Why have you got to be such a moody fucker to Mary? If I was her, I would poison your tea."

"That's why I make my own," Shane informs me. "I spoke to Brian, and he swore blind that Harry doesn't work for him. He had no idea what I was talking about."

"Well, then it must be true." My words have Shane slamming his fist against the table.

"What's going on?" Una speaks from the door, and Shane's face transforms. A smile is forced, and he unclenches his fist.

"Nothing. How did you sleep?" he asks her sweetly as she pulls out a chair beside me.

"I slept well." Her cheeks are red as she holds a coffee cup tightly in her hands.

"You smell good. What perfume are you wearing?" I lean into Una and sniff, and she laughs before taking a drink of coffee.

"I'm not wearing perfume," she tells me, and I let surprise flitter across my face.

"Really? You need to bottle that up and sell it. You could call it Una." She's laughing, as I intended, and I don't have to look up at Shane to know his blood is boiling over.

"So where did you sleep last night?" Una raises an eyebrow.

"Yes, Connor. We would all like to know," Shane says.

I don't look at Shane. "A mates," I tell Una, and she narrows her eyes.

"Boy or a girl?"

"What do you think?" I smirk, and she smiles. Now I flicker a glance at Shane. He's ready to come out of his chair. Picking up my cup, I take a long drink.

"You okay?" I ask him. "You look a little green." His chair scrapes the floor as he stands.

"I'm fine," he informs me, trying to look calm.

"Look who's home," Darragh shouts as he arrives in the kitchen, pointing to himself. He slaps me on the back. "Sorry about being a dick yesterday," he adds before sitting up on the table beside Una.

"Me too. So all good?" I ask, not sure what to say with Una sitting here, but she's munching away at her breakfast. Finn sits down opposite me with a bowl of cereal. Shane still lingers in the kitchen. I can feel him staring at my back. When I glance over my shoulder, he's watching me.

"Yeah, charges were dropped. They had nothing on me."

I take a quick look at Una again, and she doesn't seem effected at all by what he's saying.

"So that's it?" I ask.

He nods. "Yep. Yep. I am a frrreeee man." Finn rolls his eyes at Darragh's back.

"Darragh, can you not sit on the table?" Una says. "Your ass is, like, right beside my breakfast." Darragh slides off at Una's request and pulls out a chair across from her.

"I just like being beside you, sweetheart," he tells her, and I want to look at Shane.

Una doesn't respond.

"So I was wondering if it would suit you to meet Siobhan today for lunch," Finn asks me. Shane exhales loudly enough that Una looks at him. I don't know what passes between them, but he stays silent as Finn continues. "I would really like if you met her."

"Yeah, sure. I want to see who stole my brother's heart," I declare, and he grins. "Can't wait until you find someone. You won't be teasing me then."

"Maybe he already has." Shane talks as he makes his way back to the table. "Connor never arrived home last night."

"Who were you tipping?" Darragh asks, and I don't answer him.

"I was with a mate," I say, and Shane snorts.

"So you keep saying."

My eyes snap to his, and I hold his stare. I want to say that I was with Ava, but that would go down like a ton of bricks.

Shane turns his smart mouth to Finn. "You have to bring Darragh with you. Remember our agreement?"

Finn stiffens, and when he glares at Shane, I wait for an explosion. "He's not coming to meet Siobhan. She fucking hates him."

Darragh holds his hand over his heart. "She wounds me with her words."

"Then you're not going." Shane gives a final note that I don't like.

"Don't be a dick, Shane. Darragh can take care of himself. If you're that worried, why don't you stay with him?"

Everyone seems to be holding their breaths. Una stiffens beside me, but I don't give a crap.

"Shane, I'll stay with him." Una's voice carries a note of pleading.

"No, I don't want you around him. You know that."

"Jeez, everyone seems to really hate Darragh." Darragh doesn't sound hurt at all.

"Darragh, I don't hate you." Una rests her hand on his, and I'm waiting for Shane to flip the table. It's almost comical, only I don't like Shane's attitude toward Finn.

"That's settled," I tell Shane as I get up. No one speaks as I put my cup in the sink. I need a shower and fresh clothes. I leave the kitchen, Darragh on my heels.

"So I was wondering about the job we started but didn't finish." He waggles his eyebrows as he follows me into my bedroom.

"Don't you think you're in enough trouble?" I ask while pulling off my boots.

"Nah, that case was swallowed up into a black hole."

"I don't get it. They had your fingerprints in the woman's bedroom. How did that disappear?"

Darragh smirks as he takes a cigarette from behind his ear.

"Don't light that up in my room," I warn him, and he pushes it back behind his ear.

"So turns out Siobhan's aunty was the town's bike. She was doing a few young lads, mostly farmers in the area. So they didn't just find my fingerprints but others too." He bounces down on my bed as I remove my jumper.

"So I took one for the team. Said I was banging her." He shivers, and I bark a quick laugh at him.

"You're not right in the head," I tell him, getting up and slipping my phone out of my jeans before removing them.

"So am I back in?"

"Yeah, sure." He whoops.

"Now get out of my room." I enter the bathroom and turn on the shower.

"You're the best, Connor," Darragh shouts before closing my bedroom door.

* * *

I meet Siobhan in a small bistro in Kingscourt. I can see her and Finn through the large front windows. They look happy. I'm approaching the table when she looks up at me. Her brown eyes, sallow skin, and long dark hair make her look foreign.

"Siobhan?" I ask, and she smiles, flashing me a set of white teeth. She half rises and takes my outstretched hand.

"So great to meet you." She seems genuinely happy, and Finn is grinning as I sit down. Guilt churns in my stomach at seeing him happy with me here. He must have been so angry when I left.

"You too. Finn here won't shut up about you."

A small laugh bubbles up her throat, and she smiles across at Finn. "All good, I hope?"

"Every single word was praising you." She smiles softly again. She's easy to chat with, and we reminisce and laugh a lot. It makes me remember how much I missed Finn and how I don't think I can walk away and leave him behind again. And now it isn't just Finn I would be leaving but Ava too. That's becoming less of an option as each day moves by.

When Siobhan goes to bathroom, I know what Finn will ask. "So, what do you think?" He's looking for approval.

"Of what?" I get a smack on the arm for that, and I grin. "She's exactly what I thought she would be. You did good." His smile is wide now as he plays with the sugar sachets on the table.

"I'm going to ask her to marry me."

"That's a big commitment." That would be the first O'Reagan wedding.

"Yeah, I want her forever." His words are sincere, and it makes my mind go to Ava.

"You've turned into quite the sap," I tell him to lighten the mood, and he shrugs.

"What can I say?" His eyes flicker up, and Siobhan sits down.

"So what about you, Connor? Have you got a girlfriend?" Her innocent question doesn't feel so innocent to me.

"No, I can't seem to find one that will stay."

She giggles. "I don't believe that for a second." She's sweet, and I'm happy for Finn. Out of all of us, he deserves a happily ever after. We stay for a while longer before Siobhan has to get ready for work.

"It was a pleasure meeting you." I give both her cheeks a kiss and wink at Finn. But he isn't like Shane. He looks happy with my affection toward Siobhan. Finn goes back with Siobhan, and I drive my car back to the house. When I arrive, I pull my phone out and text Ava.

How is your day?

I sit in the car and wait for Ava to text back; it doesn't take her long.

Here with Nan. She's so happy you stayed last night. So am I. x Will I see you tonight?

Ah, shit. I should have checked to see if she needed to be dropped off anywhere.

How did you get there? Tell Nan I said hi. I'll be there tonight. X

Looking up, I see Shane leaning against the garage door. He just isn't going to give me a break today.

I read Ava's message before getting out.

Taxi. Nan said hi back. LOL Okay I will have food ready. What time?

"You can't be interfering in how we run things here," Shane bites out.

I slam the car door. "I'm not one of your lackeys, Shane." I move past him, and he pushes me back into the garage. I clench my fists.

"Don't touch me again," I warn him, and he raises both eyebrows.

"Darragh is a loose cannon. Finn is the only one who can keep him in line."

"I. Don't. Care." I say each word clearly. "I won't sit here as you dictate where we can and can't go."

Shane nods. "Like how you crossed into the north when you shouldn't have."

My heart stills, but I remember to breath and not let my facial expression show anything. "You're as bad as Liam. I was in Monaghan. That's hardly the fucking north."

"Belfast. Father's informant told us."

I nod. "Well, he's not doing a very good job is he? And have you actually met him?" I fold my arms across my chest. "I didn't think so, Shane. Are we done?"

"You seem to forget that I have eyes everywhere. So I do hope you're sleeping with Ava to gain information for me." His smirk has me taking a step back before I wipe it off his face.

"She knows nothing."

"Is that why she was seen at the Gardaí station?"

Bastard has eyes everywhere.

"I don't get you, Shane. Why put me on the job if you have others on it?"

"Because I don't trust you."

"Then ask one of your other brothers to do it."

He shifts and looks away before remembering himself and relaxing, but the tell was there. He can't go to them. Why, I'm not sure. "I will."

His lie has me snorting at him. "So my job here is done?" I ask, hoping to catch him, but I don't like his response at all.

"Yeah, consider your job done." He leaves the garage, and his words unsettle me. He has someone watching Ava. I just pray it isn't Brian. I shoot off another text to Ava.

I should be there around eight. If you need me for anything, just ring. X

I return to the house feeling unsettled. I didn't really think Shane would dismiss me like that. That could mean I read this situation completely wrong, or he's going to take care of it himself. The thoughts of him putting his hands near Ava has me stiffening. Panic swirls viciously inside my stomach, and when I find him in the kitchen alone, I can't help my next words. They're stupid and reckless, but I need to protect Ava. Right now, there seems to be only one thing that Shane cares about more than himself.

He looks up immediately when I step into the kitchen. I don't know what he sees in my eyes, but he's standing now.

"If you touch Ava, and I mean one hair on her head, I will hurt Una." The lie sounds convincing with how my body coils and tightens at the idea of him hurting Ava.

His response is unexpected. He charges me. I'm not ready and find myself on my back. His fists hit my face hard and fast, and I flip him on one of his pauses. I don't hesitate but make each punch heavy and fast. He gains the upper hand again as he pushes my head into the floor, his knee connecting with my back and knocking the air from my lungs.

If I don't get out of this position, he'll win. I snap my head back, connecting with his face. I'm released and standing. Shane's up too as blood sprays from his nose and makes a pathway down his shirt. Liquid drips from my ears, and when I brush my fingertips to my ear, my fingers come away slick with blood.

"That one's for free," I tell him, and he charges again, only this time I'm ready. The uppercut connects with his chin, and Shane's head snaps back as he stumbles and hits the floor. That punch has taken many men down, but Shane is getting back up.

"You want some more?" I'm egging him on when Liam arrives.

"That's enough," he warns us, and Shane seems to loosen, but he hasn't taken his eyes off me. I drop my fists.

"Yeah, I'll let you walk away this time," I tell Shane, and his temper snaps again as he moves toward me. I'm ready, but Liam wraps an arm around Shane's chest.

"Some battles you just can't win," he tells Shane, and I smirk.

"You hear that? Even Liam thinks you're weak." I watch a vein bulge along his neck.

"No, Connor, you're wrong. Shane will outmaneuver you any day. He just won't use his fists, while fists is all you have. That will fade with time, and then so will you."

"Fuck you," I tell Liam and leave the room. I want to hurt someone. His words shadow my thoughts now, and I know he will outmaneuver me when it comes to Ava. Because this is what Shane is good at.

CHAPTER SEVENTEEN

AVA

N AN LOOKS SO MUCH brighter today, and she's been a ray of sunshine since I told her about Connor spending the night and coming over again tonight.

"You be careful, birdy. That one has the armor to break hearts," she warns me, and I know she's right. I'm already falling hard for Connor. Any more time with him, and I'll be in so deep that I won't be able to get back out.

"But who am I kidding? That boy is here to stay. Just look at you, birdy. A heart of gold."

I squeeze Nan's hand. "I really like him," I confess.

"Don't I know. It's written all over your face. You're in love."

My eyes widen. "I don't think it's love, but..." It's pretty close. "Anyway, I have to get to work. I'm on a short shift, only three to seven."

"Okay, sweetheart. Now don't be coming back up here tomorrow. Take the day off, and I'll see you when you have time."

I kiss her cheek and ignore her. "I'll see you again in the morning," I tell her, and she purses her lips together trying to appear all annoyed.

"See you, birdy, and love you."

"Love you too," I tell her, and I leave the hospital ward and make my way down to the taxi rank.

I get to work twenty minutes later. I'm early, but I head on in and am surprised to find the bar and lounge empty. Normally, Paul and his friends would be here, but the place is deserted.

"Hello?" I call out as I stuff my bag and jacket under the desk.

I scream as Patrick seems to materialize at the other side of the bar. "Jesus, Patrick, I didn't see you." I'm half laughing as I clutch my heart.

"Ah, sorry, Ava. I didn't mean to scare you."

I'm waving off his apology. "Hope everything was alright the other day. I was worried."

Patrick looks away with guilt shadowing his eyes. I try to think and remember now how I left work, running out the door like the hounds of hell were on my heels.

"I forgot. Yeah, everything was fine. Don't be worrying." Now I understand his guilt. He had, after all, stood there without intervening. Patrick scratches his jaw, dark circles under his eyes, makes me want to take away his guilt. He has enough on his plate, and going up against Brian isn't exactly an option.

"Everything is fine, Patrick," I reassure him again, and this time when he glances up, he nods, desperate to believe me. "I better get to work before the boss catches me slacking," I tell him, and he smiles a little.

All through my shift, I can only think of one thing: Connor. He consumes my every thought. Paul and his friends arrive and even ask me what I'm smiling about.

"Mind your own business," I answer, but I can't stop the stupid smile that keeps creeping across my face.

I start to polish all the glasses that are never used but are mostly decoration above the bar. The dust has me sneezing, and I make a mental note not to let it get into this kind of state again.

"Ava." It's Paul's voice that has me looking down, but my eyes snap to Brian, who stands beside him.

My heart immediately starts to slam against my chest. I drop the cloth and get down off the bar. "I went to your place last night, but you weren't there. Where were you?" His blue eyes are ablaze with anger.

"You're barred!" My voice carries across the bar, but the anger I feel right now isn't containable. He might have put his hands on me, but not my nan. She raised me, loved me, protected me, and I brought him to her door.

"Get out!" My shouts make him flinch, and it gives me a sense of power. I can feel Patrick standing behind me.

"You heard her. You're barred." At first, Patrick's words give me a confidence I haven't had in a while, until Brian starts to laugh.

"Patrick, get your dumb ass in the back and close your little door," Brian says. And like that, I'm reminded of the power that Brian holds over people. Patrick doesn't move, and Brian's eyes flash with violence. I don't want to see Patrick hurt, and I bow my head, ready to give in.

"I think you should leave," Paul says. Him and his friends are holding pool sticks, all ready for action. If you ignore the slight tremble in Paul's voice, or how his friends' hands shake, you would think they could win this.

"What are you serving today, Ava? Courage? Because if everyone doesn't take a step back from me, I'm really going to lose it. You want that, Ava? You want more people hurt because of you?" Brian grips the bar like it's my neck. This is all going to end badly.

"Paul, please, it's fine. I'm fine." They move away, and they all wear a look of relief. My eyes dim, but Brian's seem to shine with victory. Patrick doesn't leave, and I don't ask him to.

"What do you want?" I grit my teeth.

"I want you to tell me where you were last night."

"At home."

His fist slams into the bar counter. "Stop lying. I checked."

"What, you can see through my door?"

"No, Ava. I got a key off Sean. Some of your clothes were gone."

I want to throw up on the counter. He was in my apartment, with my stuff, and as for Sean giving out my key without permission, he really is the worst landlord ever.

"I stayed at a hotel."

"Which one?"

"Jesus, Brian, can't you just leave me alone?" The whine in my voice comes through.

"You lied to me, Ava. You're still lying to me."

"Brian, maybe you should go." Patrick speaks behind me. The sound is odd.

"Maybe you should shut your mouth before I close it permanently." His threat has Patrick tutting, but silence falls. Now I pray for customers, but no one arrives.

"Patrick, can I take a break?" I ask, still looking at Brian.

"Yeah, take whatever time you need."

I don't turn to Patrick as I move up the bar and watch Brian follow me. I grab my bag and coat and try to make my way outside; it will be safer if I'm surrounded by lots of people. But Brian blocks the door.

"You're testing my patience, Ava." He takes a step toward me, and I take one back.

"I just want to be left alone," I tell him and soften my voice.

"Please, Brian, just let me go." My words were meant to make him remember what we had, but they don't. Instead, he throws his head back and starts laughing.

"That's not going to happen, sweetheart."

"What do you want from me?" I'm shouting again, but I can't keep doing this.

"You. I want you." He grips my arms and bile rises up my throat.

"I don't want you," I whisper to him, knowing that will bring out his anger.

"You're such a dumb tramp." His words are as effective as a slap to the face. I step away from him and don't respond. "I'm the only fucking reason you're alive." He runs his hands through his hair.

I have no idea what that means, but Brian has a vision of himself as a God. "I want to leave. Move." My throat burns, but I need to get away from him now. His hands grip my shoulders again, his fingers digging in.

"Where the fuck were you last night?" His anger is vibrating up my arms.

"With Connor." I know I shouldn't say it, but I want to see the hurt on his face, and the moment I do, I regret it.

His slap knocks me to the floor. "You're such a fucking slut, Ava."

I'm staring at gray tiles, telling my lungs to take in oxygen, telling myself that this can't happen again. I'm picturing my nan, so small in the hospital, and thinking how he put his hands on her. I'm up, and when my hand connects with his face, the sound is so satisfying. I get two slaps in before he gets over the shock. He grips my wrists, and the pain runs up my arms. I try to knee him in the balls, but he moves his leg.

"You're going to regret that," he tells me.

"The only thing I regret is setting eyes on you. You make me sick."

He pushes me against the bar, and my back erupts in pain. Everything seems to happen so fast. I glimpse Patrick behind him, a heavy crystal ashtray in his hand, and it comes down on Brian's head. His eyes widen, and he stares at me in confusion before releasing me as he falls to the floor.

"Go, Ava. You need to leave now."

I'm struggling to breathe, but I'm nodding, picking up my bag that must have fallen in the struggle.

I'm out the door. The fresh air makes me question whether that just happened. Tears burn my eyes as I run down the street while glancing back over my shoulder. My eyes scan the few people, but none of them are Brian. *Deep breaths*, I tell myself while trying to calm my erratic heartbeat. My face burns, and with shaky hands, I touch it. He didn't break the skin this time.

Patrick won't just walk away from hitting Brian over the head. I slow my pace and stop in a doorway. The step is cold under me; my legs are unable to carry me any further. My hand trembles as I push hair behind my ear. A couple walks past me and eyes me suspiciously. I wonder if they would stop if I were to ask them for help. I'm scrolling through my phone, trying to calm myself as I search for Connor's number. Reality is, he will try to pick a fight with Brian and end up hurt too. I want to scream in frustration.

"Ava." The roar of my name has me frozen on the step. Brian was always possessive, but this is psychotic. Should I run to the Gardaí station? They might not let me press charges, but surely they couldn't let him beat me. I'm up now and running around by the credit union. When he shouts my name again, I know he sees me. It's all uphill now, and he's gaining on me. Blood soaks his shirt, but I can't see where from. It must be the back of his head. A part of me wants to stop running and plead with him not to do this, but I don't think he could be reasoned with in this state.

"Ava, I just want to talk." His words are meant to calm me, but they drive a panic through my system that makes me run faster.

I'm weaving between traffic, my panic escalating. A black Mercedes stops in front of me, and I recognize the taxi man. I'm in the passenger seat looking over my shoulder. "Headfort Demesne. Please. Quickly." The taxi man doesn't ask questions, and I watch Brian grow smaller in the mirror.

CHAPTER EIGHTEEN

CONNOR

My ear is still bleeding, and I wipe blood away using my sleeve. I'm in the hall when Mary opens the door. Two detectives are in the doorway, showing Mary their badges. She turns to me and so do the two men.

"Liam," I call over my shoulder. He appears beside me. "You got visitors," I tell him. He fixes his tie and walks toward Mary. His confidence is something to be admired. I don't go into my room. My ear is killing me. I move closer to make sure I don't miss a beat. The one on the right with a shaky beard eyes me, and I give him a nod. His attention returns to Liam.

"What can I do for you gentlemen?" Liam places a hand on Mary's shoulder, dismissing her, and she scurries past me and into the kitchen. A grin spreads across my face at her large inhale. Shane must still be in the kitchen, his face a bloody mess.

A piece of paper is passed to Liam. He accepts but doesn't look at it. "What is this?" he asks.

"A warrant to search land that's registered in Michael O'Reagan's name."

Liam hands them back their warrant, and they glance at one another. "I trust you. Let us know when you're done. Anything else I can help you gentlemen with today?" They look as confused as I feel.

The one with the beard takes the warrant and places it in the pocket of his jacket. "That's all today."

Once Liam has the door closed, something changes in his posture, and he moves quickly back toward the kitchen. So everything isn't okay. I follow him into the kitchen.

"Mary, the rest of the day is yours," Liam tells her. Mary doesn't miss a beat as she moves past us, grabbing her jacket and going out the back door. Shane stands taller when I walk into the kitchen.

"Now's not the time. We just had two detectives at the door. They have a warrant to search the bog."

Liam's words have Shane's anger toward me deflating. "I've moved all the bodies," he tells Liam while getting ice out of the fridge. After wrapping ice cubes in a towel, he holds it to his face. My ear is on fire. I do the same, wrapping some ice cubes in a towel and holding it to my ear.

"All the bodies? I thought it was just the old woman."

"So you found the girl?" Liam says to Shane. No one answers me, but now that makes two.

"You lied to me. You told me you rang it in," Shane says back through gritted teeth.

"How long have you known?" Liam sounds almost impressed.

Shane looks away. "I found the body a while later."

"And dare I ask what you were doing up there?" Liam questions, and the answer is clear—burying a body. That makes three.

"Where are they all now?" I ask, and finally Shane looks at me.

"Loch Leigh Mountain."

On our back door. But they would be well hidden, and we owned land at the base of it.

"You did that all yourself?" Liam questions.

"Yes, Liam." Shane's anger is under the surface, ready to break through. I don't understand what Liam is saying that is riling him up so much. But the mention of the girl's body has the tension building in the room.

"So we have nothing to worry about?" Liam is like a dog with a bone. I remove the cloth from my ear. Blood soaks the towel, and I want to punch Shane again.

"I made sure everything was removed. Unless you buried more people and forgot to mention it?"

"No, you seem to have found them all. I'll inform Darragh and Finn." Liam leaves the room, and I'm alone with Shane.

"I think you busted my eardrum," I tell him and he glares at me.

"Good." He moves past me but pauses at my shoulder. "Get ready. We better all go down to the bog and intimidate the fuckers."

"You think that's wise?" I ask his retreating back.

"Yes, Connor, I do."

I change my shirt and hang out in the garage as I wait for the others. My phone is in my pocket on silent, but I check it before Finn arrives into the garage. Nothing from Ava. I slide it into my pocket and get into the car while Finn jumps into the passenger seat.

"This is so fucked up. This is beside were Siobhan lives." He scratches his brow as he stares out the window. "I was the one that convinced her to sell us the land." Now he faces me. "I wish I never had."

I get what he is saying. I wish I had never approached Ava under false pretenses, because now I have no idea how all this ends.

"Yeah, it seems a mess," I tell him as Darragh comes out into the garage. His eyes meet mine, and he rubs his hands together.

"You better wipe that smile off your face," Finn barks at Darragh as he climbs into the back. He's like a child ready to go on a road trip. Darragh lights up, and I let him smoke. I reverse out as Shane and Liam get into separate vehicles.

"I think it's dumb, us going down there." Darragh blows smoke in between the seats.

"I think it's dumb that you killed Siobhan's aunt." Finn swings around in the seat and faces Darragh.

"Yeah, I'm sorry, man," Darragh replies. I can't see him, but I can picture him shrugging.

"What about the girl?" I ask and move the rearview mirror so I can see him. Guilt is there across his face.

"She was a pro." He shrugs now like I pictured he had before.

"You killed someone else?" Finn yells. I tap him on the shoulder to try to get him to calm down and sit back down. He turns around in his seat.

"Jesus. I was banging her, and she was dead—I think, a junkie. So yeah, she's there too."

"Anyone else?" Finn asks, but he's growing paler by the second.

"I don't know."

We grow silent as we pull up beside the land. Shane's and Liam's vehicles pull up across the road beside the detective's cars and a forensic van. Neither Liam nor Shane get out of their vehicles, so we sit in mine as Darragh lights up another cigarette. Finn rolls down his window, and I glance at Darragh in the mirror. He grins as he blows smoke out of the side of his mouth and toward Finn.

The moment Shane steps out of his car, I grin. He has cleaned all the blood away, but his face is red, bruised, and swollen. I feel satisfied.

"You sure did a number on him," Darragh says, blowing smoke too close to my face.

"I'll do a number on you if you don't blow that smoke somewhere else." That somewhere else becomes Finn, who swings around and faces Darragh.

"Come on. Lets go," I tell them, getting out before they kill each other. I don't remember them ever fighting this much.

Liam steps out wearing a full-length trench coat. He fits the criminal mastermind bill to a tee. I want to tell him to tone it down, but it's Liam.

"What I don't understand is how they know we had land here and why they decided to check. You said all charges were dropped against Darragh." Shane questions Liam.

"Finding out we own the land wouldn't be hard, and with Darragh's connection to the aunt and Finn to Siobhan, they would piece it together. Why they're searching is the part I want to know." Liam moves forward, and we all find ourselves falling into place beside him.

No one stops us as we move across the land to where a digger is tearing up the ground.

"They're digging in the right place," Shane tells Liam. Someone squealed. The two detectives that were at the door turn to see us coming, and the one with the beard approaches us.

"You can't be here right now." His eyes flicker across all of us, but he addresses Liam.

"You got your men and equipment here fast," Liam counteracts.

"They were on standby. You need to leave, Mr. O'Reagan."

Darragh snorts, but the detective holds Liam's stare.

"David, isn't it?" Liam asks. The detective stands a little straighter. "David O'Hara?" Liam says his name slowly, and David's jaw tightens.

"My name is no concern to you." He doesn't sound so sure now.

The digger stops digging. "We got something." The man on the digger jumps down and fixes a cap on his head before going over to the hole.

David smirks at us like we're all going down. The forensics team, all in white suits, moves in. I want to see what's in the hole. One of them glances at David.

"Detective," he calls, and David gives us all a warning look. "None of you move." He turns and goes over to the men.

"What could be there?" Liam asks, and when I glance at Shane, he's grinning.

"I buried livestock around the place."

I'm grinning now as they pull out the carcass of a cow.

"Finn." We all turn as a female voice comes from behind us. It's Siobhan. Her red puffy eyes and folded arms have us all feeling a bit sorry for Finn.

He's beside her, shaking his head. "What are you doing here?"

"I heard they're digging here, looking for a body. Is that true?" Her voice rises, and Shane clenches his hands.

"It's all a mistake, Siobhan." He doesn't sound convincing. Siobhan glances up at me, and I nod, but she refocuses on Finn.

"You never told me that Darragh was brought in for questioning about my aunt."

Oh, Christ. I didn't pity him for one moment.

"He needs to get rid of her," Liam tells Shane, who turns to do that, and I step in his way.

"Leave him alone. Just give him a minute." We stare at each other. I don't want to fight, but that would make everything worse for Finn.

"The charges were dropped, Siobhan," Finn says. "Darragh is an asshole."

Darragh snorts at that. "Everyone loves calling me names," he mumbles under his breath.

"But he is no killer." This time, I believe Finn.

David is making his way back, and Liam is right. Siobhan shouldn't be here for this.

"Hi." I approach them with hands in my pockets. "They are nearly finished, but they want everyone off the land." I give an apologetic shrug. "Maybe you should take Siobhan home," I suggest.

"Yeah, you're right." Finn wraps an arm around Siobhan, and she leans into him. "I'll catch you later." Finn leaves.

"See, you don't have to be a dick to get the job done," I tell Shane.

"Okay, you all need to leave now." David doesn't meet anyone's eye, embarrassed that he didn't find a body.

"Tell your wife I said hi," Darragh says while blowing smoke toward David. Sometimes, I don't get him. Why does he antagonize the Gardaí?

"Get off this land." His shoulders tense as he approaches Darragh.

Darragh flicks his cigarette on the ground. "I was leaving anyway."

"We can use that as evidence." David points to the cigarette butt, and Darragh laughs.

"If you had my sperm inside a woman, you dumb cunts still couldn't solve the case."

That is how you get yourself arrested.

Liam shakes his head as Darragh is put in cuffs and escorted off the land by a female Gardaí he gives abuse to.

"Now, I suggest you leave before I arrest you all." David's final warning has me turning. I reach my car as the one Gardaí pulls off with Darragh in the back seat, grinning like he's off to a party.

Shane waves me over as he climbs into Liam's Jeep. The Jeep is still warm as I climb into the back.

"Someone reported us. They're digging in the exact same spot where the bodies were." Liam glances at me in the rearview mirror.

"I've never stood on that land, so don't look at me."

"I'm not, Connor. I just want you to question Darragh and find out if he did."

"Ask him yourself." I reach for the handle, ready to get out, but the door won't open. "A child lock. You think that will keep me in?" I ask Liam.

"We are having a civilized conversation. Everything doesn't have to resort to violence."

I flick the door handle roughly a few times to get a reaction out of Liam, but I don't succeed.

"Finn?" Liam questions, looking at Shane.

"No, he's too loyal, and he wouldn't drop himself into the middle of a murder investigation. Especially now, with Siobhan." Shane's logic is correct. If I put my money on anyone, it would be Darragh.

"That leaves us with Darragh." Liam looks at me again in the review mirror.

"Why don't I go bail him out and ask him," I suggest. The locks pop, and I open my door.

"They took him to Nobber Gardaí station." I don't ask Liam how he knows, but I run across the road and get into my car. The smell of smoke has me rolling down the window as I head for Nobber.

***

"I'm here to bail out Darragh O'Reagan."

The female Gardaí stares at me, her eyes dead as she focuses on her screen and types away. They have one holding cell here. I know because I sat in it many times. Mostly for fighting.

I glance around at the small reception area as my phone vibrates. As I'm reaching for it, my thoughts go to Ava.

Mark McGuiness is home alone now.

The message is from Neill, and the name is one of the guys that beat him up.

"I knew you would come rescue me."

I turn as Darragh is brought out by the bangharda. He's winking at her as she removes the cuffs. "Maybe when you're off duty, we could get a drink." She has a face that would sour milk as she pushes Darragh toward the door.

I grin, and he holds his hands over his heart. "Shot down again," he tells me as we leave the station.

"You need to control your mouth," I inform him, and he lights up a cigarette as he climbs into the car.

"I'm only having a laugh. Everyone is so uptight."

No traffic is coming, and I pull out onto the road. "So I've been tasked with asking you if you told anyone where the bodies were buried."

"They're dumb fucks," Darragh says, and I flicker a quick glance at him. "Why would I tell anyone? I don't think this face would fare well in prison. I would be a piece of meat."

I'm grinning at him. "Yeah, I thought as much, but I had to ask."

"I don't mind that everyone thinks I'm that much of a fuckup." His words are said with a smile, but something darker lingers in them.

"How about we blow off some steam?"

He's sitting up in the car now, his head bobbling. "What you got in mind? Women? Drinks?" He's working himself up.

"More like hurting someone," I say.

"I'm down with that."

CHAPTER NINETEEN

CONNOR

I HAVE EVERYTHING IN the boot of the car, so we don't need to swing by home. My phone starts to ring. It's Liam, but I hit silent. Darragh smirks. "You'll pay for that later."

"What can he do?" I ask Darragh. Their fear of Liam is nearly unjustified. I never remember him putting his hand on any of us. He never raises his voice. I know I've always felt an element of respect toward him but not fear. Yet, even Shane wouldn't disobey Liam.

"Whatever he wants." Darragh's tone is low as he faces the window.

"Like what?"

"I don't know, man. Whatever. He's just scary." His lie is delivered with a smirk.

I want to dig further, but we're coming up on Mark's house. His house is only three miles outside of Kells. I pull into an opening a few houses down. Cattle roam the fields. It's drizzling, so I hope that keeps any walkers inside.

"We'll leave the car here," I tell Darragh and get everything we need from the boot of the car. I hand him the balaclava and his bat, and he strokes her.

"Now you got to follow my lead," I tell Darragh while closing the trunk. "No killing animals at all."

He closes his eyes slightly. "Fine."

It's always a mistake to bring Darragh on a job, but he's easy to work with. We hop the side wall. Electric gates rise high into the air, but the walls on either side are low, defeating the purpose. We both move quietly along the side of the house. My eyes move quickly, checking the corner of the house for cameras, but apart from the gates, the house is easy to get into.

The double doors off the patio are unlocked, and I nod at Darragh. We pull the balaclavas over our faces as I push open the door and wait a beat before entering. Mark is messy; bundles of clothes are stacked on the table. Not just male but also female, and a pile of small children's clothing sits right in the center. Dishes are stacked up in the sink, and leftovers still sit in open takeout containers.

We move into the hall. Straight ahead are several doors, and there's one to my left. I point for Darragh to check it as I move down the hall. The first room is a utility room that stinks of rubbish that spills over the side of a bin. The next room is a bedroom. I'm not sure if it's for a male or female—everything is cream.

"You enjoying yourself?" Darragh's voice sounds loud in the silence, and another muffled voice sounds next.

"What the fuck?" I make my way toward the voices.

The room that Darragh checked is a sitting room. The rich red rug under my feet is soft, and the cream leather sofas look new. Mark has his dick in his hand.

"Nothing worse than being caught with your trousers down, huh?" Darragh laughs at him while pointing the bat at his head. I hold up my hand in warning.

Mark tucks his dick back into his pants and sits up. His white vest top showcases that both arms are covered in tats. A diamond earing flashes in the light.

"I'm going to make this really simple," I say. "We're the guys that got your friend David." His face pales a little, and I'm glad my message got around. "So you know why we're here, then."

He nods but holds up his hands. "Look, we just do the jobs we get paid to do. That's it. It's not personal. It's just a job."

I push a cushion over his face and hold him down. "His hip."

Darragh swings wide, and the crack has Mark screaming and wriggling under my hold.

"Help me hold him," I say. Darragh grabs his legs as he continues to thrash under us. "Who paid you?" I ask and lift the cushion.

"Man, you know they'll kill me."

I cover his face again, and he screams. One nod to Darragh has him swinging the bat down on his ankles. Mark's screams tear through the room, but his thrashing has lessened.

"Please stop." Drool mixes with tears as he pleads with us.

"Just tell me who paid."

He's nodding now. "Brian."

"Brian paid you to beat up Neill?" That makes no sense.

"Brian is a twisted fucker. It's possible," Darragh says while leaning on his bat.

"Look, I don't know why. All I know is he wanted him beaten pretty bad, and we told Neill it was from Brian." I believe him.

"So we're good." He's half crying, and I pat him on the head.

"Yeah, we're good." He protests as I cover his face again and let Darragh take some of his frustration out with his bat.

We leave as easily as we arrived. Neill knowing that Brian sent the men makes me question everything about him. Why didn't' he tell me?

Once we're back in the car, I check my phone. Six missed calls from Liam. I dial him back.

Liam answers the phone. "Did you manage to collect Darragh?"

"Yeah, you want to talk to him?" I ask, pulling out and onto the road.

"Did you ask?" Liam replies. I glance at Darragh. His leg is up on my dash as he stares out the window.

"Yeah, and he didn't tell anyone. Like he said, he's too good looking for prison."

Darragh snorts before lighting up another cigarette.

"Where are you now?" Liam asks.

"On our way home," I tell him. He hangs up with not even a goodbye.

"Is he always so moody?" I ask Darragh, and he grins.

***

I don't go in. I drop Darragh off before I turn the car and make my way to Ava. Why would Brian have Neill beaten up? Why would Neill lie to me about it? The security waves me on in at Headfort Demesne, and I pull up outside.

After ringing the bell four times and getting no answer, I ring Ava's phone.

"I'm at the door," I tell her the moment she answers.

"One second." She sounds strange. I can hear movement inside, and when she opens the door, her head is ducked down. Her shoulders hunch forward like they're trying to wrap themselves around her and protect her.

I close the door behind me, and she still hasn't looked up. Dread snakes its way down my spine. All I can think of is that Shane told her. Somehow she knows.

"Ava."

She looks up at me when I whisper her name. My blood turns to ice in my veins, and I'm holding her face and moving her into the light.

"Who did this?" My voice sounds calm.

"I don't know what to do anymore." Tears fall down her cheeks and make a pathway to her chin before they free fall. Her face is swollen and red, so the slap was hard, but it didn't break the skin.

"When did this happen?"

"At work."

I nod. "Let's take a look." I shrug out of my jacket and get a towel and some ice out of the freezer.

"I already iced it," she tells me, and I take a deep breath. Moving, doing something, is keeping me calm. I continue what I'm doing. She's standing at the counter. Ava inhales deeply when I press the towel to her face. I search her face for any other marks, but it seems to be the only one.

"Are you hurt anywhere else?" I question. She looks up at me from under wet lashes.

"My back." Her lip trembles, and I focus on the material in my hand, on the counter behind Ava, on everything but her.

"Can you say something?" I look into watery green eyes and clench my jaw.

"Let me see your back." She nods as I remove the towel from her face.

Lifting her top, she turns around. "Is it bad?"

My fingers gently touch the bruised skin. "No," I lie. "Is it sore?"

"I took two painkillers. It's not so bad now."

Everything inside me is climbing, scouring, and wanting out. My arms wrap around Ava as I bury my head in her neck. I don't want to say I'm sorry. That I should have dealt with this earlier. I don't want to give her excuses. So I hold her. She turns in my arms, her eyes searching my face.

"I fought back," she tells me proudly, and I place my forehead against hers. I nod, because words have failed me. I want her to stop talking. I can't bear to hear another second of it. I want to remove the pain in her eyes.

My lips touch hers, and I wait for her to kiss me back. I won't proceed if she doesn't, but Ava kisses me back with a ferocity that I match. The kiss seems to calm the rage inside me, and I slow our pace, kissing her softly. I keep closing my eyes, but each time, my mind paints me a picture of what might have happened. Emerald green eyes stare into mine.

I'm searching her face as her breath brushes against my lips. This feeling of rage mixed with something else is unlike anything I have ever felt before.

My hand finds her, and I guide her to the bedroom. Her wide eyes and swollen lips make her look innocent. I close the door behind me and take her face in my hands, kissing her lips softly. I ignore the tightness of my jeans and the hunger to be inside her, and I focus only on her.

I move my mouth across her cheek before kissing her damaged one. I want to erase the marks that he left on her.

"Your silence is a bit frightening." Ava whispers the words against my neck.

"I'm not silent. I'm just communicating in a different way." The only way I can right now. She nods her understanding. "Raise your arms."

She does immediately, and I pull her top over her head. Reaching around her, I unclip her bra and let it move down her arms. I follow it with kisses. On my knees now, I press my lips to her flat stomach and she inhales deeply, her hands sinking into my hair.

As I rise, her hands fall to my shoulders. My tongue flickers out along her collarbone, and she inhales deeply again. Her nipples brush against my chest, and my jeans tighten further, painfully. Her hands are warm when I remove them from my shoulders and turn her around. She doesn't question me as I start at her back next and trail kisses across the bruises. Her wounds feel like my wounds. I could have stopped this. Air lodges itself in my lungs, and the snake tightens its hold.

"Connor?" Ava turns around, and I'm struggling to meet her eye. "Make love to me." Her request is spoken so gently that it feels fragile, like glass that should be wrapped in cotton wool.

I'm nodding as I remove her trousers and then her underwear. Ava stands still. She doesn't try to hide herself. She allows me to see her. My jeans fall to the floor along with my boxers, and I give Ava the same time to examine me. When her eyes travel back up to mine and her cheeks are flushed, I move us back onto the bed. My hand touches her knees, and she spreads her legs, allowing me access. She's tight and wet when I enter her, and we both exhale. My arms hold me above her as I move slowly, my eyes never leaving hers. Her hands reach out and direct my face to hers. There's a pause. It's brief. Her lips move, but no words come out before she kisses me. When her tongue moves into my mouth, my control slips, and I deepen the kiss and my thrust. She feels so good under me.

"Ah, Connor." When she calls my name, I'm moving faster, pumping harder, and I keep climbing. Her soft skin brushes mine. Her breasts bounce as I push my body harder and faster, and when she screams my name, I pour my seed inside her.

***

I feel worse after. I thought it might help the rage, but it only pushed it into the cage, and now the beast is rattling its cage.

"Connor?" Ava lies in my arms, her fingers roaming across my tattoos, like she might understand them better.

"Yeah?" I answer, placing a kiss on her forehead.

"What's your favorite color?"

"Green." I kiss her nose. "The same green as your eyes."

She narrows her eyes and smirks. "Such a charmer."

"I bet yours is brown," I tease.

"Blue. Ocean blue. I find it calming."

I store away all the little snippets she shares with me.

"I keep waiting for you to run out the door." Her confession is said with furrowed brows.

I'm up on an elbow so I can see her face fully. "Why would you say that?"

Her cheeks pinken. "Just... since you met me, I've brought so much disarray into your life."

"My life was in disarray well before you came along," I tell her.

"Like what?" She doesn't seem to believe me.

"Okay, remember my brother Darragh?" She nods. "He wasn't at a party the other day. He was being held in the Gardaí station on suspicion of murder."

She's clutching the blanket.

"He didn't," I tell her. "All charges were dropped."

Her grip loosens. "I'm so sorry you had to go through that."

I'm lying back down. "It's nothing really. But just don't ever think I'm going to run," I tell the ceiling. It's her running that's the real issue. She just doesn't know it yet.

She takes the position that I just had. Leaning over me, she kisses my shoulder. "I want to know everything about you."

No, you don't.

"What do you want to know?"

She chews her lip. "Have you had many girlfriends?"

"Yes."

Her nostril's flare, but she nods. "I've had lots of boyfriends."

Her statement does two things to me. One, I know she's saying it because she's jealous, so that makes me feel a bit taller, but I also don't like the idea of anyone else touching her.

"I don't want to know." I clench my jaw so I don't say anymore. Her soft laugh has me raising both eyebrows at her.

"It's nice when you're jealous." She's still smiling down at me when her phone rings. I'm up, moving to it.

"It's Patrick," I tell her, but her eyes are glued to the bottom part of my body.

Her hand shoots out. "Let me answer. I'd say he's worried."

I give her the phone and get dressed. The reality of what happened to her is crashing back down on me. I order a pizza again as she chats with Patrick. She's thanking him for helping her.

I give her space as she chats and wait in the living area. Ava arrives into the living area wearing a pair of tiny shorts and an oversized T-shirt, but the worry in her eyes has me forgetting her tanned legs.

"What's wrong?"

"Patrick doesn't think it's a good idea for me to go back to work."

"I agree with Patrick."

"No, Connor. Why should I lose my job because of Brian? And if I don't have a job, I don't have money, and I can't do anything."

I hold her hands in mine. "Breathe, Ava. You'll find another job, and maybe that one just wasn't for you anyway." I can't mention Brian's name right now.

Her eyes continue to fill up.

"My friend Russell was saying he was looking for someone to help him out with all his rental properties."

Ava tilts her head to the side. "You're so sweet. But I know you're making that up."

I am, but I could make it real. "No, I swear." I cross my heart, and I get a smile.

"What would I have to do, clean and stuff?"

"No. No, maybe show people the properties, get contracts signed, and stuff like that."

"I'm not qualified." Ava tucks her long, tanned legs under her.

"You said it yourself when I met you. You're a people person. So this would be interacting with lots of people."

She chews her lips, but I can see her bending. "Well, if the job is going. Yeah." Her smile widens, and I kiss her gently on the lips.

"I ordered pizza."

"You are going to make me fat."

My mind goes to a child growing in her stomach, and I wipe it away quickly. The idea is way too appealing to me.

"You're perfect," I tell her as the doorbell rings. I get our food, and we sit down on the couch to eat, chatting but not talking about what happened, and it's nice. Ava's funny, and she makes me laugh. She makes talking easy.

CHAPTER TWENTY

CONNOR

L AST NIGHT, I BARELY slept. My adrenaline was running too high. I'm not used to sitting and waiting, but on this, I have to. After breakfast, I drop Ava off at the hospital. Once she's finished, she promises me she will go straight home. She won't have any problems, because now I let myself focus on Brian and what he did to her as I drive to Kells.

"Neill, I was wondering if I could drop around soon for a chat. You still at your ma's?"

"Yeah, sure, Connor. I'll be here."

"See you soon." I hang up as I pull in beside Smyth's pub. It's locked. I snagged Ava's phone when she showered this morning and got Patrick's number out of it.

"Hello?"

"Patrick. It's Connor O'Reagan. I'm looking for Brian."

Movement at an upstairs window has me glancing up. Patrick lets the curtain fall back into place.

"I haven't seen him. But if I do, I'll let you know."

"I want to hurt him for putting his hands on Ava." I know Patrick likes Ava, so he might be more willing to cooperate.

"You have my word, Connor. That animal deserves to be put down."

Cars zoom past, and I have to wait a moment before I can cross the road. "Thanks Patrick." I climb into the car before pulling out and making my way to Neill's house. His mother answers the door. She's a large woman, and only at four foot.

She shuffles away from the door. "Connor, how are you?"

I have to move one foot in front of the other as she makes a slow path to the kitchen. "I'm good, Mrs O'Reilly. You look great," I say once we reach the kitchen. I plant a kiss on her cheek, and she swipes me away.

"You'll have a cup of tea."

"I wouldn't leave without one." I tell her, and she clicks on the kettle. Her body jiggles as she continues to laugh.

"I'll have one too, Ma." Her smile remains for her only son, Neill.

"Did you sleep well?" she asks him, forcing a kiss on his lips, which he wipes off.

"Jesus, Ma," he whines as he jumps up on the chair across from me.

"Doesn't like me kissing him in front of his friends," she tells me.

"I'm more like family."

Mrs. O'Reilly gives me a cup and a kiss that I accept.

"Jesus, Ma, would you stop." Neill takes his cup, and when his mam kisses him, he wipes his cheek.

"I'll leave you boys to it."

"Thanks, Mrs. O'Reilly," I say, raising my cup in salute as she closes the kitchen door.

"So what gives?"

"I got Mark yesterday," I tell him and watch him closely.

"Ah, nice one, Connor. You're a real pal."

"Yeah. I am, aren't I?"

He puts his finger in his ear and shakes it rapidly. "Yeah, that's what I just said." He shrugs and laughs before taking a drink of his tea.

"Funny story is that Mark said Brian paid him to attack you."

Neill's complexion pales, and when he starts stuttering, I give him a warning look. I don't want to hurt him.

"Yeah, he did. I didn't want to say anything, because it's messy."

I don't speak. Sometimes when you remain silent, the other person will keep talking just to fill the silence.

"Brian hates me because I ratted him out to Shane."

"You're a snitch for Shane?"

Neill holds up his hands. "No, no. I'd do it for any of you. You know that."

"Cut the bullshit, Neill. What did you tell Shane about Brian?"

"Brian was talking to a new supplier. I told Shane, and Shane beat the shit out of Brian. So in retaliation, he got me beat up."

"You pulled me into this mess. Why not ring Shane to come and save you after you were attacked?"

Neill tilts his head to the side. "You know he wouldn't have cared." Neill was right, but that didn't soften the betrayal of him lying to me.

"Do you know where Brian is now?"

"No, I swear." Neill holds up his hands again, like that meant shit.

"I don't even know if I believe you anymore."

"Connor, come on, man."

I stand, done with this conversation.

"You're going to hurt me?" Neill has his head in his hands.

"No, Neill. I don't hurt my friends," I tell him before leaving his house. I had thought of Neill as a friend, but this is a reminder that I can't trust anyone.

I take the piece of paper out of the glove compartment. My stomach twists. I'm ringing with no news, and I hate that. My only hope is that my dad has news for me.

"Hi, son. How is everything up there?"

His voice washes over me, and it makes me feel even more conflicted. I want to go back up north, but I'm not ready to leave Ava.

"A mess, to be honest."

"Not our mess?" He questions.

"No, Da, it's Darragh." I cut off, knowing we only have a certain amount of time and that he doesn't care about Darragh.

"No sign of Bernard and no word. What about you?" My stomach twists as I wait.

"Nothing. Call me when you have news." He hangs up, and his way sometimes reminds me too much of Michael's.

I ring Russell and try not to focus on my father's similarities to Michael.

"Man, I'll fix up with you soon for the apartment," I tell him, and he sounds like he's near traffic.

"No problem, Connor. All's good."

"I'm looking for another favor. I need a job. Like an auctioneer job."

Russell laughs. "You an auctioneer? You'd scare off all my punters."

I tut. "Not me, you dick. Ava. The girl in your apartment."

"You're telling me she doesn't have a job?"

I glare at Neill's house as I speak. "She just lost it. So I promised her I would get her one. Can you make that happen?"

"Not with me, Connor, but Gunnes is looking for one. Does she have qualifications?"

"No, but she's a real charmer."

Russell laughs. "She must be since you're pulling so many favors for her. Look, leave it with me, and I'll see what I can do."

"Okay. Don't leave it too long."

I take one final look at Neill's house before leaving the estate and making my way home. I better show my face after disappearing last night.

CHAPTER TWENTY ONE

AVA

THE TAXI DROPS ME off. I'm trying to juggle my bag and pay the taxi man when my phone vibrates. "Thanks again," I say before I make my way into the apartment. Once my bag is on the counter, I check my phone. My heart deflates. It's Patrick. I was hoping to hear from Connor.

I want to send you your payment. Can you forward me your address? Hope you're keeping well.

It feels silly to make him post it out, but I'm not sure I'll be returning there anytime soon. I wish I could tell him I'd get it another time, but with everything going on, I need the money.

5 Headfort Demesne. Thanks, Patrick.

I'm trying to keep a positive mind set as I look around the apartment. It's more than I could ever have dreamed of. I just hope I get a job and am able to keep it.

My phone vibrates again.

Sure thing.

The wording is odd for Patrick, but he never texts, so maybe he's trying out some new phrases. The rubbish is only a bag, but I gather it up and take the keys out to the rubbish area. The white shutter gates are snow white. They look recently painted, and when I open them up, two large bins sit nearly side by side, one green and the other blue. I dump the rubbish into the recycling bin before heading back to the apartment.

As I clean, I keep checking my phone, hoping Connor will text. It's at such an odd moment—when I'm cleaning the bathroom—that I realize I love him. I'm in love with him. That crept up on me. Green eyes stare back at me, and I almost don't recognize the girl I see. She's smiling, yet hiding the mark on her face. My gaze drops to the floor, and I swallow the bile that rises in my throat. I'm too much work. He'll leave.

Your mother left you.

The ugly voice I shut down long ago is speaking up again, and I'm shaking my head in denial.

I repeat my nan's words. "It's her loss, not mine." My eyes water and I close them, not wanting to spill anymore tears. "It's her loss, not mine." I repeat it like a mantra until someone knocks on the door. I quickly pull myself together.

Connor.

I open the door and immediately try to slam it. Brian's hand grips the doorframe, and he forces it open. I throw my full weight behind it and slam the door on his hand. He lets go, but his roars have me rushing the door again. My head hits the wall as the door is busted open. The hallway darkens as Brian slams the door behind him. My head rings, and even as he approaches me, I can't seem to focus or move.

He pushes me into the living room, and I stumble onto the floor. I'm trying to stop the ringing in my head as Brian gets a towel for his bleeding hand. *My phone.*

I'm scrabbling, trying to get to my feet. I sway, but my hearing seems to have cleared.

"Sit down, Ava."

"Have you lost your mind?" I can't reason with this madness. He ignores me and points to the couch. I sit down, not wanting to gain any more injuries.

"It was you—" I shake my head at my own stupidity. "You pretended to be Patrick." He doesn't confirm or deny. Brian cradles his arm to his chest.

"Is your head okay?" He's a psycho.

My phone's on the counter, and I know if I can distract him for a minute, I could grab it and run.

"Yeah, it's fine," I answer, looking around the room for anything I could use as a weapon.

"Aren't you going to ask me if my hand's okay?"

I hope you bleed to death. "What do you want?"

He laughs, and I pull in a large gulp of air. "What I've always wanted, Ava. You."

"You had me, and you hurt me." Shivers race all over me as I say it. My bottom lip trembles, and I bite down to try to stop the emotion.

"Give me another chance." He's on his knees, making his way over to me. My vision blurs as I shake my head.

"Brian, please," I beg as he reaches me. Don't touch me.

"I was foolish to throw away what we had." He's looking at me like there's hope. I blink, and my vision clears fully as tears stream down my face.

"Okay," I say.

"Really?" He leans out like he doesn't quite believe me. I can only nod, and my throat closes up.

"You wouldn't lie to me, would you?"

"Of course not." I wipe my face with the sleeve of my top, trying to stem the flow of tears. "You're right. We were good together."

He's nodding, and my heart slams repeatedly against my chest. "Look at the mess you made of my hand."

Salty tears find their way into my mouth. "I'm so sorry. I just panicked."

"Yeah, you weren't expecting me. Were you expecting someone else?"

"No. I was just cleaning."

He stands now and looks around. "It's a nice place, Ava. A bit above your pay grade, but we'll make it work." My eyes snap to my phone, but I look away when he glances back at me.

"You want your phone?" he asks, and a sob falls from my mouth.

"No," I tell him. The ringing of my phone makes me jump. Brian picks it up, and I stand.

"Connor," Brian says as he scratches his head. He doesn't hang up or answer it. Instead, he places the phone on the counter.

Oh God. "Brian, we're just friends."

"Shut the fuck up, you slut!" he screams. I sit back down, rigid. "You have no intentions of getting back with me, do you?"

I want to lie down and close my eyes and pretend this isn't happening. If I say I do, he'll know I'm lying. If I say I don't, he'll lose it. I focus on the hardwood floor under my feet.

"Brian, please," I plead instead, but he's in front of me again, his bloody hand gripping my face.

"You're the only one I ever told about my childhood. You're the only person I've ever opened up to. I'm so in love with you, Ava. You have to see that." He told me about how his parents were addicts and he raised himself. Often hungry and afraid, he had to fend on his own. His story broke my heart, and all I ever wanted to do was help him. Heal him.

In a way, I did. He grew stronger, more confident. And then I became his punching bag. That, I could never forgive. I can't form the words, and I can't stop the flow of tears.

His fingers grip my hair painfully. "Answer me." Spit flecks across my face as he screams.

"If you loved me, you would have never hurt me. You're hurting me now."

His grip loosens, but he doesn't let me go. "Do you love me?"

I close my eyes until his hold tightens on my hair. My heart is jumping around my chest, making its way into my throat. I need this to end. "No, Brian, I don't love you anymore."

He releases me, and a sob tears from my throat. His blue eyes shine with tears, and I'm stiff, getting ready for the blow that he will no doubt land on me. But he doesn't. Something in him softens, and he moves into my personal space. "Kiss me."

"What?" I'm not sure I heard him right, but he leans in and tries to brush his lips against mine. My hands move on reflex and slam against his chest, stopping his progression.

"No, Brian. Just stop." Hitting me is one thing; forcing himself on me is unthinkable. He pushes against me, his lips roughly touching mine. I lash out and scratch his face, ready to bolt. I don't get to move. His large hands encircle mine as he pins me to the ground.

"What the fuck are you doing?" I'm shouting my panic, pleading with the rational part of him. "Don't do this." I can barely breathe as he leans down and kisses me again. My brain is screaming that this can't be real. Somewhere in the background, my phone rings, a reminder that this is very much real, and if I don't get up, the unthinkable is going to happen.

He's screaming, trying to pull away from me, but I've locked my jaw after sinking my teeth into his lip. My hands are free, and it's a moment of relief until his fist connects with the side of my head.

Darkness swamps me, and the taste of iron fills my mouth. I try to spit out the liquid, but the weight is still on top of me. I buck blindly, but everything gets heavier, and I slow down. The burn on the back of my neck jerks me. Cold air brushes my skin.

"No, don't." It's weak. I need to open my eyes. I need to stop this. The weight is lifted, and my stomach hollows out as rough hands tug at my trousers. My vision clears, and I'm sideways. Brian is opening his jeans.

Move, Ava.

"You're a stupid bitch and a slut." His words wake me up a bit more. I move, and he grips my bare thighs painfully. I kick out my legs and connect with his shoulder. His face is a bloody mess, but I still see the snarl as his hands dig into my legs, making their way back up to me.

"Get away from me." My throat burns as I scream and thrash under him. He grabs one of my swinging hands, but not before I drag my nails down his face.

"Fuck's sake, Ava."

"Help. Help." I can't get his weight off me. Wriggling under him is only aggravating him more, but I can't give up. This can't be it.

His face is close to mine, but he's not stupid enough to try to kiss me again. I spit at him, and pain explodes down the side of my face as his temper flares again.

I'm trying to stay awake. Brian is still on top of me, his head tilted to the side, and I don't know what he's listening to until I hear it, and my throat tightens, and my eyes blur. Someone is knocking on the door.

"Help! Please!" A sweaty hand clamps down on my face, and I bite hard, refusing to let go. Brian's roars pound in my head.

I spit when Brian tears his hand back. The knocking is now gone, and it sounds like someone is throwing themselves against the door. Brian gets off me, his eyes roaming the room. The wooden floor scratches my hands as I move backward. My back hits the couch, and I cling to it. My top is torn. On the floor, my trousers are near the door. The rattle of the door has me glancing at Brian.

He takes out a knife, and I shake my head. The world explodes as the front door shatters in on top of us. Brian moves quickly toward me, and I'm trying to scurry across the couch. My body is limp like I've been drugged, and I scream at it to move. My head whips around at the sound of running feet. I pause as a sob tears itself free from my throat.

Connor.

His pause is so brief, but my eyes connect with his, and something shifts between us, but I can't stop the crying. The sound that's leaving me doesn't sound like me. When Connor releases me from his stare, he's moving mechanically toward Brian.

Someone else enters the room, but my focus is on Connor. Brian swipes. Connor jumps back and disarms him in a second. The knife skitters across the floor before Connor punches Brian in the face. The impact seems to shake the floor under me as Brian hits the ground hard.

"Wait, let me explain. She came on to me," Brian says. Connor stands over him as he tries to crawl away. I don't turn away as a heavy boot slams into Brian's face. The crunch of his nose is satisfying. Connor's over Brian now, his fist slamming into Brian's face repeatedly. I can't take my eyes away from Connor. He's transformed. He's savage in his attack, and I don't want him to stop. I don't want him to ever stop.

"Connor." The person with Connor is trying to pull him off, gripping his arm. It slows Connor down but doesn't stop him. "You need to stop."

The other guy doesn't sound overly alarmed, but his words break through the walls Connor built around himself. He stops, his hands a bloody mess. Brian is unrecognisable under him. Brown eyes that are almost black hold mine, and Connor's moving again. Releasing Brian, he moves over to me.

"Get me a blanket," he demands. The other guy leaves the room as Connor takes me in his arms, cradling me against his chest like a child, and I release a flood of tears.

"It's okay." His whispered words are accompanied by a blanket being wrapped around me. He's standing still, holding me in his arms, and then he sits.

"What about him?"

"Just give me a minute." Connor's words rumble through his chest. My hands tighten on his top as I push my face deeper into his chest.

"It's okay," he tells me again. I stay in my safe cocoon until the other man speaks again.

"Didn't realize he was such a fucking maniac." Smoke makes its way into my safe place. Peeking out, I see the other boy is smoking. His eyes clash with mine.

"Hi." He gives me a nod. I don't answer him but look up into familiar brown eyes.

"He's my brother. He's here to help."

I nod and swallow another flood of emotions. "How did you know?" My throat is hoarse.

"Will you get me some water?" Connor asks his brother before looking down at me. "Patrick rang me when I was at home. He told me that Brian attacked him and made him get your address."

His brother arrives back with the water and hands it to Connor, who holds it to my lips. I take a deep gulp. My eyes want to move to the left, where Brian still lies, his body still, but I focus on bloody hands and brown eyes. His gentle touch is a contradiction to the savagery he just displayed.

"You okay for a minute?" he asks me.

I'm nodding, but my body is screaming, Don't go. Don't leave me. I start to tremble, and he wraps the blanket tighter around my shoulders.

"Ring Russell," he says to his brother. "Tell him we need a new front door. I'll move him." He plants a kiss on my head.

Brian is dragged by his arms across the wooden floor. His head rocks every time it hits something. But Connor doesn't slow his pace as he drags him out of the room. I don't care if he's dead. I tighten the blanket as Connor's brother gives a half smile as he rings Russell. A cigarette dangles from his mouth. I can't manage to smile back, so I focus on the door to the hallway as I wait for Connor to come back. Two hundred forty-five seconds later, he returns empty-handed.

"He'll be here within the hour," the brother tells Connor, who nods.

"He's in the trunk. I need you to make sure he doesn't get out."

"No problem." Before his brother passes him, Connor clamps a hand on his shoulder. "Thanks, Darragh."

Darragh nods at Connor. "I got you," he tells Connor, who releases him and returns to me.

Connor picks me up softly and carries me into the bedroom. After sitting me on the bed, he moves around silently, pulling the curtains and closing the bedroom door. The shower is turned on, and when Connor reappears, he still doesn't focus on me. He's rummaging through my drawers, taking out clean clothes and placing them on the bed beside me before he turns his attention to me. Removing the blanket, I shiver.

"I can walk," I tell him when he tries to pick me up. My legs wobble like jelly, but I make it to the bathroom. It feels like a dream as I remove my underwear and bra and step into the spray of water. The heat rattles my body, and I hold on to the wall. I want to scream into the white tiles, scream all the rage that's built up inside me. Soft hands touch my back, and I glance at Connor over my shoulder. He's naked behind me, the water hitting his chest.

"Let me help you?" he asks, and I nod as he soaps up a cloth and washes every inch of my skin. The care, the gentleness, nearly undoes me again after my body has felt such abuse. His hands still on each mark, and I realize there's a lot. I haven't seen my face, but it aches, and each touch burns away the roots of darkness that Brian planted. Each touch releases the knots in my chest. Each touch is making me remember that Brian didn't succeed, because Connor stopped him.

"Thank you."

He freezes, and I look up at Connor, blinking as the spray keeps interfering with my view. But the pain in his eyes catches my breath.

CHAPTER TWENTY TWO

CONNOR

S HE'S ASLEEP IN BED, and I can't seem to find the strength to leave her. But the idea of getting to hurt Brian all over again has me slipping from her room. Russell had a new door put on and is gone now. Outside, Darragh sits on the boot of the car smoking a cigarette. Opening the front door, he turns to me and walks over.

"I need you to stay with her."

"I'm not that good with women," Darragh says as he throws the fag on the ground.

"She's asleep, and I can't leave her alone."

Darragh nods. "Yeah, go on. What do I say if she wakes up?"

"Tell her I've taken Brian to Navan Gardaí station. But if she wants to talk to me, just ring me."

"You're not really taking him to Navan, are you?"

I don't answer his question but pat him on the back.

"Thanks, Darragh. I owe you one," I tell him, handing him the set of keys. He takes it with a grin. "Just be careful."

***

I drive to Kells—an old bakery that's closed down, and is owned by Michael. It was in the works to be turned into flats, but right now, it's abandoned. The locks are easy to break as I push up the shutter and back the car into the space. Pulling the shutter back down, we're plunged into the darkness. Once I'm back in the car, I turn on the car lights.

The area is open, with large cement pillars. I veer the car around. Large plastic sheeting hangs from one wall, where they started reconstruction but had to stop. Some people in the town objected to the bakery being turned into flats. It's still tied up in legal issues, but no doubt Michael will bribe whoever he needs to. My gloves sit along with my gun in the glove compartment. I remove both and put them on.

The sheet of plastic pulls away easily, and I drag it to the middle of the room, keeping it within the range of my car lights. Thumping sounds come from the boot.

"Good. Just in time," I tell Brian as I open the boot. He glares up at me, trying to cover his face. I don't give him a moment but drag him from the boot.

He hits the ground heavily, and I grab one leg and drag him toward the plastic. His cries and pleas don't make me pause. Once he's deposited on the plastic, I return to the car and get my gun before turning on the music. Country music blares from the speakers. The noise has Brian looking around him. One eye is sealed. The other darts around the space before he stares at the plastic under his hands.

"No, man." He's shaking his head. Blood drips from his face.

I kneel down in front of him, and he looks at me.

"Please." His teeth are red with blood.

"Did Ava say please?" I ask, and he drops my gaze. "You know what this is?" I hold up the gun in my hand. His one eye flickers around the space again.

"A gun."

"Well done, Brian. It's not just a gun. It's a silencer. So no one will hear when I empty it into you."

Horror has his eyes widening, and I soak up his fear. "It's not fair, me with the gun and you with nothing." I tell him while tucking the gun into the back of my jeans.

"Since you like beating on women, I'm going to give you a chance. You fight me, and I'll let you go."

"I can't win." Tears make a pathway down his face.

"You don't want to try?" I ask, taking the gun back out and pointing it at his forehead. His hands rise into the air.

"Jesus. Please, I'll do anything you want. This isn't just about Ava, is it? It's about Harry?"

I don't respond but let him talk.

"I'll tell him to back off."

I'm standing now, my finger trigger ready. "Don't mention her name again," I tell him, and he looks up but ducks his head down again while keeping his hands in the air.

"I won't. I'm sorry."

"Why did you get men to beat up Neill?"

"He told Shane I was trying to do a deal with a new guy, and Shane beat me up. So I got Neill beaten up."

"Would you do that to me, Brian? Would you hire men to hurt me if I let you live?" I'm on my hunkers again, and he's shaking his head.

"I swear I'd disappear. You'd never see me again."

"You mentioned Harry? Tell me about the deal you have with him."

He's more alert now, maybe thinking he needs to be careful. A wave of my gun has him making his mind up quickly.

"I told Harry about the body we buried in the bog."

Ah, so we have our rat.

"You helped Shane bury a body?"

He's nodding. One mangled hand reaches up and wipes blood from his chin.

"The dealer who tried to move in on his turf—they knew each other. And Brendan, I think his name was, made a reference about Shane's mother. He lost it and killed the guy."

I lean out as Brian's eye starts to close. His words send dread dripping down my back.

"Describe Brendan to me."

He shakes his head and whimpers. A slap to his face has him speaking again. "Tall, brown hair, Northern Ireland accent. I think he was attached to the IRA. Yeah. He mentioned the IRA."

I'm standing and walking away from Brian before returning.

"Bernard," I say more to myself.

"Yeah, yeah. Not Brendan—Bernard. He was his cousin or something. Look, I'll tell Harry to drop it."

I'm kneeling again as my heart tries to break free from my rib cage. "You saw Shane kill Bernard?"

He's nodding. "Look, I can unsee it. You know what I mean."

I'm standing again. Shane killed my brother.

"How did he kill him?"

Brian tries to stand, and I send him sailing back to the ground. Red splatters across the plastic as he coughs up blood.

"Answer me." He's on his side now, his breaths fogging up the plastic under him.

"Bernard made a statement about his father being with his mother. He lost it and hit him." Brian rolls onto his back, his breathing becoming deeper.

"Bernard hit his head. I think that's what killed him. It was an accident."

I'm picturing Bernard dying at the hands of Shane.

"Where did this happen?"

Brian starts to whimper again and pleads with me to take him to a hospital.

"I will. You have my word. I'll take you to the hospital. Just answer me."

"You're lying," Brian cries.

"Nah, you have my word."

"Smyth's," he tells me with a snivel.

I'm struggling to wrap my mind around this. Shane killed my brother.

"Was anything else said between them?" I ask, and Brian looks panicked as he scurries to think. I don't think Shane knows I'm Bernard's brother. But Bernard mentioning Mam and Tom together is odd.

"No, that's it."

I nod, and Brian starts crying.

"Can I go now?"

"You really think I will let you go after what you did to Ava?"

"I told you everything."

"You did. But you're still going to die."

I don't hesitate as I put three bullets in Brian's body. One in each kneecap before firing the last one between his eyes. Blood pools fast, and I move, grabbing the plastic and tightening it around his body. I grab a silver roll of duct tape from the car and tie both ends until the roll is gone. I drag Brian to the car and get him into the boot before I let the betrayal sink in.

I need to tell Da, but I also know what he would want me to do. The area looks clear as I make one final sweep of the room before getting into the car and lowering the music. I remove the gloves and gun and put them into the glove compartment. Then I make a phone call.

"How is she?" I ask the moment Darragh answers.

"She's asleep."

I'm nodding as I start to reverse up to the shutters. "Okay. I might be a few more hours. You good there?"

"Yeah, you do what you need to do."

I end the call and jump out of the car and push up the shutter. The light has me blinking after the stark darkness of the bakery. Traffic moves by in the same pattern as it always does. People walk up and down the street, and it all feels normal. Pulling out the car, I close the shutter.

Can you put a lock on the bakery shutter on John's street? My dad owns it, and I see someone broke it. I'll sort you out soon for everything, man. Thanks.

I'm driving toward home, trying to think of my next move. I need to get rid of the body in my car. I can burn out the car later. Getting Brian out of the boot is vital. The Loch Leigh Mountains spring to mind, but I think of a better place. When I arrive home, I curse myself. My hands are caked in blood, so I wash my hands in the sink, the last of the red liquid disappearing down the drain.

"Hey, have you seen Darragh?" I dry my hands while turning to Finn.

"He's on a job. Don't worry, he's fine." Finn stares at me, and now I wonder if I have blood on my face.

"You okay?"

"Yeah, just out last night." I throw the paper towel into the bin.

"With Darragh? That will give you one hell of a hangover." Finn's grinning, and I just want him to leave.

"Mother of all hangovers," I tell him. Finn walks with me as I go to my room. "Shower and some sleep." I grin, and he smirks at me.

"And you have Darragh working today?" He laughs.

I close the door and lean against it for a moment before opening it. Checking the hall confirms that Finn is gone, and I make my way back to the garage. The hum of the engine sounds like it's roaring, and I pull out of the garage and make my way to the back of the house. I grab supplies from the shed and then throw them into the back seat before I drive around the sheds and out of sight.

I sit and wait an agonizing twenty minutes. I just need to make sure no one saw me. When the twenty minutes are up, I leave the sheds and drive across the fields toward the forest. I keep to the outline of the forest until the field is cut off by a ditch. Veering into it, I drive as far as the forest will allow. I'm not very deep, but I'm hidden. This would be handy with another person, but I'm on my own.

I drag Brian across the forest floor until my arms ache and burn. When I look around me, I can't see anything but trees. Returning to the car, I get out the shovels and the black paint and brush. I pull my body up high into a large oak tree and paint a thick layer of black paint onto the trunk. It will be my only marking of where he is buried.

The burn in my arms is severe as I continue to dig. I'm only halfway down when I have to stop. A tremble has entered my hands. My limbs aren't cooperating anymore. My stomach lifts, and I close my eyes, trying to make it settle. I've never killed anyone before, and it scares me how easy it was. Brian deserved to die. The thought of him hurting Ava has me continuing to dig until the hole is deep enough. Clay crumbles under my fingers as I pull myself out of the grave. My boot connects with Brian's body as I kick and push him toward the grave. The heavy thud is satisfactory, and the plastic soon disappears under the grave of clay.

I don't stop at the house but make my way back to Ava.

CHAPTER TWENTY THREE

AVA

M Y HEART POUNDS, AND a pool of sweat sits on my chest. My mind is jumping around, not settling on anything. Water spraying on my body, gentle hands, Brian's roars, Connor's rage. I tighten my eyes to stop it all and sit up. My stomach twists painfully. My abused face screams at me, and my head pounds. I don't move as tears stream down my face. He tried to rape me. The thought of his rough fingers has me swallowing bile. I can't stay here. I'm out of the bed and pausing at the door. The smell of smoke has my stomach twisting again.

Connor's brother. It's only Connor's brother.

The door opens slowly, and I step out into the living space. Blue eyes focus on me. He doesn't speak and neither do I. I tighten my arms around my waist.

"Where is Connor?" My throat burns and I clear it. Darragh is up now, moving toward the kitchen. I don't move but watch him. I hate how I flinch when he walks toward me with a glass of water. It takes me a moment to take it from him.

"He'll be back soon." He smiles, but I nod and give him a wide berth as I move to the couch and sit down. He stays standing, giving me some space, and that makes me relax a bit more.

"Thank you." I take a deep drink of water, and it feels nice on my aching throat.

"So, you and Connor are dating?"

I shrug. I'm not sure how to answer that question. I don't know what me and Connor are. "I don't know," I finally answer, and Darragh leans against the wall.

"How did you meet?" Darragh checks his phone, and I feel his questions are to keep me occupied.

"Where I work and then later in the supermarket. He asked me out for coffee."

"Can't picture Connor in a supermarket." Darragh grins, and I find myself smiling.

"Yeah. He was buying Swiss Rolls," I tell Darragh, and he laughs. His brother being here reminds me of how little I know about Connor's life. "Do you live with Connor?"

"Yeah, in Whitewood House. None of us have fled the nest yet."

I've heard of Whitewood House. Surprise flitters through me at the knowledge that Connor lives there.

Darragh's phone rings, and I don't know which of us is more relieved. Our conversation is strained. Right now, all I want is Connor. Darragh smiles at me.

"He's here now." He leaves and opens the front door. The overwhelming urge to cry bubbles up in my throat when Connor walks into the room. His eyes land on me.

"You're awake?" He's beside me, pulling me into his arms, and I let him.

"Yeah. I feel a bit better," I say. Soft lips brush my forehead. Darragh moves across from us and sits down.

"You get all sorted?" he asks Connor, and Connor's arms stiffen around me.

"Yeah."

I'm looking up into brown eyes. "What did you do with Brian?" I really want to ask if he's still alive. He didn't look so good when he was dragged from here. Now that I look around the living area, I don't see a trace of what happened. I wonder if it was Darragh or Connor who cleaned it up.

"I took him to Navan Gardaí station."

My throat closes, and I nod. "They need me to make a statement." This is the part I hate.

"Not right now. He's being held on a list of charges. I think it will be a long time before Brian gets out."

"Did they tell you when they need me to go in? I'd prefer to do it when I visit Nan soon. Get it done and over with."

"They didn't say, but please don't worry about it."

I am going to worry about it, but for right now, I nod.

"I'm going to take the car and head home," Darragh tells Connor. "Is that okay?"

"Yeah, that's fine. Maybe you could air her out when you get home." Something passes between the brothers, and Darragh stands.

"I can do that." Darragh takes the keys from Connor. "Ava, you take care of yourself."

I smile at him for the first time. "Thank you for everything, Darragh. I don't know what I would have done if you and Connor hadn't arrived." My voice closes on the last words, and Darragh shifts uncomfortably.

"Don't mention it," he says, giving me a salute as he leaves the room. Once the front door is closed, I sink further into Connor.

"I don't want you to be scared, Ava. He's gone now, okay?"

I turn in Connor's arms so I'm looking at him. His fingers move across my cheek.

"You know what was even scarier?" My lip trembles, and I bite it. "Losing you. I'm waiting for the other shoe to drop—" My words are cut off as Connor presses his lips against mine. His kiss weaves its way through my veins, rushing all the way to my toes.

"I'm not going anywhere." His words against my lips have me opening my eyes.

My heart is galloping, and my pulse flickers in my neck. "I'm falling in love with you, Connor." I'm in love with you.

Connor's smile is instant, and it's a balm on a wound as he reaches me again and kisses me. I'm on his lap now, straddling him, and he's all I want. He's all I need.

I'm pushing my body against his, and he looks at me, his eyes a deep brown. His breath brushes my face. "Are you sure? We don't have to?"

I answer his question with a kiss. My fingers move under his shirt. Muscles coil under my touch. I let myself forget everything and lose myself in Connor.

***

We spend three days holed up in the apartment, blocking out the world, and it's perfect. Each morning, I wait for him to tell me he has to leave, but he doesn't. Every moment with Connor heals me.

"How about we get out today?" Connor is eating toast at the breakfast bar. He's a sight for sore eyes with no top on. I could handle a few more days locked in here with him, but getting out would be nice too.

"Yeah, I suppose we can't stay in here forever." I pout, and my stomach twists as Connor smiles at me.

"Did you ring your nan?" He puts the toast in my mouth, and I take a bite.

"Yep, told her I was bogged down with a new job. She's doing good."

Connor takes another bite of toast. "Speaking of jobs, my friend Russell was wondering when you can start. Gunnes has a position if you want it." I jump into his arms because he's the best.

"Thank you so much." I kiss him before stealing his toast.

"Maybe you could thank me tonight."

I'm grinning. "We'll see," I tell Connor, but I couldn't keep away from him even if I wanted to.

***

It's weird to be walking the streets of Kells. When people look at me, I think the marks on my face are visible and immediately duck my head.

A warm hand squeezes mine. "You're beautiful, Ava," Connor tells me as he stops us on the street. He's moved me into his arms now and kisses me. When we break apart, I blush knowing we're being watched. We walk around the town hand in hand. Passing Smyth's makes me stiffen, but once we're around the corner, I relax. We are coming up to the café where we had our first date.

"Connor," I say, but I don't get his attention. Connor's hand has tightened on mine painfully, and when I yank my hand, he releases me.

"Sorry." He's distracted looking at someone as they jog across the road.

When he gets to us, the guy says, "I was ringing your phone the last few days."

The silence from Connor has me glancing at him, and his eyes flicker to me, searching my face before he answers. "I saw that. I was tied up."

The other guy smiles at me. Brown eyes similar to Connor's look at me. "Aren't you going to introduce me to your beautiful friend?" The compliment is said with an outstretched hand, and I take it.

"I'm Ava," I tell him, since Connor seems to have lost the ability to speak.

"Shane. Connor's brother."

Ah, that explains the eyes. Connor said he didn't get on with Shane. Maybe that's why he's acting so weird.

"What do you want?" Connor's rude words have me releasing Shane's hand.

"Can't one brother worry about the other?" Shane widens his eyes at me, a kind smile on his face, and I feel embarrassed at how rude Connor is being.

"We were just about to grab a coffee," I say and can feel Connor's heavy stare on my shoulders.

"I would love to join you," Shane says.

"Great." I nudge Connor, and once again, my movements seem to relax him a bit more.

***

Awkward isn't enough to describe how it feels as we sit in the booth. Connor sits beside me, Shane across from us.

"So are you dating?" he asks, and I smile.

"I'm not sure." I give him the same answer I gave Darragh.

"You should really put the girl out of her misery," Shane tells Connor as the waitress arrives. We order, and Shane returns to prodding Connor. "You're all uptight, Connor. Relax."

Connor stiffens even more at Shane's words, and we sit in silence as our coffees arrive.

"So are you from the area?" Shane asks me.

"Yeah, born and raised here."

"Shane, you should leave," Connor says.

Jesus, Connor is being so rude, but it isn't my place to intervene. Shane shrugs out of his coat and pushes up the sleeves of his jumper. Something in me stills. The air feels tight, and my eyes trace the black bands on his arms. My memory snaps back to the night in the pub. My hand jerks, knocking my coffee all over the table. We all move, and I'm apologizing as my mind races.

"Are you okay?" Connor is cleaning up the spill with napkins, but Shane is watching me. I can't look up at Connor.

"Yeah," I answer. The waitress arrives and starts to mop up the coffee. My chest grows tighter. "I'm just going to the bathroom." I don't wait for their dismissal.

He was with the missing boy—Shane. Shane is Connor's brother. Connor arrived into my pub—

I'm in the bathroom, the contents of my stomach coming up. Sitting on the ground, I kick the wall and lean my head against the far wall. Connor had asked me questions about Harry and the missing boy. My stomach heaves again. When I went to the Gardaí Station, he talked me out of reporting it.

Oh my God. My hand trembles as I cover my mouth. I can't go back out there. I can't let them see what they've done to me.

I'm up on my feet and making my way out of the small café. Ducking down, I cross the open space and glance at Connor and Shane. Their conversation is low and intense. The fresh air burns my eyes, and I dip my head as I make my way down the street. What if Connor doesn't know? What if I'm jumping to conclusions? I'm slowing down. The rational part of me is telling me that of course he knew. The circumstances were stacked too high. But my heart wants to believe that we met and fell in love, and the fact that I crossed paths with his brother before is just a coincidence

"Ava. Ava." Connor reaches me and grips my shoulders. "What's wrong?" The way he questions me makes it sound like he already knows.

"Please don't lie to me," I tell him. Connor releases me and joins his hands together.

"Everything okay?" Shane arrives, sliding on his jacket.

"Can you fuck off for five minutes?" Connor snaps, and Shane loses his smile.

"Fine. But know this, Connor. You did a good job." His words are like a nail in my coffin.

Am I the job?

My stomach churns again, and I start walking briskly. Connor tries to stop me. "Don't touch me," I say. I shrug him off as I clutch my stomach.

"You have to listen to me," he pleads.

Something in me cracks, and I stop walking. I can't look up at Connor. The pathetic part of me wants him to explain this away.

"It's not how he's making it sound."

My lip trembles. *So Shane wasn't lying... I am a job.*

"Like your brother said, you did a great job." I've felt a lot of pain in life, but this is different.

"Ava, I met you, and straight away I wanted you."

I glance up at Connor as my nose burns and my eyes fill. "How could you hurt me like this?" He knew my past; he knew about Brian. My job, my home, everything. "I can't even go back to my apartment because it's all yours."

He's shaking his head. "No, that's yours."

"Stop! Nothing is mine. You've manipulated and controlled everything." I laugh through my tears. "I feel so stupid." I inhale deeply to try to settle the hysteria that's bubbling up. "I loved you," I tell Connor, but he's shaking his head.

"I can fix this."

No, he can't. I turn away from him before I crumble here on the sidewalk. I gather the small bit of dignity I have left and walk. I have no idea where to. I still have my old apartment for a few more days.

"Ava, please just let me try."

I stop walking at the credit union and turn to Connor. "You've made me feel this small." I hold up two fingers close together. I'm glad when my words make him flinch. "I want you to feel what I'm feeling." A sob tears from my throat, and Connor's eyes glaze.

"I do. I'm so sorry. Jesus. I was going to tell you, I swear. But it just never felt like the right time."

"Yeah, I can't imagine telling someone you only stepped into their life to find out information about them could slot neatly into some timeframe." I'm shouting. I don't care that people are watching. My skin feels tight.

"Get away from me." I wipe angrily at my tears.

"I love you, Ava." His words make me cry because only half an hour ago, that's all I would have wanted to hear. Those three little words would have made my world complete. Now they make me angry.

"I need you to leave me alone," I tell Connor, and he doesn't move.

"I need to make sure you're home safely. I promise I'll give you space then."

"*No.*" Then it clicks with me, and I'm really looking at him. "What happens to me now? Is someone going to hurt me?" I cover my mouth, wondering what the hell I've gotten myself into.

"No one, and I mean no one, will ever put their hands on you again. You have my word." Connor's holding my arms, and I shrug him off, but his words ease the worry in me, because they ring true to me. "Just let me get you home safely."

I'm nodding because I don't know what to do. I fold my arms across my chest as Connor rings a taxi so we can get into town, as Darragh took his car. My cheeks heat. Did Darragh know? I wonder now if they all sat around a table and laughed at the stupid girl.

"He'll be here soon."

I don't acknowledge Connor or speak to him as we make our way back to Headfort Demesne—such a shattered dream. I hold it together as I get out of the taxi. I keep strong even as Connor walks me to the door.

"I'll give you space, but I'm not going anywhere, Ava."

"How noble of you, Connor," I tell him before closing the door in his face. I'm staring at it like it might explode inwards, but when the taxi pulls away, I let myself shatter as I pour my pain across the wooden floor.

CHAPTER TWENTY FOUR

CONNOR

"T HANKS." I SLIP THE taxi man a fifty and walk up the pass to the house. I didn't want him to drop me at the door.

When I reach the house, Darragh's making his way out of the garage. He pulls up and rolls down his window. "What's up?"

"Not much." I shove my hands into my pockets. For the first time, I can't sort through all the shit that's going on inside me.

"Okay then." Darragh lights up a cigarette. "I aired your car for you."

"Thanks, I appreciate it. Now I need to find another one."

"You can use my Jeep if you want. Hate the fucking thing."

I grin at Darragh and tap the roof to let him go. "Thanks, man. I'll catch you later."

"Oh, be warned. Dad is on the warpath. That's why I'm evacuating."

I don't give a shit about Michael. I nod at Darragh and walk off as his car roars down the pass. Glancing across my shoulder, all I see is a cloud of dust.

"I can't do this anymore," I hear yelled.

If it were anyone else, I would go to my room. But it's Finn who's shouting. I find Michael, Liam, Shane, Una—who I'm surprised to see—and Finn in the library.

No one seems to notice my presence.

"Where is he now?" Michael's red face is tight with anger, and I step closer to Finn, getting Michael's attention.

"I'm fucking here, Michael," I tell him and sit close to Finn just in case.

"You're an impudent little pup."

I nod and smirk at him.

"The last time I checked, he was leaving," Finn says. "And honestly, I don't blame him."

"I have guards at my door, forensics digging up my land, yet I have four sons who can't seem to keep it together."

"Five sons, Michael." Una's voice sounds so quiet and sweet.

"What?" His voice has lowered, but it still holds a warning.

"You've five sons. You said four."

Michael doesn't answer her, but I feel all eyes on me.

"We acknowledge that something must be done." Liam speaks up, calmly and clearly. Michael rubs his face and sits down.

"This is not as bad as you think. The charges have been dropped against Darragh, and they found animal carcasses in the bog." Shane says, and I clench my fists.

"It is, Shane. Because Darragh is a loose cannon, and right now, we need a solution to this problem. I can't have guards on my doorstep. I've operated this business for over forty years, and I've never drawn their attention."

I can't stop staring at Shane, and he catches my eye a few times. *You killed my brother. You destroyed things with me and Ava.*

"If you're going to hit me, go ahead," Shane says. My message must have gotten across to him. He stands, wide arms outstretched like I'd attack him now.

I smirk at him. "Relax, Shane. I'm not going to hit you." I sit further back into the couch.

"You want to explain what's going on here?" Michael asks me, and I point at Shane.

"I'll let Shane tell you." It's like it dawns on him that my work for him was kept from his family. *Stupid fucker.*

"A misunderstanding," he says, and I laugh just to wind him up.

"You tell so many lies that you don't even know the truth." Una leans out and stares at me while tilting her head, and I meet her eye. I like Una.

"You should run," I tell her. "That's my advice to you."

"Leave her out of this." Shane's taking a step toward me, and I lean back again.

"No." I smirk again, and he clenches his fist.

"We have more important things to discuss," Michael says, and Shane steps away.

"That's a good boy," I tease him, but he doesn't bite.

Liam speaks up again. "Darragh will work for me. I take full responsibility for him."

"Darragh in a brothel?" Finn's looking doubtful.

"A Brothel?" Una says. "You work in a brothel?"

This is the first time I've ever seen Una react to something about the families work.

"Yes, I do." Liam's answer is said with a soft jerk of his head.

"Okay, I agree with that," Michael says, and Finn still looks doubtful but keeps his mouth shut. The responsibility is finally off his shoulders, and that makes me happy.

"But Finn, you still need to look out for him when he's here. It doesn't mean you can just walk away." Michael's eyes flicker to me before they return to Finn. "No one walks away from this family."

"I'm not walking away from this family. I'm getting married, and I want a life besides all this."

Michael shakes his head before looking at his two noble sons. "Family comes first." They nod like two soldiers.

Finn's face tightens as he taps his foot on the floor.

"Since I'm not family, I'm good to go." Rising, I wink at Una. I don't have to look at Shane to know it annoys the hell out of him.

Shit hurts at times. Like when you're walking down a hall and no one calls you back and says, "Stop, Connor, you are family." No, the only words that are shouted at me are from Shane.

"You're going to push me too far, Connor."

I haven't even started. Facing him makes me even angrier now, and he walks toward me with a smirk. Knowing his actions are roiling me just like I knew mine back in that room were roiling him.

"Are you really going to declare war over a girl?"

I'm smiling, telling myself to remain calm. "If you ran my dog down, that would be enough to declare a war with you. You're a vindictive, evil—" Una and Finn step out into the hall, and for them, I want to stop but for Ava and Bernard, I keep going.

"Murderer," I say the final word slowly. He doesn't like that at all. He's not shrinking away; he stands taller, like I've just handed him a knife.

"If you think I'm all that, then be careful."

"Come on, guys." Finn is trying to move in between us, but we're toe to toe.

"No, Finn, I'm not afraid," Shane says, and I push my forehead against his. I put all my anger and frustration into the action.

"Oh my God, guys, seriously?" Una says. I glance at her, and for the first time, I feel angry at her stupidity.

Stepping only a foot away from Shane, I stare at Una. "You know what they do?" Her face brightens. "Yet you still lie with him."

Rough hands grip my neck, and I'm slammed into the wall. "Stop speaking to her."

"Shane," Una warns, but I allow Shane to manhandle me.

"Una, I thought you had more respect for yourself," I say. Shane slams his fist into my stomach, knocking the wind from me. As I gasp for air, I start to laugh and cough. "You'll piss him off one day and end up in a ditch."

He charges, taking both of us to the ground. I allow each thump to my face. It fuels me. Liam and Finn pull Shane off me. I'm on my hands and knees, coughing as blood drips from my mouth and nose. When I look up, Una stares at me, a hand over her mouth as her eyes hold horror.

"I needed to show you what he is," I tell her, and Liam holds Shane back as I stand and wipe blood from my face. Michael's standing behind them all, staring hate at me.

"You must be so proud of your sons, Michael. You did a great job with them all."

"That's enough," Liam barks. His raised voice causes a lull to fall in the hall. More blood drops off my chin, and I wipe it away, but some hits the floor.

Una takes a step toward me with tears in her eyes. "Connor..." She's shaking her head, but I don't want her sympathy. I leave the front door open as I walk out of the house and make my way to the back. I need to cool down. My throat burns. No doubt Shane's hand marks are visible. I rub it, but it doesn't help.

"Connor." I want Finn to just stay inside. I don't need him coming after me. But he's there, and he's angry.

"Why did you let him hit you?"

I shrug, knowing exactly why I did it. I wanted everyone to see a monster, even just a glimpse. I wanted to put the seed of doubt into Una's head. It was a scratch to the surface compared to what I was going to do to him. No matter what, he would die. He had to. He took the life of my brother, the general's son.

"Connor, please talk to me." I stop walking and face the house. Too many windows to count look down on us. Any one of them could have an occupant.

"I wanted Una to see what he's really like."

"By letting him beat the crap out of you?"

I'm grinning now. "Darragh would have been impressed," I tell Finn, and he lets out an exasperated breath.

"Darragh would have been in the middle of it."

"Yeah, he would have. It would have been fuel on a fire."

"What happened between you two? It was never this bad before."

Stuffing my hands into my pockets, I try to stay as close to the truth as possible.

"He just messed up something good I had. With a girl. Her name's Ava."

"A girl?" Finn's smiling now, but I don't feel like smiling.

My stomach twists. What if she won't forgive me?

"Fight for her. Win her back."

"He really did a number on it," I tell Finn, and all my anger comes rushing back. Clenching my fists, I remove them from my pockets.

"Don't give up, man. Look, I have to go." Finn glances at his watch. "Siobhan will kill me if I'm late. We are going cake tasting."

"So she said yes?"

His smile is stretching. "Of course she did."

"You're a lucky man," I tell Finn, and he walks back to me and hugs me. It's quick but tight.

"Thanks, brother." Once he releases me, he leaves.

I walk further away from the house and take out my phone. Ava's phone rings out. When it goes to voice mail, I hang up. What could you say in a voice mail that could start to mend this?

I ring again, and this time, I speak. "I'm sorry for everything, Ava. I want to make this right. Just call me." Not the best voice mail I've ever left, but the most honest one.

I keep walking, knowing I have another call to make, but I don't want to. I need to make up my mind and get my story straight before I ring my da. The ringtone sends my heart pounding. It rings seven times before he answers.

"We need to meet."

"I can't today, but I'll text you a location when I have it." I'm nodding into the phone when he hangs up.

I wasn't going to tell him over the phone that his son was dead. It was a conversation I could only have face-to-face with him. My phone dings and hope surges through me but deflates just as quickly.

What did I miss? It's Darragh.

You got a job in a brothel, Shane beat me up, and Liam raised his voice.

Get the fuck out. I get to work in a brothel? You're having me on. Darragh's message makes me smile.

Yep, you're working with Liam. The decision was made.

I don't think I can accept this kind of punishment. Haha. Fools. Right, check you later.

Stuffing the phone back into my pocket, I'm still grinning as I make my way back to the house.

I need to shower and change my clothes. Entering my room, I'm surprised to find Una sitting on my bed, tears running down her face. My first thought is that he hurt her.

"You were my favorite. You made me laugh. You made me feel like I be-longed." Now she looks up at me, and bile churns in my stomach as she points at the hall. "But what you did out there was wrong, Connor. I know this family isn't perfect. I know Shane isn't perfect, but I love him so much."

She's standing now, and I hate her words. "You could have blocked every attack he made. You're stronger, the better fighter, but to push him like that... It wasn't fair." Her voice rises, and I don't know what she wants me to say. "He's damaged enough without you poking at him."

"Don't," I tell her. "Stop right there. You have no idea what you're talking about. You have no idea what he's capable of."

"But I do, and I accept it."

I'm searching her face, looking for the cracks, the lies, but she's firm. I fold my arms across my chest. "Fine, Una. Tell me what Shane is capable of."

She shifts now like she's not so sure anymore, and when I nod, she speaks. "He hurts people. He deals drugs."

I'm surprised she knows that.

"He's killed people." Her voice is so low that I have to lean in, but I heard her right. Now I'm looking at Una differently. How can she lie with him?

But didn't I kill Brian? How could Ava lie beside me if she knew the truth? Would she stay? Would I think less of her, or was this true love? You stand beside your man no matter what crime he commits.

"I'm sorry for what I did in the hall, then."

Una wipes tears from her cheeks.

"I was trying to show you what a monster he was, but you already knew."

The slap across my face stings, and I grit my teeth. That's the first time she's ever done that. Her face is bright red. I'm not sure if it's shame or anger, but she storms from my room. That went well.

I make my way to the bathroom, and the mirror confirms my suspicions about my neck—red marks circle it. A red handprint is bright and visible on my face, and my lip is cut. Swelling has started above my left eye as well. A few days, and they will all be gone. Before I get into the shower, I ring Ava again, and her phone goes to voice mail.

"Just let me know you're okay." Hanging up, I glance back up at myself. For the first time in my life, I can't fight my way out of this, and that scares me more than anything.

CHAPTER TWENTY FIVE

AVA

I'M IN THE APARTMENT, and I've just stopped looking at my phone at this stage. Each time I listen to Connor's voice mail, a lump of ice breaks away from my heart and melts. I love him, but I'm not sure it's enough. A horn beeps outside, and I grab my bag and keys off the counter.

"Hi, Gerry." I climb into the back of the taxi, and my phone rings again. This time it's not Connor. I don't recognize the number. I think about not answering it, but I do in case it's the hospital about my nan. She's getting home today.

"Hello."

"I'm looking for an Ava Smith." The formal voice has me sitting up straighter. Gerry pulls out onto the main road just as I clip in my seat belt. "Speaking."

"It's Claire from Gunnes Auctioneers. I'm just ringing to see if tomorrow is a possible start date for you?"

My stomach erupts with butterflies. A job. I could have a job tomorrow morning. The only thing stopping me is that Connor got me this job. But it would be up to me to keep it. I wasn't going to throw away an opportunity like this.

"Fantastic. What time?" I'm smiling into the phone.

"We open at nine thirty. I'll be here myself and will train you. You come highly recommended."

Guilt sways back and forth in my stomach, but I squash it down. The recommendation not being real doesn't help, but I will prove myself. "That's so great. I'll be there tomorrow morning at nine thirty," I rattle off.

"Perfect, Ava. We will see you then." I end the call and meet Gerry's smiling eyes in the mirror.

"I believe congrats are in order."

"Yeah, just got a job with Gunnes Auctioneers."

His eyebrows rise. "Very swanky." I'm still smiling when I arrive at my old apartment. I don't have much to pack, but I need to get all my stuff out. I'm skittish as I walk up the steps, fear of Brian waiting for me has me pausing and wiping sweaty hands on my jeans. I spend the next few hours packing up my life. A mover is coming for them this evening and bringing everything to my nan's.

Taking a final look around the one-bedroom apartment, I feel the loss for the girl who lived here, the girl who had a job in Smyth's. I miss the simpler times.

I miss Connor. I banish that final thought as I leave the key where I told the moving company I would. I don't want to come back here again. It isn't Gerry who drops me back to Headfort Demesne but another taxi man. When we arrive, there's a man waiting outside my door.

The moment I get out, he introduces himself. "I'm Russell, the landlord. You must be Ava."

Shit, I thought I would be long gone before I had to explain to anyone that I wasn't living here anymore. I give him a tight smile and enter the apartment. I'm still jumpy after Brian, so I position myself close to the knife drawer hold my phone. He ruffles up paperwork as he walks over to the breakfast bar.

"So I just wanted to drop this off to you." Russell isn't how I pictured him. His long hair falls to the center of his back, and as he tucks it behind his ear, I can see leather bracelets covering his wrist.

"Connor covered a year's rent." He's smiling as he tells me the 'good news' but my stomach is in my shoes. "So if you're happy after the year, we can do new contracts. Here's a set of contracts and also the rules. If you want to read through it and sign, then I'll be out of your way." He hands me a pen and turns the contracts around to me. I'm pausing, not sure what to do.

Rent free for a year?

"I have a terrible headache right now. Could you just jot down your address, and once I read through these and sign them, I'll post them back?" I'm used to giving smiles when I don't mean them. People seem to feel like they're genuine. Russell gathers up his stuff but leaves the contracts.

"That's no problem." He's smiling knowing no one in their right mind would pass up an opportunity like this. Once Russell is gone, I don't think but go through the apartment and pack the two bags of belongings I brought here. Leaving the contracts and the keys on the counter, I call a taxi to take me to Navan hospital to collect my nan.

Nan and I are only in her house a few hours when the movers arrive. Nan is so excited to have me moving back in.

"Are you sure, birdy?" She's asked me this several times already.

"I want to be here with you, Nan." She's gives a sharp shake of her head.

"As long as my birdy is happy."

I frown at her words. I'm not happy. My nan being home and safe is everything, but losing Connor took a toll on me that I wasn't expecting.

"Is Connor coming over later?" Nan asks, and I wonder how transparent I am. She always seems to ask the right questions at the right times. I haven't told her about me and Connor.

"He's working," I answer while unpacking boxes.

"That one is a keeper, birdy. I feel it in these old bones."

My throat burns. I thought the same too. But it's funny. Having him and knowing that we started on a pretense compared to not having it all seemed like a no-brainer.

"I'm glad you're home, Nan," I tell her and hug her small frame. She hugs back, her hold strong for a woman of her years.

It's later that night when I'm alone in bed that I take out my phone. I won't ring him, but I don't know... I want to let him know I'm okay without telling him.

Did you hear from the guards about me making a statement? I chew my lip as I re-read it several times. "Just send it, Ava," I tell myself, and finally, my finger hits send. So that's it. It's gone. Nothing happens. No matter how much I stare at the phone, it doesn't light up.

Fine. I lie down and reach for the light switch when my phone lights up. I'm smiling, and a giddiness rushes through me now.

No, Ava, I didn't. But don't worry about Brian. He won't come near you again. Are you okay?

My eyes blur. I want Connor to hold me now and just make this all go away.

I got the job with Gunnes. I hit send and then feel foolish, but I want to share it with him.

I'm so happy for you. You deserve this. Did you hear from Russell? Can we meet?

My poor lip takes more abuse as I re-read over Connor's message.

Yeah, he came around earlier. I better go to sleep. Have to look fresh for this job in the morning.

I'm staring at the phone again, and nothing comes in. I turn off the light and lie down but hold the phone in my hand. I hate how my stomach erupts when it lights up.

You will do great. X

I'm focused on the X, my finger rubbing across it. "I love you," I tell the phone as tears leak out of the corner of my eyes. My stomach cramps painfully, and I pull my legs up into a fetal position. The thought of losing him is causing my pulse to spike. His smile, soft hands, and kind ways torture me. Happy memories haunt me until I fall asleep.

***

The new job is great. I just show people around properties that are for rent. I close three on my first day. Claire says I'm a natural, and it does feel natural to me.

My phone rings when I'm on a break. It's Connor, but I can't answer it. Once it stops ringing, I wait for the message that I have a voice mail. Without fail, it arrives. I'm smiling like an addict as I listen to his voice. Closing my eyes, something burns deep inside me.

"Just checking in to see how the first day went. I know you will do great." A pause *"I really miss you, and it would be great if we could meet up. Just grab a coffee. Whatever suits you."* Another long pause, and I wonder if he's done. *"Let me know."*

I listen to it four more times before I stop acting crazy and put the phone down. I don't respond but finish my day's work, which flies.

Nan has dinner on the table when I arrive home. "It smells delicious," I tell her as we sit down. She's made my favorite of hers—a stew. We eat in silence, savoring each bite.

"Nan, if Jack lied to you about how he met you, what would you do?"

Nan raises her eyebrows and goes to the press under the sink, where she retrieves a box of cigarettes and a lighter. Smoking with Nan is occasional, and when she offers me one, I take it.

"Jack's been gone thirty years now. Your grandfather never lied." Nan lights up her cigarette, and my heart deflates at her words. I was being stupid even thinking of giving Connor another chance.

"But you need to spit out what you're trying to say."

"Fine. Connor lied to me. He met me on purpose to get information out of me." Those are the basics.

Nan takes her sweet time to answer, taking long drags off her fag before flicking the ashes in the sink to her back. I'm taking in the smoke but not inhaling it fully.

"Information about what?" She purses her lips, and I wonder how to explain this to her. But then I decide to just go for it.

"His brother hurt someone, and I witnessed it. So I suppose his brother sent him to find out what I saw."

"And Connor got this information out of you and then left?"

"Well, no. Things actually were going great, and I left when I found out the truth. But Connor never got any information out of me."

I'm staring at the smoke that swirls around the small room. Connor only questioned me at the start, but he never asked after that.

"Maybe you need to talk to the boy and listen to his side of things. No one's perfect, birdy." I put the cigarette out. All it was doing was burning my eyes. Nan is right. I need to at least hear his side of the story.

Once I'm in bed, I take out my phone and text Connor.

I'm free tomorrow if you want to meet up. I hit send and wait. It doesn't take long for him to reply, but his reply isn't what I expected.

A relation of ours died, so I have to go up the north for the funeral. Can we meet up after?

Yeah, sure. Really sorry for your loss.

Thank you. Can't wait to see you. X

I'm smiling again. How easily he makes me smile. I send one final message back.

X

CHAPTER TWENTY SIX

CONNOR

I BIDE MY TIME slowly and know that it's up now with Shane. He's outside talking to Una. They're smiling at each other. I wait in the kitchen, and when he arrives in, his smile tilts.

"I was hoping I could have a quick word," I say, and he gets himself a cup of tea.

"I'm busy today," he tells me with his back to me.

"Where's Bernard's body?"

The cup smashes on the floor—the reaction I wanted. Shane glances at me over his shoulder, and I can see he's trying to think quick.

"Have you heard from Brian lately?" I ask, taking a sip of my tea, and he's paling and nodding.

"What do you want?"

"Just a quick word." We leave the kitchen, and I follow Shane as he moves swiftly into the dining room. The plaque is like a beacon.

Family comes first.

I always wanted to destroy that plaque, and one day I'm sure I'll get the chance.

"So where is Bernard's body?"

"I don't know what Brian told you, but he's full of shit."

"You get one shot at this, Shane. So I'm going to tell you what I know, and then you can tell me where his body is."

Sitting down. I sip my tea, and I gesture to the seat across from me. When Shane sits slowly, I know I have him by the balls.

"Brian is dead. I blew out his kneecaps before shooting him in the head." I let that sink in. Shane's touching the band on his thumb, and I'm glad he's thinking about Mom. That's what I'm counting on. Whether he really knows what he's doing, he's doing it.

"Bernard was the son of the general of the IRA."

"I know that he was Tom's son and connected to the IRA. I just didn't know that Tom was that high up." He joins his hands now and leans them on the table. "So what, you're going to tell on me? It's my word against yours. Who's to say you didn't kill Bernard?"

I'm smiling at him. It's nearly too easy. "Because Shane, Tom will believe me. I'm his son."

His jaw tightens, and his nostrils flare as he sits back, doubt clear in his eyes.

"My da is waiting on my call to let him know who killed his son. So I can either tell him Brian did it, and that I killed him, or I tell him you did it, and then I have to kill you."

"Mam would never be with Tom."

My composure slips, and I'm leaning in. "Why? Tom never put his hand on her, unlike Michael."

He's shaking his head. "Dad never..."

"He did. But I'm not here to hash that out with you."

Silence descends on the room. He keeps looking at his hands and snapping quick glances up at me.

"Brian was the one who told Harry about the land. I told you he paid off the Gardaí, but you wouldn't believe me. He wanted you out of the picture after you beat him up."

"So you tell Tom—your dad—that Brian killed Bernard, and what? You let me walk away?"

No.

"Where's his body?"

"You need to listen to me. I swear to God, I didn't mean to. It was an unlucky blow."

I didn't need to hear his sob story. My brother was dead. How that happened is irrelevant. When I don't answer but take a sip of my now cold tea, Shane rubs his face.

"At the base of the Loch Leigh Mountains."

The thought of Bernard rotting away at the bottom of the mountains has me looking away from Shane.

"I want him in a coffin, in a hearse that I can drive up the north."

"A hearse. Where do you think I'm going to get one?"

I pin Shane with a stare. "I don't care if you have to buy me one. I will bring my brother home in a coffin."

Shane stands. He's looking a little pale now.

"I'm not finished," I tell him. Clenching his jaw, he sits back down. "In exchange for your life, you'll have to do something for me."

"I'm not agreeing to anything until I hear what it is."

"All I have to do is pick up the phone and say your name, and there will be a bullet in the back of your head. Why don't you get it? You will do what I say." I lean out and let that sink in.

When he doesn't answer me back, I proceed. What I'm about to share with him could get me killed. I lower my voice.

"Mam wasn't killed in a shooting."

Shane's hands turn white as he grips them tightly.

"Tom knew the pathologist who was taking care of Mam." Even speaking about it now is painful. I hate to think of how she really died. "The shooting was staged. She was already dead. Someone broke her neck."

Shane pushes his chair out slightly, the horror evident in his eyes. He loved her as much as I did, so for now, I would give him that bit of respect.

"The fact that someone tried to cover it up meant they regretted it. It was an accident, maybe, but it was also someone close."

"Someone close?" The denial is evident on his face, but when Tom first presented this to me, it took days for me to come to terms with it too.

"Someone must have discovered that she was having an affair with Tom," I say.

"Dad wouldn't hurt her. None of us would."

"I know what you're saying, Shane, and I get that it's painful, but the truth is, someone she knew killed her because they discovered something about her. So my logic asks, who gathers information and sends it back down the line?"

Shane's not going to get this because his mind is stuck on how she really died.

"His informant," I continue, "whoever that is, must have told whatever it was they killed her for. We find him, we find out who killed her."

"But I don't know who he is."

I'm nodding. "But that's your ticket to stay alive. Find out who the informant is, and I'll take care of the rest."

I reach my hand across the table. "Do we have a deal?" His handshake is limp, and sitting with him won't help. He needs time.

"I want Bernard's body here by tomorrow," I tell him, and he looks up at me. His eyes flicker around the room like he just woke up.

"Okay."

***

I spend much of the day packing up my bag. Da texted that we're meeting tomorrow in the same hotel in Monaghan. If Shane doesn't have the hearse ready, I can always come back for Bernard, but telling Dad face-to-face is important. My stomach churns every time I think what I have to do.

A knock on my door has me peering up. Una is half in my room. "Hi."

"What do you want, Una?" I stuff the remainder of my clothes into a rucksack.

"You're leaving?"

I glance up at her. "Yeah, I think I've overstayed my welcome."

The bed dips as Una sits down. "I'm so sorry for putting my hand on you yesterday."

I shrug "It's fine." But it's not. I've lost respect for her. Maybe time will give it back, but right now, I can't look at Una the same.

"It's not fine. I had no right."

"Una, I know you mean well, but I have a lot of shit going on. So…"

Her cheeks darken, and she stands, folding her arms across her chest. "If you need me for anything, just ring."

"Yeah, I'll keep you on speed dial."

"I'm not the enemy here, Connor."

I'm looking up at Una again. "Neither am I. I'm one of the good guys."

Her eyes mist over, and I don't want to make her cry. "It's all fine. We're good," I tell her, but she starts shaking her head.

"No, I know you. I've really hurt you." I tighten my grip on my bag.

"I'll get over it." Una stops me from leaving the room. Her arms tighten around my neck, and I can feel the warmth of her tears on my neck. Dropping my bag, I wrap my arms around her. "Don't cry, Una."

"I love you, Connor," she says to me, and I kiss the side of her head.

"I love you, too."

***

I stay at a hotel that night. I've taken Darragh's Jeep with me down to Monaghan. Shane still doesn't have everything ready, but it will be soon. When I enter the hotel, I notice two men lingering in the lobby. My eyes are more tuned in. Dad sits in the same seat of the bar. I'm not sure if it's lighting or what I'm about to tell him, but he looks older. His eyes are more wrinkled. The embrace he gives me makes me sense he knows the information I'm about to deliver. Otherwise, I would have told him across the phone.

I don't beat around the bush. "I found Bernard."

"I… That's what I thought. He's dead, isn't he?"

"Yes, Dad, he is." His face pinches up as he looks out at the sea of chairs.

"Did you get the person who did it?" Now his eyes burn into mine.

"I did. I gave him a IRA death." His large hand covers mine.

"Thank you, son."

I hate lying, but it's for the best.

"His body will be back up the north by tomorrow. We can bury him then."

"Maybe it's a good thing your mother is dead. This would kill her." Any of us getting hurt would have killed Mam.

"I'll start funeral arrangements." Dad rubs his jaw, and he's aged another five years in a matter of seconds.

"I'm going to head back, and I'll be home tomorrow with Bernard." We give each other a final embrace before I leave. Driving back has numbed me. I want to feel something about Bernard, but all I can muster up is anger toward Shane. I can't seem to find any other emotion.

The hotel room is stark, almost empty. The bed has a floral cover, and the room stinks of cigarette smoke. The thought of staying here for the night alone has me leaving the room. I ring Ava, and I'm actually surprised when she answers.

"Hi." I pause while walking down the hall.

"Hi." She sounds breathless.

"I was wondering if you wanted to meet up now?"

There's a long pause on her end, then "I'm finished in an hour if you want to meet."

"Will I pick you up?" A long pause, and my stomach tightens. She's going to back out.

"Okay."

"Okay." I'm smiling into the phone. "See you soon."

CHAPTER TWENTY SEVEN

CONNOR

I HAVEN'T FELT THIS nervous in a long time. My fingers drum along the steering wheel as I wait across the road for Ava. Everyone seems to be coming out of the office but her. Now I worry she's changed her mind and is holding up inside, or if she's slipped out the back door.

My stomach tightens as she steps out of Gunnes. She looks so good; she looks up and down the street before her eyes settle on the Jeep and then meet mine. Green eyes flare to life, and I swallow the panic that tears through me as she makes her way across the road. I don't want to fuck this up. I lean across and open the door.

"Thanks." She's nervous as she climbs in.

"You look good," I say, and she gives me a tight smile before searching her bag. She hands me a card. "It's a mass card for your friend." I take it, and it feels heavy in my hands.

"It's my brother." I tighten my grip on the mass card.

"Oh, Connor, I'm so sorry." Her small hand touches my arm, and I look at her.

"He was one of the good guys," I tell her, and I swallow the lump in my throat.

"How did he die?" She moves her body so it faces me.

"It was a bar fight. An unlucky blow." I grip the steering wheel.

When she touches me again, I face her. I want to kiss her so much, but her eyes are filled with hesitation the moment I lean in.

"I'm so sorry for lying to you," I say. "But I was going to tell you the truth." She frowns and swallows. "I love you, and I just want another chance with you."

She gazes up at me from under her lashes. "I love you, too, and I want to try again. But I can't bear if you lie to me again."

I pull her into my arms. She hesitates for only a moment before she lets me hold her. I inhale the sweet scent of Ava, and it's home to me. So familiar. "God, I missed you." I kiss the top of her head, and she looks up at me now.

"I missed you, too." When her eyes move to my lips, I don't hesitate to kiss her. Her lips feel softer and warmer than I remember, and I deepen the kiss wanting her so badly right now.

When we break apart, she smiles up at me. "We are in a public place."

"You want to go home?" I turn the Jeep over.

"Actually, I moved back in with my nan."

"If you're happy, I'm happy."

She kisses me softly on the lips. "But we could always use it to meet up, since you did pay rent for a year." Her smile has me pulling away from the curb. The car can't seem to move fast enough.

Once we arrive, Ava actually looks disappointed. "Oh, the keys are inside."

"I have a key from when we installed the new locks," I tell her and open my wallet where I keep the lone key.

"Okay." She's chewing her lip, and I lean across and kiss her. Her hands are on my face, tugging me closer, but it's not close enough. Her skin feels softer as I let my fingers run under her shirt. My touch has her pushing her tongue deeper into my mouth, and I moan.

"Let's go in." She's nodding while reaching the door handle. Her eagerness is matched with my own, and it's not just about having her now. It's hope that we can mend things. My foot kicks the door closed as I move us into the bedroom. A trail of clothes is left behind, and when we reach the bedroom, we're nearly undressed.

My fingers dive down, and she inhales sharply when I push two of them inside her. I want to watch her. My own need grows as her nipples brush my chest.

Each step toward the bed, I remove my fingers before inserting them again. She spreads her legs instantly once she's on her back. My own need soon replaces my fingers, and I don't hesitate as I pump myself inside her. Dipping my head, I take a hard nipple in my mouth, and Ava thrashes under me.

Leaving her breasts, I find her mouth. Our kisses are urgent and wet as I pump harder and faster. Our moans are mingled with flesh hitting flesh, and my release is so close. Ava's face is twisted in pleasure. Taking her nipple between my fingers, I squeeze, taking her over the edge as she covers me with her wetness. I let my seed pour into her before I slow down my thrusts.

I'm kissing her neck and face while trying to catch my breath. "I missed you," I tell her chest, and she shakes under me. When I look up, she's laughing.

"You missed my breasts?" she teases, and her smile is worth everything.

"I did." The answer has her giggling. "They are such beautiful breasts." I touch them, and she hisses.

"They're too sensitive right now."

My body wouldn't mind going again, but I need to slow my pace with Ava.

"Are you hungry?" I ask, placing a kiss on her lips.

"I think so."

I grin at her wide eyes and remove myself from her. "I'll order a pizza."

As I get dressed and make my way into the living room, the emptiness of the apartment shows that Ava doesn't live here. I order the same pizza as before on my phone before putting it into my back pocket. The contracts sit on the breakfast bar, a pen on top of them. She never signed.

I sit around for a bit until she moves up behind me, wrapping her arms around my waist. I cover her hands with one of mine. "It didn't feel right to stay here."

"That's okay. It's here if you want it."

Ava moves around so we're facing each other. "I'm going to stay with my nan for a while."

I wrap my arms around her, and she's tiny in my arms as I look down on her. "Well, we can use it to meet up."

Her cheeks darken, but her lips tug up into a smile. "I think that's a good idea."

"Me too. I might stay here for a while myself. If you're okay with that?"

"Of course. It's your place. But are you not happy at home?"

"It's crowded," I answer, and she laughs.

"I know you live in Whitewood House. It's huge. But you have a lot of family?"

I kiss her on the nose before I speak. "Finn, Darragh, who you met, and Shane." I say his name quickly and can see her flinch. "Also Liam. They're all my half brothers, but my dad is also their uncle." Yeah, this all sounds messed up. "So my other half brother, Bernard, died. I got on with him, and both families don't get on, so I just need some space."

"Sounds very complicated."

"Yeah, it is."

Ava pulls me into a strong hug. "I'm here if you need to talk."

"I know." The pizza arrives then, and I'm happy so we can move away from the topic of my family.

Once we're seated again, I ask about Nan and Ava's new job. Watching Ava talk about her job with such enthusiasm and her nan with such affection, is really nice, and I find myself relaxing more than I have in a long time.

But it doesn't last long as the topic moves on to Brian. "I know I asked you before about Brian, but I just think it's strange that the guards haven't asked me for a statement."

I don't want to lie to her, but the truth isn't something I think she could accept. "I promise you, he will never bother you again."

Ava drops her pizza. "See, what does that even mean, Connor? Does it mean you didn't take him to the guards?"

"I can tell you the truth, but you can't unhear it. So I hope you can just trust me when I say it's over. You're safe." My heart pounds as I wait for Ava's verdict. She chews her lip before she answers.

"I trust you."

Taking her face in my hands, I kiss her. "Thank you." Her saying she trusted me means everything to me. Our conversation drifts back to safe ground, and the day turns to night before we even know it. I forget about Bernard, about my mother's death. I forget about not belonging. Ava makes me feel like I'm part of something. Her smiles are infectious, and my chest tightens at the thought that I almost lost her. Her yawns are growing closer.

"We better get to bed. Are you working tomorrow?"

She's standing and gathering up our dinner that's gone cold. "Yeah, an early rise."

"Me too. I can drop you to work."

"That would be great."

She rings her nan to tell her she's safe as I get ready for bed. I check my phone.

I have everything ready.

It's a message from Shane. I'll bring Bernard home tomorrow, and we can bury him.

"Everything okay?" Ava asks. I didn't hear her enter the room.

"Just thinking about the funeral tomorrow."

She pauses getting changed. "Let me come with you." The idea of Ava with me is tempting, but I'd be bringing her to an IRA funeral. "No, it's fine. It's down the north. But thanks." She looks slightly disappointed as she slips under the covers.

"I love you," I say, and my heart gives a little kick when she says it back. I fall asleep with Ava in my arms, and it's the first full night's sleep I've had in a long time.

***

The markets area of Belfast has come to a standstill. Thousands have gathered for Bernard's funeral. I'm up front carrying his coffin. The Irish flag is covering the coffin, the colors so bright in a sea of black.

I'm front left, along with Seamus and Matt. My dad is on the right with Mark and Joe. The six of us carry Bernard's coffin. As we pass, the streets are silent. The unnatural stillness of the onlookers is a reminder of what we represent for the people.

Some bow their heads in respect. Others huddle their children away from us, like the sheer sight of us might send them down the wrong path. We are the Irish Republican Army. A force that's been protecting the Irish Catholics and trying to take our country back from the British. Our steps are in unison as we make the journey to the Milltown Cemetery where Bernard will be laid to rest in a republican plot.

As we lower his coffin, we pause just above the opening as six fighters step forward, their faces covered in green masks. Their green uniforms pressed and perfect. Guns are armed and fired into the air. Each shot makes my body jump; I keep still on the outside, but inside, my heart beats to the drums that play in the background.

We lower Bernard into the ground and step aside as the priest finishes the funeral. I keep my head bowed and don't look around me. I know the biggest names are here, along with the camera crews. I don't want to be on the front page of the paper.

Once the funeral is over, the crowds disperse.

"Thank you, son." Da walks with his arm across my shoulder.

"He went off with respect," I say.

"Great to have you back, Connor." Seamus falls into step beside me. His weather-beaten face isn't from spending too much time outside. When you lead so many men, it tends to take its toll on you.

"Thank you, sir."

"Are you staying long?" Matt asks.

I glance over my shoulder at him as he walks behind us. He's the same age as me and got on well with Bernard. "Nah, I have to go back." The longing to stay isn't lost in my words.

Seamus and Dad walk together as Matt catches up to me. He offers a smoke, and I take it.

"Fucked up what happened to Bernard," he says as he lights it up. I take the outstretched lighter and light up my own cigarette.

"Yeah, I know, man."

We leave the graveyard grounds and walk with the crowd. It dwindles until only a hundred of us are left, and we make our way into Ronnie Drew. The pub is packed when me and Matt get there. Irish music is being beaten out by a young group of singers.

"Ah, Connor you came back." Molly, Matt's sister drinks from a straw in her glass.

"Yeah, just for the funeral."

She pouts her lips and runs her hand down my suit jacket. "You look like James Bond." She winks, and I smirk at her.

"Jesus, Molly, you're like a dog in heat." Matt scares her off, and we make our way to the bar.

Matt and Molly are Irish twins. When Matt was one month old, his mother got pregnant with Molly.

"Two Guinness," Matt orders, and I have to shoulder and push my way to the bar.

"So what have you being doing?" Matt hands me a pint, and I drink half of it in one go.

"A job for Da." I can't say what it is, and he knows that.

"Shit is going down up here. You're missing all the action."

"I'm sure you can handle it," I say as my eyes clash with my dad's from across the room. "I've got to go. I'll catch you later."

I move through the crowd, and when I reach Da, he leads me to a room out back. Only about ten men are seated. Most of them high up in the IRA Da takes me to a chair in the corner.

"Nothing like a pint at home." Dad raises his pint and drinks it until his glass is empty. "He got a good send off," he says, but I can see the pain in Da's eyes. Pain he won't shed. Maybe he will later on at home, alone, but not here around these men. It would be a sign of weakness. And no matter the loss, you have to only show strength.

"Have you made any progress on your ma?" he asks.

"I will. I have Shane helping me find out who the informant is."

"Shane." Da says his name with disgust. If he knew the truth, Shane wouldn't just get a bullet in the head. He would be tortured.

"Yeah, he fucked some people over, and I found out about it. So I'm using it as leverage."

He nods, but he holds my eye a little longer, and I try to make sure I breathe normally as I pick up my drink. I hate lying to him, but I continue to remind myself that it's what's best.

Da leaves earlier, and the funeral party takes a turn around midnight. The younger members grow wild, and that's when I leave. Walking down Market Street reminds me of how much I miss this place, and when Matt falls into step beside me, I pause and stare up at the stars.

"It's getting wild in there," Matt says. He lights up a fag as I pull out my phone.

I'm staring at the stars. Are you? Once I have it sent, I realize it's three in the morning.

"Shit," I mumble, hoping I don't wake her up.

"What's up?"

"I sent a message to my girlfriend, and I just realized it's three in the morning."

Both of Matt's eyebrows rise. "Girlfriend. I'll keep that one on the down low I can already hear all the hearts breaking." I grin at Matt's over exaggeration.

I was asleep, but I'm out back now. Staring up at the stars. X I'm grinning again.

"Is it dirty?" Matt asks, leaning in. "Staring at the stars? What are you talking about?"

I push him away. **Get inside before you get cold, and I love you.**

My phone bleeps again, and Ava sends me a photo of herself, fresh faced and smiling into the camera. She's standing in the kitchen, and under the image, she's written: **I love you too.**

"She's hot," Matt says. I put the phone away and turn to him, and he holds up his hands. "What?"

She is hot, but I don't want anyone else calling her that.

"Right, I'm off to bed. Will we catch up tomorrow?" Matt sways slightly, and I help him stand straighter.

"Nah, I'm going to head back at first light. But once I'm done down there, I'm sure I'll be home for good." Matt slaps me on the back and walks off. His steps aren't the best, and I watch him until he disappears around the corner.

When I get home, the dark house isn't inviting, and I think about Ava. Maybe I could leave and surprise her, creep into her window. No, she has work in the morning. But going into the house is causing my chest to tighten. The garage is noisy as fuck as I push it open. After pulling the tarp off my motorcycle, I push her out of the garage and carry the helmet. I'll ring Da tomorrow. I don't want to linger around here for too long. It just makes it harder to leave.

Once I've pushed the bike down the road, I jump on and start it up, making the journey back.

CHAPTER TWENTY EIGHT

CONNOR

"WHY ARE WE HERE again?" I ask Ava while I balance on the thin walkway that's been laid through a bog and woodlands.

"Please, Connor. Walk properly or you're going to end up in the bog."

I do a little wobble and laugh at Ava. I open up my arms, and she walks into them. I give her a hug. It's beautiful out here. We caught a good day, and being outdoors with Ava is nice.

After leaving Belfast two nights ago, it was six in the morning when I entered Kells, so I did the proper thing and went to Headfort Demesne. I still had notions about crawling into Ava's window. But I left her alone.

Taking her hand, I face forward.

"Thank you." Her smile is wide as we walk. It's funny that we don't meet anyone here. It's like the world has decided to leave us alone.

"So I wanted to ask you…" I stop walking and face Ava again. "We have a family wedding coming up in the summer, and I would love if you came with me."

Her eyes light up, and she's in my arms. "All you had to say was a wedding, and I'm there. Who's getting married?"

"Finn, one of the youngest. We'll meet them before the wedding."

"I really can't wait to meet your family."

"Yeah. I'm dreading it," I admit, and Ava's laughter carries across the land.

"Don't. It will be fine. I'm sure they will love me."

"They'll love you. But I'm not sure how you'll feel about them." The idea of her being in a room with Liam, Michael, and Shane just doesn't sit well with me, but I wouldn't miss Finn's wedding for the world.

"I'll have to get a dress." Ava gives a small, happy clap, and I think maybe it will all be worth it. We spend the rest of the day in the bog and then eating out before going home, where we spend far more time than we intended. Spending our free time together and our nights in each other's arms makes the times I have to go home and interact with Shane easier. I know I have Ava to come back to.

***

The vibration of my phone on the bedside table wakes me up.

"Who is it?" Ava sits up beside me as I turn on a light. Darragh's nanme flashes on the screen.

"Hello ?" I kick back the covers and climb out of bed.

"Connor, I need you now, man."

I'm awake and moving into the living room. "What's wrong?"

"I fucked up!" His slurred voice has got to be caused by more than drink.

"Where are you?"

"Pool house. Yeah, I think the pool house."

I'm back in the bedroom, pulling on clothes, when Ava sits up again.

"What pool house, Darragh?"

"Ours."

Holding the phone away, I give Ava a quick kiss. "Go to sleep, it's just Darragh. He needs a lift. I'll be back soon."

She gives me a sleepy smile before lying back down. "Okay, be careful."

I'm out the door. "Are you still there?" I ask.

"Yeah. Connor, hurry up."

I try to keep Darragh on the phone, but I lose him. I'm in the Jeep trying to ring him back when I get a dead tone. The roads are empty at four in the morning as I speed through Kells. I keep hitting redial, but I still get no answer.

Why has he rang me and not the others?

I arrive at the house, and no lights are on. I turn off my own lights as I make my way around back. The pool house is lit up, and dread snakes it's way around my stomach. Pushing open the door the water reflects the lights back to me, but I can't see anyone.

"Darragh," I call out and can hear movement that seems to be coming from behind the couch. My heart picks up at each step I take, until I'm looking down at Darragh.

There's so much blood covering him, and a blond girl is dead at his feet. "I really fucked up this time, man."

***

FEARLESS

Title: Fearless
Series Number: Book Four

Blurb:

He's rich, egotistical and a womanizer. She's angry dark and sarcastic. What could possibly go wrong?

Darragh

My official punishment for messing up is working in one of my brother's hotels. The unofficial one? I'm stuck with Ciara. Angry, dark and sarcastic, she fills in my days.

Sick of being penniless, robbing a bank seems a no-brainer. That was until I got caught and I'm the scapegoat once again. Normally, choosing between my life and my friends would have been easy. Simple maths. That was until Ciara. She's making me regret a lot of my past and question most of my decisions. The closer we grow she's all I can think about. She swears she will never sleep with me, but I love a challenge. I will have her no matter what the cost.

Ciara

The streets of Dublin were all I've ever known. When Liam O'Reagan offers me a job, working in one of his hotels, things start to look up for me. That is until Darragh O'Reagan is dropped into my life and we have to work together. He's everything I can't stand: rich, egotistical and a womanizer. The closer we get the more of him I see, and I soon realize he's worth saving. But at what cost?

With the O'Reagan's the price tag always seems too high.

CHAPTER ONE

DARRAGH

"I DIDN'T MEAN IT." My hands sink further into her bloody hair. "I tried to stop it."

Connor stands over me, his chest rising and falling quickly. He moves swiftly toward me. We're now eye to eye as he sits on his haunches.

"Did you hurt her?" His voice is low, but even through my drugged state, I can still hear the threat there.

Shaking my head, I focus on the girl again, who I hold in my hands. "She was dancing and fell."

"Into the pool?"

I blink as I stare up at Connor. "I jumped in and pulled her out, but she won't wake up." I hug the body closer to me. Water and blood mixes around our feet and flows away from us.

"She was smiling." It was just the two of us, a private party, and the drugs kept flowing. First it was me giving her some, cutting it up, but I lost count of how much we took or who was cutting what. "Connor, we had so many drugs." My hold tightens even further on the girl.

"Go back to the house."

I cling to his words and release the girl. A shiver rushes me as I place her carefully onto the floor. I need a fag. The pack sits on the table in front of the couch. I grab them and light one up.

"I owe you one," I say to Connor as I leave.

He doesn't answer me, and I try not to think about what I'm leaving behind.

***

Sweet cookies—that's all I can smell as I move through the kitchen. Throwing my fag into the sink, I search for them and find a tin of cookies on the counter. I stuff two into my mouth and moan in bliss.

Taking the tin with me, I climb the stairs to my room. "You are my sunshine," I sing as I eat the next cookie. "My only sunshine. You make me happy when skies are gray."

I stuff the next one into my mouth and grin. A trail of crumbs is behind me as I enter my bedroom. "You'll never know, cookie, how much I love you. Please don't take my cookies away."

Clutching the tin tighter, I munch on two more, then I fall onto my bed. My hand roams around the tin, looking for more, but they're gone.

"Someone ate all my cookies," I tell the ceiling. My heart pounds as I picture blonde hair coated in blood.

"It's okay," I say to myself as I get up and pull off my wet clothes. "Connor will fix it," I tell myself again as I climb into bed naked. The sheets are cold under me, and my hand searches for the quilt. When my fingers grip the corner, I pull it up over me.

***

I roll and float, my eyes shooting open as my back hits a hard surface. The ceiling looks so far away, and I sit up but quickly close my eyes as my head pounds in pain. I wait until the pain subsides slightly before opening my eyes again. I'm naked on my bedroom floor.

I'm squinting against the throbbing in my head as I search the floor for clothes. Jeans and a T-shirt that smells reasonably clean will do.

The pool house. I need to check the pool house. I'm not sure if I'd been dreaming of a blonde girl. My memory jumps from dancing with her to Connor telling me to leave. No way would Connor have a go after me. It wasn't his style.

I don't bother with socks but put on a pair of brogues as I make my way out to the pool house. The light outside feels harsh, and I dip my head lower. The door is open, and when I enter, nothing looks odd.

Walking around the pool, I'm drawn to the wicker couch at the back of the room. I'm sitting on it, looking around the room, and I'm not sure what I expect to find. My pulse spikes as blood running through the cracks in the tile springs to mind. I'm up and looking behind the couch. But there's nothing, only beige tiles that stare back at me.

"Fuck it." Getting off the couch, I take a few steps to the pool. Turning my back to the water, I grin as I let myself free-fall into the water. My eyes snap open as cold water assaults my body. Rotating, I break the surface and pull myself out. I'm more alert as I walk back to the house.

"What happened?" Mary shakes her head as she stares at the water that drips from my clothes.

"Ah, shit. Sorry, Mary," I say as I pull my T-shirt over my head.

"That's not necessary." Mary sounds flustered, and when I drop my shirt and reach for my jeans, her face flushes.

"I hate wetting your floors, Mary," I say with a smile before I drop my jeans. A scream from her has me pulling the jeans back up. I'm not wearing boxers.

"My bad. I ate all your cookies last night. Can you make me more today?" I lean against the counter and smile up at Mary, but she refuses to meet my eye.

"Yes, Darragh. Just go get dressed."

"Yes, ma'am."

My phone rings when I enter my bedroom. I pull the jeans off. The chaffing from the material has reddened my skin.

"What's up?" I answer.

"Where the fuck were you last night?" DJ asks.

I find clean boxers and yank them on.

"I was going to ask you that. I can't remember. I think I was with a blonde," I say to DJ, pulling on a T-shirt.

His laughter is loud through the speaker. "Yeah, one minute we were chatting, then I go and get a drink and you're fucking gone."

"Well, women before friends," I say.

He snorts.

"I'll catch you later," I tell him. "Going to go feed my belly."

When I enter the kitchen, Mary gives me a quick once-over. Spreading my arms, I do a little twirl. "I'm dressed, Mary."

She smiles. "Sit down, Darragh."

I do as she says. I'm the only one at the table when Una arrives into the kitchen.

"You look rough," she tells me as she gathers up her red hair and clips it high on her head in a way that defies gravity.

"So do you," I say to her, and she sticks her tongue out at me.

"I was in bed early," she says.

I lean across the table. "You might have been in bed early, but I bet my sweet ass you were bumping uglies with shovel face."

Mary swipes at me, and I sit back in my seat. A fry up is placed in front of me. I stand and kiss Mary on the cheek. "I love you, Mary," I declare before I sit down and start to eat.

"Who's shovel face?" Una asks.

I grin and nod. "So you were bumping uglies with shovel face." I stuff half a sausage into my mouth and wink at Una.

Una's face flames, and she starts eating her own breakfast. She glances at the door. "I'm just not having this conversation with you."

I look up as shovel face enters the room. Raising my hand, I wait for a high five. "Una is filling me in on what you guys got up to last night."

He walks past my raised hand and sits down beside Una.

"Ignore him," Una tells Shane as he gives her a kiss on the cheek.

"I always do. But we should let him keep talking. Maybe someday he'll say something intelligent." Shane's words have Una grinning.

"Do you really think so?" Una's enjoying this.

They both look at me, and I focus on my food.

"No, I actually don't." Shane's response is quick.

"How did you even get here? Who let you out of your cage?" I ask Shane, and his shoulders tense. I'm happier now as I munch on my food. Pissing Shane off is such fun.

"Talk to you later, sis," I tell Una as I stand up. Shane's shoulders tighten. "And I suppose talk to you later, brother?" I say it really slowly to let the creepiness of that statement sink in.

Shane levels me with a stare, and I leave the kitchen laughing. *Too easy. Way too easy.*

"Don't forget you start work with Liam," Shane shouts after me, and I pause.

"What, in the brothel?" I ask with laughter in my voice. "Oh God no. Make it stop," I shout as I climb the stairs, and I can hear Una laughing.

***

The silver coating over the painkillers snaps as I gather a handful and wash them down with some coffee. Cars zoom past me, and each one makes my head hurt. I turn into Kells Business Park and drive all the way to the back. Kelly's Kitchens takes up two large warehouses, and I park my car in the front. The smoke from my cigarette blows out around me as I enter the warehouse.

"DJ!" I roar, using my hands to amplify my voice.

He grins at me before offering me a beer. "The cure," he says, and I take it, needing a cure badly.

"What's up, Fitz? I didn't see you around last night." I take the lawn chair that's vacant beside him.

His hood is up, and when our eyes meet, he can't hold my gaze. The lift doesn't go the whole way up with Fitz. He's a mad bastard, so we keep him around.

"My fucking mother found my gun and had a fit. She threatened me with the Gardaí. But I got it back eventually." He stuffs his hands into his white hoodie as he rocks the chair back and forth.

DJ pops open a fresh beer. "Yeah, but she kept his bullets." We laugh as the door opens again.

"How are you drinking again?" Art asks as he saunters over to us like he owns the place. He removes his sunglasses and places them in the *V* of his navy T-shirt. A heavy gold watch shifts as he grips DJ's hand and they half embrace.

"It's just the cure," I say to him, and he shakes his head with a grin.

"Alright, Fitz," Arrt says.

Fitz nods at Art. They have hostility between them. Art is a sneer, and Fitz doesn't like it, but it's never come to blows.

Dragging over a chair, Art sits down. "So, what's the plan?" His brown hair is dipped with highlights. He spends more time on his appearance than most women do.

Lighting a fag, I sit forward as DJ joins us. I wait until everyone is ready before I tell them my plan. I'm smirking with excitement. Already, I can feel the rush.

"We're going to rob an ATM," I say, looking from one to the other. No one looks overly impressed.

"Why? You don't need money."

"Neither do you," I shoot back at Art. He came from money, old money. His well-polished appearance and education makes it questionable why he hangs out with us. I think he likes the chase as much as me.

"So I got word that they'll fill the links close to midnight. We're talking about two hundred thousand, peeps."

DJ's eyes widen, and I've gained Fitz's attention. "We hit around four tomorrow morning. We need to rob a digger to pull it out of the wall, vehicles that we can burn, and a flatbed to take it away."

Art rubs his hands together. "I'm in."

I look at DJ. He removes his cap, runs his hand through his hair, and puts it back on. His vest showcases his tattooed arms.

"Fuck it, I'm in."

Now it's Fitz who won't say no, but we wait, all looking at him. "Yeah, I'm in."

I slap his back, and he grins at me sideways. I finish my bottle of beer. My headache is nearly gone.

"Are we good to bring the ATM back here?" I ask DJ, and he shakes his head.

"Not this warehouse. I have another one. It's small, but I don't want any connection with this one."

"Fair enough." His brothers and father are part of Kelly's Kitchens, so I get him not wanting to tie them into any of this.

"We will need an angle grinder to cut it open."

"I can do that," Fitz offers up.

Why the fuck he has an angle grinder is beyond me. I wouldn't leave him alone with kid scissors.

"So Art, can you steal a Jeep to get us there?"

"You got it, man." Art nods.

"DJ, we'll need to block the street, as well as find a way to get the digger there, which I can get."

He nods. It's a tight schedule to pull this off, but that makes it more exciting.

"So a Jeep and trailer?" he asks.

I nod. "Yeah." That should work. I get myself a fresh drink, feeling happy with the details.

"Any chance of getting a spike strip?" I ask, sitting back down.

"I could make one," Fitz offers up.

Art snorts. "This isn't Metal Work Class 101," he says, but I agree with Fitz.

"Yeah, Fitz, that would be cool. Can you have it here for tomorrow night?" I ask.

He rubs his hands on his tracksuit bottoms. "I can do that."

I raise both eyebrows at Art. "Let's rob a bank," I say and he laughs.

"Heard you had trouble over on your side with the Gardaí," Art says, and the tension in the warehouse seems to rise.

These are my close friends, but they don't know the ins and outs of my family business. "Nah, just someone who tried to get one up on us and failed," I say.

"Heard they were looking for a body." Art focuses on me.

Fitz seems to freeze beside us. We do a lot of dumb shit here, but nothing like what my family does.

"Yeah, they found three," I say. They nod and DJ shifts his gaze to Art. "Three cows," I add before taking a deep gulp of the drink as they all laugh with relief. I'm the kind of guy you just never fully know. I wonder if they actually knew me, would they stay?

"It was a vendetta against my brother, Shane. Some bent cop called it in, but he's pretty red faced now," I say before lighting up another fag.

"So, did you figure out if you pulled last night?" DJ steers the conversation to somewhat safe ground.

"I can't remember, to be honest. Had way too much of the white stuff." Cocaine was too easy of a drug to come by and abuse.

"I picked up a nice little foreign one." Art smirks.

"You tap it?" I ask, throwing my fag onto the ground and crushing it under my boot.

"Yeah, I tapped it." His voice drips with pride, and DJ snorts.

The door opens again. I don't turn around as DJ stands up and walks over to whoever has arrived.

"So what way do we cut up the money?" Fitz asks me, and Art shakes his head at Fitz.

"Equally amongst everyone," I say.

"Fuck no. He has shit for brains. What can he do?"

"Don't be an ass. He'll get a quarter," I say to Art as I place a hand on Fitz's arm.

"Guys, I want you to meet Mark." DJ walks over with Mark, who hobbles toward us on a crutch.

He nods and smiles at everyone, and when our gazes meet, I hope he doesn't recognize me.

Because I recognize him.

CHAPTER TWO

DARRAGH

M*ARK McGuiness.* His name rattles through my head as he nods at me.

"This is Darragh." DJ introduces me, and I stretch out my hand.

"What happened to you?" I ask as DJ drags over another chair and Mark sits down. DJ gives everyone fresh drinks before he joins the circle.

"Got jumped."

"Hate that," Art says. "Is it just your leg?"

I take a deep drink as I listen and tell myself not to fucking smile as I remember my bat, Rochelle, striking his hip.

"I had to get my hip replaced. The fuckers shattered it."

I'm shaking my head. "Animals," I say.

He nods. "When I'm all healed, those fuckers will get what's coming to them." He clicks his bottle with DJ's.

What a fucking moron. "You get a look at them?" I question.

"Nah, the cowards wore masks."

"So how are you going to get them back?" I take a quick drink.

DJ shakes his head at me to leave it alone.

"Yeah, if you don't know what they look like, how will you get them?" Fitz speaks up now. It's like his brain has caught up with the conversation.

"I will. They're lucky my woman and kid were gone. I wouldn't have sat still otherwise."

I snort and shut up as DJ narrows his eyes at me.

"Those dickheads will regret touching you, Mark," DJ says, and Mark clicks his bottle with him again.

"Was it sore?" Fitz asks.

Mark laughs.

"What, my leg?" His question is delivered with a silent word: *idiot.* We can all hear it. Fitz is a fucking idiot. But he's our idiot.

"Yeah, you're fucking leg," I spit out.

Mark eyes me, and I know I should really keep my mouth shut, but I can't seem to help myself.

"Your voice is familiar," he says while rubbing the stubble on his face.

"I have a pretty sexy voice," I say to him with a wink, making Fitz laugh.

"Nah, I've heard it before." Mark frowns at me now.

"Does it really matter?" DJ steps in, looking unsure.

Mark holds up his hands while shaking his head. "Just making conversation, brother."

He isn't DJ's brother. He's too ugly.

"Your voice *is* sexy," Art teases.

"Thanks, Art," I say.

Mark looks awkward at Art's compliment.

"I was once offered a job on those phone sex lines," I say.

"You wouldn't last a night," DJ says, relaxing.

"I know. I would be hunted down and raped," I fire back with a wink.

Everyone laughs, including the muppet, Mark.

My phone rings and I grin. If Mark only knew who was ringing me now.

"What's up, brother?" I ask.

"Where are you?" Connor isn't sounding very friendly.

"Where are you?" I fire back.

"Darragh, I'm warning you," he hisses.

Standing up, I cover the phone. "The woman," I say to the guys and step away. "I'm in Kells."

"Get your ass home now."

"Seriously, what's wrong?"

"I'm not discussing it over the phone."

I light a fag and hang up. "I'm out, guys. See you tomorrow night."

I wave over my shoulder and don't look back as they all say goodbye.

Throwing the fag on the ground, I climb into my car. My head still aches slightly, and I remove a few more painkillers and wash them down with cold coffee.

***

I'm not even through the front door when Connor is on me. He frowns at me. "Where were you?"

"With some friends. You need me to help you with something?" I ask, hoping we get to hurt some people.

He shakes his head.

"Come on." He walks away, and I follow him through the house and out into the yard. Dread tightens around my throat as we walk into the pool house.

"Are you going to ask me about the girl? Because you acting like last night didn't happen is disturbing."

I light up a smoke. "I don't have a clue what you're talking about."

"The girl I had to take to the hospital last night." He walks over to the couch, and my stomach twists. "Or what about all the blood I had to clean up here?"

Flashes of blonde hair covered in blood have me squeezing my eyes, and the memories slowly drip down.

"Ah, fuck. Is she okay?" I ask.

"So, now you remember?" Connor walks back toward me, and I keep the fag in my mouth as I spread my arms.

"I was high," I say, but he follows the ashes that fall from my lips. Removing the fag, I'm tempted to throw it into the pool, but Connor would have a hissy fit.

"She had to get thirty-six stitches in her head. She could have bled to death." Connor is close enough that I smell his cologne.

My stomach curls. I need food. Mary's cookies would be nice. They just dissolved last night. Funny how I remember the cookies.

"Thank God she's okay," I say, but Connor narrows his eyes at me like I'm saying the wrong thing.

"Okay? She's not okay. She got thirty-six stitches." He scratches his jaw. "You need to quit the drugs."

"You need to stop fighting," I fire back.

He rubs his neck and walks toward the bathroom door, waiting for me to join him.

"What the fuck?" I take a step back, but Connor stops me.

"You clean it up."

"Get Mary," I retort, and Connor grips my arm.

"I cleaned up your mess last night. You need to clean this up, and you don't dare ask Mary."

I yank my arm from his. "Fine, I'll do it later."

Connor shakes his head. "Now, Darragh."

"I'm not feeling so good," I say, staring at the bathroom.

Connor nudges me toward the door. There's so much fucking blood, and the bathroom looks like someone wrestled in it. Everything is scattered.

Towels caked in blood lie on the floor, and I step over the first lot of towels. The sink is filled with lumps of what look like bread. I turn my head and gag into my sleeve. Someone got sick in the sink and blocked it. I turn to tell Connor I'm not cleaning it up after all, but the doorway is empty.

He's gone.

Pushing the towels aside, I sit down and light up a fag. I'm trying to piece together what could have possibly happened here last night.

I must have used the towels to stop the bleeding. But the blood on the shower glass? Maybe she flicked her hair and blood splattered across it. Maybe that was already there from something else. She must have gotten sick. I'm not one for puking.

The powder on the top of the toilet is cocaine. We must have had sex, gotten high, and came back in here after she fell.

My phone rings, and I get it out of my pocket.

"You better have that place shining. Heard Michael saying he was going to take a swim later." Connor sounds smug.

"What are you lying for?"

"We'll see." He hangs up and I start cleaning.

We must have used every towel here. The laundry basket is full. I wipe the powder off the top of the toilet and throw my fag into it before flushing. After hosing down the shower and straightening the room, I have only one thing left to do. Clean the sick in the sink.

The toilet brush is in one hand as I face away and swish it around. I hear the water leaking out, and when it's all gone, I'm left with chunks of food. I gag again, and as I turn on the tap, most of it goes down. I get a towel and take out the rest and bin the towel along with a toilet brush.

I ring to the house using the phone in the pool room.

"Hello?"

"Mary, we need fresh towels in the pool house."

"I only stacked them yesterday."

"Yeah, I had a party," I say.

She sighs. "Okay."

"The laundry basket is full. I'll bring it over," I say.

"No. No. I'll do it."

I smile into the phone. "Nice one, Mary. Oh, one more thing. Can you get a new toilet brush?"

"When I'm out later, I'll pick one up."

"I'm going to get you a pay raise," I say.

She laughs and hangs up on me. She's well paid, but I'll slip a good word in for her.

***

"It's all done," I say.

"I'm in the bar having a drink." Connor isn't exactly a day drinker, but I won't refuse.

"On the way," I say as I head into the house.

"You know, I like having you around."

Connor grins. "I think you like me cleaning up your mess, Darragh. But this is the only time I'm going to do it."

"You know you're my favorite brother," I say.

He glances at me sideways while taking a deep gulp of his beer. "I bet you say that to all the girls."

I smirk and pop open a bottle of beer. "I'd murder a fry," I say after drinking half the beer.

"I was serious earlier. I think you should try to stop taking drugs."

The change in topic makes me uncomfortable. So to avoid it, I agree.

"Darragh, you're just throwing away your life."

I force a smile. "You sound like Dad."

"Don't insult me." His hatred toward our dad was never hidden, and it's something that makes me like Connor.

"I can stop. It's just fun," I say as Liam enters, and I know straight away there goes my fun.

"I've been looking for you." Liam walks into the room with his hands in his pockets. Sometimes I question how the fuck we're related.

"You found me," I tell him.

He doesn't grin or frown. Nothing. Nada. I wonder how large the stick is that's rammed up his ass.

"I'm leaving shortly for work, and I think a conversation about rules and such is needed." Liam moves behind the bar, tidies up our caps, and wipes down the small area.

"Would you like another?" he asks Connor.

"Yeah, sure."

He pops the lid for Connor and places it on a mat in front of him.

"What about me?" I ask.

He faces me. "Rules, Darragh. When you're in my establishment, there will be no alcohol, no drugs."

I nod.

"No smoking," he goes on.

I widen my arms. "Nah, Liam, come on."

He doesn't move. "While on your break, you can, but once you're working, it's a no smoking zone."

"Fine, I agree to all of the above." I trace my signature in the air. "You have it signed by air," I say.

"We leave in five." Liam just gives a tilt of his head.

"I can take my own car."

"You're intoxicated, Darragh. You won't be driving today." Liam moves toward the door, and I give his back the finger as he leaves the room.

"Man, I feel like I just got whipped."

"Yeah, you did." Connor smirks at me. "I think this will be fun to watch."

"What? Your brother's misery?"

"No, the rise of Darragh O'Reagan." Connor slaps me on the back as he gets up.

"If I don't come back tonight, Liam has cut me up and stashed me some-where," I call to Connor, and he just shrugs.

CHAPTER THREE

CIARA

I 'VE ONLY JUST STARTED my shift when I realize I need to get a box of gloves. I left a box on my trolley, but they're gone. You want to take your cart home with you or it gets fleeced.

"Hi, Benny."

Benny, who keeps track of inventory, has his head buried in a computer. He glances at me before he returns to his computer.

"What is it?" He taps the keyboard harshly. Friendly as usual.

"I need a box of rubber gloves," I say and he sighs heavily, like the cost of them is coming out of his paycheck. He sits back, giving his stomach a rest from being squashed against the desk.

"Listen, this isn't a free-for-all. You got a box yesterday."

"Yeah, and someone nicked them off my trolley," I say in defense.

"Yeah, yeah, you all say that." He pushes his chair back a ways and rolls to the shelving behind him. I'm praying for a wheel to snap so his fat ass will hit the floor.

No luck.

He rolls back safely with my box of rubber gloves.

Before he hands them to me, his gaze flicks to my hair. "Blue dye isn't allowed."

"Are you discriminating against my hair color?"

He sits up a little straighter. "That's not discrimination." He clutches the gloves to his sweaty chest.

"I was born like this, so it is," I say, and he narrows his already squinted eyes at me.

"No one is born with blue hair."

"Google it," I say, and hope he does on his own time. Luckily, he bypasses his computer and hands me the gloves. I sign for them.

"Nice doing business with you, Benny," I call over my shoulder, but he's buried in the computer again, no doubt Googling if someone can be born with blue hair.

"Boss is here," one of the girls—I can't remember her name—tells me as we pass each other in the hall.

"Thanks." As I turn the corner, I curse my luck. The boss stands at the room I'm meant to be cleaning. A blond-haired guy who looks like he had a few too many drinks is beside him.

"Mr. O'Reagan," I say as I approach.

Liam's gaze snaps to the gloves in my hand, and he gestures for me to enter the room. Fear skitters up my back when the blond guy enters too. Liam knows the drill. I'm a cleaner, and that's it. I flick the blond guy a look as he stares around the room.

"Ciara."

A shiver races across my body at the use of my name.

"This is Darragh, my brother, and he's here to work with you."

Darragh looks like he belongs on some catwalk, not cleaning hotel rooms, especially ones used by prostitutes.

"Okay, I'm not completely down with that," Darragh says. "You want us to be like a double act? I suppose I can do that." Darragh winks at me, and my confusion deepens. "But I won't do men," Darragh adds as he shrugs out of a suit jacket that looks like it cost my yearly salary. "Nor trannies or fatties."

I'm speechless, which isn't something that happens often. Liam closes the door gently behind him, and I take a step back.

"Darragh, you'll be helping Ciara clean the rooms." Liam waits for Darragh to absorb that information.

Darragh's mouth hangs open, and there's something almost comical about it. A part of me wants to walk over and push his chin up. But I don't. I stay close to the wall, clutching my rubber gloves and praying this will all be over soon.

"Come on, Liam. I could do other jobs. Like help get the newbies to relax." Darragh grins like he's God's gift. "Okay, if that doesn't suit, how about bar work or driving cars? I don't know, but not cleaning. I mean, do I look like a cleaner?" He looks at me like he just remembered I was here. "No offense or anything."

"None taken," I say drily.

"There are no negotiations. If you leave Ciara, she will inform me and there will be consequences." When Liam turns to me, I want to sink into the wall. He has a way of making me squirm without saying a word. "If he leaves and you don't inform me, you're fired."

That isn't fair, but I keep my mouth shut and nod.

Liam gives his brother a final nod and leaves the room before closing the door behind him.

Darragh folds his arms as he chews on a nail, and I know this isn't going to end well.

I start cleaning and my movements snap him out of whatever inner turmoil the poor rich kid was experiencing.

Pulling off the sheets, he jumps back like he might catch something. "Did someone just use that bed?" he asks.

"No, I'm pulling off clean sheets because I don't have enough work," I say in a monotone voice.

He looks at me twice before moving to the wall and sitting on the ground. The ground isn't any cleaner than the bed, but I don't tell him that. It takes forty minutes to put a room back together.

"Now we go to the next room," I inform him.

"I can't believe he's making me do this." He pats his jacket and trousers. "He took my fucking phone."

He's staring at me like I can help him. I can't. I take the dirty laundry and place it under my trolley as I move to the next room. The moment we enter, Darragh goes back to sitting on the ground.

"Are you going to help?" I ask him as I open the curtains.

"Look, no offense or anything, but I don't do this kind of work. I know you women love it, so knock yourself out."

"Wow," I say as I stare down at him. Now I can see why Liam left him here.

I move on to making the bed when he says, "Okay, I found a loophole. Liam said I can't leave you. But you can come with me."

"Genius," I say drily as I start to polish the bedside tables. I'm aware of his movements as he gets up and stands. He towers over me.

"I need a smoke," he pleads.

"Declan, I have ten rooms…"

"It's Darragh." He sounds so offended.

"I have ten rooms to clean before my shift ends. If we leave now, I won't get them finished on time."

"Don't you have breaks?" He sounds appalled.

"Yeah, but not right now."

"But can't you take it right now just this once?" He's smiling at me, trying to charm me.

"Sorry, Derek. No," I say and continue polishing.

"It's Darragh," he says.

I've left the door open, and Darragh hovers close to it. I'm keeping a close eye on him and trying to clean. This is like babysitting a moody toddler.

A brunette is walking past, catching Darragh's eye.

"Hi. You. Come here."

She's also a cleaner, and she smiles up at him as he calls her over.

"Me?" she questions while pointing at herself.

"What's your name?" He places a hand on the doorframe as he stares down at her.

I roll my eyes.

"Mandy."

"Mandy, I'm Liam's brother."

Silence makes me look up.

Mandy isn't smiling. She's walking away.

"No, don't go," he calls after her, but she doesn't stop. "Motherfucker!"

"When's break time?" he asks me.

"Once we do the next room, we can take a twenty-minute break," I say and disappear into the bathroom to clean. When I return, he's sitting on the bed I just made.

"Are we ready?" he asks, standing up.

I straighten the bed behind him before going to the next room. "Maybe if you helped, we could make break time a lot faster."

He snorts. "I'm not from your neck of the woods."

"And where is my neck of the woods?"

He looks me up and down. My mind screams at me to move, but I don't. He shrugs. "You know."

"Actually, I don't," I respond.

He runs his hands through his hair. "You're very lippy for a cleaner."

"You're very lazy for a cleaner," I retort.

He's standing even taller now, shoulders held back. "I'm not a fucking cleaner."

Talking to him is making me want to set my brain on fire. I start cleaning.

"Look, no offense," he says.

"You're fine, David," I respond.

He shifts from one foot to another. "Now I know you're taking the piss." His agitation is growing, and something tells me to stay quiet and just clean, so that's what I do.

***

He's half running down the corridor, pushing the trolley. "Come on, Ciara."

I want to smack him. If it was anyone else, I would be long gone. But when Liam tells you to do something, you just do it.

"Coming," I say sweetly, catching up with him.

"I need twenty smokes."

I open my hand, and he looks at my open palm.

"What?" His brow furrows.

"Money." I want to add the name Drew, but I don't want to push my luck.

"I don't have any on me right now. But I'll give it back."

"You better," I warn him as we reach the locker room. He's hovering over me, and I widen my eyes at him, making him back up. After removing my purse, we head downstairs. There's a fag machine in the hall.

The minute the pack falls into the slot, he reaches to get them.

"Didn't know you could move so fast," I say as he unwraps them.

"Come on." He's already walking away.

"I need to get food," I say.

He tuts. "Get it, then."

He comes with me as I get my fruit out of the small fridge in the canteen. He doesn't speak as we make our way out back.

I'm standing outside with a group of smokers that find Darragh hilarious. I've finished my banana and now move on to my apple. Sitting on the step of a door, I study Darragh and no one notices me.

His humor has picked up, and he's all laughs and smiles, telling tall tales that can't be true. Like how he took on three men at once for hitting on his woman, who he didn't keep in the end. The apple is nearly gone, and Darragh lights up another fag.

"Ticktock, Daemon. Lunchtime is up," I say, and he glances at me like I'm a dog tugging at his trouser leg. I get the attention of the three other guys. They give me a quick once-over, but I don't hold anyone's interest.

I hit the bin easily with my apple. I'm impressed but I'm the only one. One of the guys shivers and glances away, like I did something disgusting.

I walk toward the door.

"Ciara, wait. Just give me one minute," Darragh pleads behind me, but I let the door bang hard so he knows his time is up. I'm only a few steps down the hall when he's behind me.

"Do you have any friends?" he asks, falling into step beside me.

My cat. "Loads. Do you?"

"Of course I do. Look at me." He smirks.

"I am looking at you. So I take that as a no?"

His brow furrows, and he thankfully stops talking.

My job won't be worth doing if I have to work with Darragh every day. I always loved the solitude this job offered, but now it doesn't seem worth the pay.

Darragh rubs his temple. "Do you have any painkillers? My head is pounding."

"I'll check my first-aid kit," I say.

He nods, folding his arms across his chest. He does look a bit pasty.

Once we reach the locker room, I grab my trolley.

"Painkillers," he reminds me.

"I was joking. I don't have a first-aid kit," I say slowly.

"You need to ring, Liam. I'm sick."

"I can't just ring Liam. It's not allowed."

"You can, because I said so."

I'm not comfortable with this, but the idea of getting rid of Darragh has me picking up the staff phone in the hall and dialing Liam's office.

"Mr. O'Reagan."

"Yes, Ciara." I hate how he knows it's me, but then I glance at the cameras in the hall. He must be watching us.

"Darragh is feeling very ill," I tell him.

"Put him on." I hand the phone to Darragh. Time ticks by, and already, I have to shave twenty minutes off my lunch break to get my rooms finished.

Once Darragh puts the phone down, he smiles. "I get to go home."

"With pay?" I ask.

He frowns at me.

"Never mind," I tell him, and push my trolley, making my way to the next room.

It's bliss for the remainder of the day. Sometimes a wrench needs to be thrown into the works to make you appreciate what you already have.

I've come a long way.

My green Nissan Micra sits under a tree, waiting for me to return. I pat the hood before getting in. I live only ten minutes from work—another thing I'm grateful for. Kingscourt is one long strip. Every second shop is closed, but it's become home to me. I park on the street and make my way up to my apartment.

"Hello, Peaches." I pick up my cat as I close the door behind me. Taking her with me, I go into the kitchen and get her a tin of tuna. After taking a forkful first, I scoop the rest into her dish.

I saw Peaches roaming the streets of Kingscourt for weeks before I took her in. No missing cat posters went up, so I claimed her as mine. I knew what being homeless felt like.

I cut up celery, carrots, and parsnips and then boil them before adding some to a stockpot. I have twenty minutes before it will be cooked, so I take the time to shower.

My phone rings in my bag, and I root it out while trying to hold my towel up. The ringtone tells me it's Liam.

"Hi, Liam," I answer.

"Ciara, sorry for the intrusion on your personal time."

"That's okay," I say, tugging the towel closer.

"We've had a problem with a room, and I would really appreciate if you could return and help out. It would be overtime."

"I'll be there in thirty minutes," I tell him. Overtime isn't something I would ever turn down, and he knows that.

"Thank you, Ciara."

"You're welcome, Liam."

I hang up and get dressed. I don't have much time but pour myself a bowl of soup. In the process, I burn my tongue while I scarf it down.

"Be a good girl, Peaches." I rub her behind the ear before leaving.

***

The room is destroyed, but I'm not on my own. One of the other girls is helping me. She's Russian and doesn't speak a word of English, but it's amazing what you can learn from someone just by actions.

The smell of urine is the first thing that hits me. Someone has just sprayed the room. A group of men rented the room, and they sure had a party. The windows are already open, but the mattress is what's holding the smell.

Once I have my gloves on, we pull the mattress off and leave it in the hall. It's picked up within ten minutes, and we start scrubbing the frame of the bed before moving on to the floor. Glass, cans, and cigarette butts litter the floor. How could anyone in their right mind leave a room like this?

I leave the door open, but the smell is still intense, just not as strong as it was before. Laughter out in the hallway has me glancing from where I am on the ground.

Darragh's checking into the room across from me with three girls. They all laugh and smile at him. I shake my head when he pushes open the door and lets them in. His recovery is astounding.

Our gazes meet and I hope my disgust is there, but he winks at me, so apparently it isn't. I want to report him to Liam, but I tell myself this level of irritation over a stranger is unwarranted.

It takes over two hours to scrub the room. My gaze keeps moving to the door across the hall.

"How could he still be at it?" I ask the other cleaner, who stares at me and shrugs while pointing to her mouth.

"No… English."

I wave her off. "Yeah, I know. It's just ridiculous," I say and she shrugs again, repeating herself.

She takes all the dirty laundry out of the room, and I linger a little too long, keeping an eye on the room across from mine. I tell myself I'm dragging it out because it's overtime. That's the only reason I linger for another fifteen minutes before I decide that home with Peaches is where I want to be.

CHAPTER FOUR

DARRAGH

"WHY IS HE HERE?" I angle my head toward DJ.

"Come on, Darragh, he's my mate."

I glance at Mark again. "If he fucks up, it's on you."

"He won't. He'll just be a lookout." I'm not happy with bringing someone else in. Art is bouncing on his feet. He's dressed in black from head to toe, the same as me. Fitz arrives with the angle grinder and the spike strip, dressed all in white.

"Want some?" Art cuts up a few lines, and I grin at him.

"Just what I need." I take the rolled up note and inhale a straight line of powder off a small table. The rush is always instant. I pass the note back to Art as he hits up another one.

I clap my hands together. "Okay, bring it in." Mark's presence is annoying, but for DJ, I'll keep it quiet.

I gesture to DJ. "DJ, you're driving the Jeep with the flatbed. I want you to block Navan road and just stay in the Jeep."

He nods.

"Fitz, your job is to drop the spikes at the end of the Gardaí station. You got it?"

Fitz nods too. But I'm not so fucking sure he's got it. If he fucks up, we can still do this.

"Art, you're the digger driver. You get to take that bad boy out of the wall."

Art yelps his agreement.

"I'll cover you from the road. We have eleven minutes to get in and get out." I look at each person.

"What about me?" Mark asks, and I want to smash his face in.

"You stay with DJ. He's responsible for you." I want him to say something back to me so I can reintroduce him to Rochelle. But he doesn't.

"Once the safe is on the back of the Jeep, we drop it here and then me and Art will get rid of the vehicles while you open the safe." I check my watch. We have five minutes. "Let's do this, bitches."

Art walks beside me, jumping up and down, and we branch off. Fitz takes his own car to go to the police station while DJ and Mark start up the Jeep that has the digger on the back. We let them pull out first. The minute they leave the warehouse grounds, Art and I get into the stolen Jeep and pull down our balaclavas. I fix my black gloves before starting the engine.

I turn on the radio and stop when I come across some dance music. The beat has me pumped as I floor the Jeep down the Cavan Road. Art howls and I laugh.

Yeah, this is going to be fucking epic.

Shivers race all over me with excitement. I love the rush. I love the lack of oxygen and the sensation of chasing air. It's too close to discomfort, but I love it.

I slow down as I approach Kells. No one is around, but I reduce my speed to give DJ a chance to get set up. Art snorts some more coke off his hand and offers me a fresh line that he pours out onto the back of his hand.

"After. I need to keep a clear head," I say.

The steel against my back has my knee jagging. It's loaded and a scary part of me wants to use it. It's a part of me I try to keep a cap on, but it doesn't always work out that way.

I speed up as we come around the bend and approach the bank link. The Jeep and trailer are blocking the road.

"Showtime," I tell Art, spinning the Jeep.

He jumps out and races to the digger. I get out and watch the road. Removing the gun from my trousers, I keep it at the ready. The roar of the digger is going to attract attention.

Three young lads linger across the road, their phones on us. I ignore them as Art drives the digger to the wall. I check my watch. Eight minutes left. The bucket cracks the wall, and debris falls down as Art keeps smashing at the wall around the ATM. The three boys are walking closer, phones held high. My gun rises and they freeze.

"One more fucking step," I warn. I glance at DJ and Mark, who sit in the Jeep. Their focus is on Art as he gets the ATM out of the wall. I want to laugh as he swings the ATM in the air and lands it on the back of the trailer. *Easy fucking peasy.*

I walk back to the Jeep and get in, and Art jumps down from the digger. I wait until DJ has turned the Jeep and drives in front of us. Glancing at my watch, I note that we still have four minutes left.

"You did good, man," I say to Art as I stick her to the road. I have to slow down, but once we leave Kells, I floor it the rest of the way, overtaking DJ. I give him the finger.

Art snorts again. "Ease down, man. We still have to get rid of these vehicles." He rubs his nose and yelps again.

I want to join him, but we need to finish the job first.

After pulling in at the warehouse, we wait. DJ arrives and Art turns the music up full blast and has a fucking party in the back. I focus on DJ as he reverses into the warehouse and tilts the trailer. Once the ATM is inside, I turn down the music.

"You drive this one. I'll take the other," I say to Art.

He climbs into the front, forcing me to get out of the Jeep.

"You know where you're going right?" I ask him.

He blares the music, his head bobbing. I smirk and jump into the other Jeep and take off.

"Fitz, we'll be there in twenty," I say and hang up.

Art drives up beside me, still shaking his head to the music. I push the Jeep harder, not allowing him to get in front of me. He slips back in behind me as another car flashes its lights at him. The minute the coast is clear, he pulls out beside me again. Turning up my own music, I tap the steering wheel before giving him the finger. I push the Jeep to its max. Lights flutter across the hump in the road ahead. Only this time, Art isn't pulling in.

I look at him, and he gives me the finger. I widen my eyes while gesturing to him to fall behind. He gestures at me to move over. My foot is to the floor, and I'm not lifting it.

The car coming toward Art is flashing his lights. I glance at Art again and doubt has entered his features. He pulls in behind me; the car in front jams its breaks on and swerves.

"Wow! Crazy bastard." I'm hyped as I pull into the Lakeside Manor.

The hotel was shut down two years ago, and vandals have smashed nearly every window in the building. I slowly roll down to the water and jump out when the front of the Jeep disappears under the murky water. I'm not even back up when Art pulls into the hotel. Going way too fast, he jumps and hits the tarmac, and his Jeep and trailer go sailing into the water.

"Did you see that?" he roars. "I'm the next James Bond."

"That's the cocaine talking, Art. You wouldn't pull that shit sober," I remind him.

He stands up and wipes grit from his face.

A beat up Toyota slowly approaches us and we jump in. Only then do I remove the balaclava and gloves.

***

"What did I tell you?" I ask the lads as we sit around the bundle of money.

"Nearly two hundred thousand."

DJ looks up at me. I grip his shoulder. "Nice one, Darragh."

Art pats me on the arm. "Yeah, that was some fucking rush."

"So, what way do we split it?" The question comes from Mark, and his voice kills my buzz.

"Evenly?" DJ asks.

"He didn't do anything," Fitz pipes up, pointing at Mark, who rises without his crutch.

I don't move but give DJ a pointed look. He needs to put his friend in his place.

"No. Twenty percent to each of us, and ten percent to Mark." I hate giving him anything.

Mark sits down. "Yeah, that sounds fair."

I don't give a fuck how it sounds. That's just how it's going to be.

"So now can we party?" Art asks, rubbing his hands together. It's like Jekyll and Hyde with Art—once he's worked up, he's loud.

"DJ and Mark, you can get rid of the ATM tomorrow night," I say to them and go for a beer.

I hand Fitz and Art a drink as DJ gets one for himself and Mark.

"We cool?" DJ asks and I nod.

"Yeah, we're cool."

"So how much do I get, like twelve grand?"

I grin at Fitz. "Did you work that out in your head, Fitz?"

He nods.

Mark sneers and I don't fucking like it.

Art takes another line.

"Something funny, Mark?" I quiz.

"I can't seem to sneeze, but you're on my case," Mark states and glances at DJ.

"Let's all calm down and enjoy this. We just robbed a bank," DJ says while pushing his hand into my chest.

"You want one?" Art holds out a note.

"You know I don't like that shit in here, Darragh," DJ whines and I give him both fingers before I walk backward over to Art.

I blink several times after taking the line. "That's good stuff," I say to Art, but he's already bending down for another line. "Did I tell you I got a job?" I say as I walk back to the guys. Lawn chairs are in a circle, and I sit down and light a fag.

"You're working?" DJ asks.

"In a brothel," I tell them.

"No fucking way." Art sits down, wiping his nose.

"Lots of women?" Fitz asks, his eyes wide.

"Yeah, Fitz, lots of women," I say, and he laughs into his hands.

"We need to get him laid," I say to Art.

"Yeah, you need to wet that stick," Art says to Fitz.

"I already have." Fitz sits up straight, all his laughter gone.

"By who?" DJ asks.

I glance at Mark. His smirk is irritating me.

"Well, she turned out to be my cousin."

Art spews his drink on his jeans. "Get the fuck out."

I can't stop laughing.

"She had a massive pair of tits."

I can't breathe. "You're a dirty fucker, Fitz," I tell him and he grins.

"Inbred," Mark mutters under his breath.

I heard him. "Something you want to share?"

Mark stands without his crutch. "Yeah, there is. Every time you speak, your voice just bounces around in my head."

I shrug. "What, am I talking too loud for you?"

DJ stands up. "Darragh, leave it."

I don't even waste a glance at DJ. "Come on, Mark. You want to hit me?" I smirk.

He stretches his arms wide. "Why would I want to hit you?"

"You just look like you do," I tell him. He knows who I am. I can see it in his eyes.

"You came into my home."

I clap. "There we go. Took you long enough."

He rushes toward me, relying too much on one leg. I move quickly and he catches himself before he stumbles and falls. "You're a scumbag."

"Shut the fuck up." DJ pushes him back, but I'm all up for getting shit off our chests.

"Rochelle really liked you," I tell him.

Confusion coats his features.

"My baseball bat," I explain.

He charges again. DJ's grip falters, and Mark rushes me. I'm not a fighter really, but it's too easy. I punch him and it knocks him off balance. He falls on his damaged hip. A roar tears from his lips.

"Darragh." DJ stands over Mark.

"What?" I ask DJ.

"Come on, man. He has one leg."

"Yeah, but he also has a big fucking mouth," I tell DJ.

"Did you beat him up?" Art grins as he swaggers toward me.

"Yeah, while his friend held me down. Coward." Mark just won't keep it shut.

He's still lying on the ground, and I'm tempted to kick him in the face.

"You're the coward, beating up Neill. How many of you jumped him?"

He's standing now. "It was a job."

"So was mine," I say with a grin.

"Nah, you're a sick fuck. You enjoyed it."

His words rub me up the wrong way, and I step closer. "Shut your mouth or I'll reintroduce you to Rochelle."

"You think you're a god," he sneers.

I clench my fists. "I'm a fucking god!" I roar into his face.

He laughs and my blood pounds in my ears. I walk away.

"What are you doing?" DJ asks, still standing beside Mark.

I pick up the canister of petrol.

"Wow, wow." DJ walks toward me, his eyes darting to Mark.

"I'm not going to burn him," I say as I douse the money in petrol.

Everyone is moving, screaming no—all except Art, who is pissing himself laughing.

"I'm your god," I tell Mark, taking the lighter out of my pocket.

"Ah, don't, man," DJ pleads.

Rolling the lighter, a small flame flickers. I don't look away from Mark as he follows the lighter in its free fall as I drop it. His eyes grow wide as all the money goes up in flames.

CHAPTER FIVE

CIARA

"COME ON." I WAIT another few seconds before I turn the key in the ignition. Nothing happens. Resting my head against the steering wheel, I accidentally hit the horn. Startled, I lift my head quickly and stare up at the apartment. I don't know why I'm looking up. No one is going to materialize.

I wanted to go to Carrickmarcoss to do some shopping. That looks like it isn't going to happen. I quickly turn the key in the ignition again, a part of me thinking I can catch the car out. Nope. That definitely isn't happening.

People move along the footpath. I always wonder where everyone is going. At the end, we all end up in the same place. Some of us just get there quicker than others.

Only two years ago, I really thought I would be six feet under. Living on the streets of Dublin is hard. Surviving them was a fluke.

I get out of the car and lock it behind me. No one would steal it, and if they did, I would hug them if they got it started.

The charity shop is at the end of the town. Kingscourt doesn't have an actual clothes store in it, so buying clothes from the charity shop is something I've gotten used to. Large towns and crowds of people make me angsty.

I'm halfway up the street when the skies open and shower down on top of me. I'm not a pessimistic type of person, but I get that shit happens, and it isn't karma or anything like that. It's just life. I've seen firsthand how horrible and cruel the world is, so when the rain soaks right through my shirt, like I'm standing under a waterfall, I don't try to outrun the rain. I just take it one step at a time until I'm standing in the charity shop. The moment I enter, I have to allow my receptors a moment to accept the smell and move on.

I ignore how the shop assistant stares at me as I move around the store. I ignore how the other customers move away if I get too close to them. I want to shake myself like a dog. People piss me off sometimes, but I don't let them get to me. Instead, I ignore them as I browse through the clothes. Two pairs of jeans, a jumper with a small hole in the elbow, and a set of cat ornaments make up my purchase—all costing five euro.

I step back out into the pouring rain. I don't run because it seems pointless. The weather was like this the day I met Liam. I was standing outside the Mater Private Hospital in Dublin. It was always a good spot for begging. Liam, in his suit, walked past me holding an umbrella. I stood there with an empty container. I always kept my money tucked safely in my bra.

"Do you have any change?" I asked with a smile.

"Get a job." His voice was like gravel.

His words had me clenching my hand around my cup. "I would if I could, you asshole."

He stopped walking and looked me up and down before speaking. "I'll give you a job. Come on." He turned away, and I knew I was either walking to my death or to my way off the streets. It was a fifty-fifty. So I took it.

***

Peaches greets me as I enter the apartment. She rubs herself against my wet jeans, then quickly skitters off and jumps onto the couch. My wet clothes create a pile on the floor as I make my way to the bathroom.

The shower sprays my back. I know it's warm, but it's funny how I don't exactly feel the warmth. My phone rings. I step out of the shower and wrap a towel around myself.

The ringtone for my second job is the sound of someone washing dishes.

"Hello," I answer, trying to keep the phone away from my wet face.

"Hi, Ciara. Would you be able to start your shift early?"

"How early?" I ask Gerard as I walk back into the bedroom. The room is cold and goose bumps break out on my exposed skin.

"The next hour?" Gerard asks apologetically.

I agree and hang up. After getting dressed, I eat a bowl of cereal quickly.

***

One of the new girls rang in sick. In a place like this, it's a rotating door for staff. It's not an easy number. Working for Liam is a lot easier, and if I got more hours, I would give this job up.

The Europa is the most popular chippers in Kingscourt, so once the doors open, it's all go. Right now, I'm washing and peeling spuds until my hands turn red.

Time passes in a blur, and I like the solitude that the back room offers, but that's smashed when Gerard calls me up front to help serve. My stomach rumbles at the smell of all the food.

Gerard takes the orders and calls them to me, so I pack the food and hand it to him. Another guy, whom I don't know, is cooking. He hasn't spoken and neither have I, so it seems like we'll get on.

It's close to one in the morning, and my feet are sore but I'm smiling. It's closing time. The door opens and a group of noisy guys come in. I hunch down further as I tidy over the hot area.

"What can I get you?" Gerard asks.

I throw him a dirty look that he doesn't see. Thankfully.

"Give me a nice breast of chicken," one of the men says.

I roll my eyes as the children start to laugh.

"You're a fucking moron."

I freeze, recognizing the voice.

"I'm not the one with anger problems," says the guy who made the inappropriate comment.

"That's all? Just chicken?" Gerard asks, getting their attention.

"No, we'll order when we're ready." Darragh speaks up again, and I clench my jaw but continue wiping down the surface.

"DJ, you're this close to me hitting you," Darragh says, and the tension in the chippers rises.

I don't know why but I pop my head up. "Still mouthing off," I say without thinking. Everyone looks at me. There's a moment of pure anger from Darragh, but through his drunken state, his eyes widen in recognition.

"Ah, you. The lippy hotel cleaner."

I know Gerard is staring at me.

"You work here, too? Boy, you like cleaning and cooking. A real woman." Darragh winks.

"What can we get you, Darragh?" I ask.

He snorts with humor. "Four chicken breasts," he says with a slow grin. "And can you give me a tub of mayonnaise? You know, since we're friends?"

It's my turn to give a very unladylike snort. "Friends? You'll get the same tub as everyone else." I call the food order out to Gerard and get to work quickly.

"Burn." The guy he called DJ laughs and turns to the other two with them.

One has his hood up. His eyes seem to shoot around the room, and when they stop on me, the feeling leaves me unsettled. He looks like someone's stalker—hooded eyes, hunched shoulders, and his overall presence. The other guy leans against the wall and takes everything in with confidence.

"Shut the fuck up," Darragh shoots off.

I fill the chips at record speed.

DJ points at me. "Didn't think you kept company like that."

I stand straighter. "I want you to leave," I tell DJ, and it's not just him who stares at me, but Gerard gapes.

He tuts like I'm batshit crazy. Maybe I am. The guy leaning against the wall pushes off but doesn't come any closer.

"You'll have to come out here and make me." He grins, and he has every right to. He knows I won't actually make him. He's four times bigger than me.

Gerard calls back to the new guy. "Where's the chicken?"

"Two more minutes." The new guy's accent is foreign. Maybe that's why he hasn't spoken since I arrived. Maybe his English isn't great.

"You heard her. Get out." Darragh speaks up, and I know it's not in my honor. He wants to hit this guy, and I've handed him an opportunity.

"Are you serious?" DJ asks, and the two boys step closer.

I glance at Gerard, and he shakes his head at me, like this is my fault.

I'm surprised when DJ throws the first punch, and it has power behind it. Darragh stumbles back, and the guy in the white hoodie stops Darragh from falling. There's a lull in the chippers as Darragh straightens and wipes blood from his face. A slow smirk grows across his face. I'm waiting and watching for a fight, but Darragh doesn't move.

"That one's free," he says to DJ.

"Hit me back," DJ says, but he sounds afraid now, which makes no sense. He has the upper hand.

"Chicken." The thick accent comes from behind us.

I want to hush him to see what's going to happen next., but Gerard shakes his head before taking the chicken and bagging it.

"I'll hit you back when I'm ready."

"Always playing mind games," DJ shouts and storms away from the chippers.

"Get that, Art," Darragh tells the guy against the wall—the one who reminds me of a stalker. He steps up to the counter with a huge ass grin on his face and pays for the food.

I've seen lots of fights while living on the street, but this one was odd.

Art collects the food.

"See you tomorrow," Darragh sings over his shoulder.

"Yeah, can't wait," I tell him. He won't be fit for much tomorrow. Not that he was helpful the first day either.

Gerard doesn't mention anything after they leave, and we tidy up and shut down in silence.

The next morning, I'm up and getting ready for work, when I remember my car won't start. Taxis aren't exactly parked along the streets here.

I leave my apartment and go to the local shop. Above the phone is a list of all the taxi men in the area, bringing the grand total to two. I ring the first one, and the number is no longer in service. The second one answers and agrees to take me to Tracey's hotel.

After arriving to work and clocking in, I make my way to the first room.

"Hold up."

Turning, I see Darragh in the same clothes as last night—jeans and a baby blue shirt that may or may not match his eyes. He can barely keep those eyes open as he catches up with me; he squints in pain.

"Do you have any painkillers?" he asks the moment he falls into step beside me.

"Let me check my first-aid kit," I joke.

"You know you could be a little nicer to me since I saved you last night."

"Yes, you really taught DJ a lesson."

Darragh's eyes open wider, and a flash of anger storms in them.

My stomach squeezes.

"That's the last time I'll help you out of a hobble." He rubs his head as he speaks.

"I wasn't in a hobble," I say as I push the card into the door handle.

"Fuck's sake, the smell." Darragh covers his nose as he enters the room. "Can't people leave them cleaner?"

"I agree, but I highly doubt you leave hotel rooms clean," I retort as I open the curtains.

Darragh grabs them and closes them. "My head! Just let me get my bearings."

I snort. "We don't have that much time," I say.

He brushes his hand toward me but doesn't make contact. He slides down the wall and sits on the floor, holding his head. I leave him in his cocoon of self-inflicted agony and start cleaning.

CHAPTER SIX

CIARA

D ARRAGH'S VOICE STARTLES ME. It's been a while since he's made a sound. I was starting to think he had fallen asleep.

"Do you ever wish you could erase the last five years and start again?"

His question makes me pause. "Why the last five?" I ask. I wish I could erase a lot more than five years.

"Why do you have to answer my question with a question?" He waves his hand in the air, and the motion is so womanly.

"You look gay," I tell him, and he holds his hands wide before pulling them back in.

"What's wrong with you?"

I don't answer. A lot is wrong with me, but telling someone like Darragh my deep, dark secrets would do more damage to my soul than what was already done.

I continue cleaning.

"You look like a dyke with that get up."

I'm wearing the staff uniform. It's two sizes too big, but I like my clothes loose and comfortable. "Maybe I'm a dyke."

"Good fucking chance you are," he shoots back and rubs his temples.

"Are you gay?" I don't even know why I'm asking.

"Did you not see me going into the hotel room with all the ladies yesterday? Because I know you were listening to us."

My face burns, and he laughs at me. He couldn't really know I waited to see if he came back out of the hotel room.

"You're disgusting," I say.

His laughter grows louder. "I know you want me. I see how you look at me."

"You're delusional." I continue cleaning.

He continues sitting there being insulting as hell.

We get three rooms done, and then he wants to smoke. "You owe me twenty euro, and since my car broke down, I need it." I hate explaining myself, but I can't afford not to get my money back.

"Yada. Yada. Yada." He takes out a wallet and gives me a fifty. "I don't want to hear your sob story."

I rip the money from his hand before I slap him and make my way downstairs to the bar.

"We're going that way," he says, pointing in the opposite direction.

I don't stop, and when he grabs my arm, I turn and twist, pushing him against the wall. "Take your fucking hands off me."

He holds his hands in the air and nods. "Okay, calm down."

I release him. The moment I do, warmth rushes my face. He looks at me like I'm crazy.

"I'm going to get your change, and then we can go for a smoke."

"Keep it." He drops his hand and moves away from the wall.

My gaze catches the camera behind us. Damn it. I really hope Liam isn't in the office to witness me assaulting his brother.

I break the fifty, pocket my twenty, and give Darragh his thirty back. We don't speak as we go out back. I sit once again on the step and take an apple out of my apron pocket.

The lads are all over Darragh, but he's subdued. I wonder if I bruised his ego. I couldn't accept someone touching me without my permission. I remember exactly what happened the last time I allowed that.

Once I finish my apple, I stand. This time, I don't have to call Darragh. He's behind me now as we enter the building. I regret defending myself. He watches me, and it's annoying as hell. The hall seems longer today, and I'm glad when we reach the room. The moment we do, Darragh sits back down on the ground.

"Some guy hurt you?" he asks while scratching his head. So my overreaction to him touching me hadn't gone unnoticed.

"Why has it got to be a guy? Maybe a girl hurt me? I'm a dyke, after all." I strip the bed, trying to allow my mind to find that numbness I often feel when cleaning.

"If you want, I can hurt them for you."

The way he says it so offhandedly has my bitch meter rise and hit the bell.

I laugh at him. "Why would you do that? You don't give a shit about anyone but yourself. And honestly, I don't think you'd do very well. I did witness you get your ass handed to you last night, and let's not forget what just happened in the hall."

He grins, but there's no humor in it. "Forget I said anything." He closes his eyes and leans against the wall, and I hate how confused I feel. I can't figure him out for the life of me.

I go back to cleaning, but his response is irritating me. "I wouldn't know where to find him anyway. So it wouldn't matter."

Darragh plays with his lighter when I glance at him quickly. He looks at me and just nods.

"So what about you and DJ? There seems to be a lot of built-up anger there." I don't really expect him to answer, but I want to change the subject.

"I lit his money on fire," he says.

I smirk. What an odd thing to do. "How much?"

"Not sure." His eyes tell me something different, that he knows exactly how much.

"Like a fifty or a hundred?" I'd cry over a fiver. So that amount would make me fall out with someone.

"Yeah, a ton." His answer is quick.

"You could sell your jumper. I'm sure you'd get a hundred for it," I say while straightening out the bed.

"It's not about the money. I could give him his money back. It's the principal."

I'm listening now. "And what's the principal in this case?"

"That I can take anything I want from you. And you can't do anything about it."

I frown and shift my stance. Crossing my arms over my chest, I stare down at Darragh. This arrogant guy is starting to look very dangerous. His party exterior covers up a lot of anger and violence.

"This room is done," I tell him because I don't know what else to say.

We move to the next room. I expect him to leave but he doesn't. He doesn't work either. He just sits and talks until lunch comes around.

I leave my trolley in the room we're cleaning and head to the canteen.

Darragh sticks his head into the canteen, where a few other people sit. "I'm not sitting in there. It's fucking sterile looking."

Several heads turn in our direction. I give an apologetic smile.

Darragh turns away. "I want a steak."

"I have steak. Tuna steak." That's the closest I'd get to steak.

"Come on, I'm not eating in there." Darragh moves away.

"There's nowhere else to eat, Darragh," I say.

He snorts and reaches for my arm but hesitates. "There's a restaurant. We'll eat there."

"I'm pretty sure you can't bring in a packed lunch."

"I'll cover it."

I shake my head. "No."

"You're so awkward. Fine, bring your lunch. I'll sort it."

I grab my food out of the fridge, and it's intimidating as everyone watches me. Darragh taps his foot, and with each tap, I slow down until he stops.

I've never sat inside the restaurant, but I've cleaned it many times. The large crystal chandeliers are a killer to dust. I remember that part clearly.

It's odd being at the opposite side of the table as a waitress steps up. Her eyes linger on me for a second before she turns her attention to Darragh. "What can I get for you?"

He doesn't even look at the menu. "Two steak dinners with chips, and I'll have a Coke." Darragh turns to me, and I shake my head. "Make that two Cokes," he tells the waitress, who then disappears.

"I told you I have lunch," I say, patting my food beside me.

"Don't take that out or you'll get us both kicked out of here."

"You said you'd sort it," I say.

"I did. Sort it."

I sit back, folding my arms. "You know I didn't mean it like that."

"Do you fight with every guy who takes you for a steak dinner?" He grins like he knows no guy has ever taken me for a steak dinner.

The waitress returns with our drinks, but Darragh waits for my answer.

"Only the ones who trick me into it," I answer lamely.

"So you get tricked into a lot of dinners? I'm not surprised." He takes a deep swallow from the glass.

"What does that mean?" I ask, not touching mine. A part of me wants to rebel a bit longer.

"You're very hostile and snappy. The only way to deal with you is to trick you."

"You're not nice either. You're very arrogant and mean." I drink my Coke as he digests my words.

"Mean?" One eyebrow arches in amusement.

"Yes. Mean," I say.

"Give me an example."

"I have examples coming out of my ears. You called me a dyke."

"You called me gay," he fires back.

"The moment we met, you thought I was a worker," I say with raised eyebrows.

"But you are a worker." He says each word slowly.

"I'm a cleaner."

He snorts. "A prostitute. Yeah, that was a stupid mistake." He laughs.

"See, you just did it again." I sit back, so done with talking to him. He just can't help himself.

"You're confusing the shit out of me. First, you're insulted that I think you're a pro, and now you're insulted because I don't think you're one. You have to make up your mind, blue."

"I'm not explaining myself," I answer as the waitress arrives with our food.

Darragh rubs his hands together and inhales deeply.

I can't stop the smile that spreads across my face.

When he notices I haven't started to eat, he looks at me. "Dig in."

I do and the food is divine.

"So what do you do other than pretend to be a cleaner?" I ask when my stomach starts to fill up.

"I'm a farmer," he says.

I choke on a chip.

Darragh has to smack me on the back until I cough it up. *Real ladylike.*

"You don't believe I'd shovel shit or pull the tit of a cow?" He grins.

I roll my eyes. Everything is about sex with him. "You like it?" I ask. Both his brows raise in surprise.

"I'm going to a party tonight. You want to come?"

Now I'm laughing. When I realize he isn't messing, I sober up and take a drink of Coke. "You're serious?"

He nods.

"Hmm. No," I answer.

"If you change your mind, text me," he says.

I look at him sideways. "Sure," I tell him.

I don't have his number to text him, and he doesn't have mine. He's just trying to be friendly. The food is like lead in my stomach, and I put my knife and fork down.

"Are you finished?" he asks, still eating.

I nod and sit back and take in the restaurant with its amazing artwork and chandeliers that sparkle over our heads. I wonder what it would be like to have money, to be able to have an operation like this. What would it be like to burn your friend's money because you could? To have steak for your lunch or get paid to sit on the floor and watch someone clean? Life is funny.

The extremes between Darragh and I are stark. I wonder if he's put here to remind me of how far I am from a life without financial worries. The divide between us is so large.

"You okay?" Darragh asks.

I sit up. "Yeah, just thinking about Peaches," I lie.

"That your girlfriend?" Darragh smirks.

I place my knife and fork neatly on my plate. "My cat. I'm not into girls."

"Okay, calm down." He wipes his mouth on the napkin and pulls one leg up onto the other as he faces me. Being this close to him is intimidating. He's a big guy, and this close you'd think you'd find a flaw, but I can't, not even a blemish. Sitting this close makes me more aware of myself.

I take the napkin and dab my mouth.

"So you have a *pussy* cat." He keeps a straight face.

"Are you that deprived of a woman's touch that you can't stop talking about sex?"

He snorts at my question. "You saw me yesterday."

I nod. "Yeah, with two women you paid to touch you."

"I don't always have to pay them, sweetheart. Just sometimes I like to take control."

I shake my head, telling myself to let it go. "No, I bet you've never really been intimate without being drunk or high."

"You're wrong again. I actually have."

I'm not buying what he's selling. But my face is on fire, so I need to get off this topic. "Have you got any pets?"

"Yeah, lots of them." He winks, and I'm not sure what he's implying.

The waitress makes her way to our table, stopping my response. "Was everything okay?"

She looks at me a bit longer before diverting her attention to Darragh. Is she wondering what a guy like him is doing with someone like me? I'm tempted to tell her I'm only here because his spoiled ass wouldn't sit in the canteen. If his brother hadn't threatened him, we wouldn't be speaking.

"Perfect, thanks," Darragh answers and hands her his gold card.

I gather my lunch and stand up as he waits for his card. I mumble a thank-you. I know I owe him, and I don't like owing people favors. We leave the restaurant and go back to the room we were cleaning. The moment we enter, Darragh sits back down in his spot. I don't know why, but I really thought he might actually help.

"What's your number?" he asks.

I glance at him, and he widens his eyes at me while holding his phone. I recite my number to him and jump a few seconds later when my phone vibrates in my apron. I take out my phone and see an unknown number fills the screen.

"It's me," Darragh says with humor. "Just thought you tricked me. That would be your style."

I'm not sure what to say. I save the number as Man Whore and slip the phone back into my pocket.

We finish the rest of the ten rooms and pack up to go at four o'clock. There's an awkward moment as I stuff things into my locker, because Darragh just stands there.

"I'll see you tomorrow," I say, wondering why he isn't leaving.

"You need a lift?"

Yes, I do. "No. I already have the taxi planning to come."

"You sure?" he quizzes and I nod.

"Okay, blue. See you tomorrow." Darragh's voice sounds cheerful. I'm left in the locker room, unsure how I'm feeling at all.

CHAPTER SEVEN

DARRAGH

"**A**RE YOU SERIOUS?" I scream at DJ over the beat of music. I can't believe he brought Mark here.

"Look, he's ready to forget the whole incident with you beating him. I swear I'll keep him in line."

Gripping DJ by the back of his neck, I pull his head close to mine. "You better," I warn him.

He grins. "So we good?"

I smirk. "Not even close."

His grin slips, and my smile widens.

The club is full and the music vibrates through the floor. The moment Art spots me, he's up and howling into the air like a fucking wolf. High as a kite, he jumps off the couch and hugs me.

"The king is here."

My eyes land on Fitz, who's wearing the same fucking clothes he wore when we robbed the ATM. I need to replace his money. The guy needs it badly. "What's up, Fitz?"

He smiles while bobbing his head and nursing a bottle of beer in his hands. No doubt the liquid is warm. I was late to the party.

Art throws his arm around my shoulder. "You need to take a piss?"

I pause, not sure why. But another part of me thinks fuck it, and I walk with him to the bathroom.

The drugs work quickly, and I can't seem to focus on myself in the bathroom mirror. Blood trickles from my nose, and I wipe it away before washing my hands in the sink. I spot a girl in a small silver dress as she walks into the men's toilets. Art finishes up, and he stares at her as she walks past him.

"Is that bad coke?" I ask.

He shakes his head. "Nah, that's good stuff."

The girl hikes her dress up and backs her ass into the urinal and pisses. Art pulls out his phone to take photos of her.

"You're a dirty bitch," I say.

She gives me the finger. "Was busting to go." She stands up and pulls her dress back down.

I remind myself not to touch her later. She winks and walks past me, and I shudder.

"That's fucked up," Art says, stuffing his phone into his pocket.

We reenter the club. Art disappears, showing the photo to anyone who will look at it. I stay with DJ, Fitz, and Mark, who wants to be my best friend now. That shit will never happen. I drink way too much, and my nose burns and bleeds from all the coke I snort. I'm sweating, so I pull off my jumper, but my body doesn't want to cool down. My heart feels like it's skipping a beat. I sit back and clutch my chest.

"Put your clothes back on," a gruff voice sounds from above me.

I open my eyes to a large guy all dressed in black standing over me. "Fuck off. This is VIP, and I paid a grand to have the section for the night."

"You have to put your clothes back on." The hulk isn't listening.

I pat my chest to find it bare. My trousers are on, but my socks and shoes are also gone.

"I'm too hot," I mumble and close my eyes. Hands grip my arm, and my eyes snap open. "Take your big, ugly hand off me," I say.

He ignores me and pulls me up from my seat. Glass shatters across the floor, and I stare at Fitz and the broken bottle in his hand. Laughter bubbles up my throat. The security man doesn't remove his hand from mine but calls for backup.

"Let him go now," Fitz warns.

The jackass doesn't listen. I push my body weight against his, and the move is unexpected. We tumble down the few steps that lead up to the VIP area. The crowd scatters. We fall and they start cheering for us.

The noise, the drugs, and the painful thump in my chest make me feel possessed. I lace into the security man. I'm no match for him, as he's fucking huge, but I get a few thumps in before I'm pulled off and dragged outside.

When the Gardaí arrive, I'm disappointed in the security. "Can't take care of me yourself?" I sneer as two Gardaí approach me. "You got to ring in reinforcements?"

"Gardaí Síochána. Have you no real criminals to catch? Always arresting the innocent citizens."

One of the Gardaí takes a statement from the security man. Fitz is dragged past me, laughing his head off. A second squad arrives, and he's put into the back. The cold of the night is starting to hit me, and I shiver.

"Gardaí," I call.

He looks at me.

"I'm freezing. Would you mind putting me in the car?" I ask.

The fucker ignores me.

"You're useless at your job. Out here breaking up bar fights. You must not be fit to catch the real criminals. How do you sleep at night? Your wives must find it hard to get aroused looking at you two messes."

One of the officers rams me against the wall. "You'd do well to shut your mouth, Darragh."

"Oh, you know my name. I'm fucking terrified."

"I said shut up."

The security man relays his terrifying tale of his assault to the Gardaí.

"You're a pussy," I say.

The other Gardaí comes and places me into the back of the car, banging my head in the process.

"I'd hit you back, only that would be animal abuse," I sneer.

The door slams in my face, and I sit back in the seat and close my eyes.

Two more doors slam, but I keep my eyes closed.

"You're in serious trouble," one of them says.

I want to tell him to fuck off, but the rumble of the engine puts me to sleep. Cold air rushes in as the door opens again. I'm dragged from the Gardaí car and into the station.

"Take it easy, you moron. My feet—" I tell them, but they move me faster.

"You think you're funny. You will be laughing when I find out where you live." He hits me on the back of the head.

"You think you're the big man with your baton?" I push myself against the Gardaí, and he hits me back, then he pushes me back and I stumble but catch my balance.

The other Gardaí, the one with the receding hairline, pushes me forward and doesn't stop nudging me until they close the door to my cell.

The bench is cold as I lie down and hug myself. I just want to sleep.

Blood. There's so much blood. I'm staring at it on my hands, and my eyes follow the trail that soaks up into the blonde hair. The girl's head is open, and maggots crawl everywhere.

My eyes snap open as I roll off the bench and empty the contents of my stomach onto the ground. The creek of the door opening doesn't stop the assault on my stomach.

"You've made bail."

The words are spoken with humor as I bring up bile before standing straight.

"I was starting to like this place," I say, wiping my mouth with my arm. "Enjoy cleaning that up." The Gardaí's irritation makes my vomit on the floor almost seem sweet.

"Get out." His hand digs into my back as he pushes in front of him. I'm tempted to turn around and push him back.

A guy in a suit stands with his back to me. It's Liam. I'm fucked now. Liam is signing something while they remove the handcuffs from my wrists. He doesn't turn around to make sure I'm following him. We make our way to his Range Rover. He opens the door, and I climb in and shiver again as he starts the Jeep.

"I'm starting to think they're targeting me," I say, stealing a quick glance at Liam.

He doesn't react.

"Look, man, I know it's shit, you having to bail me out. But I didn't do anything wrong this time." I sound pathetic.

No response.

"Liam."

"Yes, Darragh?" Liam is focused on the road. His voice doesn't rise or fall. Nothing.

Clenching my fists, I face the window. "Nothing."

Silence fills the Jeep and seems to stretch out like the dark road in front of us. All want is a smoke, but I don't have them on me.

***

We pull into the garage, and it's then that Liam speaks. "It wasn't me. He took the call to come down and get you."

"Father?" I ask, staring out the window and into the dark space.

"We meet him in the library."

I glance at Liam. I want him to tell me it will be okay, but he gets out of the Jeep.

I shiver again as my bare feet touch the concrete floor. The smell of rust from the recent rain lingers in the air.

"Get some clothes on. I'll meet you at the library." Liam doesn't linger, and I follow behind him, taking the stairs two at a time.

When I open my bedroom door, I want to collapse on my bed. It's unmade and I move toward it. Rubbing my face, I start to look for socks, shoes, and a clean shirt. After getting a fresh pack of smokes and a lighter from my stash, I light one up as I walk through the house. I need it before I face these two.

Both of them sit across from each other, each in a suit. At this hour in the fucking morning? It has to be six, six thirty maybe.

"Put out the cigarette." Father doesn't look up at me as he speaks. I take two final pulls before putting it out in a large crystal ashtray that sits on a small round table near the couch. When I look up, it's Liam who's watching me. He points to another large couch across from him and Father. Nothing like an interrogation this early in the morning.

My ass is only just on the couch when Father starts. "I'm at a loss with you, Darragh. Each time I think you've settled down, you do something stupid." His voice rises on the last word.

"I'm sorry. It won't happen again." The lie comes easily.

"It will. It keeps happening." Father's calm voice makes me sit up straighter. I glance at Liam, who hasn't taken his eyes off me.

"I'm cutting you off." Father stands and places a hand into his pocket. He stares down at the rug as he speaks.

"What does that mean? From the family?" My heart starts to pound.

"No, Darragh."

Relief has me sitting back.

"From my money. You will have no access to any funds."

I grin, but it slips as my heart jackhammers in my chest. "How would I buy anything?" I ask through gritted teeth.

"Get a job," he snaps.

"I have one. Remember?" I bite out the last word.

Father gives me a warning look. "Sitting on the floor in each room that's being cleaned is not working. Unless you start working, Darragh, there is no more money."

"Fine. Take your money. I'll get my own," I say, standing.

Father steps into my space. "How, Darragh?"

"I'll work for Liam." I'll really just rob another ATM.

Father stares at me until I shrink a little. "I remember the day you and Finn were born." His voice hasn't softened, so I don't confuse this with a nice moment.

"You nearly cost me my wife that day. She lost so much blood."

I drop my eyes as guilt dips and swirls in my stomach.

"Are you fucking serious?" a familiar voice asks.

My head snaps up as Connor enters the study. He's holding boots and socks in one hand, and a T-shirt is slung across his shoulder.

"You're blaming a baby for Mum losing blood during childbirth?" Connor's laughter bounces off every wall.

"This is a family conversation," Father barks.

"No, this is you two bullying Darragh. Does it make you feel big, Liam?"

I want to be like Connor when I grow up. But he has nothing to lose. I have everything.

Liam stands up and takes a step toward Connor. "No, it makes me feel old. And you may feel your aggression here is justified, that you feel better standing up for Darragh, but you have no idea what goes on inside these walls."

Connor pulls his shirt off his shoulder and holds it. He takes a step toward Liam and I move. I'm not sure why or what I could do, but fear curls in the pit of my stomach.

"Exactly, Liam. All the secrets you two keep." He shoots a hateful look at Father. "You are as bad as him."

Connor looks at me. "You don't have to stay here and listen to them. You're a grown man. You can leave."

I swallow the emotion that rises. I do have to stay here. I wouldn't survive anywhere else. I know that. He knows that. So his false hope isn't welcome.

"Get out," I say to Connor.

His body goes slack with my answer.

"You heard him. Get out of our home." Father steps forward.

"That's not—" I try to explain myself.

"Shut up." Father is facing me now, his wrath growing, strangling me. I nod and I can't look up at Connor.

"I don't want you in my home anymore. You're not welcome," he shouts at Connor.

I stare into the fireplace like a coward.

Connor snorts. "I can't stand you wankers anyway." His gaze meets mine, and the hurt is there. I want to say I'm sorry, but he turns his back on me and leaves.

"I don't want him here again," Father tells Liam.

Liam nods.

My stomach tightens. "You won't hurt him?"

Both of them look at me. I don't know if it's the drink or the idea of having more guilt on my conscious, but I need to know. "Liam," I beg.

"What is wrong with you?" Father asks. "Are you on drugs?"

The tightness in my stomach travels up and closes around my chest. I need to calm down, but something in me is clawing, fighting to get out. "Answer me." I face Liam. "Will you hurt him?"

"Sit down, Darragh," Father barks at me, but I can't calm down. I can't stop looking at Liam. He won't answer me.

"Just tell me you won't hurt him. Please." I step even closer to Liam, but Father steps in front of me.

His face is red from my disobedience. "I said sit down." His final warning.

If I let this go, I won't get an answer, and no answer feels worse than Father's wrath.

I glance at Liam. "Please, Liam," I plead to the brother I know still lives inside this sociopath.

It all happens so quickly. I know the moment Father is going to hit me. He moves toward me quickly, and I brace myself for the slap that never comes.

"Don't," Liam warns him. It's one word, but it's like someone just flipped the Monopoly board. Father stands back, his fists still clenched, but he doesn't touch me.

"I won't hurt Connor," Liam finally says.

I'm not fucking sure what to make of all this. The flip in power. Father obeying Liam. I stare at Liam, not really sure what I'm looking at. A new fear creeps up on me, and I shrug as if the movement will make it go away.

"You're at work in three hours. You need to shower and get dressed."

I nod and step away from Liam. I don't look back at my father as I leave the study and return to my room.

The smoke curls around me as I lie on my bed and blow it toward the ceiling. I try to make sense of what just happened. Father listened to Liam—no, he obeyed him, like Liam was running the show. Maybe power had shifted and they weren't telling anyone.

Shane wouldn't like it. Something deep down tells me it wasn't that at all.

CHAPTER EIGHT

CIARA

WHEN I ARRIVE AT the first room, Darragh is waiting at the door. There's something different about him this morning. He's staring at his shoes. When my trolley wheels squeak, announcing my arrival, he looks up at me. He smiles, but it doesn't reach his blue eyes.

"Morning," I say and open the door. He steps in and sits on the floor. Once I have my trolley in, I move to open the curtains.

"Could you leave them closed a little while longer?" he asks, and there's something in his voice that has me agreeing. It's a tenderness I've never heard before. I start to clean the room, stripping the bed while stealing glances at Darragh. His sullen mood is a side of him I haven't witnessed yet.

"I often wonder what it would be like if my mum was still here." Darragh speaks softly, and I don't want to stop cleaning, so I get my duster and polish off the trolley.

"She nearly died when I was born." He's staring at the floor, and it's like this knowledge is eating him away.

"What happened?" I quiz and half polish the bedside tables.

"I'm a twin and she had to have a C-section. Dad said she nearly bled to death." He's frowning.

"Did she?"

Darragh's head snaps up, and he's looking at me like I just slapped him. "No, not then."

So she's dead.

"What happened to her?"

His clenched fists and quick rise and fall of his chest have me wanting to withdraw my question.

I leave him in his own turmoil and polish the TV and dresser.

"She was murdered." His words are harsh.

All the hairs rise on my body, and my hand stills on the dresser.

"I still picture her gasping for air. Her nails were painted red. Like a blood red. She always kept herself so well."

"I'm sorry," I say.

He shrugs and forces a shaky grin.

"You were there?" I ask.

He tilts his head, narrowing his eyes. He looks more alert. "No, I wasn't..." He sounds so defensive.

"It's just what you said about her gasping for air..."

"Sorry. She was shot, but I wasn't there. I had a mental night last night. My head's still all over the place. I got myself arrested." He stands now.

"You sound proud," I retort.

Darragh stares at me and it's uncomfortable. I relax when he turns away and opens the curtains, letting light stream in.

"What about you?" he asks.

I put the polish and duster away. "What about me?" I fire back.

Darragh opens a window, getting ready to light a fag.

"You can't smoke in here," I say.

He lets out a heavy breath before putting the fag back into the box. "Aren't you the rule enforcer?" he says with a grin.

"No. I just can't afford to lose my job." I grab my gloves and supplies for the bathroom. What I don't expect is for Darragh to follow me in. He takes a pair of gloves from the box and blows into them before he slips them on.

"What are you doing?" I ask.

"What can I do?"

"You want to help?" I'm surprised. His six-foot frame in the bathroom is making the space seem small. I want him out.

"My father has cut me off from the family money, so I need to work to get money." That's all it takes and I relax. "I was thinking that maybe you were doing it because sitting on the ground while I do all the work just might be getting to you. But obviously I was wrong." My words come out harsher than I intended.

"Don't sound so pissed, blue. I mean, I want to help you too."

I roll my eyes and turn my back on him. "Clean the sink," I say and then think maybe I should make him clean the toilet. Fingers coil around my arm, and my reaction is immediate.

"Take your hands off me." I rip my arm from his and square up.

Darragh holds his hands in the air. "Wow, wow, calm down."

I'm trying to control my pounding heart and tell my body he's not a threat.

"You'd be really pretty if you let your hair down." Darragh's words have me blinking.

"You're hitting on me?" My confusion works itself around my words.

"No. If I was hitting on you, you'd know about it."

"I suppose, then, ignorance is bliss," I say, but my mind is scrambling.

"Why do you take everything as an insult?" he questions.

I hate the way Darragh's making me feel. My brain is scrambled, and my mind is in chaos. I don't like it. "Because, Darragh, it usually is."

I don't miss the soft knock on the door, so I quickly evacuate the bathroom.

"Ciara." Liam's eyes scan the room. Everywhere his eyes touch, he gives a nod of approval. "I need you to come down to the club. We're getting ready for tonight's opening."

I nod. "What about my rooms?"

Darragh steps out of the bathroom.

"Darragh will finish them," Liam informs me.

I don't turn to Darragh, and he doesn't respond.

"Are you ready?" Liam isn't leaving without me.

That feels odd. I check my apron for my phone and key. "Yeah, I'm good to go." I follow Liam out of the room, and when I turn to say goodbye to Darragh, he's disappeared back into the bathroom.

***

The new part of the hotel is alive with activity. The room is nearly complete, and the last touches are being placed. A man carrying a large flower arrangement walks past me. I snort. This is going to be a strip joint. I'm not sure any punters will be looking at the flowers. Some dancers are practicing, fully clothed, but that isn't stopping the males from ogling them as they work.

I line up with the rest of the staff when Liam arrives back out. "Uniforms are ready in the changing room, so everyone should get ready and we'll start your training."

Everyone moves.

"Ciara." I hate being singled out, especially by Liam. "Your uniform size needs to be adjusted."

"I'm an eight," I tell him.

He nods. "I'll have a uniform ready for you shortly."

Great, can't wait.

Another man carrying a larger vase of flowers walks past me, and I see Liam's retreating back. I'm not sure what to do, so I just start wiping down the tables while I wait for someone to step in and tell me what I need to do. It doesn't take long before Sharon, one of the managers, comes looking for me.

"Ciara." She beckons me over with one finger. Her nails are stupidly long, but she doesn't exactly work. Delegating is definitely her specialty.

Sharon flicks her long red hair across her shoulder. "Get changed. Your uniform is in the changing room." Sharon steps away. "Derek, move the flowers. They're obscuring the bar."

I leave and find my uniform on the bench in front of my locker. I hold it up. It doesn't seem so bad. The black trousers are the same as for us cleaners. I hate how they stick to me, but they're comfortable. The red shirt is tight, and I have no choice but to unbutton the first three buttons. My chest is too large for the shirt. I leave and fold my arms across my chest as I try to find Sharon. She's still out on the floor giving orders.

"My shirt's too small," I inform her, dropping my arms so she can see for herself.

She looks me and up and down and grins. "It's perfect."

"It's not, Sharon. I feel very exposed."

She leans into me. "You'll get more tips." She turns to everyone else now. "Okay, ladies, listen up."

All the other girls have changed, and everyone's uniform looks pretty tight. No one else seems uncomfortable, but I am.

I refold my arms across my chest as I fall into line with the other girls. We spend the next hour learning how to carry a tray with one hand. A lot of glasses get broken, but toward the end of the hour, we all seem to have it. So that's what we will be here for, to serve.

"Looking good, ladies." A familiar voice rings out across the room.

I nearly drop my tray but balance it at the last minute. Darragh strolls in with a smirk on his face and a fag tucked behind his ear. His confidence fills each step he takes. He winks and grins, and when our eyes meet, his widen and he takes two steps toward me.

"I knew it." The way he says it has my face burning.

I'm praying to God that he doesn't say anything inappropriate. "I knew you were hiding this"—he points to my chest—"under all those layers."

I glance at the other girls, who look at me like I just materialized. "Did you clean all your rooms?" I fire back, hating how he's so easily embarrassing me.

"I'm on my lunch break." I thought my words would deter him from poking at me but not a bit. "Thought we might grab some food."

He's talking to my chest, and I wish I didn't have to hold the tray so I could fold my arms.

"Darragh." Sharon arrives back over and puckers her lips. Darragh's attention is taken off me, and now he focuses on Sharon. She embraces him and plants a kiss on his cheek. I hate how my stomach twists at the sight of her lips on him.

"Sharon, you look hot," he tells her, and she smiles at him.

I stop myself from rolling my eyes, knowing some of the girls still watch me.

"Aren't you a sweetheart," she says. "Did I hear you mention lunch?" She bats her eyelids, and I feel disappointed when Darragh agrees to go for lunch with her. I know I shouldn't—it's Darragh and we don't exactly know each other, but yeah, that hurts.

"Ciara, are you coming?"

I'm placing the tray on the table when Darragh asks me. I turn, flickering a glance at Sharon, who curls her lips up in distaste.

"I'm good," I say. I can't meet his eye.

"Come on. Don't make me drag you." He's in front of me now, and everyone is staring at us.

My heart starts to pound. "I brought my lunch."

He grins. "Bring it with you. I'll sort it."

I can't stop the grin that spreads across my face. "Like you did the last time?"

His own grin turns into a smile. "I promise I will sort it this time."

I don't believe him.

"Ciara is training, so she won't be ready for lunch for a while." Sharon smiles, but it's forced and she's looking very jealous.

"You want me to have a word with the boss?"

It's like Darragh knows he's winding Sharon up, and I wonder for the first time if I'm a pawn in his game. Is he trying to make her jealous? The burn of my chest has me turning away.

"I have work to do." I walk off with the burn of humiliation heavy on my cheeks.

It takes a full ten minutes before the heat leaves my face and chest.

"A word please, Ciara." Liam's voice comes from behind me.

When I turn, he walks off to the bar and I follow him. I can't think of any reason Liam is pulling me aside, unless it's to talk about working later, or maybe Darragh didn't finish the rooms, which would make sense.

"Can I get you a drink?"

The question surprises me. "Like a Coke?" I quiz.

"A Coke," he calls to the barman.

I don't want a Coke, but I don't refuse it as Liam places it on a mat and slides the mat toward me. He waits and I take a sip. He seems satisfied once I put the glass back down.

"Have you wondered why I paired you with Darragh?"

An uneasy feeling starts in my stomach. "No." I had wondered, every day since he was placed in my room.

"I selected you. It wasn't random. You, Ciara, are different from other girls." He lets that sink in.

I'm not entirely sure what he means. "Thanks," I say, but it sounds more like a question.

"Darragh has a weakness for pretty girls. He likes to break them. So with you, I knew it would work."

I grip the glass, hating what he's saying, but I'm not naïve in thinking I'm a model. But Jesus, he's making me feel like a monster. He's silent now, and the burn of my throat has me wanting to leave. "Is that all?"

He runs his long fingers across the polished bar. "Earlier, he asked you for food. I saw your face. I just don't want you to be naïve about the situation."

I pick up the Coke and drink nearly all the contents. "I'm not naïve. Don't forget where you found me," I say and stand up.

A nod of his head is my dismissal. I'm hurt, but at least with Liam, he's straight. No mind games.

The day he offered me a job and climbed into a brand-new Range Rover, I remember staring at the Jeep thinking I could be walking to my doom. He hadn't leaned out of the vehicle, but his voice reached me. "Are you coming or not?"

I walked to the car door. "I won't work the streets," I told him with a hand on my hip.

"It's a cleaning job."

"How can I trust you?"

"You can't." His honesty had me taking my chances and climbing into the Jeep.

***

I eat lunch alone in the canteen. The other girls had tried to be friends with me when I first started. I'm not a people person, and now with Darragh, I'm starting to really hate humanity.

CHAPTER NINE

DARRAGH

I WASH SHARON OFF me before heading to Kells to meet the lads. She isn't my type, but she's more than willing to relieve some of my stress, so I let her. And she also paid for my food.

A win-win.

"Did you miss me?" I ask as I enter the warehouse. I'm not sure of the reception I'll receive; everyone is here. It's DJ that comes over to me, and for a moment, we stand toe to toe. He raises his hand, and I clasp my hand with his.

"We good?" he asks, already grinning, knowing we are.

"Yeah, we're good." He releases me and takes my phone out of his back pocket and places it in my hand.

"Nice one," I say.

He also hands me my wallet. Not one card will work, since Liam canceled them all. That's why I need to get this next job done.

"Everyone ready for tonight?" I ask as I take a seat beside everyone else. Art hands me a drink and I refuse. I don't want this job to go wrong. I want to have my mind focused. Everyone looks at me like I'm a fucking leper.

"I want a clear head," I tell them, but I don't look at Mark. His presence here is good. It means I didn't piss him off enough for him to go to the Gardaí.

"There's only one thing," DJ says.

I nod. I don't want them to know how desperate I am.

"You burn our money this time and show's over, man."

I grin and shrug like I'm pretending to consider it. "Let's make sure no one pisses me off, then."

DJ turns away from me, not happy with my reply. Art snorts a laugh. He doesn't give a shit. Money is plentiful to him.

"So everyone knows what they're doing?" I ask this while looking at Fitz. He's in the same white hoodie with the hood pulled up.

"You know I am," he says, fixing the legs of his tracksuit bottoms.

"Am I with DJ again?" Mark asks.

I look to DJ. It's his call.

"Yeah, you're with me," DJ tells him.

Art snorts one line after another. "I'm with you, man," he says to me, while inhaling quickly through his nose.

I itch to join him, but I don't. Everything will be the same as the last time, only this time we're hitting Kingscourt. It's very close to home, but the layout is similar to Kells—a single street. It makes it easier to block.

Art robbed a Range Rover. The shiny black surface reflects my face as I climb in.

"You couldn't have gotten something a little more inconspicuous?" I ask.

He jumps into the passenger seat with ease and starts going through the CDs like he knows what he 's looking for. "It's my Dad's." His grin spreads wide across his face.

"Have you fucking lost it?"

"He deserved it. My Dad's an asshole." He peeks at me with a smirk before returning to the CDs.

I know he doesn't have the best relationship with his dad, but stealing his Jeep?

We wait until everyone else has left before we leave the warehouse. Art blares the music while he pretends to play drums on the dashboard.

I want to feel the high he's feeling. I hate how slick my hands are right now or how I'm thinking of all the things that could go wrong. I normally don't give a fuck. Being sober might not have been the wisest. Art takes out a small bag of powder and snorts another line up his nose.

"You want some?" he asks.

I fold. "Fuck it, yeah."

I snort the line off his hand before sitting back in my seat and letting the drug flow through my veins. The feeling of panic disappears rapidly, and I turn up the music. The tightening around my throat goes slowly, and it's replaced with the sense of invisibility. We roar toward Kingscourt as I push my foot down harder on the pedal.

***

Hot air blows out of my nose, and my face feels itchy from the balaclava. It's restricting but I'll get over it.

Everyone is ready the moment I stop the Range Rover. Art gets out and climbs up on the digger. The gun is cold in my hands as I climb out and focus on the empty street around us. Music still blares from the Jeep, making my pulse pump and pound.

Art tears the ATM from the wall and puts it on the flatbed trailer in seconds. I give DJ a wave to leave, and he starts his Jeep. Art is running toward me. I take one final look before climbing back into the Jeep.

Sirens blare and I freeze for a moment, my frantic mind wondering how the fuck we're going to get out of this. I unfreeze and race to the Jeep before jumping in and starting it. My foot pushes down on the accelerator, and smoke rises as the tires tear from the road.

Art grips his door and slams it as I take off, but the squad car in front of me blocks our way.

"Put on your belt," I say.

I clip mine in and tear toward the squad. The impact when we hit the front of it has our bodies slamming forward, but I don't stop. I don't lift my foot and zoom past them.

Art whoops and shouts as he glances out the window.

"They're following us," he shouts.

I can't stop the smile that crosses my face. "Let's put your daddy's car to the test," I say and he laughs. The Jeep roars onto Carraickmacross road. All the bends slow us down, and the Gardaí are able to keep up with us.

"You need to go faster, man," Art tells me as he snorts more coke up his nose.

"Can you hold off for five fucking seconds?" I rub my face as I look at the three squad cars who tear after us down the road.

When the bends disappear, it's only then I put distance between us and them. I can't push the Jeep any harder. The smaller Gardaí cars fall further behind, and I relax enough to pull off my balaclava. I turn down a back road. I don't slow down but keep pushing the Jeep. The roads aren't gentle to us, and we bounce around.

"Slow down before you snap my neck." Art's words have me slowing down. The night is quiet, and no sirens can be heard. I pull the Jeep into a field.

Art is out getting petrol from the boot. We douse the Jeep before lighting it up and take off on foot.

"Ring Fitz," Art says. "He'll come and get us."

I don't. Instead, I ring DJ. "You okay?" I ask, but really, I want to know if my money is okay.

"That was too close for comfort. What about you guys?"

"Yeah, we're good. What happened?" They got there too quickly. Like maybe they knew.

"Fitz rang me. The cops were chasing him, and he had forgotten to drop the spikes to slow them down."

Dumb fuck. "Where is he now?" I ask.

DJ doesn't answer, and an uneasy feeling skitters across my back. "I keep ringing him but no answer."

"Can you pick me and Art up? We're close to Dun na Ri Park," I say.

"Give me twenty minutes."

I hang up, and Art is staring at me. "Fitz fucked up. Forgot to drop the spikes."

"I'll beat the shit out of him," Art responds. His foot strikes the ground forcefully.

"He's not picking up his phone." I light up a smoke.

"You think he snitched?" When Art asks, I already know the answer.

"Nah, I just hope he didn't get caught."

***

DJ picks us up. The moment we're in the car, I know something is wrong. My first thought is Mark.

"Where's Mark?" I ask.

DJ starts the car. "Mark is at the warehouse, but Fitz was arrested."

"Fuck!" Art roars.

"Calm down, Art," I say and he sits back.

"What do we do?" DJ sounds nervous.

"I'm thinking," I tell him. "Just head back to the warehouse."

Mark is counting the money when we walk in. He pauses and looks at the three of us.

"I hope you're not pocketing any of that," I spit out before making my way to the fridge.

"Fuck you." His reply comforts me. I don't really give a shit if he does. I just need to figure out how to get Fitz out of jail.

"How much did we get this time?" Art asks, popping open a bottle.

I'm listening.

"If we split it equally?" Mark asks.

I stare at Mark before nodding.

"Ten k each." He grins.

"Scraps." That wouldn't last me long. Sitting down, I run both hands across my face before picking up my bottle and drinking half of it. I really only have one option.

I take my phone out and ring the one person who can fix this.

"Darragh." Liam's voice makes me reconsider.

"How's it going?" I ask. Everyone is watching me, so I get up and walk away.

"Are you in trouble?"

I hate how he already knows I'm not ringing for a chat. "Of course not. Can't one brother ring another?"

"I'm working, so can we continue this social conversation at home?"

"Fine. I need your help," I say.

Silence fills the line, but he hasn't hung up, so that's good.

"A mate got arrested for speeding. Could you send—"

"No. Is that all?"

"Liam, I'd owe you," I say.

"I said no."

What an asshole.

"Fine." I hang up and turn to everyone, knowing they're waiting to hear if I can fix this.

"Sorry, guys. He's temperamental these days."

Art's phone dings. "He's been admitted to Navan Hospital," Art says, looking back up. "He flipped the car. Minor injuries."

"Who told you?" DJ asks.

"Cathy, one of the nurses. I texted her and asked her about Fitz."

"Are you sleeping with her?" DJ asks really slowly.

"Of course he is." I shake my head as I grab another drink.

"She has a banging body. Not a great face, though. But it's good to have someone for information like this."

"Well, nothing we can do now, only celebrate," I say.

No one has fully relaxed. I grab a drink for DJ and Mark, and we stand together in a circle.

"A bit of a fuckup, but it could be worse," I say, and we click our bottles together before we all take a long drink.

That night, we do a lot of drugs, until bliss is everywhere.

"I love you," I tell Art as I light a fag.

"I love you too, man."

"I mean it. You're like my fucking rock. I know you got my back," I say while throwing my arm across his shoulders.

"Don't burn me." He moves away from my lit smoke, so I move it to the other hand.

"You could always buy a new jumper," I tell him.

Art grins. "But I like this one."

"You know my family is filled with pricks." I inhale again and watch the smoke fill the space above my head.

Art widens his eyes like he's trying to stay awake, before slipping away from me.

"Great talk," I mutter as I get another bottle of beer.

Sitting back on the chair, I watch as Mark and DJ hobble around to music that blares from the radio that's propped up on the wall. Both of them are stoned out of their heads. Art continues to snort too much coke up his nose, and sitting here in this shed reminds me of the fucking losers they are.

I down the rest of the bottle and leave it sitting on the ground as I get up and leave the warehouse. No one notices me as I slip out and into my car.

***

I check myself in the bathroom mirror in the hospital. My eyes are too wide. Cold water splashes my face, and I meet my eyes again in the mirror. I check my pockets for more coke; just a little bit more would settle me, but I come up empty. I must have already taken the last of it.

It's seven in the morning, and the hospital is quiet as I seek out Fitz. He's in the male ward, finally out of that fucking hoodie. The blue gown makes him appear sickly. The bruises across his face are stark, and one leg is wrapped up in a cast. The nurse's station is lit up. I can make out three of them drinking coffee and chatting, but no one is on the ward. I move quietly over to Fitz and shake him until he wakes up.

"What's up, bud?" I greet him.

His eyes flicker around the room, and fear is visible on his face.

"What did you tell them?" I ask.

"Nothing, I swear. I'm loyal to you, Darragh." His mumbling is waking one of the guys beside us.

"Shh. That's not what I asked. What did you say to them?"

"I was drinking and driving when the Gardaí followed me. I panicked and drove away. That's it."

"Excuse me." One of the nurses, who's carrying more weight than what's considered a good advertisement for the health service, shuffles toward me.

I stand to my full height and raise both eyebrows while my lips lift slightly in a smile. "Good morning, nurse."

"You can't be in here." Her cheeks tinge red as she gets closer, but she's holding firm to the hospital's policy.

"Just visiting a friend," I tell her. Fitz, the stupid fucker, doesn't back me up.

The nurse finally looks to Fitz, who nods like a dummy.

"I was just leaving." I turn to do just that, but she's on my heels.

"I'll walk you out."

"No need," I tell her, but she's still following me. "I suppose the walk would do you good," I fire over my shoulder and her face flames.

"Excuse me."

I walk faster, but she manages to keep on my heels. She's like a dog with a fucking bone.

"Look," I start, "I know you don't often get to walk this close to someone who looks like me, but you can fuck off now. I don't need a chaperone."

Her face slackens, and her washed-out eyes hold mine steadily—something I didn't expect from her.

"Security." She marches over to the reception desk. "Marcella, get me security."

I'm still walking away from her.

"Don't move, sir."

I pause. "Or what? You'll eat me?"

She shakes her head in disgust, and I turn just as 'security' enters the building. The guy in front of me can't be more than four foot six, with a bald head, decaying teeth, and a frame that threatens to fold if I touch it.

"What's the problem, Mary?" He's removing a walkie-talkie from the strap on his black trousers.

Mary, the heifer, is moving toward us. "I caught him in the male ward, and when I tried to escort him out, he became hostile and abusive."

"I was visiting a friend," I tell the security man, who's still staring at Mary. "I wasn't abusive."

"Backup to the front of the hospital," he says into his walkie-talkie. "We have an abusive man on site."

"What the fuck?" I need more drink to deal with this shit. I try to sidestep the sideshow, but the security man blocks me. I could pick him up and move him aside, but as three more enter the building, all ready for action, I decide to take a deep breath.

"What's the problem?" security man number two asks Mary.

"Have you no work to do?" I ask Mary. She's really getting on my nerves.

"Don't speak to her, sir." Security man number three, who is a similar height to my six foot, steps forward. The handlebar mustache makes it hard to take him seriously.

"I'm leaving. No harm done." When no one moves, I try to rein in my irritation. "What the fuck do you want?" I take a step toward the security man. "Money? An apology? Blood?"

"Calm down, sir," the short man says, with his hand looped into the belt of his trousers.

I try to step around them again, but I'm blocked. The third guy is out with his walkie-talkie. I can't hear what he's saying into it.

"Have you been drinking?"

"You're hospital security, not the fucking Gardaí. I see what's happening here. You all went and sat the entrance exam to become a Gardaí and failed, so this is the best you got. And fat fucking Mary here, tries to make herself feel better by helping the sick while her own sickness"—I turn to Mary—"which we know is eating, is out of fucking control."

"How dare you." Mary's wide eyes start to water.

Sweat is gathering on the back of my neck. I need a hit before I snap. I move, and when they block me this time, I push forward. The short one hits the ground, like someone throws a game in a football match. The other two shuffle in front of me with arms outstretched. They keep moving backward but don't touch me.

Once we get outside, they seem to sigh as the Gardaí pull up and two of them make their way toward me. I'm so fucked today.

CHAPTER TEN

CIARA

THE NEW CLUB IS filled with punters, but the room is kept cool from all the overhead fans. The low lights and sultry music make me want to leave and have a shower. I didn't think I would ever crave to be back cleaning toilets, but this place is making my skin crawl.

Women with bodies to die for wrap themselves around poles as the music changes to a more upbeat tempo, some singer telling them to *work, bitch*. Men lounge everywhere, their eyes wide with lust as they sit back sipping drinks and enjoying the show.

The table I serve seats two men who ooze money. The blond-haired guy has a split down the center, his hair falling to his ears. I can't keep up with the amount of times he runs his hands through his highlighted hair and flashes his pearly whites around the room.

"Two martinis," I say with a smile as I place them in front of Blondie and his mate, who didn't get picked in the looks department. His black hair is gelled back, A false tan and overwhitened teeth make his overall appearance too much.

A wink from Blondie is sent my way. At first, I straighten and check behind me. His deep laugh has me staring back at him, my eyes immediately flashing to his teeth.

"What's your name, sweetheart?" he asks.

I hold the tray loosely between my fingers and keep the smile on my face. "Ciara. Is there anything else I can get you gentlemen?"

It's like watching a peacock showcase his colored feathers. The word gentlemen seems to have that effect on Blondie, as he puckers his chest out further. His friend gives me a dismissive wave, his eyes staying trained on the pole dancers.

"Your number?"

Blondie isn't my type, but I'm pretty sure I'm not his either. That's why this conversation isn't making sense. "I'm sorry. We aren't allowed to mingle with clients. Is that all, gentlemen?"

Blondie isn't giving up. "Tell me your boss's name, and I'm sure I can sort this out."

"No, thank you." I don't wait for this conversation to get anymore awkward. I leave, but the sting to my backside has me standing up straighter. When I turn, I expect to see Blondie, but it's his friend.

"Get to work," he says while he sits back.

My chest tightens, and sweat has gathered between my shoulder blades.

"What are you looking at?" His question is taunting.

"Leave her alone." Blondie comes to my defense, but he looks uncomfortable as he runs his hands through his hair.

I move before I hit him with the tray. I'm waiting for someone to say something to me as I move back through the room. In my head, I think everyone just witnessed what happened. But as I move around the growing crowd, people are in their own conversations, smiles on their faces and alcohol filling their mouths.

Once I reach the bar, I grip the counter. I focus on the cold wood as I move my fingers in the direction where the carvings along the edge take me.

My heart falls back into a normal rhythm, and I release the tray and place it onto the bar before running my hand across the top of my head and down my ponytail. I need to pull my shit together. Looking up, I keep my eye on my table and wait for the nod that I dread.

"This place is crazy." Sinead moves beside me. Her blonde hair is up in a high ponytail, but unlike mine, hers sways perfectly. The shine of her hair reflects the light. Lips smeared in pink lipstick grin at me. "It's such fun, isn't it?" she asks me.

I force a smile. "Yeah, it's great."

Simon, the barman, moves down to us. "What do you ladies need?"

"Vodka with a dash of Coke and a beer," she orders and he moves away to get her order. I take a peek back at my table. Blondie meets my eye and nods.

"You want to swap tables?" I ask Sinead sweetly, but her own smile falls.

Her eyes narrow. "We have to stay at our assigned tables."

"I don't remember hearing that."

"Well, I do." She snaps her head, her ponytail moving quickly as she faces forward.

The crowd seems to grow closer as I hold the tray to my chest and make my way to my table.

"Two martinis?" I say with a smile to make this as quick as possible.

"Yeah, thanks, Ciara." Blondie still smiles at me.

"No. I want…" His friend takes up the drinks menu and really assesses it as Blondie smiles up at me.

I glance at the female dancer, who wraps her body easily around a pole.

"You could be like her." Blondie says it like it's a compliment.

"I'm good."

"What's this?" The asshole that touched me has his head buried in the menu. His eyes rise and meet mine, and I have to walk over to him and lean in way too close to see what he's pointing at.

"A slow screw against the wall," I say.

His lips tug up on one side, and it's creepy as fuck.

"I'll take one of those." His eyes are on my breasts as he speaks.

My breaths come in quick spouts, and my chest strains further against my shirt. I turn quickly, and the sting to my backside is like the crack of a whip. I'm moving but not toward the safety of the bar; I'm moving to him. My fist connects with his nose, and I know I've broken it. Not by his roars or the gush of blood that sprays from his nose, but by the crack. I'm smiling in victory, but it lasts for only a moment as people around us shift back.

"You broke my fucking nose."

My head snaps back to him, his eyes ablaze with fury, but I don't feel fear. I wouldn't mind round two. The pole dancer in front of us is barely moving, as her attention, and most of the room's, is on us. Security moves in from all sides.

Blondie hands his friend napkins, but they're whipped out of his hand. "I want her fucking arrested for assault."

"What happened?" Security asks, and I let the asshole scream that I broke his nose.

"He touched me," I say in my defense. I don't expect them to drop it, but I do expect them to remove him.

Instead, the second security man takes my arm. "This way."

I resist as he tries to move me without any commotion. "What about the pervert who touched me?"

The security man looks up at the guy in question. Justice would be served.

"I never touched her. She's a liar and obviously a liability to this establishment. Who's going to cover my medical expenses and my pain and suffering?"

"Your pain and suffering? I've been serving your creepy ass for the last hour. What about my suffering? Less time on the sun beds, and I'm sure that will cover the cost to your nose. It was crooked anyway." I'm nearly spitting as the security man drags me away, like I'm the criminal in all this. It's not until I'm in the hall and the music is distant that I think of my job. I can't lose it.

"Where are you taking me?" The concrete floors and sterile white walls have my stomach twisting.

Neither security man answers me. My arm doesn't come loose from their steel grip as I yank it back.

"Stop it," one warns as we turn into a room with just a table and chairs.

"What is this?" It looks like an interrogation room from a movie.

"Stay here."

I don't have a choice as the door slams behind me. I try it immediately, and it doesn't open. The room is missing that huge two-way mirror. It's not that no one is watching me; a small camera in the corner is recording my movements. The chair is hard as I sit down and put my head in my hands. I really made a mess of this.

The door opens and the security man who was first on the scene comes in. His face is still as stern as he stands on the opposite side of the table. He inspects me and I do the same to him. He's tall like all the rest, maybe a little over six feet, with broad shoulders and a wide face. His hair is cut close to his head, leaving only the shaving of hair. Green eyes observe me without blinking. There's nothing significant about him; he's average. He doesn't wear the arrogance like a lot of bouncers I know.

"He touched me," I confess, gripping both hands together.

"You don't work in this part of the hotel. What were you doing there?"

"Okay, I see you're not very bright. What, you think I was serving drinks to assholes for the fun of it?"

His grin is immediate, but he suppresses it quickly. "We don't have you on the staff list."

I shrug. "That's not my fault."

He exhales loudly. "We need to get confirmation that you were assigned to work there."

I fold my arms across my chest. "Fine, but I better be getting paid while sitting in here."

His eyes flash with humor. "You broke that guy's nose."

"He's lucky that's all I broke." My bravery is slipping. The thought of getting fired over this is scaring me, but I hold his eye.

"I'll be back shortly," he says.

I don't speak as he leaves but focus on my nails. They never grow. I've tried the nail polish that strengthens them and is supposed to be some miracle grow formula, but no, my nails always remain short. Fake nails aren't something I can wear in my line of work. Still, I would at least like them a bit longer so they look more feminine.

The door opens and my stomach squeezes. My heart beats faster as Liam steps into the room. He frightens me. It's his unemotional state. Even now, everything is precise as he closes the door gently behind him and moves to the table.

He carefully pulls out the other chair and sits down so we're very close and eye to eye. I swallow and the small bit of bravery I felt shatters across the concrete floor.

"I'm sorry."

"For what?" Liam always takes each movement in. I haven't been in his company much, but when I am, I often feel like he observes others reactions and movements, like he's learning. It's unsettling.

"For causing a scene." I don't say for breaking the guy's nose, because I'm not sorry.

The way he holds my gaze causes my chest to rise and fall quickly again. The strain on my buttons has me trying to calm my heart. Liam doesn't look down at my chest; his focus is on my face.

"Life is cruel, unkind, and most often, our decisions are based on what life shapes us to be. So you strike out at a customer for touching you. In one sense, it's justified." He pauses before continuing. "But can you imagine if everyone acted on their instincts, acting with brutality? What kind of place would this be?"

Heat rushes to my cheeks. It's how I survived on the streets. Well, at the start not so much, but I learned fast. It was a kill or be killed kind of world.

"He touched me," I repeat, but my words fall flat. I'm going to get fired.

"He won't be in this establishment again."

Surprise flitters through me. "But what about his nose?" I ask stupidly, and then kick myself. I need to shut up.

"It will heal." Liam rises and places the chair gently back in its place.

I don't know what I'm waiting for—the other shoe to drop, maybe. This all seems to have gone so well.

"Ciara." My name has me looking at Liam. "You've been warned now. The next time you act without thinking, your time with us will be up." And the other shoe falls.

I nod.

"If that happens again, you report it to security and the person will be removed."

I swallow the emotion that rises inside me.

"You can go back to work," he finally says.

I'm standing on shaky legs. When I leave the room, I don't return to the floor. Instead, I go to my locker. I just need a minute. The water feels nice on my burning throat. Liam is fair, but his words seem to swim deep and take root inside me.

Every unwanted touch, every slap rushes me. I take out my phone and search for a distraction and am surprised to see a missed call from an 049 number, which is local. I ring it back just to distract myself.

"Navan Gardaí, how can I help you?"

"Hi. I have a missed call from this number."

"What's your name?" The Gardaí asks, sounding half-distracted.

"Ciara Michaels." I chew my lip as I hold the line. I have no idea what this is about. But after breaking someone's nose, it's looking like the creep has reported me. My stomach twists. What would happen if someone filed assault charges? I could end up with a criminal record. A fine.

A familiar voice fills the line then. "Ciara, you gem. I need your help."

It takes a moment for my fizzled mind to catch up. "Darragh?"

"Yeah, so I'm in a bit of a situation. I got arrested last night and need you to bail me out."

"Why me?" I ask, utterly confused.

"You're my friend."

I snort. "You're such a liar. Anyway, I can't. I'm in trouble here and can't leave."

"Why, what happened?" His concern sounds genuine.

"I broke some guy's nose."

He's laughing. "Did you get fired?"

"No, but I need to get back to work," I say.

"Hold on. Seriously, I need you to bail me out."

I chew the inside of my mouth. "I'm finished in a few hours. I can do it then."

"I can't survive another few hours."

I close my locker door, aware of the amount of time I'm wasting. "Darragh, it's a few hours or nothing. Which is it?"

He lets out a heavy breath that holds no humor. It's filled with exhaustion. "I'll let you know."

Guilt gnaws at my stomach as I finish the bottle of water and make my way back onto the floor. A few people give me looks, but I serve my new table while ignoring them. The men smile at me, so the news that I was violent hasn't spread yet. It's an easy shift, but my mind is stuck on stupid Darragh and his pitiful voice. I know what sitting in a cell feels like. I know what it feels like to not have anyone come sign you out. The Gardaí usually just got sick of me and let me go.

I make a stupid decision as I ask Sinead to take over my table.

"We already talked about this." Her voice fills with bitchiness.

"They tip really well and it's all yours."

"Even the tips you've made already?"

I force a smile. "Yeah."

"Fine, but you owe me."

I don't have a clue how she figured that one out, but I nod and get off the floor. I'm questioning my motives in what I'm about to do. I can only assume that fresh wounds have come to the surface for me today, and I hope I'm thinking straight as I knock on Liam's door.

"Come in." His voice gives me pause.

After turning the knob, I step in. "I was wondering if you have a moment."

He points at the chair in front of him. The door closes behind me, telling me there's no going back. The chair is comfortable and I sink into it, but under the circumstances, I don't want to get comfortable, so I sit forward.

"I got a call from Darragh. He's at Navan Gardaí station and needs someone to bail him out."

"And he rang you?" His eyebrows rise slightly.

"I'm as surprised as you," I say.

"Thank you for letting me know."

I'm getting up, but I pause behind the chair. "So... are you going to get him?"

"Does my brother's welfare concern you?"

"No," I answer too quickly. "I was just curious."

Liam stares at me, and I shift uncomfortably.

"Okay." I'm not getting an answer. I leave the office and feel no further along.

Now, a different kind of guilt churns in my stomach. I feel like I've dumped Darragh into a mess. He hadn't rang Liam, and maybe there's a reason for that.

CHAPTER ELEVEN

CIARA

I'M BACK ON THE floor, and the work is a great distraction. The club is alive, and no one looks at me strangely. I'm serving tables and time flies.

After a while, I get that feeling like someone is watching me. When I look up, it's Blondie, who's sipping a beer at the bar. I raise a brow at him, and he raises his drink. He's alone at the bar, but I feel uneasy with him here. I continue serving drinks and try to ignore his eyes, which seem to burn into the back of my neck. Three security men are close to me, and my shoulders loosen. I just need to be aware of where they are.

Sharon moves around the room. She offers nods to servers who are doing a good job and raised eyebrows to any servers who aren't moving quickly enough. When my customers leave, I tidy up their table.

"You can keep the bar area clean and check the floor for any rubbish," Sharon says as she scans the room again before she meets my eye.

"Of course," I say.

When she leaves, I do as she asks, and the closer I get to Blondie, the more irritation claws up my back. I hate being watched. I pick up some glasses and move right beside him as I wait for Simon to come and take them from me.

"What do you want?" I ask, not looking at him.

"Your number?"

Now I look at him. "No. Not because I'm not allowed, but because I don't like you." I say it quickly as Simon arrives and takes the empty glasses from me. "Leave me alone or I'll hurt you," I warn him.

His easy smile is gone, and the saying 'birds of a feather flock together' comes to mind. But I don't wait around for a response. I'm back on the floor, weaving through bodies as the beat has the dancers wrapping themselves tighter around the poles and the men moving a little closer to the stages.

When my shift finally ends, I just want to wash it all off me. I want to go back to cleaning rooms. This isn't going to work well for me. I just know it.

I check my phone—no messages from Darragh. I consider ringing Navan Gardaí station to see if he was bailed out, but I remind myself that this is none of my business.

I grab my bag and leave work.

Outside, I inhale the fresh air. The sound of the music still beats away in my ear. I need to ring a taxi. My car is still broken, so I need to get it fixed as soon as possible. Taxis in Kingscourt aren't readily available. I ring the one number I have, and it goes straight to voicemail.

"Great." I walk away from the hotel and out the front gates. Cars come and go, but one slows down beside me. I keep walking, but I'm aware of it.

"I was trying to be nice to you." Dread curls in my stomach at Blondie's words.

I hold my phone tightly in my hand. "If you don't go away, I'm ringing the Gardaí," I threaten, but his car still rolls beside me. My pace quickens, and he easily finds a stride beside me.

"Come on, get in. I'll give you a lift."

"My lift is on the way," I say, considering walking back to the hotel. But it's bright and lots of cars are coming and going. I don't think he's going to hurt me. He's just trying to intimidate me.

"I know you're lying." His words hold a smile.

I stop walking and face him. He stalls the car. When I look inside, I see the other guy. "What do you want?" I ask.

"You broke my nose, bitch. You can't get away with that."

I laugh at him as his face reddens. "What are you going to do?"

Blondie is out first, and I try to hold my stance.

"Make you pay." His nose is bandaged, and bruises blossom under each eye. There's no blood on his shirt, as he wears a fresh white one.

"Get back into your car before I hurt you again." My threat doesn't sound so great now as they move closer. Cars whiz past and that's what's keeping me calm. It's daylight. They won't hurt me while the world watches, but something has me moving away. Sharp stone bites into my back, the hotel boundaries stopping me from moving any further.

Blondie is the first to touch me. His fingers wrap around my arm. I quickly pull it free and start dialing 911 on my phone. The screen cracks as it hits the ground.

"You're not ringing anyone, *Ciara*." The way he says my name has me thinking he's more dangerous than his friend, who's moved around the car and is closing in on me.

"You want money? I can get you money," I say.

"Do we look like we need money?" Blondie opens his arms and points at his car. It's new and flashy.

"Everyone always wants more," I say, my eyes snapping to my broken phone.

The other guy reaches me, and I move back out of his way, causing the stones to bite into me painfully.

"Look, you two freaks. Fuck off now before I start screaming." My voice rises.

The cars that move past us are going at high speed, the noise drowning me out. Their grins tell me they know no one will hear me. I dash to the left. Fingers grip my hair, painfully whipping me back.

My reaction is immediate. I start swinging, and my fist connects with Blondie's jaw the same time the other guy takes a swing at me. I can't avoid it, and the impact is worse than I remember. It's been a while since I've taken a hit. My ears ring and my heart slams painfully against my rib cage. It's like waiting for a gun to fire, and when it does, it either makes you freeze or move. My fist collides with him over and over again, until I'm dragged backward.

"Stay the fuck down," Blondie tells me before his foot connects with my stomach.

I gasp for air as he walks away from me and picks up his friend while dragging him to the car. Loose pebbles burn into my palms as I push myself off the ground.

The air is still thin as I try to catch my breath. My broken phone is beside me. I pick it up along with some loose stones and fire them at the car. Glass shatters and Blondie ducks for cover.

I don't stop but keep picking up whatever is accessible to me. I'm down to just pebbles, but I continue to fire them at his car. Small scrapes and dents are visible, and it feels like victory, that is until security comes running down the hill and out the front gates of the hotel. My first reaction is relief, until they reach me.

Hysterical girlish screams tear from Blondie's mouth. "She jumped us and beat up my friend."

"They attacked me first. They waited for me outside." I'm touching my face, which seems to ache even more now. My hands tremble. Shock is starting to settle in.

"She vandalized my car," Blondie roars as he holds his phone to his ear.

"Everyone needs to calm down." The security man holds out a hand toward each of us.

I'm calm as I gather my bag off the ground. The ringtone is loud as Blondie rings the Gardaí. While he's occupied, I get my phone off his front seat. I'm surprised when it switches on. The screen is cracked, but it still works. The other security man moves around the car. Moans erupt from behind the car as Blondie's friend starts to sit up. Cars slow down, catching glimpses of the commotion.

It doesn't take long for the Gardaí to arrive. The moment they do, Blondie is on them like a fly on shit.

"You need to arrest her..." He's pointing an accusing finger at me.

I stand hunkered, clutching my bag, hoping the whole 'little ole me' part comes across and that the Gardaí don't arrest me.

"Calm down and give us a moment." They approach the security men first to see if they saw anything.

I'm asked next. "You want to tell me what happened?"

Blondie throws a wobbler. "She attacked us," he roars.

"You need to calm down."

I can't hide the small smile of victory I feel as the Gardaí speaks to Blondie.

"Look at my car."

"Sir, last time. If you don't stop, we will take you all down to the station."

My smile is gone now. "You can take his statement first," I say quickly, just wanting this to end.

"She broke my nose." The other guy moves around the car, his face a mess. Blood drips from a cut on his lip. I don't remember getting his mouth. I was just hitting out blindly.

"I'm taking her statement first." The Gardaí gives everyone a final look, and when no one says any more, he turns to me.

"I work in the hotel." I keep my voice low, quivering. It's not that I'm lying, but I need him to believe me. "I was serving these two gentlemen, and when I turned down an advance, this one slapped me on the behind." I point to the asshole who did it. "I ignored it and continued working until he did it again. The second time, he hurt me."

"She's a fucking liar. She was coming on to me."

"Okay, arrest them all." The Gardaí pockets his small notepad.

My heart slams heavily against my chest. "No, I didn't do anything."

The two men are handcuffed and placed into the back of the car. The click of the cuffs on my wrists is familiar. I hate it.

"You can't put me in the back with them," I protest, my soft voice gone.

The Gardaí ignores me and makes me bend my head as I'm placed into the back of the squad car.

We don't speak as we're driven to Navan Gardaí station. The heat in the car has carved a path down my spine.

"I don't understand why I'm being arrested." I lean forward as I speak to the Gardaí.

"Assaulting people. Destroying their property," Blondie barks beside me.

If my hands weren't cuffed, I'd elbow him in the face. The Gardaí don't answer me, and I sit back.

***

Thankfully, we're separated once we enter the station. The room I'm taken to is small. The Gardaí that arrested me is the one who removes my cuffs and sits down with a clipboard. I rub my wrists, mostly out of something to do. They aren't really sore, but the bonds aren't normal.

As the Gardaí looks at his clipboard, I observe him. He has day's-old stubble on his face, some hairs a soft gray coloring. He's only in his forties, but the gray doesn't look bad on him. Blue eyes flicker to mine.

"Your full name?"

"Ciara Marie Michaels," I say clearly.

He writes my name down, but I don't like his furrowed brows. His eyes snap up to me, and he looks at me differently now. "We spoke on the phone today."

That's why his voice was so familiar. I couldn't pinpoint it earlier. "Did we?" I ask with a smile and tilt my head.

"Yes, we did. Darragh O'Reagan rang you to bail him out."

I sit back in my chair, my pretend smile gone. "Look, I barely know him. I work for his brother..." Something tells me I'm digging a huge hole for myself.

The Gardaí sits up straighter with interest. "Which brother?"

"Liam O'Reagan. I thought I was being questioned about what happened today."

"I ask the questions, not you. So what exactly do you do for Liam O'Reagan?" The Gardaí sits forward in his chair. There's eagerness in his stance.

"I'm a cleaner. I clean hotel rooms," I say slowly, and I get a sense of comfort when the Gardaí deflates.

His eyes scan the form in front of him. "How do you know Darragh?"

I want to ask if this is necessary, but I answer his question instead. "He works with me."

A look of disbelief stretches across his face. "Darragh O'Reagan cleans hotel rooms?"

I don't know these people, but even I know how doubtful this all looks. "It's the truth."

"Okay, you want to tell me what happened?"

Finally. I tell him exactly what happened from start to finish, but as I get to the fighting outside, it all starts to sound sketchy. Like how I managed to fight off two men. Knock one out and wreck a car. I'm small, so I can see in his eyes it isn't adding up.

"That's the truth," I finish up with.

"Just like Darragh O'Reagan cleans hotel rooms." His eyes narrow slightly.

I want to say something smart, but I fold my arms across my chest and look away. This is all starting to look and sound pointless.

The Gardaí leaves and I try not to stare at the two-way mirror behind me. I hate the idea that someone is watching me. I wait for fifteen minutes, and when no one returns, I can't sit still any longer. My mind won't allow me to pause on what will happen if they don't believe me.

I face the mirror. The left side of my face is swollen and my shirt, which was already revealing enough, is missing three buttons. Great. I look like a slapper. I untie my blue hair, which is falling out of its bobbin, and retie it again.

Walking closer to the mirror, I stare at myself. Blue eyes nearly the same blue as my hair stare back at me. Cupping my face with my hands, I try to look through, but it's not possible. I sit back down and wait. I'm not sure how much time passes when the door finally opens. This time, two Gardaí step in. Both of them sit down, not speaking.

"I'm Gardaí Bernard Brady." This new Gardaí gives me half a smile, while the one who had questioned me focuses on the stupid clipboard.

"Can I go now?" I fold my arms across my chest, trying to cover myself.

"We just have a few more questions."

I let out a heavy exhale. "I'm tired and injured. I'm the victim in all of this."

My words cause Gardaí Brady to grin. "They look far worse than you."

"That doesn't mean I'm not the victim." I'm not fucking smiling.

His grin disappears quickly. "You said the car approached you outside the hotel grounds?"

I nod.

"You need to speak."

"Yes, that is correct," I say slowly.

"What were you doing walking along the road?"

"My car is broken, so I rang a taxi."

"Who swung first?"

"Blondie," I say.

"He swung at you first?" The question is said slower now.

"No, he pulled my hair, and I swung," I answer.

"So you swung first."

"In self-defense." I'm looking from one to the other, trying to make sense of this.

"Ciara, just answer our questions. When you smashed the car, where were the men?"

"Behind it." I say it low in hopes it goes unnoticed.

"So they weren't threatening you then?"

I'm shaking my head. They're twisting my words.

"Just answer the question, Miss Michaels."

"No, they were cowering behind it," I answer.

"See, this isn't looking so good for you." Clipboard guy finally looks up. "Why's that?"

"Their stories match. Both claim you attacked them, and then they hid behind the car that you continued to smash up."

I'm rolling my eyes now. "They're full of shit."

He nods and stares down at the clipboard.

Gardaí Brady takes over. "You're looking at an assault charge."

My pulse flickers in my neck, and the air grows thin. The silence in the room isn't helping. Both of them watch me.

"But..." Gardaí Brady starts. Hope blossoms and it feels cruel. "If you help us with something, this can all go away."

"Help you with what?"

"Liam O'Reagan. We believe not everything he does is above board. So if you give us some information, this will be reduced to a minor assault, and then it will disappear."

Running the brothel isn't above board, but I'm not going to be the one to reveal that to the Gardaí.

"He uses really cheap soap in his hotel rooms..."

Gardaí Brady sits up sharply. "This isn't a game."

"No, it's not. It's my life. I clean hotel rooms. That's it. I don't know what you want me to tell you. I get a pay slip, lunch breaks, and everything is normal."

They're both getting up, and my heart hammers against my rib cage. I want to scream for them to come back, but I try to sit still as they leave the room. The breath that leaves me is shaky. What have I gotten myself into? I should have just gone right back to the hotel.

It takes them another hour before they return, and I'm feeling like a caged animal at this stage.

"You get to make a phone call to get someone to bail you out."

I'm staring at Gardaí Brady. Someone has to bail me out? This is a clusterfuck. I have no one to ring. My eyes burn. "I need my phone."

"You can use the station's."

"What, does the station have all my contacts?" I ask.

Gardaí Brady narrows his eyes, and he opens the door further. "This way."

I follow him down a small hall before coming out to the front desk. He gets my phone out of an evidence bag. I scroll through it as my mouth waters. I have no one to ring. My heart is fluttering in my chest as my eyes continue to burn.

"Problem?" the Gardaí asks, and it sounds smug.

"Nope." I pick up their receiver and dial quickly before I change my mind.

"Hi, I'm at Navan station and need you to come get me."

His laugh is deep. "You're joking."

I take a quick glance at Gardaí Brady, who watches me closely. "No. I wouldn't ring you if I had another option."

"Ah, so I ring you to bail me out, and you didn't come and get me. Instead, you told Liam, and now you want me to come and get you?"

It isn't worth groveling for. They can't keep me here forever.

"Fine. Forget about it," I bark and slam the phone down. I look at Gardaí Brady. "You need to return me to the room. No one is coming for me."

With a raised eyebrow, he takes me by the elbow and leads me back to the room.

"What am I being charged with?" I ask.

"Aggravated battery."

"What does that mean?"

"You could be looking at jail time." He moves to close the door, but I can't be left here with my thoughts.

"How long?"

"Anything from three to 264 days." He closes the door, my sentence still undecided.

I sit down and try to wrap my head around this. Instead, the tears come and they don't stop. I'm still crying when the door opens a while later.

"You've made bail."

CHAPTER TWELVE

DARRAGH

"W E HEAR YOU'RE WORKING in a hotel."

I'm signing my name to get Ciara out. After she slammed the phone down on me, I couldn't just leave her. Liam is going to be pissed that I skipped out on work, but fuck it. I can't just leave her here.

"Yep." I hand him back his pen. Tom takes it, but I hold it firm and his grin slips. "I hear your daughter's fit." I release the pen, and he doesn't stumble back like I'd hoped he would.

"Don't make me arrest you." His warning means fuck all.

I give a quick laugh that has his nostrils flaring.

"Stay here." He moves around the desk to get Ciara. It's nice being the one bailing someone out. It's always me being bailed out. The sound of footsteps has me turning back around as Tom arrives back with a very upset Ciara.

The left side of her face is swollen, her clothes are dirty, and her shirt is missing a decent number of buttons. The puffy red eyes have me looking at Tom.

"What did you do?" I'm taking a step toward him. Ciara crying doesn't seem possible.

"We arrested her for aggravated battery." His bullshit words have me looking at Ciara, who gathers her belongings.

"Are you okay?" I focus on her.

She looks at me, and I'm glad when she holds my stare. She nods.

"You'll get a notice in a few days for your court date for sentencing," Tom informs Ciara, and he sounds so fucking smug.

I'm ready to hit him as I watch Ciara tighten and stiffen.

"We'll see about that," I say before wrapping an arm around her. She lets me and that seems even worse. Every other time I've touched her, she's reacted badly.

"Look, don't worry about it. We'll sort itout ," I say while opening the car door for her.

Once she's in, I look back at the station. Three of the Gardaí are out front, staring at us. I hate how they smile, like they have somehow discovered my weakness. I won't let Ciara pay for my crimes. I give them a grin and the finger before getting into my Audi and tearing out of Navan. I can see the dust in the mirror.

"You've got to say something, Ciara." I light up a fag as I hold the steering wheel with my legs.

"Thanks for bailing me out."

I take a quick look at her as I take the steering wheel back in my hands. She's staring out the window.

"You want to tell me what happened?" Rolling down the window, I blow out the smoke.

"It wasn't my fault."

When I look at her this time, she's staring at me. Her blue eyes are no longer sparkling, like they had been back in the station. Now, they burn with anger, and that makes my shoulders relax.

"They waited for me outside the hotel. I was walking along the road..."

"Wait, why were you walking on the road?"

Ciara shifts and faces me more. When I glance at her, all I see is boobs. Her shirt has really taken a beating.

"My car broke down, so I rang a taxi."

"You should have rung me," I say, but once the words leave my mouth, I know how stupid they sound.

"What, you're running a taxi service as well as a cleaning one?"

I don't answer her as I inhale deeply and blow smoke around the car instead of out the window.

She clears her throat. "Anyway, they cornered me. Blondie pulled my hair, and they were going to hurt me, so I reacted."

I'm grinning. I shouldn't be, but I wish I'd been there to see it. "Look, let's get the footage from the hotel."

"They have cameras outside the grounds?" Hope fills her words.

"Yeah, I'm heading that way anyway, so may as well kill two birds with one stone. I was working and Liam's been ringing nonstop."

We're close to the hotel now. After throwing the fag out, I roll up the window and take another peek at Ciara.

"We need to get you a shirt, Ciara."

At my words, she clutches her chest.

Pulling into the parking lot has me feeling slightly apprehensive. Liam won't be happy.

"You shouldn't have left work." Ciara speaks when I turn the car off.

"What, and leave you in a cell?"

Her cheeks turn red. "I'm sorry I left you."

Taking out the keys, I unbuckle my belt. "I know you couldn't leave."

Ciara stares back at the hotel, and as I study her side profile, I can see how scared she really is.

"We'll fix this," I say, and her attention comes back to me. Her eyes roam my face, and it's odd but I shift under her full stare.

"Why are you doing this?" she questions. Her eyes flicker from my lips up to my eyes. "I won't sleep with you," she fires out before I can answer.

"Talk about shooting a guy down." I grin at her. "You're my friend."

She shakes her head and looks away. "Be serious, Darragh."

I touch her shoulder gently, and she looks at my fingers, which I remove before she finally looks at me. "I am serious. You don't owe me anything. I just want to help."

"Why?"

"Why can't you just say thank you?" I can't understand why she's resisting help.

"Because nothing comes for free. Everything has a price tag."

"Ciara, if you don't want my help, fine. But I'm just trying to be the good guy here." I open my door and hope she gets out too. When she does, the relief is immediate.

"Come on."

She keeps her arms crossed over her chest as we walk into the hotel.

***

We're in Liam's office watching the footage from outside the hotel. Liam wasn't happy when we entered his office, but he's obviously willing to help Ciara since we're watching these two scumbags follow and corner her. Watching her being manhandled has me looking at Liam.

"Do you have their names?" I ask him, and he doesn't answer me with words. We watch to the end, and once Liam switches it off, I sit back down.

"I will forward the footage on to the police. They will drop the charges once they see it was self-defense. And you should go home." Liam stands.

I try to protest, but he raises a hand a warning to me that I heed. Liam picks up his phone and orders a taxi for Ciara. I want to protest again—I can drop her home—but I keep my mouth shut.

"If you need some time off, Ciara, that can be arranged."

"No, thank you. I'll be back to work tomorrow. I really appreciate you sending on the footage."

Liam nods and Ciara stands up.

"Thanks for everything." Her words are directed at me, but I hate how Liam is watching me, so I just give her a nod of my head. When I can't resist any more, I look at her. She's staring at me, and her eyes shine with hurt. Her lids flutter down, cutting me off, and she leaves Liam's office.

"Why her?" Liam asks as he removes the footage from the recorder and places it into a plastic cover.

"What?"

"You left work to bail her out. Why?"

"She's a girl, Liam."

Liam shakes his head. "Who's broken beyond repair. No good will come from that Darragh. Leave her alone."

"I bailed her out. I didn't propose to her. Relax." My neck itches with a fresh coating of sweat. Ciara is broken, but so am I. I'm not going to sleep with her. I just want to help her.

"You're lying. Maybe you're lying to yourself. You need distance from her. I'll assign you to someone else."

I stand because this is Liam's controlling bullshit. It isn't about Ciara.

"No. I'm working with Ciara, Liam. I'm not working with anyone else. Me and her have a system," I say.

"I know. You sit and watch her clean."

I'm staring at Liam. "There are cameras in the rooms?" Of course there are. It's Liam.

"You never know who will be using our services. You can go back to work now."

I'm dismissed.

"I stay with Ciara." My words don't sound as strong.

Liam agrees. "For now."

I head outside for a fag and ring Connor. He's been churning around in my head, and when he doesn't answer my call, I don't blame him. I sold him out. We hurt each other all the time, but no matter what, we have to forgive each other. But isn't that the O'Reagan way? No matter what, we have to forgive one another and stick together.

I don't put the phone back in my pocket but send a message to Connor, hoping it will break the silence. **I have a job if you're in.**

***

When I arrive to work the next day, Ciara is already there, pulling a bed apart like it did something to her. "What did the bed do?"

She startles, turning quickly. "Darragh, you can't creep up on me like that." Her anger dissolves by the time she reaches the end of the sentence.

"I work here too."

She continues stripping the bed. I take a pair of blue rubber gloves from her tray and blow into them before slipping my hands inside. They barely cover my hands. The pillow I pick up has a white case over it, which I yank off and toss onto the pile Ciara made on the floor. I know she's watching me, wanting to ask me what I'm doing, but I continue removing pillowcases.

"That wasn't so bad," I say with a grin.

She laughs. "Now we have to remake it, polish, vacuum, check the wardrobe, and refill the tea and coffee before we move on to the bathroom, and then it's the next room. When that's done, all the rubbish and laundry have to be sorted. So let's see by the end of the day if it's that bad."

"Has anyone told you that you're very cynical?"

"No, you're the first," she says it with a straight face.

Ciara takes out fresh sheets and spreads them out. They wave across the space, and I grab my side. When the sheet settles, she's looking at me, smiling, and my heart gives a thump.

"What?" I ask.

"You're being very helpful lately. First you bail me out of jail, and then you get Liam to help me, and now this." She tucks the sheet down along the side.

"So you owe me," I say, balling up the sheet and stuffing it with all my force under the mattress.

Ciara sees what I'm doing and moves around to me. She pulls it out and shakes her head. "I'd hate to see your room." As she speaks, our shoulders brush.

"Is this reverse psychology because you want to see my room?"

She's laughing again. "I told you. I'm not sleeping with you."

"Yeah, so you keep saying." I'm not grinning now. She keeps saying it like it will never happen. "My brother is getting married in a week."

She shoos me out of her way so she can fix the other corner of the bed before she grabs the duvet.

"Which one?" she asks.

"Liam," I answer. The disbelief on her face has me smiling. "I'm messing with you. It's my brother Finn. We're twins."

"Liam getting married just doesn't seem possible. Can you imagine the pictures?" she says.

"Leave him alone. He just has a resting bitch face."

She's smiling again as she puts on the duvet cover. I let her work at that one alone. I don't want to have a used duvet that close to my face.

"Anyway, I need a date. So are you free?"

"Nope. Sorry." Her answer is immediate, and she doesn't even flinch.

This is so fucking strange. "You don't even know what day it is."

She throws a pillow at me, which I catch. The force behind it tells me she isn't as unaffected as she wants me to believe.

I take a step toward her, and her lids flutter closed. "I don't like weddings."

"Me neither. But I need a date. I can't go on my own."

"I don't own a dress." She's bending.

"I can sort it," I say.

She shakes her head, tightening the pillow to her chest. "I can't dance."

"Me neither." I take another step toward her. I don't know what the fuck I'm doing, but she's getting flustered and I like it.

"Let me think about it."

I pick up a pillowcase and give a quick nod. "By the end of the day," I say. She agrees.

We finish the bedroom in silence, and once we start into the bathroom, I'm not feeling as hopeful about her coming.

She's scrubbing the toilet with her back to me. "If I do say yes, I'll need a bag and shoes."

"So it's a yes."

She glances at me over her shoulder, and my smile has her standing straight. She's still clutching the toilet brush, pointing it at me.

"Put the weapon down," I say, holding my hands up.

She points it toward the ground. "I'll go. But I swear, Darragh, this is a favor. I'm not sleeping with you." Her conviction is stitched into each word.

"Why would you think I would sleep with you?" I cross my arms over my chest.

Her cheeks redden. "I don't. But I'm just saying."

"Why are you so adamant on it? I'm curious."

"I saw you with those girls, and Sharon talks. It just seems that you would 'do' anything."

Her words are light, but I fucking hate them. "Don't worry, Ciara. I won't do you." The hurt that flashes across her face has me stepping towards her. "If you don't want me to," I quickly add.

Her face flames, and she turns her back to me and starts scrubbing the toilet again.

"So you're coming." I need to confirm that I haven't fucked it up.

"Yes. I'm a size eight. Shoe size five. Don't get me anything too revealing."

"Noted."

My phone dings and I slip it out of my pocket.

It's Connor. **What do you need?**

You're the best, Connor. I need to scare someone. You free tonight? I shoot back.

His response is quick. **Yeah, I'll pick you up at the house at midnight? See you then.**

CHAPTER THIRTEEN

DARRAGH

I T'S FREEZING OUTSIDE. I walk down the driveway, keeping close to the bushes with my bat in hand. Looking back at the house, I hope I'm not as visible as I feel.

I take out my phone and my heart deflates. It's twelve fifteen. He's not coming. The day back in the library has me understanding why he isn't coming. I stood there while they told him never to come near the house again.

Car lights shine in the distance, and when Connor's car pulls in, I'm jogging over to the passenger door and getting in.

"Thanks for coming," I say while placing my bat at the side of my leg.

"Beating someone up is what got me."

I smirk at Connor's response. "So are we good, man?" I gently punch his arm.

He reverses out onto the road. "Yeah. So where to?"

"Kells. We aren't really beating anyone up."

Connor slams on the breaks.

I hit the dashboard. "What the fuck?"

"Why aren't you wearing your belt?"

I rub my head as I sit back and clip in my belt.

"You said we were hurting someone."

"We're scaring someone. My friend DJ hit me and I owe him, so I thought two guys with bats showing up in his room would be a lesson."

Connor's stares at me for a moment before he sits forward and starts driving again.

"So you all set for Finn's wedding next week?" I ask.

"I can't wait."

I smirk. "Yeah, it seems everyone's holding their breath. Finn invited Auntie Trish."

"She's still alive?"

I'm laughing as get my smokes and lighter out of my pocket. "Yeah, I know. That bitch got nine lives."

"Who else is coming?" Connor asks as we move silently down the road.

I spark up the fag and inhale deeply. "All our relations. It's going to be one hell of a party."

Connor glances at me. "What, like even Michael's side?"

I roll down the window and blow the smoke out. "I'm pretty sure."

Connor focuses on the road, but his hands have tightened on the wheel.

"What's wrong?" My question has him loosening his hands.

"I just didn't think they spoke."

"Well, you know Finn. He's a goody two-shoes. He'll try to build bridges."

"Should be fun to watch them all burn down," Connor says.

I agree. Nothing good could come from this.

We roll up close to DJ's house, and I'm excited. I can't wait to see the little prick's face. We have our balaclavas on, and I pull Rochelle close to my side.

"He lives with his family, so we can't be too noisy. He sleeps downstairs. It won't be too hard to get in," I say as I tighten my hold on my bat and get out of the car.

We make our way around the back of the house, and I try DJ's window. It's locked. Connor takes over and pops the lock on the back door. We're in.

We step in on wooden floors, so we have to really watch our step as we make our way down the hall. The last bedroom on the left is DJ's. I can't wait to see his face. This will teach him not to touch me again.

Pushing open the door, I step in and Connor follows silently behind me. The room is empty. I glance around the room, the disappointment immediate.

We leave the house as quietly as we entered. I'll just have to reschedule for another night. I hate how pumped I am. Adrenaline still flows through me, no doubt through Connor too. We need to find something else to do.

Connor closes the back door soundlessly. I'm ready to leave, when low voices from the bottom of the garden have me smiling. I move toward the shed, and Connor follows me across the grass.

This is DJ's hangout spot away from his family. The closer we get, I start to recognize the voices. Fitz, Art, and Mark are here. Disappointment courses through me again. Tonight isn't our night. I can't do anything with everyone here.

"I'm not doing it, man. I'm not hanging him out to dry." Fitz's voice is close, and I move to the side of the shed. Connor is beside me. His eyes meet mine, but I focus on the conversation.

"He's the one that got us into this. If you don't sign the deal, we all go down."

"I can't do this either." DJ speaks up.

My heart stutters in my chest.

"I'm signing the deal." Art's words hold conviction. I know him. He'll sign whatever deal he's talking about.

"I thought you and Darragh were best friends." Fitz jumps to my defense.

At the mention of my name, Connor moves toward the shed. Gripping his arm, I shake my head. He doesn't come back, and my pulse spikes. If they see us, we can't stop what's happening.

"Fuck you, Fitz. I'm not going to prison for him. The bank jobs were his idea. So if they offer us immunity for him, I'm all in."

Fucking traitor.

I'm aware of Connor staring at me. No doubt the bank job part didn't go unheard.

"You can count me out." Fitz's voice floats away, as if he's moving.

I sink further into the shadows. Someone shuffles around.

"You can't leave, Fitz." Mark's voice has me clenching my fists.

"Leave him alone, Mark." DJ jumps to Fitz's defense.

"You're either with us or against us, Fitz. Or I'll make sure your name goes along with Darragh's." Art. I hadn't expected him to betray me. "Same for you, DJ. I have no problem dropping you in it."

"I'm not doing it." Fitz makes me proud.

"You really are retarded," Art sneers. "You're going to get raped daily in prison."

"Art, shut the fuck up." DJ's voice has risen.

Connor pulls on my arm. I know we've heard enough, but I'm waiting for Art to say he's made a mistake. That handing me over isn't an option.

"Are you in, DJ?"

"You know I'm in," Mark says.

"I need more time," DJ says.

"You fucking tell him, and you're a dead man." Art's threat has me clenching my fists again.

"Two weeks. That's all you have before we have to give our answer. If you don't do this, we all go down."

Connor pulls me again, and this time, I leave with him. Once we're in his car, I pull off the balaclava. I'm waiting for Connor to rip into me over the bank jobs, but he doesn't.

"You need to tell Liam." Connor clips in his seat belt.

I light a fag as Connor pulls out from the roadside. His suggestion has me looking at him.

"What? You know he's the one that will make this go away."

He's right. But I don't want 'this' to go away. He would have them all clipped.

"Darragh, this isn't a walk in the park. You're looking at ten plus years," Connor reminds me.

I inhale deeply while blowing smoke out the window. "Yeah, I know."

Connor pulls the car in on the hard shoulder, and I nearly hit the dash again.

"You need to listen to me." He's facing me now, and I'm listening. "They die or you die. Which is it?"

It sounds pathetic, but they're my only friends. "They die," I mumble while inhaling more smoke.

"You need to tell Liam." Connor grips my shoulder, enforcing each word.

Telling Liam would make it so definite. "I will. Just give me time." I glance at Connor, and he releases me.

He shakes his head. "No. You do it now."

"We have two weeks. Next week is Finn's wedding. We don't need this shit right now."

Connor slams his fist into the steering wheel. The horn rings loud across the open night. "You're the one behind the ATMs."

"Only two." I shrug, not sure what he wants. I don't regret it. If I could, I'd do it again.

"I wonder about you, Darragh. You don't need the money."

"Yeah, I do. They cut me off. I'm fucking cleaning rooms for my money." I reel my anger in. Connor isn't the target here. I'm not exactly sure who is. Liam, Father, or me.

"I'll take care of it, I promise. After the wedding, I'll tell Liam. Or in the meantime, I'll find a way to convince the guys not to sell me out."

Connor is shaking his head again, pissing me off. I throw the fag out the window and roll it up.

"They'll sell you out. Who else can they blame?" Connor starts the car and pulls back out onto the road.

I know he's right. If they don't hand me over, we all go down. I wouldn't fair too well in prison. "I'll tell him. I promise," I say again.

The house is dark when I get home. I go straight to my room and let the betrayal sink in. Out of everyone, I really thought Art would be the one who would have stood beside me. I got that so fucking wrong.

The bottom drawer of my bedside locker holds a half bottle of whiskey. I take it out and unscrew the cap. The burn is immediate, and I drink deeply. Telling Liam would get them clipped. I don't care about Mark, but Art dying doesn't sit right with me. Liam wouldn't let Fitz and DJ walk away either. I can't let them all die.

The whiskey sloshes in the bottle as I place it onto my bedside table before picking up my fags. After lighting a smoke, I lie back on my bed. The red tip glows in the dark room. Smoke billows over my head, and I try to just focus on it. But Art's betrayal is too fresh. I drink until I pass out on my bed.

"Oh my God. You need to clean this place up."

Opening one eye, I look up at Una. She's standing over me with her hands on her hips as she stares down at me.

"What are you doing in my room?" My head pounds as I speak.

Una moves out of my line of sight. Light burns my eyes. "Close the curtains." I bury my head in my pillow.

"You texted me last night." Una glances around my room, wriggling her nose. "This place reeks, Darragh."

"I texted you last night?" I'm sitting up even as my head and stomach protest.

"Yes, you did, asking me to go dress shopping with you. I didn't know you cross-dressed." She's smirking.

I'm struggling to function right now. "I need painkillers and coffee," I mumble through dry lips. I pick up the bottle of whiskey and drain the final three drops to try to moisten my lips.

"You know, you have a problem." Una's voice isn't playful this time.

I don't need a lecture. "Yeah, my head is banging." I get up, pulling the blankets aside.

"Oh my God!" Una's shouts don't help my head.

"What's wrong?" I ask, but she won't look at me. Her hand is covering her eyes.

Looking down at myself, I nod. "Ah, shit. I don't even remember changing."

"You're naked."

"Yeah, I know," I say, glancing at her back.

"Put some clothes on, Darragh."

I tug on a pair of jeans. "I'm decent," I tell her.

She turns around and her face is bright red.

"I think you like what you see," I tease and bend to pick up a T-shirt, but my head screams at me, and I stand again.

"You really need help."

"Get me a T-shirt?" I ask with one eye open. Una tuts but still rifles through my drawers and pulls out a clean blue T-shirt.

I throw it over my shoulder as we leave my room.

"So do you still want to go dress shopping today?" Una sounds cheerful now that we're out of my room and making our way downstairs.

"Yeah. It's for Ciara. I have to get her a dress and shoes and stuff for the wedding."

Una's squeal hurts my head. "You have a girlfriend. This is a first for you."

Mary is in the kitchen when we enter. "Morning, Mary," I say while pulling her into an unexpected hug.

"Oh, Darragh." Mary swats me away.

"What?" I ask, pulling on my T-shirt.

"You smell of drink. Sit down until I get you some food."

"Mary, I'm really considering marrying you," I say and she smiles.

"That would be unfair to your new girlfriend," Una sings as she sits down at the table.

"You have a girlfriend?" Both of Mary's eyebrows rise with surprise.

"No, just a friend who's a girl," I clarify as I sit down.

"So a girlfriend." Una is enjoying this too much.

Mary gives me two painkillers and a glass of water, which I take instantly.

"Tell me about Ciara." Una is bouncing beside me.

"Am I going to regret this?"

"Of course." Her laugh has me smiling. "Just describe her."

"She has blue hair. She can kick anyone's ass. She's hostile and violent."

Una frowns at my description. "She sounds like a keeper."

I laugh. "She's cool."

Una tilts her head. "If I didn't know you, Darragh, I'd say you liked her."

Mary has been listening, and she hands me a cup of coffee and some advice. "If she makes you smile, then she's worth it."

I take Mary's advice as I sip on my coffee. "I wouldn't say smile," I respond. "She amuses me."

"Okay, I need her body stats."

"She's five foot four, small build, big boobs." I grab my chest with my hands, and Una rolls her eyes. "She's a size eight in dresses and a five in shoes."

"Wow, what did you do measure her?"

"She told me her measurements, and that she wasn't coming unless I got her a dress and shoes."

Una laughs. "I can't wait to meet her."

"Meet who?" Shane enters the kitchen, and Mary immediately returns to the stove.

"Darragh has a girlfriend," Una tells him. I don't correct her.

Shane sits down beside Una, taking her hand like he still needs to make his mark on her.

"God help her." I ignore his words as Mary places a fry up in front of me. I give her a wink before I dig in.

"I'm going shopping with Darragh to buy her a dress." Una is spilling her guts to Shane. I don't interject but continue eating my fry.

"I don't know, Una," Shane starts.

I just want to eat my breakfast in peace. "Shane, go take your sister and entertain her yourself. I'll go shopping myself."

Shane's chair hits the floor, and he's over me.

"Shane, don't!" Una's standing too.

I continue to eat my fry.

"You're pushing me too far, Darragh."

I glance up at him. "What, you can insult me, but I can't tell you a truth?"

The air leaves me as my back collides with the floor. The chair screeches and stops as it hits the wall. Shane's over me, veins bulging. Una and Mary are frantic, and their noise has me closing my eyes. Sounds muffle and when it returns, so does the air and pain. My lungs refill and I choke.

"Shane."

I continue to cough as Liam's voice seems to dance across everyone else's, and silence falls on the girls. "Let him up."

Shane's still over me. I can see the struggle he's having letting this go, but I don't want to. I don't want to just let him be saved again by Liam. I don't want to be saved by Liam.

"Be a good boy and do as you're told." My words get the reaction I knew they would. His fist collides with my face. The pain races up into my already sore head.

Copper fills my mouth, and with the pain comes something else; it's a tide rising slowly, a rush, and I let it free. My own fist connects with his face, and the rush that I was deprived of last night at DJ's fills me. I get three good strikes in, and I know if I had Rochelle, I would make bits of Shane.

He's strong as we wrestle on the floor, knocking over chairs. Finn and Liam pull me off Shane. As I rise, he kicks out, connecting with my stomach, taking the air from my lungs. I throw my leg one final time and impact with his face. Una's screams bash my ears as I try to catch my breath. My body aches and the earlier rush is gone. Now I just feel fucking exhausted.

"What is wrong with you?" Finn's speaking, and when I glance at him, I see it's directed toward me.

"So it's my fault?" I ask him, but I'm aware that Shane is standing up while Una frets over him.

"Is it?"

"What does it matter? I'm wrong no matter what." I yank my arm free from Finn. Liam has already released me. Mary is standing at the kitchen sink, a cloth clutched to her chest, the water soaking into her white blouse.

"I'm sorry you had to see that Mary," I say before I leave the room.

CHAPTER FOURTEEN

CIARA

No matter how many times I try to forget about the two guys, I can't. My mind won't slow down. I keep thinking they'll be waiting for me around every corner. I've started to carry a knife and pepper spray in my bag.

I hesitate as I stuff it into my locker. Should I remove it and take it with me? I push the bag into the locker. I'm no longer working in the strip club. Since the incident, I've been assigned to cleaning rooms only.

A scream tears from my throat as Darragh pops up out of nowhere.

"I don't look that bad," he says around a swollen lip and a black eye.

"Should I ask?" I close the locker door as my heart falls into a steady pattern.

"It was just a family disagreement."

I can't look away from his battered face. "I'd hate to see what happens when your family has a serious row."

"Someone normally dies." The way Darragh says it has me narrowing my eyes at him.

"I'm joking," he says. "So let's start work."

I get my trolley and make my way to our first room. "Are you okay?" He seems to be leaning more so on his right leg.

"You want to nurse me back to health?" His grin returns.

"I think I'll pass." I slide my card into the room door.

The moment we enter, Darragh sits on the floor in his usual spot. "Can I sit this one out? Since I'm injured?"

"You'll have to tell me what happened." I don't really expect him to tell me, and when he looks away, I start to strip the bed.

"The second eldest of us, Shane, he just hates me."

I take a quick peek at Darragh. He's studying his hands, so I continue to clean.

"When we were in school, if anyone annoyed one of us, they had to deal with us all. Family came first, no matter what."

When I steal another glance at Darragh, there's a sad smile on his face.

He shrugs to the floor. "Family still comes first, even though it's all fucked up now. But back then, we really had each other's backs. We were brothers."

I'm so aware of each word, and something is telling me that Darragh doesn't share too much. For me, if anyone asked questions now, I would know they were listening, and I would shut down, so I continue cleaning the room, slowly and quietly to allow him to keep speaking.

"You know, it was all pretty great until our mother died." His brow furrows, and the pain in his eyes has me stopping and breaking my own rules.

"I just lost it…" He looks up at me, and there it is. He knows he's sharing. He shifts.

"Death isn't easy," I say.

He scratches his beard and looks around the room. "I went mad on drugs. I really gave my family a hard time. I don't remember much of it, but I was sent someplace to dry out. My memory is fuzzy. It felt like a prison. It was always so silent and cold."

I'm sitting on the bed now, piecing Darragh together.

"When I came back, everyone was different. Cold. Shane hated me most of all. He said I bailed when they had to face it all. He was right. I took the easy route. It wasn't just us that was different. It was the house, the smell, even the noise."

Darragh trails off, and I find myself on the floor in front of him. The strain on his face barely holds back his pain.

I slowly touch his hand. "I'm so sorry, Darragh," I say. My touch has his eyes flickering up to mine.

"I don't know how to fix anything. I just seem to have a habit of breaking things."

Liam's words about him breaking pretty things floods my mind, and I remove my hand. "Maybe cut back on the drink," I say. "You reek."

He gets off the ground. His hand fills my vision, and I take it as he helps me get up. He doesn't release my hand until my eyes settle on his.

"What about you?"

I can't hold his eye. "What about me?" I easily remove my hand from his and start making the bed.

"I spill my guts out, and you won't tell me about you."

"I didn't force you." I glance at him.

His grin isn't filled with humor. "Fine." He stomps to the cart and gets a polish and duster. The side table is assaulted by his large hands. My heart races in my chest. I don't want him to be mad at me, which is a crazy feeling to have.

"They're dead," I say.

Darragh stops abusing the furniture. "What happened?" My stomach squeezes, and I search the room for words. I don't talk about it.

"My mum overdosed." I keep my head high and wait for the judgment.

"Fuck, that's intense."

"I found her," I blurt out, blood pounding in my ears. Saying it out loud makes it too real.

"My dad was a junkie too. He also overdosed." I'm nodding, just trying to tell myself to keep it together.

"Ciara." The way Darragh says my name has me turning away.

"It's fine," I say quickly as I go to my trolley. I don't know what I'm looking for. I freeze as strong arms wrap around me.

"What are you doing?" Fear clogs my voice.

"Just let me. Please." Darragh turns me in his arms and holds me. I can't respond as my arms hang loosely at my side.

"What are you doing?" My voice trembles again as I keep staring at the door. I won't close my eyes. I can't. If I close my eyes, I don't know what will happen.

"I'm hugging you." He explains to my hair, and God does it feel nice to have this contact. But I don't know what to do with it.

I want to push him away and put my walls back up, but I can't move. My hands seem to rise on their own accord, and I'm wrapping them around his back. I'm all in now, but closing my eyes will break me.

"I've been living on the streets with my father since I was sixteen." I tell this to the door, and Darragh tightens his hold on me. I don't blink. "He died three days after my seventeenth birthday. So I've been on the streets until your brother found me."

A kiss is planted on the top of my head, and I want to ask Darragh to stop. I want my tongue to stop moving, but it doesn't.

"I learned to protect myself. I had to," I whisper.

Too many memories slowly flood my mind, and I close my eyes against them, only to fill up with pain that has me clutching Darragh. I'm a sinking ship and Darragh can't swim. I know losing myself in him is dangerous, but I can't stop the pain. My hands push against his chest as I try to stop this, but he holds me.

"It's okay, Ciara."

"No, it's not. Just let me go."

Darragh does, but I don't step away from him. His frame is a shield from reality. I just need a moment to pull myself together.

"Look at me," he says. I do as tears create a path down my face. "It's okay to let someone in."

My hands still rest on his chest. The heat and the heavy beat of his heart has my own beating to a new dance. One I'm not familiar with. I'm looking at him, and it feels like too much.

Darragh moves closer, dipping his head, and I'm not sure what's happening between us. I don't want to lose myself. He moves closer, his large hands cupping my face as his lips touch mine.

I'm kissing him back with an uncertainty, like he'll change his mind in a second, but he deepens the kiss. I'm moving fast; the air is thinning, and I feel like I'm drunk. I break the kiss. Darragh's heavy breaths brush my face.

"You can't kiss me," I tell his chest. "You can't... just..." I lick the salty moisture from my lips. "Do that. You can't just kiss me." Each breathless word is painful, and I want to lash out. I move away from him, and I can't look up at him. "You have no right."

"You kissed me back." His words have my focus snapping up to him.

Blowing air through my lips, my vision wavers. "This isn't right."

"We're two adults who kissed. Don't make it sound like a crime."

"Don't ever do that again." My angry words come out calmly, and Darragh snorts.

"Fine, Ciara. I was just trying to comfort you."

"By sticking your tongue down my throat," I bark back.

"You're twisting this. You kissed me back." Darragh walks away from me.

"Yeah, well, don't do it again."

He looks at me over his shoulder and shakes his head but doesn't answer me.

"I'm cleaning the bathroom. Alone." I'm stumbling, gathering supplies I don't even look at. Once I close the bathroom door, I move to the sink and run the taps before sinking to the floor. My hands cover my mouth as I try to push everything back in, but it won't go back down. Everything haunts me, all the ghosts. Biting my hand keeps some of the pain at bay. I want to hurt Darragh. Why him? Why the hell did I open up to him?

"Ciara." Darragh's voice and a knock at the door brings me to the surface.

"Five minutes," I choke out, but the door is opening. "Oh my God. Just give me a minute." My lip trembles as I speak.

But he isn't leaving. "I don't know what to do here, Ciara."

"Are you deaf? I said leave. I don't want you here." My anger rises like a tide, and I'm on my feet. The tears stop.

His laugh has my anger boiling over. The blood that pounds through my veins feels red hot. "You find this funny?"

"No." His stupid-ass answer is said with a grin. "I've just never felt this unsure before." It's in his eyes—the pain, the strain he carries daily. He's tired, and just like that, my anger deflates like a burst balloon, and I give a wobbly smile.

"We can pretend today never happened," I say as the lid goes back on my emotions.

"Is that what you really want?"

What kind of question was that? "Yeah, it is."

He nods.

I don't stand around, allowing myself to break again. After splashing my face with water, I pat it. Darragh still stands behind me, and I refuse to meet his eye in the mirror.

"We better get this room finished. It's taking too long." I turn around and face him.

"What if I don't want to pretend today didn't happen?"

"Tough." I move past him, and a part of me lights up as he grips my arm, but another says I'm too tired for the feelings he's making me feel.

I'm waiting for him to speak, and when he doesn't, I glance up at him. Our eyes clash and he releases me.

I finish the room robotically.

The rest of the day is a blur of work. I eat my food, but I don't taste it. I don't pause until the laundry is dropped off in the laundry room. I pretend I don't notice how Darragh hasn't left my side, even as I clock out and make my way down the hall. But as we reach the last hallway, I know I have to say something.

"Why are you following me?" I ask the empty hall in front of me and the looming presence beside me.

"I'm not." He's right, he's not. We're both going to the parking lot.

I root out my phone, remembering I need to ring a taxi.

"I can give you a lift," Darragh says.

I take a quick peek at him, and he isn't looking at me. He seems distant and that comforts me. "Are you sure?"

"I wouldn't offer if I wasn't." This time, he looks at me. His face grows serious.

"Thanks."

His Audi doesn't fit in with all the staff cars. "For a cleaner, you're doing pretty well," I tease.

He grins. "I have other jobs."

I get into his car. "Like what?"

"Stuff that would have you curling up in your bed at night."

It's not what he says but how he looks at me when he mentions my bed. The air catches in my throat, and I put on my belt to distract myself. I'm overthinking everything.

"I didn't picture you doing something gentle," I say.

He starts up the car. "If you had to guess, what do you think?"

I look at Darragh now. He's very well put together—his hair is shiny, his skin flawless. He takes care of his physical self. He could be a personal trainer, but he would be too selfish.

"I don't think you do anything else, only just whatever you want."

"What does that even mean?" He sounds so offended.

I smile as I lean back into the heated seat. "You've always had money. You're a privileged child. You've never had to work for anything. You also wouldn't understand hunger or cold. Those ideas would be foreign to you." Now I look at Darragh. I'm expecting him to be clutching the steering with anger, but he isn't.

"Yeah, that sounds pretty right. But now I've been cut off, so I have to work."

"So the job is covering your Audi payments, tax, insurance, and all that? I don't know where I'm going wrong." My sarcasm has him smiling.

"A wise woman once told me that if a woman can make you smile, then she's a keeper."

I'm not sure how I feel about his statement. "Was it your mother?"

His smile slips. I think I make him frown more than smile, but I keep that to myself.

"No, my cook."

I laugh. "Your cook?"

"What? Mary is the best."

"Yeah. You're privileged," I say.

He grins, but it slips from his face. "Fuck."

I want to ask what's wrong, but I don't. A checkpoint up ahead is waving us down. The guard who meets my eye is Gardaí Brady.

"Fuck is right."

CHAPTER FIFTEEN

DARRAGH

O NCE THE CAR STOPS, I roll down the window.

"License and registration."

I wonder which one of them offered my friends immunity to put me behind bars.

My license falls onto my lap as I flip down the visor. Picking it up, I don't hand it to him straight away. "What's this about?" I ask.

Ciara clears her throat beside me, getting the Gardaí's attention.

"Your license, Darragh." Tom speaks to me while looking at Ciara.

I hand it over to him, and he finally looks away from Ciara and at my license.

"How many of you does it take to read my license? Oh, actually don't tell me," I say to Tom.

His smile holds his secrets, as if I don't know my friends are ready to sell me out.

"Miss Michaels, I see you're keeping some fine company." Tom leans in.

I'm very tempted to roll up the window on his face.

Ciara doesn't answer him, and he leans back out. I'm handed my license back.

"Tell me what they pay you. Five hundred a week, maybe six hundred?" I'm grinning as I turn the key in the ignition.

"You'll get what you deserve soon." Tom taps the hood of my car.

"We'll see. I'll let you lads get back to your minimum watch job while I go home and wipe my ass with one hundred-euro notes." My smile has both of them standing back from the car. I'm waiting to be pulled out and arrested, but when they both stay silent, I know I won't get arrested today.

"See you soon, Darragh." The warning is there in his voice.

I roll up my window and drive off, foot to floor.

"Is that necessary? Are you trying to get arrested?"

I lift my foot off the gas pedal. "They always fucking target me."

"Yes, Darragh. You are such a victim. I mean, you insulted them in every way possible."

I glance at Ciara. "You have no idea what they're like."

"They're the Gardaí. They aren't going to be all friendly."

She has no fucking idea.

"Yeah, you're right," I say to end this conversation.

"Don't be an ass. You don't mean it, so don't say it."

I face the road. "Fine, I fucking hate them."

"At least you're honest."

When I glance at Ciara, her plump lips tug up. I want to kiss them. How had I not noticed her lips before? I keep looking at her. I thought she was pretty from the moment I set eyes on her, but now she's fucking gorgeous. How does that shit happen?

"So are we still good for the wedding?" I ask.

"Yeah. Just remember, I'm not going to sleep with you."

I grin. "Can I put money on it?" When I look at her, she isn't smiling like I expected.

"Do I look like a hoe?"

Fuck. "Of course not."

"Of course not? Like me being a hoe isn't possible?"

I look at her again, wondering if she's messing with me. No. She's serious as fuck.

"You're confusing the fuck out of me, Ciara. You could be a hoe if you wanted. I'd pay."

My words have her shaking her head, and I'm glad when Kingscourt comes into view. No woman has ever made me feel so stupid. I've never questioned myself as much as I do with Ciara. I pull up outside her place, and she's ready to jump out.

"All I'm saying is," I start. "I'd sleep with you."

She pauses and then turns around and kind of smiles. I think it's a smile. It could be a grimace. "A thousand," she says.

"A thousand what?"

"That I don't sleep with you."

I smile while reaching across the open space. "You have to shake on it."

She takes my hand, and I'm tempted to pull her in for a kiss just to see what she would do. Her hand slips from mine quickly, and she closes the door in my face. I watch her until she disappears behind her door.

***

When I arrive home, I'm not expecting a welcome home committee.

"What?" I ask, closing the door behind me. Una's standing in the hall with her arms folded.

"Your dad has called a family meal tonight. You have to be there, no exceptions."

"You mean our dad," I fire back and regret it.

She closes her eyes and shakes her head. "Why do you do that? Sabotage yourself all the time. Are you afraid we might love you?" Una takes a step toward me.

I fold my arms across my chest. "Are you hitting on me?"

"God damn it, Darragh, stop. I'm trying to help you."

"I don't need help. You and Shane do." I don't mean a word I'm saying. But I also don't need an intervention.

"See. I know you don't mean that. You're deflecting."

"Una, I've had a rough fucking day. So can we hit pause on this and pick it up another time?" I'm walking around her and up the stairs.

"Dinner's at eight." Her words follow me all the way up the the landing.

The moment I get into my room, I light a fag. I need a drink. I open the bottom drawer and remove a full bottle of whiskey. I'm staring at the reddish-brown liquid, but all I hear is Ciara telling me not to drink. The bottle is placed back into the drawer.

My bedroom is a bomb scare I try to ignore as I pull my shirt off while trying not to burn it. My phone dings.

What's up, man? Want to hang out? The text is from Art.

I want to smash the phone at his betrayal. Maybe he deserves to die. I put the phone down and head for the bathroom. I throw my fag into the toilet and flush, but it won't disappear. After three flushes, it finally goes down.

Once I'm in the shower, I let my mind wander back to Ciara. She can be my distraction. There's no betrayal from Art or fight with Shane. Connor is still here, and my father isn't an asshole. Right now, there's only Ciara, and she wants me.

Closing my fingers, I take my shaft in my hand and start a slow stroke. I'm picturing Ciara lying on a hotel bed, her blouse open, her black bra full. I try not to go too quickly with my strokes, but my body demands it. I skip ahead until I'm buried inside her.

My pace quickens as I slam my free hand against the tiles. On tippy-toes, I push my body faster as I picture her coming over my cock. My seed sprays the white tiles of the shower. The release allows me to relax and sink back down to my feet. That was good. It was quick, but good.

"Darragh." Finn steps into the bathroom.

"I could have been jerking off," I say while firing a look over my shoulder.

"Are you?" Disgust fills his voice.

I rinse myself down. "No. But can't I have a fucking minute?"

"Sorry, I'll wait in your bedroom."

I finish my wash quickly and get out of the shower.

"I'm very popular today," I say when I enter my room. Finn is sitting on my unmade bed.

"Did you talk to Shane?"

I run the towel across my head. "No, Una was waiting for me when I got home. Why, does Shane want to make up?" I grin as I search for clean clothes.

"What's going on with you?" Finn's decent, and I know his concern is genuine. I'd normally tell him. But his wedding is a few days away.

"I drank too much last night. I'll make up with Shane." The relief is immediate on Finn's face.

"Thank you." He exhales heavily.

I turn and drop the towel. The boxers and jeans go on quickly, and I turn back around.

"No problem. So, we're having a family meal?" I get out a new black shirt. May as well get some wear out of them. Pulling off the tags, I check myself in the mirror.

"Yeah, I think Dad just wants to warn us all to be on our best behavior for my wedding."

"You mean warn me." I meet Finn's eyes in the mirror.

He can't hold my stare. "Please, Darragh. Don't make this about you."

What the fuck did that mean? "I'll be on my best behavior."

"Like I haven't heard that before." This time, Finn's voice carries a playful tone. "I'll see you downstairs."

Once Finn leaves my room, I sit on my bed with my phone. I don't feel like pretending tonight, but I have to.

What's up? I'm good. Just hungover. Having a family thing tonight, so I'll have to skip. Might have drinks tomorrow night. Maybe just us two like old times.

Once I send the message to Art, I get on my shoes and socks before leaving my room.

No one is in the dining room yet, so I head for the kitchen. I'm starving and the smell that wafts from it has me heading in that direction.

"Mary." I kiss her on the cheek.

She smiles up at me. "Are you okay?" It's whispered, and that's when I see Una and Shane sitting at the kitchen table. I can't stop the smile that spreads across my face. Shane looks far worse than me.

"I'm okay. You should see the other guy."

Mary giggles, then remembers herself and gives me a half-arsed stern look.

I sit down across from Una and Shane. Una stiffens, but Shane stares at me like the devil just sat down.

"I'm sorry about today," I say to Shane. Una's eyes light up. She wraps her hand around Shane's open fingers and squeezes like she's trying to get a response out of him.

"It's not me you need to apologize to. It's Una."

"I'm sorry, Una," I say to her.

"I forgive you." She smiles wide. Shane doesn't, but he doesn't look ready to kill me at least.

"Okay, all into the dining room." Mary ushers us out of the kitchen. "I'm ready to start dishing this out shortly."

"Wish me luck," I say to Mary, and expect her to smile at me, but I'm surprised when she makes me stay behind.

"You don't need luck, Darragh. You're the kindest of them all. Don't keep letting them hurt you."

Her words have me kissing her softly on the cheek.

"As kind as Finn?" I ask with a raised eyebrow.

She smiles. "Always with the last word." She returns to the stove.

I pause at the door. "Thanks, Mary."

"For what?" She's smiling sweetly at me.

"For believing in me."

"Always, Darragh."

Everyone's in the room when I enter. It's always the same set up. Liam to Father's right, Shane to his left. This time, Una sits beside Shane—that's my spot—and Finn sits beside Liam. I opt to sit beside Una, so I don't have direct sight of Shane.

"I'm glad everyone came." Father raises his glass.

Not everyone, I think as I pour a glass of water. Connor isn't here. When I look up, I wonder if I've spoken out loud.

"What?" Shit, I hope I hadn't.

"Nothing." Una speaks up and fires a stern eye around the room.

As I lift the glass, Finn smiles. I stare at the glass in my hand, and it dawns on me. Everyone is staring at me because I'm having a glass of water.

"I'm just trying it out," I tell them, and a part of me hates how fucking proud they all look, especially Finn.

"Maybe you could consider not drinking the day of Finn's wedding." Father's voice rings clear across the room.

Bang. There we go. All I need to do is remain calm.

"I'll give it a try," I say in a big fuck-you voice.

"We would all really appreciate that." His words are clipped as he sips his wine.

"You don't have to do that," Finn says.

I take a gulp of my water. "I don't mind."

"He does have to do it, Finn. Darragh is too unpredictable with alcohol. You don't want him ruining your wedding."

My eyes snap to my father, and I'm wondering if he's trying to start a row. He focuses on Finn like I'm even not here.

"He said he would try, so let's take his word for it." Liam speaks up, and he meets everyone's gaze before stopping at me. A curt nod from him, and the conversation about me fucking everything up ends.

I want to ruin this meal for my father. I'm considering bringing up Connor. I know that will kick off a row.

"Where's Connor?" Una asks innocently from beside me.

I smirk.

"He's working," Father says, and smiles sweetly at Una.

"He got a job?" I ask.

My father lands his full stare on me. "He has a job just like the rest of you."

"Father is trying to cover up something that doesn't need to be covered up." Liam meets my eye before speaking to Una. "Connor struggles with the family. He wanted space, so we gave it to him. He's safe and fine, and we will all catch up at the wedding."

I take a peek at Una, and she's drinking up his lies like it's a fine wine.

I wonder when we became so good at lying to other people and each other. I glance at Finn, and his clenched face and hard eyes tell me he knows what really happened. Connor must have told him. When he looks at me, my stomach twists with guilt.

"I met him recently and he's fine," I say to Una, but I'm also telling Finn. I need him to know that things are fine between me and Connor.

"What did you do?" Finn asks, and it's like he knows I asked Connor to help me hurt someone.

"Just hung out with some friends." Art's betrayal is there in the front of my mind. I'm glancing at Liam and find him watching me. I have to tell him what happened, but not until after the wedding.

"So is Siobhan all set for the wedding?" Una slides in her question with a smile, and the conversation shifts to a comfortable ground. The wedding becomes everyone's focus. Mary brings in our dinner, and it's the only redeeming thing about this meal. I feel like everyone is watching me, waiting for me to fuck up by either saying something inappropriate or taking a drink. So I eat and keep my lips sealed.

"I can't wait until you see her in her dress, Finn. She's going to blow your mind."

"She blows my mind anyway." Finn's smiling like a drunken sailor, and I'm happy for him.

When I look at Liam, I don't see happiness at all. He knows I'm watching him; his eyes meet mine, and it's me who looks away.

"Before the wedding, I just wanted to say a few words." Father rises and takes his glass with him.

"The day you were born, we nearly lost your mother. I remember being called in. The chaos in the room was frightening, but then you cried and everything melted away for a moment. Big blue eyes looked up at me and you stopped, Finn."

I'm wondering where I was since me and Finn are fucking twins.

"Your mother believed she was going to die, and she just asked me to promise her that I would love and care for you all." His eyes touch each of us, and I want to salute him for failing fucking miserably.

"Thankfully, she pulled through and raised you all. I'm not sure what way you would have turned out otherwise. I'm proud of you, Finn." He holds his glass higher, and everyone follows suit.

"You've always been a good son, a good brother, and now you will be a great husband." Father drinks and we all do the same to close the speech.

"To family. May it always come first."

I'm already getting sick of drinking water. A beer would wash his bullshit down.

Una's clapping beside me like a happy fucking seal. I grin when I look at Finn. He's so happy with Father's praise.

The conversation continues about the wedding, and I'm glad when Mary arrives in with dessert. This is coming to an end.

CHAPTER SIXTEEN

CIARA

"So you still good to go to the wedding tomorrow?" Darragh's been asking me the same question the last few days like I'm going to back out of it. I've thought about not going, but things have fallen into a comfortable pattern with us.

We work together, have lunch, and Darragh drops me home and picks me up. I enjoy his company, and we haven't mentioned the kiss. Yet I can't seem to forget about it.

"Yes. So when do I get to see my dress?"

He grins at me as he puts on a fresh pillowcase. He's still using my rubber gloves, which are way too small for his large hands. "You can try it on for me after work."

Going to the cart and getting polish and a duster gives me a moment to hide my burning face. The idea of Darragh standing in my apartment does funny things to my stomach. "You'll just have to wait until tomorrow."

"Fine. When I drop you home, I'll give it to you. I have it in the car."

"It better fit, or I'll have to wear my trousers and a shirt." I'm teasing.

Darragh puts the final pillow on the bed. "If you want to wear your trousers, I'm cool with that. Whatever you're comfortable with." He's being serious.

"Nah, I never get to dress up."

We move onto the next room. Thinking about the wedding tomorrow is making me nervous. The sad reality is I've never been to one. I've never worn a dress. I don't share this with Darragh. I don't want to make a big deal out of it.

"So... my family is pretty intense." Darragh isn't looking at me; instead, he's checking the wardrobes to make sure the previous guests didn't leave anything behind. His tense shoulders and the fact he won't look at me tells me that he's worried. "They don't agree with my lifestyle and pretty much think I'm going to fuck it up. So if they start, you have to ignore them." He closes the wardrobes.

"Okay."

Darragh looks at me, searching my face. "Okay."

"I don't think you're going to fuck anything up." I'm finding it hard to meet his eye. I believe what I'm saying, and that confuses me. Since when do I believe in someone?

"Trust me. If anyone will make a mess of the wedding, it will be me. So I'm going to try not to drink."

Darragh moves toward me, and my heart rate picks up. He makes me feel small, and with each step, my breath lodges in my throat. Is he going to kiss me? Would I stop him?

Darragh's eyes shine, and his lips tug up slightly as he leans around me. When he moves back, he's holding a pair of blue gloves. I die a little as he grins like he knows what I was thinking and knows the effect he just had on me. He moves away and starts stripping the bed. I pick up my brain and lady parts off the floor. What the hell is wrong with me?

"I won't drink either," I say as I strip the quilt. I can feel Darragh's focus on me, and when I look up, it's confirmed.

"You don't have to do that."

"I know," I answer.

He seems stunned for a moment. "It's going to be one boring wedding with both of us sober."

I tut. "With me, I'm a joke a minute. I don't need a drink."

Darragh's grin reappears.

After work, Darragh keeps to his word and drives me home. Once we reach the apartment, he hands me a bag that has my dress and shoes in it.

"Thanks." I wrap my arms around it. I'm so nervous to see what he picked for me.

"If you need help with your hair or makeup, just let me know."

"What, you have more hidden talents?"

Darragh laughs at my remark. "My stepsister would gladly help."

My stomach flips at the idea of his sister helping me. I shake my head. "I'm good, but thanks."

"So I'll pick you up around twelve in the morning."

"I'll be ready." My nerves are kicking in. I can feel the tremble rise all the way into my hands, so before I start shaking, I get out of the car and don't look back.

Peaches is waiting for me when I enter my apartment. I rush to get her some food and milk before bringing the bag into the bedroom. I'm staring at it, afraid to look. I hate how much this means to me. I want to savor every second of the unwrapping. My first dress and I let a guy pick it.

"Here goes," I tell myself as I open the bag.

The dress I pull out has my pulse spiking. It's a blue I see all the time. It's the same as my eyes. I've often been told they're electric blue. The satin runs over my hands. The full-length dress had a generous slit that goes up my thigh while the halter neck has a plunge line. It's stunning. But for me, I'm not so sure.

The doorbell ringing has me placing the dress onto the bed before returning to the living room.

"Hello?" I speak into the intercom.

"Hi, Ciara, it's Bernie."

"Come on up." I buzz Bernie in and open the door.

I've never met her before, but as she rounds the corner, I notice she's a lot younger than I thought she would be. Her buzz-cut hairstyle and baggy clothes aren't what I expected from a hairdresser.

"Hi, Bernie," I greet her as she reaches the top step.

"How do you climb so many steps?" She's puffing as she steps into the apartment.

"I suppose I just got used to them." I'm nervous about getting my hair done.

"So I'm going to set up here. Is that okay?" Bernie asks as she places her bag on the counter.

"Work away."

"Are you sure about this?" She smiles.

I sit down on the chair she points to and let her remove my hair tie.

"Yes. I think so." I'm smiling too.

"What's your natural color?" she asks while parting my hair. "Ah, I see it's blonde." The blue is starting to leave my roots, showing some of my natural color.

"Yeah white blonde. Can you remove all the blue?"

"I can do anything. Just relax and let me work my magic."

***

It takes three hours, and when Bernie is finished, I'm starving and a little surprised with how I look. I'm in the bathroom mirror, and it's been so long since I saw *me*. The me that I hide from the world.

My stomach twists, and I want my blue hair back. It was the thing that made me stand out but also made me look dangerous, a warning not to mess with me. Now I look innocent, and innocent attracts the wrong kind of people. That's why I changed my appearance so much. No makeup, blue hair, baggy clothes, so I'm not worth looking at.

My looks before had brought so much unwanted attention, and not one ounce of it was good. My reflection disappears as I close my eyes and try to take some calming breaths. I'm going to be fine. I'd be with Darragh, after all.

My smile is shaky, but it's there as I picture him seeing me with blonde hair. Blue eyes that look larger stare back at me.

My phone pulls me away from my reflection.

Do you like the dress? Need a hand getting in or out of it?

I picture him in a mansion surrounded by servants or maybe at a party with the elite. If he was, he wouldn't be texting me. So maybe he's just bored.

It's nice.

I go back to the bag and remove the dress again. It causes a lump to rise in my throat. It's stunning. The shoes are also electric blue, with some stones placed at the front where the material gathers.

Just nice??? I picked it myself.

The idea that Darragh selected my dress causes my stomach to tighten.

It's stunning. Thank you, Darragh.

The reply is immediate and makes me smile. **Can't wait to see you in it, blue.**

He won't be able to call me blue anymore. My fingers run through my hair again. It's going to take a while before I get used to the new me. Well, actually, the old me. I look like my mother. The longer I stare at myself, the blurrier my vision grows.

Peaches rubs up against my leg. After rubbing my eyes, I pick her up and focus on her instead.

DARRAGH

We never had a stag for Finn—he didn't want one—but tonight we're meeting up in Cabra Castle for a few drinks, all organized by Liam. He has a big pull there. He hosts most of his 'private' meetings there. He could own the place for all I know. Liam is a closed book, like always.

"You got an invitation?" I say with a smirk, when I spot Connor at the front desk.

He grins when he sees me. "I'm doing this for Finn," he says, moving away from the desk.

"Me too. I could think of lots of other places I want to be."

Glancing around the area, I see we're the only one's here. "Are you early? Or are they late?"

"They're upstairs. I said I'd wait for you."

"The wait is over." I'm waiting for it, and it doesn't take long. I've only got my foot on the first step when Connor speaks.

"Don't forget you have to talk to Liam or I will."

"Fuck's sake, Connor. I know. Why does everyone feel the need to babysit me?"

I don't expect his laughter. "Because you know you need someone to look out for you. You're a loose cannon." When Connor says it, it's with humor and not the vindictive way I'm used to hearing it from the rest.

"Well, you'll be glad to know I haven't touched a drink in six days."

Connor throws me a sideways glance as we head up the stairs. "It's a girl, isn't it?"

We reach the second floor and walk past a tin man that would creep me out if I wasn't sober.

"No, I'm just sick of listening to people's shit," I say.

He grins. "Nope, we've been at you your whole life, so why now?"

Is he right? Is it Ciara? No. It's to shut my father the fuck up.

"I'm sick of always being the disappointment."

Connor stops walking and grips my shoulder. "Don't ever say that again. I know you might think that, but they all think a lot of you. Why do you think they protect you so much? If they didn't care, they'd say nothing, like they do with me."

"What's this, see who Father hates the most?" I joke.

"He's not my father." Connor's serious tone has us walking again, and I'm glad when we reach the private room. I'm also glad when I see it's just us brothers.

Finn's face lights up when he sees Connor, and he embraces him like he hasn't seen his brother in ages. I look at Liam, wondering if he'll reconsider the ban he put on Connor.

Finn slaps me on the back. "You guys are so late." He sits down, and I check my phone.

"By twenty minutes," I say and pour out a glass of water. This time, no one says anything.

"A toast to Finn, the first of us to marry. He may also be the last." Connor makes the speech, not caring about how Liam and Shane watch him.

I join in. "Last night of freedom. You can always run now," I tell Finn.

He smiles. "I'm good," he says and we drink.

"So what's on the menu tonight?" I ask Liam since he organized this. When he lifts the menu, I sneer.

"I was talking about entertainment. Did you bring anything home from work?"

"Finn wouldn't approve." Liam continues to stare at the food menu.

Finn looks sheepish "What? I don't want that."

"Yeah, but what about the rest of us?" I ask.

"There's only you and Liam."

I can't even look at Liam. I'm not sure what he's into—men, women, maybe both, maybe none. He shows no interest. But now my interest is piqued.

"You want to hit a strip joint later, brother?"

Liam's lips twitch. "You seem to forget I own several."

Finn steers the conversation away from strippers and back to us. It's nice to have just us brothers here. No matter how much we fight or hurt each other, we all come back to each other in the end. We all protect each other. Family comes first, no matter what.

CHAPTER SEVENTEEN

DARRAGH

IT'S THE MORNING OF the wedding, and my stomach tightens and twists. I need a drink. I'm fixing my tie and failing each time when a knock sounds on my room door.

"Come in," I call, not looking away from the mirror as I pull the tie off for the hundredth time and try to retie it. I pause when I meet my father's eye in the mirror.

"I'm still sober. No need to check up on me." It's out of my mouth before I remember who I'm speaking to. "Sorry," I add quickly.

He nods. "I'm not here to check up on you, but it's great to see you're sober."

I turn around, and Father walks toward me. He's a large man. Even at his age, he still scares the crap out of me.

"Let me fix your tie. Your mother taught me." He speaks while he places the tie around my neck.

I'm uncomfortable waiting for him to tighten it until it cuts off my air supply. Sweat gathers between my shoulder blades as I watch his hands move. He doesn't strangle me; he just makes the knot in my tie.

"I know what you did. As do other people." The knot moves into place a little too tightly, and when I clear my throat, he loosens it. "It's important that you don't say anything out of place. These people will hang us the moment we step out of line."

Father steps back and brushes my shoulders. "You've grown into a man," he says, but my mind is stuck on what he's saying.

"I don't know..."

"It's your brother's wedding. I don't want to hurt you. So just listen and shut up. You know what I'm talking about. Unless you've been up to worse than robbing banks like you're some low-life criminal."

The blood drains from me, but I hold myself firm.

"Just give your family this one day."

I nod.

His hand lands with some force across my face, patting my cheek. I don't move until he leaves my room.

I loosen the tie straight away before going to the back of my wardrobe and removing a small bag of coke I keep hidden. My hands are sweaty as I take it to my bed. I pat my jacket pocket and remove my wallet. Rolling up a fifty, I take out my card. A knock at my door has me sitting on top of my stash.

"What do you think?" It's Finn. He does a twirl.

"The suits okay, but that face blows my fucking mind."

He grins while checking himself out in the mirror. His gray suit is tailored to perfection, the same as all of us. We're all in gray with a white shirt to tie in with Siobhan's dress.

As he checks himself out, I'm hoping nothing's stuck to my ass. I grab everything and stuff it into my pocket and wipe my bed quickly. I'm sweating as I turn to Finn.

"Are you nervous?" I ask him.

He looks away from the mirror, his eyes trailing around my room. His brows furrow deeply. "I think I'm more nervous that your room is clean."

"You and me both." Being off the drink gives me too much time on my hands.

"Let's hope she shows up," I say.

Finn widens his eyes. "Don't say that, man."

Like it was a possibility.

He swallows his nerves. "We better head down."

"I'll see you at the church. I've got to pick up my date." I don't look at him as I speak.

"Yeah, this mysterious date. Did you pay her?"

"I kind of did," I say honestly.

Finn's face falls. "You're bringing a prostitute to my wedding?"

I'm laughing at the insult. Ciara would hit him for that one. "No. But I had to bribe her to come with me. She wasn't exactly on board."

"But she's coming willingly?"

"Ha ha." We leave the room and part ways. He's joining Shane and Liam in the study, so I don't envy him.

The minute I'm outside, I light a fag and just sit on the steps, letting the air cool me down. The front door opens and Liam steps out. I want to roll my mother fucking eyes.

"I've already been warned. So don't start."

He pauses on the steps. "I'm just going to get the car."

I take a deep drag of my fag.

Liam watches me. "What did he say to you?"

That he knows I robbed a bank. "Just not to drink," I say, standing up. My movement causes the small bag of white powder to fall onto the step. We both look at it.

"I wasn't going to use it." I stare at the bag.

Liam bends at the waist and picks it up. "Good. You won't need it, then."

I say nothing as he slips it into his pocket and walks away. A part of me feels lighter to have the temptation out of my way. But it has also made me feel better knowing it was in arm's reach if I wanted it.

"Fuck." I throw my smoke onto the ground and go get my car. I need to pick up Ciara.

***

Ciara isn't like other girls. When I ring and tell her I'm outside, her door opens. She doesn't keep me waiting. A woman steps out wearing Ciara's dress, and I can't look away. A blonde bombshell, but it's the eyes that I've looked at every day that has me realizing it's Ciara. The keys rattle in my hand as I pull them from the ignition and get out.

Ciara looks at me from under her thick black eyelashes, making her look so innocent. So beautiful. She's something to protect. But from firsthand experience, I know that's not true. She's well capable of protecting herself. She always had an air of innocence about her. Before, it was buried under a smart mouth and anger; now, there's nothing to hide it.

I watch her as I move around the car and meet her at the door. The rise and fall of her chest shows how nervous she is. The plunging line showcases perfectly firm breasts.

"I have an idea," I say and she smiles, but it's strained. I've never seen her this nervous. "Let's go back inside so I can peel that dress off you."

She laughs, and it does the job I intended it to do. It makes her relax. "I'm never sleeping with you." Her comeback doesn't hold the normal amount of belief it normally does.

I really want to tell her how amazing she looks, but that would scare her off.

"So that's a no, then?"

"Yes, it's a no." She's still smiling, and a light blush kisses her cheeks.

"Are you sure?"

She laughs again and nods. Stepping aside, I open the car door for her and she slides in. The dress splits open, and I see so much fucking skin. The cold metal of the car door is the only thing that keeps me from leaning in and kissing her. I focus on the feel of the door.

"I'm in," she tells me.

I've been standing here too long. After closing the car door, I race around to my side and slide in.

"You look really good." Her words have me grinning.

I fire up the car. "I know," I tell her as I pull out and she smiles. "You look good too." Her smile isn't as wide, so I keep any further compliments to myself.

I can't stop stealing glances at her. "Who knew you were blonde."

She touches her hair. "What, this? No. I'm naturally blue. Just thought I could do with a bit of a change."

"Well, it suits you. I think you look hot." I kick myself for letting it slip, but she smiles up at me.

"Really?" She isn't fishing for a compliment. She really doesn't know how gorgeous she is.

"I'd sleep with you," I say and my heart beats faster. I mean it, and something in her posture tells me she's picked up that this time it's different.

"That's an odd compliment. But thank you."

"You don't want to return the compliment. Tell me how you're undressing me with your eyes."

Her laughter fills my car. That's what I've been doing since I saw her—undressing her with my eyes.

"Yes, I can't stop picturing you naked."

"Oh, tell me more," I tease. The blush on her cheeks makes me wonder if she really is picturing me naked.

We pull into Kells, and I don't drive down to the church grounds knowing parking isn't possible. Instead, I park at the back of the Headfort Arms Hotel. It's another one of Liam's establishments.

I check my watch. It's a quarter to one. The wedding starts at one.

"So I have to go up top with my family, as I'm one of the groomsmen, but I'll leave you with Una."

"You don't have to do that." She looks so pure, making me want to taint that purity with a kiss.

"I know." I get out and move around the car to open her door. Once she's out, I pull the shawl around her shoulders.

"Thank you for doing this for me."

Ciara holds my gaze before reaching up and brushing her lips to my cheek. "You're welcome." The words are whispered against my ear.

I reach out my arm, and Ciara takes it as we leave the parking lot and make our way across the road to the church. The lot is as packed as I expected. With four hundred guests, the church will be full. Some people are still outside smoking or having a last-minute chat. I spot my Father having words with a man who looks similar to him, Uncle Tom. The words are heated but controlled. They wouldn't let themselves down in front of a crowd.

I grip Ciara tighter as I make my way into the church. The walk up the aisle is long, and the seats are filled with a lot of people I don't know but who seem to know me. Being identical to the groom is a bit of a giveaway. I get a lot of nods, smiles, and hellos. Occasionally, someone knows my name.

Liam, Shane, Connor, and Finn are standing at the front of the church. "Those four guys at the altar are my brothers."

"Jesus Christ, you all look like models."

Surprise at her words has me looking down at her. "You think I look like a model?"

She grins up at me but doesn't answer. Liam spots us first, and his eyes slide to Ciara. I see it the moment it happens—the moment he recognizes her. His eyes snap to mine and he nods. I'm not sure if it's approval of who's with me or just the fact that I showed up. Una's fiery red hair is like a siren. She's only three people in and close to the top.

I stop at her row of seats. "Una, this is my date, Ciara. Can I leave her in your hands?" Una takes in Ciara, and she smiles at her. "You can sit with me and Ava."

Ava gives me a smile.

"Nice to see you again," I tell her, and Una seems surprised that we know each other. Beside the three girls is an older woman who is watching us. Most certainly not Liam's date. I'm curious about who he brought.

"You okay?" I ask Ciara before I have to leave.

"Yes, I'm fine. Go on." Her smile has me making a quick decision. I lean in and plant a soft quick kiss on her lips. She looks startled as I leave her and join my brothers.

"You're cutting it close." I ignore Shane's words and pull Finn into a quick hug.

"You can still bail," I tease.

He grins, but it's strained. "Not a chance. I just hope she shows up." He's watching the door like her not arriving would actually happen.

Liam steps closer to me. "You brought Ciara?"

I don't look at him as I speak. "Yes, she cleans up nicely, doesn't she?"

"That she does." I don't like Liam agreeing with me. He steps away as I turn to him.

"You brought the rings?" Connor asks me, and I'm shaking my head, my spine tightening.

"No, what? No one said for me to bring the fucking rings." I'm getting loud, but I didn't fuck this up.

Shane shakes his head at me, but Connor is grinning. "Of course you didn't. I'm the best man."

I want to punch him.

Shane leans in a little too close. "Could you try to watch your mouth? We're standing in a church."

"Move back before I deck you," I say to him through a smile.

"Please remember this is Finn's day." Liam speaks up while glancing out over the crowd.

Finn is staring at the altar, and I nudge Connor. "You're the best man," I whisper, and he steps toward Finn and whispers a few words in his ear.

Music starts and every head whips to the closed front doors.

My own stomach goes for Finn. Taking our places quickly, I find Ciara watching me and I wink at her. The doors open and Siobhan steps in.

I take a quick look at Finn. Tears brim in his eyes as he stares at Siobhan. A veil covers her face, but the dress is stunning, with a train two meters back that has four girls lifting and fixing it at each step she takes.

Father is giving her away. He walks with an air of a man who knows his worth. Head held high, he nods to people as he passes them. When he gets closer to us, he looks at each son, and pride shines in his eyes. I smile as Siobhan reaches Finn, and when he gets to push back the veil, his face transforms as their eyes meet.

The mass is an hour long, and I spend most of my time watching Ciara. She's crying along with Una and Ava. When she meets my eye, I suppress the smile that threatens to appear.

"I now pronounce you husband and wife." The words are music to my ears. The mass is finally over. Finn doesn't waste a minute before he takes Siobhan in his hands and kisses her. The church erupts in cheers.

The bells ring as Finn and Siobhan walk hand in hand down the aisle. A hand lands on my back. It's Connor. "Thank God that's over," he whispers and I agree.

I can't wait for a smoke. As we follow behind, Ava falls into step with Connor and Una with Shane. Ciara looks unsure, but I hold out my hand and she takes it, slipping out of her seat. I check behind me, but Liam walks on his own.

"That was beautiful." Ciara's voice is still clogged with emotion.

"Yeah, it was long," I say.

She squeezes our linked hands. "You can't say that didn't do something to you." She's really emotional, and it's sweet.

"It made me realize I'm really addicted to fags. And I don't like staying in one spot too long."

Ciara narrows her eyes at me.

"Fine, it was beautiful," I say, and she seems satisfied as we step out into the sun. Connor and Ava come over to us.

"Ciara, this is my brother Connor and his girlfriend, Ava." Connor takes Ciara's outstretched hand. Ava and Ciara smile at each other.

"We already met," Ava says.

"Thanks for letting me sit with you."

"I'm as new as you. This is my first time meeting the family." The girls move closer together, bonding over being new.

"I see Liam doesn't have a date," I say to Connor as I spark up a fag.

"I didn't see him come in with anyone. Makes you really wonder about him."

I'm nodding. "Did you see Uncle Tom is here? Father was having words with him earlier."

Connor doesn't look at me as he speaks; his eyes scan across the crowd. "I didn't see him, but they have a bad history, so I'm not surprised."

"Over the shooting?"

Ava and Ciara look up at us. "The bird shooting," I tell them with a smile.

"Here comes Father," I say to Connor and his face tightens. "I mean Michael," I say just for him, and he relaxes.

"Well done. You both did a great job," he tells us. I know we are the fuckups.

"Thanks," I say.

Connor doesn't speak, and I'm grateful that he doesn't. He normally has nothing good to say.

"Are you going to introduce me to your dates?" Father smiles, and he looks like such a sweet and doting father.

"This is Ciara. Ciara, my father." Ciara takes Dad's outstretched hand.

"So great to meet you." Her smile is sweet, and she blinks up at him.

"And this is?" he questions, releasing Ciara's hand. Connor isn't speaking.

"Ava, Connor's girlfriend," I say.

Father steps toward her. "Isn't he a very lucky man?" Father says while taking her hand.

She looks nervously at Connor. His silence isn't helping.

"Okay, family photo, Darragh." Father walks away, and I hate that he got a dig in. How he didn't mention Connor.

"He's such a fucking asshole," I mutter.

"I know, man. But just for Finn, let's make today go smoothly." Connor gives Ava a quick kiss.

"I won't be long," I say to Ciara, wondering what the hell she's making of our family, but she smiles like today is a great day.

An hour of photos and repositioning is bad enough, but with crowds watching us, it's draining.

Three photographers are directing us.

"Okay, can we just have the brothers?"

We all stand together. "Maybe move closer and wrap your arms around each other." We do as instructed. "Now Darragh look at Shane, Liam face forward, and Finn, you look at Connor."

We do that. I'm looking at Shane and its all kinds of awkward.

"On the count of three, say something to each other. One, two, three."

"You're a prick," I say to Shane as the cameras snap away. I'm smiling at him, his face rigid. "That's going to make a great photo," I say as we finally finish up.

"Why didn't you smile?" Una questions Shane, and I'm grinning as I step away.

"What did you say to him?" Connor asks.

"I just said to smile. But he refused."

Connor snorts.

CHAPTER EIGHTEEN

CIARA

I CAN'T TAKE MY eyes off Darragh. He just seems to draw me in. Watching the photoshoot is captivating. Each brother looks like they're modeling wedding clothes. Each one is so different but equally good-looking. Normally, there's an ugly one in the family. But not the O'Reagans.

"So have you and Darragh been together for long?" The question has been asked several times, but I smile at Una. She hadn't asked yet, but I knew she was dying to know.

"We're friends."

Both her eyebrows raise and she smiles. "Ah."

I want to ask what 'Ah' means, but Darragh is walking toward us. A part of me is still reeling from the kiss he gave me in front of everyone. It distracted me and I just couldn't fully enjoy my very first wedding. My lips still tingle, and I wonder why he did it. The first kiss we had was me in tears, telling him my past, but this time he didn't have to kiss me.

"We can start making our way to Cabra." Darragh lights up a cigarette.

"I'm starving and honestly these shoes are cutting into my heels." Una winces as she speaks.

"Yeah, mine too. I should have gotten smaller heels," Darragh says.

Una narrows her eyes at Darragh before smiling at me. "See you at the castle."

Shane arrives then. He doesn't smile much, and he levels Darragh with a stare. I find myself taking a step toward Darragh, not liking his hostility at all. His eyes snap to me and his face softens.

"Can't wait to see the photos. They might have to edit you out." Darragh's words are delivered with a smirk.

Shane's face tightens again. "See you at the castle." He turns and Una gives us an apologetic look.

"So she's your stepsister?" I ask.

Darragh blows smoke into the air. "Yep."

"And he's your brother. So she's also his stepsister?"

"You're preaching to the choir."

"I'm not saying there's anything wrong with it. I'm just curious," I say, not wanting to judge. They aren't related. It's just the title that makes it seem kind of weird.

"I didn't get to meet your date." I startle as Finn comes up behind us. He's Darragh's identical twin, but the more I look at him, I don't think he's like Darragh at all. He's too soft and polished.

"This is Ciara. Ciara, Finn."

"Lovely to meet you, and congratulations."

He smiles sweetly. "Great to meet you too, Ciara. We're going to go to the hotel now. I'd say everyone is starving."

I was hungry, but I didn't say. Finn pats his brother on the back, and we leave together.

"Why did you kiss me?" I ask as we wait to cross the road. Keeping my focus on the traffic allows me the bravery of asking the question.

Once we get safely across the road, Darragh speaks. "Did you like it?"

"You can't answer my question with a question," I tell him.

"I wanted to." He shrugs and throws his fag onto the ground like it's no big deal. Like he didn't leave me stunned and thinking about it through the whole ceremony.

We reach the car, and Darragh opens my door but stands in the way. "Can I do it again?"

My heart starts to race. I want him to do it so much, but I'm scared.

"I think we should keep this platonic." My words don't tether him at all.

His smile is slow. "I think it's a bit too late for that."

Yeah, it is.

He steps aside, and I get into the car.

***

I've never been to Cabra Castle before, but already, it's stolen words from me. This is like a fairy tale. "So, this isn't my doing, but rooms were booked for each of us."

I unbuckle my belt. "Okay?"

"I mean, couple wise. We're sharing a room."

"Oh." The idea of sharing a room with Darragh is heating up my blood.

"Look, I'll sleep on the floor. Scout's honor." Darragh crosses his heart like I might believe him.

"Or we could just ask for a spare bed to be brought in," I say.

"I can organize that."

I grin. "No, let me." I don't trust him one bit.

"So about this platonic relationship. What are the rules?"

"What do you mean rules?" I'm smiling.

Darragh's eyes light up. "Like, can we dance?"

"I won't be dancing, because I can't," I reply.

"But we can dance?"

I laugh. "Yes. We can dance."

"Hand holding?"

"Depends on what the situation is."

His lips tug up into a smile. "A kiss on the cheek?"

"Acceptable."

Darragh moves in and my heart gallops, my grin dissolving off my face. The smell of his cologne fills my lungs, and I can't look away from him. His lips graze my cheek, warm breath brushing my neck, and I shiver. Moist lips touch my neck, and it takes a lot of control to stay still. Each kiss he plants moves closer to my lips. If he reaches them, I'm not sure I can stop him.

A knock on the window has me jumping away from Darragh. He doesn't move away but groans before turning to his window, where his brother Connor grins at him. The burn of embarrassment rushes across my cheeks.

"The happy couple is about to arrive," he informs Darragh before looking at me and grinning.

The heat travels across my chest, and I'm glad when the cool wind blows around me as I step out of the car. Warm fingers wrap around mine, and my head snaps up to Darragh.

"You said hand holding was okay."

"I said it depended on the situation," I answer as I allow myself to relax into his touch.

"So I made an executive decision and decided this was the perfect situation."

We join everybody else as Siobhan and Finn arrive. White petals are lifted by the wind and swirl around the couple. I can't stop looking. There's such a magical feel to it. Regret at not going to a wedding before rises inside me. I never knew what I was missing out on.

Men on either side of the door play the tin whistle, the sound romantic but haunting. The castle inside is even more enchanting. The money this must have cost... I can't even begin to think about it.

Once we enter the main room, I'm separated from Darragh. He has to sit at the head table with the rest of his family, but I've been placed with Ava, and since she's 'new' too, we stick together.

We're seated with mostly Northern Ireland people. Their accents fascinate me. I could listen to them for hours.

"How do you know the bride or groom?" The place name in front of the man is Tom. He looks very similar to Darragh's father, and I wonder if they're related.

"I'm here with Darragh. He's the groom's brother."

"Ah, Darragh, nice bloke. They sure have some fine women down this end of the water."

I grin at the compliment. "Thanks."

"What about you, love?" he asks Ava, and I take the time to start on my soup.

"I'm here with my boyfriend, Connor, also a brother to the groom." It's funny how Ava's response gets everyone's attention.

"You're Connor's woman?" a young lad asks.

"Matt, watch your tongue." Tom's response is sharp, and Matt apologizes to Ava.

It's awkward, but Ava waves it off. I'm glad when the meal part is over and we no longer have to stay at the same tables. My heart lifts as Darragh makes his way over to our table.

"You want to check out the room?" he asks me in front of everyone. Darragh focuses on my company, and he smiles at Tom.

"Uncle Tom, didn't think you would make it." They shake hands and don't release them as they speak to each other.

"Didn't think I would be invited, but Finn was always the softest." There's a strain in the conversation, and when I glance around the table, Matt is looking at me and gives me a soft smile.

"Sorry to hear about your son."

"You weren't sorry enough to come to the funeral." Their words are delivered quickly. Darragh releases his uncle's hand.

"I didn't think we would be wanted," Darragh fires back and faces me. The strain in his shoulders and around his eyes has me standing.

"Let's check out the room," I say, getting up.

I don't like leaving Ava alone. "Want to come take a look at our room?" I ask her.

"Don't worry, we don't bite." Tom speaks up, but I ignore him and focus on Ava.

"No, I'm good. Just going to find Connor." She uses the moment to stand, and I'm relieved that I'm not leaving her with them. Right now, Tom seems so hostile.

As we leave the main room, Darragh doesn't look up from his phone. His fingers race across the keys.

"Is everything okay?" I ask as we climb the stairs.

He finally looks up and stuffs the phone into his pocket. "Yeah. Sorry about that. So you want to take a look at our room?"

"Just a look." I take a peek at him and he's grinning.

Our room is huge, like stupid huge. The four-poster bed dominates the room, along with the claw bath that sits in the middle of the room.

"Well, a bath is out of the question," I saym running my hand along the off-white ceramic.

"I won't look. Promise."

I laugh at Darragh.

"I promise." He does a little cross over his heart, and I shake my head at him, but I can't stop smiling.

The windows drop to the floor, and I step closer. We're overlooking a garden that's filled with guests, and beyond that, fields and even further out is a forest.

"It's stunning," I say as heat against my back has me catching my breath.

"Not as stunning as you," Darragh whispers into my ear.

I'm so tempted to turn and look at him, but I'm just not that brave. The heat is replaced with cold as he walks away from me. His footsteps are cushioned on the luxury beige carpet under our feet. I stay in the window for a little while longer before I gather some courage and turn around. Darragh's sitting on a clawed legged chair, watching me. My breath swirls and stills in my chest.

"Why are you looking at me like that?" My breath seems shallow as Darragh rises without answering me and steps toward me. I want to fidget or look away as he continues his walk to me. He stops, leaving only inches between us. His eyes flicker to my lips.

"I've never met anyone like you. I've never met anyone who's made me feel like this."

I wet my lips at his words. "What way do I make you feel?" I can't look away from his lips.

"Content. I've never felt that before. I'm always chasing something I can't reach, but with you, I don't mind standing still."

My lips touch his. His surprise lasts only a few seconds before he returns the kiss. We're moving, and soon, the bed sinks around my back.

Darragh moves his tongue into my mouth, his excitement brushing against me, and wetness starts to pool between my legs. Breaking the kiss gives me a moment to think clearly. Darragh trails kisses down my neck, and when he kisses my breasts and runs his tongue across my nipple, I stop him. My halter dress is untied. I didn't even notice him undoing it.

"We need to stop," I say.

He stands with his hands in the air. "I've stopped." He says each word a little breathlessly.

I sit up and hold the dress in place before retying it.

"You started it this time, not me."

I nod while trying to compose myself. "I know I did," I answer as I run my hands across my hair.

Darragh sits on his hunkers so he can see me as I duck my head. "You sound upset."

I shake my head. "No, just guys like you don't normally like girls like me." I'm honest with him. He's scaring the crap out of me, and I don't scare easily. I've seen so much in my life, and I've been hurt pretty badly, but with Darragh, I'm not sure I'd bounce back.

"You have no idea of your worth." He takes my hand in his. "Let's just go back to the wedding and enjoy ourselves. We don't have to figure out everything right now."

He's right.

"But we could say this is our first date." He starts to rise as he speaks, pulling me with him.

"A real date?"

"Yeah." He grins as he twines our fingers together, and we leave the hotel room. "Like boyfriend and girlfriend kind of date."

"Wow, that escalated quickly," I say. His laughter is husky, and my stomach responds by tightening.

"We could be married by the end of the night."

I glance at Darragh sideways. "At the speed you're going, anything is possible."

We enter the ballroom that's been transformed once again. The lights are dimmed, and candlelight casts most of the light around the room. No one is dancing, but soft music plays out.

Darragh isn't slowing, and the horror of what he's thinking of doing has me trying to pull discreetly away from him.

"I don't dance," I hiss.

Darragh throws a grin over his shoulder. "Neither do I." He twirls me unexpectedly. My dress spreads out around me. My free hand presses against a solid chest as Darragh pulls me into him and we are swaying.

"What the hell was that?"

"Just a move I picked up." The heat of his hand in mine is making me forget that we're the only ones on the dance floor.

Glancing down, I try to follow his footing.

"Just let me lead."

When I glance back up, his eyes search my face before landing on my lips.

"Okay," I say. We spin and move around the floor, and I feel like a ballroom dancer. Each twirl has me laughing as I spin, and all the faces merge into a blur. Darragh's smiling face reappears each time as I try to let the dizziness go.

"You're an amazing dancer," I say, trying to catch my breath.

"So are you."

The music softens further, and he pulls me into him until our bodies are flushed. His warm breath brushes my neck. The slow movement allows me to see that we're being watched, and my nerves kick in. Closing my eyes, I bury myself deeper into Darragh and allow myself to enjoy my first dance.

DARRAGH

"Smile, ladies."

Ciara, Una, Ava, and Siobhan are sitting together at a table. They look up and smile as I capture the picture. Looking at it on my phone, Ciara's smiling face and her bright blue eyes have me smiling.

"Let me see." Finn slides in beside me. "Can you send me that?"

I quickly attach it and send it out to each brother. "Sent."

"Are you coming out for a smoke?" I ask Finn, and he nods before giving Siobhan a kiss.

"We're just heading out for a smoke," I say to Ciara. She's watching me, and I want to kiss her but I restrain myself.

"Go. I'm fine here."

I wink at her before heading outside with Finn.

"Where are you going?" Connor falls into step beside us.

"I need a smoke," I say as we head outside. Everyone wants to talk to Finn. So we move into the parking lot, where none of the guests are. I light up a smoke and hand the box and lighter to Connor. He lights up one too and passes the box to Finn.

"It's someday," Connor says and I agree with him.

"Yeah, it's perfect. Just can't believe it's all gone without a hitch. I can't thank you both enough."

"You can take us out for drinks when you get back from the honeymoon," Connor says.

Glancing back at the hotel, I allow myself to relax and enjoy this moment. "Where's the honeymoon, anyway?" I ask.

"A cruise around the world." I'm not much for boats, but a holiday is something I might think about taking soon.

"How are you doing?" Finn asks after a moment of silence.

"Yeah, I was going to ask too." Connor walks over to a cigarette bin and puts out his fag.

"I'm good. It's funny. I feel great," I say to both of them.

Finn smiles. "You look happy," he says.

"I am."

"Do we have to thank Ciara?" Connor's smirk has me nudging him.

"This is all on me," I lie and put out my fag. We go back into the hotel, where the dance floor has filled back up. I spot Shane and Liam drinking together.

"You ever wonder what they talk about?" I ask Connor as Finn gets swallowed up by his guests.

"All the time."

Connor's answer surprises me. I thought it was only me. "Let's go over."

"Don't start anything," I warn and it feels weird. Normally, everyone is warning me. Not the other way around.

Screams start from the side of the room and seem to trickle throughout the crowd. Connor and I pause halfway across the dance floor. I'm searching for the source of panic that's spreading rapidly. Everyone is running as the first shot rings out. I hit the ground hard and cover my head. We're sitting ducks. Connor lands beside me and grabs my arm.

"Move." He's crawling across the floor.

People are running in their panic to get away, and an elderly woman slams into me and hits the floor, the crack of her head making me pausing. The bang of another gunshot has me moving again.

Once we reach the tables, I can't stay down any longer. I need to see what's happening. Standing, I can't see anything through the stampede of people. Climbing onto the table gives me a better view.

"What are you doing?" Connor tries to pull me down. Five men in balaclavas hold shotguns they repump. They're searching the room; they aren't shooting blindly.

A hand grips my leg and pulls my trousers. I see the moment the shooter looks at me. Our eyes meet as he pumps his gun. *I'm going to die.*

Connor's standing, blocking me from the path of the shooter. The gun fires.

CHAPTER NINETEEN

DARRAGH

I'M STARING INTO MY brother's wide eyes. Looking over his shoulder, I see the gunman still staring at us. The screams in the room block out everything else.

"Get down now," Connor warns, and this time, I let him drag me under the table, where a couple and an elderly man are hiding.

"He missed," I say as my eyes roam Connor. He looks away from me. My brain is screaming that he didn't miss. He just didn't shoot us. "They didn't shoot you." I'm rambling.

Connor grabs my arm roughly. "Go find the girls. I'll find Liam and Shane."

Does the shooter know Connor? I'm looking into the eyes of a stranger who shakes me again. "Now is not the time, Darragh."

I pull my arm from his grasp and pause as three more shots ring out. The screams of pure horror are close to me, and I push ahead, one voice striking a chord deep inside me.

Ciara's screams and her cries tear at me, and I no longer crawl. I'm standing, jumping across people and chairs. I halt the moment I see what everyone is screaming for. Siobhan is sprawled out, her dress soaking up the blood that seeps from a bullet wound in her stomach.

She's dead. Ciara is holding her hands over the wound, blood rushing through her fingers. I drop beside them, and Una grows frantic the moment she sees me.

"Oh my God." She's trembling, but I check Siobhan for a pulse that I know won't be there. I spot Ava huddled under a table, her head buried in her knees.

"What do I do?" Ciara's eyes are wild.

I hate that I can't do anything. Shaking my head, Una starts roaring again. It doesn't matter. Everyone seems to be frantic. People are rising slowly, half-bent at the waist.

"Ciara," I take her face in my hands. "She's gone."

Tears trickle from wide blue eyes, and she buries herself in my chest. I'm staring down at Siobhan, her dress rapidly turning red.

"Siobhan!" Finn's voice has me releasing Ciara.

"Just stay here," I tell her before I stand and spot Connor and Finn. I don't see Liam or Shane. Connor meets my eye. His face pales as he stares at my chest. Ciara's bloody hand marks are imprinted on my shirt.

"Are you okay?" Connor reaches me first, and I stand aside.

"Finn." I can't get the words out as he moves closer to me.

"Ah, no. Ah, no." Finn moves past us and falls to his knees beside Siobhan.

Connor looks at me, and I can't hold his stare. I pray to God he had no dealings with this.

"Stay with him," I tell Connor.

Finn is bent over Siobhan, crying as I leave to find Liam and Shane.

"Liam. Shane!"

Arms grip me and I look up into my father's face. "Your brothers?" His fear is gripping him, choking him.

"Finn and Connor are fine. I need to find Liam and Shane."

"I'll help you."

I nod and we both call them. I'm walking toward the last place I saw them sitting. "Siobhan's dead," I mumble to Father.

"Darragh." It's Liam, and he's safe. I embrace him. I want him to fix this. He can fix things.

"Whose blood is on you?" Liam asks, and I can see he's shook.

"Siobhan's."

He nods. "Is everyone okay?"

Father pats him on the arm. "Shane. Where's Shane? He was with you."

"The minute they fired, he raced off, looking for Una." The screams in the room have fallen to cries of despair.

"Shane," I scream again and my voice carries across the room.

"Over here." Uncle Tom is standing, and the strain on his face has me running toward him, with Father and Liam on my heels. *Please God, don't let him be dead.*

There's so much blood. Shane's tie has been removed. I find his pulse and Father is beside me, but he isn't fussing over Shane. "He has a pulse, but it's weak."

"If I find out you had anything to do with this, I will kill you," Father threatens Tom.

"I've been here the whole time."

"Shut the fuck up." My roar silences them. Shane is bleeding to death. Now is not the fucking time. "Someone ring an ambulance."

"I've done it already." Liam joins me, and I move, letting him press his coat to Shane's wound.

"Go be with Finn," Liam tells me and I nod.

I don't want to. I have no idea what to do. Standing up allows me to see the room. It's carnage. The doors open again, and the room is filling with an ambulance crew and the Gardaí. I meet Una near where Siobhan was. Her eyes are red and puffy.

"Have you seen Shane?"

"Una," I say, and she's shaking her head.

"Don't you dare." She's struggling to breathe, her eyes filling with tears. "Don't you dare," she says again, gentler this time.

"He's alive, but he's been shot."

Her hand slaps against her trembling lips. "Where is he?"

I take Una to Shane. The ambulance crews have arrived and lift him onto a stretcher.

"I want him to have the best of care." Father is gripping one of the paramedics by his collar. Two Gardaí put their hands on our Father. Liam and I move at the same time.

"Get your hands off him." I push the closest one back. Gardaí Brady stares at me.

"Don't touch him again," I say and he doesn't speak back.

"Dad, let him go." I pry Father's fingers off the paramedic. "You're delaying them leaving." My words have my father releasing him.

The other Gardaí isn't as quiet as Brady. "Take your hands off me, or I will arrest you."

Liam releases his neck but still stands close to him.

"Liam, come on." I pat his arm, getting him to come away.

"Shane, please stay with me." Una's cries drift away as she leaves with Shane.

"Dad, go with Shane."

Father nods and moves to leave, but the Gardaí that Liam grabbed stops him.

"No one leaves this room."

"This is our family." Liam's composure slips.

"This is a crime scene." The Gardaí moves toward Liam.

"Don't make me arrest you."

"Philips. Leave it." Brady steps in, but Philips is really new to this.

"No."

Una's shouting at the top of the room. They won't let her leave with Shane. I go to join her, but Connor is there, trying to calm her down.

"You will pay for this." Liam's threat is low, but we hear it.

"Turn around and put your hands behind your back." Philips removes the cuffs, but Liam doesn't move.

"I will have your job for this if you don't get him to step away from my son." Father is speaking to Brady, who pales and moves to Philips.

"They just lost family, Philips."

Philips isn't heeding him, and two more Gardaí arrive. Liam raises his hands.

"Fine." Liam turns around, and Philips places his hands in cuffs before patting him down. When he takes his hand out of Liam's pocket, he shows the officers my bag of cocaine.

"That's mine," I say immediately.

"It's mine," Liam barks.

"Possession with intent to sell. You could be looking at a long spell behind bars."

I have no idea what to do. Connor moves toward us, and he doesn't stop as he throws his weight against Philips, taking him to the ground. It's been a long time since I saw Connor fight. All his rage is released as four more Gardaí try to stop him, but he's tearing them down.

"Uncuff him." Father grabs Brady, who pales and uncuffs Liam. The bag of coke is kicked along the floor, and I scoop it up and empty it into a glass of champagne beside us before I join Connor.

I'm throwing punches. My knuckles aren't used to the abuse. Immediately, they crack and I don't stop until I'm pulled off a Gardaí. Connor is restrained too. He did a lot of damage. The Gardaí are rising, but each one has sustained injury.

The room is filling with more Gardaí, and Connor, Liam, and I are pulled to our feet. I'm looking for Finn, guilt churning in my stomach at having left him alone.

"Dad," I call and he moves in front of us. "I'm here with Finn. Don't worry." His words are filled with sorrow. But he gives me a nod.

I'm looking for Ciara but don't see her as we're removed from the room.

A Gardaí van is outside, and we climb in silently. Once the door is closed, I look at Connor. I won't question him in front of Liam, but the fact that he won't meet my eyes makes my theory that the shooter knew him seem more solid.

"It was stupid to attack them." Liam is facing Connor.

"We did it for you." Connor sits forward, but the strain of the handcuffs on his wrists has him sitting back.

"I was getting arrested anyway," Liam fires back.

"Yeah, but I got rid of the coke." I grin at Liam, but he doesn't look pleased.

"That should have never been there in the first place," he says, and I look away this time.

"Poor fucking Finn," I say, not caring about us getting arrested. The charges would be assault, but it was better than Liam going down for possession and intent to distribute. Which was bullshit. There were only a few lines in the bag.

"This will destroy him," I add.

"He will survive."

I look at Liam. "Just once, try not to be so fucking cold."

"You're reckless and emotional. I'm only saying the truth."

"Are you ready for a road trip, boys?" Philips opens the back door. A black eye is already blossoming.

Connor growls at him.

He sneers. "Hold tight, boys, the road is pretty bumpy."

"Motherfucker." I slide off the bench and hit the ground hard. I can't even protect myself from the fall, as my hands are cuffed. When the van finally stops, we're all on the floor.

"I'm going to kill him." I glance at Connor as he tries to sit up. The doors swing open, and Philips smiles at us.

"Everyone okay back here?"

I grin. "Yep. Couldn't be better. How's the eye? Your woman won't like that, now will she?" I hadn't a clue if he was married, but the tightness around his eyes tells me I've hit my mark.

"I bet you're all about missionary. Maybe I need to visit her and really give it to her hard." I get dragged out first, and the concrete floor greets me. Blood fills my mouth, and I spit it out onto Philips's shoes. He dances back, but the damage is done.

"Or maybe your daughter would like my cock." I brace myself for a kick I don't receive. When he kneels down, his grin fills his face.

I spit again. "Sorry, I meant your son." The tightness around his eyes is back as he pulls me up. Two other Gardaí get Connor and Liam out of the van. They aren't manhandled like me.

"It will be a long time before you'll be out of here." Philips moves me to the exit door.

"But the moment I do, I'm going to slip into your son's room."

He doesn't bite but pushes me through the exit and into Navan Gardaí station. I've been booked so many times that I do everything before they ask. Once Philips leaves, I try to get the attention of a female Gardaí.

"Excuse me. I've been assaulted by one of your colleagues. Who do I complain to?"

She glances up at me and raises a brow.

"You can file it with Gardaí Philips. He will be interviewing you."

Fuck.

"But he's the one who assaulted me."

She lets out a heavy breath while pushing my finger into black ink before pressing it against a page.

"You like touching me?" I grin at her, and she releases my hand before looking up at whoever stands behind me.

"Take him to interview room twenty-one." Fingers tighten around my forearm as I'm escorted to the room. The corridor is tight as we pass another Gardaí who's walking in front of Art. I pause when our eyes clash.

Fucking Snitch.

"You okay, man?"

"Yeah, fuckers got me in on an overdue parking fine." I smirk. The Gardaí with Art doesn't comment on him calling them fuckers.

"You need any help?"

"Move along, Mr. O'Reagan." My own Gardaí isn't as patient, but I plant my feet firmly on the ground, refusing to move.

"You don't look like you're in a good position to help me," Art says back, and I want to hurt him.

"I'll be out soon. Don't worry about me. You need anything, just let me know."

The Gardaí have enough of our conversation, and I'm pushed along. I let the Gardaí move me. It's hard to look Art in the eye and not want to hurt him.

I'm left in the interrogation room alone. I want to know how Shane and Finn are. Jesus, Ciara must be terrified. I can't let these thoughts seep into me now. I need a clear head.

The door opens and Philips arrives in with a file. He takes a seat and points at the chair across from him.

"Sit down, Mr. O'Reagan."

I just want this to end.

He's shuffling fucking papers, spreading them out across the table like I'm not here. I want to sit still and not allow him to see my impatience, but I need to get back to my family. I slam my hand down on a piece he's reading. Philips looks up at me and grins. His dark eyes hold a smile. The bruising around his eye is expanding.

"Are you in a rush?" His fingers are perfectly manicured. He's a pencil pusher. I wonder what took him out of the field.

"Nope. Just bored." I lean back in the chair and fold my arms across my chest.

"You assaulted five officers. How do you plead?"

"Not guilty and I don't want to talk to you anymore since you assaulted me. I'll wait for my lawyer."

His lips form a straight line, and he sits back.

"I'm going to be honest with you, Darragh. Can I call you Darragh?"

"Go for it, Philips."

He joins his hands on the table, a move I've seen before. It's making him look relaxed in his delivery of what must be very bad news for me.

"Liam will be released since he didn't assault anyone. The possession charge won't stick since the drugs are missing." He's smiling and I want to smile too, because for me, that's good news. He can get me a lawyer and check on our family.

"Connor, on the other hand, has been released, which is hard to wrap my head around. I can't seem to get answers of why he hasn't been charged with assault."

I don't speak. I have no clue why Connor has been released. He did the most damage. But I don't feel comfort at the idea of him leaving. Especially if he had anything to do with this.

"So Connor knows people, or he's just lucky. But you... You're not so lucky. The five accounts of assault rest on your shoulders."

I stay quiet.

"You see, your family has left you to take the fall."

I glance away, not biting, but the seed of doubt with Connor has already been planted and is growing rapidly.

"Even your friends have betrayed you." I glance at Philips now.

"What do you want?" Everyone wants something. He isn't wasting his time going through this with me unless he wants me to do something.

"Nothing, Mr. O'Reagan. I'm simply informing you of what you're facing. Which is a very long time in prison." He gathers up the pages and puts them back into the file.

"You can't charge me with anything. Where is your evidence?"

He stands and smiles down at me. "Your sister-in-law is dead. Your brother is fighting for his life, and you will soon go to prison. How do you think your family will fare with all this?"

I keep my mouth shut.

"I don't think they'll do so well." He leans in close to me. "One by one, I will take down your family. Paying off the Gardaí will no longer happen."

I grin back. "Let me know how all that turns out for you."

He steps away, but I want to fucking hurt him.

"One thing I know. You won't be able to keep your promise about my family. But I'll keep mine about yours."

The tightness in his shoulders gives me satisfaction as he leaves the interview room.

CHAPTER TWENTY

CIARA

"**D**RINK THIS." MR. O'REAGAN hands me a glass of brown liquid. It's so cold in the hall that someone has placed a jacket around my shoulders. I can't even remember who.

"Thank you." I take the glass.

Mr. O'Reagan sits beside me. "You saw what happened?" His voice is low as he leans into me.

I meet his eye and nod. My bottom lip trembles, so I take a deep drink of whiskey. "They just shot her."

It was chaotic. We were moving while trying to stay together, and I looked up to see a man pointing a gun in our direction. I froze. I hadn't been able to run or scream like some of the others.

The shooter had hesitated and then pulled the trigger. The bang resounds in my head, and I close my eyes.

"He didn't care." I remember how he reloaded the gun. The red cartridge he'd emptied hit the floor. After all that, all I saw was blood.

"I tried to stop the bleeding." I speak into my glass before finishing it off.

"Did he say anything?"

My shoulders hunch forward. The Gardaí asked me the same questions. I wish I had something to help them. "I'm sorry, Mr. O'Reagan. But that's all I saw."

He pats me gently on the back. My eyes wander to the area still soaked in blood. Siobhan had been removed. Oh God, poor Finn. He was allowed to leave the room with her.

I want to ask about Darragh and Shane, but I don't. No one is allowed to leave the room, so no information is getting in or out. Ava and Una huddle together at a table across from me, both of them still crying.

"Una," I say more to myself.

When the gunman raised his gun, he had been pointing it at Una, but Siobhan moved in front of her and got in the way of the bullet. I saw the slight hesitation in the shooter's stance, but then he'd pulled the trigger anyway.

"It's nothing," I say now.

"No, tell me." Mr. O'Reagan leans in again.

"It's just, the shooter pointed the gun at Una, but Siobhan got in the way. He hesitated like he wasn't sure. But he shot her anyway. I'm sorry. I don't think that makes any difference."

"Maybe it does."

Mr. O'Reagan rises as the door opens, and Liam steps into the room. I'm trying to see if anyone trails behind him, but he's alone. Liam scans the crowd, and his eyes land on his father. He's walking towards u and I stand.

"How's Darragh?" I ask.

Mr. O'Reagan looks at me, but I don't let Liam's gaze go.

"He will be fine, Ciara. He's still being questioned."

Liam walks away and his father follows. I sit back down. Una follows them. "How is he?"

"I don't know. I came straight here."

"Why? He's alone and hurt." Her tears fall faster now. Her hands tighten into fists.

"Go be with Ava," Liam tells her, but she stamps her foot.

"No!" Her voice carries across the room. "You can leave. Go and find out what's happening with him."

Liam is aware that everyone is watching. His eyes flicker across the room quickly before they settle back on Una. This time, I can't hear what's being said. But after some words, Una turns on her heel and returns to Ava.

The Gardaí are still gathering bullets and evidence from around the room. No one is watching the door. I stand and shiver out of the jacket. No one seems to notice me as I move along the wall. My heart pounds when I reach the door. Sweat gathers on my neck and palms quickly.

The doorknob is slick in my hand, but the click sounds like freedom.

The hall is empty as I make it outside. Two Gardaí are outside, but they look at me and say nothing. They must assume I've been let go.

I take out my phone and ring a taxi and ask for them to collect me at Dun na Ri Park. It's only ten minutes from here.

"What are you doing?" I don't stop walking as Liam falls into step beside me.

"I don't know. I just know I can't stay in that room another minute longer."

Liam's fingers touch my bare skin. It's brief, but it makes me stop. "You can't help him right now, Ciara."

"Maybe I just want to go home and wash all this blood off." We stare at each other until Liam finally nods.

"Let me get my car. I'll drop you home. You're better off waiting here and not drawing any more attention to yourself."

Once Liam leaves, I wrap my arms around myself and stay on the side of the road that leads to the gates.

Liam's Bentley rolls down the drive at such a slow pace, like he doesn't have a care in the world. The car slows down beside me, and I get in.

"Are you okay?" I ask him once I've strapped myself in.

He hesitates in answering. "Yes."

He doesn't ask me if I'm okay. "I'm not okay," I say as I watch the green fields and trees pass us.

"I've watched people die. But it was for drugs or money. Watching someone in their wedding dress being shot is unthinkable. And for what? It was meant to be the happiest day of her life." I laugh now. "It was the happiest day of my life." I can't seem to cry anymore. "Why did someone do that?" I face Liam.

"I don't know." His answer is clipped, and it's the first time I've heard emotion in his words.

"You don't know why someone would hurt your family, or you don't know who did it?"

His eyes slide toward me. "I don't know."

His answer has me sitting back. We pull up into Kingscourt, and the thought of being alone causes my heart to beat rapidly.

"I don't want to be alone," I tell the window as tears blur my vision.

"Unfortunately, I don't have time to sit around and babysit."

My tears dry up quickly, and I get out of Liam's car. I don't have the door closed before he pulls away.

Taking the steps two at a time, I race to my door. My keys jangle in the door from trembling fingers. It takes me several attempts before I get it open. I spill onto the floor, unable to contain the horror of the day.

I wait for the onslaught of tears that seem to rise through my body, but they don't come. Peaches weaves through my arms as I try to hold myself up. I kick out my foot, and the door shuts behind me. The purr of peaches is what I focus on as my stomach roils and reels.

I dig into my bag and remove my phone and dial Darragh's number. Pushing myself up, I lean against the wall as his phone just continues to ring and goes to an automated voicemail.

"Hi," I say. "It's me. Are you okay?" Peaches makes her way onto my lap, and I stare at the ceiling as I speak into the phone. "I'm not. I'm at home now. Call me when you can."

I hang up and sit for a while, trying not to picture Siobhan with a hole in her stomach.

My stomach lifts again, and I rush to my bathroom just in time before I empty the contents of my belly into the toilet. I have to hold on to the toilet bowl as I rise. I don't know the girl I meet in the mirror. There's blood on her chest and neck. My hands have their own coat of blood on them.

Blood that gushed through my fingers as I pressed down on Siobhan's wound.

The blue dress slips to the floor, and I step out of my shoes before shedding my underwear.

No matter how many times I seem to wash my body, more blood twirls down the drain. I close my eyes as I picture his arm hanging over a black sack. That was the first thing I saw. The needle he had used to inject himself with still hung out of his arm. Each step I took further down the alleyway revealed a bit more of my dad. His eyes were still open, devoid of life.

The worst part was, I hadn't tried to perform CPR on him. I sank to the ground across from him and just stared. I didn't want him to live, but seeing his death did something to me. Maybe knowing I was kind of happy he was dead made me feel like such a bad person.

Drops of water make a path down the shower doors. My wriggly fingers touch the moisture as I follow it down and onto the shower tray. I meet it at the bottom as I let the water pour over my head. I sit there until the hot water turns cold and goose bumps coat my body.

I finally get out and wrap myself in a large towel. I turn on the TV and leave it on a random station, as right now I just want the noise. It has someone being interviewed about climate change. I leave that station on and get Peaches some fresh food before returning to my room and getting dressed into trousers and a top.

The buzzer rings and I can't get to it quick enough. It could be Darragh. Maybe he got out.

"Hello?"

"Ciara Michaels." The formal voice has me hesitating. "I'm Gardaí Philips and have a few more questions to ask."

I exhale loudly. "I've answered all your questions."

"This will just take a moment."

I buzz him in. I did leave the hotel when I shouldn't have, so maybe answering his stupid questions will make him leave me alone.

Philips is waiting at the door when I open it. "Miss Michaels, this won't take long." He looks over my shoulder, and I step aside and let him in.

I mute the TV.

"I thought there was a crowd in here."

Folding my arms across my chest, I sit down on my couch.

Philips sits across from me. "You were allowed to leave Cabra Castle?" he asks and I just nod.

"I'm here on a different matter, Miss Michaels. Recently, you were involved in the assault on two men." His words are clear and said with a hidden smirk.

"Yes. But all charges were dropped."

He nods and gives a sharp smile. "I know. The funny part is, I couldn't find the men who had originally pressed charges against you."

I shrug, but my heart starts to pound. "Maybe you need to brush up on your detective skills."

"Hmm." His focus is drawn to Peaches as she saunters into the room and over to me.

"This isn't your first assault case."

"I'm tired and I've just been through a very dramatic day, so really, what is this about?" I rub Peaches.

"What's your involvement with the O'Reagans, besides dating Darragh O'Reagan?"

News travels fast.

"I work for Liam," I answer.

"Cleaning rooms, I believe." Philips doesn't even blink. His brown hair is cut close to his head, like someone you'd see in the army.

"Yes."

"You have no idea what happened to the men who claimed you assaulted them?"

"No."

He nods now.

"Is that all?" I want him out of my home.

"For now."

I can't wait to close the door on him. He has one foot out when he stops and turns back to me.

"I'm not sure if you're very good at playing dumb or if you really have no idea what you got involved in, but if you don't want to end up like Siobhan, I'd advise you to get away from the O'Reagans."

I don't answer him, and he finally leaves. I don't want to think about what he just said, but now it's all I can think about. When I got the call to say the charges were dropped, I assumed Liam had shown them the footage or sent it to the Gardaí station. What if they hurt those men? Killed them? I feel no remorse and that means I don't have a good moral compass to be the judge of this situation.

Picking up my phone, I consider ringing Liam and asking him. Immediately, I change my mind. Now isn't the time. I'm not sure if there ever would be a good time, but now isn't it. Instead, I ring Darragh again. Nothing will have changed, but I just need to make sure. It goes straight to voicemail.

"Hi. It's me again. Hope you're okay. Ring me when you can."

I hang up and sit back down on the couch. I need to do something. Sitting here and ruminating isn't going to help me. After grabbing a pair of runners and my purse, I leave the apartment and ring a taxi.

CHAPTER TWENTY-ONE

DARRAGH

I'VE BEEN LEFT IN this fucking room for the last few hours. No one has come to check on me. When the door finally opens, it's my solicitor, Eric. "About time," I say.

He sits down across from me. "You're looking at five accounts of assault—"

I wave him off. "Eric, we don't pay you for a recap. Just make this all go away," I tell him.

"I'm trying." His eyes shift around the room, looking for cameras.

The door opens again, and Philips steps in. "Ah, your solicitor finally arrived. We can conduct the interview now."

Eric gets up and sits beside me. "My client won't be answering any questions."

"You don't even know what I'm going to ask. There's no need for such hostility."

"What is my client being charged with?" Eric asks.

"Assault, for now." Philips glances at me before refocusing on Eric.

"And the witnesses?" Eric asks.

Philips leans back in the chair and spreads his hands. "Come on, Eric. I have a room filled with four hundred people. Also, four other Gardaí who were assaulted."

I go to speak, but Eric holds his hand up. "I can tell you now those four hundred people saw the O'Reagans assaulted and intimidated just after the death and shooting of two family members. You used the chaos to assault my client."

Philip's jaw clenches as Eric shuffles some pages and stops on an A4 that has four names.

"Gardaí Brady, Gardaí O'Rourke, Gardaí O'Neill and Gardaí Curran have all dropped assault charges against my clients. So yours just looks false, and frankly, even vindictive."

I want to pat Eric on the back for a job very well done, but I sit still as I watch Philips's case crumble in his hands.

Eric rummages through more paperwork before taking out four sheets. "These are their signed declarations."

Philips doesn't even look down at them. "How can you sleep at night knowing you work for criminals?"

"Very well and on Egyptian cotton," I answer, just to piss Philips off, but he's focusing on Eric.

"When was all this done?"

"When you were seen going through my client's phone and leaving the station. You know it's a criminal offense to touch his property."

"His phone was ringing. I simply answered."

"Who was it?" I ask. I want to know if there was any word on Shane.

Philips smile is sly. "Ciara. She was very upset. So I paid her a little visit."

Eric clamps down on my forearm as I move toward Philips. "He wants a reaction, and right now you're in the clear," Eric informs me.

"Her cat liked me."

I reach across the table and grab both his arms.

"If you do this, Darragh, I can't make it go away." Eric hasn't let me go as he pleads for me to stop. "We are being watched, and there are cameras in the room."

"She was just out of the shower when I arrived." Philips's grin is wide.

I want to ram my fist down his throat, but I hear Eric's rational words and release Philips.

"Can I go now?" I ask.

"Let me go and get your paperwork written up." Philips leaves and I stand before I punch something.

"He's trying to get a reaction out of you."

"Well, it's fucking working. I want out of here now, Eric."

Eric gathers his papers.

"Anytime today would be fucking nice."

He moves faster, and I'm glad to be left alone.

***

I light up a fag the moment I'm out. "Did you bail Connor out?" I ask Eric as we leave the station. It's dark outside. It's close to three in the morning now.

"No. Just Liam. I have no idea who bailed him out." Eric walks to his car.

"Any word on Shane?"

"Sorry, Darragh, but I haven't heard from anyone."

I nod as he climbs into his car. I leave the station and walk through Navan. I get out my phone and dial Liam.

"I'm only out now," I tell him the moment he answers.

"Where are you?"

"Just making my way up to the hospital."

"You won't get in. I'll pick you up in five minutes."

"Is he awake?" I ask, feeling frustrated.

"No." Liam hangs up.

I keep walking. I'm walking down the street when his Bentley comes into view. I throw my fag on the ground before I get in.

"Eric sorted it for now, but I don't think Philips is going to let this rest. I have a bad feeling about the guy."

"Right now, we need to focus on Finn."

I rub my face. "How is he?"

"I don't know. I've been helping Eric get you out and also trying to find out how Shane is. He's stable, but he hasn't woken up yet."

"Jesus Christ. Any idea who did this?" I'm so tired. I can barely think straight.

"Not yet. But Ciara said the gunman was aiming at Una, and Siobhan stepped in the way."

"Did Ciara tell you that?" She was that close? My weariness feels like it's seeping into my bones.

"She told Father." Liam drives home.

I don't want to go in. I don't want to look at Finn and what this is doing to him.

"It tells me that the target was Shane and Una, so we need to figure out who Shane has pissed off."

I'm nodding at Liam. He's right.

Every light seems to be on in the house, or maybe that's the fear talking. I was hoping everyone would be asleep. Once I'm out of Liam's car, I spark up and take out my phone.

"You have no new voice messages." I opt in to listen to old ones, and Ciara's voice has me closing my eyes briefly. So Philips had listened to my voice messages.

I don't want to ring her at three in the morning, so I just text.

I'm home now. I hope you're okay. I'll ring you tomorrow.

"Are you coming in?" I hadn't realized Liam was waiting.

"Yeah, I'm just going to finish this." I show him my smoke before inhaling a deep drag.

"I'll be in the library if you need me."

I nod at Liam and he leaves. I light another cigarette up the moment I finish the first one. I'm trying to put off going in. Throwing half a fag on the ground, I finally head inside.

I check the kitchen before heading up stairs. Finn's room is empty, but the lights are on. He was here. His suit is laid out neatly on the bed, his wedding band sitting beside his outfit. Fear has me moving through the house quicker. Liam is in the library, as he said he would be.

"Do you know where he is?" I ask.

"He's in your room."

I nod and leave, not rushing to my room. Why my room? I open the door and have to turn on the lights. Finn's sitting on the ground, a nearly empty bottle of JD dangling from his fingers. His eyes are red and puffy, and when he looks up at me, he squints before drinking from the bottle. I have no clue what to do, so I sit down beside him and light up a fag. He doesn't take the one I offer him.

"I couldn't find drink anywhere. I knew if anyone had some, it was you." Finn's words are sober for a man who has drank nearly an entire bottle of JD.

"Yeah, you never know when you'll need a drink," I say.

"Do you remember the first day we met her?" Finn's smiling.

"Yeah." It's vague, as I was high, but I remember it was at her father's wake.

"Straight away, she captured me." Finn's brows furrow, and he bites his lip before drinking from the bottle. "I wish I could talk to her one more time. You know?" His eyes shimmer as he looks at me.

"I'm sorry, man."

"How beautiful did she look?" His smile wavers.

"She was beautiful."

The cigarette is burning away in my hand. Ashes fall onto the floor, and I brush them away before getting up and putting the fag out in the ashtray on my bedside table. Sitting back down, silence encases us for a moment before Finn speaks.

"I should have never left her side."

"You know that shit will do you no good."

He laughs. "She fucking died on her wedding day." Finn stands and his words grow in sound and power. "Because of fucking me." He hits the bottle against his chest. "I should have left her alone that first day, and she would still be here."

I stand up too. "You don't know that."

"Of course I do!" he roars, causing veins to bulge in his neck. "She was doomed from the moment she met me." Tears trickle down his face.

"This isn't your fault." I'm not good at this. I wish I could be anywhere else. Cleaning toilets in the hotel would be more desirable than watching my brother fall apart.

"I pulled that trigger the moment I fell in love with her." The bottle sails from his hand and smashes against my wall.

I don't move. I wait until he seems calmer. I approach him and take his face in my hands forcing him to look at me. "The best thing you can focus on right now is finding the bastard who killed her and shot our brother."

Finn pulls away from me roughly. "I'm not like you. I don't want revenge. I just want my wife back. But you couldn't possibly understand that."

"Look, you're grieving…"

Finn takes a step toward me. It's frightening what loss can do. I've never seen him look so wild or out of control. Not even when our mother died.

"This isn't grief. It's guilt. I let my guard down with our family, and it cost me my wife." His fist hits his chest as he dances on the spot with anger. "She didn't deserve this." He goes still as his eyes shimmer again and his shoulders fall forward. "She didn't deserve this."

I reach for him, and he doesn't stop me as I pull him into a hug.

"She didn't deserve this," he says again as he starts to cry.

The door opens, and Father walks in. I've never been so happy to see him in my life. He looks like a wreck, as I'm sure we all do.

"How are you, son?"

I step away from Finn so he can talk to him.

"Fine." Finn speaks while looking away and wiping his eyes.

Father looks at me and I shake my head. He sits down on my bed, and I stay standing, not sure if I should leave or stay.

"I remember the day your mother died. I felt like a piece of me died too."

Finn is facing the wall, staring at the broken bottle on the ground. His shoulders shake from silent tears.

"And it did. A piece of me is gone, and I have never gotten it back."

I glance at Father. This isn't helping. Finn turns around and wipes his face.

"I know how wide and empty it is, Finn."

"Does it get easier?" Finn's words are filled with hope and despair, and I want Father to say the right thing this time. Tell him time heals all wounds, and that it will get easier. That he'll find love again.

"Never. Some days it feels even harder."

I sit down at the end of the bed, facing away from both of them, and light up a fag.

"But you learn to live with it. You will live again, but she will always be missing."

I glance at Finn as he cries into his hands. Father stands and places a hand on each of his shoulders. He doesn't pull him into a hug but pats him twice before leaving the room, leaving me with a bigger fucking mess.

"He's wrong," I start.

Finn runs his hands down his face. A spark in his eyes surprises me, and he takes my box of fags and the lighter off my bed. He lights it up and inhales deeply.

"No, he's right. I don't ever want to forget her. I'm also sick of being told that time heals everything. I don't want to heal."

We sit in silence and smoke our fags. The bed dips as Finn rises. "I'm going to try and sleep." He puts out the fag. "I'll clean up the bottle tomorrow. Sorry about that."

"I got it. Don't even worry about it."

There's that awkward moment where I don't want to hug him in case he breaks down again. As I pass him, I touch his back and he nods.

"See you in the morning," he says.

"Yeah, sleep well," I say as I extinguish the fag. Once he's gone, I grab my bin and start to pick up the shards of glass. I don't feel much like sleeping. Ciara has left me a message on my phone.

I'm still awake if you want to ring.

The message was from an hour ago.

Are you still awake?

Her response is immediate. **Yes**

I check on Finn, who seems to be asleep, before I get my car keys and make my way to the library. Father and Liam are still sitting up, both having a drink.

"Finn's asleep. I'm going to go check on Ciara."

"You did good today, Darragh." Father's words have me standing a little straighter. His praise isn't something I'm used to.

Nodding at him, I leave the room.

***

"Can you open the door?" I ask the moment Ciara picks up the phone.

The door lock clicks, and I push it in and climb the stairs to her apartment. She's standing at the door, and her oversized T-shirt and black tracksuit bottoms seem to consume her. She looks tiny and fragile. She's left her blonde hair down, hiding some of her face.

I reach her and pause at the door before pulling her into a hug. Her body shakes in my arms as she starts to cry. My fingers find their way into her hair, and I tuck her closer to me. Her trembles subside and she peeks up.

"You don't have to be here."

"Yes, I do," I say and step into the hall, closing the door behind me. I don't think about it. I just take her by the hand.

"Which room is your bedroom?"

She points to the door on the right. Her place is nice. It's small but clean. Her bed is unmade, the quilts twisted like she's been tossing and turning all night. The lamp on her bedside table is on, and it casts some light into the room.

"Into bed," I say and kick off my boots. She follows my movements as I pull my T-shirt over my head. She swallows.

"We're just going to sleep," I say.

Her wide blue eyes focus on my chest. I open my jeans and let them land on the floor. Ciara still hasn't moved, and I let her take me in as I stand in my boxers.

Her hand is warm as I slip mine into hers, but she pulls away and takes a step back. I'm surprised when she pulls her T-shirt over her head. Her blue bra is full, and I can feel my boxers tighten. When Ciara steps out of the tracksuit bottoms, I'm surprised at the girl who stands before me. She's perfect and sleeping beside her doesn't seem like such a good decision.

I'm considering the couch when she takes a step toward me and slips her hand back into mine. This time, she leads me to her bed and I follow. I lie down and Ciara pulls the blanket over me and lies down beside me. There are a few inches between us, both of us facing the ceiling.

"I think we need to be honest. Neither of us are going to sleep like this." I glance at Ciara, and she faces me now, the blanket tucked under her arms.

"You're right."

I'm surprised once again when Ciara pulls back the blanket and places herself on top of me. She's sitting up on me, and my boxers grow even tighter.

"I'm not complaining here, Ciara. But what are you doing?"

Her eyes seem to devour me, and I rest my hands on her hips. She shivers and closes her eyes briefly.

"I've wanted this for a long time now, and if what happened today has taught me anything, it's that life is too short." Ciara runs her hands up my chest, her face getting closer to mine.

"I've never been with anyone when I'm sober," I confess.

Ciara smiles. "So I'm your first."

I laugh. "That would be a bit of a stretch."

My hands leave her hips, and I grab her face. Her eyes grow wider as she looks at my lips. I move her closer, and she pushes against my chest, stopping my progression.

CHAPTER TWENTY-TWO

CIARA

I 'M STARING DOWN AT Darragh, and my heart pounds, threatening to come out of my chest. I'm not normally nervous, and this feels so right. I've played this moment out in my head more times than I care to admit, but having Darragh under me now and knowing how inexperienced I am is making me second-guess myself.

"I... haven't done this much," I say. My heart beats rapidly in my neck, and I'm tempted to touch it and cover it up, but I don't move.

"You don't have to do this." Darragh's words are said softly.

I nod. "I want to."

Closing my eyes briefly, I tell myself I'm not afraid. When I open my eyes, Darragh is waiting, and I answer with a kiss. Being on top of him makes me feel powerful. His body is sculpted and perfect. I push against him, and he groans into my mouth. I deepen the kiss, and a panic takes over me. I want this so badly.

Our kisses grow frantic, and Darragh flips me so I'm on my back. I bite his lip, and he pulls back but grins before kissing me again. Being under him has an entirely different feel. I'm small and desirable. I'm his.

His warm mouth brushes kisses along my throat, his teeth grazing the skin. The pain and pleasure have me pushing against him. I manage to shimmy out from under him, and he grabs me around the waist, but I push his hands away and kneel up. My chest rises and falls as his hungry eyes focus on my breasts.

Reaching back, I remove my bra and let my breasts hang free. I hiss as his mouth covers my nipples. His bites have me digging my nails into his back. Darragh moves back up my neck, and when his lips brush mine, he keeps his eyes open. There's something so personal about watching each other. My hand finds his erection, which grows as my fingers slide over the head of it.

Releasing his cock, I turn away from him and arch my back, cocking my backside in the air. Darragh's large hands grip and squeeze my ass, and pain radiates up my back. Looking at him over my shoulder, I can't wait any longer.

Holding myself up with one arm, I reach back and take his cock, directing it to my opening. He doesn't need any more encouragement. Darragh fills me, and at first, I feel like I'm stretched too far. He eases back out and slowly reenters. Burying my head in the quilt, I groan into my sheets.

"Faster," I plead.

His strong body pulses and pushes against my ass. He grips my hips as he pumps faster and harder.

"Faster." My shouts and groans have his flesh slapping against mine until I release all over his cock.

Darragh trembles behind me as he empties himself, his movements slowing down to a stop. He gives a final two thrusts before pulling out of me. I lie back down, and Darragh flops beside me.

"That was so fucking good."

I'm smiling at his words. "At least you'll remember it," I say, closing my eyes. I'm ready to go to sleep.

"It's not possible to forget you, Ciara."

I open one eye and smile up at him.

"I'm going for a fag." Darragh gets out of the bed and pulls his boxers back up.

"Be careful of Peaches," I say, half-asleep already. The quilts are pulled up on my body, the heat lulling me into a sleep. I've been afraid all night to close my eyes. Each time I do, all I see is Siobhan's empty eyes, the red soaking into the dress. If that didn't haunt me, it was my father's body. I sit up as Darragh arrives back into the room.

"I keep seeing her," I whisper to my fingers. The bed dips as Darragh climbs back in. "I keep seeing my dad too."

Darragh tips my head back so I'm looking at him. "It happens to me."

My lip quivers at his words.

"I allow each face to pass, and then that's it. Don't give them permission to stay." Darragh wipes away a tear.

We lie down and he pulls me into his chest. "I'll keep all the ghosts away, Ciara. You just sleep."

I believe him and allow myself to close my eyes. If anyone can take this away, I know it's Darragh.

***

"I have to go." Words are whispered close to my ear.

"Okay," I say, not wanting to wake up. A soft laugh has me becoming more alert. *Darragh.*

Opening my eyes, I stare up at him. "Morning. Well, is it morning?"

"It's more like dinnertime."

I rub my face and sit up, taking the blankets with me. "How did you sleep?"

"The best sleep ever." Darragh leans in and kisses me softly. "I'll be back later. I'm just going to go to the hospital and see how Shane is."

Guilt rises up. I hadn't even asked about Finn or Shane. "How's Finn?"

The moment I say it, I can see the pain in Darragh's eyes. "He lost someone he loved. Right now, it seems like he'll never be himself again. But with time, he'll be fine."

I take his hand in mine. "He has you, so he will be fine." I kiss Darragh's fingers.

"Can I do anything?" I ask when I look back up at his handsome face. My stomach tightens.

"Keep doing what you did last night, and I'm sure I'll be fine."

I laugh at his answer. "I can do that."

Darragh plants another kiss on my lips. "I better go."

I watch him get dressed, soaking in the perfection of Darragh O'Reagan.

Once he's dressed, he climbs back up and gives me one final kiss. "I'll ring you later."

"Yeah, let me know how Shane is."

"I will."

Once the door closes, I sink further under the quilt and can't stop the smile that coats my face.

DARRAGH

Shane has been moved to the Mater in Dublin. I grab a sandwich and coffee from a deli on the way up. Finn is with me, but he's refused food, and the heavy sunglasses on his face are to help with his hangover and grief.

"Father said Shane woke up last night." Finn stares out the window as he speaks.

"Yeah, I was talking to Liam this morning. So that's good news," I say and glance at Finn. He's still staring out the window.

"I went to your room last night. You weren't there."

Guilt churns away at my stomach. "I went for a walk," I tell him and start to slow down as we enter Dublin.

"All night?"

When I stop in traffic, I look at Finn and see my reflection in his glasses.

"Yeah," I lie and he faces forward.

***

Una is holding Shane's hand. Her back is hunched as I stare in through the large glass window. I want to give them time, but Finn pushes open the door and Una turns to him. The pain on her face is immediate.

Releasing Shane's hand, she walks to Finn and hugs him. I use the moment to slip into the room. Shane's eyes track my movements and I smile.

"You're alive," I say and regret my words straight away as Shane shifts his attention to Finn. "What are the doctors saying?" I try to cover up my previous statement as I sit down on the chair Una vacated.

"I'm lucky. The bullet tore clean through my shoulder. I'll be out soon."

"How are you feeling?" Finn has removed the sunglasses.

Una still keeps an arm around his waist like he might fall down. He looks like he could do with a bed beside Shane.

"Like I got shot," Shane says, and Finn's eyes crinkle at the sides.

"Anyone know who did this?" Shane asks mem and I shake my head.

"I think right now everyone is focusing on your recovery and... Finn's." I say his name low.

"The funeral is in two days. They're releasing her body." Una squeezes Finn's hand as his eyes shimmer.

"Why don't we go get a coffee?" Una smiles up at Finn. I'm so grateful when they leave the room.

"How bad is it?" Shane asks the minute they leave.

"Really fucking bad," I say and rub my face. I feel exhausted again. "Imagine losing Una." I shrug. The thoughts of Ciara being hurt is painful. But loving her, marrying her, and then losing her... I think I would be hell-bent on revenge.

"We need to find out who did this." Shane's jaw is clenched.

"We will, brother. Once we bury Siobhan, we will find out who did this." I'm not sure why I'm telling him this next part, but I feel he should know. "Ciara was standing beside Siobhan when she was shot."

"Is she okay?" Shane asks.

I grin at his false concern. "She will be. She doesn't believe Siobhan was the target."

Something like fear flickers across Shane's face. "What do you mean?"

"She said the gunman was aiming at Una, but Siobhan got in the way."

Shane's pulling himself up, pulling at his drip. I grab it before it falls over.

"Okay, calm down," I tell him before he hurts himself.

"Why am I only hearing this now?"

I sit back down. "Because you've only just woken, Shane. But it does make this look like revenge toward you."

Shane looks away, and my eyes are drawn to the black bands on his arm. I know what they mean, and maybe now one of those bands is coming back to bite him in the ass.

"So who did you piss off?" I grin when he looks at me to try to lighten the mood.

"The wrong kind of people apparently." Shane's face is pale, and I wonder if I should have left this alone until he recovers. "Liam and Father know, so they're on the case."

When Finn and Una return, the conversation is strained, and I decide it's best we leave. The awkwardness isn't helping anyone.

"I'll try to get home tomorrow," Shane tells us.

"No, you will not. You will wait until you're discharged." Una slaps a hand on her hip, and it's so great to watch Shane be schooled.

"Of course, if the doctor says it's fine."

I snort at his lie and he grins at me.

"You need a lift?" I ask Una.

She shakes her head. "I drove up, so I'll stay a few more hours." Una gives me a hug, and I hug her back.

The hug she gives Finn is longer, and I raise an eyebrow at Shane. He shakes his head at me, but I can see the ghost of a smile there.

The drive back feels quicker. "How's Ciara?" Finn asks.

"She's good."

"Is that where you went for a walk last night?" Finn's voice has a touch of humor in it, so I answer honestly.

"Yeah, I stayed the night," I say and glance at Finn.

"You get it on?" I can't see Finn's eyes, as he has the sunglasses back on, but he isn't frowning so I grin.

"I don't kiss and tell."

"I'll take that as a yes." When I glance at him again, he's looking out the window.

"Yes," I say just for him, and when he looks at me, his lip tugs up slightly.

"I'm happy for you, man."

***

The morning of the funeral comes too quickly. Finn insists Siobhan be waked in her own home. The irony isn't lost on me as I stand out back looking out on the old cattle sheds.

"What are you doing out here?" Ciara comes over and links her arm with mine.

"I don't know if I ever told you, but me and Finn met Siobhan at her father's wake. In fact, she was standing right here when we first saw her." I think back to that day and how insensitive I was to her. But all I wanted was to close the deal for Father and get drunk or high afterward.

"No, I didn't know that."

I glance down at Ciara. "It feels like a lifetime ago. I didn't ever think I would stand where she stood, only it wouldn't be her father in the coffin but her."

Ciara squeezes my arm. "We never know when our time is up."

"I know that."

"Do you remember that day?" Finn's voice startles me, and this is a memory I don't want him to have. I nod. He's smiling.

"The moment I set eyes on her, I thought she was so beautiful. I just never thought I would be so lucky to marry her." Finn comes closer. "You were an asshole to her," he tells me, and the fire in his eyes has me holding his stare.

"I know," I say. Ciara seems to be clutching me tighter. "But I made you look good. Otherwise, she could have fallen for me if I was nice."

Finn smirks at my words. "I highly doubt it."

Ciara relaxes beside me.

"I was wondering where you went." Shane arrives, his arm still in a sling. It's a relief to see him up and walking.

"Just needed some fresh air," I say. And some alone time. Which is something I'm not going to get today.

"I'll just see if the ladies need a hand in the kitchen." I plant a kiss on Ciara's head as she leaves.

"She's too good for you." Finn speaks the moment she's gone. His anger isn't like him, but for now, I'll let him say what he wants.

"I know."

Shane squeezes Finn's shoulder. "All our women are too good for us."

When I light a smoke, Shane and Finn take one each.

"No one told me we were having a meeting."

I grin at Connor as he saunters over to us and throws his arm across Finn's shoulder. He's been avoiding me the last few days, but once Siobhan is laid to rest, he won't be able to avoid me any longer.

"A smoke?" I offer and he takes it too.

"I feel bad now. Think someone should tell Liam?" Shane says, and we all say no together.

"I'm glad you all feel that way." Liam materializes and walks toward us with his hands in his pockets. I offer him a smoke and he declines.

"We were messing," Shane says to Liam, who focuses on Finn.

"She has a beautiful home." Finn frowns but thanks Liam. There's that part of all of us that doesn't know what the hell to say. We're afraid to make it worse by saying the wrong thing.

"So what brought everyone out here?" Liam asks.

I notice how we're all standing in a circle, all smoking except for Liam.

"I came out here to have a moment alone," I tell Liam.

Connor smirks at me. "That looks like it turned out well."

"I came out here because this was the first place I saw Siobhan." Finn's looking at me, that same anger in his eyes. "It was her father's wake."

"I saw you from the kitchen and thought a smoke would be nice." Shane looks from me to Finn, picking up on his hostility.

"Ciara told me you were out here," Connor tells me.

I can imagine what she really said. She doesn't like Finn being mad at me, and I've told her how close me and Finn are to Connor. I nod at him and throw my fag on the ground.

"I came out because they're closing the coffin. It's time." Liam's words are like a bomb. We knew it was close, but for Finn, this is it. His final time to say goodbye to Siobhan.

CHAPTER TWENTY-THREE

DARRAGH

THE FUNERAL IS BEING held in Kells church, the same one they got married in only a few days ago.

We all carry Siobhan up the aisle. Finn and Liam take the lead, Connor and I are at the back, and Father and Shane are in the center. The walk feels so long. I can't imagine how Finn is feeling. The idea that this will end soon is the only thing that's getting me through the funeral.

Once we rest her coffin on the stand, we sit in the front row. I don't listen to the priest. I'm stuck thinking about our mother. I have no memory of her funeral or her wake. I have no idea what they buried her in or what prayers were said over her coffin. I wonder now if I was even present, and if I was, did I cry?

I look around me, wondering if all these people stood at my mother's grave. No matter how hard I try to imagine her funeral, I just can't. Bells ring and I look up as the priest moves behind Siobhan's coffin as the two hearse men push it down the aisle. We fall in behind them. Outside, a black carriage awaits her coffin, with two black horses ready to pull it.

They slide the coffin into the back of the hearse. The silence is eerie. The only disturbance is the church bells ringing.

Even the traffic seems to be at a standstill. I can see why now. Gardaí cars have stopped the traffic, allowing us the full use of the road. No doubt bought and paid for.

Ciara walks beside me as we follow the hearse to the graveyard. Her arm links with mine, and I twine our fingers together. No one speaks as we walk the fifteen minutes to the graveyard where Siobhan will be laid to rest.

When her coffin is lowered into the ground, Finn starts to cry, Connor steps forward, placing an arm around his shoulder.

"Raglan Road" is sung, with just a tin whistle accompanying it. I swallow down my own emotion as Finn clings to Connor. Liam, Father, and Shane stand firmly together.

Once the first shovel of clay is put on Siobhan's coffin, the crowd starts to leave and make their way back to Headfort Arms Hotel, where food awaits them. None of us are going. We can't risk our family being targeted again.

I spot Art, DJ, and Fitz in the crowd. DJ gives me a nod when our eyes collide. Today, I don't want to see them. But I nod back. They're a reminder of what I must face soon. Standing here with my family and Ciara reminds me that I'll sacrifice every one of them so I can stay here. I look away and step closer to my family. Una and Ava have joined us. Mary stands off to the left alone.

"I'll be a minute," I whisper to Ciara and release her hand. Mary looks up as I walk over to her. Her smile wobbles, and she pulls me into a hug.

"I'm so sorry, Darragh." Her words are low, even though the funeral is over and most people have left.

"Me too," I say and kiss her on the cheek. "Come over with us."

She shakes her head. "Stephen is taking me back to the house. We will prepare a meal for the family."

I nod and give her a final kiss on the cheek. "That sounds great," I say. "Mary." I stop her from leaving and step closer. "Was I at my mother's funeral?" I feel stupid asking.

Mary looks sad as she touches my face. "You were there but not present."

"Like I was drunk?" I question.

She frowns. "No. You were medicated. You weren't doing so well."

I nod now and Mary leaves.

I return to Ciara and we stand for a while longer before Dad tells us to make our way back to the house. I leave with Ciara, and the minute I'm in my car, I light a fag.

"That was fucking torture," I tell the roof.

She squeezes my leg. "The worst is over."

I look over at Ciara as I lean my head back on the headrest. "Thank you for being there."

She moves closer, her hand leaving my leg and touching my chest. "Of course I'm here. There's nowhere else I'd rather be than with you."

She's looking at me differently and I move closer. The kiss she plants on my lips is featherlight, and she lingers there. "I love you."

Her breath brushes my lips quickly. I lean out to look at her, but she's focused on my lips. Tilting her head back, I make her look at me.

"No one has ever said that to me before," I whisper. "I never really thought about how that would feel." My fingers brush her cheeks. "It feels good." I smile and she mirrors it. "It feels really good," I add before kissing her.

Shane and Una move past my car and get into Shane's.

"We better go." Ciara is still smiling. She's not angry that I didn't say it back, and it makes me want to say it to her. I've never told anyone I love them, apart from my mother.

Ciara leans out and puts on her seat belt. I do the same and start the car.

"I know you met my family at the wedding, but coming to our home is going to be a bit different." I try to say my words carefully without scaring the shit out of her.

"Okay." I can hear the smile in her voice.

"It's only family, so it's small and anything is liable to happen."

Ciara nods.

"I hope you're still smiling when you leave."

She laughs. "The idea of getting to see your home, and maybe your room, outweighs any uncomfortable thoughts I may have."

"My room?" I grin at her. That's one place I would make sure to show her. I cleaned it this morning to have it ready for her.

"Only if you want to." Her shy response has me reaching out and taking her hand.

"That's the only thing that has been keeping me going," I tell her honestly. "Picturing you naked on my bed, screaming out my name."

Ciara laughs while retracting her hand. "We will see."

I grin at her response. "Yeah, we will. You want to bet on it?" I ask her as we drive through Nobber. My stomach tightens as we get closer to home. I hope my family doesn't make an absolute ass out of me.

"I already owe you a grand, so all bets are off the table."

"When are you going to cough it up?" I glance at her.

She's grinning. "I suppose I could pay you with IOUs."

"You mean sexual favors? That sounds good to me."

Ciara's hand slips between my legs, and I nearly lose control of the wheel.

"That's not a good decision." I relax into her touch. "Or maybe it is." She moves her hand in a circular motion. "Should I pull over?"

Ciara removes her hand. "No. Keep driving."

I'm looking at her and taking quick peeks at the road. "Why are you stopping?" My erection wants her back.

"It was just a taste." She smiles at me sweetly.

"You're a tease."

"Maybe I am."

I rearrange myself as we come close to my house. The gates normally open with a clicker on our arrival, but Father had it disabled. The new gate man who is stationed outside the gate in a small booth peers out. Rolling down the window, I try to make his job easier for him.

"It's me. Darragh."

He hesitates.

Ciara sniggers beside me. "Maybe we have the wrong house."

The gates are open, and I salute the new guy as we move up the drive. Ciara is silent and I take a look at her. She's wide eyed, staring up at the house.

"Impressive, isn't it?" I say, looking at it through her eyes.

"It's like right out of a fairy tale."

I snort. "Or a horror movie."

Thankfully, Father didn't alter the garage doors, and they rise as I pull my car inside.

Once the car grows silent, I turn to Ciara. "Okay, we might need a safe word."

"For sex?" Her question is said so genuinely that I can't stop the laugh that bubbles from my lips.

"No, for my family. But a safe word in sex never hurt anyone."

Color blossoms in her cheeks. "What about peaches?"

"Your cat? What if you're just talking about your cat?"

She nods. "De De."

"De De?"

"Yes. De De. It's easy to remember."

I'm not exactly convinced, but I don't want to be late for the meal. "Fine, De De is our safe word. If you need to get out of the room or are really uncomfortable, just say De De."

Ciara leans in with a slow smile burning across her face. "We still need to think of one for the bedroom."

"You look so innocent," I say, holding her face, and she smiles wide now as I plant a kiss on her cheek.

"We better go in."

I'm nervous as we leave the safety of the garage. I want to hold Ciara's hand, but I also don't want to remind Finn how alone he is in the world right now. I find everyone except Liam in the dining room.

Una smiles up at me and Ciara as we enter and pats the seat beside her. I let Ciara slide in, and I sit next to her. Connor and Ava are across from Shane and Una, while Finn and an empty chair are across from me and Ciara. Father arrives and smiles at each of us. Liam follows behind and sits beside Finn.

"I love your dress," Una whispers to Ciara, but with the silence in the room, we all hear.

"Thank you. Yours is pretty too." Ciara sips water and looks around the table. My hand rests gently on her leg that keeps rocking. She's nervous and I don't blame her. This isn't your normal funeral.

Father rises with a glass in hand, and we all reach for the glasses that are placed in front of us.

"To Siobhan O'Reagan. She will always be remembered as one of us. We will live for her and remember her in happy times." Father takes a drink, and we all follow suit.

Finn looks up and nods at Father. It doesn't matter how Finn really feels once Father is around.; he will put on a show. And maybe that's not a bad thing to force him to do.

Shane stands now. "Siobhan was a lady, and I was happy to call her my sister-in-law."

We drink to his words. Good job it's just water, or we'd all be pissed. Una says nice words about Siobhan, as they were close. Ciara remarks on her beauty, and now it's my turn.

"Siobhan had great intuition. She hated me." That gets a snort out of Finn. "From what I knew of her, she was strong, honest, and loved my brother. To Siobhan."

We drink to that and Connor stands. "Siobhan had a great sense of humor and the patience of a saint, with our family as well."

A ghost of a smile crosses Finn's face. Ava says all the right things also, and Una's in tears across the table. I once again touch Ciara's leg that keeps rocking. I want to tell her this awkwardness is nearly over. The sad reality of it is that we didn't really know Siobhan. We didn't bother getting to know her. I glance at Ava, realizing I've never given her time either.

Liam stands now, with his glass in hand. "Siobhan may be gone to us, but for Finn, she will always be alive within his heart. I hope your memories of her are vivid. I hope her smell still lingers, and remember that one day you will join her. To Finn." Liam drinks, and tears fall silently into Finn's mouth as we drink to him.

When the food arrives, no one is hungry. The talk is so small that I want to scream De De at the top of my lungs. I excuse myself for a smoke and offer Ciara to come with me but she stays.

Outside, a soft rain has started to fall, but I don't mind getting wet. Sitting on the front steps of the house, I light up my fag and loosen my tie. The atmosphere in the room is choking, and I've wanted to drink so much, but now isn't the time. Now that the food is nearly over, maybe we can separate. No one wants to be in that room together.

"I didn't know that Liam was a poet." I grin as Connor sits down and takes a fag.

"Me neither. He had no idea what to say."

"None of us did."

"Maybe it would be nice if we did something together." I glance at Connor. He raises both eyebrows. "Me and you."

"With Ciara and Ava," I say and crush my fag under my shoe.

"Yeah, I can do that." I sit as Connor finishes his fag.

"Did you get to talk to Liam yet?"

"Yeah, yeah, we spoke at the burial," I say and stand, stuffing my hands into my pockets.

"Don't get all defensive. But tell him today." I nod, knowing Connor is right. I dragged it out long enough. The last thing the family needs is for me to get arrested.

"I will," I say and we head back in. Finn isn't at the table, and neither is Liam or Dad.

"Finn is tired," Una says when we enter.

"I'm going to get changed. You coming?" I ask Ciara and she stands. "Talk to you later."

"Be good," Connor calls after us.

Once we're out of the room, I twine my fingers with Ciara's. It feels weird for her to be here but really good too. Ciara looks all around her as we climb the stairs, and I'm forced to see this house through her eyes. The large winding mahogany stairs wraps around the walls before expanding onto a large landing. The oak floors under us are covered in a long red rug that runs the whole way across the landing. Paintings and mirrors that took three men to hang line the walls. Once I open my room door, Ciara returns her focus to me.

"This place is like a museum. It's amazing. I want a tour."

I remove my jacket. "We could start with a tour of my room," I say, kicking off my shoes. Ciara removes her shoes and moves toward my bed, where she sits cross-legged while taking in every detail of my room.

I pull off my shirt, and her attention snaps to me.

I smirk. "I can leave it off," I say.

She bites her lip. "I think I would like that very much." Her wide blue eyes and loose blonde hair make her look so innocent, yet her words aren't.

Stepping out of my trousers, I move to my chest of drawers.

"This is where I keep all my socks and boxers," I tell her and open a drawer.

"Over here is my mirror." I point before pulling off my socks. "That door leads to my bathroom, and that one to my closet."

"I'm impressed, Darragh. I really am." Ciara hides a laugh behind her hands.

"These are my curtains," I tell her, raising a brow while whipping them closed, and she giggles.

I drop my boxers and stand back up as I approach Ciara, who isn't giggling anymore. "And you're on my bed."

"Will I be punished?"

My erection grows as I crawl to her quickly. "Severely."

Her smile is back as she tugs me down onto my back. She straddles me as she pulls her dress over her head. The black number she's wearing is stunning on her.

"We have to be quick," I tell her between kisses.

"I can be quick," she says before biting my lip.

Ciara takes the lead, brushing her underwear aside and placing me inside her. Her body rocks against mine, and I'm tempted to move her under me, but watching her with her eyes closed as she moves rapidly against me has captured my focus. I let my fingers touch her clit, and her eyes snap open.

"That's so good," she says, and I move my fingers faster as she grinds into me harder.

My own release is so close. I want to grab her hips and drill her down on me, but my fingers work her clit until she's panting and moving faster and harder on my cock. We both release at the same time. Ciara crashes down on top of me, a slight coating of sweat on her face and body.

"You are so hot," I say.

She kisses my chest. "That was good."

We lie in silence for a while. Ciara randomly places kisses on my chest, and I can't stop touching her hair. Her smell is something I'm getting used to. Like when she climbs into my car and I smell it, it makes me happy. She makes me happy. I never thought I would find anyone like her.

"You make me happy," I say, and when she looks up at me, I kiss her softly on the lips.

"You make me happy too."

"I'm addicted to you."

Her laugh fills my room. "I'm not sure I like being your addiction." When she rolls back in, she kisses my shoulder.

"Fine. Fine. I'm using all the wrong words." My heart picks up speed. "I love you." I finally say what I want to say.

Ciara's eyes shimmer as she sits up. "Like for real?" Her lip pulls down like she might cry.

I sit up, my fingers touching her lips. "For real."

Her lips tug up into a smile, and tears fall from her eyes. "I love you too."

Taking her face in my hands, I kiss her. Salty tears flow into our kiss.

We lie back down, and I just hold Ciara. It's been such a long time since I've been this happy. I kiss her head again, and she shuffles in closer to me, her small warm body pressed against mine. I allow myself to close my eyes and just relax.

CHAPTER TWENTY-FOUR

DARRAGH

Later that night, I slip from the bed and leave Ciara sleeping. For a funeral, the day seemed perfect in one sense, but now I know I need to talk to Liam.

Connor, Shane, Ava, and Una still hang out in the dining room. They're all drinking, and I'm tempted to join them.

"Anyone see Finn?" I ask from the doorframe.

Una frowns now. "He still hasn't come out of his room."

"No one has checked on him?" My question is answered with lots of guilty faces.

"I will." Connor gets up and I'm grateful.

"Anyone see Liam?"

"The last time I spoke to him, he was in the library," Connor says.

I tap the doorframe and head for the library. Connor falls into step beside me.

"Are you going to have that talk?" he asks. We separate at the stairs.

"Yes, so you can stop pestering me about it." I grin as I head toward the library, but it soon leaves my face as I think of the complications of what I'm about to tell Liam. Also, for the first time, I don't want to go to him with a problem for him to fix. I want to help fix it.

Sticking my head in, I'm glad to see Liam alone. He's nursing a glass of brandy.

"How are you holding up?" I feel guilty kicking off with something like that, but launching into the real problem doesn't feel right.

"I'm grateful our family is still here, in one piece. For now anyway." Liam drinks from the glass, and I sit down across from him.

"Yeah, knowing Shane will be okay is a relief."

Liam is watching me. He knows me and I hate this.

"I hate doing this right now, Liam. I really mean that. But I've got myself into a pretty serious mess this time."

A ghost of a smile shadows Liam's face, but it's gone so quickly I wonder if I imagined it. "Don't keep me in suspense."

I grin at Liam. His attitude feels different. "I robbed two bank links with friends of mine. One of them got caught, and now they're all going to give my name up to get immunity."

"How long have you been sitting on this?"

"Not long. It just never felt like the right time. Two of the guys are decent and undecided. But I honestly don't think they will be a problem. It's Art and Mark who are going to sell me out." Art's betrayal still hurts.

Liam nods now. "What is it you want me to do?"

I shift in my seat. "I honestly don't have a clue. I just need you to help me."

"I tried, Darragh, remember? I cut you off and gave you a job. But you decided to rob a bank." Liam finishes his drink, and I look away from him. I've never felt like more of an idiot than I do right now.

"Look, forget it. I got it." I stand and fix my trousers.

"Tell me how you will fix it." Liam sits fully back, his legs crossed. The glass rests on his thigh.

"I'll talk to them, convince them not to do this."

"Okay, and if they agree, what happens then?" Liam asks, and I hold on to the back of the Queen Anne chair.

"We all go down," I say.

"Exactly. So you can't win this one."

"What, you think I should go down for this?" I've done so much bad shit and gotten away with it. I know I deserve punishment, but not now. Not when I'm trying to be better.

"Of course not." The bite in Liam's words surprises me. "We need to remove them."

This is what I expected to happen. My stomach twists and tightens and I nod. "I know. Art and Mark—"

Liam stops me. "All of them except one."

"No, Liam. Fitz and DJ are good people."

"You want to go to prison or not?"

I squeeze the chair in front of me, and Liam repeats his question.

"Of course not. But DJ and Fitz don't deserve to die."

"Only one of them. You decide."

I'm shaking my head. "What happens to the one who lives?" I ask.

Liam finishes the drink. "He'll go down for the robberies. Someone has to pay the price, Darragh."

"I can't do this," I finally say. Hurting Mark and Art is hard enough, but DJ and Fitz too?

"Fine. I'll pick for you." Liam gets up.

I'm holding up my hands. "No. Just give me more time. I'm sure I can talk them out of this."

"You don't seem to be listening. The only way out is with three dead bodies and one in prison."

"I said no." I take a step toward Liam. I'm not strong enough to go up against him, but hurting DJ and Fitz? I can't live with that.

"The moment you stepped into this room and told me, that was the moment the decision was already made for you. I'm being kind and giving you a choice of whom to save. For me, it's simple."

I need to warn them. I can't let this happen.

"So pick one, Darragh." Liam places the glass on the bar. "When I leave this room, the decision will no longer be yours."

Clenching my fists, I close my eyes. "Fitz. Don't hurt Fitz."

Liam doesn't face me but nods. "I'll take care of it," he says before leaving.

I don't have much time. I need to get DJ and Fitz out of this before it all goes south. I still have time to fix this.

I will fix this.

***

HEARTLESS

Title: Heartless
Series Number: Book Five
Blurb:
She once was my prisoner. Now I want her to be more - no matter the price.

Svetlana
Liam O'Reagan once my captor, was now my everything.
My savior.
But lately I was starting to realize he wasn't bulletproof.
And now I'm sending not just Liam out to war, but the O'Reagan family.
My uncle would have me back no matter what blood is spilt.
This war is for me, one I hope we win.

Liam
Svetlana, she's breathed life back into me and my heart is pumping again.
I'm starting to feel guilt over things I have done.
I know I'll have to come clean to my family about our mother's death.
But, as the attacks on Svetlana's life grow, my sole focus becomes keeping her safe.
And to do that, I have to go to war with her uncle.
But I'm not standing alone, I have my brothers at my side.
This is a war that will change the face of the Irish Mafia for all time.

CHAPTER ONE

SVETLANA

M Y BARE FEET SINK into the lush cream carpet as I pace inside my cage. Blood that dried in hours ago still coats my chest. My long brown skirt gathers and swishes around my ankles as I continue to pace the room.

I want out.

I need to get out.

My fists collide with the large white door.

"Open the door now." My shouts and bangs finally get someone's attention. I move back quickly as my uncle enters the room. His black mustache is brushed perfectly. The shine from his black hair carries all the way down into his beard.

"Svetlana, you have been causing more problems again." He wiggles his fingers at me as if I'm five again and I've smashed some expensive vase within the house. Folding my arms across my satin blouse draws my uncle's attention to my chest. Dropping my hands doesn't make him look away. That uncomfortable feeling I get around him as I continue to grow and develop skitters across my skin.

"Uncle please. I just want to get out of this room," I plead with him, while dropping my head slightly in obedience.

"Svetlana."

I peek up into his open arms, and I have no choice but to walk into them. I hide my revulsion behind the need to get out of here. "Andel is dead." His words are meant to make me feel remorseful. But I'm not. Frankly, I'm glad he's dead.

"He tried to rape me, uncle," I remind him as he strokes my hair. Andel had broken into my room and tried to force himself upon me. I was lucky that I slept with a gun under my pillow. I was also lucky that I knew how to use one.

"You could have shot him in the arm or called for help. Hmmm Svetlana, don't you think that's more reasonable than killing him?"

No I didn't. He deserved to die.

"If I called for help and IF someone heard me, I might be saved this time but what about the next?" I'm trying to break free from his hold to see if my words are penetrating his false concern but I'm pulled back into a hug. Uncle wears too much cologne, the smell burning my receptors. His hands move to my hips and I tell myself not to react.

"My men want your life."

Something inside me stills and then shivers. I try to look at my Uncle but he pulls me harder against his chest until it becomes harder to breathe.

"I hold you now and I don't think I can take your life, Svetlana." He sounds angry. The air is being cut off from my brain and I start to struggle against him as he tucks my head deeper into his chest. My lungs scream for air as his words rush my ears. "I loved you like you were my own daughter." My fists grip his leather jacket as I try to push him away from me.

"I love you so much." His words sound tortured, my hands turn into fists and I try with my final bit of energy to hit him on the back. Each slap gets weaker and I stop fighting him.

Air fills my burning lungs, and a cough rises from the back of my throat. My uncle releases me fully and I tumble to the floor unable to hold myself up. Air continues to slowly fill my lungs as I place my hand over my hammering heart. He's looking down at me and I hate the look of finality that's on his face.

"If you had been here-" A cough cuts off my words. "-I know I would have called for you." I finish and try to swallow the cough that tickles my throat. "You've always protected me and I'm so grateful for that." I crawl to his legs and hug them. Self-preservation has fully kicked in, overriding the scorch of embarrassment. When my uncle doesn't answer me I look up at him, still clinging to his legs. "I'm sorry uncle," I say and tears burn the back of my eyes as I watch the conflict play out across his features. I swallow my tears of hope as he kneels down making me release his legs. His eyes quickly travel to my chest that rises and falls rapidly. Hands that I don't recoil from, stroke my face. "When your father asked me to keep you safe, I was so honored." I nod now, trying to calm my frantic mind that's screaming at me, he just tried to kill me, but I choke down that thought.

"You have always been my pride and joy. The heir to your father's throne. The one I keep warm for you, Svetlana."

"I don't want it." I repeat the same words that I have used since I was a child. *I didn't want it.* I wanted none of it. I just wanted to be a normal college student. Not the daughter of the most notorious gangster in the Czech.

My uncle's hand leaves my cheek and trails down to my neck. "Your beauty stills my heart, Svetlana."

I drop my eyes and focus on the floor to try and stop the shiver that wants to overtake me at his touch. I had no religion, I was never baptized, but I believed in a god, he had kept my uncle's hands off me this whole time; I prayed once again that he would help me. "Thank you, Uncle," I whisper and he releases me before standing quickly. I'm rising with him; a panic in me has me standing and gripping his hands, in fear that I have lost his favor. I'm tempted to kiss him, just to stay alive, knowing that's what he has desired the moment I started to grow curves.

I can't.

"I will have to think about what happens next."

My heart gallops around in my chest. "Can I use the bathroom?" I ask as tears burn my eyes.

"Of course Svetlana. We aren't animals."

I force a shaky smile. "I know Uncle," I say.

He smiles while rolling his eyes. He widens his arm for me to leave the room and use the toilet. I'm across the hall in a few strides. I close the bathroom door behind me and clamp my hands across my mouth trying to keep in the screams that claw at my chest. My hand trembles as I lock the door and race across the bathroom to the window. I'm only two floors up. I could jump. I look out onto the green expanse of grass that's laid before me. Freedom. That's all I smell is freedom.

"Svetlana you okay?" My uncle's voice penetrates the door.

I try to calm myself by closing my eyes. "Yes uncle. Just a minute," I say and don't waste another second.

I jump out the window. I land on my bare feet, bent at the knees. I don't rejoice that nothing feels broken, instead I tear across the meadow, the grass soon grows longer brushing my shoulders and I start to slow down. I have no idea where I can go. I'm recognized everywhere. Cutting my long black hair won't hide my identity. My face is too recognizable amongst my father's people. Now my people.

"Svetlana!" My uncle's roar lights a fire under me and I'm pushing my body harder. I can hear the buzz of the jeeps. It sounds like they are coming from all sides but I don't stop to listen. I keep pushing aside the long grass until I burst out into a field that's recently had the grass burnt. I curse as three jeeps appear from all sides. Running back into the grass crosses my mind until my uncles voice carries across it. Whistles are blown alerting everyone that I've been found. Sinking to my knees I cover my head with my hands and wait for my uncle to arrive. In my cocoon of darkness I try to draw strength from my mother's voice. Her soft singing soothes my aching heart.

She had bought me a mirror on my tenth birthday. It covered a large portion of my wall. It was the same one from the movie *Snow White*. "Mirror, Mirror on the wall who is the fairest of them all?" My mother would question while standing behind me, her hands on my shoulders, the mirror would shimmer and an image would appear of just me.

My mother would clap her hands. "You are the fairest of them all." She would whisper in my ear.

But as I grew up the image still remained the same, the magic of it soon lost to me.

"Svetlana." My uncle's voice pulls me from the memory. His hands grip my forearms and I look up into his face.

"I had a flashback," I say quickly and his wrath eases off slightly. "I thought it was Andel banging on the door."

Confusion takes over my uncles features. "You are lying!" It's said with anger.

I shake my head. "No. No. I got confused. I thought he was going to hurt me." Tears fall from my eyes as I confess the lie. The tears are real. He was going to kill me if I didn't convince him not to. "I panicked. But when I heard your voice, I stopped running and sat here, waiting for you to save me." I'm clinging to him, pleading with him to believe me. He looks at the men who stand up in the opened roofed jeeps.

"She did stop and sit." One of them says and his face will be forever embedded in my memory. I will owe him my life, because his words save my life. My Uncle drags me to my feet, still angry but his anger isn't as lethal as I've seen it before. I have only ever tried to run once before when I was fourteen, and it was my last attempt until today. I learned that there were far worse things than dying. I had prayed for death but it never came. All I have ever done since then is fight to survive. Lie, manipulate, until I don't know who I am anymore.

He opens the passenger door and I climb in with my head down and my heart bouncing around in my chest. My uncle climbs in and all the jeeps roar to life as we return to my parents' house. I had always felt like a princess and this would be my kingdom. Now it was my prison. I had read the fairy tales about Sleeping Beauty. Once I had believed that maybe, just maybe, my Prince Charming would come and rescue me from my cruel uncle, but no one ever came. Glancing at my uncle I'm trying to gauge if I should speak or if my silence would fare better.

I opt for silence. I am too tired to try to sort through my emotions. Once we reach the house, the idea of being placed back in my room is welcoming.

My uncle grips my arm as we move to the front of the house. Two of his men step aside as we enter. We don't speak but fear lodges itself in my throat as we reach the second landing. I see Holic waiting for us. His bleach blond hair is animated against his dark skin, with a wide nose and crystal green eyes; he stands out from the rest of us and not just for his looks. He is my uncle's right-hand man. His thirty years on this earth, I'm sure, have been filled with blood, pain and torture. That's what he does. He tortures my uncle's enemies. I've only ever been to his room once, and that's when I'd prayed for death.

"Holic, you have weakened at your job." My uncle's words cause Holic's grin to slip. His eyes shoot to me and I take a step back.

"Svetlana did not learn her lesson the first time." I'm shaking my head at my Uncle's words. "She tried to run away again."

He didn't believe me when I told him I had run because of Andel. "No not from you Uncle, from Andel," I say.

Sharp blue eyes focus on me. "Ghosts don't chase people."

Falling to my knees is the only way I know I will survive. "I swear on my mother's grave that I wasn't running from you Uncle." Tears splash my joined hands as I beg for his mercy.

He's kneeling with me, covering my joined hands with his. His eyes roam my face and he brushes my cheek with a gentleness that has me believing it will be okay.

"I don't believe you." He rises and Holic grabs my arms. Fighting is useless but I kick and scream and spit and bite. I scream the whole way to Holic's room. I stare at the closed door and I can't breathe as my top is torn from my body. I scream and scream until time is lost and at moments I fear I am too.

***

"Jan." I search the house for my golden retriever. "Jan." I move through the house and enter rooms that I have access too. I slow down at Holic's door, my body frozen as screams that aren't happening now fill my ears. It has been weeks, and I'm still recovering. The marks might fade but the memory never will. "Jan," I whisper allowing myself to step away from the door. The clothes that brushed my back still hurt me but I didn't show any pain around my uncle.

A fake but automatic smile stretches across my face as my uncle walks towards me. His smile is full of love and adoration for me as if I was his daughter, and him a doting father, and not some twisted uncle.

"Have you seen Jan?" I ask sweetly still smiling.

"Svetlana you look like sunshine today."

I smile shyly. Well I hope it looks shy, I do practice every day. I grip my long yellow skirt and hold it out. "Thank you, Uncle."

He pats me on the hand. "Jan is down in the kitchen."

I widen my smile as I skip past him. The minute he passes me I drop the smile and make my way to the kitchen.

I stop at the door.

"You want some more." Holic's voice skitters across my damaged back, like nails digging into my wounds. My feet want me to step away but Jan is in there with that monster. Now I wonder if my uncle sent me to the kitchen with the knowledge that Holic was here.

"Jan," I call him and he comes to my side.

Holic's eyes rise from the bacon in his hand to me. Crystal blue eyes focus on me. "Svetlana. Nice to see you."

I swallow the growing saliva that pools in my mouth. I'm not stupid enough to anger him, but I'm not strong enough to speak. I nod and leave the kitchen with Jan.

"You know not to talk to strangers," I scold him the moment we enter my room. Rubbing him behind the ear I kick off my shoes and sink to the floor. "You're a good boy," I say while planting kisses on his head. Jan lays his head in my lap and I let my fingers run through his coat as I stare at the door. I'm wondering when will it open and who will it be. What was my fate here?

CHAPTER TWO

LIAM

COLD METAL RESTS IN my palm, I weight it from one hand to the other. A groan falls from the man's lips as he raises his head. Gregor shifts behind him, but I keep my focus on the man who's strapped to the chair in front of me. His panic is immediate when he realizes he's restrained. He's pulling and yanking but stops. Through his panic he can see me, his eyes moving from my black polished shoes that show him his fear, all the way up to my eyes.

He's shaking his head, pushing back further into the chair, his eyes snap to the nine inch nail in my hand before snapping back up to me.

"Mr. O'Reagan..."

Gregor moves behind him and Andrew cranes his neck back to get a better look at Gregor. Andrew's nostrils flair trying to force air into his lungs. Sweat coats his forehead as he turns back in his chair. Gregor keeps his arms folded over a wide chest, his hands are clenched, each knuckle is tattooed, one hand says the word love, the other hate.

"Andrew, I am sure you are aware of what you are doing here." I start the interrogation.

I'm nodding as Andrew starts shaking his head violently. The denial is useless, but expected.

"I swear Mr. O'Reagan I've done nothing wrong." He's watching me but also trying to see Gregor over his shoulder.

"But you have Andrew." I kneel down in front of him. He's new to the security team that we hired for Finn's wedding. In his twenties with too much to prove to the world, he was a perfect candidate. That was until our security team sold us out. Opening my hand, I allow him to see the nail. Sweat drips down the side of his face and he's shaking his head again.

"How many images have you seen of Jesus?" I ask him while placing the nail on the floor. He's focused on the nail as I unbutton my shirt sleeves.

"Focus Andrew," My words penetrate his foggy state.

Swallowing, his eyes skitter around the room. "Lots."

I roll up my left arm, making each fold equal to the next. "Not one image got it right. They all show Jesus nailed to a cross, by his feet and the palms of his hands." I roll up the other sleeve before picking the nail back up. Rising, Andrew follows my every move as I stand over his left hand. It's been strapped firmly to the chair, palm up. His fingers wriggle as I place the nail in the center of his palm.

"It is impossible for his body to be held up in such a way. If it was the case-" I glance at Gregor and nod. Andrew is trying to see what Gregor is doing when he should be focused on me.

"-the nail would have ripped through his palm." I move the nail to the wrist and the cold steel against his skin has him trying to yank his arm back. "-but placing the nail here, the bone would have supported his weight." Gregor reappears and hands me a hammer.

"Ah no. Mr. O'Reagan. I'll tell you anything you want." Saliva drips from his lips. The blood has stopped pumping to his hand as he yanks on it forcefully, trying to rip it from the strap with no avail.

"Yes you will Andrew." I put all my force behind it as I drive the nail through his wrist. Blood immediately pools from around the nail, the initial impact squirts some blood onto the floor. Andrew's roars fill the basement. I glance at Gregor again and nod. He leaves. Andrew doesn't notice as his body leans towards his damaged wrist, his screams bubbling out of his mouth.

Andrew's body shakes and trembles as his screams lessen. He can't look away from his mangled wrist. His sobs are accompanied by drool that's pooling around his chin.

"Please Mr. O'Reagan." His words this time are echoed around the space. Gregor hands me a pair of pliers.

"Removing the nail is more painful than inserting it." I say.

Andrew's head rests on his chest as he gulps for air through his cries. "I'll tell you anything."

I kneel again and he's looking at me. "You know what I want Andrew."

He swallows his pain, while shaking his head wildly. "The wedding." His words are quick; his wide eyes are filled with horror and pain. "Some girl gave us three grand each. She said take a piss for ten minutes and that was it." Andrew starts to cry, his wild eyes looking at his wrist again. Blood continued to seep out of it.

"What did she look like?"

"Tall, red curly hair. Freckles."

I stand and press on the pliers. "Anything else Andrew?"

"Please Mr. O'Reagan that's all I know." His tears fall from his eyes and I glance at Gregor. He was like a human lie detector.

"He's telling the truth." Gregor confirms, his deep voice rattles through his chest like he needs to cough.

Andrew hears his words and starts to cry with relief. His body slumps but his arm is held tight. "I'm telling the truth Mr. O' Reagan." The alarm in his voice rings loud.

I move to his wrist with the pliers in hand. "I know," I say.

He's shaking his head. "Don't touch it."

His hysteria has him trying to move his body away from me.

"When Gregor takes you to the emergency room, what will you tell them?"

"Whatever you want." He's watching his wrist.

"You can tell them you are bad at DIY," I say and tighten the pliers around the nail.

Andrew's pleads are screams across the space, and when I pull, the final roar turns into sobs and cries. The bloody nail I hold up to the light, the surface glistens with red. I walk to the small sink. The sounds of Gregor removing his restraints are drowned out as I turn on the water and wash the blood from the nail. Turning off the tap I pat it dry and move to the long wooden table that holds a single black case. Opening it, I place the nail back into its pocketed home.

When I close the case Gregor has left the basement through the small tunnel that will lead him outside the premises and to an awaiting car.

Blood splotches along the front of my shirt has me peeling it off. While moving into the private part of the basement, concrete gives way to an oak floor. A black dragon catches my eye as I pass a wall of mirrors, it flexes and stretches above the muscles on by back. The mirror catches the room as I open it and remove a clean white shirt. Once it's on, I clap my hands once and start to button up my shirt as my system comes to life.

"Good morning. What would you like me to do?"

"Good morning Wanda. Can you ring the front gate please?" I finish off buttoning up my shirt as the ringtone fills the room.

"Hello?"

"Stephen. I want you to keep me informed of who leaves and arrives at the gates," I say as I put on a black tie.

"Like every time Mr. O'Reagan?"

Removing a black waistcoat from the mannequin in front of me I put it on. "Yes Stephen. Has anyone left since last night?"

"Shane and Una left last night. Also so did Mary, but she came back this morning."

"Very good. I would like an update every time someone comes or goes. You can message it to me."

"Just you Mr. O'Reagan?"

"Yes, just me, Stephen."

"No problem." Stephen ends the call.

"Wanda," I say as I gather my car keys and wallet from the side table.

"Yes, Mr. O'Reagan."

"Lock down the basement," I say as I start to leave.

"Lock down commencing in one minute."

I make my way to the steps that lead out of the basement. "In fifty seconds."

The countdown continues as I leave the basement and enter a small hallway that arches off into the main one.

Entering the kitchen I pour myself a coffee. "Good morning Mary."

She gives me a tight smile, like she always does. Mary is as unsure of me as most people are. Yet, she would never try to have a conversation with me. Taking my coffee I join Finn at the table. He's sipping his own coffee while wearing sunglasses, they don't hide his disarray.

My phone vibrates and I remove it from my pocket.

Your father has left the premises. It's from Stephen. I push the phone back into my pocket. There really is only one person I'm concerned about leaving and that's Darragh. I can't let him leave the premises. If I do, he will go straight to his friends and try to save them. Which isn't possible.

"I don't know what to do," Finn speaks up.

I'm not entirely sure if he's looking at me or not. But being the only one at the table with him I feel obliged to answer him. "You should work. Keep your mind occupied."

"I don't want to work."

"There is a difference in knowing what to do and not knowing what to do. Right now you just don't want to do." I drink my coffee.

Finn whips off his sunglasses. His angry eyes remind me of Darragh. "You have no idea what I'm feeling." He's shaking his head at each word.

"I'm not pretending to understand," I say while standing.

"You're not even pretending to care." Finn's sharp words have me pausing.

"I do care," I say.

His snort is loud as he slaps his sunglasses back on and leaves the kitchen. Placing my cup near the sink I make my way to the garage and slip into my Bentley.

Starting the car Wanda comes to life. "Good morning, what do you need today?"

I reverse out of the garage, the door rising on my departure.

"When is my next appointment?" I ask driving down the pass.

"In fifteen minutes at *Cabra Castle*." Wanda's robotic voice fills my car.

I find comfort in her. "Thank you Wanda."

"You are welcome."

Slowing down, I approach Stephen. He's hanging out of the box that shelters him. "Mr. O'Reagan."

I pause at his window. "If Darragh tries to leave, I want you to keep him here until I get back."

He's nodding but his eyes tighten with how uncomfortable my request is making him. "I'm not very strong Mr. O'Reagan."

"I'm not asking you to restrain him. Just tell him there is a problem with the gate."

His smile is quick with relief. "I can do that."

"The barrier Stephen," I say as I face forward and he scurries to lift it so I can get out.

***

I enter Cabra Castle through the side door. "Shane," I say the moment I set eyes on him. I focus on his arm that's still in a sling. "I told you to rest."

"I know what you told me. It would look weak if I didn't show." He was right, but he looked even weaker with his arm slung up.

"You will be a reminder that we aren't safe. That they aren't safe." I remind him, that they were more important. They were our survival.

Shane groans as he removes his arm from the sling. He stuffs it under a cushion on a chair beside him before standing up straight. His arm hangs loosely at his side and the pain is too evident on his face.

"Try not to look like you're in pain," I say and turn knowing he will follow me. We move towards the back of the castle where a set of double doors come into view. A gold plaque has been placed on the door, the words *'Mens Club'* scrawled across it shines at us now like some kind of beacon.

Gregor is at the door. His large bulky form doesn't flinch as we arrive. I don't have to ask if he did his earlier job, because I know he did. He was one of my most loyal men. He opens the door and we walk in.

"Judge Cody." I take the eager and outstretched hand of the Navan Judge. "Did you get a drink?" I ask ignoring the glass that's in his hand. He raises it and the ice cubes rattle around the empty space. Catching the eye of one of the servers, she approaches us.

"A fresh drink for Judge Cody," I say and she takes his empty glass. Being an alcoholic and a judge proves fruitful for us.

"I hear you had a family situation." His words are delivered with a smile.

I find Shane in the crowd and point at him, Judge Cody follows my finger. "We are all fine. An exaggeration to frighten our most powerful and important clients." His ego grows at my measured strokes. I leave him and move deeper into the room. Catching glances of Shane I'm impressed with how good he is acting. He appears relaxed, and his laughter floats across the room as he entertains our guests.

"Gardai Brady. I'm glad you are here." I say approaching him at the back of the room. He's sitting with two other Gardai that are on our payroll. I had thought he might jump ship, so him being here was one less person for me to dispose of.

"Of course Liam. But I was wondering if I could have a private word."

I nod. "Of course. I will seek you out once I've finished my rounds," I say, and he sits back in his seat.

"Eric." I greet our solicitor who hunkers at the bar. He likes our money but not the association. He comes because he has to but the moment the meeting ends he will disappear.

"You did a great job on the assault case," I say as I sit beside him. He looks shifty for a solicitor. His nerves are why I picked him. He wasn't nervous enough to mess things up, but he was nervous enough to be smart and not to get caught.

"Thanks Liam, but it was your money that bought off most the Gardai." The bitterness is there as it always is.

"Yet, it was your skill and education that executed the plan," I say but he isn't seeking my approval only my money and the power to bury secrets.

"I have a new case for you that won't be easy, but a challenge will do you good."

Eric doesn't look at me as he nurses his drink. A pat to his back has me returning to the room and making sure everyone knows their worth.

CHAPTER THREE

SVETLANA

THE FAN THAT WHIZZES in my face isn't enough to keep me cool. Sitting at the double doors that open onto the patio gives me a little relief from the sweltering heat we are experiencing. I keep my fingers buried in Jan's fur as Holic walks past us with a bottle of beer in his hand. His eyes are heavy on me and when he pauses, I try to look out to see if my uncle is watching. He was the one who hurt me the most, but he was also the only one who could protect me.

"You must be hot."

I don't look up at Holic as he speaks. His bare feet come into view as he steps closer. "I'm good," I say. The trail of sweat that drips down between my cleavage makes me itchy.

"If it's the marks, don't be ashamed of them."

My head snaps up at his words. *He was a monster.* It was one of the reasons I was sitting here in a long white dress that covered my damaged back. *His marks.*

Air lodges itself and my ribcage tightens. The urge to wrap my hands around my middle has me tightening my fists. Jan shifts under me and I loosen my grip on him.

"You earned them, they ..."

I couldn't sit here. I knew he wasn't right but his words had bile climbing up my throat.

"Jan," I call as I leave the kitchen.

"Svetlana."

I stop and swallow the horror that's choking me. My uncle calls me two more times before I find some composure and turn to him with a smile. "Yes Uncle."

"What did you say to Holic? He seems upset." My uncle isn't angry, he seems curious as he takes a step toward me; his head tilts to the side as he runs his tongue along his teeth removing whatever greasy food he was eating.

"Nothing."

He smiles and wags his free hand at me as he sucks the grease from his fingers. "Come now, Svetlana. I know when you lie."

No you don't.

"He just asked me if I was hot. I simply told him I was good."

My uncle studies me, and I hold still even as his eyes drag across my body.

"Maybe you are too hot." Alcohol has lightened up his eyes.

I drop his gaze and shake my head. "I was just going to lie down," I say. One of the guys comes into the kitchen and gets more beers; the rattle of the glass distracts my uncle.

"Okay Svetlana. Go lie down."

I'm moving before he changes his mind.

"Svetlana."

I swallow again before turning to him. He is pointing at his cheek with his index finger. I let out a strangled laugh and walk back to him. Planting a kiss on each cheek, he seems satisfied as I leave. I walk up the stairs slowly as I know he still watches me. Once I disappear around the bend, I'm taking the steps two at a time.

My room holds no air and I immediately feel bad for dragging Jan with me. Opening the windows as wide as the steel bars will allow I close my bedroom door. The only way to lock my room is from the outside, and when my uncle says so. The need to strip off has me pushing a chair under the door handle.

I stand at the window in my bra and underwear and smile as the breeze, which lucky enough is blowing in my direction, kisses my sweat soaked skin. Holding my hair up I let it touch my neck and I shiver as cold meets hot. Jan lies at the foot of my bed and I smile at him. I stand still and allow the air to cool me down, it's only then I dare step away and get a clean dress from the wardrobe. I see a hundred images of myself stare back at me from my cracked mirror on the inside door of my wardrobe. I have never let my uncle see it. It was after my first punishment, I couldn't look at myself or the marks that Holic had inflicted on me. It was the only mirror in my room and I couldn't bear to look at myself. My fingers run across the cracked glass but I jump away as Jan barks. Someone was coming. Pulling out a clean dress I pull it over my head before racing over and getting the chair away from the door. The knob rattles and I quickly sit down on the chair, out of time to move it further away.

Beda narrows his eyes before they slitter around my room. "What are you doing?" He's young, younger than me, and his age makes him dangerous. He's always eager to please my uncle.

"I don't understand the question," I say sweetly as he steps into my room. He would never touch me, it's forbidden. My mind goes to Andel. It was forbidden for him to touch me too, but he had tried. Under the disguise of night he had slipped into my room. I push the rest of that night away.

"Your uncle wants you." He looks at the chair like he knows it shouldn't be there, yet he had no proof that I was doing anything wrong. Standing I tap my side and Jan immediately comes to me.

Beda steps out of my room and I follow him back through the house and outside to where my uncle and his men sit. I can feel Holic's eyes on me the moment my bare feet touch the hot slabs under me.

My uncle stands and comes to me wearing a huge smile. Everyone is looking at me and I feel a change in the air. The men are excited. My fear rises and I tell my heart to still.

"What is it that men truly want?" My uncle asks his own men as he reaches me and places his hand on the small of my back making me walk further out onto the patio. I let my hand hang telling Jan not to follow. I don't know what's going to happen and I can't let him get hurt. I hate how Holic watches me, sees my movement and stares at Jan. If he hurts him, I would kill him.

"Money." Beda speaks up and all the other men drink to his words.

"Yes. Money and women. But not just any woman but a beautiful woman." My uncles hand leaves the small space at my back. He pushes my hair back away from my face and touches my cheek, looking at me as he speaks to his men. "And not just a beautiful woman, but one who is untouched." My skin burns at his words and I breathe deeply through my nose.

"She will be our bargaining chip." He releases me and my legs wobble.

"What?" I speak before thinking. I'm waiting for my uncles wrath but he smiles at me far too sweetly.

"You always want to get out of the house don't you? Well, now I'm going to take you to Ireland."

My stomach twists painfully, the air grows hotter and I shift my burning feet on the slabs beneath me.

"Don't look so afraid Svetlana." My uncle laughs and his men join him. The only one who isn't laughing is Holic, his eyes burn as he stares at my uncle.

"You will only be on loan as good faith. Do not worry you will not be touched."

I'm shaking my head. "Uncle I love it here. I don't want to go." I try to keep the fear out of my voice and force a quivering smile.

"Go rest as we leave tomorrow." He turns his back on me and I'm taking steps away from them, the moment I pass Jan he's beside me and I can't see the stairs as my eyes blur. I don't make it fully up the stairs before I crumble on the steps. I was being handed over like ... a gift. What would happen to me? I'm standing as I hear footsteps in the kitchen, and race the rest of the way to my room. I could try to escape again. Closing my eyes the tears fall, I know how useless that would be. Running only led me to one place. Jan barks and I turn as someone enters my room.

"What are you doing here?" It's Holic. Crystal blue eyes bore into me and I take a step back. "You can't be in here." He has never come into my room, but the room doesn't hold his interest, I do.

"Are you going to run?" he finally asks.

"No. I want to run to get away from this place. But I won't. Because if I do, I have to be in your presence and that thought alone turns my stomach." My pulse spikes as I lash out at him with my words.

"I want you to run." He takes a step deeper into my room and I want to move back away from him.

"Now I won't run. I will go to Ireland where you nor my uncle can hurt me anymore."

Holic's jaw clenches along with his fists, my words are hitting a nerve. "They will treat you bad Svetlana. You belong here with us."

Laughter bubbles up my throat and leaves along with angry tears. "You're sick and twisted and I'm not like you. I don't belong here with you. Get out of my room." My voice rises but Holic doesn't flinch.

"I know you will come back to us." Are his parting words that I refuse to accept.

"Yes I will-" I shout after him as salty tears find their way into my mouth, "-in a box."

He's back in my room, he's too close but I've lost everything. "I will die over there."

"No, your uncle assures your safety."

"I will push so hard that they will kill me."

His brows furrow and he shakes his head. "You want to die?"

"No. I want to get away from you. If that means death, I'll take it before I let you near me again." More words have him flinching. I never saw it before, I always saw his anger, but in his twisted mind he didn't just enjoy hurting people, he enjoyed hurting me.

"You are not going."

His words confirm my theory and I laugh at him. "You have no power Holic. You are as good as my uncle's dog."

His anger ripples under his skin and he marches from my room. The moment he slams my door and I hear the lock slide into place, I slide to the ground wondering what the hell I just did that for.

***

The clouds are large, white, and puffy and I focus on them as I stare out of the plane window. The further I get away from the Czech, something in me starts to stir and come to life. After staying in my room last night I started to think that maybe, just maybe whomever I was being handed to might be kind to me. I might even like them. I take a quick glance around my uncle's private jet. All his men are here. Holic is sitting across from me, a cut on his face has recently been stitched. I wonder if that is the work of my uncle. Did Holic really go to him refusing to let me go to Ireland? I'm smiling now at the thoughts of him being hurt. I just wish I was there to hear him cry out. But I don't think he would have, he would have held it all in. Holic enjoyed the cries of pain, so he wouldn't allow someone to have that joy from him.

Hope is a dangerous thing but I can't stop it from filling me as we touch down in Dublin airport. I take down my carry-on bag from overhead and stand in the aisle as I wait for my uncle.

We leave the plane and the air bites into my bare skin. I shiver.

My uncle smiles at me. "I told you Svetlana, it is cold here."

He had, but I didn't think it would be this cold. Taking a jumper out of my carry-on bag I tug it on over my dress and catch up with my uncle. A row of black jeeps wait for us and I climb into the one with my uncle and Marek. Once the door is closed, the vehicle moves under us and fear starts to clutch at my chest. What if I'm beaten worse than when Holic does it? What if I'm raped? I close my eyes and push that thought down. I don't want to ask my uncle about the man he is handing me over to, frankly I haven't spoken to him since I went to my room last night. I had heard him laugh saying I was sulking like a princess. The other part of me says I actually might get to escape, I could start over. Ireland's beautiful from the pictures I had seen, but so far I wasn't overly impressed with the drab weather and grey buildings we move past. I wasn't expecting buildings; I was expecting countryside and cottages. Like the pictures show you.

"Mr. O'Reagan." My heart pounds and my attention is on my uncle as he speaks to someone on the loudspeaker. I wonder if this is the man who I am being given to.

"Mr. Novak. I believe you've touched down in Dublin." The voice of the man is deep, clear and well spoken. But it holds such detachment.

"Yes. Thank you for the vehicles. We are now en route to the hotel. So when will we be meeting?" My uncle looks at me and I sink deeper into the seat.

"Tomorrow, Mr. Novak. At noon."

"I look forward to it." The call ends and my uncle smiles.

***

The hotel isn't what I expect either. It's as fancy as the ones we have back home. I was picturing something smaller, more personal, but this is modern and cold. I have to share an adjoining room with my uncle. I don't like the idea that he can come into my room, but I don't have a say in how it makes me feel, our how being given to a man in a foreign place makes me feel.

Sitting at the vanity table I'm staring into frightened blue eyes. What would my mother tell me right now? Alert the hotel staff that I'm here against my will? My uncle would defuse the situation and I would disappear. I knew being handed over to this man was my best chance of escape. If I was obedient, I may be allowed to roam free. Maybe he would help me? I grit my teeth at my reflection. "Or maybe he will beat you and rape you, Svetlana." I speak in English my accent strong around my words. I stand up now as a waiter arrives at my room. He smiles softly at me but I don't return it as he pushes in a trolley that's filled with food.

"Your evening meal Miss Novak." He starts removing plates, placing them on the table. His eyes keep flickering to me and he smiles again. I try a smile back at him and his widens. What if he would help me? I look behind him at the open door. I could run. My heart starts to gain in speed.

"Anything else I can get for you Miss Novak?" He's waiting still wearing the smile that shows off his dimples.

My freedom.

My eyes snap up to Holic who appears in the doorway. I drop my gaze and the waiter looks behind him.

"Leave," Holic speaks in Czech and the waiter looks lost.

"I have everything. Thank you," I tell him and he glances at Holic before giving me a final nod and leaving. Holic stands in the doorway so the waiter leaves it open. I march across the small space and slam the door in Holic's face. It feels good.

CHAPTER FOUR

LIAM

"S TEPHEN GO AHEAD."

"Darragh is at the gate and he's not happy that I won't let him out."

"Stephen, just give me a moment." I say and stand pulling on my suit jacket. I take the tunnels out of the basement and come out not far from the gate. Pushing the overhang of ivy aside I walk down the pass. Darragh sees me in his rearview mirror. He shakes his head before jumping out of his car.

"Are you serious right now?"

"You can't stop this," I warn him as I reach his car.

He slams his car door with unnecessary force. "Liam these are people. People I care about."

He just couldn't grasp the severity of this situation. "I want you to come inside and we can speak about it."

Darragh seems surprised by my offer and nods while stuffing his hands in his pockets. "Right, but you'll listen to what I have to say."

"You have my word."

He nods and removes his hands. "I'll park the car."

I step off the pass as he reverses back up the drive. I enter the house using the front door. I've been left with no alternative with Darragh.

He comes out of the garage and I walk away knowing he will follow. Slipping into the small hallway that leads to the basement door I turn the handle and descend. He pauses at the top step and I don't turn around to see if he will follow. Darragh is too curious not to follow me. I clap my hands twice and the basement lights up. The area we step into is carpeted and comfortable, the design is meant to surprise and relax. When I turn to Darragh, I can see it works.

"Jesus I thought I was stepping into some concrete and creepy spot. But this is nice." He's glancing around the space.

"Thank you." I gesture to the seat across from me and he sits. Opening my suit jacket I sit too. "Tell me what you were about to do?" I ask and sit back.

My mind has already been made up. I know the outcome of this conversation. I know Darragh's fate.

"I know Art and Mark are going to sign those contracts so in a way they are signing their own death sentences and I can live with that." He pauses and scratches his beard.

I nod.

"But DJ is decent, Liam. He's been there for me through the worst of it. And Fitz," Darragh lets out a long breath. "Fitz wouldn't harm a fly. I can't do that to him."

"But you're not, I am."

"This doesn't feel like we are talking, this feels like you're telling me." Darragh's irritation grows, and he's shifting where he sits. Pulling one leg up he holds it as he taps his other foot on the floor.

"No matter what way you see this play out in your mind, someone has to go down for the crime. I'm not sure your understanding that part," I say.

"I am. Can't you kill Mark; blame it on Art and let DJ and Fitz walk away."

"Art is selling you out; they will take him sending you down, over me sending him down. Eric is a great solicitor but with this new Gardai our hands are tied a little tighter on this matter Darragh."

"Christ." Darragh stands up now.

I rise too. "Walk with me."

He does through a door that leads to a different part of the basement. The chair that I had tied Andrew to sits in the center of the room. Darragh slows down and gives it a wide berth.

"What is that?" He asks.

I keep walking. "A chair."

"A torture chair? What the hell do you do down here?" His words trail off as his eyes dart around the room.

I open the final door and he walks over to the small room. I have a moment of anticipation but Darragh simply steps in.

"What's this?" He looks around the small room that has only a bed.

I step away from him. "This is for your own good." Closing the door I lock it.

It takes a moment for Darragh to start knocking. "Come on Liam, this is stupid. Open the door." His words aren't panicked but annoyance soon fills them.

I clap my hands once. "Wanda, play Galina Vishnevskaya."

"Playing Galina Vishnevskaya." The space fills with the sounds of classical music drowning out Darragh's banging.

Removing my jacket and waistcoat I start to scrub the blood on the floor beside the chair. Once I'm finished, I put my jacket and waistcoat back on before going back into the entrance room. The sound of the music disappears behind the sound proof walls.

"Wanda," I call as I gather my car keys and wallet.

"Yes Mr. O'Reagan."

"Lock down the basement," I say as I start to leave.

"Lock down commencing in one minute."

I ring Gregor as I walk to my car. "I am going to send you three names and addresses. I would like you to dispose of them."

"No problem."

Hanging up, I leave the house. Stephen is quick to let me out and I give him a curt nod before driving to Tracy's hotel. Business is booming, the brothel scene more profitable than I had ever imagined. With the demand growing, I didn't want to do business with my own so Mr. Novak caught my attention. He was a very powerful man in the Czech Republic. He ran all the brothels and strip clubs over there. His reach impressive. Having him onboard with our operation would increase our income four fold. His price was high, but it was one I was willing to pay.

***

Staff move quickly around the hotel as I make my way to my office. It's there I send Gregor the three names.

"Eric, that job we spoke of before will be ready to go ahead tomorrow. I'm going to send you the name and address of the person that you can present to the Gardai." I leave the voice mail and email him the details of Barry Fitz, the one who will pay the price for my brother's error.

A knock on the door has me pausing. "Come in."

"We have a bit of a situation with one of the girls." I check my watch. I still had another meeting today once Sharon gives me a brief on how the hotel was running.

"Where is she?" I ask standing up and taking my phone with me.

"Room 212."

"Thank you Danny." Danny seems surprised that I knew his name, but it's something I try to do and remember all my security members' names. They worked harder for you if they thought they were important to you.

"What's her name?" I pause at the door.

"Marcella."

I nod and open the door to room 212. Marcella is sitting on the floor and when she looks up it takes a second for her to get to her feet.

"Mr. O'Reagan."

I hold up a hand to silence her stuttering. "What is the problem Marcella?" I ask.

She fidgets with a large hoop earing. "I refused a customer and Danny obviously reported me." She's pointing at the open door and I know Danny can hear her. "Yesterday was rough on me Mr. O'Reagan. One of my clients got a bit rough." She shrugs and I'm looking at all her skin that's on a show to see if there are marks. There are none.

"Did he mark you?" I ask.

"No but he was rough."

I nod like I understand and Marcella gives me a nervous smile.

"This job is by no means for the faint hearted. But, you are not being forced to do anything Marcella. So if the job is too rough for you, I suggest you vacate your room and I will have another girl fill it in a minute."

She's shaking her head. "No I want my job..."

I cut her off. "Good. So I'll send in your next client?"

She looks out the door and nods. "Yes Mr. O'Reagan."

"Send in her next client and come to my office afterwards Danny," I say as I return to my office.

My phone buzzes. Home appears on the screen. "Father, I hope we haven't run into anymore problems?" I answer my phone.

"I'm worried about Darragh. I can't find him and he's not answering his phone."

"Don't worry about Darragh. Is that all?" Danny steps in and I point at the chair in front of me.

"He needs to be found Liam. Not just for my sake but yours too."

"I have him somewhere safe," I say and glance at Danny who's looking around my office.

"Where?" Father's word is biting, his temper flaring.

"Like I said, he's safe. Is that all?"

Father hangs up and I turn my attention to Danny. "Marcella claims that her previous customer roughed her up. I want you to find out what she means and who the client was."

"That's no problem."

"Also keep an eye on her." Danny nods and I dismiss him.

The knock on my door comes immediately after Danny leaves, it's Sharon. I check my watch she's two minutes late.

"I was waiting outside," She explains.

I nod. "Let's start."

It's nearly two hours later by the time I leave the hotel and make my way to my next meeting.

The ringing of my phone tells me how late I am and I don't like being late. "Stephen."

"Mr. O'Reagan, there's a John Cummings at the gate."

"You can let him in, I'll be there soon." It's been five years since I've seen John. He left to join the army. We had spoken on the phone over the years but seeing him would be different. We both had changed so much.

I arrive at the house and Stephen lets me in. After parking my car I head straight for the basement and turn on the lights. Opening the door off the entrance music still plays and I leave it on before closing the door behind me. I open the door to the tunnel. A tall figure looms there, and I let John in. The years haven't been kind to him. His face is scarred, pocketed in so many places. His arms immediately go around me as he hugs me tightly.

The embrace doesn't last long when I don't return it. He leans back and looks at me. "You've changed a lot Liam."

"So have you John." His red hair is tainted with grey. The curls bounce as he steps in and I follow him.

"I like what you've done with the place."

I go to the small free standing bar and pour both of us a whiskey. Handing him a glass he sits down, but he hasn't taken his eyes off me since arriving.

"How has life treated you?" I ask and sit back while cradling my glass of whiskey.

"I got married."

That surprises me. "Consensual?"

He grins. "Not sure, she divorced me a year later after we had our first." He shrugs like it's no big deal. But I've been looking at pain for far too long to not recognize it.

"I'm sorry." I tell him.

He grins into his whiskey before taking a deep drink. "You didn't bring me here to ask me about my life. So what can I help you with?"

I liked his straight forward approach. I hated small talk. "It's Darragh. He's remembering."

John finishes his whiskey and sits the glass on the small table beside him, before running his hands across his face, when he looks at me his eyes are haunted. "I've fought in foreign countries, watched my friends die, held some of them while they died, but I have a clear conscience because it's war and that's what we do in war. But what we did to that boy-" He leans forward, and the anger pours from him. "-wasn't right Liam. I knew one day it would come back and haunt us."

"I did it to protect him."

"Bullshit and you know it is. You did it to save your ass. Honestly I did it so you wouldn't kill him. But I think we did far more damage."

I place my own full drink on the table beside me. "You don't know what damage was done. You left, remember?" The anger that rises inside me, I push back down and refuse to let it come out.

"You have no idea what being an addict does to you. It destroys your soul. But that was my choice to get high and leave this place. It wasn't Darragh's.

We made him an addict, so yeah I left. Living with what I did with firsthand knowledge was too much."

"You shouldn't have done it then John if it gave you so many sleepless nights."

Johns stands up. "You're a cold bastard. I don't remember you being this cold."

"So you won't help me again?"

He barks an angry laugh. "No and neither will you."

I nod. "He's in far more trouble now."

"Because of you?" John asks, but he's accusing me.

"I did everything to protect my brother."

John shakes his head. "We both know why you turned him into an addict and it had nothing to do with protecting him. Goodbye Liam." John walks away and I don't like it. No one walks away from me. Especially not with the knowledge he has.

"He's here again. Locked in that same room."

When John looks at me now, I try to ignore the twinge I feel deep in my stomach. He's moving through the room and I stand in his way. "Liam, get out of my way."

"He robbed a bank and got caught. He will go to prison if I don't keep him here. He's trying to take the high ground and save his friends."

"Let him. Then at least it will be his choice." John tries to move around me and I side step him.

"The choice has already been made, he only has to remain in there for two more days and the deal will be done."

Johns face crumbles. I had no idea that what I had asked him to do five years ago had imprinted itself on him so heavily. "We took him down here against his will, strapped him to that bed and injected him with heroin for weeks..."

I cut him off. "I don't need a recap. I was there."

"You have no idea what we really did to him." He's eyes fill with shadows of the past.

"When he recovered he believed he was in rehab. He has no recollection of that night. There was no other way."

"Of course there was." John's eyes shimmer making my decision for me.

"I will let him go tomorrow. If he remembers so be it," I say.

John's tense shoulders relax. "You're lying." He sounds unsure.

"You might not respect the decisions I make for my family, but I'm not a liar," I say and that seems to have John accept what is happening here.

"Take care of yourself John," I say and he drops his eyes looking deflated with hands hanging at his sides. A part of me thinks I've hurt him more than I will ever know.

CHAPTER FIVE

SVETLANA

I KNOW SOMEONE IS in my room. I'm aware of the closeness of the person, but I remain still, hoping my still form will make them leave, but they only come closer. Air brushes my face and I snap my eyes open. My uncle is too close for comfort. He's kneeling at the side of my bed, his face as close as the bed will allow his body to go.

"I am changing my mind beautiful Svetlana. I think I will keep you." His words brush my face and I can't stop the shiver that assaults my body. I wasn't anyone's to keep and staying with him, returning to Czech, seeing Holic again, my odds seemed better in this foreign place with foreign people. I don't speak or react. He doesn't seem pleased with my silence.

"We will have breakfast together and I will make my final decision."

I was a mouse dangling from the cat's mouth, its belly too full to have me but refusing to let me go.

My uncle gets up off his knees and I roll trying to calm my hammering heart that threatens to smash through my chest like it's porcelain.

I don't want to get out of the bed in my small nightdress but my uncle isn't leaving. His back is turned to me and I use the moment to scurry out and wrap myself in a silk nightgown. When I turn around his hungry eyes soak up any bare skin. He makes me feel naked and my face flames with his horrible thoughts that shine through his cruel eyes.

I walk across the carpeted floor keeping my focus on the table that has been set for two. I hadn't heard the waiter come in. When I sit down, I wonder how long my uncle has been in my room. He smiles while pouring out tea. I'm not hungry but I know better than to skip a meal with my uncle. He would never starve me intentionally but sometimes he forgot that I needed to eat. Biting into my toast I'm surprised when he gets up and opens the door. "Holic." The toast feels heavy on my tongue and it takes a large drink of tea to wash it down as Holic steps into my room. His eyes immediately find me. I dip my head and focus on buttering bread that I don't think I can eat.

"I want you to stay here while we eat." My uncle sounds happy as he sits back down and I'm confused why Holic has to watch us eat. I'm uncomfortable with having his eyes on me. My back grows tight and I wonder if that was the idea behind my uncle's decision.

"I'm in two minds about keeping you, Svetlana. So I need to be convinced that you should stay."

Holic shifts at my uncle's words.

I keep my focus on my uncle. "I'm not sure of my worth uncle," I say.

He laughs at me before dabbing his mouth with his white cloth napkin. "Oh, Svetlana." He leans across the table and I hold still as he touches my face. The gesture is loving and gentle. "Not you. Holic, will convince me."

This time I look to Holic, the anger in his crystal eyes freezes me. "You know he has a crush on you." Uncle laughs.

My heart thumps away like a rabbit's leg in my rib cage.

"Come closer Holic." My uncle's laughter is gone as he speaks. Holic moves on my uncle's command. I heard the warning and so did he. "Don't be shy. Save her."

Right now sitting here I wasn't sure which one of them was the bigger monster, but pity crawled into my heart for Holic. The memory of the pain he inflicted on me erases it quickly and I take a bite of bread before looking up at him.

"She is Czech," He says and my uncle nods.

When Holic doesn't continue he pauses before drinking his tea. "You were more convincing yesterday. Have you changed your mind Holic?"

Holic looks at me as he answers. "No I still think she must remain with us."

My hands coil around the knife. He has no right to say what happens to me.

"You are making Svetlana angry." Uncle's words are sung, he is enjoying the discomfort he is causing.

I relax my hand feeling tired.

"She belongs with her people. She will one day be their Queen." My heart stills at his stupid treacherous words. What was he thinking? I jump as uncle throws down his knife and fork, his plate cracks under the assault. The pepper spills over and tea pours onto the floor. Fear lodges itself in my throat.

"I warned you!" The roar has me gripping the table as I keep my eyes closed.

"I cut your face as your warning, was it not enough?"

"I'm sorry." Holic's words don't hold an apology and I open my eyes as my uncle steps closer to him.

"Svetlana come here."

I'm shaking my head. I can't move. When he sees I haven't moved, he comes across the small space and pulls me from the table, the contents on the table rattles as I'm pulled from it. I stand in front of Holic nearly toe to toe.

"Do you see his face?" My uncle asks.

I nod. When he shakes me I speak up. "Yes uncle."

The room shifts as he spins me around until my back faces Holic, the dressing gown is ripped from me and the burn in my throat is so sudden that I cough. My uncle is gentle as he moves my hair aside and lower's the straps of my night dress.

"Do you see her back?" He asks Holic.

Hot tears make a path down my face.

"Yes." Holic's word is low.

"You want to touch them?"

I stiffen at the thoughts of his fingers on my skin.

"No."

Holic's reply has me catching my breath with relief.

"I put these marks here because she disobeyed me. You think they are your marks. But they are mine. Just like the mark on your face, I might not have put it there, but it was on my command. So if I tell you to hurt her, not to hurt her, don't look at her. Don't call her a Queen. Jump up and down. You will do it."

"Yes boss," Holic answers and a part of me feels such sorrow for him.

"Cut off your finger." He commands Holic.

I'm turning and my uncle tightens his fingers on my neck pushing me to my knees. Holic doesn't hesitate as he places his hand on the table and takes out a large knife that's strapped to his leg. Spreading his fingers I try to look away but my uncle shakes me. "Watch my power." The knife detaches Holic's finger within a split of a second and I choke down on a scream. Holic cries out, sweat coats his face as he grabs a napkin and tries to stop the squirting blood. All I see is red.

"That is my power Svetlana, not yours. Remember you have none." He releases me roughly and walks out of the room. Holic's legs give way and he crumbles to the ground. I crawl to him taking his hand in mine. I have no idea what to do, but it's like watching an injured animal. I just can't walk away.

"What do I do?" I ask blinking several times as the napkin turns from white to red like I'm a witness to a magic trick.

"Nothing." Holic is watching me like he's not bleeding out on the floor, like my uncle didn't just make him cut his finger off.

His face softens and his free hand touches my bare arm.

I stand and move away from him. "You need to get someone to look at that, I can't help you." I pull my tattered night gown around me as Holic stands up and takes his finger with him. He casts me one final long filled look that sends a tremor skittering down my spine. When the door closes behind him I cover my mouth with my hand pushing down the screams that threaten to pour from me.

***

My uncle has sent up a box that's wrapped in a large blue bow. The hotel staff member leaves it on the end of my bed. The shower I take is long, and I don't want to come out of it and back to this nightmare. My new night gown is tightened around my still wet body as I walk to the box. The satin bow opens easily at my touch. Moving the paper aside I take out a red jump suit. I don't think about why he picked red, or why red lipstick is sitting on my bedside table. I'm a gift. I push the fear aside and focus on getting dressed. At least I don't have to wear anything revealing. The jump suit is loose on my legs and comfortable and tighter from my waist up. I don't admire myself in the mirror but brush out my hair and apply the red lipstick. I try not to meet my eyes in the mirror. Lately, I find each time I see myself in the mirror I am becoming more and more like my mother. The pain of her memory still squeezes my heart.

The door opens and my uncle walks in. Dropping my hands to my sides he walks towards me with outstretched hands. I walk into his open arms as he places a kiss on my cheek.

"Svetlana you look breathtaking."

His compliment is salt on a wound, but I force a smile. "Thank you uncle."

"We are ready to go."

I don't think but slip on the red heels that he has also gifted me. I have nothing else. I refuse to think of my only friend that I left behind. I refuse to think about what is waiting in front of me. I refuse to feel. Instead I focus on the carpet under my heels. I focus on each man as they fall into step around me. I even focus on Holic as he joins us. He is home, no matter how cruel it was. He is home, and I hate him for that. His hand is bandaged fully, but he shows no signs of a man who has just lost a finger.

The jeeps are lined up in an underground carpark. As we walk across the concrete floor, the sound of my heels ring through the space. My heart seems to jump to the sound. My uncle opens the door and I slide in. He joins me, and Holic joins us as well. I have no idea why he has to be around so much, but it didn't really matter anymore. I keep my eyes on the window and pretend that I am here for a holiday. Mother and Father ride in the jeep ahead of me. Jan is with one of our servants. Everyone is safe. Everyone is happy.

The illusion bursts like a bubble as my uncle speaks. "I've made up my mind Svetlana."

I don't want to look at him; I don't want him to be here.

"You will be staying here for a short time. Once my business is done, I will take you home."

This time I look at him. The heaviness in my chest starts to grow; it's like a wave that wants to consume me.

"Home?" I repeat. I didn't have a home. He had taken it all away.

"Yes with me." He sounds almost confused.

I nod before shooting Holic a look, he's been staring at me since he got into the jeep while ruining any happiness that I try to find.

"Stop looking at me," I tell him and he does.

My uncle laughs and I stare out the window.

"Daddy slow down." The wind whips my face and I'm flying but it's too fast. My father's laughter rumbles through his chest. "Don't worry princess, you're safe." Glancing back at him, I laugh. He will keep me safe. He could throw me into the clouds and catch me. He could run so fast that no one could catch him. Right now the basket that I sit in is wide and attached to the front of his bike. The long grass bends towards us as we race down the open path. The heat of the sun is warm on us and even at five; I remember it so well. I remember thinking we were flying, that my father was invincible. That once I was with him nothing bad could happen.

The image washes away as bombs of rain splash the window that I stare out of. My throat burns and I take a peek at my uncle. It douses the memory and along with it the longing. All I feel is the hate and pain; I cling to that feeling for the rest of the journey. It feels like we stay in the jeep a long time. The scenery changes to what I expected of Ireland. Green fields and trees seem to move fast past the jeep. The rain comes and goes, sometimes it's no more than a drizzle.

When the jeep slows down my heart picks up. We pull into a field where one lone car sits waiting for us. Five jeeps in total pull in after us and I'm not sure if I'm going to get sick.

"Stay here." My uncle steps out of the jeep and Holic hesitates but I stare out the window. Once the door closes, I shift forward trying to see the driver of the Bentley. Is this the man I was being handed to? I can't see anything through the black dividing panel, and the jeep is parked at an odd angle that doesn't allow me to see out.

I twist my fingers together while I wait for my fate. My mind keeps jumping to the worst possible scenarios. When the door finally opens its Holic, his jaw is clenched as he stares in at me. "Your uncle wants you to come out."

My heart slams against my ribcage and I want to cling to Holic and beg him to help me. The jeep starts to feel smaller now and fear tightens around my throat.

"Svetlana. Everyone is waiting."

Everyone, as in the man who was going to take me. After inhaling three deep breaths I move to get out of the jeep. Holic reaches out his hand for me to take but I don't accept it. I step out into a field of green. I'm staring at the ground as I take each step. It's cold but I don't feel it completely. The tremble in my body alerts me to the air temperature or maybe it's fear.

"This is Svetlana." My uncle says as I finally reach him. The field spins as I raise my head and look into soulless eyes.

"She is my pride and joy and as good faith she will stay with you until our deal is complete."

The man in the suit nods, but he isn't focusing on me. My uncle nudges me to walk across the field to him. I feel sick as I take a step. I stare back at my uncle and he gives me an encouraging smile like I'm riding my bike for the first time without stabilizers, not that I'm walking to a strange man who's taking me away. Holic breaks form and moves across the field to me.

"Holic!" The anger in my uncle's voice doesn't stop Holic. He reaches me and grips my arm. "If you don't come back. I'll kill Jan slowly."

I don't know what I was expecting but for him to threaten Jan isn't it. He moves back quickly as I find myself in a daze stumbling the rest of the way. A larger man takes me by the arm and places me in the back of the car. I can't breathe as the reality starts to sink in.

CHAPTER SIX

LIAM

"I THINK TWENTY PERCENT is more of a reasonable number, since you now have the most precious thing that I own." Mr. Novak looks at my car where the precious cargo sits.

"Ten percent set-up costs, Mr. Novak. We have already discussed this. You are more than welcome to retrieve your niece whenever you want." I didn't want her. But returning a gift would be an insult.

His smile is wide as he rubs his hands together. "How did you know she was my niece?"

"I'm sure you've researched me as much as I have researched you. So I understand her importance not just to you, but your people, and I'm grateful for the gift."

His smile is gone; I know mentioning her power would annoy him. I didn't like anyone trying to change our contract at this stage. My trust for him was limited already and now I had zero faith in this man. The blond-haired guy with him had disobeyed him too easily and marched across the field to whisper something to Novak's niece. He had no control over his men and that didn't sit well with me.

"I suggest we all start our work and I will be in contact Mr.Novak." I nod and turn my back on them making my way to my car. Gregor is driving and I slide into the passenger seat. My eyes flash to our cargo in the back. She's staring at me, ice-blue eyes that are fueled with hate.

"Do you speak English?" I ask while watching her in the rearview mirror.

She shakes her head. "No English." Her accent muffles her words and I look away from her, but I understood what she said.

"You need to have Sam keep an eye on Mr. Novak." I tell Gregor. I didn't trust the man one bit. He was good at what he did, I just needed to make sure he didn't screw me over.

"What about her?" Gregor asks looking at Novak's niece in the mirror.

"I'll take care of it," I say.

We arrive home and Gregor stalls outside the hidden arch that leads into the basement. I can't take the girl into the house. Opening the door for her, she doesn't move, and it takes me to look at her before she steps out. Her head stops at my shoulder as she walks beside me while glancing around her. Pushing back the ivy, I open the door and she steps in hesitantly. Once the door closes we are plunged into darkness. Clapping, the tunnel comes to life one light at a time. It's not strong lighting, but it's enough for us to see. The girl still hasn't moved.

"Keep going," I tell her, but she doesn't move.

"Prosím, nech mě jít." Her words are heavy with her accent. Touching the small of her back she moves forward. Each step she takes echos loudly in the tunnel. I had given Darragh food before I left, I needed to get him some more. He was still very angry but his rage was easy to deal with.

We enter the basement and the girl stops walking and takes in her surroundings. But I don't pause and move deeper into the basement. She follows me as we move through the more sterile part of it until we enter my own private quarters. No one has ever stood in here but she will be kept out of sight. I'm not happy with anyone else touching my stuff. The large space we step into has an open area. A living space and a large kitchen fill it. She's looking around her but I move her to the bedroom. She hesitates at the door before turning and looking at me with wide frightened eyes. "Prosím." Her red lips release the one word and I step back and close the door. I don't lock it.

"Wanda."

"What can I do for you today?"

"Lock down my private quarters," I tell her as I leave and return to the entrance room where Gregor waits for me.

"Sam is on it now," he says the moment I step into the room.

"Thank you Gregor. I have two more jobs for you. I need you to feed Darragh and the other one I will discuss with you later."

I return to the main house and find father in his study.

"I've been ringing you," he says it with an air of authority that he doesn't own.

"I know. I had several meetings today."

"With the Russians?" I'm not surprised he knows my business. He just didn't gain that knowledge from me.

"They are from the Czech," I correct him while sitting down.

"I don't care Liam. I care about Darragh. Where is he?"

"You don't care about him, so let's stop pretending you do."

My father's fist hits his desk, but I don't react or move.

"I do. But of course I'm also concerned with what he remembers."

I don't respond and he picks up a pen. "I saw John leave the premises. He looked upset."

"He was upset and soon he won't be here anymore."

"Son." My father's voice softens, and he places the pen back on the desk. "You can't keep disposing of people like its nothing." He stands now rubbing his jaw.

"Of course I can and I will. He knows too much, he's as big of a liability as Darragh is, and he isn't family."

"He was your friend." I'm confused as to why my father is defending John, or why he even cares.

"You let your own brother go to prison for a crime he didn't commit. So please, don't lecture me on family or friendship. I just came here to reassure you that Darragh is safe and I'll have his mess cleaned up in two days." I rise.

"How is Finn?"

"His wife died, how do you think he is?" I lean in on the desk and my father sinks back. "Your wife died." I remind him and he swallows. "Be with your son, comfort him."

I leave his office and make my way back down stairs. Voices ring out from the kitchen. I pause before entering. The effect I have on the room makes me want to leave. Everyone stops talking and Mary bustles back to the stove and away from table where Shane, Una and Finn sit. I didn't expect to see Ciara in our home. She stands up the moment I enter; she is the only one who doesn't look afraid of me.

"Hi Mr. O'Reagan." Her chirpy tone rings out in the silent kitchen. "I arrived a while ago, I was looking for Darragh." She doesn't sound worried, but she was rambling and I knew that was a nervous tick of hers. "So I just said I'd drop in and make sure everything was okay."

"I'm curious where he is too." Finn states from the table. He's still wearing sunglasses.

"He's away on business for me." I tell the room and Ciara's mouth forms a small O. I have no idea what Finn is thinking but Shane just nods. I turn to leave regretting coming into the kitchen.

"When will he be back?"

"In a few days. It was nice to see you, Miss Michaels." I keep it formal letting her know not to follow me. She doesn't but Shane does.

"We had a problem at the club. But I took care of it." Shane falls into step beside me.

"Good." I answer.

"Aren't you curious what it was?"

I glance at Shane. "No."

"Where is Darragh?"

I stop walking and face him. "He's safe don't worry. I need to clean up a mess he made."

Shane nods. "Yeah, Father told me about the bank job. He's an idiot." I didn't like him knowing this, not since he had grown close to Una.

"How is Finn?" I ask Shane.

He stuffs his hands in his pockets. "When I ask him he says he's fine. But he drinks every night and the sunglasses don't come off his face during the day."

Finn was soft, and I always said that his softness would slowly destroy him. He needed to take his anger and focus on finding out who killed his wife, not cry about it.

"You did well at the meeting," I say to Shane. His arm is back in the sling, but I was impressed with how easily he had moved around the room like him being shot was a silly rumor.

"Thanks brother," Shane pats me on the back and I leave going back down into the basement. Gregor is waiting in the entrance hall as I arrive.

"He started shouting again."

Darragh wasn't giving up. "It is fine I'll talk to him." The moment I open the door I hear Darragh's shouts, he's banging the door rapidly.

I open the small slot at the top and am face to face with his anger. "You need to calm down," I say.

His fist sends vibrations through the steel door. "I've been locked in here like some fucking animal and you're telling me to calm down. This is unforgivable."

I wait until his rant is over. "You have only two more days and I will let you out."

He throws his body at the door. "Let me the fuck out now Liam."

"No, and if you don't start talking to me in a more civil manor I'm leaving."

"Civil? Civil? Who does this? Who locks their own brother in a fucking cell?"

I can't see him as he walks away, but he comes back into view. He seems calmer.

"I'm going crazy in here; please Liam just let me out."

"I can't but I'll get you something to watch."

"Has anyone asked where I am?"

"Everyone thinks you are on a business trip for me."

His anger returns and he tightens his fists. "You're so fucking sneaky." He runs his hand through his hair. "What about Ciara? Have you thought about her for one fucking second?"

"She's actually upstairs right now, with Shane and Una. I reassured her you would be back shortly. And honestly Darragh you should have thought about her before you robbed a bank."

His fists slam against the door again. "I wasn't with her then."

I wasn't staying here much longer to hear him throw a tantrum. "I will have Gregor organize some entertainment for you."

"Wait." He stops me before I close up the slot.

"What?" My patience is slipping.

"You're a fucking wanker." I close the slot before he sees the amusement on my face.

CHAPTER SEVEN

SVETLANA

T HE DOOR CLOSES, AND the man disappears. There's no sound as the blood thrashes against my ears. My clammy hands tremble as the finality of this situation sinks in. I'm stepping back with jerky movements. Black spots grow at the corner of my vision. I've stopped moving. The tips of my fingers reach down and touch silk. Spinning too quickly I'm facing the large dominant bed that's covered in black silk sheets. I keep checking the door waiting for someone to storm in, waiting for that man to come and hurt me. It's only a matter of time I tell myself. The tremble is immediate and grows in my arms and legs.

I hold my breath; I thought I heard a noise outside the door. He's coming, and he's going to hurt me. I'm scurrying away from the bed moving towards the wardrobes. They are built in and small gaps allow me to slide in and hide. My breathing quickens as sweat gathers at the back of my neck. I think I hear another noise outside the door. Pulling open the large wardrobe door I stumble back. Rows and rows of suits are hung perfectly, starting from a black and reducing in color like a color card. A sob bursts from my mouth and I push it back with my hand. This was his room. I was in his bedroom. Where he slept. My eyes move to the bed. What would happen when he returned? Would he rape me? Hurt me? I sink to the floor as the fear starts to choke me.

I'm standing up again and my single minded focus is Jan. I need to return to Jan. He would be my focus; he would be my strength, my anchor.

Opening the bedside tables gives me nothing. They are both empty. There are no lamps, not even an alarm clock. Nothing to pick up and throw. A half mannequin sits in the corner of the room, a suit jacket hangs from its shoulders. The lighting in the room is built into the walls making you forget that you're underground. My chest tightens and I try not to think about where I am. I need to find a weapon. The room was dominated by the bed. Lying on my stomach shows not as much as a piece of fluff under it. The wardrobes are the final piece in the room. I wait and listen around my pounding heart for any other noises. I don't think I hear anything. I open the second wardrobe, it's just rows of shoes, all polished. All in perfect order. After searching the room I find nothing. The only door in the room is the one I came through. I move towards it and place my ear against the door. I hear nothing. Wiping my clammy hands on my legs I touch the door knob. A part of me just wants to back away and find a corner to sit down in and wait this out. But if there is a chance of getting out, or a chance of finding something I can defend myself with then it was worth the risk. Turning the knob my heart jumps around as the door opens. The slight click has me holding my breath as I open the door further and peek out into the living space. The lights are on but I don't see anyone. The kitchen is open plan and my mind is conjuring all the knives that are at my fingertips. I move to take a step out of the door but remember my heels. Kicking them off I swallow before stepping out onto the tiled floor. The imprint of my feet appears but disappears as I step forward. Sweat coats my body as I reach the kitchen area. Opening the first drawer it's filled with tea towels and cloths, I close it quickly.

The room dims and I'm standing straight as a strange red hue flairs to life. The blare of an alarm has me frozen to the spot. My mind can't understand what's going on. Black spots dance across my vision again. I need to leave now. Someone was going to come. I race across the kitchen but pause. What if this was my only chance of finding a knife? What if from here on out I was locked in that room? Locked in his room? With a sickening twirl of my stomach I race back and quickly open more drawers. Please, please God. The blare of the alarm cuts off and I feel a presence in the room. I'm spinning around trying to spot the danger that I feel. He's standing at the end of the counter, his black eyes consuming my fear. My hands grip the counter as I try to move around the kitchen and away from him.

"Byl jsem hladový," I tell him I am hungry in a shaky voice. He blinks and moves towards his kitchen. His eyes are calculating as he glances over each drawer, press and counter. I have no idea what he is searching for.

"Why are you in my kitchen?" His voice is deep as he speaks. I try to calm my racing heart and think. *Think.* Glancing away from him gives me a moment to process my thoughts.

I try to give him a confused look and shrug. "No English." I say as broken as I possibly can. He takes a step closer and I sink against the marble worktop. My eyes dart around. I could run to the room. But there was no lock on the door. My eyes shoot back to him as he takes another step towards me.

I rub my stomach. "Hladový," I say. His eyes follow my hand movement and I drop it. I want to get away from him. Something about him unsettles me but I can't put my finger on it. He was well dressed, well groomed, but there was something in the way he moved. He was a predator. I'd been around enough of them to recognize one.

In his eyes there is such a heavy black that I can see his iris fully. I shiver as sweat trickles down my back.

"Go back to your room and don't leave it again."

I don't move. I want to. I want to run to the room and hunker down and never have to be in his presence again. But if I do, he'll know I understand him. I rub my stomach again. "Hladový," I repeat. My hand trembles too much as it touches my stomach.

He steps closer to me and with two fingers touches my arm. I move away from his touch and bump into the cooker handle. Jumping away from it I nearly walk into him. He directs me like you might try to control a wild bull. Moving so I move in the direction he wants me to move in.

He points at the bedroom. "Stay in there and don't come out again." I hear the warning. It sends dread skittering down my spine. I move towards the room. When I step in I'm ready to crumble to the ground but he doesn't close the door like I thought he would instead he enters too. I'm backing away quickly towards the corner of the room. My eyes dart to my heels that sit at the door, a weapon that I hadn't thought of. He isn't looking at me, he's opening his wardrobe. He's back is towards me like I'm not a threat. My muscles tense as I take a step towards my shoes. My stomach twists and tightens as I quicken my steps. I move too fast, and like startling an animal, he moves too quickly and is blocking the door. I stumble away from him and nearly land on my behind.

My chest rises and falls rapidly. "Obuv." I point to my shoes with a shaky hand. He looks at the red heels for a spilt second before picking them up and I'm shocked when he hands them to me. I take the weapons and clutch them to my chest as I back away from him again. He goes back to his wardrobe and I huddle against the wall until he leaves with a fresh suit, shirt and shoes. He closes the door without a word and I sink to the floor holding my shoes tightly. I sit there for a long time just trying to calm my racing heart down, when I finally do the trembles slowly leave and the exhaustion has me closing my eyes. Just for a minute I tell myself.

The sound of the door clicking has me opening my eyes. My shoes lie beside me and I reach for them as my eyes dart and dance around the room, landing on a tray of food beside the door my stomach grumbles. No one else is in the room. Putting down my weapons I take the tray back to the corner and examine everything on it. The spoon could be useful. I stuff it into my pocket. The sandwich I eat without tasting. The plate could be used but if it's missing he would be suspicious. So the only thing that I can take is the spoon. The tea is warm and I drink the full cup down. The thirst I feel burns my throat. I eat only one half of the sandwich when I start to feel sick. Panic consumes me as I pull the other part of the sandwich apart. I'm taking off lettuce, cucumber, tomatoes, and some chicken. After smelling the bread and sniffing nothing unusual, I sit back. I'm afraid of being poisoned but that wouldn't make sense. My appetite vanishes quickly and I push the tray away.

Resting my head against the wall the heaviness that pulls against my eyes is too much and I know it's not natural. I'm fighting it as the door opens and his legs appear moving towards me. I'm trying to sit up but my body slides down onto the ground. I refuse to close my eyes. Each blink gives me a smaller view.

"Please." I mumble my brain fuzzy, telling me I've made a mistake. One hand wraps around my waist and the other under my legs. I'm airborne. My head rolls until it's pressed against a solid chest. His heart beats calmly, the beat making me close my eyes fully. My sense of smell kicks in and I inhale him deeply, he smells of leather, shoe polish and his cologne. His breath brushes my face as he lowers me onto the bed; the smell of whiskey has me half opening my eyes in alarm.

Uncle.

His hand leaves my waist and I'm trying to move. He comes into view, not my uncle but the man.

"Stop fighting it," he tells me, but his tone suggests he doesn't care either way. A whimper leaves my throat as my eyes flutter closed. The bed dips and I know if I fall asleep now whatever happens I won't be able to stop.

"Please," I whisper again as moisture leaks from the corner of my eye.

***

Someone has stuffed my mouth with cotton and rammed it down my throat. Sitting up I'm yanked back. My arm stings as I pull it again. Through my confused state I try to grasp what's happening. I'm handcuffed to the bed by one arm. Panic shoots through me and I'm sitting until my arm twists painfully. I'm pulling at the handcuffs not caring of the damage I'm doing to my arm. When I don't make an impact but only hurt myself, I stop thrashing and take stock. I'm still in my clothes. My body feels fine, as far as I can tell over the adrenaline that rushes through it. The door opens and I don't have time to prepare myself or get away.

His ink filled eyes focus on the poster of his bed that I'm handcuffed to. "Don't damage my bed." He carries a tray as he moves towards me and I shuffle back but my god-damn arm prevents me from moving away from him. He places the tray on the bedside table. He had drugged me yesterday. I turn my head away from the food letting him know I wasn't eating. His fingers quickly work as he un-cuffs me. I pull my aching wrist to my chest.

"Get up." He holds the cuffs in his hand and I follow his movements as he puts the key back into his pocket.

"No English," I repeat, but something tells me I might have messed up. When he reaches me I move back until my back hits the headboard. His fingers aren't tight on my arm, but I feel the pressure of his touch and I'm off the bed and standing. He keeps directing me by touching the small of my back when I pause. I hate the feeling. I glance at him over my shoulder but he's focused on our destination. A bathroom, the moment I step in I close the door. But it doesn't close fully his foot is stopping the door. I'm shaking my head. I was not doing my private business in front of him.

"The door stays open," he says, his coal-black eyes soaking up any light in the room until I step back away from him. The toilet is slightly deeper into the bathroom and to the right so he wouldn't be able to see me. Each time I peek at him he has his back to me. After releasing myself of a full bladder, I wash my hands and face. The sound of the running water has him stepping in to the bathroom making the space feel too small. I'm frozen watching him having no idea what he is doing as he opens a vanity door and takes out tooth paste, a tooth brush, soap and a cloth. He holds the items out to me, his long fingers and large hands easily holding the contents. The cold tiles under my bare feet take away some heat that burns through me. I take each item from his fingers, confused by his kindness. But Holic was kind at times, yet his cruelty was animalistic.

I quickly step away and turn to the mirror. He's still behind me watching me and I try to ignore the burn of his eyes on my back. I brush my teeth in record time. I don't use the soap or cloth. Once I turn off the tap, I gather up my supplies and hold them close to my chest. He nods and touches the small of my back as I'm directed back to the room.

"You can put your things in the bedside table," he says and I want to tell him to shut up. That's what I was going to do but now that he said it I need to pretend I don't understand. Going to the corner of the room where my shoes lie I hold my toiletries. He moves to the bedside table closest to me and opens it, points at my things and then at the drawer. I give myself five seconds of looking like I'm trying to figure out what he is saying before I step towards the drawer where I lower the items.

He points at the food after closing the drawer. "Eat. I'll be back soon."

I don't move as he leaves the room, once the door closes I move around to the food. My stomach rumbles but I don't touch it. It could be laced with sleeping tablets again; instead I go to the corner and sink to the floor.

CHAPTER EIGHT

LIAM

"WANDA."

"What can I do for you today?"

"Lock down the living quarters." I leave the area to let the girl eat her breakfast. She hadn't eaten much yesterday, but she ate enough that my sleeping pills worked. I had added the same amount to her breakfast. Keeping her sleeping while she was here would be easier for everyone.

"Gregor, how is everything moving along?"

Gregor rises from the couch as I enter the entrance area of what I like to think of as my domain.

"Unfortunately Art overdosed last night, he had a very heavy drug habit." I'm always impressed at Gregors skills and delivery of his work.

"And the other two boys?" I ask.

"Mark and DJ both died after their car veered off the road and into the lake. I was present when they recovered their bodies."

Always so thorough.

"I'm meeting Gardaí Brady today to give him up the final boy and then Darragh is free to go. I will let him know now. I have another job for you, but just let me finish this up first."

Gregor nods and I leave him to see Darragh. Opening the slot the sound of a car chase and guns firing reach me. Looking in he's lying on the bed watching a movie from a portable device on his lap. Plates are stacked up around him. When he notices me he pauses his movie.

"Am I allowed out?" hope fills his voice.

"It depends on you," I tell him.

His jaw clenches.

"Art overdosed last night," I say.

His face crumbles but he tries to hide it. "What about DJ?" Regret fills his eyes, he wants to know but doesn't. He needs to.

"DJ and Mark died in a car accident last night."

He's at the slot staring at me with pleading eyes. "Why didn't you just shoot DJ. Did he suffer?"

"Does it matter?"

"Of course it matters." Darragh's back to hitting the door.

"Your behavior is telling me you're not ready to come out yet."

He swallows and fights to compose himself. "I am. I know it's over and there is nothing I can do."

I nod. "I have to meet Gardaí Brady now. Once Barry is in custody, I will inform Gregor to let you out."

"Liam." Darragh comes close to the slot so I can only see half his face, but he's shaking his head. "I can't live with doing this to him."

"You'll just have to." I close the slot and walk away as he continues to throw himself uselessly against the door. The alarm sounds from my apartment and I'm not surprised she's out again.

The bedroom door slams the moment I enter the living quarters. She didn't wait around to be caught this time. Opening the bedroom door she's in the corner again. Her back plastered against the wall, her eyes dart around the room as I step in. She hasn't eaten her food.

"Eat," I say.

She looks at the food but then she shrugs and frowns very unconvincingly. "No English."

She was fluent in English, I knew this when I researched Mr. Novak. She was well educated and clever. I was comfortable pretending she didn't understand me. But right now I couldn't sit around and babysit her. Walking to her food I lift the tray. "Eat," I say again and she widens her eyes as if she understands. When she reaches the food, I expect her to take the tray, but she shakes her head.

Lowering it down I take the cuffs out of my pocket and see the moment she decides to scurry away. Moving quickly, I Wrap my fingers around her small wrist. I don't think about the feel of flesh under my fingertips. She tries to resist, but she's not very strong. I close the cuff around her wrist and quickly move to the post of the bed, I'm ready to close it when she rolls unexpectedly, and the cuff comes free from the bed. I move quickly onto the bed and grab both her arms, she thrashes as I force her arms down pinning them either side of her head. Leaning my body against hers finally stops her. Feral ice-blue eyes filled with fear stare at me and for a moment I wonder why she's so afraid. She's breathing heavily, the pulse in the side of her neck flickering wildly. Her slim throat works as she swallows and I loosen my grip on her wrists. Heat burns from her skin penetrating my suit and I shift my fingers until they touch the metal of the cuff. Releasing her I pull the cuff until she moves towards the post understanding that fighting is a waste of her dwindling energy. I close the cuff around the post and get off the bed. The tray sits on the bedside locker within her reach.

"You should eat."

She looks away from me as tears trickle down her face. Leaving the room I lock down the living quarters in case she manages to get out.

***

"Gardaí Brady." I greet him as he sits waiting for me with another member of the Gardaí.

"This way gentlemen." They both rise as Gregor and I make our way to the gentleman's club. The room is empty and the two men follow me. Gregor stays on the door making sure we have full privacy.

"Can I get you a drink?" I offer and both decline.

"Mr. O'Reagan this is Gardaí Weldon. He's new on the force and has shown great judgement with situations." Gardaí Brady uses his words carefully as I sit down and push across the file that I had Sam make on Barry Fitz.

"Gardaí Weldon we shall see your worth," I tell him.

He gives me a nervous smile.

"Here is everything you need."

Gardaí Brady touches the brown file but doesn't open it.

"This is an open and close case." I remind him.

He opens the file and looks through the information that will put Barry behind bars.

"I'm impressed," he says looking up at me.

"All you have to do is go to that warehouse and you will find the ATM's and a lot of money. The warehouse is registered in Barry Fitz name." I point at the next line. "Location of two of the vehicles that are covered in his finger prints and some hair samples. He didn't act alone. You will also find traces of Darren Jordan, Art Bell and Mark McGuiness."

The new Gardaí frowns. "Darren Jordan and Mark Mc Guinness were pulled from the lake in the early hours of this morning."

"How unfortunate," I say and focus on Gardaí Brady. "The evidence is all there Gardaí. You have Barry's address. I can assure you he's at home."

"Is he alive?" The bite in Gardaí Brady's voice tells me he isn't happy about the other's being dead. But I wasn't here to make people happy.

"Yes."

"What about Art Bell?"

"I assume he is Gardaí Brady. But I can't guarantee anything. The boy after all had a serious drug addiction." I stand to let them know this meeting is over. "I want word when Barry Fitz is arrested. I want him behind bars as quickly as possible. Set bail at a million. He is after all a flight risk," I say.

Gardaí Brady nods at everything I say.

"In the warehouse, there is a black bag behind the ATMs that's for your service."

They both get up and Gardaí Brady takes the file with him. I've been avoiding the next job on my list but I know it's time. I can't allow myself to regret my decision. If someone chooses to force my hand then it is no longer my choice.

"Gregor." He enters the room and stands close to the table that I stay seated at.

"John Cummings recently retired from the Army. He had a heroin addiction ten years ago and has remained clean." I stand before I say the next part. I've never felt conflicted before but this was the world I was forced into. The one of impossible decisions and an ever ending circle of violence. "He needs to return to his old habit, and he needs to die with a needle in his arm."

Gregor nods his understanding. He never shows any discomfort or hesitates no matter what I ask him to do.

"Also tell Sam to give me a report on Mr. Novak's movements and I will release Darragh myself."

The door closes and I get up and pour myself a drink. I can't allow myself to think about John. He had too much knowledge. He was the one who knew all about heroin and the correct dosages. He had injected it daily into Darragh's arms for weeks. I drink a full glass of whiskey before I pour another. I had trusted him not to hurt my brother, and he had lived up to his word. I knew asking him to do it again wouldn't be easy on him, but I didn't think he would say no. A part of me wished he had just agreed.

***

The minute I get word from Gardaí Brady that they have Barry in custody I go to Darragh. Opening the slot I'm surprised when he stares back at me.

"I've been waiting for hours," he barks.

I pull back the lock not prolonging the inevitable. The door hasn't fully opened when he storms out like a bull released from a cage.

"Where are you going?" I call after him.

"For a fucking shower." He slams the door as he leaves the area.

"Wanda."

"What can I do for you today?"

"Unlock the living quarters," I say as I pull my tie off.

"Living Quarters are unlocked."

I enter and scan the area but nothing has been disturbed. Opening the top button of my shirt I move quietly across the room and push the bedroom door wide open. She's awake and is making good work of cutting through the poster of my bed with a blunt knife. She holds it out to me. Her food still sits on the tray.

"Wanda."

"What can I do for you today?"

"Shut down the basement except for the living area."

"Shutting down the basement."

I walk towards her and a tremble in her hands vibrates down into the knife.

"I'm going to uncuff you so you can make yourself some food." Her clothes are wrinkled and she looks like she could do with a wash. She looks away from me before returning with the frown she uses to make herself look confused. I turn my back on her and go to the wardrobe. I don't have much to offer her but a white t-shirt and a large pair of black jogging pants.

"I don't have anything else but you can shower and get changed." I place the clothes at the foot of the bed.

She's still holding the knife refusing to lower it. "You can either put the knife down and place it on the tray. Or I'm coming over there and I'll remove it from you myself." The knife rattles as it hits the tray.

"Your understanding of English has evolved so rapidly that I'm impressed."

Her cheeks tinge with a pink hue and she drops her gaze.

I uncuff her. She cradles her hand to her chest.

"If you try anything I will recuff you," I say.

She doesn't look at me. "No English." She can't even look at me as she lies poorly. I don't correct her but leave the room. I'm removing every sharp object from the drawers as she enters the kitchen. Her footsteps are unsure.

"Make whatever you want, just clean up after yourself."

I use a pillow case to gather up all pointy objects. I leave her in the living space as I check the cabinets in the bathroom. Her moving around in my kitchen has me tightening my jaw. She's touching my things, and I don't like it at all. I take everything back out to the living area where I place them on a table and start up my laptop. I check in on all the hotels and back-end business. My mind goes to John again wondering if Gregor is now with him. Is he dead or high?

The food smells lovely and I glance over at the girl. She's still nervous, her eyes darting around the room. She notices me looking at her and drops my gaze. The tremble in her hand is making it difficult for her to cut up onions and especially with a blunt knife.

My email dings and I open the report from Sam on Mr. Novak. *He's been down in Kilkenny, Longford and Athlone,* it's the next three places I wanted to open up my new ventures. Nothing was out of the ordinary.

Good job Sam. Stay with him.

The smell of food is to my right. The girl stands there and I close my laptop that she is staring at. She's left a plate of food beside me, noodles with chopped peppers and onions. The sauce smells like a mushroom and she gives me a quivery smile before handing me a knife and fork. She walks away and the nervous tick in her walk has me looking at the food.

"I want you to take a bite."

She pauses her stride and turns to me and shrugs.

I pick up the knife and point at the food and then her, it was unnecessary but I would keep up the pretense. "You eat."

"Ah... Hmm.... You." She points at the plate and then at me.

"You," I say. I can see the moment she knows she should just taste it. She walks over and takes the fork from my fingers, her pulse flutters in her neck as she takes a very small amount of noodles. I stop her before they reach her lips.

"More," I say the word strongly and her nostrils flair.

She drops the small amount back onto the plate and takes a large fork full.

"Eat it all," I say standing.

"No... hmmm. You."

Her attempt at broken English is almost amusing. I go to the counter where her plate sits and I pick it up while getting a clean fork. She watches me nervously as I start to eat hers. She pauses eating mine.

"All of it," I repeat and I enjoy the results. Her eyes drop closed, and she fights it, trying to pretend that she didn't scrape the remainder of the tablets off her breakfast and into my dish. I finish my own food and walk towards her just before she slides off the side of the couch. Lying her down, I pull her arms to her side and brush her hair out of her face.

She was clever I had to give her that.

CHAPTER NINE

SVETLANA

MY HEAD HURTS AS I slowly open my eyes. I'm sideways. A slick black laptop sits on a coffee table in front of me. A black object under the table catches my attention. Opening my eyes fully I don't move as I focus on the gun that's strap to the base of the table.

Footsteps have me sitting up too quickly; I hope my face doesn't portray what I just saw. I hold on to the arm of the couch as he places a glass of water in front of me.

"You fell asleep," he says. At this stage I think he knows I understand English. My parched mouth won't give me a second, the water looks so good. I gulp the full glass down as he stands over me.

"Would you like another?" He asks his hand reaching out for the glass. I glance up at him and into ink black orbs. I have no idea if I've angered him or if he's feeding me water to drug me.

"Ano." I refuse to speak English but hand over the glass. I watch him as he moves across the floor, his broad back shifts under the fabric of his tailored suit. He fills the glass from the tap; I don't see anything being added to it.

I gulp it down and this time when he watches me I'm more conscious of him. Was he waiting for me to relax so he could punish me for trying to poison him? What would my uncle have done? He would have sent me to Holic or worse. Placing the glass on the table I wrap my arms around myself. My mouth dries up as he slowly descends before me until he is on his hunkers. I want to sink back into the couch but my hand has gripped the arm of the couch and I don't move.

"You tried to drug me."

My stomach roils and flips at his words.

His eyes tighten ever so slightly as he continues to speak. "I know you understand what I'm saying. So understand this. I will let it go since you didn't succeed. But the next time you try to do anything like that, there will be consequences." He rises and fixes the sleeves of his suit jacket.

My heart palpitates as he stares down at me.

"Consider this your final warning." When his back is to me my hand flutters to my chest, trying to keep my heart in place.

"I have business to attend to. I would suggest you get fed and washed before I return." He turns back to me each step has me sinking into the couch. I wish time would speed up as it feels like he's walking towards me forever.

He picks up the slick black laptop. "Wanda."

"What can I do for you today?" The robotic voice comes from speakers that I can't see but seem to be all around us.

"Unlock the basement," he says as he walks from the living space. He disappears out a large door and I'm tempted to follow him to see where he goes. But I don't move from the couch. I'm trying to calm down my frantic mind. I wasn't sure how long he would be gone but a shower sounded good and maybe more food.

I'm hesitant to remove my clothes. There is no lock on the bathroom door. There is nothing I can move to push against it either. Returning to the kitchen I pull in one of the large stools under the breakfast bar. It weighs a ton, but I manage to get it into the bathroom and push it against the door. It won't stop anyone from coming in, but it will take force to get in fully and I will hear it. I quickly strip down and jump into the shower. I don't want to think that this is his shower. Opening up the shower gel, it reminds me of him, a kind of minty smell with a hint of grass. The night he picked me up it was there under all the other smells. I wash myself quickly not lingering in the bathroom too long. I should have brought in my clothes. I find towels in a press. None of them are very big. One wraps around me but cuts off well above my knee. Wrapping myself in it, I try to find a bigger towel but come up empty. Holding the towel with one hand I pull the stool away and nearly topple it on my toes, luckily I catch it before that happens. Goosebumps rise over my bare skin as I step out of the steamed up bathroom and into the living space. I want to run through the space and into the bedroom but I force myself to walk. I remind myself that I'm fine, no one is here. The clothes that he has given to me still lay on the bed. The t-shirt is brand new, the lines from the packaging still available to see.

"Turn around slowly."

The hair lifts on the nape of my neck as I clutch my towel and turn around slowly.

I'm staring at a black gun that's pointed right at me. I can't blink or look away. My whole body tenses as the gun slowly disappears. The man still holds it but he looks into the bedroom both hands clutching the gun. It's pointed at the floor but he looks like he knows what he's doing.

"Where is he?" His green eyes shoot to me, and beads of sweat start to form on my lip.

"No English." My lip and voice trembles.

He's still looking at me. His red curly hair is tight to his head, but streaks of grey give away his age.

"Are you alone?" He asks, and the gun seems to be rising.

I nod my head.

"Don't dare move," he warns as he moves into the living space. My whole body starts to shake and I'm looking around the room. I have no idea what for. When he reappears he keeps the gun pointed to the ground but he's not letting it go.

"Get in here."

Licking my lips I hold the towel tight feeling so vulnerable right now with just a towel on. I sit on the couch and he stands over me. Taking out his phone he rings someone.

As he's occupied with his phone, I consider the gun I saw earlier strapped under the table. My heart starts to jackhammer in my chest at the thought of using it. I don't get a chance as he hangs up and his focus returns to me.

"What's your name?"

"Svetlana," I say.

He continues to look around the space like he's waiting for someone to arrive.

I clutch my towel with one hand and wipe the other on the very small piece of material. My wet hair clings to my shoulders and back. Drops of water slowly crawl down my skin making me shiver.

"Where is he?" His voice rises and I jump at the unexpected amount of anger. I'm shaking my head as he takes a step to me. The side of my face erupts in pain as he lashes out, hair whips across my face painfully and I stay huddled under my curtain of hair as my face burns.

"Let's try that again. Where is he?"

Holding my breath, I push my hair off my stinging face. "I don't know," I say and gulp down air as he walks away. My hand trembles as it touches my face. Blood covers the tips of my fingers. My stomach feels like a rock landed in it as I watch him pace. I try not to touch my face but the burn feels like it's getting worse. When he looks at me again, I look away and try to make myself small.

"Ring him," he demands and dread trickles down my spine. "Ring. Liam. Now."

"I don't have a phone."

This man had no idea that I was here against my will, but if I tell him that, he wasn't going to help me. Maybe he would dispose of me understanding how useless I was?

He hands me his phone. "It's ringing."

I take it and listen to the ring tone.

"John. I hope you're keeping well." Liam's voice fills the phone and I quickly look at John.

"It's Svetlana. You need to come home."

John rips the phone out of my hands. "Don't take too long Liam. I don't like to be kept waiting, and you don't want me to hurt her now do you?" He hangs up and stuffs the phone in his pocket. Using the sleeve of his army green jacket he wipes sweat from his forehead.

"Don't move," he says as he lowers the gun and starts to move towards the kitchen. He's opening drawers, running his hands under the stools and counters. I don't know what he's searching for. I think of the gun again and shimmy forward on the couch.

"What are you doing?" He's in front of me, his strides filled with anger.

I sink back. "I ... I need to use the bathroom." I stumble across the words. He wipes his forehead again before glancing at the bathroom door.

"Fine, make it quick."

I'm up and moving across the space quickly. He doesn't follow me and I close the bathroom door calmly. I have no idea what to do. The stool is still here and I shift it behind the door. Opening presses I search for a weapon. The knock at the door has me jumping.

"Hurry up." His bark penetrates the door. There is nothing in the bathroom. Sweat trickles down my back. I catch a glimpse of myself in the mirror, the cut on my face isn't as big as I thought but covers half my cheek. A small amount of blood has gathered around the opening.

The door handle rattles as he tries to open it. "Open the door now."

Squeezing my eyes shut I try to think. "Just give me one moment."

The chair starts to rock as he pushes the door in. I take one final panicked look around the bathroom and the only thing is the glass soap dish. Picking it up I wait until his head pops in. I throw it and when he screams, I rush back into the shower. I've hit him but now as he pushes open the door fully, the chair scatters against the wall, I see I've only angered him. Grabbing the door of the shower I throw my weight behind it as he tries to open the door. Blood trickles fast from the cut on his eyebrow. The gun comes into view and he points it at my head. "Open the door or I'll pull the trigger."

I release the door and the moment it's open, he grabs me by the arm and drags me back out into the living space. His fingers dig painfully into my arm as he pushes me onto the couch. Clutching the towel I just about keep it covering my body.

He keeps his narrowed eyes on me as he walks backways to the kitchen. Taking a towel from the drawer he presses it against the gash on his eyebrow.

He stuffs the gun into the back of his jeans as he opens a black bag that's placed on the table. He takes out a small black box and opens it. My leg hits the table as I fumble to move back. A large needle and a bottle of white liquid are the only contents in the pouch.

"It's not for you," he says but his words aren't to comfort me. He takes the red soaked towel away from his face and winches in pain. If it's for Liam and he kills him, what did that mean for me? Would it be my opportunity to escape from here or would he kill me after killing Liam? Did I want Liam to kill him first? Any outcome for me wasn't good. Unless they killed each other or Liam killed John and then in that moment I could get the gun and kill Liam. That seemed like the best plan. But I wasn't sure if I could move, the risk had my heart hammering in my chest.

I touch my face again as the burn returns, the bleeding had stopped but I can feel the swollen skin under my fingertips.

The door to my right opens. I don't hear it but see the movement at the corner of my eye. John is closing up the small black pouch. I move my head slowly and my pulse spikes, the sound of my heartbeat thrashes in my ear. Liam is here and I don't see a weapon in his hand. He walks across the floor like there is no danger here. He hasn't looked at me his focus is solely on John.

"John, sorry for keeping you waiting."

John removes the gun quickly and efficiently from the back of his jeans and points it at Liam. Liam doesn't stop walking, he moves like there is no gun. I don't know if he's crazy or brave.

"Are you surprised to see me?"

For the first time Liam glances at me. "It would be in both our interests to let her leave the room."

"She's going nowhere."

"Did you do that to her face?" Liam asks him when he reaches the table. He's close enough to me that if he reached out he could touch me.

"I had to keep her in line." John moves away from Liam. "You sent a hit man to kill me?"

"I see Gregor failed." Liam doesn't deny trying to kill John and hurt flashes across the man's face before it tightens with anger.

"He's dead, and that's on you."

"What do you want?" Liam asks him bluntly. They are focused on each other and I think of trying to get out of the room but I know I wouldn't get two feet without being noticed. Sitting here and keeping quiet could be the only thing that might save me for now.

"I would never have come after you like that." John's brows pull down as he speaks while hurt tightens his words. He keeps the gun on Liam as he picks up the blood-soaked towel and dabs his eyebrow taking away fresh blood.

"Pick up the needle and fill it." His attitude changes as he points the gun at the cases. My mind takes a moment to realize he's talking to me.

My hand trembles as I reach across and pull the pouch towards me. It's hard to get it open with one hand, but I refuse to let my towel go. I've never filled a needle before but I've seen it on TV. The needle is huge as I remove it from the casing. I quickly look to Liam but he's watching John.

"You should have run when you had the chance." Liam's words are so calm.

John takes a step towards him and points the gun at his head. "I'm the one with the gun Liam; you think I won't pull the fucking trigger?"

My body tenses and I'm frozen as I wait to see if he will pull the trigger. Liam doesn't answer him and I find myself being the target of John's anger again.

"Fill the needle now. Or I'll shoot you."

My hands tremble too badly and I drop the needle. While trying to pick it up my eyes blur from pure fear. The bang of the gun rattles the couch as John pulls the trigger.

CHAPTER TEN

LIAM

FEATHERS RAIN DOWN AS the cushion explodes from the impact of the bullet.

"Fill up the needle now." John has the gun pointed at me as he shouts at Svetlana who hasn't recovered from the shock of nearly being shot. She's clutching her towel, her head bent and I'm not sure if she's breathing. She wasn't shot but I think she's holding her breath as her body is too still.

"Let me do it," I say to John. "Shooting at her isn't going to make her any calmer."

John looks between me and Svetlana before wiping sweat and blood from his head. He's high. Gregor must have started the job but never got to finish it.

"Fine."

Kneeling down, I pick the needle up from the ground. I glance at Svetlana, she looks at me through her curtain of hair and it's like she remembers to breathe. Her body starts to shake, and she slowly raises her head with her eyes on John.

"Hurry up," John shouts.

The irritation in his voice is growing, and that makes him very dangerous. I glance at him from under my arm, he's wiping his face again with the sleeve of his jacket and I use the moment.

Taking the gun that's strapped to my ankle I don't rise as I aim the gun between his eyes and pull the trigger. Svetlana screams as John falls to the ground. The wall behind him is splattered in blood. I don't rise but place the gun back in its holder and turn to Svetlana. She's trying to catch her breath as she stares at the wall.

Her face is swollen, a cut etched into her cheek. Taking her face in my hands I make her look away from John and towards me. Her breath brushes my face as she tries to suck in air. The cut on her cheek isn't deep. My fingers prod closer and she hisses in pain.

"It's okay. It's over now," I say not sure if my words will reassure her, but some part of me wants her to know that she's safe. I need to get something to clean her face.

I rise but her hands shoot out and grab my arms. "Don't go." She inhales deeply and exhales a sob. She hasn't released me and I sit down on the couch that has a bullet hole in it. She leans into my chest and cries. She's still holding my arms but releases them and grips my jacket like I might leave her. I've never been in a situation before where someone seeks comfort from me. I'm normally the cause of the distress. I slowly allow my arm to wrap itself around her and the other finds its way into her hair, my touch makes her cry harder and her hold on me grows tighter. My thumb grazes her back, the skin lumpy and scarred. I stop the movement when she freezes under me, her sobs ceasing. She withdraws instantly moving away from me and wrapping her arms across her chest. Now she won't look at me and I'm unsure what I have done.

"Go in and get dressed," I say.

Ice-blue eyes that are filled with anger focus on me. Her anger is for me and I'm not sure why. Her legs knock together as she rises and goes into the bedroom.

Picking up the needle and glass bottle I place them back in the pouch before putting it in the bag that John had brought with him. Stepping between his open legs I bend down and pick up the gun. I disarm it and place it in the bag also. The hole between his eyes had killed him instantly. He was a friend, and I felt I had given him an honest death. Pulling back the large screen TV, I enter the code to open my safe. After stuffing the bag in I go to the bathroom, glass crunches under my feet and the bathroom is disheveled. Taking down the first aid kit I take it with me to the bedroom and open the door slowly. Svetlana has changed into the t-shirt and jogging pants that I had left out for her. Her knees are pulled up to her chest as she sits in the corner of the room that she has favored since arriving here. She isn't crying and when I step in her eyes track my every movement. Removing my suit jacket I place it on the bed before I go to her with the first aid kit. Sitting on the floor in front of her she continues to stare at me.

"Have I done something wrong?" I'm curious as to what happened for her to place such anger on me.

"Besides kidnap me."

Her words surprise me. I knew she could speak English but hearing it was different. Opening the first aid kit I take out an anti-septic wipe. "This might sting a little," I warn her in advance. Taking her face in my hand she pulls away from me. "I'm trying to help you," I say before I proceed. This time when I take her face she holds still but her eyes are still burning with hate. I dab the area and she doesn't blink.

"I didn't kidnap you. You were given to me," I remind her. She doesn't reply and when I look at her she swallows and looks away.

"What happened to your back?" I ask while getting a clean antiseptic wipe. She doesn't answer me and I finish cleaning her face. "Are you hurt anywhere else?"

I ask and her anger melts away she shakes her head, "No."

I repack the first aid kit and get ready to leave.

"I ran away, and my uncle got Holic to punish me. He favored a whip. That's how I got the scars on my back." She clutches her hands together as she speaks. She won't look at me and I'm surprised at the level of anger that rises inside me. Getting up I take the first aid kit with me and go into the kitchen. Pouring two whiskeys' I glance over at John. Why did he have to kill Gregor? He was one of my best men.

"Wanda."

"What can I do for you today?"

"Ring Gregor." I take a drink as Gregor's phone rings. I'm hoping he answers but when he doesn't I finish the rest of the whiskey and take the second glass into Svetlana. She's still sitting where I left her. I don't kneel down but reach the glass out to her.

"You're in shock, it will help," I say.

She turns her head away. "I don't trust you. I'm sure you've laced it with sleeping pills." Her recent shock is making her very brave.

My hand grips around the glass. "Your English gets better by the second. And I don't trust you either; don't forget you tried to drug me too." I place the drink on the bedside table feeling more annoyed than I should be with her.

Leaving her I go back into the living area and remove my waistcoat and tie, I roll up my sleeves and start by washing the blood off the wall.

"Mr. O'Reagan." Gregor walks into my living quarters, he's never been in here before but he doesn't look around, there is relief on his face when he looks at me. His struggle with John is evident on his face.

"He tied me up. I couldn't get here to warn you."

"It's okay. I'm glad to see you're alive," I say.

He comes and stands beside me.

"Can you get rid of him?"

"On it." He goes to leave but after thinking he was dead and realizing he wasn't makes me appreciate him more. I continue to clean the walls and Gregor works around me. Once John is gone, I easily wash the blood from the wall. Getting a black sack I remove the burst cushion and clean up the smashed glass.

Svetlana comes out of the bedroom holding an empty glass. I don't comment but I'm pleased that she drank it.

She's looking at the floor where John had been. "Was he your friend?"

Taking the black sack I leave it in the kitchen area and start to clean up all the feathers. "Yes."

"Why did you kill him?"

"He was going to kill me. What happened to my bathroom?" I fire back not liking her questions.

She sits on the couch, pulling one leg under her. "I was hiding from him. Should I clean it up?" There is a nervousness in her that wasn't there a moment ago and I try to figure out what was going on. She drops my gaze and tightens her hands on her leg.

"I'll do it," I say and walk away. From the corner of my eye I see her move.

Her movements are quick but I don't turn around. "I just want to leave."

I reach the kitchen and pour myself out a whiskey. Looking up at her, Svetlana is standing beside the couch, holding my gun that is kept strapped to the base of the coffee table. I take a slow drink.

Her eyes shift around the room. "I'll shoot you if you don't let me leave." She moves towards the door and I take a step out of the kitchen area. I don't put my drink down.

She stares at it in confusion. "I will shoot you. Don't test me." Her hands tremble.

"You know you can't leave," I say and finish my drink. "The only way out of here is if you kill me."

Her eyes fill with tears and she blinks letting them fall down her cheeks. "I just want to be free. I don't want to hurt anyone."

I don't move or react to her words.

"You can tell him I escaped," she's pleading now.

I move back slowly towards the counter and place my glass on it. "Just put the gun down." I give her a final warning.

She shakes her head.

I see the shift in her stance.

"I'm sorry." She tells me before she pulls the trigger.

It takes a lot to surprise me but she just did. She looks at the gun like she can't figure out what just happened. She points the gun back at me as I walk towards her and continues to pull the trigger. Each click has her eyes filling with tears. I reach her and take my gun from her hands.

"You think I would leave a loaded gun in a place you could easily access?" Once I have the gun in my hand she moves away from me. But every step she takes I mirror it. I'm angry that she so easily pulled the trigger. I didn't expect her to do it and I don't like surprises. She's panicked. I can see it in the shift of her eyes. The moment she darts to the left, I let her get a few steps ahead of me. She's trying to make a break for the door. I catch her easily and she screams as I wrap my arms around her waist and lift her off the ground. She's kicking and screaming, reaching back and trying to claw at my face. Once I reach my bedroom, I deposit her on the bed and she scurries back to the headboard.

"I'm sorry."

"Useless words, Svetlana." My calm drives her panic and I'm glad. She just tried to kill me.

"Please," she begs as I move around the bed, she tries to dash away from me and I grip her arm, pulling her towards me. I'm ready when she strikes out at me, grabbing her other arm I hold them together.

"Let me go." Her words are growing frantic and as much as I want to hurt her, another part of me wants to calm her. Pulling in her into my chest I hold her and she struggles but finally she stops.

"I'll let you go when you calm down." I speak to the crown of her head. She's dangerous and it has nothing to do with her ability to kill me. She's dangerous because I didn't want to let her go. She doesn't speak and I don't release her. Her body soon sags in my arms and I come to my senses and I let her go.

"I will arrange for your return to your uncle tomorrow," I say standing up.

"No. No. Please. He'll kill me."

"Like you just tried to kill me?"

"Tie me to the bed. I won't protest." She's shaking her head, tears falling from her eyes. "But I'm begging you don't send me back. Holic will make sure this time I don't survive."

I turn my back on her, and she jumps off the bed.

"Liam, please."

Her words scorch me but help me make a decision. I face her now.

"No I've made up my mind. I don't want you here anymore." I close the bedroom door and leave her. My phone rings and I close my eyes trying to pull myself together.

"Yes Una," I answer.

"Finn's missing. No one can find him."

"He may have needed time away," I tell her.

"No Liam. This is different. His wedding band, phone and car keys are here."

"I'll be up in a minute." Hanging up I stuff the phone in my pocket.

"Wanda."

"What can I do you for you today?"

"Ring the front gate."

The ring tone is immediate and Stephen answers. "Did you see Finn leave today?" I ask him.

"No Mr. O'Reagan." That meant he was still on the property.

"Wanda lock down the whole basement." I tell her and grab my keys before leaving.

"Locking down the basement."

CHAPTER ELEVEN

LIAM

I FIND SHANE IN the kitchen waiting for me. I want to tell him I don't have time for this.

"What's happened?"

"Finn's missing and so is Darragh. Both of their phones are here. It just doesn't feel right to me Liam."

The minute he mentions Darragh's name, something uneasy slithers up my back. *Had I made a mistake letting him go?*

"Where have you searched?"

Shane shrugs. "Everywhere."

"Did something happen?" I'm going around in circles.

The back door opens and Una comes in with her hair frizzy and damp from the start of fresh rain. "Stephen saw Darragh go into the forest a while ago and Finn was following him."

A tingle starts in my chest and I have the urge to rub it. "I'll go, stay here both of you in case they come back."

Shane narrows his eyes. "I'll go with you."

"No." I needed to get out of this kitchen. "Just stay here."

The urge to get out of the house isn't eased when I step out into the rain. Walking to the yard, I'm picturing the worst possible outcome. Darragh being in the forest again isn't a coincidence. I take the quad to get there faster. I don't allow my mind to go to that night. That night that destroyed each one of us in a different way.

The time that Darragh had left with the gun and Una and I searched for him in the forest, that day I thought he had remembered. He was standing in the spot where it had happened. But he hadn't. I hope I get lucky again today.

I reach the tree line and stop the quad. I try to listen over the soft rain and the chatter of birds but I don't hear voices. Getting off I start the short walk to where I hope they aren't. But hope doesn't make the image of Darragh and Finn disappear. I can't hear them but they are where I thought they would be.

They don't hear my approach and I put my hands in my trousers pockets to look calm and collected. For the first time in a long time I'm rattled. Dealing with John and Svetlana hasn't helped but this right here, was something I had fought hard to bury.

"Darragh you are causing quite the stir back at the house." I step out from behind a large oak tree. Finn spins around and faces me. He's not wearing his sunglasses; his eyes are haunted and filled with pain. I hope its Siobhan's loss and not something Darragh has said. My eyes move to Darragh who's soaked to the skin. He's hunkered down while touching the forest floor.

"I used to dream of that room." He looks up at me now, and I don't see hate or anger. These are the emotions Darragh wears the most but right now he looks as sorrowful as Finn.

"Come back to the house, everyone is concerned about you," I say.

He's rising and Darragh's never looked as tall or as threatening. "I want the truth." He takes a step towards me and Finn moves closer also.

"The truth about what?" I remove my hands from my pockets. An ache has started in the back of my throat that I ignore.

"Why was I in that room?" His tortured voice wavers.

"You robbed a bank Darragh and ...."

"No, before. I was in that room before." He's shaking his head, running his hands through his hair, like he can pull out some memory.

"What did you do to him?" Finn speaks for the first time.

"You should go back to the house. Una is very worried about you." Finn doesn't answer me but stays exactly where he is.

"I dreamt of that room for so long. But that's all I thought it was, a dream. While in there I remember I carved my name into a wall. It's still there Liam." Darragh takes another step towards me. "Tell me why I was in that room." His anger grows with each word.

"I was helping you get clean." I have the urge to rub my throat again but refrain from moving.

"Who is John Cummings?" When he asks me this question there is something in his eyes, he already knows.

"I'm not standing in the rain debating this nonsense. We need to return to the house." I look at Finn and he takes a step towards me.

"You drugged me. He told me what you did to me." Darragh's brows furrow and the look of betrayal on his face rattles me further.

"Why would you do that?" His disgust fills each word.

"Did you do that to him, Liam? Our brother?" Finn looks at me like I'm the monster I am.

"No."

Darragh's face changes. It goes slack with hurt before curling up with anger. He lets out a cry as he races towards me. I'm ready for his anger.

"I don't want to hurt you," I warn him but he doesn't slow down. I hunch slightly taking the impact of him to the left side of my body, before swinging out and gripping his neck. I slam him into the ground. The air is pulled from his lungs but I hold him down.

Finn's moving and I don't release Darragh as I look up at him and he pauses.

"Let him up now." Finn demands.

"I will when he calms down," I say to Finn. Darragh is thrashing under me and I use both hands to hold him down. The air returns and he gasps, his face red.

"Get the fuck off me." His roars only make me tighten my hold on him.

I'm keeping an eye on Finn too but he doesn't move. "You need to calm down."

He's shaking his head, pushing his body up. "Fuck you. You're a liar. That's all you do."

The weight on my chest keeps growing as I hold Darragh down. I've held him down just like this before. My hold falters and he gets out from under me. Darragh doesn't pause for a second and I'm not ready when his foot impacts with the side of my face. The impact rolls me onto my back. I'm trying to stand; I can't hear anything and black spots fill my vision. Finn is holding Darragh, but he won't be able to for much longer. Darragh is like a man possessed. He wants to hurt me. I'm standing and stumble, a tree that I cling to stops me from falling. I feel the shift more than hear it. Turning my head, Finn has lost the battle to hold Darragh back. I hold the tree for support until the last second. Turning I shift until I'm behind him and grab him by the neck. I push his body against the tree roughly.

"Calm down," I say. My voice sounds strange I only have hearing in one ear.

"Did I watch her die?" Darragh's face crumbles and once again I'm faced with the decision I made that night.

"What is he talking about?" Finn is pacing.

The rain is coming down heavier on top of us all.

"He must be high again," I say.

Darragh losses control under me. My control over this situation was slipping.

"You go back to the house Finn." I raise my voice.

Darragh slows down his fight against me while Finn takes a step back.

I think he's going to go, but he doesn't. "Did you find out who killed my wife?"

Closing my eyes I try to compose myself. "Finn. Don't you think I have enough to handle right now?"

"You always put him first Liam."

"You sound pathetic." I can see the hurt my words inflict. "Go home."

"I know I'm not the strongest, but I'm not damaged like you. So I'm not the pathetic one."

"I said go home Finn." This time he does with hunched shoulders.

I wait until Finn is out of sight before I focus on Darragh. "Your mind is playing tricks on you. You need to let this go." I shake him hoping I'm drilling each word into him.

"John told me what you did to me." His lips turn into a snarl. "Just fucking admit it, you are so weak." His roar is laced with venom that pierces my skin.

I shake him again, slamming him into the ground. "I'm the only thing holding us together." My chest tightens again and I don't know what's happening to me.

"I. Don't. Believe you. I saw my name on that wall."

"Yes you were there before, to dry out." It doesn't matter what I say he's shaking his head, blinking rain out of his eyes.

"No Liam. You drugged me because I saw something I shouldn't have seen."

My hands release him and I sit back. I need to remove my tie. I can't breathe properly.

Darragh is standing over me now. "Just tell me what happened. I can take it." Darragh continues to plead.

I open the top button of my shirt but it doesn't give me the relief I'm craving. "I don't know what you're talking about." My words are choppy and I use the tree beside me to stand. I need to get away from here but Darragh is in my face, his hands grip my shoulders.

"I'm begging you Liam. I can't have this going around in my head all the time." The pain in his eyes radiates towards me.

"You are better off not knowing," I whisper, the fight in me leaving.

Hope blossoms dangerously in Darragh and he grips me tighter. "I need to know. Please. I can't live like this anymore. I keep seeing her Liam. I keep seeing mam."

"Stop." I try to walk away; the air seems to be thinning at an alarming rate.

"No. I can't stop. I see her dying face. She's gasping for air."

I push Darragh away from me and take a step back. "I said stop."

"Did she die here?" He's pointing around him wildly. "Is this why I keep coming back here. Did she die in this forest? On the ground?" His frustration is growing as he spins around. "Tell me!" his roar carries across the forest.

"This is the final time I'm saying this. Leave it alone." I walk away from Darragh. The rain batters down heavier now like it knows our voices need to be kept hushed.

"No!" Hands slam into my back and I stumble into a tree. Hugging it I use it to try to get my guard back up.

My anger rises like a tide and I want to contain it so I try to walk away. But he pushes me again. "Tell me now. I want to know. Did you hurt her? Did I see it?"

I swing around not able to control myself. "I am the only person who has protected you, so stop this. It won't end well." I warn him but I know he won't listen. His mind is frantically searching for some explanation of what he thinks happened.

"I need to know." Right now I'm not sure if it's the rain or tears that trickle down his face.

"There is no going back Darragh if you go down this road."

He steps closer. "I'm already standing on the road brother."

I hate him for this; I hate him for not letting it go. But most of all I hate him for what he is making me do. "Fine you were there when she died."

He stumbles back like I've just struck him. He looks at me from the corner of his eye as he takes in deep breaths while shaking his head. "I didn't..." He can't finish the sentence and I don't finish it either. He spins around with his back to me before lowering to his hunkers. "Oh God, no." He's pleading with someone that isn't there. "Oh no. No." He's standing again and this time I know it's not the rain that wets his face. He's looking at his hands now before looking back at me. His brow furrows and he lets out a strangled sob. "Ah Liam, no." His voice chokes.

When he moves, he looks like his balance is off. I can't hear what he's muttering as he looks to the sky. An uncontrollable cry releases from his mouth. His pain is tearing at me as his steps falter like he's drunk. He's back on his hunkers shaking his head repeatedly. His eyes dart around the floor of the forest before he crumples. His hands sink into the wet mud and he cries.

I can't move, I can't comfort him. A wave of cold assaults me and I know what I am doing is unforgivable.

"Darragh." My voice doesn't carry across his cries.

Shouts in the distance have me rushing the few steps to Darragh. "You need to listen to me. It's over. It's buried. We are the only ones who know." He won't look up and I get down on my knees. I'm holding his face in my hands as he tries to pull away.

"We need to tell them." His broken voice has me reeling back.

Panic rushes through me. My hand collides with his cheek. "You need to pull it together now. They are coming. You need to pull it together."

"Darragh, Liam." Shane's voice is closer now.

I grip Darragh again. "You will keep it together, or they will kill you," I warn him and he's nodding like he's waking up. "My neck is on the line too." I shake him and start to rise. My suit is covered in mud. I need to fix my appearance. I button up my shirt and fix my tie as Shane comes into view. Darragh gets up, but he's still not fully present, his mind still shattered in a million pieces.

"I found him, call off the search party. Just another case of Darragh being Darragh." I give Darragh a warning look but he's not even looking at me.

"Are you on drugs?" Shane's anger ignites as he steps towards Darragh.

Darragh's head snaps up and the pain in his eyes has me stepping in front of him.

"Leave him," I warn Shane and he tightens his fists.

"Why do you always protect him?" I don't answer the question that I'm always asked.

"You better return and tell everyone he's fine," I say but Shane tries to look around me.

"He needs help Liam." Shane leaves, and the relief is short lived as I turn to Darragh.

He's staring at me. "How can you look at me?"

"Let's get back," I say and let him walk in front of me. His steps are so unsure; his hands hang at his side. He holds himself like a man who has given up.

CHAPTER TWELVE

SVETLANA

Hours pass, I don't know if the day has turned into night but it feels like forever that I wait in Liam's bedroom. I'm kicking myself for being so stupid, now I would pay a hefty price. I shiver again just thinking of my uncle. What would he do to me this time?

My head snaps up as I hear movement in the living space. I rush to the door but don't dare open it. Someone is moving around. Pressing my ear to the door I try to listen. Footsteps sound heavy and they are coming towards the bedroom door. I rush back and I clear the area as it opens. Liam drips water onto the floor. His brow is cut and his jaw red. Mud clings to his clothes and I take another step back as he steps into the room. I want to ask what happened, but he goes to his wardrobe and removes his suit jacket. His tie follows it onto the ground before he unbuttons his shirt. I'm holding my breath as he pulls his shirt down. His tanned wide back is covered in a huge tattoo of a black dragon. It shifts under his muscles as he removes the shirt. I'm waiting for his trousers to be removed but he pulls out a black t-shirt from the press and pulls it on. His hair is still damp. It's like he remembers I'm here and he glances at me but I'm dismissed so quickly that it stings.

He takes out a pair of black jogging pants, gathers up his damp clothes and leaves me to my thoughts. It's the last place I want to be. I want to know if he rang my uncle. It's not like I'm going to get sent to my room by my uncle, he was going to kill me. A pain starts in the pit of my stomach and no matter how tight I hold myself it doesn't go away. I wait for another ten minutes before I open the door. Initially it looks like the living area is empty.

Liam drinks from a bottle and I move around the couch. He's sitting on the floor between the couch and the coffee table, a bottle of whiskey is his comfort from whatever happened. His face looks sore. It's normal perfect appearance makes the marks appear starker.

He glances at me before drinking from the bottle again. "Don't even try to leave. I'm in no mood."

I wasn't planning on running. My only concern right now was finding out if he rang my uncle. I go to the bathroom because it's where I assume the first aid kit is. I'm nervous as I take it back into the living room. Liam doesn't react as I sit at his bare feet and open the kit. Taking out an antiseptic wipe just like he had done with me I rip the packaging.

"This is going to sting," I say and he looks at me from the corner of his eye. The depth of the blackness has me focusing on the wipe in my hand. I have to lean in to get to the cut near his eyebrow. He watches me until I'm aware of how close we are, how my breath brushes his face. How his hands that hold the whiskey bottle brush against my thighs. I'm hyper-aware of his smell and how much larger he is compared to me. When I make contact he hisses. "Sorry," I whisper, but he doesn't acknowledge the apology.

"When I was younger, I wanted to be a vet." I can sense his dark eyes on me but to keep myself calm as I continue to clean the cut that's started to bleed, I go to my childhood. "I once nursed a bird back to his full health. He had broken his wing." I'm smiling now, not at the thought of the bird but my Father. He had made a bed for the bird; he had helped every step of the way. My kindness came from him. He wouldn't hurt anyone or anything.

"You should have broken its neck." Liam's cold words have me sitting back so I can look at him. "You were cruel," he adds.

The pain in my stomach erupts at his words. "No, he lived because I helped him, that doesn't make me cruel."

"A bird who can't fly, is a dead bird anyway. You just made him understand that, with each day you kept him earth bound."

"I don't see it that way." I hate the quiver that has entered my voice. I try to return to cleaning his cut.

Fingers curl tightly around my wrist stopping me. "Well that's how I see it." He pushes my hand away roughly. "Get away from me."

The sting of his words plasters red across my face. "Nesnáším tě." The words tumble from my lips but thankfully he doesn't understand me. I rise after telling him I hate him.

"A tak bys měl." I'm frozen as he speaks Czech back to me, telling me that I should hate him.

"You speak Czech?"

He looks exhausted as he glances up at me. "Go away."

I know I should, but I can't. "Did you ring my uncle?"

His laughter is cruel and I take a step back as he rises. "Ah, cleaning my face, telling me about your childhood. When really all you cared about was if I rang your uncle." His words are coming out in a snarl.

I'm shaking my head denying what he is saying.

"Do I have to hurt you, is that the only language you understand."

I take a quick glance at the bedroom door but he's in front of me, towering over me and I see my mistake, I took him letting me help him as a sign that maybe he was kind. Not answering is all I know. I fear no matter what I say that it will anger him further.

His hand slips around my neck. "Do you want me to hurt you?" I move back and he takes a step with me not allowing me to get away. He isn't squeezing but his large hand could crush my windpipe at any second if he wished.

"No." The word leaves me quickly as my back hits the wall. Liam's too close: too close to me, too close to losing it. His breath rushes across my face. Black orbs bore down on me.

"Why are you here?" His nostrils flare as he speaks, his hand tightens around my throat.

"What?" I had no idea of what the question meant but I didn't like how tight his hand was getting.

"Don't lie to me." His roar has the air halting in my throat. I don't know what he sees, but he loosens his hold on me. "Did he place you here to distract me?"

My stomach hollows out. "Distract you?"

He bares his teeth. "Don't act innocent."

"I don't know what you're talking about." I squeeze my eyes shut as his hand strikes out and hits the wall over my shoulder. A small startled scream bursts from my lips. The muscles quiver in his arms that are now planted either side of my head. Heat radiates off his body in waves, making the space smaller. His eyes roam my face and settle on my lips. My mind stutters and falters, was he going to kiss me? My breathing grows heavier then his head dips. My heart was ready to come out of my chest. "Liam."

He pauses, his eyes snap up to mine, his eyes tighten now, and he pushes himself away from me. "Get out of my sight." The disgust in his voice has tears burning my eyes.

I walk stiffly into the room and close the door behind me. I don't know what just happened, but I felt disgusted with myself. I had wanted him to kiss me, just not like that. I'm trying to wrap my head around the idea that I wanted him to kiss me when the door to the bedroom bursts open and Liam's anger pulses from him.

Humiliation burns my neck, and I want to hide with how he looks at me.

"I want you out of my room." His monotone is back, any emotion gone, and it makes me question if I had imagined it. When I don't move straight away, he takes a threatening step towards me.

"Did you ring my uncle?" I want to grab the question and ram it back down my throat. Liam's eyes darken and he's in front of me fingers curling around my arm.

"Don't touch me." My warning halts him and I try to yank my arm back but his grip is too tight. My senses heighten, his smell, his warmth that's all I notice.

"Are you sending me back?" My question is whispered this time, my fast pulse making my words sound breathless, and my Czech accent heavy on each word.

"I don't know. That depends on you." His eyes flicker to my lips again.

What did that mean? I'm too afraid to ask.

Liam releases me but doesn't move away. My hand drops to my side. The cut over his eye still looks pretty bad.

"He'll kill me," I blurt out and hold my head high. I refuse to let the tears fall. I can only hope that whatever flicker of kindness I keep seeing in this man will fully ignite and he won't send me back. I'm not naïve in thinking I'll never go back. But to be sent back now would be a death sentence.

"You're sleeping on the couch tonight." I hate how he won't answer me, but I take the fact that I'm still here for the night as a good sign.

***

Being in the living area is like starting fresh again. I was just getting used to the feel of the bed, now I would have to adjust to the couch. I remind myself that anything right now is better than being with my Uncle and Holic. At least I could make a cup of tea. I glance at Liam's closed door before going into the kitchen space. I check all his presses quietly as the water boils. It's a little too organized for me. There isn't much in the presses but what is there is lined perfectly. A tin of peaches catches my eye and I take it down. Pulling the tab off the tin I get a fork and sit at the breakfast bar. I'm half way through it when the door opens. I clutch the fork stopping it from slipping from my fingers. There's a blond boy standing in the doorway, he looks around him before his sad eyes land on me. Both of his eyebrows rise.

"Hmmm, not what I was expecting," He says taking a step into the room.

I'm off the stool still holding the fork. A need to run nearly overwhelms me until he holds up his hands.

"I'm Liam's brother Darragh. I'm sure he's told you some wonderful things about me."

My eyes flicker to Liam's door. I'm trying to think quickly, is he a threat or could he be my saving grace?

Darragh's blue eyes land on the fork again. "I'm just here to see Liam. I'm not going to hurt you so you can drop the weapon." A grin spreads across his face.

"No English," I say.

He nods. "That makes sense. Liam's not much of a talker."

My face flames at his insinuation.

Darragh takes a step towards the bedroom door and I make my decision. I take a risk and go to ask him for help. My mouth opens the same time as the door opens and words fail me. Liam fills the doorway; he's not wearing a t-shirt now. His tanned solid chest has the ability to scatter my brain. The ding of the fork as it hits the floor has both men looking at me.

"Go into the room," Liam tells me, but he's looking at his brother who should be very afraid now. Black orbs seem to swirl and grow with an anger that has his muscles rippling. When I don't move his eyes snap to mine and the warning there is enough for me to move. He's still filling the doorway and I take one final look at Darragh who looks unsure now.

"I needed to talk to you." Darragh starts but Liam doesn't answer.

Once I'm in the bedroom, my vision is filled with Liam's back. I had seen it earlier today but this close I'm drawn to the black dragon that seems to move across his flesh. The dragon disappears as Liam grips the door handle and closes the door without looking at me.

My ear is plastered against the door as I try to listen. When Liam speaks it's too low and muffled but Darragh's voice carries through.

"I'm going crazy, I need more answers." He sounds upset. Liam's mumbles are getting further away until finally Darragh's words aren't understandable anymore.

The bed looks tempting and I give in and move towards it. My hand touches the still warm sheets and I stand back, feeling like it's an invasion on him. I'm sliding into the bed and pulling the sheets up over me. It doesn't take long before I'm drifting into a sleep.

The river close to my house is babbling, and it's a hot day. Jan is running on the opposite side and he keeps barking at me. I'm running along with him on the opposite side. The day is perfect but I can't understand what he's barking at. He stops running, his barks growing louder.

"Jan." I call. He moves forward towards the river like he might jump in, like he might chance swimming to me but something in the long grass behind him grabs his attention. Dread reaches out and curls its bony hands around my neck. I'm shaking my head, words lodged with the tightening grip. Holic stands over Jan, a large blade in his hand and I know he's going to kill him.

"I'm sorry Jan," I tell him closing my eyes and refusing to watch.

"Wake up." The voice I recognize but I refuse to open my eyes, I can't see Jan's body, and it would undo me to see him hurt.

"Svetlana." The use of my name has me opening my eyes and staring into two inky pools that threaten to drown me. It's Liam, he's hanging over me and I struggle to control my breathing.

His hand reaches out and I sink deeper into the pillows. After dreaming such violence I'm waiting for it but Liam's fingers touch the corner of my eye. He examines the moisture on his fingers like it's something foreign to him.

"You were dreaming," he finally says, and it's like I get permission to acknowledge that it was just a dream and that Jan was still alive. I start to rise and it forces Liam to move back out of my personal space. Pushing back the blankets I'm ready to climb out of the bed but Liam stops me.

"Stay here, it's almost morning anyway."

"No it's fine."

"I said stay." His voice rises with frustration and I'm tired so I don't try to leave the bed again.

"Who's Jan?" He questions with a level of uncertainty that I have never heard from him before.

I don't want to cry. Thinking about Jan is painful but talking about him is too much. I can't look at Liam. "He's important to me," I say. No one would get it, that he was my only friend, the light in the darkness. He kept me sane. So saying he was a dog just didn't cut it for me. He was my safety net.

Liam gets up off the bed without a word. He doesn't say anything to me as he walks out of the room.

CHAPTER THIRTEEN

LIAM

J AN NOVAK, I TYPE into my laptop and hit search. Three results show up and I'm clicking on the first. A ninety-year-old man, who lives over three hundred kilometers from where Svetlana lives. So I rule him out. The second one is young, too young thankfully. He's a twelve-year-old boy and once again the further I dig he bears no relation to Svetlana. The third has my hands tightening. A twenty-two-year-old. I open his image; he isn't what I thought Svetlana would like, blond hair and brown eyes. He wasn't very tall for a man, maybe five foot five and he had a slim build. Was this the Jan she was talking about? The one she was calling out in her sleep? I close the laptop and rub my eyes as I release a growl. My muscles feel too tight so I get up. This shouldn't bother me; I had no idea why it was bothering me. I had more important things to focus on. The burning sensation in my chest has me rubbing it again. I had no idea what was wrong with me.

The spray of the hot water loosens some of my tightened muscles.

I can hear the phone ring from the living space. Grabbing a towel I wrap it around my waist and enter the living area. Svetlana is leaning over my phone, she hasn't touched it but it's soaked up all her attention that she doesn't notice my arrival. A small startled yelp falls from her lips as I pick up my phone. Her cheeks deepen and she glances away from me.

"Sam, I hope you have some news," I say as I go into the bedroom.

"Mr. Novak's doing what he's supposed to do. He hasn't done anything else only what you requested him to do."

"Good. Don't leave his side."

"I won't boss."

"Just one more thing, can you listen in their conversation?" I close the bedroom door and drop the towel as I move to the wardrobe.

"I could with one of them tonight. He likes a drink in a local pub here. I don't know why, it has a few farmers in it. No women."

"Bug them and let me know if any important conversation arises." Taking a suit out of the wardrobe I lay it on the bed.

"I can do that."

I pause. "If the name Jan is mentioned you'll let me know."

"No problem." I end the phone call and get dressed. When I return to the living area Svetlana is sitting at the breakfast bar, she's holding a cup of tea, and another sits beside her. When I move closer, she slides the mug towards me. "I made you a cup of tea. I wasn't sure if you took sugar, so I didn't put any in it."

"Do you take sugar?" I ask.

"No." Her fingers are wrapped around the mug, but I easily detangle them much to her confusion. I raise the mug to my lips and take a drink while sliding my cup towards her.

"You can never be too careful," I say.

Her blue eyes sparkle. "No you can't." She takes a deep drink and I'm waiting for her to collapse onto the breakfast bar but she doesn't. I wait until she drinks all of the tea; I wait a few minutes after just in case the drugs are moving slowly through her body. The fall from the breakfast bar would hurt her. Her eyes are clear. I finish my tea.

"Thank you for the tea," I say placing the mug in the sink. When I gather my wallet, keys and phone I can see the stiffness settle around her shoulders. I pause and frown at her. Why was I pausing? I had a meeting in fifteen minutes. Her eyes widen the longer I stand there, it looks a lot like hope.

"I'm locking down the apartment so don't try to leave," I warn her, my words louder than I had intended.

Her shoulders slump forward in defeat and I tighten my fists.

"Wanda," I call.

Svetlana doesn't look at me.

"What can I do for you today?"

When I don't respond immediately, she repeats the question. This time Svetlana looks at me.

"Why are you looking at me like that?" I ask Svetlana.

"I'm sorry. I don't understand the request." Wanda's robotic voice fills the space and for the first time since I had her installed I want her to shut up.

"I'm not looking at you like anything." Her soft-spoken words ignite something in me.

"Go into the room," I say.

She doesn't move.

"Now."

Her cheeks darken and she slides off the stool. I watch as she walks across the floor with tightened fists and closes the bedroom door behind her.

"Wanda," I say more calmly now.

"What can I do for you today?"

"Lock down the basement except for the living quarters."

"Lock down commencing in one minute."

After taking one final glance at the bedroom door I leave the basement and return to the house.

Shane and Finn are in the kitchen when I arrive.

"Are you ready?" I ask Shane. We had another meeting in Cabra Castle, new recruits were arriving so we had to give them the standard welcome.

"Yeah."

Once we are in the hall, I can sense that Shane wants to say something. "Say what you want to say Shane."

"It's Darragh. He's acting ... strange."

We enter the garage and the lights come to life.

"Isn't he always acting strange?" I fire back as I get into my Bentley. She smells familiar, and it reminds me of who I am and who I need to be.

"What happened in the forest?"

"We have a meeting-" I check my watch "-In eight minutes. This will have to wait until later."

Shane nods and closes the door. Darragh arriving last night in my apartment was unexpected. He wasn't keeping it together like I thought he might. I had promised him more answers, so I needed to avoid him. The whole truth I could never tell. But I could tell parts of it and hope with enough truth that he would fill in the blanks like he had in the forest. My chest tightens and the unexpected shift has me rubbing it.

***

Gregor is at the door when I arrive.

"Everyone on the list is inside." I enter the room that holds only ten people. But I hope its ten people who join us. Their talking ceases as I step into the room. Shane arrives only a moment after me. His smile is immediate. Two of the guards on the list shake my hand eager to impress. I selected one from Nobber and one from Kells. Most of our guards that we had on our payroll were Navan. So it never hurt to have them from different areas.

"I want to thank you all for coming on such short notice." I start and Shane makes his way up to me. His arm still isn't fully healed, but he has smartly gone without the sling, and his suit and smile give him the polished appearance that we want them to see.

"We know you are all new to the area." I make sure my eyes touch each member; some might work, others won't. Judge Harper is new and his stern face and hard grey eyes are filled with suspicion.

"So we wanted to introduce ourselves. I'm Liam O'Reagan and this is my brother Shane O'Reagan." I give Shane a moment to look at each person. "We run most of the hotels, and other business in the Co. Meath, Co. Cavan area."

"That's what you asked us here for, to brag?" It's the judge that I knew wouldn't be easy.

"To connect, Judge Harper. It's always good to know your neighbors."

"And your enemies," he says back.

I nod at him. "Of course." I move on not entertaining him. We had three judges, another would have been nice, but I wasn't wasting time on him. My research said he had two young grandchildren that he cared for. Their mother was in rehab for a drug addiction, this was knowledge I felt I could use.

"So if you ever need a hotel to stay in or someone to talk business with we are here." Six, I count six that will work. That looked happy, that can read between the lines.

"Now enjoy the refreshments." A buffet of tea/coffee and some pastries is set up.

"Talk to the two guards and give them the run down. They are in. Mr. Jordan the solicitor has a drink problem so when you speak to him don't forget the brandy." I glance at two others. "Peter is a barrister and his partner in the workplace and outside is George. Their wives don't know. Can I leave you with them?"

"I'll have every one of them on board."

He will because I just gave him the easier ones. My first to approach is Judge Harper.

"We are very grateful you came," I say. He's helped himself to a coffee, so maybe he's not as eager to leave as he might like us to think.

"I wanted to meet Liam O'Reagan. I've heard a lot about you." Placing my hands in my trousers pockets I keep my voice low.

"I have also heard a lot about you Judge Harper. How is your daughter?" His hands rattle as he places the cup and saucer on the table. "I hope rehab is helping her, with two small children left behind, times must be very hard."

He doesn't answer me and when he goes to pick up his coffee, I touch his hand briefly. "You can leave that there. Thank you for coming." I hold out my hand and he takes it. I like the fear that flashes across his face.

"I'll let you out."

"I was actually enjoying the coffee." How I love when people back track.

"It didn't seem sweet enough for you."

"It's sweet enough." His words are dry but we are finally on the same page.

"Good. Then stay and finish it."

As we move around the room, only two seem rattled by us and we don't need anyone unsure. We either want people who are afraid of us or want to impress us. The ones who are unsure just won't work.

Once the room is empty, I sit down.

"I know there is something wrong Liam. You seem - different." Shane sits across from me and I'm unsure of what is wrong. I always had a lot going on, but it's all starting to slip through my fingers.

"You really want to ask about Darragh," I say not focusing on him. His concern wasn't for me. It was for Darragh.

"Yes, but I also want to know what's going on with you."

"Nothing is wrong, and Darragh will be fine."

The door opens and Gregor looks in. "That's ready for you boss." I nod at Gregor.

"I'll see you at home," I tell Shane. He doesn't answer me and I don't look back as I leave with Gregor. We move down through the staff quarters of the castle. The deeper we go, the less people we see, until it's cobwebs and dust. "Has he spoken?" I ask as I hunker down through the tunnel.

"Yeah, too much."

I'm standing to my full height now as I enter the lowest level of the castle. Four archways circle us and I let Gregor lead.

"Barry." I greet him and he tries to look at me from over his shoulder, but his restraints won't allow him to see me fully. Stepping into his line of sight I glance at Gregor to explain all the marks on Barry's face.

"He tried to run, twice."

"I don't know who you are but I didn't do anything." Fresh blood still drips from his trembling lips.

"I'm Liam O'Reagan, Darragh's brother and you skipped bail Barry."

He's trying to look behind him again. "Darragh," he calls.

"He's not here. In fact he doesn't know you're here."

"I have money."

I nod and pretend like that is an option. "From the banks you robbed."

His brows furrow. "I didn't do it. I wasn't even there. I have a cousin in England, my mam has arranged for me to go there. I won't be trouble to no-one."

"You're a problem for me Barry."

"Where was he when you found him?" I ask Gregor but I know already.

"On your property Mr. O'Reagan."

Barry sinks back into the chair.

"That doesn't sound like you were going to England."

"I was trying to warn Darragh."

"About what?" I stuff my hands in my pockets.

"About the guards knowing we did the bank job."

"Ah so you did do it."

He shakes his head in denial. He was a half-wit. How much had he spilled to the wrong person? If we handed him over he would be tried and sent to prison, but how much would he say. If he ended up dead? Well, the dead can't talk.

"So England is it?"

"Yeah, my cousin Rodger is letting me stay in his room. He has bunk beds."

"Sounds fun Barry." I cut off his restraints.

"Can I go?" He asks once he stands.

"Of course. Safe journey."

His smile is wide as he takes one final look at Gregor while wiping blood onto the sleeve of his jacket. I wait until he is a few steps away before I give Gregor the nod. They disappear under the arch but I can hear it all. The moment Gregor tightens his arm around his neck from behind. The struggle to get away, the kicking of his runners. The gasping for air. The small thuds could be him trying to hit Gregor. They shift and the thuds grow softer before they cease. The loud thud is the body hitting the ground and I walk towards the arch.

Barry's open eyes stare up at the brick ceiling.

"Bury him and send word that he was seen on a boat for England."

My phone bleeps in my pocket, removing I stare at the warning and growl.

A breach in the basement.

CHAPTER FOURTEEN

SVETLANA

I HATE BEING ALONE, and I miss Jan more than ever. I start to clean. I don't know what else to do. It takes me thirty minutes to put the space back together. I go through all the presses looking for anything that might help me but I don't find a thing. Liam was really thorough when he removed anything that he considered a weapon. I want a shower but after the last time I decide to just brush my teeth and clean my face. I don't let the water run, but only turn it on when needed. I want to be able to hear anyone coming. I finish cleaning over the bathroom and return to the bedroom. His suits are all in the same perfect order that I saw in the kitchen. Top row is shirts nearly all white, the second half is suit jackets, below them is trousers and the final slot was reserved for shoes that looked identical to me. The side of the wardrobe was kitted out with shelving that held t-shirts and jogging pants in an array of colors. Closing the door I open the second one to see his more personal stuff. He's a boxer's man; nearly all his socks are black or navy. Nothing is out of place, everything is perfect. I have the urge to ruffle it up. Closing the doors I move to the bed where I lie down. I don't know how he lives down here with no windows. The AC is on but everything feels so artificial. The lighting dims during the day but it's still there. Lying here lets my mind roam to my parents, my country, even to my uncle. I get back up and go into the living room. The door that leads out of here looks so large now.

"Wanda," I call and my pulse flickers waiting but she doesn't respond. I try saying her name in a deeper voice. But she isn't fooled. I keep trying but nothing happens only I make myself laugh as I try to do Liam's serious voice. I eat another tin of peaches and tidy up after. Lying on the couch I close my eyes. Grey clouds fill my vision, roaming fields that surround my home are all around me. I inhale deeply, but it's not the smell of freshly cut grass, or the smell of the sun as it dries up the rain. I smell Liam. Opening my eyes, I stare at the ceiling.

The wail of a bell has me sitting up and moving off the couch. I lie flat on the floor as the door opens and someone bursts in. It sounds like more than one person. I try to remain still. Clamping my hands over my mouth I try not to breathe too loud. Whoever is here couldn't hear me anyway over the wail of the alarm. I can't hear them move, so I'm not sure if they have left. I don't want to sit up and ask for help, whoever broke in here won't help me. I might become a target. Liam seemed to have a lot of enemies. I doubt my uncle knew this before handing me over, or maybe he did.

The sound of the alarm stops and I'm all too aware of my breathing. So is whoever is in the room. Footsteps are slow but they are moving towards me and I've nowhere to go. A woman appears above me.

"Found her," she calls over her shoulder but doesn't take her eyes off me. "It's okay. We are here to help you." She smiles softly at me.

A man appears and stares down at me. "Good work, now let's move before he gets back." Their accents are different from Liam's. It's the girl who reaches down and helps me off the floor.

Her short blond hair is cut neatly to her head, but she wouldn't be mistaken for a man. She has curves were they should be. I'm up on my feet and she gives me a reassuring smile, I'm thinking that everything might be okay, maybe they are saving me. I'm returning her smile, mine is a little shaky.

The world goes black as something is pulled over my head. I try to rip it off but my hands are restrained. The ground leaves from under my bare feet and I claw at the hands that tighten around me.

"Stop it." His voice is close to my face.

I start to scream. "Help!" Flesh clamps over my mouth and muffles my words but I don't stop. Arms tighten around my legs and the chaff of a rope is painful as it's tightened. I wriggle trying to get free.

"Keep her still." The woman's voice is abrupt, and she sounds like she's under pressure. I use all my strength and continue to wriggle and kick as I continue to scream. The air in the sack is hot and I try not to focus on how sweaty it feels or how dizzy I'm getting. I'm airborne now and blood rushes to my head. A large shoulder digs into my stomach. Using my fists I hit as hard as I can until my arms are yanked painfully together and my hands are tied.

"Get her into the van now." We are moving, light flickers across my eyes and disappears. I'm trying to control my labored breaths. The moment fresh air touches the sack I know I am outside. I start to scream. I hit the ground hard, the air knocked from my lungs. Hands grip me under the arms and I land heavily on another hard surface, the light is gone and I'm plunged into darkness. Doors close and I move back until my back hits a wall. The floor under me rattles as the van starts up. Shuffling to the back of the van, I throw my weight at the doors but nothing happens. My fingers search for a handle but I can't find one. Rubbing my face with my joined hands I try to get the sack off my head, but it won't budge. A primal scream claws up my throat as the van shifts under me. I throw myself against the door again in blind panic.

"Help!" My screams start to reduce along with the air. Lying flat I try to control my breathing. I didn't want to pass out. If I did, I feared what I would wake up to. Why were these people taking me? I should have ran into Liam's room and tried to block the door. I had thought for just a moment that they were going to help me. The van stops.

"You need to sign here." I can hear someone speak. I move until I'm in a sitting position. "Help!" I shout but my voice is low and breaking. This was my only chance. "Help." I shout louder and start to move to the front of the van to get closer to the man's voice. "Help me!"

"Is someone in the back?"

"Rats that we caught." It's the woman's voice. "Larry go check and make sure none of them got out of their cages."

"No I'm a person. Svetlana." The van shifts and light comes from my right and I rush to it, but large hands wrap around my neck pushing me back in.

"Yep, one got loose," Larry shouts.

No air is getting to my burning lungs as his fingers tighten around my throat.

"Maybe you should stay in the back." The woman suggests and I'm released as he closes the door.

"Scream again and I'll snap your fucking neck." He keeps a hand clamped down on my chest and I couldn't scream even if I wanted to. Right now I'm struggling just to stay alert.

"I hate rats." I focus on the conversation and Larry growls in frustration at the delay.

"Yeah we better get going before the rats start to chew on Larry." The woman laughs, and the man joins her. A phone rings.

"One moment."

"Everything okay in the back." The woman hisses low.

"Yeah just stop talking to him. What's taking so long?"

"Just stay calm. He's just answering the phone."

Larry tuts and I swear his hand feels heavier on my chest.

"What company did you say you worked for again?" The man asks and I can hear the nervousness in his voice.

"Rat Killer's" The woman answers.

"I just need to check your paperwork."

"What paperwork?" Larry growls above me.

Even I know he is delaying and that meant that Liam was coming.

"Hold on." The woman warns before the van moves quickly back. I slide along with Larry to the opposite side of the van; we stop and start to slide back towards the front. We collide with each other; my head hits the floor hard. I fight off the darkness. Larry lands on top of me cutting off the last bit of air.

"He knows. I had to ram the barrier." The woman's panicked voice reaches my ear. We are sliding again.

"Slow the fuck down," Larry screams.

"I can't. We're being followed." I hit another steel wall; this time my left arm takes the brunt of the impact. The burn starts at the shoulder and runs into my fingers. I hiss in pain and try to brace myself as the woman screams at us.

"Hold on." Her shouts are filled with alarm and I reach out searching for something to hold on to but I find nothing. I'm floating in the air, my arms raise on their own accord and the moment only lasts a second as I impact with the floor before I'm flying again, but I brace myself for the impact that happens quickly. My body slams into the glass that shatters on top of me. The sting grows, a million small needles pierce my leg before I hit a hard surface and everything stops. A horn sounds. I think it's ringing in my ears but as my hearing clears, I recognize it as the sound of the van horn. Moisture starts to pour around my hands. It's cold, and it soon covers my hands completely and continues to spread up my arms. I need to move. The gentle gush of water tells me it's pouring into the van and filling it up fast. My legs scream in agony but I need to move. I don't know which way is up or down.

"Help." My throat burns as I scream. The horn still rings and the water level continues to rise. "Help." The creak of metal has my head turning in that direction. Light burns my eyes but I'm screaming reaching out to it. "Help me. Please." A shadow casts across the sack, taking half the light with it.

"Take my hand," Liam's voice is above me and I look up but I can't see him. I reach out my tied hands, the pain in my wrist has me crying out but I keep my hands outstretched. Water fills around my feet and rises quickly to my knees.

"I can't reach you," Liam's words have me trying to jump higher, my leg burns and throbs and I fall down into the water. It feels like the van shifts as I push myself upwards.

"Svetlana."

I break the surface of the water.

"I can't reach you," Liam says again and I can hear him shift before a loud splash sounds in the water. He left me. He left me to die here.

"Please don't leave me." I jump up again trying to grab onto something but my nails drag down the metal. "Liam!" My legs give out again and water rushes over my head. The world tilts and I push back up to the surface but hit a wall. My tied hands run along but there is no break in the wall. I can't find a gap. My legs stop kicking and I'm sinking, my lungs ache and burn for oxygen as the last bit of air leaves my mouth. I fight not to inhale but my mouth opens and I drag in a mouth full of water and the world explodes as my body pulses and trembles to try to exhale water that can't be exhaled.

CHAPTER FIFTEEN

LIAM

I'M IN THE LAKE trying to open the side door so I can reach Svetlana. The van is disappearing at an alarming rate. I take a deep breath before I go under the water. It's cold and murky and I have to use my sense of touch to find the door. I try to pull it open but it doesn't budge. I keep trying until my lungs burn and I have to return to the surface.

"Boss I can't swim." Gregor is still on the bank. Useless to me. I swim back and climb onto the back of the van that's still jutting out from the water; it's easier this time as more of it is submerged in the lake. I don't see Svetlana. I take another deep breath before I jump in. She's not the only one down here; I push the body of the man and find Svetlana, my hands touching the sack over her face. Something loud bangs and the light dims. One of the doors must have closed. I'm swimming towards the door pulling Svetlana with me. The door rushes towards us as the van sinks quickly.I pass it gripping Sveltlana and we break the surface of the water. The moment I do I pull the sack off Svetlana's head. She isn't breathing. I swim as fast as I can to the bank and Gregor is there, he pulls her up as I climb onto the grass and start pressing on her chest. After compressing I hold her nose and blow into her mouth. I repeat this again. "Come on," I beg her as I continue to press on her chest. She coughs and splutters up water and I pull her up while turning her on her side. She continues to bring up water. It leaves her in gushes.

"Get me my phone," I say to Gregor and he takes off running towards the car. Svetlana continues to bring up lake water. Her leg is bleeding pretty badly and I lay her down on her side when she stops getting sick. Removing the rope from her hands causes her to hiss.

"Liam."

I'm right back up near her head. "I'm here," I tell her.

She looks at me with lids half closed. "Thank you." A smile graces her face. "I thought you were going to leave me."

"You are no use to me dead," I say the words easily as I move down to her feet and untie the rope. I take more care; her leg is in bad repair. Gregor hands me my phone and I take it. "Get her into the car." Gregor bends at the knees to pick her up. "Be careful with her," I warn him as I rise and ring George. He answers straight away.

"I need you to get to my house right now." I hang up not giving him a moment to deny me. Gregor has Svetlana in the car.

"You drive," I tell him as I climb into the back. Lifting up her head I rest it on my lap. A moan leaves her lips. My hand goes to her hair and I start to stroke it, trying to soothe her as we drive home.

"Shane there is a van at the bottom of Whitewood lake. I need you to get the bodies out of it, and bring them back to the house."

"I'm on it."

"Bring Darragh with you." *It will keep his mind occupied.*

"Is that really necessary?" Shane questions.

"Yes." I hang up and ring Stephen.

"Mr O'Reagan."

"We are coming now. Have the barrier up. Also George Watson is arriving soon; don't delay in letting him in."

"The barrier is broken, they crashed through it."

"Get someone out to repair it straight away."

We arrive only a moment later and I tell Gregor not to slow down. The car bumps across the broken barrier. He pulls into the garage and I lift Svetlana out. She groans and I try to be as gentle with her as possible. Cradling her to my chest, I'm trying to stop her from moving too much. Shane and Darragh pause in the hall when they see us.

"Don't stand there. Go and do your job," I say as I pass them. Gregor opens the doors and we move into the basement.

"Stay outside and wait for the doctor."

Gregor parts ways and heads back up as I carry Svetlana into the bedroom. She's shivering and I hate the color of her skin. Sitting her up I peel the t-shirt off her. Her skin is already bruising in several areas. Laying her back down she moans again, she's trying to cradle her left arm to her side. I dump the top onto the floor and start to remove her trousers; they pull down easily to her knees, but her right leg is a mess. I leave her and get a scissors from the bag of knives that I had taken from the kitchen.

When I get back she's trembling. Taking the blanket I wrap it around her. "Stay with me. The doctor will be here soon," I say and focus on cutting the trousers from her leg. Every hiss has me clenching my jaw. When the material falls apart I lift her leg by the heel and pull out the material.

Footsteps have me breathing a bit better. "George her leg looks bad," I tell him the moment he enters the room. He moves the blanket back and her shivers continue. I'm tempted to pull it up around her but I let him do his job.

He takes a look and she cries out as he moves her leg. The cold has seeped into me also and I strip off my suit jacket and tie before going to the side of the bed.

"It's okay. He's going to help you." I try to comfort her but she continues to cry out.

"Can you put her out?" I ask him and he doesn't glance at me. He has a magnifying glass strapped to his head as he examines her leg.

"I didn't exactly have time to prepare." He moves back to his bag and puts on gloves while taking out some white bandages and what looks like a large tweezers.

"You better stay up there with her this is going to be sore." I take a moment to pull off my shirt.

"Give me a minute," I tell him and kick off my shoes before stripping off my trousers and boxers. Taking a pair of jogging pants I pull them over my wet skin and slide on a t-shirt. At least now I can sit on the bed. Once I'm beside Svetlana, this time I take her head in my lap and hold the one hand that doesn't seem sore. I give George a nod and he starts. It takes everything in me not to jump off the bed and hurt him. It takes another thirty minutes of Svetlana crying out, twice she loses consciousness.

"She's very lucky it's more surface cuts, she didn't do any real damage." He moves up now to check her arm. When he touches it she stirs. "I think it's broken but I'd need to x-ray it."

"No. you figure it out here. She can't go to a hospital."

George looks at me for the first time. "I can strap it, but I need to go and get some things."

"She swallowed a lot of water," I say.

He nods before getting his steth-o-scope. "You need to sit her up."

I do slowly and she opens her eyes. "Leave me alone." I ignore her protests and hold her body against mine. Pulling her wet hair away from her chest I let George listen to her heart. The red lace material that covers her breasts is wet but I'll let her remove it.

"It's nearly over." I murmur in her ear.

"You need to lean her forward so I can check her lungs." I do as he says holding her away from me. It feels like he takes longer before I can pull her back against my chest. I pull the blankets up over her chest and she shivers.

"Her lungs sound fine, but honestly she would be better in a hospital. Things can change quickly."

"That's not an option," I say again and hope I don't have to repeat myself any further.

"I'll bandage her leg and go and get the strap for her arm, and some painkillers."

Svetlana wakes up as he moves her leg. Brushing her hair back I try to soothe her. When he's finally done, she relaxes against my chest.

"Gregor will let you out," I say to George as I let Svetlana lie fully down on the bed, I'm careful with her arm as I move her.

"Please don't leave me." Her good hand is reaching out to me.

"I won't." I'm able to pull the blankets over her bandaged leg now and all the way up to her neck before lying beside her. "I'm here." I whisper to her but she's already asleep.

***

"Mr. O'Reagan." I open my eyes, my hand reaching under my pillow where I usually keep my gun but I don't touch the cold metal that I've become accustomed to.

"The Doctor is back and so are your brothers." I nod before glancing at Svetlana. She's asleep, her breathing is deep. My movements are slow as I get out of the warmth of the bed and meet George in the doorway. "She's asleep and I don't want her woken up."

He's clutching his black bag that bulge's with equipment. "I can come back later."

"No. just sit and wait for her to wake up." My request isn't taken kindly but George goes into the room.

"Get him a chair," I tell Gregor as I get some clean socks and runners.

***

Shane and Darragh are in the entrance area; both of them are in dry clothes but their hair is still wet.

"Where are they?"

"You want them down here?"

"Yes," I answer Shane. Darragh mutters as he leaves to help Shane with the bodies. I open the door that leads into the more sterile part of the basement.

"Wanda."

"What can I do for you today?"

"Light up the basement."

Lights flicker to life one after the other. I move around the chair that's cemented into the middle of the floor. That will have no use today. A butcher's block is pushed up against two large pillars. Taking it, I roll it further into the room and cover it with black sacks.

"Where do you want it?" Shane asks.

"Here."

"What are you going to do?" Darragh questions.

"I don't know," I say as they place the body on the wooden slab. They've wrapped it in a bed sheet and we remove it. It's a male. His beige coat doesn't cover his gut.

"He wasn't very fit," I say. The smell of smoke assaults my senses and I flicker a glance at Darragh who leans against the pillar watching me while smoking a fag.

"Can you start at the feet?" I ask Shane and he removes the man's Nike runners. I check his jacket pockets but there is nothing in them. Opening his checkered shirt there is no tattoos on his body.

"Feet are clean," Shane says.

"Yeah so is his chest," I mumble, while checking his neck.

I open the belt of his trousers and we pull them off, Shane lifts the legs to help shift the material off.

"He's a briefs man," Darragh states with laughter in his voice. "Always reminds me of a pedophile. Especially the ones with big bellies."

"So you think he's a pedophile?" I ask as I search his pockets, my fingers touch the leather of a wallet.

"Who the fuck knows," Darragh answers me as I open the wallet and remove the ID.

"Larry Wheelen." I read his name out loud. The image on the ID card matches his.

"Legs are clear," Shane tells me.

I nod.

"Didn't Dermot Wheelen recently die?" Shane quizzes.

"The name sounds familiar," I remark.

"Did he live at the crossroads on the way to Nobber?" Shane walks to the sink and starts to wash his hands.

"Yeah, he was huge. When he did his weekly shopping he would first get a cooked chicken and eat it while he did the shopping." Darragh extinguishes the cigarette on the floor and I walk over and pick it up.

"It's a concrete floor."

"It's my home," I say.

He snorts. "It's like a serial killers nest if you ask me."

"I didn't." I place the butt in the bin before washing my hands.

"Let's redress him and get the next body in here." I'm surprised when Darragh helps me dress Larry.

"What will we do with the bodies after?"

"Burn them. Our DNA is everywhere. Micky Heffernans funeral home in Trim will burn them for us."

"So what we just drop the bodies off?" Darragh buttons up Larry's shirt as I put back on his socks and shoes.

"He opens for fifteen minutes each night. You have to be there between twelve and twelve fifteen and he will burn the body, he charges 10k a body."

"That's day light robbery." Darragh remarks as he lights up another cigarette.

I wrap Larry back up in the bed sheets.

"Mr. O'Reagan." Gregor stands at the door but hasn't come into the room.

"Yes Gregor. You can speak." He's hesitant in front of Darragh and Shane. Gregor wasn't something I shared with my family.

"She's awake and looking for you."

"Tell George to give her something to help her sleep." I clench my jaw hating leaving her after what just happened but finding out who did this was important.

Gregor leaves and I can feel their questions brush the nape of my neck.

"No, she is not my girlfriend. Yes, she is staying with me. I'm not sure for how long but her life and mine are tied." I finish turning to my brothers. "If she dies, I will be killed."

"What can we do?" Shane is always ready to help.

"Put him back in the van and bring the next one in." They do and I want to rush this body. I want to get back to Svetlana. We repeat the process only the woman is clean no ID, no wallet or anything to identify her.

"She's pretty." Darragh has decided to lean against the pillar again and watch us as he smokes.

"At least we have his ID." Shane remarks as we redress her. I had hoped she would have some ID on her or a mark that we could tie her to a gang. But she looks like a normal woman who might have kids and a nine to five job.

Once we redress and re-wrap her Darragh and Shane take her to the van. I wash my hands after picking up another of Darragh's cigarette butts.

Svetlana is playing on my mind but I promise myself I will get to her soon. Leaving the basement I go up to where Darragh and Shane are just finishing loading the van.

"You can get rid of them tonight?" I ask Shane.

"Yeah, I think I have cash." I expected it to be dark when I arrived back up out of the basement but the sun is still shining in the sky.

"Darragh I need you to check in tomorrow on the hotels." I've never handed this responsibility over to anyone but leaving Svetlana right now wouldn't be wise.

Darragh seems to stand a little taller and I hope I don't regret my decision in sending him.

"Yeah what do I do?"

"Do you have a suit?"

He smirks. "Yeah and I look pretty hot in it too."

I don't look away and his smirk melts off his face. "I need you to be serious. You need to be the boss."

"I can do that." He's nodding with a serious expression.

"I'll email you a list of each manager. It will be just a short meeting with each of them. Find out if there are any problems. They will give you printouts of the month's figures and any formal issues. Just bring all the paperwork back to me. I can work from here. Can you do that?"

"I can do it."

"Good."

Shane still lingers and I can see all the questions in his eyes but right now is not the time.

"What about Larry Wheelen?"

"I'll take care of it," I tell Shane and descend down the steps into the basement. Gregor and George are in the living area; the minute I step in they both turn to me.

"How is she?"

"She's been asking for you, but right now she's asleep. I splintered her arm and wrapped it." He rattles a brown bottle of pills. "Give her two of these three times a day."

"You'll be back tomorrow to check on her."

"If you want."

"I insist."

He gathers his bag. "I'll be off now."

"See you tomorrow George." Once he leaves I pour myself a whiskey and drink it down quickly.

"Larry Wheelen, he's from this area. He might be related to Dermot Whee-len." I remove the ID card from my pocket and hand it to Gregor. "Find out everything you can about him."

"No problem. Is that it boss?"

"Yeah." Gregor leaves and I fill my glass before drinking it all down. I had no idea who knew she was here and why they would want to kidnap her. The only logic to it was to start a war. If I lost her Mr. Novak would kill me. But who sent them? And they weren't professional's. Someone was sloppy.

Svetlana groans and I leave the living room and enter the bedroom.

CHAPTER SIXTEEN

SVETLANA

I'M SINKING DEEPER AND *deeper, the black water pulling me under. I no longer have a sack on my head, and I can see Liam. He grins at me before shrugging.*

"Don't leave me," I plead.

He starts to laugh.

The sludge around my legs starts to pull me under. "No, no. Please don't leave me."

"I'm here. It's okay you're safe now."

The warmth of a body beside mine has me whimpering with relief. I move closer to the source of the heat. My leg burns and I hiss.

"Try not to move." The words are spoken softly and close to my ear but I don't listen. I want to get closer to the heat. I'm so cold. My arm touches something solid and warm. It disappears for a moment before it moves tightly against me. So close I can lay my head on the warmth. The beat of a heartbeat soothes me back into a sleep.

***

My hand skims warm flesh. It feels solid and flexes under my hand. I move my hand again and it tightens. Burying my head deeper into the chest allows me to move my hand further up. Anywhere my hand touches the muscles shift and flex under them. A part of my brain is telling me to wake up but I like this dream too much. My hand stops above the fluttering of a heart beat and I inhale the smell of cologne, leather and shoe polish. The smell is familiar but my brain has shut down, as my hand moves back down over a six pack that coils under my fingertips, each bump is tantalizing, my hand stops at the band of his trousers. I'm nearly giddy as my fingers slip under the band, a hand covers mine stopping me from exploring any further. My eyes snap open. My heart sky rockets. The burn of humiliation splashes across my cheeks as the smell registers with me.

Liam.

I slip my hand out of his and rest it on my hip.

"Are you in pain?"

I want to die. Why couldn't he just pretend to be asleep? I think about his question to give my mind something else to focus on. The pain in my arm and leg is there constantly and niggling at me. I focus on that pain.

"A little," I answer and swallow before looking up at him. Instantly I regret it. His eyes suck me in; they are no longer black but a deep brown that's filled with a longing, with a want that I want to fill. I've never been with anyone; I've never felt this way. I drop his gaze and am glad when he shifts under me. I raise my head from his chest and he slides out of the bed. The moment he's gone I lie back down and snuggle into the warm sheets. I'm inhaling the smell of Liam when he arrives back into the room.

"Here's some water and painkillers."

I die all over again and hope he didn't just witness me sniffing the sheets. I must have banged my head pretty bad. Sitting up I don't meet his eye as I take the water with my good hand, the other one is stiff and bandaged. I don't remember being in a hospital. Liam takes the water back and places the two tablets in my hand, once I pop them into my mouth he hands me the water and waits until I drink it all down.

"Larry-" I look up at Liam, he's watching me carefully. "- Larry was the man's name."

He nods. "Did you hear the woman's name?"

I try to think hard but I don't recall her name being mentioned. "She just said she was going to help me." I had been so stupid. I should have fought harder. The bed dips as Liam sits down. His fingers brush mine as he removes the glass, I wonder if it was intentional or if for some reason my body was hyper aware of everything.

"I heard them say they worked for Rat Killers." I'm searching my memory but nothing stands out. They hadn't spoken. "Was it you chasing them?"

Liam's jaw is clenched, and he nods. "Yes, they hit a bank, and the van flipped before landing in the lake."

The memory of being airborne has me tightening my eyes. I don't want to remember the pain of slamming into the frame of the van.

"What happened to them?" I ask while keeping my eyes closed.

"They are dead," Liam's voice is void of any emotion.

I'm looking at him now. "What did they want with me?"

His jaw tightens again his fingers clenching around the glass. "I don't know. But I'll find out."

I believe him when he says he will find out. I'm tired again, my body demanding more rest. I start to lie back down and Liam moves quickly putting the glass on the bedside table. "Let me help you." With one arm it is a bit tricky. Liam lowers me down until I'm flat on my back looking up at him.

"You weren't breathing." He's frowning as he speaks. "I thought you were dead." The confusion in his voice is growing as his frown deepens and all I can do is watch in fascination as he tries to figure out what he's feeling. "I didn't like it." He finally looks me in the eye his frown disappearing. "I didn't like it at all."

My heart is picking up speed. "It sounds like I'm growing on you." As much as you are growing on me, I don't say it out loud but it's there. There's something about Liam that I'm drawn to. Under his cold demeanor I see a kind man.

"Get some sleep." His voice is impassive as he rises and I don't want him to go. Biting my lip I keep the words in.

He takes the glass with him and leaves the room. I know I won't sleep. What if someone else comes for me? I only feel safe in his arms. I can't even toss that much, my leg burns. My full bladder starts to press on me and I pull the blankets back. Liam hasn't closed the bedroom door and I try to look out from the bed but I don't see him. All I can see is the back of the couch. I get my good leg out of the bed before I slide out the bad one. Using my one good arm I sit up. Sweat gathers on my lip and forehead. The blankets slip away fully and I die a little, I'm in my bra and underwear, my clothes gone. How the hell had I not noticed that? Pulling the surrounding blankets I try to stand, my leg protests the moment I put pressure on it. I can't hold the blanket around me and hobble.

"Liam." I don't have to wait long before he walks into the room.

"What are you doing?" He looks so large as he walks into the room, it grows smaller with each step he takes.

"I need the bathroom."

"You need to call me; you can't just get out of bed yourself."

"I don't seem to have any clothes on." I say and this time I look up at him.

"We had to cut your clothes off to get to your leg." He walks away as he speaks.

"Why didn't I go to a hospital?"

He opens the wardrobe and takes out a white t-shirt. "You didn't need to. We have our own doctor here." I don't believe him but I let it go as he hands me the t-shirt. He doesn't leave but stands in front of me crossing his arms over his chest. I have to let the blanket go to get the top on. I get one arm in easily but the one that's bandaged isn't easy.

Liam unfolds his arms. "Let me help you. You need to take it off and put it on this arm first." He speaks as he takes the t-shirt off again.

When he doesn't put it back on straight away, I peek up at him. He's focused on my chest. My movement has him putting on my t-shirt but he won't meet my eye. It's easier when he puts it on the splintered arm first and then my good one.

Taking my good arm Liam helps me stand. The t-shirt covers all my important parts. "Wrap your arm around my neck and put your weight on me." I do as Liam instructs his arm snakes around my waist as he walks us slowly towards the door. After three steps the pain has me stopping.

Liam doesn't give me a moment before he lifts me into his arm, his other arm holding onto my bare thighs. I'm so aware of where our bodies touch; I can't relax as he fingers sprawl out along my thigh. Holding my breath I don't breathe until we reach the bathroom and he puts me down.

"Can you manage?"

My head snaps up to Liam. "Yes."

Having a man help me go to the toilet wasn't something I would allow and most certainly not a man like Liam.

Liam waits outside. It's painful but I manage to go to the toilet and hobble the short distance to the tap. My toiletries are here instead of in the drawer where I left them. I glance at the door that is slightly ajar but I can't see Liam. I finish up brushing my teeth. Getting a brush through my hair just isn't possible. It needed a good washing. My energy is dilapidated. I had done enough. Rubbing down the sink with my washcloth I'm delaying, the idea of Liam's hands on me again is elating but also terrifying.

"Are you okay?"

I couldn't delay it much longer. "I'm finished."

The bathroom shrinks to nothing when Liam steps in. He doesn't look at me as he carefully picks me up. I want to snuggle into his chest but resist the urge that wants to consume me. It's like there's another person inside me fighting to have her way. I assume it's because I never experienced anything before. Maybe this was how girls felt when they hadn't done anything. I really had no idea.

We reach the bed quicker this time and Liam lowers me slowly. He makes quick work of pulling up the blanket.

"Don't go." I feel childish for asking but I really don't want him to leave. I won't sleep wondering who will crash through the door. With him here I will be safe. I can sleep.

He's nodding before he removes his footwear and climbs in. I'm lying on the broad of my back not brave enough to curl into him.

"I was in a car accident when I was younger." I remember the red car, the crunch of the tires as dad veered around the deer. "We had struck a tree, I was ten. I broke my nose."

"It healed well."

I glance up at Liam a smile tugging at my lips. "Thank you." He's a head taller than me and I'd love to turn on my stomach so I can really see him. But my arm and leg restricted the movement.

"Have you ever been in a car accident?" It's funny how much I want to get to know him.

"No. But I broke two fingers when I was younger." He holds up his left hand.

"They healed well." I say not seeing a blemish on his long fingers. When I peek up at him, his lip lifts ever so slightly before it falls back into place. He must feel my eyes on him as he glances at me.

"You should sleep."

At his words I yawn. "Will you stay?"

"Yes."

I let my eyes close slowly. "Liam." I'm mumbling now.

"Yes." He sounds alert.

"Thank you for not leaving me."

He doesn't answer and I feel the need to clarify. "For not leaving me in the van."

His fingers sink into my hair and I gravitate towards his touch. "I wouldn't have left you."

"Because my uncle would kill you?" I smile sleepily at my words.

"Go to sleep." His command has me sinking further into a heavy sleep.

***

Fingers are sprawled against my stomach and it's my turn to wake up and try not to move. I sneak a quick peak up at Liam. The sharp definition of his face has softened now that he sleeps. He looks beautiful, almost peaceful. With his eyes closed I can examine him without feeling intimidated by those black orbs. I shift slowly his hand moving to my hip, this way I can see him properly. The urge to trace his lips with my fingers has me raising my hand but I stop as he stirs. I shift up closer towards his face. I don't know what I'm doing but I can't seem to stop. I want to kiss him and see what it feels like. I've never been kissed. Wetting my lips I lower my head towards his, my heartbeat is like the hind leg of a rabbit, beating rapidly and uncontrollably in my chest. This wasn't right, I needed to lie back down and not be so creepy, but would I ever get this chance again? Once I go back home, I knew who would take my first everything. A shiver assaults me at the thoughts and I take my chance while I have it. I'm a hair breath away from his lips when I pause his breathing seems to have changed, but he doesn't stir and his eyes are closed.

I wet my lips again and press mine to his. His are warmer and softer than I expected. I open my lips and press them harder against his. His fingers tighten on my hip and I pause until his hand relaxes. My face burns with the thoughts of what I was doing, kissing a man while he slept. I was as bad as molesting him. I lie back down quickly and try to control the fire that rages inside me. My fingers touch my lips and my eyes burn.

My first kiss. I stole my first kiss. A tear escape's the corner of my eye and I close them tightly trying to fight the onslaught of emotions that ride quickly through my body. Liam's fingers move again and I hold my breath. If there is a God, he won't wake up yet. I needed to get some control over myself.

"Are you okay?"

There was no God.

"Yeah." I can't look at him.

"Why are you crying?" He moves his hand and I feel the loss immediately. I still can't look at him.

"Just my arm pinched a bit," I lie and close my eyes so it looks like I'm falling asleep.

"I can get you pain killers."

I glance up at him, my eyes flicker to his lips. Do they look swollen? Will he be able to tell that someone has been kissing him while he slept? Oh God. Humiliation sweeps across my cheeks and I look away.

"No thank you."

"I'll make us some food."

I nod in agreement. The distance could do us some good.

CHAPTER SEVENTEEN

LIAM

THE KISS STILL LINGERS on my lips. I had no idea why she did it. Was it nearly dying that had her wanting some human contact? The omelette sizzles and I turn it before setting the breakfast bar for our food. On second thought, getting her out here might be a problem. Once the food is ready, I set it out along with some tea and place it all on a tray. She's sitting up looking conflicted. Her lip tugs in between her teeth but she releases it as I set the tray down. Her focus is on my lips and guilt lights up her cheeks. I sit on the edge of the bed and place the tray beside her. Taking my own plate I keep it on my knee.

She doesn't speak as she starts to eat and the silence is uncomfortable. "Did you work back in the Czech?" I cut more of my omelette before looking at her. I want her to relax again. Her body is held too tight.

"No. I was studying psychology."

"That's a dangerous profession," I tease.

She smiles. "I'm not analyzing you." Her shoulders relax and she picks up her cup of tea, it pauses at her lips. "Did you drug it?"

"If I did do you think I would tell you?" I eat my omelette and her attention is drawn to my mouth. I want to know what she's thinking.

"No, I don't think you would tell me." She takes a drink of tea. I hadn't drugged it, not this time anyway. She wouldn't be going anywhere now until she fully healed.

"I miss learning." Her confession is said into her mug. "I miss it as much as I miss the daylight."

I hate the guilt that churns in my stomach but I finish my omelette.

"Would you like me to make more?"

She's cleared her plate, but she shakes her head. "No thank you."

A somber mood settles around my room and I don't like it. But I don't know how to remove it.

"I studied engineering." I offer up the knowledge freely.

Her eyes light up slightly. "Are you an engineer?"

"No. I'm a hotelier."

She sips her tea, her attention back on the contents inside it. Taking the tray I place our plates on it and my cup leaving her with her tea and thoughts. I feel like I can breathe better in the kitchen. This wasn't going to work; I couldn't stay down here with her and take care of her. She's making me feel itchy in my own skin. Who would I leave with her? Gregor had too much to do. Darragh had seen her, but I didn't like the idea of my brothers near her.

"Shit." Her voice carries through to the kitchen.

Leaving the kitchen I go to see what has her upset. She's trying to get out of bed again. "I told you to call me." The white bandage has flecks of red soaking through it. "Svetlana." I growl. She should have called me.

"I'm just sick of lying here." She tries to run her hand through her hair but it gets snagged on each knot. "My hair smells like lake water."

My phone starts to ring in the kitchen. "Can you just stay here for a moment?"

"Yes," Her answer is said to the wardrobe doors as I leave the room.

"Sam, go ahead."

"He's heard that his niece nearly died. They are on their way to you." I glance back in at Svetlana. She's still sitting on the edge of the bed. A look of frustration crosses her face.

"They?"

"The other guy is called Holic."

"Thank you Sam." I hang up and ring Gregor.

"Any news on Larry?"

"Nothing yet boss. He is local. So far nothing odd about him."

"Okay keep looking we might have trouble on the way. Mr. Novak has found out about Svetlana being hurt and he's on his way here."

"You need me to come back?"

"No. I can manage it."

Looking in at Svetlana this time she is looking out at me.

"I'll call you if I need you." Ending the call I step into the bedroom. "Tell me about Holic?"

Svetlana hunches forward her eyes widen and I hate the reaction his name brings up, but I also need to know what I'm up against. When I had researched him he was the one with the least amount of information on him. I knew he was brought up in the foster system in Czech and got into working with gangs.

"He's ... cruel." She blinks several times.

"Your uncle has heard the word that you got hurt." I don't know why I'm telling her this.

The remaining color slowly drains from her face. "He's coming for me?" She's nodding while she speaks. She's waiting for me to confirm.

"Yes."

She covers her mouth with a trembling hand as her eyes dart around the room, like some magic door will appear and she can run out of it.

"Holic is coming too."

Her eyes snap to mine and widen further. They sparkle and shine. "I didn't do anything wrong." A sob strangles from her throat but her tears don't fall. Watery eyes stare at me and I hate how she looks at me.

"Are you going to let them take me?" Her lip trembles.

"I don't have a choice." My words come out harsher than I intended.

"Everyone has a choice." Tears fall down her face as her voice rises. "You just choose to let an innocent person die." She tries to stand.

"What are you doing?"

"Don't touch me." She holds out her arm to make me stay back as she takes in a deep lungful of air. I have no idea what to do. "You could hide me." Her suggestion is spoken with desperation and I clench my fists.

"No."

"No you don't want to, or no you can't." She takes another unstable step towards me.

"No." I bark this time.

"They are going to kill me, how can you live with that." She takes another step, and the strain is visible on her face, her forehead starts to shine with sweat.

"You're hurting yourself. Go back to bed."

Her laughter is taunting. "I'm not even close to hurting compared to what they will do to me." She's nearly reached me and I don't want her this close to me. "They won't just punish me Liam." Her lip quivers again, and she glances away as tears trail down her face. "They will hurt me in the worst way possible."

"You are forgetting you're not mine. You have to go back no matter what I want. What you're asking me to do is unreasonable."

"I just don't want to die." Her whispered words make their way into my heart. I want to comfort her and tell her she's safe, but I won't lie to her.

"He won't kill you; you are too precious to him." Her eyes snap back up to me. I wasn't sure anymore who I was trying to comfort.

"There are worse things than death and more than one way to kill a person."

"I can't help you." I start to walk away.

"Please don't." A thud has me turning around. Svetlana is sprawled out on the ground.

I try to pick her up.

"Don't touch me," her angry words are filled with pain. I ignore them and pick her up carrying her back to the bed.

"If you try to move again, I will handcuff you to the bed."

My warning has her face tightening. "You're just like them." Angry words lash out at me.

I stand up.

"I hate you." Her shouts carry too much pain and I slam the bedroom door to block out her words but they follow me.

"Wanda."

"What can I do for you today?"

"Lock down the basement except for the living quarters."

"Lock down commencing in one minute." I leave not looking back, there is a pull on me each time I take a step towards the stairs that leads out of the basement. A pull I ignore until I'm back up inside the house.

My phone rings. Its Mr. Novak. I walk to the study where I can take the call in private. My stomach tightens, it's an odd feeling that I push back down.

"Mr. Novak. I hope everything is going well." I close the door behind me.

"On our end we are keeping up our end of the bargain, but I don't know if you are."

I slide into the chair and pull it close to my father's desk. "You will have to expand on your accusation Mr. Novak."

"Word has gotten to us that Svetlana has been hurt."

"You never stated what I can and can't do with her."

His laughter is tinged with an unbalance that makes him the best at what he does.

"So you claim you were the one who hurt her?"

"Mr. Novak if you want your niece back, by all means just say the words and I will have Gregor deliver her to you. Right now I have lots of work that demands my attention."

"I am demanding your attention." There is a pause as I tighten my fist. "We need to re-negotiate."

"Do we?" I question.

"Svetlana was given as a good will gesture. I don't like the idea of my niece being hurt."

"I find that hard to believe Mr. Novak. I have seen the marks on the girl's back." I know I should keep my mouth shut, but he's pissing me off.

"She tried to run away. Any loving uncle would do the same thing." His justification of whipping her made it clear he had no love for her, she was a toy that he was using, but for what I wasn't sure.

"I don't want to hear she was hurt again."

"Agreed." I state.

"Mr. O'Reagan she is pure and must remain that way."

"I have no intentions of doing anything with your niece."

"Good. But if we hear she's been harmed again, I won't be happy."

"Is that all Mr. Novak?" Relief that I hadn't expected swirls through me at the idea that I didn't have to figure out how to not hand her over. It wasn't until his name came up on the screen that I knew I couldn't give her back.

"We will be in contact." He ends the call.

I ring Sam.

"Are they still on their way?"

"No I was going to ring you. They've stopped on the outskirts of Longford in a small pub. Do you want me to go in?"

"No, just keep an eye on them from a distance."

"No problem."

"I'll be in touch." I hang up as the alarm from my basement flashes up on my screen.

"God damn it." My anger is rising; she just can't manage to do what she is told. A second thought has me moving faster, what if someone has broken in again? I punch in the code and take the steps two at a time, the last three I clear as I race to the living quarter's door. I stop abruptly and reach out grabbing Svetlana before we collide with each other.

"Going somewhere?" I want to shake her, but she already looks like she needs to lie down. She's barely fit to walk. Yet she made it out of the bedroom and to the door.

"Wanda."

"What can I do for you today?"

"Unlock the basement."

"Basement is unlocked." The alarms stop and Svetlana leans into me, exhaustion taking over her limbs.

"You're a stupid girl," I tell her while picking her up carefully. Her head rolls back as I carry her into the bedroom. Lying her down on the bed I brush her hair away from her face, she moves away from my touch. Even now when her body needs to shut down, she keeps fighting. Taking the blankets I pull them over her and sit for a while. I was regretting my decision with getting involved with Mr. Novak. He wasn't as trustworthy as I had first thought. He was making millions off this deal, yet it didn't seem to be enough. I needed to find out what he wanted and what he thought he could achieve by placing Svetlana in my care. I look at her now. The rise and fall of her chest is gentle. Was she part of his ploy? I was good at reading people and her fear of him seemed plausible.

Getting out fresh clothes, I go for a shower. I opt for leaving the bathroom door open so I can hear if she decides to leave again. I wasn't sure how far she would get. Maybe outside and end up passed out on the lawn.

Stupid girl.

When I'm finished showering, I wrap myself in a towel and check on her, she's still asleep.

"Incoming call from the front gate." Wanda informs me.

"Receive."

"Mr. O'Reagan. Doctor Watson is at the front gate."

"Let him in."

Stephen was proving to be very thorough and I liked that. It made me think of the reason he was here. To protect our family. I needed to talk to him about how the van got in on our property without been stopped.

I've put on my trousers and a shirt when George arrives.

"She's asleep." I say putting on my tie.

"You want me to wait?" He sounds irritated.

"No wake her up."

He passes me and goes into the bedroom. Another thing is bothering me is how Mr. Novak knew that Svetlana was hurt. Both people were dead, the van at the bottom of the lake. No one knew only my family, Gregor, George and Stephen. So someone had betrayed me.

"Svetlana," George shakes her gently and I step into the room.

"Start changing her bandage I'm sure that will wake her up." I was angry with her for being so stupid. She had made clever decisions since she arrived but trying to leave, while injured wasn't wise. She could have fallen down the stairs, being found outside by someone else. Even been taken again.

George is stalling so I pull back the covers and she stirs. "Svetlana wake up." Her eyes snap open at my words and they snap from me to George, it takes her a few seconds to recognize him, and she relaxes but when her gaze returns to mine she tenses.

"George is going to change your bandages so be still." I leave her with my departing words as I return to the living space. She hisses and George apologies a lot.

It takes a bit of time before he arrives back out to the living area.

"She's doing well. Her lungs are still clear and I don't think the arm is broken. It may have been a sprain. But I've still kept it splintered."

"Can she wash with the bandages on?" I ask.

"Yes, they are waterproof. You want me back tomorrow?"

"Yes."

He has his bag in hand and gives a final nod before leaving. I don't trust him; I need to test his loyalty.

CHAPTER EIGHTEEN

SVETLANA

I can't look at Liam. He's dressed in a suit, dressed for business. There is a detachment that I saw when I first met him and it's back again. His mind is made up. I was going. If I got to go home, I'd get to see Jan again. That is the only thing I hold on to.

"Do you want to go for a shower?" So he was cleaning me up before sending me back. The doctor had re-bandaged me and now he would re-package me. I don't know why I was surprised or hurt. I knew I would be going back. It was a foolish part of me that had hoped for more in my life.

"Yes." I still can't look at him even as he picks me up in his arms. I try to keep my head as far away from his chest as possible. One part of me wants to lean in and enjoy the remainder of my time with him, the other wants to go so this will end.

We enter the bathroom and he doesn't put me down, the time stretches out until I finally peek up at him. He's looking at me and my stomach flips.

"Why did your uncle give you to me?"

It's not a question I expected but one I give fair weight to.

Liam places me carefully on the ground but does a bizarre thing and places two fingers over my flickering pulse.

"What are you doing?"

"I'm asking the questions." There is a warning in his tone. "Why did your uncle give you to me?" he starts again and I want my arm back but I don't pull away.

"I don't know." My pulse spikes.

"You're lying." His brows rise slightly.

I yank my arm back but he won't let it go. His fingers dig painfully into my wrist and we are moving backward until my back is against the wall. I'm cornered with nowhere to go.

"Tell me why?"

"I'm not sure why." My face burns as I think back to the conversation in the patio area, the day I found out I was being given as a gift.

"You're lying." Liam's closer now his body against mine.

I have to look up at him. My heart is pounding, and it has nothing to do with the questions. "I don't know." I shout wanting him to step away. "He had said men wanted women." My face burns.

"But why you?" his eyes that are inky black now search my face. His fingers are still pressed firmly against my wrist.

"I don't know," I whisper dying a little at the memory of that conversation. We are moving towards the shower. "What are you doing?"

Cold water sprays down on top of me and I squeal with shock. Liam fills the small space that the shower has, his fingers still pressed to my wrist.

"Let me out!" I try to push him but he won't budge. "Are you crazy?" He was standing in the shower in a suit, the water soaking through his clothes. I shiver from the cold water that keeps assaulting me. "Because I am untouched," I don't lose eye contact as I him tell the humiliating fact about me.

"You're a virgin?" There is an element of disbelief in his words.

I shiver against the cold of the water. "Yes."

Liam lets me go and I stare at his chest as it grows closer to me, his arm moves behind me and the water turns from cold to a nice heat that causes me to shiver more.

My heart still beats to a heavy drum in my chest. "What are you doing?"

Fear lodges itself in my throat as Liam removes his tie and jacket. "I'm going to help you get washed." He doesn't look at me as he kicks off his shoes that are filled with water. I'm frozen as he strips down to his boxers.

"You can't touch me," I warn him as he takes a step towards me. "My uncle will kill you." I move back as he moves towards me. The edge of the tray pushes against my spine. Liam hasn't taken his eyes off me as he reaches around and takes down some shampoo.

"I'm just going to wash your hair. I don't think your fit to do it with your arm."

I wasn't, but my mind is still caught up that I am in a shower with a man, a half-naked man, a very attractive half naked man. I can't seem to move or form words.

"Turn around."

I do as it's easier to try to calm my raging mind. "Can you take off the t-shirt?" Having it on in the shower was weird and now that my back was too him it made this easier. It takes him a moment before his fingers grip the bottom of my t-shirt. Everywhere his fingers touch, I shiver. The material is pulled over my head. His chest presses against my back as he removes each arm carefully. The top falls to the shower tray with a splash of water. Liam doesn't step back, his fingers run along the back of my neck before he lifts all my hair to the side. His touch is gentle and I remember what's on my back. Spinning around, I let my hair cover it. I can't bear for anyone to see that part of me. I'm looking at a solid chest and my eyes won't drift up, his head is bent and I can feel his eyes on me.

"It's okay." His words brush my face and something inside me cracks a little.

"It's him, it's his mark on me and I hate it." I let my eyes drift up to his. "I hate my uncle for making him do it to me." My chest tightens and my hand touches it as if it might be able to untangle the knots that are choking me. "I hate you for sending me back." I step away from Liam.

"You say it like I have a choice."

I'm close to the spray and brush water out of my face. "When is Holic coming for me?" I notice how Liam clenches his fists, and it annoys me. He has no right to get mad. He has no right to feel angry at me. I was the one who was disposed of again.

"They aren't coming." He doesn't sound happy.

My heart jumps. "I can stay?" Hope grows inside me, like the air inside a balloon.

Liam brushes water off his face. "Yes." I hear the unspoken part 'for now', but I had more time.

I step back into the spray and let the water wash my tears away. I don't want Liam to see my heart so I turn my back on him. It takes a moment before he moves closer to me. His fingers touch my hair as he massages the shampoo into my scalp.

His touch has weakened me. I hold on to the tiles taking as much weight off my leg as possible. He moves even closer to me.

"Lean against me," I do as he says.

He works quickly washing my hair and I wonder how he hasn't got some shampoo on his face with how close we are.

Once he is finished, his fingers touch my shoulders. I tense at his touch but soon relax into his chest.

"Do you want me to wash your hair?" I ask. The rumble through his chest shakes my back and I turn around, surprised to find Liam laughing.

"You want to wash my hair?" He's smiling now, and it softens all the sharp plains of his face.

My heart gives a heavy thud and I smile back. "I've never washed anyone's hair before." I admit. But it wasn't about that.

His smile grows quiet, and he nods before picking up the shampoo. "Okay."

I take it and feel unsure now. Liam is smiling as he bends his head and I lather up my hands before dropping the bottle heavily onto the floor. I can only use one hand but I try to massage his head as best as he did mine. I enjoy the feel of his hair running through my fingers. Stepping closer I inch around to the back of his head. His hand moves around my waist and I stop briefly, surprised at the contact. His arm holds up most of my body weight and gives relief to my leg as I continue to massage his scalp. I don't notice how close his face is to my chest, or every place our flesh touches. I don't notice how tight his fingers are getting around my waist.

"Can you go under the water so I can wash it off?"

Liam spins us not letting me go until we have reversed positions. I close my eyes as I run my hands through his hair, and rinse off all the shampoo. I don't open my eyes for a few minutes just enjoying the feel of our bodies, when I do Liam is looking down at me, our faces only an inch apart. My breathing quickens and my gaze flickers to his lips. His kiss had been really nice, now I was trying to imagine what that would feel like with him awake and willing. *Willing*, the word has my stomach churning with guilt. My hand touches his face and when he doesn't stop me I let my fingertips glide over his lips that part for me.

"I've never been kissed," I admit. He doesn't react; the only tell is the tightening of his fingers at my waist. "I ..." I glance away before getting the courage to look back at him.

"I kissed you when you slept." My face burns at my confession but I also feel a sense of relief at being honest. My fingers still linger on his lips and he kisses them, my heart jumps.

"I know." His words sweep across my face.

"You do?" I had been certain he was asleep.

"Yes." His lip tugs up slightly at my discomfort before they fall back into their normal arrangement. "Would you like to try it now that I'm awake?"

My heart slams against my rib cage. This is different. If I kissed him now I felt like there was no going back, or maybe that is the naïve virgin in me talking. Girls kissed and even slept with loads of guys, but with Liam I didn't think any girl would really walk away from him, he did the walking away. I was taking too long and overthinking this. I might never get this chance again. My fingers move to his cheek and I move my head closer, flickering my gaze between his eyes and lips. I close my eyes and tilt my head as my lips touch his. At first it's like in the bedroom when I kissed him the first time, that is until he kisses me back. His hand tightens further around my waist and he moves us. My back is pressed against the cold tiles and the contrast of his warm body has me shivering. My eyes snap open and I stop kissing him as his manhood presses against me. He still holds me but leans out slightly to see what's wrong.

He's a bit breathless. "What's wrong?"

I shake my head feeling embarrassed. He's still pressed against me and the feelings that are swirling through my body are overwhelming. I needed air. I wanted him so much but fear had me wanting him to step away.

"Nothing." My pulse is beating in the most unexpected area. Heat sears my face. I swallow knowing I was making this worse. I move in to kiss him again but he stops me.

"There is something wrong. You need to tell me. Did I hurt you?"

"No." I focus on his chest, my fingers trace the water flows through the groves of his muscle. "I've just never felt anything like that, it surprised me." Now I look up at him. His free hand holds my neck as he pulls me into a kiss. This time it is different and so much better which I didn't think was possible. His tongue finds its way into my mouth and I moan in surprise. I follow his movements with my own tongue and his manhood seems to grow and press heavier against me. I want to squeeze my legs closed as it throbs. My head spins and I'm moving my other hand to his neck, the pain doesn't stop me as I cling to him with both arms. He breaks the kiss and I bury my head into the nape of his neck and stare at the beige tiles. My body feels like I am going through the aftermath of being electrified. Every nerve end jumps and I feel frazzled.

Liam reaches around me and the water stops, his hand reaches under my legs and he carries me out of the shower. I'm still buried in the nape of his neck, not ready yet to allow this feeling to go. I want to cling to it a bit longer. Liam lowers me and I glance up as he sits me on the toilet before wrapping a towel around my shoulders. He has my full attention as he wraps a towel around his waist and then removes his boxers I watch them slip from under the towel and all the way onto the floor. Strong arms wrap around me as Liam carries me out of the bathroom. His towel holds up, firmly secured to his waist. He settles us on the bed and my pulse spikes.

"Have you ever had an orgasm?"

The question has my cheeks blazing and my thighs tightening. "Yes."

His lip tugs up, and I bite my lip. "I mean by someone who isn't you."

A nervous laugh bubbles up my throat. "No," I answer honestly.

"Then let me." Liam's serious words have my laughter ceasing abruptly. I'm terrified, yet excited, and he moves me back on the bed until I'm lying flat on my back, he hovers over me before planting a kiss on my lips. I return the kiss but my mind is too focused on the orgasm. *Would it be different from when I do it?* "You need to relax." His words enter my mouth between kisses, but I feel his fingers trail down the towel; I pull in my stomach on reflex as his hands move across it. He is still on the outside of the towel and I inhale a sharp breath as his fingers touch my bare thigh, his hand moves closer to the area that throbs and begs for him to touch it. Pushing myself closer to his hand he deepens the kiss with his tongue. When his fingers slip under my underwear I open my eyes, he's watching me and my body seems to jump.

Long fingers touch the rim of my entrance and I tense. Liam's other hand parts my towel and when his hand brushes my breast I close my eyes in wonder and push my tongue deeper into his mouth. I want to touch him, but I'm too afraid so I keep my hand firmly on his shoulder. His fingers dip into my wetness and I push my body harder against his hand forcing his fingers to go deeper. When they fully enter me I moan into his mouth as shots of electricity pour through me. My hand leaves his shoulder and moves down his chest. I don't stop until I feel the towel and beneath it his manhood. Fingers move deeper inside me and I arch my back while spreading my legs even further giving him as much access as possible. My fingers move under the towel and touch him, it jumps at the contact and Liam moans. He keeps his rhythm plunging his fingers into me before bringing them back out. His thumb flicks across my clitoris and I'm holding back the orgasm. I run my own thumb across the head of his erection and he groans breaking the kiss and shifts himself away from me before moving his fingers faster, his thumb hits my clitoris harder and I can't hold back any longer. His lips crash down on mine as I release over his fingers and cry out his name.

CHAPTER NINETEEN

LIAM

I WATCH HER AS she releases all over my hand. My own need pulses but I focus on her. Her wide eyes and swollen lips make her look even more desirable. When she had said she was a virgin, I couldn't resist. Who could? I know now as I look down at her that she's mine, and I wasn't giving her back. Removing my fingers from inside her warm and wet flesh I put the towel back in place.

Her eyes flash with uncertainty as she glances at my towel her hand moving in that direction.

I stop her. "I wanted to do that for you," I say.

"I want to do the same for you. I know I haven't much experience, well actually none, but I'd like to try."

My self-control was slipping, but I needed to remember that this was all new to her. "You can, but just not now."

She lies back and the disappointment rests on her shoulders. I lie with her for a while and just watch as her face transforms as she smiles at me. Blue eyes shine at me like I gave her the world. My lips tug up into their own smile and I plant a kiss on her swollen lips. "I'm going to get dressed."

She nods while looking at me shyly from under her lashes making it hard for me to leave. One final kiss and I make myself push off the bed and get dressed into a t-shirt and a pair of jogging pants. Glancing back at Svetlana she still lies on the bed and guilt churns in my stomach. I had no idea how I was going to make this work. How would I keep her safe, I couldn't keep her hidden down here forever? At the back of my mind the name Jan niggles at me. She told me he's important. Was he important enough that she would return to him if she could? Taking out a fresh t-shirt I bring it over to her.

"I'll get you some proper clothes tomorrow," I say as I take her hand and pull her up gently into a sitting position.

"Maybe I could go with you." She's smiling but I'm not.

"I can't allow that."

Her smile falters and she won't meet my eye now. "I know." She shrugs and frowns. I let her remove her bra, she's quick using one hand. Holding the surrounding towel I pull on the t-shirt and she slowly lowers it not allowing me to see a thing. I leave her to remove her underwear and get her a fresh pair of bottoms. She opens her hand to take them.

"I can help you."

"I want to do it myself." She still won't look at me as she speaks. I place them beside her and leave the room.

***

For the next three days Svetlana avoids me. She withdraws into herself and I have no idea how to get her to come back. She eats the food and uses the restroom but she won't leave the bedroom. I've noticed she's moving around more but she never joins me. I bought her new clothes and made space in the wardrobe but she hasn't changed out of the clothes I had given her three days ago.

"Anything yet?" I ask Gregor as I meet him at the entrance of the basement.

"Nothing with Larry but we have found the red haired woman." Gregor hands me a file and I take it. Opening it up I study the image of the red haired woman that we had been searching for.

"Margaret Murphy," I say out loud. She's twenty seven and her brother Matt Murphy has an involvement with the RA. She's from Belfast.

"Do you know where she is now?"

Gregor nods looking pleased with himself. "She's been seen in the Nuemore Hotel in Carrickmacross and guess who she was meeting?" I don't guess and Gregor gives up the information quickly.

"Connor."

"Can you bring her in quietly?"

"She's not alone. Her brother Matt is with her along with a few other associated members of the RA. But the first moment she's alone I'll bring her to you."

"She's your number one priority." Her tie with the RA told me that it was an RA job. But why kill Siobhan and try to kill Shane? That was the information I wanted to get out of her. If her brother was deep in the RA, she just might know why she was told to get rid of the security the day of the wedding. I don't return to the basement but lock it down before going into the house.

Darragh is showing great intuition and working hard at overseeing the hotels for me. I hope to return to them next week but right now the situation with Svetlana is niggling at me.

I find Finn and Shane in the bar playing pool. It's nice to see Finn smile, but it slips when I enter and the game pauses.

"Please don't stop on my account," I tell them but both of them don't resume.

"I'm going for a walk." Finn leaves the room and I look to Shane for an answer.

"He's pissed that you are doing nothing to find Siobhan's killer."

"You think I'm doing nothing?"

Shane picks up a pool ball and weighs it in his hand before putting it back down. "No. But you need to talk to him, reassure him the killer will be found."

"I can't give him that reassurance," I say honestly placing my hands in my pockets. "Have you a theory on why you were targeted?"

My question catches Shane off guard, he's about to pick up another ball but pauses before completing the action. "I have no idea. Just someone doesn't like our family very much."

I nod and don't call him out on his lies. I don't like Shane lying to me but I would find out exactly what happened no matter how deep I had to dig. "I was actually looking for you for a different reason."

His brows rise as he waits to hear my request.

"I'm looking for a psychology teacher to come here for a one on one."

"Yeah I can ask Rachel, she works in the labs in Dublin but studied in UCD so she might know of any free-lance psychology teacher."

"Good if they could be here in the morning at nine I would appreciate it."

"I'm not sure I can organize it that quick."

I remove my hands from my pockets. "I have full faith in you that you will."

My phone rings as I step out of the room.

"Sam have you news for me?" I continue on down the hall and to the basement as I speak to him.

"The pub they stopped in was owned by Ciara Cunningham. Who's married to Larry's sister."

"Interesting," I say as I punch the code for the basement.

"So I got talking to Ciara, and she likes to talk. Larry has special needs, and she said he was always led astray by other kids. Right now he's missing but they aren't worried saying he will return as he left with an old family friend."

I enter the basement and am surprised to see Svetlana sitting on the couch. She glances at me but looks away.

Removing my jacket I place it on the back of the chair.

"Get this, the family friend was Claire Rodgers who was into some dodgy things, but Ciara didn't expand on dodgy."

"Did you find out anything on Claire?" I ask and Svetlana is listening. I can tell by how she leans towards me. I go into the bedroom and close the door.

"Yeah, she's part of a local group that sells drugs and even for the right price will kill someone. I found the group and none of them were willing to give up too much information. But one of them said that Russians had been around a few days previous and spoke to Claire."

"Great work Sam. Stay on Mr. Novak." I end the call and let the information slide into place.

Mr. Novak was playing me. He had arranged the kidnapping that's how he knew about it. He was trying to maybe take what I had built, accusing me of losing Svetlana or even killing her. How far would he go? And when would he strike again?

The bedroom door opens and Svetlana steps in and she looks as uncertain as she had the first day she arrived.

"Who's Claire?"

"None of your business." I get up off the made bed, she had been keeping the living space clean. Boredom was setting in heavily on her.

"Do you touch her like you touched me?" She crosses her arms over her chest; I'm surprised by her level of jealousy.

Removing my tie I don't answer her.

"I'll take that as a yes."

I glance at her and hope she sees the warning in my eyes, if she does she ignores it.

"I want to speak to my uncle."

I open the top button of my shirt. "No."

"I'm demanding it."

I stand now and she tightens her arms across her chest. "It wasn't long ago you were begging me not to let them take you. Now you want your uncle."

"I'm always going to be a prisoner with you. I'm just waiting until you send me back and its torture. So maybe I should make that decision of when I go back." Tears brim in her eyes as she speaks.

"You have no say. When he wants you he will come for you." She knows this; her struggle for control was a battle she would lose.

"I hate it here." She speaks through gritted teeth. I try not to react to her words but my body reacts and I clench my fists.

"You think I wanted you here? You are the first person to have ever seen where I live and since you arrived, I've had a string of people in here."

"I'm sorry for being such an inconvenience."

"I don't know what you want from me." My loud words have her hands falling to her side and her eyes widen.

She doesn't answer.

"You don't even know what you want, do you?" I take a few steps towards the door knowing I need to leave before I lose my temper with her. She was asking for something I couldn't give her.

"I just want to be happy." Her watery half smile has me stopping. "I just want to know that tomorrow my time isn't up. I want to be free."

Frustration rattles through me. "You tell me how I can do that for you. You tell me how I can win this?"

"You can't win against him." Tears stream down her face. "But you could let me be free. You could pretend ..."

I'm shaking my head already. "I can't let you go."

"Why not?"

My hands grip her arms and I shake her. "I want you to stop this. I'm not letting you go, that is the end of this discussion."

"Not until he clicks his fingers."

My hand moves up to her throat and I force her to tilt her head back. "I'm not letting you go," I repeat, her lips are parted and I bend my head and kiss her. At first she doesn't respond but it takes a moment for her to kiss me back. My thumb rubs her neck where her heartbeat pulses under it. Her hands slam into my chest, breaking the kiss and surprising me with the force she uses. I take a step back, her lips are swollen again her cheeks coated in a pink hue.

"Don't ever kiss me again." She marches over to the bed and I leave her to cool down.

CHAPTER TWENTY

SVETLANA

LIAM WALKS OUT OF the room with clenched fists and a part of me wants to go after him. But being here, locked in this place, is breaking me down. Each touch is making me fall deeper for him and soon I fear I will give up the sun just to have his touch. That of course is until my uncle wants me back. There is something in the way that Liam had said 'I'm not letting you go' that sounds so final. But I'm not naïve to think my uncle would just release me after so many years of being his prisoner.

My eyes go voluntarily to the wardrobe and guilt churns in my stomach. Over the last few days I've tried not to even make eye contact with Liam for fear he would figure out what I am doing. So far I had managed to get four hundred euro from his wallet, a knife that he had left out after making us food, and I know the gun is still strapped to the underside of the coffee table. All the clothes he had bought me are unnecessary, but I have an outfit picked out, all black and easy to move in. Liam has started to trust me, I'm not sure if he is aware of what he is doing but he stopped locking the basement. Normally he is only gone for a few minutes but that's all I need. I just have to wait now for the perfect opportunity.

He passes the bedroom door and glances in at me, the kiss is still burning on my lips. I look away and move back to the corner of the room that I had favored at the start. My red stiletto heels still sit in the corner. I don't know why but they make me think of Jan. Maybe because they are the last things I wore. If I ran, Holic would kill him to spite me. My plan was to first get away from Liam and get home to the Czech. I had no idea how, but with money someone might help me. It would be my best chance at getting Jan since my uncle and Holic where here in Ireland.

"Is it night time?" I shout out at Liam. My fuse is short lately. I hate not knowing if it is day or night.

He appears in the doorway. "No."

Always with one-word answers. I turn my head away from him.

"Claire is the girl who tried to kidnap you."

I quickly look at Liam, he hasn't entered the room, and instead he leans against the door frame like we are having a casual conversation. He's opened two buttons of his shirt showing off some of that tanned skin.

"What?" I'm too distracted when I look at him.

"You asked me if I touched Claire liked I touched you."

My face flames at his matter of a fact tone.

He continues. "The answer is no. I was inquiring about her because she was the woman who tried to kidnap you."

"What did she want me for?"

"I'm still trying to figure that out." He pushes away from the door frame as he speaks and steps into the room. I feel so vulnerable sitting in the corner of the room as he moves towards me. When he reaches me he kneels down until he's on his hunkers in front of me. "Why are you sitting on the floor?"

"Am I not allowed?" I fire back.

Liam exhales loudly like I'm being some awkward teenager that he has no idea how to help. "Yes you are allowed Svetlana. You just don't have to."

Turning my head away from him I face the wall. His eyes pull me in and strip me bare and right now I need to keep my barriers up.

"Well I want to. It's the only thing I have control over."

"You have the full run of my home. I haven't mistreated you." His words are said through clenched teeth. "Have I harmed you?"

Now I look at him. "Am I meant to be grateful that you haven't hurt me?"

A muscle flex in his jaw. "That's not what I am saying. You're acting like ..." He trails off.

I sneer. "Like what Liam. Like a prisoner."

He's standing now and I fear I've pushed him too far. My plan was to keep him on my side so he would continue to trust me but I couldn't seem to control my mouth around him. His hand appears in front of me and I look at it.

"Take my hand."

Looking into his eyes is like looking into deep pools of ink, they show no emotion and I hesitate but eventually I take his hand and he helps me stand.

Once I'm standing he releases me and I follow him into the living room. When he opens the door that leads out of this room I hesitate.

"Where are we going?"

He doesn't answer me but steps through the door. I follow him. The room we walk into sends a shiver up my spine. I'm not wearing shoes but the cold that spreads through me has got nothing to do with the cement floor under my feet. It's a chair that is the center of the room. It's bolted to the floor. The large wooden contraption has straps for the feet and arms; I'm stepping away when Liam focuses on me.

"Sit in it." He says.

I'm shaking my head.

"You said you were a prisoner." His anger grows too quickly.

I take another step back. "I want to go back to my room."

"That's not your room. That's my room. Sit on the chair."

I glance back at the door, the beat of my heart is loud and thrashes against my ears. Fingers tighten around my arms, I hadn't heard him move. A weakness enters my legs.

"I said sit in the chair." He pulls me over to it and I'm in it, shaking my head. He seals the straps on my feet and then my hands, my stomach curls in on itself and I close my eyes. All I see is Holic. He would make me strip from the waist up; his eyes had burned a path into my naked flesh. The first time I had thought he was going to rape me, but when he had told me to turn around and kneel I had felt relief and fear. The anticipation of not knowing what was going to happen had driven me to scream at Holic. "Just do it." Whatever it was I couldn't wait any longer, he hadn't hesitated at my words. My skin had split open easily as the whip had connected with my flesh. Pain like I'd never experienced before, even when I broke my nose, or broke my heart when my parents died, lashed out across my back. My roars left my throat raw; my cries for help ceased and turned to sobs of agony. No one came, no one would now.

"Just do it," I say to Liam keeping my eyes closed. I had no idea of what he was going to do with me. But I refused to look at him. I refused to wait. I refused to let fear control me anymore. Nothing happens and I slowly open my eyes and glance up at Liam.

"When people disobey me, I hurt them." He kneels down now so we are at eye level.

My vision blurs but I force back the tears.

"When someone questions me, I remove them." His words ring with truth and I can't look away from the black abyss of his eyes that hold a coldness that I haven't seen before.

"I've never come across a problem I couldn't fix." A long finger touches mine, I can't move as my wrists are strapped. The feeling isn't unpleasant; I'm just waiting for him to hurt me. "Until you." His eyes roam across my face before his attention goes back to my hand as he continues to run his fingers in-between them.

I swallow when he pauses while waiting for the blow. "If you want to be a prisoner, I can treat you as such, but if you don't, then this is a final warning Svetlana."

His focus is back on me and I hold still almost not breathing.

A final warning.

Words fail me so I nod.

He touches the strap on my wrist but doesn't release me immediately. "I need to hear you say it Svetlana." There is a touch of triumph in his eyes.

"I will obey you."

His standing, I'm very aware of how he isn't unbuckling me. "I don't want your obedience." He's leaning in now, gripping the back of the chair and he's too close. His breath brushes my face and I try not to turn my head away from him.

"I don't want to be a prisoner." My words come out in a growl.

Liam's lip tugs up slightly. "You're strapped to a chair and you're giving me attitude." Why does he sound so amused, yet his body still leans in towards mine in a threatening manner contradicting his tone?

For the first time I look away from him, I don't know if I should be brave or afraid. I wasn't sure which way he would tip his hat. A heavy exhale is released from his lips drawing my attention back to him.

He moves down into a kneeling position again. "You are not making this easy."

Once again I bit my tongue not allowing the remark that wants to burst from my lips to form.

His eyes flicker to my lips before he leans in, the smell of him surrounds me as he presses his lips against mine. He doesn't close his eyes and neither do I. There is a challenge in his stare, push him away and he wins, let him kiss me and he wins. He continues to press his lips against mine and when I don't respond he breaks the one sided kiss.

"Are you enjoying yourself?" I ask and kick myself immediately knowing I should stay quiet.

"You kissed me while I slept. You're alert and have the capability to turn your head away. But you didn't."

My face burns. "I didn't kiss you back either." My heart beats faster as he leans again, his lips barely touching mine.

"But you want to."

Did I? Was he right? I knew the answer deep down. He hasn't moved and like he said before, I didn't turn my head away. I don't want to and I hate him for that. Black orbs like the bottom of a lake pour into me and I can't find the ability to look away. The ground trembles under my feet and I think it's my body's way of dealing with Liam's full attention. The tremble rises up my legs and Liam moves back. Small stones bounce along the concrete floor and then the sound of several alarms blare in the room. I'm pulling at my arms trying to get out. While my eyes snap to the ceiling looking for cracks that I can't see.

"Let me out," I squeal as I continue to pull at my arms. The trembling has stopped but the alarms continue to blare.

"Stay here." Liam isn't looking at me and dread worms its cold fingers around my spine.

"Please Liam untie me, don't leave me like this." He pauses and curses before coming back to me. He can't untie me quick enough, the thoughts of being buried alive has me taking terrified peeks at the ceiling.

"Go back to your room and don't leave." I nod as I fold my arms across my chest and gladly leave the concrete box behind me.

"Svetlana." I pause and glance at Liam, my stomach twists. "Don't even think of leaving."

I nod again because that's all I've been thinking about. He disappears out of the room with a look of uncertainty on his face. I don't linger any longer but know this is the best time to put my plan into action.

CHAPTER TWENTY-ONE

LIAM

"WHAT'S HAPPENED?" SHANE ASKS as we meet in the hall and continue outside. Finn is standing in the courtyard and we all pause. A large cloud of smoke is visible.

"Darragh took the quad." Finn frowns as he speaks.

We start making our way across the field. If Darragh had only gone now at least that ruled him out of causing whatever this was. The closer we get the wearier I feel.

One of the outbuildings is a pile of rubble, Darragh looks up as we approach, and he's holding something in his hands. His clenched jaw and drawn eyes tells me this isn't good. Taking the device from his outstretched hands, I stand out of a stream of smoke that's blowing in our direction now with the change of the wind.

I'm turning it over in my hands when Shane appears over my right shoulder. I take a quick look at him before handing him the device.

"It's a timer," he says glancing up at me and Darragh.

"For what?" Finn asks as he swipes smoke away.

"Considering we are standing beside a pile of rubble my guess would be a bomb."

"You don't have to get smart Darragh." Finn shoves his hands in his jeans.

"It's a warning," Shane's not focused on any of us as he speaks. His eyes are drawn to the forest.

"A warning for what?"

Shane hands me back the device and starts to walk away. "I'm not sure." He fires over his shoulder.

"What aren't you saying?" Darragh steps up beside me and Shane stops and turns to all of us, guilt churns heavily in his eyes, as his eyes flash to Finn before returning to me. "Whoever shot me, has come back to finish the job."

I'm examining the device again, it's definitely a bomb, the warning is clear. "You need to get more security on the ground."

Shane nods and turns away again. I'm staring at the rising smoke wondering how many other people heard the bang or even felt the tremble. "We need to keep the Gardaí away from this. No doubt someone has informed them already." My phone rings. "I think we are too late." I say before answering to Stephen. "Delay them for about ten minutes, then you can let them in."

Hanging up I hand the device to Finn. "You need to hide this." He sprints off across the field clutching the device.

"Was there anything else you saw?" I ask Darragh as I try to see beyond the smoke and rubble.

"No, but it's still pretty hot."

"You hit a gas pipe," I inform Darragh.

"Why is it always me?"

"Do I look like I would hit a gas pipe?" I question.

He grins. "Liam making jokes." His smile falters and he squints out across the field.

"Is that...?" I turn and follow his line of sight; someone dressed in all black is racing across the field.

"God damn it." I'm moving as fast as my legs will allow me. The small frame is female and there is only one who I know would be running away from me. She's fast as she disappears into the forest. I should have locked down the basement. I curse myself as I slow down and listen for movements. She's noisy as she crashes through the forest and is easy to follow. Our distance closes in and my anger is growing. I had given her, her final warning and yet she still disobeyed me.

A part of me doesn't want to catch her yet, the chase is pushing the blood quickly through my veins. She's three trees ahead of me, her heavy breathing and loud footsteps make me pause and allow her to get a little further ahead. I catch up with her easily again, a flash of red hair has me springing out from behind a tree and I clamp a hand over her mouth before pulling down the black hood. Red curly hair frames her face. Green eyes stare up at me before she sinks her teeth into my hand.

The pain has me immediately releasing her but her teeth don't leave my hand. Twisting her other arm behind her back, I push it until she screams and releases me, but I keep pushing her arm, just stopping before it breaks.

Blood seeps from the four small wounds on my hand that's already swelling. Releasing her arm I grip her head and direct it towards the tree, they collide with a heavy crash and she slumps. I grip her before she lands on the ground and sling her over my shoulder. My hand throbs with pain and I hold it away from myself while I balance her using my good hand. I don't step out of the forest but lay the girl down as I search for blue lights or some movement but I don't see anything. Taking my phone out of my pocket I ring Darragh while keeping my eye on the sleeping form at my feet.

"What's happening?" I ask him.

"I'm just informing the selective rapid response team about my re decorating accident."

"Don't get arrested," I warn him; no doubt they heard every word he was saying.

He snorts. "I'll try not to."

"I've some baggage to bring in to the house."

He shuffles before speaking again. "How much time do you need?"

"Fifteen minutes."

"No problem. Mary is just about to put on the kettle." I hang up and leave the Gardaí in Darragh's hands.

My hand seems to be getting worse as I hoist the girl up on my shoulder. I move in a hunched sprint across the fields. The smoke from the outbuilding stills bubbles into the air, it would block anyone from seeing me from the house. I stay in the field that runs along the front of the house. Stopping a few times I dump the girl onto the ground. Her pulse flickers in her neck, and I focus on it as I hunch down in the grass and do a quick sweep of my surroundings. Blood still oozes from my hand. Wiping it in the grass I bit the inside of my jaw before picking up the girl and hoisting her over my shoulder again. Shrubbery that grows thick in the front gardens gives me cover as I make my way to my secret entrance. There is a gap, its short but I still need to be careful. I use my injured hand to get my phone out of my pocket; I try to ignore the pain as I ring Darragh.

"Are you still entertaining?"

"Yeah I'm about ready to break out in dance."

"Good." I hang up and shift the girl so she's in my arms; her head rests against my shoulder as I carry her across the few paces towards the entrance. Once I clear the door, I move quicker.

Each step is filled with a thrill and fear. I've never felt this kind of fear before. If Svetlana is still here when she had an opportunity to leave, my heart picks up at the thought, but sinks when I think about her not being here, while I was chasing this girl maybe she was getting away.

I'm moving faster. The body on my shoulders starts to stir as I enter the entrance room. Her moans have me moving faster until I move into the next space. I pass the chair that I had strapped Svetlana too before opening the door to the small room that I had kept Darragh in. Dropping her on the bed, her eyes open wide but I'm out the door before she can start protesting. Closing the door I go into the living quarters. I don't call her name as my eyes quickly scan the empty living space. The bedroom is empty. Her corner is vacant.

She left.

My chest grows tight with an ache and I rub it with a clenched fist trying to untangle the knots that threaten to suffocate me. Moving deeper into the room I try to remove this feeling but it seems to grow. My limbs are heavy as I make my way to the bathroom. Turning on the taps I use both hands to capture the cold water before splashing it on my face. The cold liquid feels good.

Glancing up into the mirror movement behind me captures not just my attention, but it tugs at something deep down inside me. Blue eyes stare back at me, fear makes them wide and tears have left marks on her face.

My skin tingles as I dab it with the towel before turning to Svetlana. She's still standing in the shower, still staring at me without saying a word.

"It was an outbuilding that collapsed." I explain the earlier tremors.

She nods and blinks. "I thought it was an earthquake." Her voice trembles as she speaks. She wets her lips and swallows before taking a look around her again. She seems distracted.

"We don't have earthquakes here."

She steps out of the shower. "Good."

Wrapping my fingers around her wrist stops her departure from the bathroom. "Are you okay?"

Her blue eyes snap up to mine. They search my face, her mouth opens and closes several times but she finally looks away and slowly removes her hand from mine. She doesn't step away from me. I want to know what she's thinking or what really has shaken her up.

My body stiffens. "Is someone here?" I ask her moving her behind me immediately. Reaching for the gun in the band of my trousers my fingers don't touch cold metal only the fabric of my pants. I had removed it earlier.

"No just me." Her small voice comes from behind me. She still looks rattled. I hate it. I want to remove the worry from her eyes. Was it the chair? Had I scared her too badly? My phone rings and all she does is look up at me with doe eyes.

"I frightened you?" I question wanting to find out what was bothering her.

Her lip rises slightly but her eyes still hold such weight. "No."

Taking a step closer I want to touch her. My phone continues to ring but I ignore it. "You look afraid." She swallows and folds her arms over her chest. Standing over her she appears so small but I know she isn't fragile. The marks on her back tell me her strength, her defiance shows me her bravery and that makes me want her more than I have ever wanted a woman before.

"I'm just tired." Her head dips and I hate not seeing her eyes. Touching her chin gently I raise her face until she is looking at me, this time her eyes are different. The fire is back in them. Her desire has me looking at her lips.

"Don't lie to me," I move my head closer.

"Never," She whispers but she sounds as distracted as I am. I want to kiss her. But I also want her permission.

"You are a very bad liar." I focus on her eyes and they smile up at me briefly before they darken again.

"I want you to kiss me," I tell her.

The rise and fall of her chest has grown rapidly, her breast brush against my chest. I continue to hold her face gently as I wait for her to either step away or give into the desire that is clearly there between us.

My phone starts ringing again.

"You should get that." She steps away from me and I take the phone out of my pocket and walk into the living space not allowing her rejection to affect me. I never had to ask for a woman's affection, so a dismissal had never happened before.

"They are gone. They bought my story." Darragh sounds happy with himself. "What took you so long to answer?"

Svetlana moves past me quickly and into the bedroom, her bare feet move silently across the floor. I watch her until she disappears out of view.

"Are you there?"

"Yes. I had my hands full." I leave the living quarters.

"Who was running across the field?" Darragh sounds like he's moving too.

"That's why I have my hands full; I think she's the same one who bribed the security at Finn's wedding."

"Did she say that?"

"No." I move towards the door and open the small slot so I can see her she's awake and pacing the small space. She pauses and looks at me but doesn't speak. I close the slot.

"Then how do you know?"

"She has red hair and green eyes, just like the description I got off one of the security men and Gregor found out who she was. Margret Murphy. Her brother is with the RA."

"I'm on my way." Before I can protest Darragh hangs up. I wasn't going to interrogate her yet. I would let her stew.

When I reach the entrance room Darragh is already there.

"I want to let her sit for a while." I tell Darragh.

He rubs the back of his neck. "Is she in that room?"

I nod seeing how uneasy he appears. There is a shift in the room and I can almost feel the tension that ripples under Darragh's skin. I never wanted to be alone with him.

"I have other jobs that require my attention." I hope my dismissal makes him leave.

"I know. But…" He frowns before ramming his hands in his jeans pockets. "Was it quick?" His eyes grow heavy with pain. The truth weighs on me.

"Yes." Strangling someone is a slow and painful death. Her panic that night, her fear and confusion had suffocated me. I had never frozen before but that night I had and it had cost me my mother.

"Did she beg me to stop?" His brows pull down and I know he is fighting with himself not to cry. Removing one hand from his jeans he rubs his nose and sniffles. "Don't answer that."

I honor his request and remain silent. "The spreadsheets I asked you for from the hotels, did you get them?"

He blinks before running his hand over his face like he's stepping out of a dream. "Yes," his voice is shaky and unsure but his eyes are drying up.

"Good. Can you check in with them over the next few weeks?"

"Liam..." His voice holds too much pleading.

"If you can't, just tell me, I can find someone else."

"No of course I can do it for you." He shrugs before stuffing his hands back in his pocket.

"Good. Get me the reports today." He nods and I turn away from him, the shadow of my mother hunches over me causing a shiver to race down my spine.

I am cruel.

CHAPTER TWENTY-TWO

SVETLANA

MY HEAD WON'T STOP pounding. The pain seems to be radiating down my legs. I've barely slept and refused to sleep in the bed. Last night Liam had been angry when I wouldn't move from the corner of the room but he eventually left me alone.

Standing up now I kick out my legs trying to get some life back into them. "Are you ready for breakfast?"

My heart leaps at his voice and my stomach twists when I set eyes on him. A black t-shirt is stretched across broad shoulders. The black the same color as his eyes that assess me now.

His lips tighten and I sigh before he can start a threat that lingers on his lips. His mouth relaxes slightly as I walk past him, the smell of aftershave wafts from him and I try not to inhale like some hungry animal.

He's made an omelette. This was starting to look like his signature dish. A napkin has a knife and fork resting on top of it. As I sit down on the stool, I pick them up. The smell of aftershave encircles me as he moves past me. His wide back fills my vision as he pours out two cups of tea. The spoon rattles against the mugs.

"I have someone I want you to meet today."

The fork halts at my lips as he turns around to me. His face wasn't giving anything away. I don't eat until he's seated, and he pushes a mug towards me.

I chew slowly but now the fluffy omelette feels like lead on my tongue.

"It's a good thing," I glance up at Liam; his voice sounds so exasperated, he isn't looking at me as he starts to eat.

"Who is it then?"

His smile is quick and catches me off guard. I can feel the burn on my cheeks at the surge of emotions that one action elects in me.

"You'll have to wait and see."

I focus on my food and he sighs heavily but I don't look up at him.

I'm still so angry with myself. Last night I had the perfect opportunity to leave. I had money, I was dressed, and no one was watching me. I had made it to the end of the tunnel and paused. My heart had been beating so fast that it drove tears to my eyes, my palms had grown slick with sweat. I didn't want to go. The realization had filled me with self-disgust. I was falling for him and that made me so pathetic. I had turned around and came back to my prison. I had no one to blame but myself now.

I push my plate away, my appetite gone. Taking the cup I cradle it in my hands. I feel cold; I know the tiredness isn't helping and Liam's gaze on me is making each second sitting next to him almost unbearable.

"Why don't you go and get dressed."

The suggestion has me finally looking at him. I hate how my body is reacting to him. I push away from the counter and leave the barely touched omelette behind me.

I'm staring into the wardrobe of clothes that still all have labels on them. Irritation has me slamming the wardrobe door. I march back to the bedroom door and Liam is where I left him, finishing his tea like there isn't a prisoner in his home.

"I'm not sure what to wear. Am I going home to my uncle? Or am I being handed over to someone else? Should I be sexy?"

It's my last question that has him looking at me, the look reminds of an intelligent animal after its prey.

"Wear something comfortable."

"So a plane journey?" I hate how my voice cracks. I was a fool for not running last night. What was I thinking that I would stay here and live happily ever after with my captive? It just showed how much I knew about love.

"You're not leaving my home." The depth his words carry have something deep inside me stirring again. *Home.*

My throat burns and I don't want him to see the effect his words are having on me so I turn away and run back to the wardrobe. I'm getting dressed without thinking. Selecting the underwear has heat splashing across my face but I quickly put on the fresh black set before picking a simple pair of black jeans and a long red shirt that's cool on my skin. When I place my foot inside the boots Liam steps into the room. The timing is unsettling, and I wonder had he watched me get dressed. Once again his face portrays nothing.

"Are you ready?"

Running my fingers through my hair distracts me for a moment, but the knots that tie themselves in my stomach make me give up.

"I would like to know what I am walking into."

"You will just have to trust me," His lip tugs up slightly. The hidden smile changes the inky black from his eyes and fills it with a chocolate brown. The transformation chips away at my wavering uncertainty. I do trust him. But I don't tell him that.

"Lead the way."

Liam's back muscles rise and fall as he walks, it reminds me of a cheetah from a wildlife documentary. His suits keep him so structured but with the t-shirt it really allows me to see all the muscles and curves of his body. It's distracting me so much that I pause only when I'm standing in a very grand hallway. The wooden floor under my feet is covered in a red rug that runs the length of the never ending space.

A shadow looms over me. Liam's cornered me close to the wall his back a black sheet that hides me.

"I think it's time we had a chat." The voice belongs to an older man and I'm tempted to peek out from behind Liam's back but his tense structure keeps me still.

"We will, just not right now." Liam sounds formal, and it really makes me want to see who he's speaking to.

"You're busy?" The curiosity in the other man's voice is clear. The black wall moves and I'm looking into the face of an older man. He's dressed in a suit and the resemblance to Liam is uncanny.

"Well hello." His surprise raises both his eyebrows.

I glance at Liam but he doesn't meet my eye. His tense jaw and stiff frame has me looking between him and the older man he looks like.

"We better go or we'll be late." Liam's hand touches the small of my back ushering me forward. I glance back over my shoulder to find the man watching us. Liam shifts blocking me off from looking back and moves me to a door on our left.

Inside an old man in a tweed brown suit looks up through a pair of heavy-rimmed glasses.

"Mr. O'Reagan." He moves quickly from behind a large writing desk and reaches out his hand to Liam, who takes it. I don't know what I was expecting, but this wasn't it.

A stack of books on the writing desk are opened and look used. I allow my eyes to wander around the stunning library.

"You must be Svetlana." It's the elderly man who speaks. I take a step towards him as Liam watches us now. I still have no clue what I am doing here.

"Yes," I say and flicker a quick look at Liam. His chocolate brown eyes are drinking up my reaction to a situation I don't understand.

"I will be tutoring you in psychology. Mr. O'Reagan has informed me you studied it back in the Czech."

Soft green warm eyes smile at me but I'm speechless as I glance from Liam to my new tutor. He did this for me.

"Yes," I finally answer.

"Shall we." I walk to the chairs at the desk and sit down. "You can call me Sam." Sam smiles again. His facial hair has turned gray and hides most of his face but his eyes smile with him.

I nod at Sam before turning to Liam who's now sitting on an emerald green couch. His stare consumes me and the urge I have to get up and go to him has me gripping the arm of the chair. A smile that I can't contain spreads quickly across my face and he smiles back, my stomach does somersaults and a soft laugh bubbles from my lips widening his smile. He looks breathtaking.

"Thank you," I mouth as emotions keep my voice hidden. A soft nod of his head lets me know he heard me.

"Shall we start?" I turn to Sam who has sat patiently waiting for me.

"Yes I'm ready." I'm the perfect student. I soak up every bit of information that Sam shares with me. We read over textbooks and he breaks down anything I don't understand. The session ends too soon, and it feels like I'm waking up when I glance to the emerald couch. Surprise flitters through me. Liam is still there, still watching me.

"I will see you in two days." Sam starts to tidy up and I nod eagerly. This wasn't a once off.

A brown leather worn bag is tucked under Sam's arms as he leaves a neat stack of textbooks on the writing desk.

"And after that?" I ask.

"Three days each week. That is the agreement with Mr. O'Reagan."

I glance at Liam again before returning to Sam. "Thank you."

"Thank you. You are a fantastic student." His praise has me basking in his words.

Liam walks with him out of the room and I'm left in a space filled with knowledge. I know the moment Liam steps back into the room. I wonder is that normal to just feel someone's presence?

"I'm jealous of you." I skim my fingers along the spines of the books as I speak. "Growing up I was obsessed with fairy tales and stories about happily ever afters." I take a peek at Liam. He's absorbing my words like they hold secrets about me. "My father..." I have to look away as a familiar friend squeezes my heart at the thoughts of the man who loved me like nothing else. "He told me he would build me one. He never got to." His life taken before it should have been.

I refuse to cry and turn this moment into something sad. "Can I stay here a bit longer?" I don't look to Liam as I ask, I'm afraid of the disappointment I will feel when he tells me no.

"Stay as long as you want." Closing my eyes briefly at his soft words is the only way to keep my emotions closed off.

"Thank you," I whisper leaning closer to the books.

"You're welcome." His breath brushes the back of my neck and I stiffen before allowing myself to lean into him. Strong arms wrap around my waist and I drop my hands to cover his, the touch is intimate and penetrates through me.

"Why are you doing this?"

He reaches up and brushes my hair back from my neck. I shiver as his breath caresses my skin. "You are." His answer confuses me and I turn in his arms fully facing him.

His hands find their way into my hair as he brushes both sides back and continues to hold my face. "I can't seem to find myself with you."

I'm feeling even more confused, and he looks away now unable to hold my stare. "That doesn't sound like a good thing."

His focus is back on me, black orbs consuming me and I shiver in his hands. "It is. I think I like being lost." He dips his head, and the air leaves my lungs. "Will you kiss me?"

I answer him by pressing my lips against his.

His large hands hold my face. The heat and pressure has me sinking into the kiss. A storm starts circling inside me, I can feel the tingle in my toes and it races up my body lifting emotions I didn't understand, while sending my head into a spin. Liam takes my lower lip between his and kisses me leaving me breathless. Books press into my back; I hadn't noticed we'd moved. My body is flush with Liam's and I want his fingers inside me again. I moan as he sucks softly on my bottom lip. A commotion behind us has Liam breaking the kiss, but he doesn't step away from me.

"You owe me a ton, told you he was into women." I recognize the voice. When I peek out from behind Liam, I see three men standing in the doorway. Two resemble each other with blond hair and blue eyes.

"And she doesn't even speak English," Darragh winks at me and my face burns.

"How do you know that? You cheated." The other blonde argues back.

"What do you want?" Liam's voice stops their chatter.

"We need a word." The taller and more serious one glances at me but focuses on Liam now.

"About?"

Once again the taller brother looks at me and I step out from behind Liam. Now they all stare at me and I want to step back behind Liam.

"My wedding." There is a somber tone to the blonde boy's voice and sorrow fills all their eyes. I glance up at Liam but he nods like he doesn't see their pain.

"I'll be back shortly." Liam holds out his arm formally for me to walk and I do as the three men watch me.

"Nice seeing you again." Darragh fires another wink at me.

"Nice seeing you too Darragh."

His mouth hangs a little and I don't smile until I'm out of the room and can hear the other man laugh.

"She can talk you moron."

When Liam steps into line beside me I'm waiting for him to say something about me speaking out.

"They are my brothers."

"They seem nice." I take a look up at him and our eyes clash.

"They can be." We've stopped walking, his stare holding me into place.

"The older man from earlier?"

"My father."

I nod. That made sense. "You have a nice family."

Something passes Liam's eyes, and he starts walking again hiding whatever he doesn't want me to see.

When we reach the basement Liam goes straight into the room and pulls off his t-shirt. I watch him until my face burns and turn away. I notice how he doesn't lock the area down anymore. Or how he let his family see me, or how he brought me into his home.

I'm sitting at the high stool my mind still reeling. He had got me a tutor. My throat burns again but I clear it as Liam returns in a suit looking perfect. The grey suit is tailored to his tall and broad frame.

"I have some business. But I'll be back later." He isn't looking at me as he speaks. So my nod isn't seen.

"Okay."

He picks up keys, his wallet and a phone before looking at me. I can't tell you what I see but he's conflicted about something.

"It won't always be like this."

I pretend that I don't understand his words. "What me hanging out in a bachelor pad, getting private tutors and a personal shopper." I point at my clothes.

Liam walks to me, each step has my heart hammering. "You won't be locked away. You will be my equal."

This time when my throat burns I can't stop the tears that rise. "Please don't promise me something that you can't do." Hope is always a good thing, too much is dangerous. Right now too much of it was coming alive and blossoming inside me.

His smile is short lived. "I'll check on you later." A soft kiss on my lips has me parting my legs so Liam can step closer. My fingers curl around his large shoulders and I pull him in as I deepen the kiss with my tongue.

The kiss ends too quickly.

"Don't leave." His departing words sound more like a plea than the warning they once carried. The sad part is I know I won't leave. I had a chance, and I didn't take it.

CHAPTER TWENTY-THREE

LIAM

OPENING THE SLOT OF the door I look in, a pair of green eyes stare back at me.

Once again she doesn't speak but stares at me. The door behind me opens but I don't turn around as Darragh and Finn enter.

"Are you both sure about this?" They had insisted on being here for the interrogation.

"Yes." It's Darragh who answers so I open the door. The girl doesn't struggle or plead as I put her in the chair. She examines Darragh and Finn. Finn's uneasy, he shifts from foot to foot and she sees his weakness. As I tighten the straps, the girl looks at me.

"You want to start with your name?"

She smiles through cracked lips and turns away from me. I already know her name but hearing her confirm it would be start.

"You know I'm going to hurt you," I tell her tightening her hands.

"I didn't think we would be hugging."

"So you've been interrogated before?"

She looks away quickly but not before I catch the fear in her eyes.

"No, you've never been interrogated before but you've been trained in it and from your accent I'd say you're from the north." I don't mention the RA. I keep the knowledge to myself.

Her eyes flicker to me for a split of a second.

"They didn't train you very well." I say standing up fully. "I can smell your fear."

Her heartbeat flickers in her neck but she's holding her body calmly.

"Did you kill my wife?" Finn starts, his voice holds his pain as he steps towards her. His question is silly and pointless but I let him proceed as I get my tools.

"What's her name?" Margret asks.

"Siobhan."

"Can't say I remember her." She is playing with him.

"It was her wedding day, and you animals gunned her down." Darragh's voice is rough and angry.

"I don't know what you're talking about."

"Please. I just want to put my wife to rest. Just tell me why?"

"Finn I know you're distressed. But if you want to be here, this is done my way," I tell him as I roll out my black tool bag so it's open on the wooden slab allowing me to see all its content. I remove a long silver knife, one polished and that allows me to see my reflection in it. A moment's hesitation passes me as I think of Svetlana, but this girl isn't innocent. She had taken part in trying to kill my brother and now she was on our property after setting off a bomb. I turn to her and its Finn's eyes that widen the most.

"I can be very creative but I'm sure you are very well versed in all torture methods."

Her hands are relaxed but she can't hide the fear in her eyes.

I kneel down before her and allow her to see the knife. "Have you heard of the expression 'death by a thousand cuts?'"

She doesn't answer.

"It's known as 'slow slicing' or 'Ling chi'. It was used as a form of execution in China." I press the cold knife to her hand and she holds still.

"What were you doing on our property?"

She doesn't answer. I don't expect her to.

"In China the condemned was tied to a post and bits of skin and limbs were gradually removed. Shall I start?"

No response.

I glance at Darragh and Finn now letting them know they can leave but both of them hold firm. I'm not sure how long Finn is going to last. He doesn't look well at all. I nod before pushing up the sleeve of her top. The first slice has her hissing. I don't press too deep, just enough to break the skin and allow the red liquid to flow.

"What were you doing on our property?"

I don't wait for a response but cut her again. Finn folds his arms and shuffles. After six slices her arm is coated in blood.

"What were you doing on our property?"

She looks at me now, the first sign that she might be bending.

"Fuck you." Warm liquid splashes across my face. Taking out a napkin I wipe her spit away.

As I stand I put away my napkin, and she's bracing herself for my temper. But I keep it in check. Pushing up her other sleeve I make two deep cuts and she howls in pain.

"Jesus Liam." I don't look at Finn as I speak to him.

"You can leave."

He doesn't.

"What were you doing on our property?"

Her chest rises and falls rapidly as I clean the knife on the piece of cloth that I picked up off the slab where my other tools sit.

"It was only a warning." Blood drips from the chair and onto the floor, sweat gleams on her face as she tries to keep her panic at bay.

I return with my clean knife and pull up her trousers legs.

"A warning about what?"

She's shaking her head, her eyes shooting around the room. "I didn't kill his wife." Her shouts tell me we are breaking down barriers.

"I never said you did." I slice quickly across her leg and her screams fill the room again.

"Please. Please tell him to stop. He's killing me." She's screaming at Finn and he steps forward his face pale.

"Stop! This isn't right."

I clean my knife again. "Was it right that they killed your wife on her wedding day?"

"She didn't. You heard her, now let her go."

"She paid the guards to turn a blind eye while five gunmen entered your wedding and killed your wife and tried to kill your brother."

Finn looks at her now.

She's shaking her head. "I didn't. I swear."

"Finn." Darragh steps up to him. "Go upstairs."

"Are you telling me you think this is okay?" Finn faces off with Darragh and I can see the spark of hope in the girl's eyes but when her eyes settle on me it disappears quickly.

"Are you going to tell me what the warning was for or am I going to have to get started." I leave her to ponder on that and get out my nine inch nail. She squirms back in the chair.

"Oh no." It's Finn protesting again.

"Take him upstairs," I tell Darragh.

"This is one of my favorites," I say as I retrieve a hammer. "What was the warning for?" I ask again as Darragh pushes Finn from the room. The girl strains to see them leave.

"Now it's just me and you."

"I didn't kill that girl."

"Wrong answer." I hold the nail over her hand and she starts screaming.

"I want to speak to Connor."

CHAPTER TWENTY –FOUR

LIAM

Wild green eyes stare up at me. I push the tip of the nail into her palm.

"Get Connor!" Her fear is growing and I devour it.

"I don't take orders from the likes of you." Color drains from her face as I raise the hammer.

"I'll tell you everything." Fear chokes her words.

"Liam." I don't remove my focus from Margret.

"What is it Shane, can't you see I'm busy." Now I look at my brother.

"You." Something almost feral enters Margret's voice. Craning her neck back, she's trying to see Shane behind her.

"You. You killed Bernard." She's struggling and pulling. Her words don't put Shane off as he steps forward.

"You. You killed Siobhan and tried to kill me." Shane tells her with as much hate in his words as she seems to carry for him. I still hold the nail, but step back to let Shane closer to her.

Spit flies from her mouth but it doesn't reach its target, Shane side steps it.

"They are coming for you." Angry words turn her face red as she threatens Shane, my brother, my family. My fingers close tighter around the nail. The movement is so minimal, but it grabs her attention. Her eyes flicker to my hand before returning to Shane.

"She's demanding to speak to Connor." I watch Shane's back stiffen. "But maybe you are enough of a substitute." Shane faces me and I hate the guilt I see there, I wanted to be wrong but the truth was etched into his face.

"What did you bring upon our family?"

"Death," Margret's voice fills the basement and Shane flinches before he reacts. His hand connects with her face, blood splashes on the floor from the impact. Both of them seem to be breathing heavily and when Margret looks up at Shane, a promise shines in her eyes.

"Will I get Connor?" I ask to Shane's back again. His shoulders rise and fall and when he doesn't answer me, I take my phone out. It rings three times before Connor picks up. "I have Margret Murphy, a member of the Irish Republican Army strapped to a chair in our basement. If you're not here in twenty minutes, I'm slicing her throat." I hang up, not giving him a moment to answer.

Shane glances at me over his shoulder.

"You've been lying to me," I say.

"Withholding the truth." His voice is low.

"There's a difference?" I ask, but shake my head in disgust.

"That girl died because of you." Margret taunts Shane and once again I observe.

Shane grips the chair, his knuckles turning white as he leans into Margret's face. "That girl died because one of your people took her life." He pushes away and takes a quick look at me before walking towards the door, but he doesn't leave.

"You want to tell me who killed Siobhan?" I know she won't answer, but we have time to kill.

"I hear you have the niece of the Czech's leader here." Her words catch me by surprise.

I laugh. "Now, now Margret. Is that a threat?" twirling the nail between my fingers catches her attention.

I walk away from her and wash my unused nails and hands. Checking my phone after I see only ten minutes have passed since I rang Connor. "Only ten minutes left Margret," I tell her while placing the phone in my pocket. She looks away from me. Shane moves around the room but avoids all eye contact with me.

"You can leave," I say to Shane as I get a knife out of my bag.

"That would be great." Margret's response is quick.

I glance at her and she showcases a grin.

"I'll wait." Shane glances at the door as it opens and Connor steps in. His eyes immediately flicker around the room before landing on Margret.

"You're a fucking traitor." It wasn't the reception I was expecting Connor to have, since she asked for him.

"Be quiet." His words are quick as he steps into the room.

"No. If I'm going down, so are you." She's angry, angry on such a personal level that I wonder what exactly he is to her.

"What are you doing here?" He faces her, but his eyes shift to me and then Shane.

"Just hanging out with your real family. You know the ones that mean more to you." Hurt laces her words.

The door opens again and Darragh steps in. Closing the door behind him, he doesn't ask questions but lights up a fag and leans against one of the pillars.

"Just let her go." Connor finally speaks to me.

I take a step towards him. "Just like that?" I hold the knife higher.

"You've tortured her and she clearly isn't speaking." Blood still oozes from all her cuts.

"I've only just started Connor. She's going nowhere and neither are you."

"I killed one of their people." I'm surprised when Shane speaks up. His voice is low as he steps closer to me. "They retaliated."

"You didn't think we should have known that the RA had put a target on our backs?" Darragh crushes the cigarette under his boot, his temper flaring.

"I was under the impression that it was sorted." Shane speaks to Connor now, who stands straighter.

"It was." Connor bites back.

Margret spits from the corner of her mouth, blood and saliva splash the floor. "We aren't stupid."

"Who killed Siobhan?" Darragh lights up another cigarette as he moves around the room.

"Fuck you." Margret's getting braver now that Connor is here. Her hostility to him is hurt, but she still trusts him.

"Maybe Connor would like to share that knowledge with us," I say.

Everyone is staring at Connor as his shoulders hunch forward, the strain on his body rolls down into his clenched fists.

"Maybe you could tell us who killed our mother?" he fires back at me.

I smile, it's slight but make sure he sees it clearly. "You already know," I say. Darragh's shifting from foot to foot, and the urge to look at him so he will stop moving is almost overwhelming. But I hold Connor's angry eye.

"I want to hear you say it." Connor takes a step towards me and I place my free hand in my trousers pocket and relax my posture.

"What are you doing?" Shane steps towards Connor but he stops when I flicker a warning glance at him. His betrayal hurt more than any of the others.

"I'm doing what I asked you to do." Connor answers Shane.

"Not like this." Shane doesn't heed my warning but steps in front of Connor stopping him.

"Do you know who fucking shot me?"

"Yes." Connor answers and Margret starts squirming in the chair.

"Was it her?" I point at Margret.

"No."

"Don't you fucking dare? It was me. I did it." Margret's fear is expanding and turning into panic.

"Shut up!" Connor's own composure is slipping.

Darragh leans against the wall and I take the moment to look at him. He's pale, too pale.

"What do you think would be a fair punishment Margret?" I ask her and Shane turns to look at me as Connor takes a step towards Margret.

She's looking at Connor like he might save her.

"I asked you a question." I hold the knife a little higher.

"I don't know." She finally answers. The door opening announces Finn's arrival. He looks at each of us before slipping into the room.

"Did she reveal anything?" His innocence often intrigues me. How did he grow up in the same house as us and remain so naïve to things?

"Yes, a lot actually. We know that Shane killed a RA member, so in return they attacked," I answer frankly.

"Siobhan was a revenge kill." He staggers backwards like someone pushed him.

"Finn, I didn't know this was going to happen," Shane tries to defend his actions.

"You could have warned us." Finn stares at the floor before glancing at all of us. "He could have warned us." I nod in agreement.

Surprise flitters through me as Finn launches himself at Shane. He was no match for Shane. Finn easily takes him to the ground and unleashes his hurt and pain onto Shane who covers his face but doesn't retaliate. We all stand and watch but it's Connor who finally breaks them apart. Darragh helps to hold Finn back.

"You killed Siobhan." Finn's angry words are said as he pushes Connor and Darragh away from him, they finally release him.

Shane gets off the ground, wiping blood from his face. "I'm so sorry. I didn't know this would happen. It was sorted." Once again, he glances at Connor.

"Connor, you seem to be the man with all the answers." Everyone looks at me. "You know who killed Siobhan; it's someone close to Margret." I glance at Margret, who struggles in her chair.

"You know who killed Siobhan?" Finn's hurt pours into his eyes as he stares at Connor. They were close and the hurt of the betrayal is evident on his face. He doesn't give Connor a moment to answer.

"What about you, do you know?" He questions Shane who's still nursing a bloody nose.

"No, of course not." Shane sounds tortured now and I don't want the attention taken off Connor.

"Finn, Shane didn't know. But Connor does," I say it frankly, capturing everyone's attention again.

"You of all people. I fucking hate you." Tears burn Finn's eyes but he doesn't attack Connor, it's like everything in him has given up. Like the weight of betrayal is too heavy on his limbs.

"So tell us Connor, who killed Siobhan," I say.

"You're such a shitty brother." His reaction doesn't surprise me. He never could watch his mouth.

"Just tell us." Darragh's anger swipes out across the room. Color has re-entered his face, but I want him subdued and silent. He's too volatile.

"Tell me who killed my mother and I'll tell you who killed Siobhan," Connor says. Margret starts pulling at her restraints like she might be able to break free and shut Connor up.

"A group of unknown men killed our mother, Connor. We all know this," I say.

"Bullshit."

"What do you expect me to say?" I move towards Margret slowly.

"You did it."

I laugh at Connor's accusation.

"Stop it Connor." Shane sounds deflated but irritation still growls in his voice.

"No, I won't stop until I know the truth."

"The truth?" I step closer to Margret.

"You are the one who can't seem to tell the truth. You claim you are family, yet you know the person who killed Siobhan and tried to kill Shane, but you protect them."

I move swiftly, it's not fast, but it's efficient until my knife rests on Margret's neck. "Does she mean more to you, than your own brothers?"

"You're making a huge mistake. If you kill her, they will come back here."

I nod in agreement. "The difference this time is that we will be ready." I flicker a glance at Shane.

"We can be prepared."

"Prepared for a war, Liam?" Connor questions.

"Yes." I answer before exhaling heavily. "This is the final time I'm going to ask both of you." I glance at Margret and Connor. "Who killed Siobhan?"

"Don't you dare!" Margret's screeches fill the room. The snap of her restraints is loud as she tries to free herself.

"I already told you, I'll tell you when you tell me who killed our mother."

"It was me. I did it." Margret's hysterical answer has the room growing still. I nod at Margret and a silence pours into the room as I run the knife across her throat. It's quick and does the job as blood pours down her chest. She's choking, gasping.

I step away as Connor grabs the wound and tries to stop the bleeding. "Jesus Christ."

He won't save her. Turning my back on him, I wash the knife down.

"She didn't do it!" His roar is close now.

Dropping the knife in the sink, I face him. "Of course she didn't." Drying my hands on a cloth, I glance at Margret. Her head has fallen back, blood still oozes from the wound but she's dead.

"What did you kill her for?" His roar grows with each step and I don't look away, but can feel the shift in the room as my brothers step closer to me and Connor.

"Because I could." I sidestep his angry blow. Connor is a fighter, but when he is angry, he doesn't think correctly, making him a sloppy fighter.

"I could take your life right now and no one would stop me." I was hoping everyone was angry enough at him not to contradict me and I'm right as he glances at each brother.

Connor deflates and faces me again. "I tried to protect this family." He points at Margret. "But you just put them all in danger."

Dropping the towel on the table, I roll down my shirt sleeves and button them. The sound of Darragh lighting a cigarette is the only sound in the room.

"You placed every one of us in danger. We all know this. So you can twist your words, but they are still your words."

"Who killed Siobhan?" Finn is starting to sound like a broken record. But I allowed it, to see if it would poke at a different part of Connor.

"It doesn't matter anymore."

"What? Siobhan doesn't matter?"

Connor rubs his face. "That's not what I'm saying. This..." He's pointing at Margret again. "This is going to cost us, one death won't be enough this time."

Connor reaches for the binds on Margret's wrists.

"What are you doing?" I ask him.

He doesn't stop.

"She's my kill." I state.

He's in my face. "Do you know you sound like an animal? She's not a kill. She's a person who didn't do this."

"A person you chose not to save, she obviously meant very little to you." I retort.

"Fuck you Liam."

"Get away from him." Shane clamps a hand on Connor's shoulder. "He's right. You did nothing to save her."

"You did nothing to save Siobhan." Finn's emotions start to run his mouth again.

"She wasn't the target. Una was," Shane's voice rises.

"Then why isn't she dead?"

"Finn." Darragh places a hand on Finn's shoulder.

He shrugs it off. "Why did my innocent wife have to die?"

"Una is innocent too." Shane's retaliation is taking this conversation down an emotional road.

"This isn't about who is more innocent. Right now we need to prepare for a war that is coming." Connor steps out of my way as I untie Margret.

"It was her brother Matt who carried out the shootings." I untie her legs before standing and facing Connor.

"You could have saved us a lot of trouble if you just told us that earlier, Connor."

"Fuck you!" Connor storms away.

Finn blocks him from leaving the room. "Are you going to warn him? The man who killed Siobhan? She really liked you."

"I'm sorry, brother."

"I'm not your brother." I know that will hurt Connor. He's always been an outsider, but not to Finn.

"Let him warn his friends. It will do no good." I tip Margret forward until her body hits the floor with a loud thud. I watch Connor's reaction, his eyes fire up as he stares at me.

"I'm not warning anyone. I'm going to try to stop this from spreading. You're like a disease, Liam."

"You can't stop this Connor," I called after him.

The slam of the door is loud in the room and the mood is subdued. I stare at Margret's body that lies at my feet. I wasn't sure what to do next but I knew this thing with Connor wasn't over. He knew more about our mother's death then he was willing to share, and I had a feeling he wasn't going to let it go.

CHAPTER TWENTY-FIVE

SVETLANA

THE AIR ON MY cheek is what stirs me awake. I don't open my eyes. Holding my breath, I wait but whoever is there doesn't speak. My lungs burn, my muscles tighten painfully, and I try to relax. Once I do, I can smell shoe polish and I open my eyes. Dark black ones focus on my face, moving from my lips and now to my eyes.

"Is everything okay?" I ask Liam. I feel vulnerable under his stare. He's changed since I last saw him; the suit has been swapped for jeans and a black snug t-shirt.

"It is now." His full lips capture my attention. My heart does a small jump as he leans in closer.

"As opposed to it wasn't before?" I know he won't answer me. I want to know where he went, what he was doing. I want to know Liam.

"You were dreaming." Liam sits back and the surge of disappointment rises within me. But I try to focus on his words and sit up against the headboard.

"Yeah I was dreaming about my parents." When I dream of them it's in color, it's a memory.

"Do you want to talk about it?" Liam searches my face.

"It was just a memory." I shake my head as if I might knock the smiling faces away.

"I have memories."

I can't stop the smile that spreads across my face. "You want to share?"

"It will cost you." Liam's serious.

My smile slips. "What will it cost me?"

"A kiss." His eyes flicker to my lips, but he remains serious as he waits for my answer. The idea of kissing him has my blood bubbling with excitement.

"It seems like a fair trade," I answer.

His lip tugs up slightly. "I remember having a friend. He was from the local estate. They were a poor family, but I liked them."

His formal way of speaking would make anyone question the truth of the story. But I was starting to understand Liam and could tell that this meant a lot to him, it is in how rigid he holds himself as he speaks.

"I went to his house one night. I didn't knock on the back door, instead I looked through the window and just watched. His family was sitting down eating a meal. They laughed and smiled a lot." There is a sadness to his words that make me want to reach for him, but I don't.

"They had nothing but each other. Their happiness lit up the room." He looks at me now. "That's how I feel sometimes with my own family. Like I'm watching it through a window, like I'm not here."

My chest tightens. "That sounds lonely," I whisper.

"No. It was just an observation. I just realized at a young age that I was different."

Something in me twists for him. It was like he can't connect with people, like he can't connect on an emotional level.

"Now you owe me a kiss." My heart does a full three sixty as he moves closer. Licking my lips I don't move as Liam moves close enough until our chests nearly touch. My hands rest on his solid shoulders.

"With you, I don't feel like I'm looking through a window. I'm not watching." Air lodges itself in my throat as his lips brush mine, extracting the air in a quick whoosh. "I'm participating," he whispers against my lips. His hands hold my face and I wonder if he knows the effect he has on me.

Pushing my lips against his, I take the kiss. Warm hands slide away from my face and down my arms, leaving a trail of raised hairs. My fingers tighten on his wide shoulders and I'm pulling him back down onto the bed with me. The duvet separates us briefly until Liam lifts it away. I break the kiss, my body protesting immediately. Liam doesn't move but holds my stare as his breath brushes across my face. I lift my hands into the air, not looking away from Liam. It takes a beat before Liam touches the hem of my top, his fingers brush my stomach, my muscles tighten at the contact. Slowly the material is raised until I can no longer see Liam. The moment it passes my head and lands on the floor, I close the distance and kiss him. I'm burning, my skin feels like it's actually caught fire as his hands roam down my sides but not moving past the band of my trousers. My chest swells and the pain that's ignited inside me, I need it to stop. A moan escapes my lips as Liam kisses my neck. My fingers tug on the bottom of his t-shirt and he pauses his assault on my neck to allow me to remove it. My heart pounds and seems to jump around my chest as I gaze at his hard, muscular chest. His shoulders appear even wider now that they are bare, and my moment of studying him is gone as he leans in close, our lips a fraction away. His focus has moved to the strap of my bra that he unclips with ease. The material drops from my chest and Liam takes it the rest of the way down. His eyes soak up my bare breasts just like I had soaked him up.

Another moan is ripped from my lips as he brushes his thumb across my hard nipple. The feeling is painful but also pleasurable. I want him to feel what I'm feeling, moving closer I dip my head before I change my mind and flick my tongue out brushing his nipple, his intake of breath has me pausing, wondering if I have done the wrong thing.

"Don't stop." His husky voice has me recapturing his nipple in my mouth as he continues to knead my breasts. Taking his nipple between my teeth, I bite slightly and his moan has me biting harder. Liam's hands leave my breasts as he directs my face back up to his, the kiss is rough as I sink back into the bed. My fingers pull at the band of his trousers and when he doesn't stop me, I push them down off his hips. I don't push down his boxers, instead my hand reaches in and when he exhales loudly I tighten my hold on him. I'm unsure of what I'm doing and he feels so large that it scares me a little. My hesitation causes Liam to break the kiss, it's brief before he consumes my nipple in his mouth, the warmth of his tongue and the sharpness of his teeth has me closing my eyes and throwing my head back. The pool of wetness between my legs seems to grow to the point of wetting my trousers.

Trousers that I want off, I start to shift under Liam and it's like he knows. Leaning back, I release his manhood as he removes my trousers and panties in one sweep.. Black orbs trace along my skin, I have a moment of being aware of myself but when Liam parts my legs, with a gentleness that has my nerves skittering, I can only focus on the crown of his head. The first touch is his lips to my thigh and already I feel like I'm going to come undone, each kiss gets closer to my wetness and I jerk under him. His hand rises and touches my chest, at first I think it's to keep me still but when he squeezes a nipple, the same time his mouth descends on the part of me that aches the most, I exhale a moan loudly as my eyes open wide. My fingers sink into his hair as his tongue dips inside me.

Oh my God.

Liam's fingers tighten around my nipple painfully and I want to tell him to stop as I grip the sheets on either side of me.

"Harder," I scream instead and he obeys. His tongue delves deeper inside me before coming up and sucking my clitoris, the action grows in speed and I can feel my release building inside me until I shatter with Liam between my legs. His name is called out loudly as I close my eyes. My body seems to jerk in the aftermath of my release.

Liam releases my aching nipples but continues to gently lick between my legs, each lick still sending electrical short shocks up through my body. When he finally raises his head, the aftershock subsides. Liam shifts between my legs, but I keep my eyes closed, trying to breathe evenly. The soft click of the door has me quickly sitting up and glancing around an empty room. My exposed skin feels chilled now that he's not here. I finish getting dressed when he arrives back into the room. He hasn't put a shirt on and I can see the bulge that still sits in his trousers. My cheeks heat as I take a step towards him. I'm more aware of myself now then I've ever been. He doesn't move until I reach him.

"You taste so sweet." His words have my cheeks burning with excitement and embarrassment. The words are said so seriously from Liam's red, swollen lips.

"I want to taste you," I say as my heart beats fast.

"Liam." A banging on the bedroom door has me stepping away from Liam.

"Liam, I need to talk to you now." It's one of his brothers, I think Darragh. Liam doesn't hesitate but moves past me and picks up his shirt.

"Liam..." More bangs pound the door.

Liam doesn't answer his brother but stops in front of me. "Just give me a moment." I nod as he plants a soft kiss on my lips.

I wait for a few seconds after he leaves before going to the door and pressing my ear against it.

"I can't do this to them Liam." It's definitely Darragh and he sounds distraught. His voice is raised and it's tinged with hysteria. I don't really need to have my ear to the door to hear him, but it's Liam's voice that keeps me in position.

He speaks lower and with that same calmness he always possesses. "Do what Darragh?"

"You know what. I'm going to tell them what I did." Pain radiates through Darragh's words.

"Don't be so stupid. You think that will make this go away."

"If I give myself up, they might tell us who killed Siobhan." Darragh's voice rises again.

"Are you that daft?" A different emotion has entered Liam's voice.

"Liam, that information could stop all this."

A bang against the bedroom door has me jumping back and covering my mouth.

"Nothing is going to stop this. It's already in motion. Now this conversation ends." Liam's voice is clearer. "Go into the lobby. I'll be with you in a minute."

I move back as quietly as I can away from the door and sit down on the bed just as the door opens. I know I look as guilty as sin.

"Everything okay?" I sound so stupid, but Liam doesn't falter in his steps as he comes and sits beside me.

"You know it's rude to listen to someone's conversation." My heart beats wildly in my chest and I slowly raise my head to meet his dark eyes. I have no clue how angry he is. I don't deny it.

"He was very loud."

"Is that why you had your ear to the door?" I'm sure I can hear a slight amount of humor in his question.

I shrug. "Is everything okay?" I ask again.

Some of the darkness has left his eyes. "It will be, but I need to take care of some things."

I want to moan and whine. I was going to be locked up again and the thoughts of being alone were really starting to get to me.

I nod and try to hide my disappointment. Focusing on the floor makes it easier than looking into his face.

"It won't always be like this." Words he had told me before are spoken again and I do believe him. I just want to know when.

His warm fingers take my face in his hands and he makes me look at him.

"You have my word Svetlana. I'm really trying."

I nod again. "I know."

CHAPTER TWENTY-SIX

LIAM

"I HOPE YOU'RE CALMER," I say to Darragh the moment I enter the lobby, but I can see he isn't. His foot drums along the floor as he inhales his fag, one puff after another.

"It's a mess." He shakes his head as he blows smoke out into the air. "Connor is going to tell them you killed Margret." When I don't respond, Darragh throws the fag on the floor and stamps on it. "What the fuck is wrong with you? Why aren't you more alarmed? It's the RA, Liam."

Darragh's raised voice has me stepping closer to him. "I've sorted it. So when you decide to calm down, you can help me with the body." I leave him and go back into the room where Margret still lies on the floor bleeding out.

"We need to clean her and wrap her," I tell Darragh without looking behind me to make sure he has followed me. His heavy footsteps stop as he reaches Margret's body. We lift her onto the large wooden butcher's block. I start by washing as much blood away as possible.

"I have someone tailing Connor, so if he does anything funny we'll know." I don't look up at Darragh as I feed him this information. "I'm going to give Margret over to the Czech explaining that the RA tried to kill Svetlana." Now I look up at Darragh.

"You're setting up the Czech against the RA?"

I nod as I grab some fresh sheets to wrap the body in.

"But what about Connor?" Darragh has stopped cleaning and lights up another fag.

"What about him?" I throw the sheet across the body.

"What if he tells the RA that you killed Margret?"

Using a large piece of cloth, I tie it firmly around Margret's neck to try to stop the bleeding.

"There is a very good chance he will, but I noticed that Margret had no love for Connor. So he messed up. I'm hoping he will either be wise enough not to say anything, or if he does, that they won't believe him." I tighten the sheets using string around Margret's legs, mid-section, and head.

"Are you going to help?" I ask Darragh and he puts out the fag and helps me lift the body.

"That's a lot of ifs and buts," Darragh says as he stands holding the top part of Margret's body.

"Just help me get her into the van."

I'm glad when we have the body packed and I send Darragh away. He is a problem, and one I didn't have time for right now.

Svetlana's uncle answers on the first ring. "I need to see you," I say the moment he answers the phone.

"About what?"

I don't like his question. "Not over the phone."

It sounds like he's chuckling, but I can't be sure.

"Fine. Will I come to you?"

"No. I'll go to you."

He hesitates before responding and rattling off the address I know he is already at. The moment I hang up I can only pray that this will work.

***

Two hours later I pull into a farmyard. Lights illuminate from several sheds that are shuttered with large doors. No one comes out to greet me, I assume that's part of their intimidation tactic. I sit in the idling van, lights shining on the steel doors, they slide open, a man wearing a white vest and a cigar hanging from his mouth waits until I pass. I notice the machine gun that's strapped to his back. Sheets of black plastic cut off a large portion of the shed. But the portion I drive into has a few men sitting around a table. None of them are Svetlana's uncle. The man who let me in knocks on the hood and I turn off the engine.

"I need to search you." His Czech accent is thick as I step out of the van. He searches me and once he's satisfied, he whistles loudly. Svetlana's uncle moves from behind one of the plastic hanging curtains, a large smile on his face.

"You can never be too careful." His black clothes are decorated with silver swirls and buttons. My eyes trail all the way down to his black pointy boots with silver tips.

"I have something for you," I say, returning to the van. I can feel them shift behind me, but I can't do anything about it. I don't think they would attack me, it would be a very stupid mistake.

Opening the back sliding door, I haul out Margret's body before dumping it at Svetlana's uncle's feet. A hush falls across his men as they stare at the body on the cement ground.

"What is this?" Svetlana's uncle doesn't sound so sure anymore.

"We were attacked in my home."

He shrugs. "What has that got to do with me?"

"Svetlana was attacked," I say, getting his full attention.

"This is who attacked her?"

I nod as he leans down and tries to remove the binds, I don't help him, but he nods to two of his men to open it as he rises. We stare at each other as they unwrap the body. One of the men laughs.

"It's a woman." He sneers.

Svetlana's uncle doesn't acknowledge his man, instead he focuses on me, his face held rigid.

"Who is she?"

"Have you heard of the Irish Republican Army?"

He nods. "Of course."

"She's a member and she tried to kill Svetlana."

The disbelief is immediate and I know I need to make sure I say the next piece right.

"Why would she do that?" He questions.

"I ask myself the exact same question. One of your men", I now look away from Svetlana's Uncle and towards his men who don't shy away from my stare. "tried to rape a woman who happened to be RA."

"You lie." Svetlana's uncle's voice raises and the wildness in his eyes makes him a very unpredictable man.

"Don't call me a liar." My words cause him to smile.

"How would you know this?"

I push my hands into my pockets and glance at his men. "The same way you know things about me."

His smile widens. "So you have someone tailing my men."

I nod, allowing his words to sink in amongst his men. The one who had let me in shifts nervously, the snake tattoo that climbs along his neck was the marker I had. I point at him, but not feeling completely comfortable with how easily he could take the machine gun from his back.

"He's the one," I say.

Svetlana's uncle stares at the man I point out.

"He's lying, Boss."

Svetlana's uncle raises two fingers and indicates for the man to come over. He does slowly, but the uncertainty is in each step he takes. He looks back at the other men, but none of them move.

"Don't lie. You know I hate lies. Just tell the truth and this will all go away." Svetlana's uncle grips his man by the scruff of the neck, pulling his head close to his own.

"I swear, Boss." I can hear the plea. I didn't expect him to admit it, it wasn't exactly true, but I knew enough truth to mix it carefully with lies.

"The West Wing last week, you were there?" I direct my question to him and hate shines in his dark blue eyes. His blond hair is slicked back in a tight ponytail.

"Yes, so what?" He spits on the ground beside Margret.

"The girl was found in the ladies bathroom shortly after you left."

His eyes shoot around the room. I wasn't lying, she just wasn't RA.

"I want you to think very carefully, Juf."

Juf looks at me with fear in his eyes. I hold his stare, but I'm aware of all the other men who've stepped closer. I'm also keeping a close eye on his hands. I don't want him to get too excited and start shooting at me.

"I swear boss, I didn't know she was in the Irish Republican Army. She looked harmless."

"Harmless enough to rape?" I interject and his jaw clenches.

"You nearly cost Svetlana her life. You're lucky I was there to take care of this one." I point at Margret, whose dead eyes stare up at us from the ground.

The execution of Juf is quick and I don't move as the bang of the gun resounds in the shed. My eyes follow the pistol back to its owner. Svetlana's uncle. Juf joins Margret on the ground.

"I won't accept lies. Let this be a warning to all of you." He faces his men and with his pistol still raised in the air. My eyes trail across Juf's body. The wound in his head still oozes blood. The machine gun still strapped to his back.

Svetlana's uncle faces me. "Is she okay?"

I don't ask who. "Yes. I got there in time."

He steps towards me, placing the gun in its holder behind his back. His hand reaches out to me and I don't want to touch him but I do.

"Thank you."

I nod.

"I just wish you hadn't killed her." He doesn't release my hand.

"I didn't have time; it was kill her or let her kill Svetlana," I answer, gripping his hand tighter. He stares at me for a moment before releasing my hand.

In Czech he calls his men, and my eyes go to the machine gun once again. Three of them pick up Juf's body and take it away, two drag Margret's behind the large plastic sheets.

I take a step towards the van. "I need to get back," I tell Svetlana's uncle. He doesn't answer me and I continue until I'm sitting in the van. He doesn't look away as I turn on the ignition and reverse slowly out of the shed.

I ring Gregor once I'm on the road. "Make sure that body can't be found."

"Already taken care of, Boss."

I hang up and focus on the road. I can only hope that Svetlana's uncle bought my story. It was half-truths but I didn't want any bodies lying around. They would soon discover it was just a local girl who Juf got too handsy with.

But she needed to be removed from the equation, so there was no question about her identity.

CHAPTER TWENTY-SEVEN

SVETLANA

I'M EXCITED TO START my lessons again. Every time I'm here with Sam, so is Liam. At first I had thought it was to keep an eye on me, but now I realize that Liam likes to watch me learn. I don't mind him being here. It's nice knowing how much he cares. I look away from Liam, and focus on Sam's words.

"It is so important to understand that things are never black or white. That there is no good or evil."

I nod. "There's both in everyone."

Sam smiles at me. "Exactly, Svetlana. But it takes circumstances to either bring out one or the other in us. That is how so much evil is formed. Evil doesn't just exist, it's created, but it stems from within."

"Like a serial killer?" I ask.

"It doesn't take someone to kill to be evil. Our thoughts can be evil but once they become more than thoughts, our actions define us. Just like a serial killer."

"So if we could change someone's thought pattern, you think we could stop people from hurting each other."

He nods. "Of course, but some people can't erase the road that has already been laid in their mind. We can only hope it never gets put there in the first place and if it does, that we might be able to lay a road beside it. But we can never erase it."

I had evil thoughts at times, about hurting my uncle. I'd killed a man. Did that make me evil? I didn't like how this lesson was making me feel.

"I think she has had enough lessons for today." Liam speaks up, pulling me out of my thoughts. Was I that transparent? Before I can tell Sam, it's fine, he's already packing up his books.

I wait until he leaves before turning to Liam, but he's already up off the couch.

"Come on."

I take his outstretched hand and love the feel of his fingers wrapped around mine. I keep stealing glances at Liam as he leads us back downstairs, but instead of going to the basement, he leads me towards the back of the house. I want to ask him where we are going, but instead, I focus on my surroundings. The house is old, everything is well polished, and there is so much wood. Wooden floors, wooden doors, the dark wood frames each doorway and the high skirting boards give that sense of grandeur that this house deserves. We move through a large kitchen and outside into a courtyard.

"We are outside," I say in bewilderment, looking at Liam.

His lips tug up slightly. "You are very observant, Svetlana."

The teasing in his voice has me smiling. "Very funny. What are we doing outside?"

This time Liam looks at me. "Just getting some fresh air." The air is tinged with cow dung, straw and damp grass. I love each smell I take in. We move past stables that hold some horses and walk out towards a field.

"You seem troubled with what Sam was saying today."

"I just question good and evil so much." I trail off, not sure how to put into words what I feel. We walk for a bit more before Liam stops.

"Is it me?"

Surprise filters through me. "Is what you?" I search his handsome face.

"Good and evil. Did it make you question me?"

"You're a good person, Liam." I hate that he thinks it's about him. "It was my own thoughts that made me question the whole good and evil thing."

Liam's shoulders relax. "Tell me your impure thoughts."

My cheeks heat up. The way Liam said impure, just made me think of what we did yesterday, more like what he did to me yesterday. I still haven't gotten to return the favor.

"I think about hurting people," I say honestly knowing what he's asking me.

He nods. "Everyone does Svetlana, that is normal."

"I would kill," I answer. I already had.

"Good." Liam takes my hand in his and starts walking again, leaving me bewildered.

"Good? Good that I would end a life."

He glances at me sideways. "Yes. If you hesitate, it could be your life. So I'm glad that you would take a life, to save your own."

"That's not what I said." We stop walking again and Liam faces me.

"I want to kill my uncle. He wouldn't have to be doing anything, I would just like to kill him."

Liam takes hold of my shoulders. "Because he's hurt you. You have every right to want to hurt him."

I wasn't so sure. I felt like my mind was a bit warped thinking like that. I didn't want to see him punished or anything else, I wanted him dead. I didn't think that made me a very good person.

"I will kill him because he hurt you; I don't need a better reason than that."

My heart pounds at his words. He had said will, not would. Before I can protest, Liam kisses me deeply and my body responds to him immediately. The thoughts of him killing my uncle for me has my heart swelling. I loved Liam, and now that love seemed to grow deeper.

"Who is Jan?" Liam asks, the moment the kiss ends.

I have to think for a moment as my head clears. "Jan?" I repeat the name.

"Yes, you spoke of him before. You sounded very affectionate when you spoke of him. I was curious." I hold Liam's stare. His curiosity wasn't just mild, and that made me smile.

"My dog."

"Your dog," Liam repeats.

"Yes, my dog Jan." A pain that I had buried rises to the surface. "He was my sole companion. My best friend and he's back in the Czech. Holic threatened to kill him, if I didn't return."

Liam stands stiffly, and after what feels like a few minutes, he nods. A soft kiss is planted on my forehead and we resume walking. I'm not sure what just happened or what Liam was thinking, but an ease has settled on him.

My chin connects with the soil and grass covers my face. My ears ring from the loud bang and I can't breathe. Weight is lifted off my back and I turn to see Liam standing up. Grabbing his leg, I try to tug him back down. I know that sound; it was a gunshot.

"Get down," I hiss at him, he has his phone out and my pleas don't make him come to me. I spit out grass and some blood that had filled my mouth.

Whoever Liam rings doesn't answer. He pockets the phone and reaches down for me, pulling me close to him. His fingers grip my chin as he examines my face. "I'm sorry for shoving you. I'd thought for a moment that we were the target." He tilts my head from side to side. "It came from the house." He continues to speak as his eyes roam my face.

"I'm okay, Liam." He releases me and faces the house again. Taking out his phone, he makes another phone call, this time someone answers.

"Did you see anything?"

I can't understand the voice on the other side of the phone.

"Stay where you are and don't move. I'll go check."

My fingers clutch Liam's. I don't want him to go and check. I'm waiting for him to tell me to stay hidden, but to my surprise he doesn't. Instead we walk quickly, half hunkered to the front of the house. We stepped into the opening he had taken me down through, when we had first arrived here. Liam's living quarters are empty and he moves me quickly into the bedroom.

"You need to stay here." I didn't want to stay here, but chasing after Liam wasn't an option.

LIAM

My fingers move quickly over the number pad on my safe. I remove two guns and place them in the band of my trousers. I leave through the tunnel and circle around to the back of the house. Movement close to the shed has me withdrawing my gun. Slowly, I inch closer. Footsteps sound from the shed that holds all the guns. Closing my eyes, I wait, listening. The rattle of the cabinet door that's locked has me moving from my hiding place. Whoever is in the shed would have their back to me. I cock the gun as I step into the shed.

"Darragh." I lower my gun as he spins around. His eyes darted from the gun to me.

"Don't fucking shoot me." His wild eyes and raised hands make me question if he's on something.

Placing the gun in the band of my trousers, I leave the shed.

"You're not going in there." Darragh grabs my arm, stopping my progress.

"A gun was fired. One of our brothers could be bleeding to death right now." My words have the intended effect and Darragh releases his hold on my arm.

We move slowly through the back door. The house is quiet. Darragh isn't light on his feet, but he's safely behind me. Downstairs is all clear. Moving upstairs, I pause on the stairs knowing we need to split up. The second gun sits neatly in my hands but I pass it to Darragh, without a word he takes it, clicking off the safety. Once we reach the landing, we split up. I take the left side of the house while Darragh takes the right. Five bedrooms later, I've seen no one at all.

My back presses firmly against the wall as I approach my father's study. The door is slightly ajar. Closing my eyes, I listen. There's a faint sound, moans maybe. Using my foot, I push the door open slowly before stepping into the room. Father's on the ground, a pool of blood around him. The flickering pulse in his neck gives me little comfort. His fingers reach towards me but I move around the study, checking behind the desk and chairs. The rooms are empty. Kneeling down, I study father's wound. A gunshot to his side still bleeds heavily.

"Is the person still here who shot you?" I grip his face, making him become more alert.

His moans are a waste of time, I shake his head and his eyes snap to me.

"Is the person still here?"

"No." He closes his eyes and I release him before leaving the study. The rest of the rooms are empty, so I retrace my footsteps until I meet Finn and Darragh.

Placing the gun in the band of my trousers, I indicate for both of them to follow me to the study.

"He's still alive," I say as I push open the study door. Finn and Darragh run to him.

"George. Are you at work?" I turn away from Finn and Darragh as they try to see where father has been shot.

"Yes, but Liam, I really can't leave."

"I don't want you to leave. I'll be there shortly and have your team on standby." I hang up.

"Did you ring an ambulance?" Darragh's standing now, his hands tainted in red from father's blood.

"No, you and Finn take him. He's been shot in the side. George will be waiting for your arrival. I'll follow you there." Darragh doesn't question me but rushes back to father. Finn hasn't spoken, his hands now cover the wound as he tries to stop the bleeding.

Lifting him up, he groans loudly and I leave them to get him downstairs. I need to check on, Svetlana.

I take out my gun as I take the final steps into the basement. A scream from Svetlana has me wanting to run to her, but instead I slow down and listen. She's crying, another squeal erupts from her. Pushing open the door slowly, I can see Svetlana. She's kneeling on the ground with her back to me. I scan the room but I don't see anyone else. She shuffles back and the brown box that sits in front of her comes into view. I make a small noise and she spins around. Placing my finger over my lips has her swallowing her cries.

I point for her to stay where she is as I move towards the bedroom.

"There's no one here." She confirms, and I lower my gun before marching towards her. Sitting at her feet is a box that has a pair of large hands in it. One hand tattooed with the words LOVE, the other HATE.

"Gregor," I say, as I place the gun in my waistband. This was a warning, I just wasn't sure if it was from Svetlana's uncle or the RA. Did father catch the intruder in the house and that's why he was shot?

I reach out my arm for Svetlana and she stands immediately, coming to my side.

"That's a pair of hands." Her voice trembles.

"Did you hear anything?"

She swallows and blinks before shaking her head. "I don't think so."

"I need you to think, Svetlana."

She nods again. "Yeah, yeah." Now she looks at me. "That's why I came out. I thought maybe it was you."

"How long ago?" That meant the intruder could be still on the grounds.

"A minute ago."

"Stay here," I tell her, racing to the tunnel. Whoever did this didn't leave through the house. The door is ajar, confirming my suspicions. Removing the gun again, I race down the dark tunnel. He wouldn't linger and whoever did this has a few minutes head start.

Taking out my phone, I ring Stephen but get no answer. The air outside is still warm and I slow my pace as I move along the grass. The box at the gates looks empty, moving closer I look in and see Stephen on the ground. No blood is anywhere to be seen. Pushing open the door, I check for a pulse and find one. He's just been knocked out. Finn's jeep rolls up and I open the gates, letting them out. They don't look in but speed past. Stephen groans as I step over him. Whoever did this was gone.

"Stephen, wake up." I nudge him with my foot a few times before he finally wakes up.

"What happened?" He slowly stands, while touching the back of his head. "Someone hit me from behind."

Useless information. "You didn't see anyone enter or leave."

"Sorry Mr. O'Reagan." He shakes his head.

"Get your head seen too." I say, leaving him and returning to the house. Svetlana is still there staring at the hands.

"Did you get him?" Her skin is very pale.

Pouring out two whiskeys I hand her a glass.

"No, not a trace." I drink the full glass. Svetlana sips on the whiskey, her eyes keep drifting to the box.

The glass clicks as I rest it on the marble counter. "I'll get rid of them." The flaps on the box have been cut off so I grip the sides and take it out into the area that's reserved for this kind of thing. I'm glad when I return to find Svetlana sitting on the couch still nursing her whiskey. Her hands don't seem to tremble as much.

She glances at me as I sit down beside her. "Why would someone do that?"

I pull her into my side and hush her. "I don't know. But I'll find out."

CHAPTER TWENTY-EIGHT

SVETLANA

T HE IMAGE SEEMS TO be embedded in my head, hands severed at the wrist. The large masculine hands once belonged to someone. Was he awake while someone sawed his hands off? I shiver at the thought. Liam's refilling our drinks, but he seems calm. I wonder how many times he had to deal with something like this. Nothing seems to faze him.

"Was he your friend?" I ask, as he hands me the glass. He pauses before passing the glass to me. I take another burning sip of whiskey.

"Yes, he was." Liam sits back down and drinks half the glass of whiskey. "He was a good man."

I hold my glass up. "What was his name?"

"Gregor."

I nod. "To Gregor."

Liam clicks his glass with mine before emptying all the contents, this time I do the same, and when he offers me a refill, I deny it. My head feels fuzzy and my blood warm.

"I want to give the house one more final check."

I didn't want to be alone. "I'll come with you." Liam stares at me for a moment, and I'm surprised when he agrees. It's a short nod of his head, but I'm standing with him.

He removes a gun from the back of his trousers and hands it to me. Taking it, the steel feels heavy in my hands.

"You know how to use it?" A slight pull raises his lips. No doubt he's remembering me holding him at gunpoint.

"I'm sure I can manage," I say while checking to make sure the safety is off. Liam waits patiently until I'm satisfied that the gun is ready.

We move silently through the house, checking windows and doors. Seeing the enormity of the house doesn't surprise me that they didn't catch whoever broke in. There are so many entry points that you couldn't watch them all.

"Do you have cameras?" I ask, when we return to the basement. Liam locks down the area and it feels safe down here.

"Father never permitted them."

There is a bitterness to his words that I've never heard before.

"Right now I'm sure he's regretting it." Liam dismantles the gun and I hand mine over to him.

"Did anyone get hurt?" I wanted to add beside Gregor, but I don't.

"It was my father who was shot."

My hand rises to my mouth. "Oh no, I'm so sorry."

"Thank you." Liam's words rattle me. He doesn't sound sincere or upset.

"You don't care that he's been shot?"

Liam removes his suit jacket carefully, and places it on the back of one of the chairs.

"I'm not entirely sure." His honest answer startles me.

"Was he a bad father?" I'm getting too personal but I want to know everything about Liam.

"No. He's a good father."

I frown, confused.

"He wasn't a good husband." Liam removes the three steps between us. His thumb rubs the lines between my eyes making me relax.

"I'm going for a shower."

My heart picks up speed.

"Would you like to join me?"

I smile at his question. "Okay."

Liam unbuttons the sleeves of his shirt as he walks to the bathroom. I don't strip but watch him as he pulls the shirt from his back.

"Why a dragon?" I ask, as I step up to his back. My hand hovers over the large black dragon that seems to move and coil as his muscles bunch together.

"After my mother died, I wanted something to remind me of her. To remind me to stay strong."

My hand touches the dragon's head and its wings come closer as Liam tenses under my fingertips.

"The dragon is a sign of courage and strength."

"It's a beautiful creature." *Just like him.*

My hands continue to trail across the dragon before moving around to his stomach. Muscles shift and tighten beneath my touch, and it makes me feel powerful. Liam hasn't moved and I press my face to his back, inhaling his scent. He doesn't question what I'm doing, but he just allows me to have this moment. My fingers grip the bottom of his shirt and I pull it from him fully. A heavy thud resounds in my chest as I move around Liam. Black orbs focus on me, they trail my movements. The belt rattles as I unbuckle it. Liam doesn't stop my progression as I push his trousers and boxers down his hips. I pause when his large manhood springs to life. Swallowing the fear that starts to swirl in my stomach, I don't give myself time to think. I take all of him in my hand. Liam groans and it's encouraging. Wrapping my hand around his shaft,

I pump really slowly. Taking a peek at him, has color filling my cheeks. Liam's eyes gleam with a hunger. I hold his stare as I stroke him again and his lids half close. I return my attention to pleasing him when his hand wraps around mine, stopping me. He removes my hands and steps out of his trousers. He had taken off his shoes earlier and all that he wears is socks that he pulls from his feet, before reaching for my top. He isn't as slow as I was, and all my clothes form a neat bundle at our feet. Taking my hand, Liam leads me into the shower. The first spray of water is cold and I jump back until it heats up.

The hunger in Liam's eyes hasn't left and when his arm snakes around my waist, I shiver. Nothing separates us now. It's flesh and water, and my body seems to mold perfectly against his. His erection presses against my stomach and I want to touch it again. Liam tilts my head back making me look at him and there is something in his eyes that causes my stomach to twist and dive. I don't overthink it as his lips crash down on mine. A hunger grows inside me, I want this, I want something I've never had, and I want it with Liam. My hands grip his face pulling him closer. My legs move apart, craving him.

He breaks the kiss. "Are you sure?" He asks, as his hand trails to my thigh. "Yes."

He nods, and lifts my leg high, with his other hand he directs his erection to my entrance. Once he has himself positioned, he takes my other leg and wraps them around his waist. The erection brushes my entrance and I'm wet and eager. Liam's hands grip my ass, holding me up, and the anticipation has me slamming my lips against his again. He eases in slowly. The burn is instant and tears burn my eyes. It's painful, but the deeper Liam moves inside me, a pleasure starts to build. Liam pauses in his gentle stride.

"Don't stop," I say against his lips and he pushes deeper, spreading me, until I take all of him. Once he's in, he slides back out. I hold still as the burning pain recedes and each stride starts to bring pleasure. Liam keeps his strides slow, moving his full erection out of me before filling me back up. Throwing my head back, I let out a moan that's building inside me. Gripping Liam's shoulders, the tightness of his body starts to show his strain.

"Go faster," I say.

Liam slides out of me before slamming back in, his movements grow faster, almost frantic and I'm not sure what's building inside me. My teeth sink into his shoulder and he hisses, pounding into me faster. I release his flesh and let my head rest against the tiles. Liam's body pounds mine against the wall and I've never felt anything like this. I want to let go, but I don't want this to end.

"I'm going to come." His confession brings me to my own climax, and as he thrust his final few thrusts, I shatter with him, while calling out his name.

I can feel the warmth of his seed pour inside me and my body responds by releasing more juices. I'm kissing his shoulder where I bit him, the marks clear. Liam twitches inside me, the sensation has me looking at him. He's watching me and I can't stop the smile that spreads across my face.

"Hi."

His eyes are a light brown with darker swirls, and when he smiles at me, he looks so young and free.

"Hi to you too."

His response has me laughing. I bite my lip as his eyes trail across my face before landing on my lips.

"Are you okay?" He asks, between kisses.

"More than okay." His smile against my lips sends my heart racing.

He slowly removes himself from me, before setting me down on the shower tiles. My legs feel stiff and I'm grateful when he holds me tightly around the waist.

"Was that nice for you?" I ask, a bit shyly. I hadn't done anything, but now that it was over I wondered how I compared.

"Yes."

I glance up at Liam. He's still holding me, looking at me with wide eyes.

"The biting was different." His lip tugs up slightly.

My cheeks heat. "I kind of marked you." I say, running my fingers over the bright red teeth marks that still look stark against his perfect skin.

"I like that you marked me."

My heart gives a heavy thud with pride. He had marked me too, only his mark was permanent. No matter what happened, Liam O'Reagan took my virginity and I was glad I gave it to him. I gave it to someone I loved. I don't want him to see my face, so I kiss him softly and he closes his eyes. His hands creep up my back and my own snake around his waist. The kiss slowly dissolves and Liam just holds me under the spray of water. His chin rests on the top of my head and I listen to the steady beat of his heart.

My body is sore as I sit at the breakfast bar and watch Liam make us an omelet. He looks good in the kitchen with no top on. His stance is relaxed and when he looks at me, he smiles. My heart swells and grows each time our eyes clash. I don't want to eat; I want Liam inside me again. The thoughts make me shift on the stool.

"It's almost ready."

It does smell divine, but I'm struggling to stay focused. All that skin is making me remember what it feels like against mine. "What will we do after the food?" I ask as Liam places a plate in front of me.

"What would you like to do?" He sits down and sprinkles some pepper on the omelet.

"I can think of a few things," I mumble as I start to cut up my omelet.

"Like what?" Liam speaks around a fork full of food.

We aren't on the same wavelength here. "We could go to bed," I say, hoping my face isn't burning.

"You're tired?" he asks seriously.

If that's how I got him into bed. "Yes, exhausted."

He chews another fork full of food. "Okay, we can do that." He really doesn't hear the double meaning. My body tightens and relaxes with excitement. I eat the omelet quickly and have to wait for Liam to finish his.

"Do you have to eat so slow?" I ask, feeling a sense of impatience grow.

"You in a hurry?"

My cheeks flame, was I going to have to spell it out for him? My silence has his eyes widening.

"I'm finished." He pushes his stool back and takes my hand, leading us to the bedroom.

"Tell me what you want, Svetlana," Liam speaks while removing his trousers, his erection is there in all its glory, as he stalks towards me, I move back.

"I want you inside me." I hold his fierce gaze and he gives a wicked smile that I've never seen before.

"I won't be gentle this time." His fingers circle my wrists and excitement has me clenching my legs.

"I won't be gentle with you either." I hold my head high and watch Liam's smile grow.

"Good." He whispers, before pushing me onto the bed. The way he moves over me has me praying that I didn't bite off more than I can chew.

CHAPTER TWENTY-NINE

LIAM

"I CAN'T JUST PUT him in an induced coma." George's words annoy me, I glance at my ringing phone. It's Connor, I was wondering when he would ring.

"You will, George," I say, as I leave the hospital. Keeping father asleep would keep him out of this mess. If he woke up, I had no idea what meddling he would get up to.

"Yes, Connor."

Svetlana looks bored in the car. She was excited to get out but I couldn't bring her into the hospital. Soon she would be free. I hated caging her, she wasn't meant to be caged. When her eyes settle on me, she smiles. No one has ever looked at me like that before.

"Is he okay?"

"No. He's in a coma fighting for his life," I answer bluntly.

"Jesus, you know it wasn't us."

I stop at the driver's door and don't get in. "I don't know that, Connor."

"Tom, wouldn't kill his brother," Connor says.

"But he would kill his nephew?" I open the car door and climb in. "Margret was handed over to the Czech and they killed her. Maybe that's knowledge you would like to pass on to your father."

"I haven't told them anything."

I start the car up. "Good. Now you know what to say." I hang up, and turn to Svetlana.

"How is he?" Her concern for my father's well-being is nice.

"I'm sure he'll live," I tell her to ease any worry she might have.

We drive back to the house where Darragh, Finn, and Shane wait for me. What I don't expect is Connor being there.

"Brothers." I greet them, but they all seem more interested with who's with me.

"I'll just go make some food," Svetlana says.

I nod my thanks to her. No one speaks until she is out of the room. I wait until I hear the click of the door that leads down to my quarters.

"Is there a problem?" I ask.

"This wasn't the RA." Darragh speaks up, standing shoulder to shoulder with Connor.

"Okay," I answer.

Darragh's shoulders deflate.

"Okay as in you're not going to retaliate," Connor asks.

"You don't want Michael avenged?"

Now Finn and Darragh look to Connor.

"It wasn't the RA."

I nod. "Did you pass on my message?"

Connor's jaw clenches. "Yes."

"Please send my condolences as well."

Darragh moves to the fridge and gets a bottle of water. "Anyone want a drink?" He offers. We all decline except for Finn. I wait until Darragh's finished guzzling down the water.

"Is that all?" I ask Connor as he seems to be in charge.

"Tom wants to meet you." Connor confirms my suspicions that this wasn't a simple matter.

"No Liam, you can't." Finn jumps in. These are the first words he has spoken.

"What does he want with Liam?" Darragh sounds suspicious of Connor now, and I lean back against the wall and let them squabble it out. It was pretty perfect. It was something I was going to demand, to see Tom, so having Tom reach out was ideal.

"It's just to let him know that he didn't do this to Michael." Connor opens up his hands as he speaks.

"What about my man, Gregor? Someone sawed off his hands, and left them in my living room."

Finn visibly pales. "What the fuck?"

"Jesus, why didn't you say something?" Darragh questions quickly, while taking a cigarette from behind his ear, and lighting it up.

I answer neither of them, but wait for Connor to answer me.

"I don't know Liam. You must piss off a lot of people," Connor fires back.

Finn sits down, while running his hands through his hair. "Was that girl down there when it happened?"

Finn, always so soft. "Yes. Svetlana, was the one who found them."

"Can't you send her home?" Finn shakes his head, while pointing at the table.

"No."

"Tell Tom I'll meet him," I say to Connor. "Today." I add as I leave the kitchen.

***

After spending some time with Svetlana, I leave her with Finn. She doesn't want him around and he doesn't want to be there, which makes them a perfect fit.

I hadn't far to go before I reached Carrickmacross where Tom was waiting for me. I clocked six men as I walked through the lobby, and into the hotel restaurant, that was closed this time of day. Tom doesn't rise as I enter.

"How's your father?" He asks, the moment I open my suit jacket and sit down.

"Critical." I don't expect the sadness that I see in his eyes.

"Michael is strong, he will pull through."

No, he won't. I don't reassure Tom with lies.

"We didn't do this Liam."

"Did Connor tell you about Margret?" I say, and see I've hit a cord.

Tom clenches his fists. "She was such a good girl. Her mother is devastated."

"She was a very clever bomb maker as well." I state.

Tom sits back. "I've wondered why the Czech have taken Margret."

"She attacked one of their people who's under my protection."

"Svetlana," Tom says, and I'm not surprised he knows who she is.

"They took Margret, and I wish I had been able to stop them."

Tom laughs, but it holds no humor. "You're very like Michael, great at talking your way out of situations. I'm just not sure how much I believe."

I didn't need him to believe everything I was saying, I just needed to plant enough seeds so doubt would grow and grow.

"Honestly, Tom. If I had gotten my hands on the girl, I would have killed her." Mixing the truth with lies was also a tactic that worked. "After all, someone tried to kill my brother and succeeded in killing my sister-in-law."

"That debt isn't cleared." Tom stamps his finger onto the table.

I needed to steer him away from Shane. "Are you sure it wasn't your men who attempted to kill Shane, but shot my father instead?"

"Listen to me boy and listen good. I had nothing to do with my brother. No one would touch him."

"Either way, he's fighting for his life, Tom." I sit back and take a quick count of the men in the room. The three of them are carrying guns. Mine are stashed in the glove compartment in the car. I didn't want to risk bringing them in. I didn't think that Tom would harm me.

"The Czech reassure me that they had nothing to do with my father, they are quite convinced that you are the one behind my father's attack."

Tom's fist comes down hard and fast on the table, but I don't flinch. "Those bastards are trying to set us up against each other."

I raise both eyebrows in response. "So what do you propose we do, Tom?" I tilt my head to the side and wait for him to come up with the plan that I've already laid out.

"We attack together, Liam." Tom raises both eyebrows.

"I work with these people," I remind him.

"You have my word that I never touched Michael. They did. Otherwise why point the finger at me." Tom drums his fingers on the table.

"How do I know this isn't a set up?" I pick up two pint mats and place them together.

"You could be setting me up," Tom fires back.

I place the mats back on the table. "I'm not," I answer simply.

"You have my word." Tom reaches out his hand for me to take. "Do we have a deal? Let's take care of these Russian bastards once and for all."

"What about my family?"

Tom closes his open palm. "Shane took my son's life." A deadness enters Tom's eyes.

"You took my sister-in-law's life, and continue to attack my home." I release the mats now, and take a quick glance around the room. The men are still in the same positions.

"There will be no more attacks. I want this resolved with the Czech then we can talk more."

It was fair enough, but I pretended to ponder on it for a bit longer. This time I reach my hand across the table and Tom takes it immediately.

"We have a deal," I say.

***

Connor leans against my Range Rover.

"What happened?" he pushes off the passenger door and faces me.

Unlocking the Jeep, I climb in and I'm not happy when he gets into the passenger side. I lock the doors and his eyes shoot to his own door. He shifts, stuffing his hands into his jacket pocket before facing me again.

"Why not ask your father?" I don't start the jeep but slowly put on my seatbelt.

"I'm asking you, Liam."

I start the jeep. "Is that all?"

"I'm not Darragh, or Finn." He's moving closer to me, but I don't flinch.

"No you're not—what is it that you want Connor?" I ask, removing my phone from the inside of my jacket pocket and sitting it in its dock.

"I want to know if he told you who shot Shane?"

He had my attention, but I continue to set my phone up. "Why?"

His silence has me glancing at him. "No, he didn't."

Connor nods. He takes a quick peek out his window before returning his attention to me. "I'll give you the name if you tell me who killed mam."

"Why don't you give me the name of the person who tried to kill Shane and I'll consider it."

"No. I want mother's killer first."

I sit fully back in my seat now. "Why are you so convinced that I know it?"

Connor shrugs. "Someone in our house did it Liam. You seem to know everything, so you're my best bet."

"I'm going home now. Are you coming with me?"

Connor shakes his head and exhales quickly. "That's not my home." He pulls the door handle but its locked. Without facing me he speaks through clenched teeth. "Could you open the door, please?"

"Of course." I open the door and Connor jumps out.

CHAPTER THIRTY

LIAM

I check my rearview mirror, to see Connor walking away from the hotel that I had met Tom in. The ringing of my phone fill's the car. Finn's name flashes up on the screen.

"Yes Finn." I pull back onto the road and leave Carrickmacross.

"Are you nearly home? It's Darragh, he's been arrested."

I feel as exasperated as Finn sounds. "Which station is he being held in?" I take a right out of the town and start towards home.

"Navan. He was really drunk and shouting about stupid stuff."

"What stupid stuff?" I ask, driving faster.

There's a long pause. "Finn?" I control my voice.

"I think he ... hurt someone. Like really badly."

"Did he say he did?"

"Not in so many words. But he just kept ranting about how he didn't mean it."

Darragh was becoming a huge problem. "I'm on my way to Navan. Are you still with Svetlana?"

"Of course. She kind of witnessed Darragh's meltdown."

"Why was he arrested?"

Finn breathes deeply into the phone. "He rang the Gardai himself, saying he hurt someone, and when they got here, he gave them nothing but abuse."

"I'll be home shortly." I hang up.

***

I sign the slip to get Darragh out of jail. "What's the charges?" I ask Gardai Weldon. He was on my payroll.

"Nothing much. Wasting Gardai time mostly."

"He didn't say anything when he got here?" I push the clipboard back to him.

"No, he had withdrawn his previous claim of hurting someone, saying he was messing with us."

I nod.

Gardai Weldon leaves to get Darragh.

I don't have to wait long before a smiling Darragh appears in front of Gardai Weldon. They don't remove his handcuffs until he is in front of me. His disheveled clothes and bloodied nose has me glaring at Weldon.

"Was he touched?"

"No. He arrived like this." Gardai Weldon's casual response, and Darragh's snort have me relaxing.

"Thanks for bailing me out." Darragh was high, and right now I couldn't look at him as he climbed into my jeep. Once I'm in, I don't start the jeep but lock the doors.

Darragh snorts. "What's this? An attempted kidnapping?"

"No Darragh. This is a warning." I look at Darragh now.

He no longer smiles. "Why did I do it?" his voice breaks.

"Where is Ciara?"

Darragh's eyes widen in surprise before they dim. "You think I hurt her?"

It was a possibility with Darragh. "No."

"She broke up with me." Darragh takes a box of cigarettes and a lighter out of his pocket.

"Don't light that up in my jeep. You think she'll want you back now."

"How the fuck should I know." His foot strikes out kicking my dash and I let him have his tantrum. Gardai Brady walks past the jeep and I salute him.

Once Darragh calms down, I speak again. "Do I need to sign you in somewhere?"

"What? Hide the fuck up away?" Darragh throws his fags at the dash. They bounce off easily and land on the floor.

"I don't exactly have time for your outbursts. Is it possible that you could try not to attract the attention of the Gardai?" My temper is slipping and it isn't something I am used to.

"I don't know, Liam." Darragh's eyes waver.

I start the jeep.

"I destroy everything," he's whispering now.

I leave the Gardai station and Darragh picks up his fag box. I'm aware of him removing the fag but I don't stop him, as he lights it up.

"Why did I do it?" he asks while blowing smoke out the window.

I loosen my tie and flicker a glance at him. He's staring out the window, one of his feet is on the leather seat. I'll have to get my jeep cleaned.

"How did I do it?" He's holding his hands in front of him and the gesture is obvious to me. His hands are wrapped around an invisible neck. "Why won't you tell me?" He looks at me now.

"I need you to stop this."

"No!" My dash is abused as he kicks it several times. His fag sends sparks around my jeep and I jam on the brakes, stopping in the middle of the road. A car blares behind us, but I just want Darragh and his madness away from me. I lean across and open the door. He's bewildered until I push him out onto the side of the road. He lands in a ditch and I'm breathing heavily as I throw his half-lit cigarette at him. The car behind us continues to blare. Sitting up straight, I stare at the driver in my rear-view mirror and he takes his hand off the horn, and moves past us. We glare at each other and once he's gone, I grip the steering wheel, I close my eyes. Taking a deep breath in through my nose I release it through my mouth, I repeat this several times. Movement sounds and the jeep dips. I glance at Darragh as he closes the door and puts on his seatbelt, not saying a word. I put back on my own and start driving again.

My phone has ashes on it and I brush them off before dialing Sam's number. He answers on the third ring.

"Has there been any movement?"

"Nothing unusual, Boss," Sam says.

"Be careful that they don't spot you. They spotted Gregor." I inform Sam, turning down the main street of Navan.

"Is he okay?" Sam asks.

"I received his hands in a box. So I'll say no."

"Fuck sake."

I glance at Darragh, as he stares silently out the window.

"Keep me informed of any movement."

"Yes, no problem boss."

I end the call with Sam and pull into the carpark of Navan Hospital.

"Have you visited father?"

Darragh looks at me like I materialized from thin air. "No."

"Well, now you will." I unbuckle my belt and get out of the jeep. Darragh's still in his seat and stares at me. I rap my knuckles against the window and he gets out.

"I don't want to see him."

I ignore his attempts at sulking and enter the hospital. Father's been kept in a private wing of the ICU.

The room is silent except for the machinery that he's wired up to. Everything is keeping him in a coma. Darragh closes the door softly behind him. Pulling the blind back, he glances out the window.

"What are you watching for?" I ask as I move around the bed and stare down at father. He looks peaceful.

"I got into a bit of trouble here a while ago."

"Of course you did." I close the top button of father's pajamas.

"Look what they have done to our family, Darragh." Opening my suit jacket, I pull a chair over to father's bed and sit down.

Darragh shifts uncomfortably at the door, half of his attention still on the staff and visitors who move past the window.

"Darragh."

He lets the blind go and looks at me, and then at father. "I don't like hospitals."

"Nobody likes hospitals, Darragh. I want you to really think about your actions. You could be trying to help us figure out who tried to kill our father instead of roiling up the Gardai."

Guilt finally shines in his eyes. "I fucked up."

I raise a hand.

Darragh exhales loudly.

"Am I boring you?" When he doesn't respond, I continue standing up. "I brought you here so you can see first-hand what they did to our family. An Chlann." I move closer to Darragh. "They are picking us off one by one." I take another step. "They won't stop until there is nothing left and all of this will have been for nothing."

Darragh shakes his head, so I grip the back of his neck to keep him focused. "I need you." I release him and step aside. "He needs you." I point at father.

The door opens and Shane steps in. His eyes linger on me and Darragh before he glances at father and shuts the door.

"How is he today?"

"I haven't spoken to the nurse yet." I walk back to the chair and sit down.

"Are you okay?" Shane glances at Darragh, but his voice holds more contempt than care.

"Yeah. I'm just going out for a smoke." Darragh leaves quickly, and I hope even a small amount of what I said sinks in.

Shane pulls a chair up the opposite side of father. "I heard he had gotten arrested again."

I stare at Shane, wondering how well I really know him. "I think you should be more concerned with your own actions."

He sits forward. "Is that so?" Both eyebrows raise high.

"Yes, Shane it is. I want to know about this boy you killed. Why you killed him? Why you kept it from our family?" I could keep listing questions for him, but I had made my point.

Shane runs his hand across his mouth. "I didn't mean it."

"Oh well, that's all that matters." I sit forward joining my hands together trying to keep my composure. "I trusted you above them all and you lied and betrayed me." I sit back as surprise lights up Shane's eyes at my outburst.

"I'm sorry, Liam. I thought I had made the best decision at the time. It was an unlucky blow. I hid the body with Brian and Connor found out. He killed

Brian, and told me if I did something in return for him he would tell the RA it was Brian. So I agreed."

Shane looks away now, and I'm wondering what exactly he had to do for Connor. When he doesn't offer up that bit of information, I have to ask.

"What did Connor have you do for him?"

Shane stands and so do I. He isn't getting away that easily.

"Find out who killed mam." His words are low.

I laugh, really laugh.

Shane looks so unsure now. "Liam."

I hold up my hands. "Am I your number one suspect?"

Shane rubs his mouth again while tilting his head. "Come on Liam, don't say that."

"I want to hear what my brother Shane has been conspiring behind my back."

Shane plays with his ring on his thumb finger, something he often does when he thinks of her. "Connor said that father was beating her."

I deflate at his words and remember who I am. Buttoning up my suit jacket, I compose myself.

"He wasn't lying," I answer.

Shane pales further. "You knew."

"We were children." I answer, knowing it's really no defence.

"I would have killed him." He's pointing at father in the bed.

"Really?"

His brows furrow. "Yes, really Liam. Why didn't you say something?"

The door opens and a nurse steps in. She glances from me to Shane with a forced smile.

"I'm just checking on Mr. O'Reagan."

I step further away from the bed. "Of course."

Shane moves closer to the door and he doesn't look away from me. We stare at each other as the nurse checks Father's vitals. I can see how uncomfortable we are making her. She drops the blood pressure pump twice and nearly knocks the stand over. After a few moments and some notes in a chart that rests at the bottom of the bed, she excuses herself with a tight smile and red cheeks.

"You should have told us." Shane picks right back up where we left off. He was right, I should have told someone, but she had made me promise not to. I was the eldest. I had to protect her secret.

"She always said it wouldn't happen again, or he didn't mean it."

Shane moves quickly over Father's lying figure.

"Do you want to hurt him?" I ask.

"It won't bring her back." He finally answers after a few moments of silence.

"You need to distance yourself from Connor."

Shane's head snaps up. "I don't exactly hang out with him."

"Tom is going to have you killed one way or another." I point at father, "He might be our only hope of saving you."

The door opens again and Darragh arrives looking a little more grounded. He's tidied himself up a bit and more color has entered his cheeks.

"Are you ready to go?" I ask Darragh.

He nods eagerly.

CHAPTER THIRTY-ONE

SVETLANA

THE COUCH DOESN'T FEEL as comfortable as it normally does. Maybe it's the fact that Finn's here and he's trying to make small talk, but failing miserably. He doesn't want to be here and every time his phone bleeps he happily leaves to answer it. Liam's been gone for hours and each time I hear Finn's phone ring, I'm praying it's him.

"Are you hungry?" Finn asks for the tenth time. Each time I've said no.

"Yeah, actually I am."

Finn looks relieved. "What can I get you?"

"Rice with red sauce would be nice." My stomach grumbles. It's something I love having but haven't had it since arriving in Ireland.

"Rice with red sauce?" Finn repeats and his lip curls up in disgust.

"It's fine if you don't have it." I pull my feet up on the couch closer to me.

"No, I can do that." He moves towards Liam's kitchen.

"He doesn't have rice." I inform Finn.

He gives me a shaky smile. "I can go upstairs and cook it for you. I'll only be ten minutes."

"Take your time," I say with a genuine smile. He's out of the room quickly. *Poor guy.*

I lie back on the couch, and it's funny that I like the silence that this space offers. I thought I hated it, but what I hate more is small talk. I wasn't very good at it. Especially with one of Liam's brothers. They looked at me like I was some alien. They looked at Liam in a pretty similar way.

The sound of footsteps has me ready to bang my head against the wall. "No rice, I take it?" I ask, sitting up.

Crystal blue eyes stare down at me and my throat tightens as I scurry into a sitting position. "What are you doing here?" It's whispered, but Holic hears me.

"I was worried about you." He hasn't moved. I can't see his hands, they're stuffed in his pockets. I try to focus on him.

"Did my uncle send you?" The shock of seeing him is starting to wear off. Each thud of my heart sounds loud. I don't want to glance at the door, the fear of Finn walking in here is making it hard not to.

"No. I wanted to make sure you're okay." Holic shifts, it's the first time I see insecurity in his stance.

"You've seen me and I'm fine," I say, and his eyes shoot around the space, he steps back away from me, allowing me to breathe a little.

"They have you hidden in a basement." His sharp eyes shoot back to me. "Is no one watching you?"

I shake my head and pull the sleeves of my jumper down over my whitening knuckles. "You need to leave now, Holic."

His brows draw down. "You don't want to come with me?"

"Of course I do. It's just that I can't."

Holic takes a step closer and fear wraps around my spine. I hold perfectly still as he removes his hands from his pockets. His missing finger is a reminder of his disobedience. He grips my face and a whimper leaves my lips.

"Holic please."

He taps my face gently but repeatedly until my heart threatens to come out of my chest. "Why are you lying to me?"

"I'm not. I swear."

"You don't want to leave." The accusation has him tightening his fingers on my face.

"I can't leave. You know that." I say as my vision wavers. Holic's fingers tighten on my throat. "Please Holic," I beg again.

"You're different."

My cheeks flame. That's not possible, he couldn't tell that I was no longer a virgin. I hadn't changed in any other way. But him knowing that, wasn't possible. A new fear skitters up my back and drapes itself across my shoulders.

"It's me, Svetlana."

Holic loosens his grip on me. "No, it's not Svetlana. What have they done to you?"

My heart pounds until black spots start to fill my vision. A cold sweat forms on the back of my neck. "Nothing. It's me."

"Did they interfere with you?"

I pull away from Holic's hold. "You're being paranoid and you need to leave."

Something changes in his stance and his hands curl around my shoulders, forcing me down on the couch. His crystal blue eyes shine with a madness that has me pushing against him.

"Get off me," I demand, but he doesn't budge.

"You gave yourself to them?"

"Get off me."

"You gave yourself to them? Was it so they wouldn't force you?" My skin is crawling with Holic this close to me, and he sounded insane, like he was trying to rationalize this situation.

"My uncle gave me to them. So let me up." I remind him, but he's shaking his head, his hands seem to sink deeper into my shoulders.

"They shouldn't have touched you. You are coming with me."

I'm on my feet in one sweep movement. Holic's hand grips mine and I can't help but focus on the missing finger.

"He'll kill you."

"I don't care." Yanking my arm, he walks towards the door that opens. My bowl of rice bounces off the floor as Finn looks at Holic.

"Holic please," I plead, knowing that it wouldn't matter to Holic. "Let's just go. You and me, he's a nobody."

Holic doesn't speak but stares at Finn, who slowly raises his hands.

"Look buddy, I don't want trouble, but you can't take her."

Holic shoves me behind him. Two knives slip from their holders on his back.

Finn pales, and I'm ready to throw up on the floor.

"Is he the one who touched you?" Holic speaks in Czech to me. Finn's nervous eyes flicker around the room.

"No. Please Holic, let's just go." I speak in English.

"I can't let you leave with him." Finn widens his arms and tilts his head like he has a chance of stopping this. Holic moves closer to Finn.

"Holic, my uncle won't be happy." My stern words have him pausing. I widen my eyes at Finn, he needs to run, he has no idea who he is dealing with.

"He robbed you from me."

I swallow as Holic faces me, turning his back on Finn.

"I'm still here." I answer. "We can go now." I force a smile.

Finn shifts and I lose Holic's focus.

"First, I must kill him." Holic speaks in English.

I take a step towards him. "You're wasting time. We should leave now."

Finn hasn't moved, his hands still outstretched as Holic advances on him, with a knife in each hand.

"If you touch him, I'll never forgive you," I shout. It's Liam who would never forgive me and that I couldn't live with.

Holic pauses. "You have forgiven me for far worse things." His smile has my heart skyrocketing and I move quickly, standing in front of Finn. "Just trust me," I whisper quickly before turning to Holic.

"You'll have to hurt me first." I hold my head high.

Holic grins, and to my amazement he puts the knives away. "With pleasure." His words spoken again in Czech, take a moment to register with me. He has a grip on my forearms and I'm sailing. The impact with the counter is painful, my shoulder takes the brunt of it and I scream out.

LIAM

"I recognize you." Holic spins around, knives drawn. Finn's pale face grows slack as he stares up at me. I don't look at Svetlana, who's on the ground cradling her arm.

"I recognize you too."

Holic moves away from Finn so he can keep an eye on all of us. Darragh steps out from behind me.

"It's three against one," I say, stepping into the room while loosening my tie.

"I've had worse odds."

I grin. "I'm sure you have. But I'm a fair man, so let's make this fair. Me and you." I open the top button of my shirt.

Holic laughs. "When I kill you, then I kill them." He points his knives at my brothers before looking at Svetlana.

"Don't look at her," I warn him. Something stirs inside me.

Holic looks at Svetlana again, who now stares up at me. His brows furrow. "You." The word is released along with a knife that sails through the air. I move, anticipating the action since I stepped into the room, but not fast enough. The knife nicks my cheek, drawing blood. No one moves as I reach up and touch my cheek.

"Holic stop this." Svetlana is standing now and she is getting too close to Holic for my comfort.

"You want me to die?" He asks her while keeping his eye on the rest of us. He speaks in Czech but I understand what he's saying. Darragh moves and Holic turns to him. "Stay where you are."

"Darragh," I warn.

"You are a man of your word?" Holic asks moving closer to me and further away from Svetlana.

"Of course." He's still holding the second knife, it's tucked under his hand. He bends his head slightly while scanning the room. I didn't expect a man of his size to be so swift on his feet, but three large steps, and he's swinging the knife in a wide arch. I bend back as far as my body will allow, the knife cuts through air where my neck once was.

I dance back and he has to scan the room again to make sure no one else is going to attack him, it's the only opportunity I need. Curling my fist, I put all my strength behind the punch that strikes his side. The impact has him jerking back and I strike out again into his ribs. I meet his swinging hand that holds the knife, the force behind it has wavered as his body hunches from where I've hit him. My fingers tighten around his wrist trying to make him drop the knife, his hand bends, the knife nicks my fingers. I keep my hold even against the pain. My other hand goes to his throat and his mirrors mine. Using his hand, I force it closer to his face, forcing the knife closer to his eye. There is movement that catches my eye. Holic roars out and his knife falls to the ground. I don't let him go as Svetlana pulls a knife from his back. He's trying to turn around and see who's stabbed him, but I hold him tightly by the neck. My eyes meet Svetlana's, hers filled with a darkness I've never seen before. She plunges the knife into his back again. His roar isn't as loud, his strength dwindling, and this time I let him glance over his shoulder, so he can see who did it.

"I love you." My hand tightens on his throat, cutting off any further words.

"You tortured me." Svetlana pulls out the knife.

"Jesus Christ, that's enough." Finn is standing directly behind Svetlana, the horror shining in his eyes.

"You scarred me." The knife plunges into him again as tears trickle down Svetlana's face. This time she doesn't take the knife out but lets it go. I release Holic and he topples to the ground, where he takes his final breath.

Svetlana walks from the room, closing the bedroom door behind. My eyes meet Finn's and his are wide, staring at me like I've lost my mind.

Darragh's sniggers come from behind me. "She's definitely your girl-friend."

"Don't leave this room, either of you," I say, stepping over the body on the floor.

She's sitting in the corner of the room, her knees drawn to her face. She hasn't looked up and I take slow steps towards her. Kneeling down in front of her, I wait for her to look up at me. Her hands have blood on them. I never wanted that for her, but I think it was something she needed to do.

I don't ask her if she's okay. She isn't.

"I hate that I enjoyed that." She sniffles into her arms, still not allowing me to see her face. "I hate that he made me do that." Her body shakes with sobs and I move closer and touch her arms. She springs, nearly knocking me back, but I hold my balance and tighten my hold on her as she cries. Each time her body shakes, I want to go out there and plunge the knife into Holic's still form. His death was too clean for what he deserved, but I wasn't taking it away from Svetlana.

"I know this is hard but I need you to do something for me."

Svetlana looks at me for the first time, tears continue to stream down her face. I take her face in my hands. I can't protect her here, and that reality has me afraid.

She's nodding now, waiting to hear what I want from her.

"I'm going to send you to stay with my brother for a while."

"No." She's shaking her head. "I'm not leaving you."

"Svetlana, I can't protect you here."

Her lips tremble as tears make a pathway down her face and into her mouth. "I'm safe with you."

I wanted to remove my tie again. A tightness was making the air in the room limited. "No. You're going." I release her and stand up.

"You can't make me." She's standing too.

I smile at her boldness and take the two steps back to her. Taking her face in my hands, fear flickers across her face. When my lips touch hers, she kisses me back with a ferocity that shows her turmoil. Salty tears mingle with our kiss that I break. "I'll make the call." I release her quickly before I change my mind. I go back into the living room.

Darragh is lying on the couch, while Finn is standing over Holic staring at his body.

"Finn, tell Mary there is a dead body in the house and she needs to call the Gardai."

Both Darragh and Finn start to protest, and I raise a hand to silence them.

"Finn. Do as I say and then leave the house." Finn's jaw tightens, but he leaves the room.

"Want to tell me what fuckery you are up to?" Darragh is off the couch. I don't answer him as I take my phone out and ring Shane.

"I need Svetlana to stay with you and Una for a while. Darragh's taking her over now."

"We are here. I'm assuming you will explain later."

I glance at Darragh, who's waiting for answers too.

"Of course."

Placing the phone in my pocket, I turn as Svetlana steps out of the bedroom. Her earlier upset is gone.

"I need you to take Svetlana to Shane's." I turn to Darragh. "I'll explain everything later."

Darragh nods at me.

"Are you ready to go for a ride?" Darragh's boyish grin accompanies his words. For the first time, I'm grateful for his upbeat banter. I don't turn as they leave the room. Reaching down, I pull the knife from Holic's back and keep it held in my hand.

With my other hand, I pick up Holic's knife and take a deep breath before plunging it into my side. The pain that tears through me brings me to my knees. I bite down hard as not to shout out, but still a growl forces its way out. I take three more deep breaths and pull the knife from my side. Blood flows freely from the wound. The room tilts, but I need to stay alert. I push the knife that I just stabbed myself with into Holic's hand. The other knife I hold tightly and don't let it go as I wait for the Gardai to arrive.

CHAPTER THIRTY-TWO

LIAM

THE BLEEP OF A machine rouses me, I don't open my eyes straight away. I allow myself to adjust. My side aches, the tight stitches have me carefully exhaling. Taking shorter breaths I listen beyond the door to the hustle of the hospital before opening my eyes.

The weight of the metal on my wrist, has me pulling my arm causing the handcuff to rattle against the bar. No one was in the room but I could make a shadow who stood outside my door. The Gardai, no doubt. With my free hand, I push down the quilts and raise my top. The neat stitching on my side is commendable. A steady hand and a sharp eye. Whoever did this didn't rush, they really took care in stitching me. I drop my top as the door opens.

"Gardai Weldon." I yank on my restraints. "Is this necessary?"

He removes the set of keys from his pocket, as he makes wide strides over to my bed. I don't look away from him as he uncuffs me. His hands shake slightly, he's nervous.

"Why was I handcuffed?" I question while rubbing my wrists. Gardai Weldon still hasn't looked at me, and I'm starting to wonder what I am missing.

His eyes snap up to mine. "There was a dead body found in your home."

I nod. "Don't you want to take my statement about what happened?"

He swallows and looks away. "Gardai Brady wants to take it."

My spine straightens at that interfering man's name. He was a job I needed to move up to the top of my list.

"You will take my statement, Gardai Weldon," I say it carefully.

He fumbles, taking out a notepad and pen.

"That man broke into my home, stabbed me, so I retaliated."

He hasn't written anything down. His eyes dart around the room. "Retaliated? He was stabbed four times in the back."

"Maybe he fell on something. I acted in self-defense."

Gardai Weldon pockets his little notepad.

"So that means we are done here, Gardai Weldon. It's a case of self-defense."

He nods and exhales before he leaves the room. I sink back into the pillow as my exhaustion can't stay hidden anymore. Sweat makes a path down my back, my mouth feels dry. There is no water on my bedside table. I reach for my phone. The names blur slightly and I squeeze my eyes tightly before opening them. The contact names become clear. The door opens and a nurse steps in.

"Mr O'Reagan, you need to rest." She tilts her head as she approaches me. "You need to lie back down." She checks the monitors as she speaks.

I do lie back into the pillows, but I don't take my eyes off her as she jots down my stats. "I need water."

She flicks me a glance. "I'll get some now, you just have to rest. Is that a deal?"

I wasn't sure how to react to her words. They sounded almost playful. I wanted to tell her to just leave and get my water, but my silence seems sufficient for her as she gives me a soft smile and leaves.

Bringing the phone back up to my face, I have to squeeze my eyes again to focus.

"Did she get to you, safely?"

"Yeah, she is fine, Liam. Darragh said you killed one of the Czech people and rang it in. I'm starting to wonder if I'm missing something here."

"Was she upset?"

Shane exhales and he's moving around. No doubt pacing with impatience. "Yes. Una is with her. She's safe."

His words give my body permission to relax. I had no idea I was so wound up.

The door opens again and I'm glad the nurse has finally come back with my water. Glancing at the door, my whole body wakes up.

"I will ring you later," I say before hanging up.

"Mr. Novak." This I hadn't expected. I sit up, the burn in my side blurs my vision, but I continue to sit up fully and try not to react to the pain.

"Flowers? For me?"

He steps into the room and places the flowers on the table at the end of my bed.

"You are a very lucky man Mr. O'Reagan." He's wagging his finger at me, a sadistic smile on his face.

"I don't feel very lucky, Mr. Novak."

We stare at each other, he still stands at the end of my bed, and I can't wait to kill him.

"Where is she?"

"She's safe. He tried to kill her." I flinch as my body tightens and jerks towards him.

"Holic would never hurt her."

I clench my jaw and stare at him. He was delusional. "He tried to kill her. Are you calling me a liar?"

I dare you.

"Of course not, Mr. O'Reagan. But getting the Gardai involved wasn't a very smart move."

I nod in agreement. "It wasn't me, I had collapsed and our maid had found us, she rang it in."

His sharp blue eyes flicker across my face, searching for the lie.

"You killed one of my men Mr. Novak." I throw in my curveball and he blinks.

"That is a very serious accusation."

"I received his hands."

Mr. Novak shrugs. "Only his hands?"

"Yes."

"So he may be still alive." His eyes smile at me and I want to cut them out.

"Without his hands?" I bite out the words and the smile leaves his eyes.

"I'm not a doctor. Maybe Holic killed him."

"Maybe he did. I would like his body back." I wanted to bury Gregor. He deserved more than rotting away in some ditch.

"I will most certainly keep an eye out for a handless man."

The door opens again and the nurse steps in with a jug of water. She pauses as she takes in my visitor.

"I'm sorry, no flowers are allowed in the hospital." She gives Mr.Novak an apologetic smile.

"I will place them on my mother's grave." He smiles at her sweetly and she gobbles it up, before filling me a glass of water.

"I pray for your swift recovery, Mr. O'Reagan."

"Thank you."

He gives me one final look before leaving. The minute the door closes, I sink into the pillow and allow my body to scream.

"You're burning up." Water touches my lips and I accept it. The nurse fidgets with her machine and takes my blood pressure, but my body refuses to stay alert, and no matter how hard I fight I fall back into a deep black hole.

The bleep of the machine is the sound I wake up to. I keep my eyes closed as I listen. I'm not alone. Someone is sitting to my left. I stir and they stand.

"Liam?"

"Connor, how nice of you to visit me." I open my eyes. Connor is standing over me, his stance hostile, but it normally is towards me.

"You played your cards well."

I want to sit up. My side throbs, but I refuse to appear weak. I pull myself up.

"Let me help you." Connor steps closer and I'm tempted to accept, but I wave him off.

"I'm fine." Once I'm sitting up, I try to control the trembling that enters my body.

"What did your father say?" There was no point beating around the bush. I prayed my decision paid off.

"You won them over. Any doubt about your intentions is gone."

I feel triumphant. "You need to warn Tom that he has a rat in his high ranks."

Connor clenches his jaw. "Why is that Liam?"

"It was retaliation for me telling Tom about who hurt Margret. Someone told the Czech about it and they put a hit on me. I'm not safe now because of the foolishness of Tom's men. So they need to act fast."

Connor grins and sits down. "You should really stop while you're ahead."

"Why's that?"

"Tom is giving you his full backing. So I would leave it at that. You're smart Liam, but just not as smart as you think. Like why was Mr. Novak visiting you?"

"Was he? I didn't have any visitors."

He laughs. Its sharp and ends in a growl. "Finn said you weren't stabbed, he seemed rather confused when he was asked about it."

My whole body stalls and I try to keep my face impassive. "Finn is fragile." I pause and he clenches his jaw. "You know this. I think for our brother's sake he shouldn't have to answer questions. He has a tendency to get confused."

The chair scrapes as Connor stands abruptly. "You should be proud of yourself. You have won this battle."

I knew I had, but I needed to win the war.

"Did you speak to Darragh?"

Connor's ready to leave but pauses at the end of my bed. "About what?"

"About what happened."

He sneers. "His version was pretty impressive. He seems to have amnesia about the details. You really did a number on our brother."

I can't stay still this time, my body temperature jumps. "Everything I do, I do for my family. For my brothers."

He shakes his head. "You're a poison to them Liam. If you thought anything of your brothers you would leave them alone."

"You have no idea what you're saying." I bark at Connor and his eyes widen slightly at my unusual outburst.

"You might not hurt them directly, Liam, but you hurt them. You know what's the worst type of poison? A slow one."

"What about you Connor?"

His shoulders slump. "I don't blame you for anything that happens to me. It's on me."

"But do you not hold some responsibility to the downfall of your brothers?"

He stands up straighter, brows furrow, his head dipped. It's Connor's signature for when he's getting ready to lose his temper.

"I mean, you left them and it broke a part of Finn. Who picked up the pieces then?"

His fists tighten, his lip curls up. "It was hardly you."

I nod. "That is true, but like you said, I don't directly impact them, but I like to think I steer them all in the right direction. I had Shane watch over them."

"Is that all you wanted to say?" Connor's eyes bounce around the room, his anger and frustration growing around him.

"Just keep protecting them, Connor. No matter what you think of me."

He shakes his head before leaving. The door hits the wall as he storms from my hospital bed. The same nurse comes in and stares wide-eyed at Connor's receding form.

"Is everything okay, Mr. O'Reagan." She's facing me now.

"A family squabble," I say.

She refills my water and hands it to me. I drink it down whole.

"Are you in any pain?"

"No," I answer quickly. "Can you remove everything, please? I'm ready to leave."

She snorts a laugh as if I'm joking, but when she sees I'm not, her face grows serious.

She starts shaking her head, "Mr. O'Reagan, you could have died."

I take the drip out of my arm. "You either unhook me or I will do it myself." She starts to remove everything as I've requested. My stay here had filled its purpose. I had pitted the RA against the Czech successfully, now I just needed them to hurry up and wipe each other out.

***

The house is empty. Stephen is on the gate and he's the only life around the house. I pull the tape off the door that leads down to the basement. Holic's body is gone, but the area is still stained in blood. The knives are gone, but otherwise the space looks untouched.

The bed is unmade and I try to ignore the tightness in my chest. My home wasn't mine anymore. I'm sweating when I pull out a bag to pack some clothes in. Sitting on the bed, I take the painkillers that the doctor reluctantly gave me on my departure. The longer I sit, the thoughts of getting up grow more distant. My body is screaming for rest, my side aches, but I need to leave here.

Getting up my body protests, but I stuff clothes for me and Svetlana into the bag.

CHAPTER THIRTY-THREE

SVETLANA

I'm hovering at the door waiting for Liam to arrive.

"Where is he?" I bite my lip as I fold my arms across my chest. Shane steps out of a room to my left. He looks troubled and my heart squeezes.

"Is he okay?"

His head snaps up to me. He wasn't aware I was standing out here. But sitting in front of a TV trying to pretend that any of this was okay was killing me.

"Yes. He's recovering."

My body relaxes to hear he's fine. "Recovering from what?"

Shane looks away while stuffing his phone in his pocket. "I'd rather not say." He sounds unsure.

"Where is Liam?" My throat burns. Has something else happened? My accent is thick and when Shane doesn't answer me, I'm afraid he didn't understand, so I repeat myself. "Where is he?"

"Shane, tell her." It's Una, she's been really nice to me since I arrived, but I don't know these people. It's been two days stuck in this place waiting for word on how he is.

"Una." Shane's warning towards Una is half filled with begging.

She folds her arms across her chest and he sighs heavily.

"He's in hospital, but he's recovering well." Shane states.

I feel the room tilt. The idea that anything could hurt Liam seemed unreal. He seemed so untouchable, so the word hospital had me dredging up horrible images.

Una takes a step towards me. "Are you okay?" Her hand touches my arm and I move away, my focus back on Shane.

"What happened?"

He looks at me with confusion. "I thought you were there?"

The front door opens and my heart leaps into my throat, only to return to its resting place.

"How did you get a key?" Shane's snarl has Darragh removing his key from the door with a grin on his face.

"Relax, Una gave me one." He pockets the key and winks at Una.

"Are you going to tell me what happened?" My patience is slipping.

"Why don't we all move into the sitting room."

The hall was starting to feel cramped and the air thinner than before, but I just wanted to know about Liam. I'm in the door first and the moment Shane steps across the threshold I'm ready to hear.

"What's going on?" Darragh asks while throwing himself down on the couch.

Shane glances at him and his jaw clenches. "Can you sit on the couch correctly?"

Darragh sits up and crosses his legs while resting his hands on his knee. He looks ridiculous and Una laughs.

"Tell me now." My patience snaps and everyone turns to me like I'm mad. "He was stabbed."

I stumble back and reach for some support, but my hand only touches air.

"It's odd that you don't know this. Since you were there." Shane takes a step towards me and I blink, wondering what was going on.

"She was, but she's in shock and her English is pretty poor so she mixes up her words." Darragh has moved in front of me as he insults me while saving me.

"I don't need her words Darragh. It's written all over her face that she didn't know."

Darragh flickers me a glance over his shoulder. "Fine her English is better than mine, but seriously just leave her alone." Darragh returns to the couch, lying out across it like he had the first time. "Or he will kick your ass." Darragh grins up at Shane.

"Are you okay?" My attention snaps to Una, who has taken a step towards me. She was just trying to be nice and I wasn't making this easy.

"Yes. Thank you."

"Where was he stabbed?" I ask Shane, trying to keep some of my emotion in check.

"You got it bad for him." Darragh teases me from the couch, but I'm not entertained. I've sat here for two days thinking Liam was being questioned. I had remained quiet not asking questions but now to hear he was stabbed, had me wanting to run from here. I needed to see him.

"In the side. Svetlana, he is fine."

I cover my mouth with my hand, still reeling that someone stabbed him.

Finn, the quietest of all the brothers steps into the room. His eyes meet mine and he gives me a soft nod. The atmosphere in the room changes. Everyone smiles when they see him.

"You heard from Connor?" Darragh quizzes from the couch.

Finn seems to pale. "No. Why is he okay?"

"Jesus. Everyone needs to lighten up. He's grand." Darragh sits up straighter and takes a pack of cigarettes from his pocket.

"Don't fucking dare light that up in my house." Shane's strained and it's like he's ready to break at any second.

"Shane." Una warns.

"Yeah, relax. I wasn't going to spark it up." Darragh's grinning as he puts the fag behind his ear.

"No smoking in my home." Una reinforces and Shane glances at her.

Finn sits down across from Darragh.

"Why is it okay for you to say it?" Shane questions Una.

She smiles. "Because sweetheart. I ask nicely." She takes a few steps towards him and places a kiss on his cheek, it's like water on flames. He relaxes into her kiss.

"How are you holding up?" I startle at Finn's voice. Everyone watches me now and I hate it.

"I want to speak to Liam." I lay out my demands.

Darragh grins. "I still can't believe you have the hots for Liam."

My cheeks redden and I focus on Finn. He seems the most reasonable. "He was stabbed." I add and guilt fills Finn's eyes.

"Isn't it odd how she didn't already know that?" Shane's voice is tight. "You know, since she was there. I hope someone decides to tell me what's going on."

"You need better security. I was able to walk right in."

We all turn. Liam fills the doorway and it's like everything shrinks around him. He's there, standing in front of me. He's dressed all in black and right now he looks even more divine than he ever has. I exhale a shaky laugh before I go to him. I don't care who's looking as I wrap my arms around his neck. It takes him a moment to react. His strong arms wrap around me and I want to cry into his chest. His heart beats fast and it's another reminder that he is alive. I lean out so I can see his face. Tilting my head back, I touch his cheek where Holic had cut him. It's healing already.

"I missed you." I search his face, deep black eyes bounce from my lips to my eyes.

"I missed you too."

My face nearly splits in two at his words. I rest my head on his chest again and close my eyes. He was safe. He was here.

"I don't think I'll ever get used to it." Darragh's voice brings me back to the room. I had forgotten briefly about everyone else. I know I need to let Liam into the room.

"Don't be a dick." It's Finn who speaks up, and I know I have to release Liam. Sliding my arms down Liam's chest, he hisses and it reminds me of what Shane said about him being stabbed. When I had seen him standing in the doorway, he looked perfect. I was hoping that Shane had been wrong.

"What's wrong?" I step away, not wanting to hurt him any further.

"I'm fine."

I'm already shaking my head because I know he's not.

He removes the space between us and takes my face in his hands. "I promise. I'm fine." He places a kiss on my forehead that scorches my skin and worms its way to my heart.

"Shane said you were stabbed." I look up into Liam's eyes, but he's glancing behind me.

"I thought she was there?" Shane speaks from behind me.

"Let the man sit down." It's Una, always the diplomat.

She's right, he needs to sit down, a sheen of sweat is gathering on his forehead. I step away to let him and am startled when his fingers brush mine, before he takes my hand in his.

Darragh's on the couch and sits up as we approach. His eyes shine with laughter as he stares at our hands and I have the urge to tell him to stop, but these are Liam's family. I don't look at Shane with his angry eyes or Una with her sympathetic ones. Finn is the easiest person to focus on. We sit down and Liam releases my hand. He's struggling and no one says it as his face tightens. I bite my tongue but once we are alone, I won't stay quiet.

"Can I get anyone a tea or coffee?"

Shane smiles lovingly at Una.

"Tea would be nice." Liam speaks up and everyone seems surprised, but Una nods and leaves the sitting room.

"I'll go help her." Darragh's off the couch and Shane watches him as he leaves the room. His eyes are filled with distrust as he stares at his brother.

"How are you feeling?" It's Finn who speaks. His voice is calm.

"I'm fine. No one has to worry. How are you?" Liam asks and his voice sounds staged. It's odd, but Finn doesn't seem to notice.

"I'm here." Finn lets out a shaky laugh, that carries pain that has me looking away from him. I feel like I'm invading a very private moment and I don't want to.

Shane is standing at the fireplace and I glance up at him to find him watching me. My fingers search for Liam's hand and I find it. Shane's scary and angry and I sense he doesn't like me so much.

"I'm hoping you can explain things now." Shane plays with a ring on his finger.

"Not now, brother." I glance at Liam and fight a smile. It's so nice to hear his voice. It's so nice to see him. Feel him. My fingers tighten on his hand and he glances at me. It's brief, but it's enough to send my heart sailing.

Darragh arrives into the room with a tray. He seems to wear a permanent smirk that's filled with cockiness.

"Would you like some sugar?" He asks me and I swear he's fighting a smile.

"One please."

Once Darragh hands me the tea, I relax. I don't like letting Liam's hand go, but he's here right now in the warmth and safety in the room. With Liam at my side, I felt lucky.

"So how long am I putting you all up for?" Shane asks.

"Shane." The warning from Una is expected; even as she delivers it, she still gives Shane a smile. They were opposites but seemed to work so well together.

"You are all welcome here, but when will the house be safe for you to return to it?"

Shane's eyes widen. "You did it again. You asked what I just asked."

"I asked in a nicer way."

For the first time, I can't stop the smile that spreads across my face. Una catches my eye and smiles at me.

"Soon." That's all Liam says and they accept it as an answer.

"I'm kind of liking this spot. I think I might crash a little longer." Darragh takes his tea and biscuits over to the fireplace where he places them. Shane moves to the left to give Darragh room, but he looks at him like he's the bane of his existence. Darragh dips his biscuit into the tea before winking at Una. "I think Una doesn't want me to leave."

Una smiles at him and it's filled with a fondness and an understanding that he's just jesting.

"You're the first one out the door." Shane steps away from Darragh and sits down on an empty chair to his left.

After I place my empty cup on the coffee table, I lean back and close my eyes as the voices of the Irish brothers wafts over me. The sense of freedom and contentment I feel right now has a lump forming in my throat. It's been such a long time. Too long. The pain inside me escapes from under my lashes and runs down my cheeks even as I smile. My emotions are such a contradiction of each other. The brothers stop talking and I know there is a good chance that they see me smiling and crying, but right now, at this very moment, I refuse to apologize. Fingers tighten around mine and I open my eyes and look into Liam's dark ones.

"You're safe."

Salty tears make a path into my mouth. "I know. That's why I'm crying."

Liam faces me and runs his thumbs under my eyes, wiping away more falling tears. His hand leaves my face and he takes my hand, helping me off the couch.

"I will speak to you all tomorrow."

No one asks where we are going or says anything about me crying. There isn't even a smart remark from Darragh. Liam doesn't speak as we climb the stairs. Once we reach the landing, he pauses, unsure where to go now. I take the lead and bring him to my room. Opening the door, I feel nervous as we step in. Liam just has the ability to do that to me. I glance at him as he closes the door. I had told myself I wouldn't apologize for crying but right now I wonder why he isn't speaking, if maybe I embarrassed him in front of his family.

"I'm sorry for crying." I start and he closes the distance between us. My heart skyrockets, as he takes my face in his hands and presses his lips against mine. The kiss drops into my shoes and makes its way slowly back up through my body. My fingers hungrily cling to his wide shoulders. I'm panting when he breaks the kiss.

"I missed you," he says, like he's trying out a new language.

"I missed you too." I smile as my heart catches up with his words and decides to keep racing.

My eyes burn as I look into his. I love him. I know this, like I know I'm standing in this room. A part of me hates it. It's another form of a cage. I was sick of cages.

Liam leans in and his kiss this time is softer. My hands move to his stomach and he hisses in pain. I don't ask but raise his top. His right side is covered in a bandage and it's a reminder that he isn't immortal.

My eyes flicker to his. "Who did this?" I'm terrified in case it's my uncle, that he discovered that Holic is dead. "If it was my uncle, I'll tell him the truth. That I killed Holic." I look at my hands now and it's a reminder of what I did.

"Your uncle knows Holic is dead. But he didn't stab me. I did this to myself."

I take a step away from Liam. "What?" That made no sense, who in their right mind would do that to themselves and why.

"Why?"

"For you." He closes the distance again. "So I can keep you and keep my family safe."

"Keep me?" I'm parroting his words. I hear what he is saying, but nothing is sinking in.

He smiles and my heart leaps into my mouth.

"Yes. That is if you want to stay?"

My eyes and the back of my throat burn again. "I don't think I could walk away even if I wanted to." I speak the truth.

I rise up on the tips of my toes and plant a kiss on his lips. "Thank you for stabbing yourself to try to keep me." It sounds bizarre, and Liam lets out a soft laugh that rumbles through his chest and rattles my nerves.

I take his hand and bring him to the bed. "You need to lie down." I don't have to say it twice as he lies on the bed. I remove his shoes and his socks. Liam watches me as I move around the room and the power his stare holds is nearly crippling. Drawing the curtains, I kick off my boots and climb into the bed beside him. My body wants him so badly, but I move carefully beside him and give him a soft kiss on the cheek.

"Do you think it will work?" I ask, leaning up on one arm so I can look down on his handsome face.

"Time will tell."

I kiss his cheek again before lying down beside him. I'm careful where I place my arm. The love I feel for him is almost painful, and I never knew it could hurt like this.

CHAPTER THIRTY-THREE

SVETLANA

IT'S BEEN WEEKS THAT I've been in Shane's and Una's house. I get free rein of the house which is lovely and my lessons have resumed which I'm due to attend soon.

I empty the contents of my stomach into the toilet for the third time this morning. This is my morning routine and it scares the life out of me. My fear is what it means.

"Are you okay?" Sweat gathers at the nape of my neck .Flushing the toilet, I get up off the floor. "Yeah, just a second." I respond to Una. What was she doing in my room?

Facing the mirror, I wash my face only to have my stomach lift again. I make it to the toilet and get sick two more times before my stomach finally settles. I listen but can't hear anyone in my room. Washing my face again and brushing my teeth, I leave the bathroom.

"Are you okay?" Una is sitting on my bed.

"Yeah. I just ate something funny."

"Every morning?"

The blood drains from my face. "Please Una."

She holds up her hands and gets off the bed. "Svetlana, I'm here to help you. You can trust me."

Trust. What a powerful word. It was something that had the power to destroy people. But right now I had no one else. My vision blurs, but I swallow down the tears.

"I think I might be pregnant." Which was crazy. I didn't know it could happen after only a few times.

She's nodding like she already got that. I hadn't noticed she was holding anything until she steps towards me.

"I keep a few in my bathroom just in case."

I take the pregnancy test from Una and hate the shake that has entered my hands.

"You won't..."

She cuts me off. "I won't say a word to anyone."

"Are you scared?" She asks.

I give a shaky laugh. "Terrified." The funny thing was, I wasn't terrified to have a kid, being a mother would mean the world to me, and having Liam's baby made me love him even more. But I wasn't sure how he would react. We didn't know each other very long, and I had never thought about getting pregnant.

"Do you want some privacy or I can stay?" Una flicks her gaze to the pregnancy test.

"I'm good. Thank you."

"If you need me, I'm here." Una turns to leave and fear grips me.

"Maybe stay."

She smiles as she returns to the bed and sits down. It's awkward when I go to the toilet and pee on the stick. I'm not sure if I should sit in here and wait or go out to Una. It says it can take up to five minutes. It's only been a few seconds and already I can't stay calm. I open the bathroom door and Una stands up.

"I'm still waiting," I tell her and she sits back down.

"Do you have family?" She asks.

"No. It's just me and my uncle."

The thoughts of him frightened me even more now. "If he found out he would kill all of us."

Una pales. "He's really dangerous." She whispers.

I nod. "He will want me back." I'm shaking my head. "He won't stop." I'm talking out loud as I sit down on the bed beside Una. "If I'm pregnant." I touch my stomach and stand up abruptly, the thoughts of what he would do has me going to the bathroom. I left the test on the rim of the sink. Picking it up my stomach lunges and I half laugh, half cry as I hold on to the sink.

"Well?" Una sounds breathless as she stands behind me.

I hand her the test and she stares at it before she glances at me.

"Congratulations." She hands me the test but doesn't smile.

I stare down at the result window. I was pregnant.

Una steps out of the bathroom and I look up at her in confusion.

"You won't say anything."

She pauses at my bedroom door. "You have my word I won't." But something in her eyes is telling me a different story, one I have no idea how to decipher.

I hide the test at the back of the bathroom cupboard. I can't stop the onslaught of emotions I feel as I make my way to my lessons. One part of me feels like I'm walking on clouds, yet the other feels like it's dodging trip wires.

"Svetlana." Sam greets me with a warm smile.

I try to stay focused, but it's hard when my mind continues to wander to what's growing inside me. I had no idea how Liam would take it or when I should tell him. He had so much going on, I didn't think now was the right time.

The door opens to the study and my stomach twists as Liam steps in. He's wearing a gray suit and he looks amazing. I smile at him, but worry still lingers.

"Please continue." he instructs before unbuttoning his suit jacket and sitting down. He does this sometimes, just sits through my lessons and watches me. It's distracting as hell, but I normally love it. Today however, I fear he will see my nerves.

"You seem distracted." I kick myself. I had forgotten about Sam.

"Yeah. I didn't sleep so well," I tell him.

"You didn't?" This comes from Liam, who stares at me.

"No." I wasn't sure what else to say.

"Our lesson is over soon but I'm sure this once, that it is okay to finish a bit earlier." He's looking at Liam, asking his permission. Liam must give a nod of approval as Sam starts to gather up his books.

"Get some sleep." He tells me before leaving. Once the door closes I can sense Liam's eyes on me.

"You want to tell me what kept you awake last night?"

I can't face him. "Nothing."

He's moving and I close my eyes as he rests his hands on my shoulders gently.

I reach back and place my hands over his strong ones. My heart beats faster and I feel the want to tell him burn a pathway inside me. My hands automatically want to reach for my stomach, but I keep them on Liam's.

"Do you want to talk about Holic?" His question throws me as he releases my shoulders, my hands slide down into my lap. I focus on him as he walks around the table and sits down so he's facing me. My heart skips a beat when he's eyes bore into mine, prodding, curious and unsure.

"He's dead. What more is there to say."

Liam nods. "My thoughts exactly." Why did I feel disappointed in his answer? His brows furrow and it's an unusual expression on Liam who always seemed so put together, so controlled and untouchable, I was starting to learn he was none of those things and I loved that about him.

"But.. that is my thoughts on it. I don't believe that it's yours." He's trying to piece together a puzzle. It's like he knows it's not meant to sit in the box, that you are meant to make it up. He's a child learning to deal with not just emotions but understanding other people's. Right now, holding back my thoughts on Holic wasn't an option. I wanted to show him that he was right, that this is deeper, even if I didn't want to talk about Holic.

"You're right."

His eyes look a lot brighter at my response. So I continue. "Holic was home. That might sound dysfunctional." I glance down at my hands and a small laugh falls from my lips. "It is dysfunctional but even his cruelty was home." I nod as I swallow down the tears. "He loved me in his own warped way, and my uncle did that to him. He made him that way." My lip trembles and I swallow again. Liam hasn't as much as blinked, and I have no idea what he is thinking.

"I always hoped that I would never become like them, you know?" I swallow again and exhale as my eyes burn. The truth is rooted into my soul and I wish I could uproot it. "I'm not proud of what I've done." Tears fall and with them some of the pain. "I've become them."

Liam shakes his head. "You did what you needed to do to survive."

He didn't understand. "I enjoyed it, Liam," I confess.

"A part of me wishes you hadn't killed him either." His words are like a slap in the face and I flinch back.

"So I could have torn him apart, from limb to limb." His anger that he had held back through this conversation is there like something tangible in the room. It's fascinating watching him trying to reel it in. It's a glimpse of the darkness inside him, and I hate how much more I want to see. He scares me when he's like this, but I know he would never hurt me.

Liam stands up and comes around to me. Looking up into his eyes, my stomach squeezes and I think of the baby. Was it a tiny dot? Did it know that it's mother and father were here in the room? Would I raise it at home in the Czech amongst the lush green grass or would it be here with the O'Reagans?

Liam reaches out a hand and I take it as he helps me out of the chair. "I want you to feel safe here with me."

His words have a smile growing on my face. It's like him saying he loves me. The fact he wants me to feel safe with him, it really was a big step for Liam.

"I do." I rise up on the tip of my toes and plant a kiss on his lips. "I always feel safe with you, Liam." I kiss him again, he hasn't closed his eyes and neither have I. It's there on the tip of my tongue to tell him I love him.

"I don't think you are safe with me." I place a kiss on his jaw line. I inhale sharply as he places his hands on my hips, the heat of his hands burning my flesh.

"Why is that, Svetlana?" My name on his lips has my stomach twisting.

"I want you," I say and my heart beats a little faster.

"You have me." His hand leaves my side and touches me face, his eyes roam my face and my breath hitches in my chest as his lips tug up into a half smile.

I kiss his half smile and his lips mold around mine. I'm still gentle with him as he's healing slowly. The kiss grows deeper, his tongue demands entry that I grant. My body hums for him and I wonder if this feeling will ever leave or even fade. My body responds to Liam like it's the first time his hands touched me. I never seem to have enough of him. His fingers flitter along the hem of my jumper and I don't want him to hold back.

"Will we go upstairs?" I ask as his lips leave mine.

"You don't like this room?" He asks with a straight face and I giggle, Liam smiles and I want to tell him I love him but I don't as the door opens.

"Do you have a minute?" Shane asks and I step away from Liam trying to fix my clothes.

"Go ahead." Liam's response has Shane's eyes darting to me before they settle on his brother.

"Gardai are looking for you, you need to go down to the station."

I grip Liam's hand like I might be able to keep him here with me.

"It's alright. It's only standard questions." Liam explains. He leans in and kisses me softly on the forehead. I can almost feel Shane's irritation and I think it's towards me. When I look up, he's staring at me, and now I wonder if Una lied to me and told Shane. His gaze flickers away from me.

"I'll be back soon." Liam releases my face and I just nod. Once he steps away from me, I fold my arms across my chest. Liam pauses at the door and looks back at me.

"Get some sleep."

I force a smile. "I will. Be safe."

I have the urge to run to him and kiss him, but he leaves with Shane heavy on his heels.

When he gets back, I would tell him about the baby. My hands flutter to my stomach and I can't stop the smile that spills across my face. He will be an amazing father. I wish right now my parents were alive. What would my mother tell me right now? I had no idea what I was doing. I'd never changed a nappie or cleaned a runny nose. Fear clutches my throat and I try to loosen it by leaving the study and making my way upstairs. I needed to rest. Maybe some rest would help and when I woke up, I prayed that Liam would be back home and I would tell him that he was going to be a father.

CHAPTER THIRTY-FOUR

LIAM

I DON'T WANT TO leave Svetlana. Something doesn't feel right with her. When she spoke of Holic, my fear was that maybe some part of her loved him too. That thought, I couldn't bear.

"You will take care of her," I speak to Shane, as I climb into my car. Once I'm seated, I look up at him.

"Of course." He didn't seem to like her, but I didn't care about that. All I needed to know was that he would keep her safe. "Like you would with Una," I state.

His eyes widened slightly. "For you, yes."

That's all I needed to hear. I close the door and reverse out of Shane's garage.

***

"Peter," I greet my solicitor as we make our way into Navan Gardaí station.

"My advice is the same as always. Try not to respond." Peter's advice is said as we arrive at the front desk. Gardaí Weldon is there, ready and waiting for us. He's nervous and it's a reminder that I need to employ more Gardaí, ones who don't look like they are working with the enemy.

"This way, Mr. O' Reagan."

I follow him to a room off the left. It's a basic interrogation room. Peter and I sit facing the wall while Gardaí Weldon sits down across from us, the chair beside him empty. Maybe that's why he is nervous.

"Are we waiting for someone else?" I ask.

The door opens and Gardaí Phillips arrives. His intelligent eyes meet mine.

"Gardaí Philips. It's been a while," I state. He doesn't respond, as he opens his file and takes out a pen. He wasn't on my payroll. This wasn't going to be easy. But, at least now I understand what made Weldon so nervous.

Gardaí Philips was an Army sergeant, now he was over the Criminal Assets Investigations of Ireland, or the CALL.

"Liam O 'Reagan," he says my name slowly, and he sports a smile that I want to wipe off his face. "It has been a while. How is your brother? The one who lost his wife?"

"Great. Thank you so much for asking. I didn't realize that this was a personal chat, Gardaí Philips, but since it is, how is your wife and son, Luke isn't it?"

He bristles. "Darragh has been asking after him. I do recall at your last meeting you had a personal chat about it."

Anger tightens his fist. I knew it wasn't wise to poke at him, but I couldn't help it. It normally was wise when it rattled some of them and they stepped away. With Gardaí Philip I could tell it was going to push him forward in his quest to destroy my family, as he had once promised.

He returns his focus back to the file.

"Holic Cerny was found dead at your premises four days ago. He had multiple stab wounds to his back. A knife with your fingerprints was found at the scene." He's reading what is written in front of him.

"You want to tell me what happened?"

Peter places his hand in front of me, his cue for me to remain silent.

"He broke into my home and attacked me. I acted in self-defense," I answer.

He checks his notes. "I don't see anything here about someone breaking and entering."

Peter's hand once again rests in front of me.

"The house was unlocked. But I did inform Gardai Brady about the events. Maybe your staff need to become more thorough with their work. "

Gardai Philips smiles and he closes the file. "Why don't you tell me your fairytale of the night's events."

"Gardai Brady took my statement already. I suggest you go find it." I speak to Gardai Weldon who starts to get up.

Philips stops him. "Sit down."

When he doesn't, Philips stares at him. "I pay your wages, not him. So sit down." There it was, he knew he was on my payroll. Gardai Weldon sits back down.

"Please, just tell me what happened."

Peter's hand appears in front of me again and for the first time I'm thinking about heeding his warning to stay quiet.

"What are you charging my client with?" Peter asks.

Philips doesn't look away from me. "I've got a list of crimes."

"Ones that you can prove?" I question.

His smirk is quick, nothing more than an angry flash. "This interview is just to clear up a few formalities in your statement."

"So you have read my statement."

"It was three lines, so using the word statement is a stretch. What were you doing before Holic Cerny allegedly attacked you?"

"I have nothing to say." I could have given him a million things. Eating, resting, watching tv. But now I didn't want to cooperate.

"Mr Cerny, was a highly trained member of the Czech gang run by a Mr. Novak who is in this country. Do you know anything about Mr. Novak?"

"I have nothing to say."

He smirks again, that quick one that tells me he's getting irritated.

"To think a highly skilled man only managed to stab you in the side, it seems so unprofessional. He doesn't seem like a man who was inaccurate with knives."

I just stare at Philps.

"And to think he was stabbed not once," His fist hits the table. "Not twice." Again it slams down, but I don't look away or flinch. "But four times."

Now he starts to laugh. "And to think you still haven't been arrested. That you are walking around like you did nothing."

I speak very calmly and slowly. "I told Gardai Brady that I acted in self-defense."

His fist hits the table again. "Is he another one you have bought?" He's out of his seat, leaning across the table.

"This is harassment of my client." Peter speaks up as the door opens.

"Philips." The man that speaks from the door I don't recognize. He doesn't look at me. Philips looks at him from over his shoulder and he pushes away from the table, and leaves the room with the other man.

I'm left with Gardai Weldon. "Who was that?" I ask him. He points at the door and I nod.

"He's the head of our department. Mike Gordon."

I nod.

"Does he outrank Philips?"

"Yes." Weldon looks nervous now.

"I would like for you to arrange a meeting with me and Mike Gordon, I would like to discuss the harassment I've been receiving from certain members of the Gardaí Siochana."

"I can do that."

Weldon sits there looking from me to Peter.

"Now please."

He stands up but pauses before leaving. "You know, this won't stop Philips."

We will see about that.

I don't respond and he leaves.

"You need to start listening to me, Liam. When I say don't speak..."

I cut him off. "When you say don't speak I will consider your advice. I may not take it, Peter."

I turn to him now and he nods in understanding of what I am saying.

***

It takes another two hours before I'm released without charge. Having Mike Gordan on our payroll was something that could stop these over-achievers, who rise from nowhere, and decide that the O' Reagans will be their trophy.

I drive to the house just to make sure no one has come. I don't like the idea of anyone being inside our home. I had the locks changed, even against Peter's advice. Stephen lets me in and I notice immediately that I'm not alone. Finn's jeep is parked out front, I had no idea what he was doing here after I forbade them from entering, until I got rid of Mr. Novak. I leave my car parked behind Finn's jeep and go in the front door. I don't call out but make my way through the downstairs of the house. I find Finn sitting at the head of the dining room table. My eyes immediately go to the plaque that hangs over his head.

Chlann is the singular word on it. The meaning of it is Family. It's what everything we do is for. Family.

"What are you doing here?" I ask from the door. When Finn looks up at me, his eyes gleam with tears that he fights not to spill. His fist is placed over his mouth that he removes now.

"I thought I'd sit here and see if the men who killed my wife came back to hurt us. In my head..." He looks away from me. "I kill them for taking her." Now he looks at me and it's not just pain I see in his eyes, it's alcohol too. "But it won't bring her back." He blinks and tears spill down his face.

"Do you know what the worst part is?" He's standing now as he wipes his face roughly. He's far more intoxicated than I thought. "I'm a coward and I couldn't even take their lives if I wanted to."

"That makes you brave, Finn," I tell him.

His roar fills every space in the room. Pain amplifies it and rips at him. "I'm weak. I hate how powerless I am. She's gone."

He takes another unsure step towards me. "I lost her." His pain is crippling him and I don't put myself in his shoes. I try to keep the same distance I've always kept from this kind of emotion. It was weak and would do him no good.

"You are weak," I tell him.

He seems to stand a bit straighter and he gives me the strangest look; I can't decipher it.

"You just said two seconds ago I was brave, now I'm weak?"

"You are brave for not killing those men, because it won't bring her back and that's what I'm here for. I'll take care of them. But right now, you're weak and she would hate to see you like this."

His shoulders slump forward.

"Go home."

He sniffles. "I actually thought you were Connor. I rang him to pick me up."

The doorbell rings on cue. "I'll get it."

Finn sits back down at the table as I leave him. My hand goes slowly to the gun that's in the waistband of my trousers. I open the door, ready for whoever it is. It's Connor.

"Is he okay?" He's trying to bust past me but I jam the door with my foot, making Connor take a step back. "One of your friends killed his wife and you are refusing to give the name of that person. So no, your brother isn't in a good place." I remove my foot and he isn't so eager to enter now.

"Maybe if you tell me who killed our mother."

I let him in and close the door. "I didn't kill her Connor," I say and he sneers.

"What? I'm just meant to take your word for it?"

"Yes. You seem to forget that I was the first born. I loved her just like you." He doesn't respond.

"Now, you can take your over-intoxicated brother out of the house and try to keep him away."

He still doesn't move. "You never see me as your equal. You think because I was born from the affair that that makes me less."

"I knew of the affair. You being born from Tom didn't bother me, Connor. It was your own disregard for this family that made me dislike you, but no matter what, you are family. Even Tom lives by that rule." I pause. "Or he once did. But I swear to you if you help me keep our family safe, I will help you figure out what happened to our mother." I put out my hand for him to take, the conflict rattles across his jaw that flexes, but he takes my hand.

Connor steps away and once he takes Finn out to his car, I lock up the house and leave too. I'm anxious to see Svetlana.

Returning to Shane's house, I try not to give in to my instincts and push my foot down on the peddle. Two Gardai cars are parked out front of the house. Had they changed their mind about me and decided to arrest me? I would work my way out of it, but Svetlana was here and that terrified me more than anything. I leave my gun in the glove box before getting out of the car.

Shane meets me at his front door. He gives me a nod and something in me relaxes. He was telling me it was okay.

Two officers are in the sitting room. I look around quickly, but they are the only occupants of the room. Opening my jacket, I sit down.

"Earlier today a body was discovered in the Headfort Arms in Kells. We believe the hotel is registered in your name."

I nod and glance at Shane, who has joined us.

"The hotel has been closed as forensics investigate it. It is now a crime scene."

God damn it.

"Of course. I will comply in any way necessary," I say and the Gardaí nods.

"How was she killed and was she a member of my staff?"

"A Bernie Hughes."

She was a prostitute.

"Her knee caps were blown out and a kill shot to her head after."

I glance at Shane and his jaw tightens. The R.A. They were sending a message, shutting down my business. Cutting off my money. It was clever but wouldn't make a dent in my operations. Still, the fact I had believed to have them on my side set this whole thing back.

"I do appreciate you coming out to tell us."

We all stand and they place their hats back on their heads before leaving.

"What are you going to do?" Shane asks as Connor steps into the room.

"Finn is in bed," he says. "What were the Gardai doing here?"

I look at Connor now, really look at him. He had so much inside knowledge. He had access to both sides. Access to the head of both families.

"There was an attack on one of my hotels."

I stare at him and Shane.

Connor shrugs. "What did they take? Money? I'm sure you've plenty stashed away."

I take a step towards Connor. "They killed a girl, shot out her knees before killing her."

His face falls slightly, but not enough for my liking. "But you knew that already."

"Connor?" Shane steps forward and I stop him.

"You've conspired with him once, so my advice to you is to remain silent."

I turn back to Connor. "This is war and you are standing on the wrong side."

"I didn't do this." Connor for the first time is looking panicked.

"Liam, I just swore to protect our family. Why would I do this?"

"You may not have done it yourself, but you know who did."

His silence is my answer.

"You betrayed us?" Shane sounds hurt and it's naïve of him to even think of trusting Connor.

"This is what separates you from us," I say.

Connor sneers. "Fuck you, Liam. I'm not your lapdog. I don't take orders."

"But you do."

"No. This was nothing to do with the R.A. This was a one-man job. I swear. I tried to stop him, but he's hell bent on revenge. "

"Who? Tell me who and prove your loyalty to your brothers."

Connor turns away from me and I can see the conflict on his face. "I can't."

Shane moves quickly and grabs Connor. He could never win a fight with Connor. None of us could.

"You've never considered me family, Shane. Now let me go." Shane releases him and steps back.

"Here is the warning you can take back to your family. I will be attacking." I close the button on my jacket and walk past Connor.

"Don't Liam. I'll tell you who did it."

Something in me breathes. I've relaxed since I discovered this person acted alone. It meant the plan with the RA will still go ahead, and we can wipe out Novak. The second thing that allows me to breathe is Connor is loyal to us, he just fights it too hard.

I stop but don't turn around.

"It's revenge for his sister, Margret. He's like a brother to me, Liam."

Now I turn around at the pleading in his voice. "He jeopardized my business. They have closed my hotel. No doubt questioning my staff."

"You and I both know that can be mended. He's had his revenge and he will stop."

"What are you asking?" Shane sounds disgusted.

"Spare him." Connor looks at me.

"I want his name."

Connor is already shaking his head, a look of defeat in his eyes. "Please, Liam."

"His name or I will retaliate."

"Matt... Matt Griffin."

CHAPTER THIRTY-FIVE

LIAM

CONNOR LEAVES AND SOMETHING inside me tugs. Shane hasn't spoken and I can see the weight on his shoulders. When I look at him, he shrugs. "What happens now? Are you going to kill Matt?"

"I don't know," I answer honestly. I didn't want to act on emotion, I needed to think about what was the most effective way to proceed with this.

"We will talk later." I leave and go upstairs, seeing Svetlana is the only thing that is keeping me going. She's what this is all for. To keep her. I open the bedroom door and feel a pang when I discover it empty.

"Svetlana?" I call as I push the half-open door into the bathroom. It's empty. I remove my suit jacket and tie, before going back downstairs. Shane is still in the front room, standing at the fireplace.

"Have you seen Svetlana?"

"She could be asleep."

"No. I've just checked her room." Something stirs in me.

"She could be with Una."

I nod and go to the kitchen. Una has her back to me, while she washes the plates. When I step in, she turns to me.

"Hi." She sounds off, like her voice is raised too high. "You okay?" She sounds like herself again and I shake off the odd feeling.

"Have you seen Svetlana?"

She smiles and nods. "Yeah, she's in her room."

I'm staring at Una and she stares back, water dripping off her yellow rubber gloves onto the floor.

"You're dripping water onto the floor," I say.

She gives a laugh. "Are you okay?" She asks again while removing her gloves.

"Fine." I turn and leave her to check the study, but Svetlana isn't there. I pass the front room again, Shane looks up at me.

"I can't find her." My voice is low as I turn for the stairs and take it two steps at a time. Each bedroom door I open, I know she isn't in.

"Svetlana," Una calls. We pass each other on the landing and she squeezes my arm. "It will be okay."

I appreciate her helping. After searching upstairs, we move downstairs. Each empty room has my stomach plummeting.

"Ring Connor and Finn. I'll call Darragh," I say to Shane.

I try to remain calm as Darragh's phone rings out.

"Is Svetlana with you?" I ask and try to remain calm.

"No. Why? Did she finally get a grip and run?" He's joking, but deep down that is the fear. I hang up on him. Shane's finished too.

"Una is asking Finn now. He's still asleep and Connor said no."

"Someone took her."

He's shaking his head. "No one took her, Shane. There is no way anyone got into this house without my knowledge."

Una steps into the room. "Finn hasn't seen her either."

My heart is pumping too fast in my chest.

Una takes a step towards me and her eyes soften. "Maybe she ran away," she says softly.

"Did she say something to you?"

She swallows and looks away.

"This is no time to keep secrets, Una," Shane says, and she looks up at him and nods.

"You're right. She hadn't said it, but I knew she missed her home and she was afraid of her uncle. She was afraid that he would find her."

Something deep inside pulls at my heart. "I told her she was safe. She had no reason to be afraid. I would protect her."

Una's eyes water. "Oh, Liam." She reaches out and touches my arm. "I'm so sorry." She blinks and her tears fall.

A part of me didn't believe that she ran away, but she had every reason to run. I hadn't exactly kept her safe.

"She wouldn't leave me," I say the words out loud and step away from Shane and Una.

I race up the stairs again, my heart pounding faster at each step I take. I enter our room and open the wardrobe. Pain sears me and it feels so physical. Some of her clothes were gone. She really had left me. I don't know how long I've been staring into the wardrobe, but when I look up Shane is there.

"I want you to find everything you can on Mike Gordon."

Shane steps into the room and I gently close the wardrobe door.

"Liam, you need to talk to me."

"I just told you what I need you to do. What do you want me to talk about?" I pick my tie up off the bed and put it on.

"About Svetlana. I know she meant a lot to you."

"She decided to leave. What can I do?" Once I have my tie on, I pick up my jacket.

"I don't know but..."

"I'm not like you. I don't break down on a whim. Do as I've asked."

Shane's eyes widen briefly as I pull my jacket on. By the time I close the buttons, his composure has returned. He gives me a brief nod and leaves the room.

Taking out my phone, I step onto the landing and glance around me. A part of me remembers her unease earlier. I knew she was hiding something, but leaving me wasn't what I thought it would be. Taking out my phone, I hit Sam's name.

"Mr. Novak's niece has run off, no doubt she may go back to him." As I speak the words into the phone I know they aren't true. She was terrified of him.

"If you hear anything regarding Svetlana, you let me know straight away."

"I've heard nothing. But if I do, I'll ring it in, Boss."

"Thank you, Sam." I hang up and slip my phone back into my pocket. My legs won't move, they won't obey me. I loosen the tie around my neck. It didn't make sense to me.

Leaving the house, I pull the tie off completely and fold it before putting it in my pocket. It's a long walk down the gravel driveway from Shane's house. How far could she have gotten. Every fiber of my being wants to start searching for her and bring her back to where she belongs. I reach up and open the top button of my shirt.

The hut near the entrance comes into view. The surrounding greenery has grown around it and ivy hides it from one side. As I walk around to the window, Jim, Shane's gate man, stands up and pushes the window open.

"Jim. I'm Liam O'Reagan, Shane's brother." Jim looks behind me no doubt wondering how I got here.

"I thought a walk would be nice." I answer his unspoken question.

He nods his head. "Once it's not raining, it's not so bad," he answers while sitting back down.

"Today, from when your shift started. Can you tell me who has come in and out of the property." I knew the chances that Svetlana walking out the front gate were zero, but my mind wouldn't let it go that someone may have taken her. I watch Jim's reaction while he answers me.

I focus on his eyes, body language. I'm searching for a nervous tick, a sign that he's lying.

"The only person who left was Una, that was a few hours ago."

I hate that he's telling the truth. I want someone to blame for her leaving, but I know who to blame. Myself. I couldn't keep her safe. Una spoke the truth.

I return to the house with the intentions of questioning Una again. I want to hear the conversation she had with Svetlana, word for word. I can't find either herself or Shane.

The interior of Shane's pool room that acts as a bar isn't that much different from father's. A lot of the house has that same décor. I don't think Una was the designer. No one is in here and searching upstairs wasn't something I was going to do. Removing my suit jacket, I place it on the couch and open another button on my shirt. The air seemed thin. Pouring myself a glass of brandy I drink it down and it washes away some of the burning that I now associate with Svetlana. It's pain, pain I have never felt before.

I pour another glass while walking to the window and opening it wide, allowing some of the air into the room. My mind springs to Svetlana's smiling face before jumping to my mother's dead one. I drink the glass down while looking at the pictures that Una and Shane have hung on the wall. One of our family has me pausing. It's a few years old. We are all standing around our father who sits on a high-back chair. I'm directly behind him, Shane to his right and Finn to his left. Darragh is beside Shane and Connor beside Finn. Not one of us looks happy. Darragh is smirking into the camera, but it's fueled with chaos. Shane stands proud, but something in the way he holds his shoulders shows his discomfort with the photo. With being a part of something bigger than him and I. Connor, I find my lips tugging up, he was the strongest of us all. He wasn't fully like us and sometimes I envied him for that.

The glass feels heavy in my hand as I stare at my father's eyes. He is proud, proud to have his family around him, arrogance shines from him and I tighten my hold on the glass. I leave the picture and refill my glass, the oxygen level in the room seems to be returning to normal. I sip the drink as I continue to look at pictures of Una and Shane, most of them are Una with horses, but one of her and Shane lying on the ground, the picture taken from above shows me a carefree Shane, a side to my brother I've never seen. He looks ... happy.

I finish my drink and fill another. The buzz in my head is nice.

"Liam?"

I don't turn as Una enters the room. I finish my drink before turning to her. She halts in her steps. The nervous twitch she always displays around me is there. Right now it seems worse. She swallows as her eyes shoot to the glass.

"I didn't peg you for a drinker?" She's forcing a smile. The strain has me quickly watching her body language. She was too tense, too still. Her eyes flicker to the left.

"I want to hear the conversation you had with Svetlana," I say.

Her hand flutters to a necklace that dangles a half heart on the end of it. "Just that she was afraid."

I shake my head. "I want a word-for-word conversation."

She swallows again. "She was afraid that he would find her."

I shake my head. Irritation growing too fast. "Where were you when this conversation took place? What was she wearing? How did the conversation start? I want a full description, Una."

Her eyes glisten as they fill with tears. "I'm so sorry, Liam. But this won't do you any good."

I look over Una's shoulder as Shane steps into the room. I'm the enemy, I can see it in his eyes. He hasn't blinked or taken his eyes off me as he makes his way to Una. She jumps as he places his hand on her shoulder. When she turns to him, he looks away from me, instantly his whole body language softens.

"It's okay." He rubs tears from her eyes and something in me twists. I refill my glass and keep my back to them until I hear the door close. I know Shane is still here.

"She told you everything. Don't forget, we opened our doors to Svetlana. We aren't the bad guys here."

I finish my drink and reach out for the bottle that disappears. Shane comes into view holding it.

"What? I'm the bad guy?"

He shrugs. "I don't know, but what I do know is that you drinking yourself into a state isn't good for this family."

He was right. I knew he was. If one of them acted out like this, I wouldn't have it.

"Finn coming home drunk is bad enough without you starting." He puts the lid on the bottle and removes my glass. I don't stop him.

"Jim. How well do you know him?"

Shane glances up at me as he places the bottle back on the shelf. "Everyone who works for me has been screened by me personally. He's loyal."

I want to find a kink in Shane's armor. I wanted someone to be responsible, but it was still looking like it was coming full circle.

I was the reason she left.

"Liam. We need you." Shane's leaning over the bar and I nod. I don't feel the dedication I usually feel, but I knew I had to be there for my family. We both look up as the door opens and Darragh steps in.

He raises both eyebrows. "Bad time?" He quizzes.

I stop Shane from speaking. "No."

He nods and steps in.

Shane leaves the room and Darragh watches him go with narrowed eyes. "What's up with him?" he asks, going behind the bar and getting himself a drink, oblivious to my turmoil.

He takes a bottle of beer out of the fridge. Kicking the door closed with his foot, he opens the bottle. His movements are always so carefree. The lid of the bottle hits the bar and he leaves it there. When he looks up to find me watching him, he raises the bottle to his lips and drinks deeply.

"You want one?" He asks the longer I stare at him.

"No."

He grins now. "Are you drunk?" He moves around the bar and sits down. "It must be the apocalypse." He takes another long swallow and I envy his carefree manner, yet the darkness that haunts him is in his eyes, a darkness that I have the power to remove.

"Just needed a drink," I finally say.

He raises both brows before taking another long swallow. "Yeah, me and you both." He puts the half empty bottle down on the bar.

"You didn't kill her," I say without blinking.

His brows furrow and Darragh grips the bar stool tightly. I can see the immediate shift in him. "What are you talking about?" he's whispering.

"Mother," I answer.

He flinches before looking away from me. He picks up the bottle and drinks more down. He places it back on the counter and when he looks at me, he shakes his head. "You said I did." His words are shaky, like someone standing on the edge of a cliff during a storm. One wrong word and it would all go over the edge.

"I didn't. You said it. Not me."

"Are you fucking with me?" He stands up abruptly and the stool wobbles as he gets up but doesn't fall over. "You said I fucking strangled her." He holds out his hands. A vein throbs in his neck. "With my hands." He holds them up. "These hands." His roar rushes across my face.

"I never said that, you said all that. I just never corrected you." I stand now as he takes a step towards me.

"Why are you doing this to me?" Pain fills his words.

"I'm telling you the truth." I want to end this conversation. I step away, but Darragh blocks me.

"If I didn't kill her, did you?"

I don't answer him.

His laughter is sharp and quick. "Is this the part where I fill in the fucking blanks? Again." His fist smashes into his open palm.

"You didn't do it. That's all that matters."

His hands slam into my chest. I stare at Darragh in surprise. I didn't expect that. "We're done." His words aren't filled with anger or hurt. They are filled with pain. Just pain that blurs his eyes as he turns on his heel and storms from the room.

I stare at the door. "That went well," I tell myself as I go behind the bar, and take back down the bottle of Brandy that Shane had put away. I pour myself a drink, and try to drown out all the voices that want to haunt me.

CHAPTER THIRTY-SIX

LIAM

T HIS TIME TOM MEETS me in Cabra Castle. Danny, one of the security men, is holding the door open for me. Straight away I think of Gregor. Funny, but I miss him.

After Darragh left me, I drank until … until I don't remember what happened. I woke up on the couch in Shane's house with a blanket over me. The moment I had woken up, I'd reached for Svetlana, who wasn't beside me.

"Tom," I greet my uncle as I step into the meeting room. He stands. I glance around, he is alone as I had requested.

"Searching me wasn't necessary," he states straight away.

He was right it wasn't, but it reinforced my distrust of him.

"I'm afraid it is." I open my suit jacket, and sit down.

Tom stares at me, his eyes so like fathers. He sits. "The boy who did this is from a good family."

When I don't respond, Tom continues.

"He was trying to avenge his sister, Margret. He acted alone."

"Margret was killed by the Czech. You know this Tom." I place both hands on the table. "This boy Matt, is he the one that killed Siobhan?" I ask.

"Yes. When we find him, we will hand him over."

I force a grin. "Find him? As in he is lost?"

How very convenient. They were lucky I had other plans for Matt. "When he is found, he is mine." I declare to Tom and reach out my hand to his.

He takes it and we shake.

"See you soon." Tom releases my hand and leaves the room. My phone rings, the sound louder. I wince with the pain in my head. Taking out my phone, I exhale as I see Connor's name flash up on the screen. Tom wasn't even out of the building.

"You are quick."

"What did he say?" Connor speaks like he expects an answer. Normally I would be careful with my words but by the end of this I don't think anything would remain hidden.

"He told me that Matt is responsible, and that he acted alone. I know he killed Siobhan, and he will be handed over to me."

Connor curses down the phone.

I leave the meeting room.

"Liam. He's not a bad person."

"Why don't you tell that to your brother, Finn?"

"This won't bring her back," he barks.

I stop walking. "What will keeping him alive do? It will be a reminder that you can hurt the O' Reagan's and nothing happens. What then? Maybe they will target Darragh next?" I start walking again and leave Cabra Castle.

"Just promise me when you get him you'll let me talk to him before anything happens?"

"No." I end the call.

Outside in the cool air, I inhale deeply as I pull off my tie. It was becoming irrelevant wearing them lately. They spent more time in my trousers pockets, than around my neck. I return to Shane's house. Jim opens the gates to allow me to drive in, I don't move past the hut and he pops his head out the window.

"Yesterday, are you one hundred percent sure that only Una left the premises?"

"Yes." His answer is so definite. I hate it.

"What time?"

He picks up a clipboard and stares at it. "Twelve fifteen."

"You record it all?"

He nods. "Shane's orders."

I enter the house. The smell of cooking from the kitchen has my stomach heaving. Another beautiful effect of drinking.

Any news to report? I text Sam. He has no news. If he did, he would have rang me. But I needed to feel like I was doing something.

The smell of bacon is strong as I step into the kitchen. Una is at the cooker and she glances at me over her shoulder. She wasn't expecting me, I can tell by how her face drops but she recovers.

"Hi Liam."

"Una." I move around her and make a cup of tea. She doesn't speak as she flips the bacon, but a slight tremble in her hand catches my attention.

"I'm sorry about yesterday," I say.

She glances at me. Her eyes soften. "It's okay." She gives a little shrug before refocusing on the bacon. I make my tea in silence, but I keep snatching glances at Una. She's snatching glances at me too and something isn't right.

"I just was worried in case I had missed something." I sip my tea but glance at Una over the rim.

She shakes her head without looking at me. "No. I told you everything."

She was lying. The tea turns sour in my stomach.

"Would you mind telling me again?" I open the top button of my shirt. The air feels thin.

"Why aren't you answering your phone?" The demand comes from Connor, who enters the room with Shane.

"We have nothing more to discuss."

"Like hell we don't. You hung up on me." Connor is filling the room, his anger growing faster than his steps that he takes towards me.

I glance at Una, who's watching us. "I would like to hear the conversation again," I say to Una.

"I told you everything," Una says.

Shane kisses her on the top of the head before looking at me. "I told you to leave it," he says to me.

"I'm asking her a question." I step around Shane and when he stands in my way, I take a step back.

Una turns around from the frying pan. "Maybe it's a good thing she's gone."

Her outburst has Shane glancing at her.

"What do you mean?" I'm staying calm, but now I know she knows more.

"What if he comes here looking for her? You put her in my home, Liam. You put us at risk by placing her here."

Each word that leaves her mouth has me tightening my fists. "What did you do?"

I take a step towards her without even being aware. It's not until Connor and Shane block me.

"I'm asking her a question. I'd advise both of you to move right now."

"She was ripping this family apart. She was a danger." The accusations that pour from Una's lips choke me.

"You need to calm down." This comes from Shane and for the first time I take three steps away from them, because right now I'm not sure what I'm capable of.

Connor stares at me wearily as Shane turns and walks back to Una. "Sweetheart." Shane takes Una's face in his hands. "It's okay, but you have to tell us."

"I had to."

My heart pounds rapidly in my chest. "Is she dead?"

Una's eyes widen. "No, I would never do that."

I exhale loudly and run my hands across my face. I had expected to hear that she was. "Where is she?"

Una shakes her head. "She's safe."

I take a step towards her. "Speak now, Una. Where is she?"

Connor moves into my line of sight again and I try to keep it together.

"I hid her. She's safe."

"Did you both plan this?" Shane asks and he looks dumbfounded that she could keep something like this from him.

She doesn't answer but tilts her head. It was taking every ounce of strength I had to stand here and wait until she was ready to speak.

"No. I forced her."

"Jesus Christ. What were you thinking?" Shane asks and he looks a little stunned. Connor hasn't taken his eyes off me.

"Just tell me where she is and I will let this go."

"No." Una blinks rapidly.

"Una. What are you doing?" Shane shakes his head in confusion. The fire alarm rings and the smell of cremated bacon fills the kitchen.

Shane reaches behind Una and takes the pan, throwing it into the sink. I clear the three spaces that separate me and Una. Connor is beside me, but doesn't touch me. Shane's eyes flash and he's moving.

"Where is she?" I'm toe-to-toe with her. Pleading with her. Something I have never done.

Una's eyes fill with tears. "She caused so much, Liam."

I tighten my fists at my sides and hold them there. All I want to do is strangle the truth from her.

"Where is she?"

Una jumps at my raised voice and Shane pushes me away from her.

"He would come here for her, Liam." Una pleading and crying doesn't matter. I don't care if she bleeds on the floor in front of me. I want to know where Svetlana is.

"When he finds out, he will kill all of us. She said it herself that he would kill all of us."

"I want you to listen to me. We all need to calm down." Shane's voice I focus on right now. He's holding my face and over the ringing alarm and my own heartbeat, I focus on his words. "I promise Una will tell us where she is. Right now, everyone needs to calm down." He nods and I nod back.

The fire alarm ceases and Connor jumps down from a chair with the battery in his hand. Our eyes clash, but I refocus on Una.

"I need you to listen to me. I did it to protect us." I didn't want to hear her speech. "Her presence in my home..."

"I'll take her away from here," I say through gritted teeth, my control slipping.

"Una." The warning comes from Shane. He glares at her and I can see my brother now. It was about time.

"She was pregnant. Do you know what that means?" She's shouting at Shane and it's like someone has hit me in the gut. "Liam has put us all in danger." She's pointing at me, but I can't seem to wake up.

She's pregnant.

"Do you hear yourself?" Shane grips her arms. "This life is dangerous. You can't hide her because you're afraid."

"I love you. I did it for us." Una's cries have Shane releasing her.

I was going to be a father. Me.

"Liam." It's Connor who has taken a step towards me that snaps me out of my frozen state.

"How could you have been so silly?" The disappointment in Shane's voice has Una taking a step away from him.

"What did you think would happen when Liam found out you took her?" Shane's speaking like I'm not in the room and right now I don't feel present. I'm watching them like an act being played out on some stage and I got a front-row seat.

"You should fear him more than Novak. You know this." Shane's shouts have Connor moving closer to Una.

"Stop shouting at me." Una's raised voice is filled with anger and tears.

I was going to be responsible for a child. A child that was part of me, that notion has me already pitying the creature. The child would be part of Svetlana, I focus on that and become present.

"This is the final time I'm going to ask. Where is she?"

The room falls silent as I speak clearly.

CHAPTER THIRTY-SEVEN

SVETLANA

THE WOODEN SPOON SNAPS in my hand and I pound the small square window. I didn't think I could have fitted through it anyway, but I had to try to get out of here. I was in another basement, only this one was bare with just a bed that was pushed up against a concrete wall.

A scream rips from my throat as my chest tightens. My hands automatically flutter to my stomach. I needed to calm down. Stress wasn't good for a baby. Would it feel what I was feeling? Tears burn my eyes as I move away from the window and sit on my creaky bed. I couldn't believe Una would do this to me. She had convinced me to come with her and get pregnancy tablets for the baby. I should have never listened to her, or followed her down here. I knew it was off, but I've seen shops in stranger places.

I dab my face with my hands as tears continue to make a path down my face. I needed to calm down. It had only been a day, and I just hoped that Una returned soon.

I start to hum a lullaby that's haunting, yet calming. I sing for my baby; I sing to ground myself. I try not to think about my parents or Liam. A sob tears through my lullaby and I pull in a deep breath as I try to piece it back together.

Closing my eyes tightly, streams of warm liquid pours down my face and into my mouth. I swallow as I continue to hum, and hold my belly. My baby.

I was still terrified of how Liam was going to react. Now I wondered if I'd get to tell him. I shouldn't have trusted Una. I didn't think another woman would do this to a pregnant one. It had been a whole day and night, and she hadn't left me so much as water. Was she going to just let me die down here? I'm moving around the space again and I pick up the broken wooden spoon; it was the only thing I had found. Using it, I try to wedge it into the corner of the window. With all my force, I push down. Pain sears my hand as it snaps again and cuts into my hand. Blood immediately flows as I pull the piece of wood from my palm. Dropping the bloody splinter, I return to my bed with the intentions of pulling off the pillowcase to wrap my wound.

The rattle of the door has me freezing halfway across the floor. I'm not sure if I'm seeing things. I'm staring at Liam as his eyes seem to scorch every part of me. He's beside me in a few strides. He doesn't look at me as he takes my damaged hand in his large one.

"You're hurt." His brows pull down and I've never heard Liam sound so unsure. He's holding my hand like it's some broken bird. I think of the bird that I had helped once. I had told him that story, and now I feel like he was remembering what he had said. How he would have snapped its neck. Tears burn my eyes again. Was I some broken bird to him? Never to fly again.

His eyes finally meet mine and my stomach tightens. It is like watching someone in a tug of war, he's pulling for dear life and now he just releases the rope.

But he is not giving up.

He is giving in.

"I love you." His words swallow me whole and when he bends down and rests on his knees, I have no idea what to make of this. Was he going to propose? When he looks up at me, his eyes are the softest brown I have ever seen them. His hands release mine gently and he moves them aside. Every part of me freezes as he leans in and kisses my stomach.

He knows.

"I love our baby too." He looks up at me and I'm not sure how I'm still standing.

I was good enough.

As he rises, so does my temperature. My heart feels like it sings. "You're okay with this?"

Once again he takes my damaged hand gently in his. "I'm so lucky to have found you." His eyes roam my face and the soft tug on his lips has me smiling through tears.

"Like in the basement or in general?" It was meant to be funny.

His small smile dissolves. "This will end tonight. You will have nothing more to fear."

His words have my fear spiking and I'm all too aware now of everything. For the first time, I'm aware that we aren't alone.

My eyes clash with Una's and I can almost feel fire at my fingertips. "You have no idea what I'm capable of," I speak my threat in Czech to Una, who tightens her hold on Shane's hand. She might not understand my words, but she understands my body language. "You will regret locking me down here."

When I look at Liam, he's smiling and I can't fathom why. "I know what you are capable of," he says through his smile. I had forgotten he understands Czech. Now he speaks in English.

"I will never forgive her," I glare at Una speaking English now. "You left me here with no food or water. You knew I was pregnant."

Guilt swamps her eyes.

Liam touches my arm. "You never have to forgive her, what she did is unforgivable." His jaw is tight as he speaks.

"Liam." The warning comes from Shane.

Liam turns to him, shielding me. "No harm will ever come to Una, not by me or Svetlana." I bite my tongue as Liam continues to speak. "But, if Una finds herself in harm's way. I won't help."

No one speaks as Liam takes my hand in his and walks me out of the basement. I don't look at Una as I pass her. Liam opens his car door and helps me in. Once I have the seat belt on, Liam gets into the driver side, he doesn't start the car but opens his glove compartment. He takes out a white handkerchief. Taking my hand, he places it gently in it. "Tighten your hold on it."

I close my fingers around it before looking up at Liam. My stomach twists and my free hand touches it. Liam follows my movements with his eyes, they flash with something, I'm not sure what but I want to know.

"Are you afraid?" I ask.

"No. Are you?"

His quick fire answer has me smiling. "Not anymore."

He reaches out and takes my face in his large hands. "I need you. I've never needed anything before. But, I need you." He's nodding as he speaks.

I turn my head and kiss his open palm. "I'm here."

A knock on the window has Liam looking away from me, he doesn't release my face as he turns to Shane. Rolling down the window slightly, Shane gives me a half smile that I don't return.

"Can you open the door?"

"Ring a taxi." Liam rolls up the window and Shane steps away from the car.

"You can't leave them stranded," I say to Liam as he lets my face go, and starts the car.

"They'll manage."

I tighten my hold on the white handkerchief and watch it slowly turn pink. "Svetlana."

I glance at Liam, he's alternating watching me and the road. "I'll keep you safe. I promise, no one will hurt you again."

His fierce words reach deep down inside me. I had no doubt he would do everything to keep me safe, especially now that I carried his child, but you couldn't move a mountain just because you willed it. So we had too many enemies and when they started popping up in your own home, it was always a deadly dance.

Liam turns back to the road and a muscle tightens in his jaw. Now I wanted to tell him that I believed him just to ease the tension. But no one could really make a promise like that. My hand tightens across my belly, knowing that my number one job now was protecting my baby.

Our baby.

I reach out my hand to Liam without looking and he takes it, like I've just presented him with a lifeline.

We don't return to Shane's home. Instead, Liam takes me to a castle. It's a hotel and the interior is amazing. It's like it hasn't been touched since it was built. We don't have to stop at the desk. A man is waiting with keys that he hands to Liam on arrival. We are also met by the doctor George, who had cared for me before, and another man in a suit who follows behind me. Liam wraps his fingers around my uninjured one.

"Danny is security here in the hotel. He will be watching over you." Liam informs me as I steal glances over my shoulder. I try to feel like I'm not being kept in a cage again. My movements have always been watched, but this time it was for the right reasons.

I glance up at Liam to find him watching me.

"Okay."

We stop at a set of double doors that are opened for us. We step into a large sitting room, my eyes are drawn to the roaring fire at the end of the room. Two doors are closed on either side.

"Can I take a look at your hand?" I turn to George, who has set his bag on a small round mahogany table that holds a single lamp. I sit down on the coral colored couch, the fabric looks like it's been brushed. I observe Liam as George removes the handkerchief from my hand. He's talking to Danny, who drinks up all of Liam's words.

"It's not too deep."

I return my focus to George. He doesn't ask how it happened. "Thank you."

He peeks up at me before returning to cleaning my hand. "This is going to sting."

I nod and look away. The sting is instant and I suck in a sharp breath while biting on my lip.

"I'm nearly finished," George says while Liam kneels down beside me with a glass of water. I take it with my good hand and sip slowly.

"I've ordered food, it will be here soon." The concern tightens the corner of Liam's eyes.

"I'm okay." I want to reassure him. I know he has enough to worry about.

"All done."

I focus on George, right now it's easier. "Thank you, George."

"I'll leave you some painkillers." He gets up to rummage through the bag.

I feel awkward as I glance at Liam, who still kneels beside me. "Are they safe in pregnancy?"

Georges turns quickly and surprise flashes across his face. "Yes. They are just paracetamol."

I take the tablets from George. "Congratulations."

He's the first person to say that and I smile at him. "Thank you."

"I'll need you to organize a nurse and midwife, everything necessary for her." Liam's rising now as he speaks to George. "I want Svetlana to have the best of care."

George nods while giving me another look. "I'll set it up."

The door opens and our food is wheeled in. The smell has my stomach rumbling loud enough that everyone glances at me. Liam's fists tighten and I drink down the remainder of the water to stop the noise.

Liam silently takes the food off the tray and places it on the table while everyone else leaves the room.

The steak smells and looks divine, Liam sits across from me but he has nothing in front of him.

"Why aren't you eating?" I slow down my bites, feeling conscious now.

"I'm not hungry."

"Eat some chips," I say and am surprised when he picks one up and starts to chew on it slowly. I can't stop the smile that spreads across my face while watching him.

"How are you feeling?" Liam's eyes flicker to my stomach.

I stuff another chip in my mouth before answering. "I'm good. I'm excited and a bit scared to be honest."

"There is nothing to fear. You will be an exceptional mother."

My throat closes slightly and the chip feels heavy. Washing it down with a glass of water, I focus on cutting my steak as my mind takes a wander down a road I don't want to go down.

"Svetlana."

I swallow before looking up at Liam. His head is held high. I think of a lion standing on the edge of a cliff, looking down over the world. Over his world. That's what I see now.

"Your strength is something I never expected. Honestly, I never expected anyone like you. If our child has half its mother's strength, I will be a very proud father."

My vision blurs and I swallow down the emotion that threatens to pour. I refocus on my food and slip a piece of meat into my mouth, after a couple of chews I feel more composed and glance up at Liam who continues to watch me.

There is power in his stare, he makes me want to sit straighter, and be proud of myself, but also slump, because I know I'm safe with him.

"Are you full?"

I yawn. "Yes."

Liam stands and walks around to me, reaching out his hand like he wants to dance, I take it. Tingles race through me at the touch as he leads me to a door on the left of the roaring fire.

We step into a spacious bedroom with a large fairytale four poster bed. "You need to rest." Liam pulls the curtains as I make my way to the bed and strip off my clothes until I'm in my underwear. A shower would be nice after being in the basement, but I needed to sleep. When I glance up Liam is watching me, his focus on my stomach, a look of awe and I see fear in his eyes. He doesn't speak as he makes his way to me. Each step has my heart racing a little faster. He hesitates for a moment before he touches my stomach and then his eyes shoot up to mine before darting to my lips. On instinct my tongue flickers out and moistens them for him. I had wanted to kiss Liam from the moment he stepped into the basement.

"Miluji tě." My heart soars as I tell him I love him in my own language. His widens briefly before he takes my face in his hands.

"Také tě miluji." His response has me pressing my lips to his. The warmth and softness of his lips have me groaning into his mouth. I reach up and push his suit jacket off his wide shoulders. My pulse spikes when I look into his black eyes that drink me up. He doesn't help as I unbutton his shirt and push it down his arms and it floats to the floor. I lean in and inhale Liam while pressing my body against his. My skin bursts into goosebumps at the contact with his. Large hands run down my arms and don't stop until he threads his fingers with mine. I rest my cheek against Liam's chest and listen to his fast beating heart. Looking at him he seems so unaffected. A kiss to my neck has me pushing my body harder against Liam's, turning my head I catch his lips with mine.

The kiss this time isn't gentle, it's as if we are crashing together. Both of us are oxygen to each other. Liam moves us to the bed and releases my hands, I easily move back onto it. Lying down, he holds himself up over me as he continues to deepen the kiss with his tongue. The warmth of his kisses have me pulling his large shoulders down so his body is nearly flush with mine, but he still holds himself above me.

Liam breaks the kiss and I use the moment to reach down and open his trousers, eager to have him inside me. He helps me by kneeling back and pushing his trousers and boxers down, letting his erection spring free. My core tightens and my light panties grow damp.

I'm grateful when Liam kicks off his trousers and resumes his position above me. Reaching down, I take him in my hand and place him at my opening. Liam pushes in while pressing his lips to mine. I exhale loudly, feeling a sense of completion as he pushes fully inside me. I push my tongue into his mouth as he pulls out before moving back in, each movement grows quicker and I grip his shoulders while widening my legs more, wanting him to have full access to me. Taking Liam's bottom lip in mine, I suck before releasing it, and throwing my head to the side for air, as he continues to rock back and forth inside me. I allow the feeling to take over all my senses.

Liam takes my hands in his, my focus returning to him, as he places my hands on either side of my head, our fingers entwined. Looking at him as he moves gently inside me has my heart ready to explode. I can't look away from

him, yet staring into those black orbs has me feeling like I'm on the edge of
something. One blink and I'll fall. Liam moves faster but not harder, it's his
gentle, yet powerful strokes that have me groaning. It's the most vulnerable
I've ever felt, he's seeing me at my rawest, I'm giving him the purest part of
me, not just my body but my soul. I need this to end; I need to come down off
the wave I'm riding. Liam's face tightens and I can tell he's close to coming,
so I let myself go with him. I let him take me over the edge and I cry out my
release along with him. His seed fills me again and the need to cry overwhelms
me. I'm glad when he buries his head in my neck, it gives me a moment. Liam
stays like that for a while, and I find myself drifting off as I continuously run
my fingers through his hair.

"It's so soft," I say out loud and he stirs. His eyes are heavy like he was asleep.
His lazy smile has my stomach tightening.

"What's soft?" He places a kiss to the corner of my mouth.

"Your hair."

"I'll tell you my secret for a kiss."

I can't stop the smile. "Always a trade off with you?"

"I always seize an opportunity."

A laugh bubbles up my throat at his playful tone. I press my lips against his
and the kiss lingers for a few seconds. When I lean out, he still wears that lazy
smile like God made it just for his handsome face.

"I'm just lucky, "he says when the kiss ends. "My hair has always been soft."

His playful eyes shine a stunning brown and I reach up and touch his hair
again.

We are silent for a moment.

"I have to go." Liam speaks softer than I have ever heard him speak before
and fear slowly snakes its way into my bloodstream.

"Why don't I like the sound of that."

Liam doesn't respond but removes himself from me. I'm too tired to move,
so I just move up in the bed and pull the blanket up on me as I watch Liam
get dressed.

"Everything will end tonight and you will be free. "His words should have
made me happy, but they don't.

"You're putting yourself in danger. "A lump catches in my throat.

"My life is dangerous. Svetlana. Tonight is no different."

"It is. You are going against my uncle. "I shake my head. "Liam. I don't
want you to do this."

He smiles as he returns to me fully clothed.

"Your concern is lovely, but I will be home." He takes both my hands in his
and kisses my left one first. "I will be home to you-"he kisses my right hand "-
and our child." The kiss sinks into my skin and it feels like it touches my heart.

I nod. "Okay."

I had to believe that he would return to us. We stare at each other for a moment before Liam releases my hand and leaves me to count down the time until he returns.

CHAPTER THIRTY-EIGHT

LIAM

"**A**RE ALL YOUR MEN ready?"

Tom walks me over to a shed of cattle and I follow. The yard is clean. The concrete base beneath my feet had recently been swept. When we move closer to the cattle they take a step back deeper into the shed. Tom stops and I follow his gaze as he reaches down and opens a large green army bag. Inside, it's filled with guns.

"They won't know what's coming." He had enough to take out the Czech.

"How many men?" I ask Tom, while stepping away from the shed. I've already clocked three of them, watching me with weary eyes.

"We have ten ready to go."

I nod and turn to Tom. "For Michael," I say, stretching out my hand.

"For Michael and Margret," Tom says while taking my outstretched hand. The three men around the yard shout out for Michael and Margret.

***

Shane is waiting in the car for me. I have my reservations about bringing him along, but I need someone I can trust.

"What happened?" Shane's staring out the window, up at the shed where Tom and his men are loading into a black van.

"We are leaving now," I say while starting the car.

"I do trust you, Liam. But, are you sure you can trust them?"

I start driving out of the farm yard. "No, I don't trust him at all."

"You know Darragh is pissed at being left behind."

I glance at Shane. Darragh obviously hadn't told anyone what our argument was about, but I didn't want him with us. He was too emotional, and that was a dangerous thing around people like Novak.

"I need you to have a clear head Shane." I glance in the rearview mirror to make sure Tom is following me. The large black van keeps two paces behind me.

"I do." He sounds offended.

"You don't. Stop worrying about Darragh's feelings. You need to remember that the RA still has a hit on you." Now I glance at Shane.

His eyes meet mine. "I know, Liam."

I didn't think he understood the full implications of what that meant. If Tom survived this, he would want my brother's head. Yet killing him would cause a war between me and the RA. I just needed to hope that after Tom and his men wiped out Novak's men, that I could wipe them out. I had two guns in my glove compartment. They had ten men, I hadn't that many bullets.

"You brought a gun?" I ask Shane, and he nods while staring out the window.

We drive for a while in silence, but I can sense Shane's unease beside me.

"I rang the hospital this morning."

I turn onto more back roads. Dust fills my rearview mirror but I still catch glimpses of the black van.

"Dad's still in a coma." Shane continues.

If Tom had lied about having more men, I wasn't exactly sure if I could pull this off, but I knew this was my best hope of freeing Svetlana and my family.

"I think we should try to wake him up."

"He's in a coma for a reason, Shane." One I didn't plan on letting him wake up from.

"Because he was shot?" Shane sounds doubtful and I don't glance at him. I can feel his eyes on me.

"Exactly," I lie as I push my foot heavier on the accelerator.

More silence follows, and I know Shane is thinking again. I glance in the rearview mirror to make sure we are still being followed, we are.

"About Una."

"Shane. I need you focused. Right now you aren't." I glance at him and he nods.

"We will talk about it later."

I wasn't so sure if there would be a later for all of us. I slow down as I come close to the turnoff that will lead us onto the road that Novak is staying at.

"Don't leave my side," I tell Shane as I pull in alongside some old broken down fencing. I didn't want to drive too close to the yard that Novak was at before I allowed Tom to see Shane. I didn't want him to get a surprise and get all trigger happy when I needed him to focus.

Getting out of the car, Tom and his men pull up behind me. The moment Tom sees Shane, I see his eyes flash with anger.

"He's not to be touched," I say to Tom who refocuses on me.

"For now."

I grit my teeth at his answer. "I'll go first and distract him. You attack on my signal."

Tom nods and he returns to this van.

"You're driving," I tell Shane while circling around to the passenger side. I climb back into the car with a weary Shane.

"You want to tell me what we are doing?" I can hear the irritation in his voice.

"No." I answer as he pulls out. "Remove any weapons and leave them in the car."

Shane doesn't act straight away, and when I glance at him he shakes his head, but removes his gun from its holder that's strapped under his jumper; he hands it to me. I open the glove compartment and put Shane's gun in along with my own.

The moment we pull into the yard, two of Novak's men, armed with machine guns turn to us.

Shane rolls down the window as we move closer.

"I'm here to see Mr. Novak," I say while keeping my focus straight ahead, like I'm waiting for them to pull the gate back. I don't give them my attention. The one beside me speaks into a walkie talkie.

"Open it." His broken English is roared across the yard as the gate starts to open. Shane drives on.

The moment we pass the gate, we stop dead in a large open shed. Once again a few men sit around. There is no sign of Novak. Shane turns off the ignition and I step out of the car. Shane follows suit. I keep my hands raised as I'm patted down. The man pauses at my side and I hiss.

"Go easy." I tell him and he eyes me for a moment before he finishes.

Shane follows my lead and allows Novak's men to pat him down. Once we are checked, another man who's been watching, speaks into a walkie talkie. It doesn't take long for Novak to arrive.

"Mr. O' Reagan. What a nice surprise to see you walking around." He claps his hands together, a large smile on his face.

I move towards him favoring my right side, one of his men steps towards me.

"Leave him." Mr. Novak's words have his man stepping away from me.

"I'm glad you're here. I actually have something for you." His smile is still there, but I know to be very careful. I don't speak as he claps his hands to two of his men. They leave the shed.

"And who is this?" He takes a step towards Shane.

"My chauffeur. Driving with my injuries isn't easy. He can stay in the car." I offer.

"No, he can stay here." Novak's attention is back on me and I nod.

His men arrive dragging a body bag with them.

"Holic, buried him deep in the ground."

The bag lands at our feet, Novak stands waiting, but I don't react.

"Do you not want to open it?"

"Would you mind? I'm still tender."

He isn't smiling now and nods at one of his men. "Open his shirt." He speaks in Czech to one of his men, and I open my arms wide before he approaches me. As he opens my shirt, I focus on Novak.

"How is my niece?"

"Alive."

My answer has him smiling. Once my shirt is open, his man steps back to let Novak see the bandage that covers my side.

"My men felt something I needed to check." He nods at me and I close two buttons as he leans down and zips open the body bag. I don't move back, even as the smell assaults me.

"I'm assuming that's your man, as he has no hands."

I nod as my eyes meet Novak's. His shine. He did this. I know it.

"I would punish Holic, only ..." He shrugs while smiling "he is already dead." His laugh spreads across his men who laugh with him.

"So what brings you here?" His serious tone has silence falling around the shed.

"I want to discuss another matter."

I glance at his black shirt pocket. "Could I have a smoke?"

He takes the packet out of his pocket. "I didn't know you were a smoker."

He hands the pack to one of his men who gives it to me. He was still weary. I take the pack and remove one cigarette. His man hands me a light.

"I wanted to discuss, Svetlana."

"You couldn't speak across a phone?"

I light the cigarette while blowing smoke into the air.

"No. You never know who is listening."

The cigarette tasted like burning bushes, I felt slightly light-headed and decided the second time not to inhale. I knew Shane was watching me, maybe wondering what I was doing.

I inhale again and blow the smoke out. I'm tempted to glance around. Me lighting up the cigarette was the signal to attack. My stomach lurches. Novak looks shifty, he knows something is going on.

"What about Svetlana?" His accent is heavy. He seems impatient now.

"How much?" I didn't think the conversation would ever get this far. Why wasn't Tom attacking?

"You think you can just come here, and buy my niece."

I inhale one last time before dropping the cigarette to the ground. I crush it under my foot.

Guns being fired in the distance has everyone's attention. He didn't leave me. Novak starts shouting in Czech, telling his men to go check it out. Most of them leave.

I don't hesitate but pull open my shirt and tear off the bandage. I rip some stitches that burn instantly, along with the warm liquid that flows down my torso. I grip the small blade and take the three steps to Novak. His eyes widen as I wrap one arm around his neck like I might embrace him before I plunge the knife into his neck. I continue to sink the knife in three times, blood covers my hand and I let Novak sink to the ground. A gun is fired close to my head. One of Novak's men drops only a foot away from me.

I release Novak and turn to Shane, who has a gun in each hand. He fires them again and I duck down, using Novak's body as a shield as his men return fire. The impact of the bullets I feel as they tear into Novak's back. I move towards the car and drop his body as I crawl across the seat. A shot through the front windshield shatters the glass. I cover my head as it rains down on top of me, cutting into my hands. I wait for more bullets, but none are fired.

"Liam," Shane's voice has me looking out through the shattered windscreen. I move out of the car slowly.

Shanes hands are raised above his head. I count four men with Tom, who has a gun pointed at Shane.

"This wasn't part of the deal," I say as I step out of the car.

"Yes, it was. I said we would deal with it after the Czech were dead. They are all dead."

I glance around at the bodies that are littered across the floor. He must have lost men in the crossfire as only four of them are with him now. I can hear the sound of a van approaching, the black one that had followed us here.

Once it stops, the driver gets out and opens the back door. Matthew is tied up.

"I promised you Matthew."

His man pulls Matthew from the van.

Once Matthew is on his knees before us, Tom's men move towards Shane and I step in their way. The gun that Tom holds points at my head.

"We had a deal, Liam."

"I want to make a new one."

"The only thing I want is the man who took my son's life."

"What about the man who took our mother's life?"

Tom's jaw tightens and his brows pull down.

"You had Connor looking into it, so I know what this means to you, and I know who did it."

I can feel Shane stir behind me.

"Who?" Tom barely speaks and right now I feel like the whole world is holding its breath.

"Shane gets into the car behind me, and drives away, and I give you my word that I will tell who killed her."

Tom lowers his gun and I can see he's bending.

"Boss." One of the men speaks.

"Shut up. I'm thinking."

He glances at me. "If you lie to me."

I hold up both my hands. "You will kill all of us. I know." There is another tense moment as I wait.

"Leave," he barks at Shane and something in me breathes.

"Not without you, Liam."

I turn to Shane. Now wasn't the time for his heroics. "Go." He still stands, and I'm afraid Tom will change his mind.

"Now," I shout and Shane snaps his eyes from me to Tom, before he steps towards the car. I keep an eye on everyone as Shane closes the car door, the engine starts and he drives out of the shed.

"Tell me now."

"He found out about the affair. He was so angry."

The pain that floods my mouth I could nearly chew on it. "She told him about Connor."

Tom's hands hang at his side, the gun still in his hand, but it hangs limply as he listens to each word like it's a dying man's final confession.

"He couldn't control himself."

Tom looks at me from the corner of his eye. He doesn't want to believe me. "How could you know this?"

This was the part I hated the most, the part that I had buried for years. "I was there." His gun is pointed at my head now.

"If you were there, why didn't you stop him."

"I froze." I had. I had never frozen before at anything in my life, but watching your father strangle your mother can do that to you. Darragh had walked in on it, and keeping him calm had become my focus. Later, I had tried to bury the truth by drugging him so my father could live.

"You froze?" The gun is closer to my head now. I didn't like Tom holding a gun and being this irrational.

"You know the truth and now it ends," I say as calmly as I can but the gun isn't removed from my face.

"If you were there and you froze, then you are responsible too."

Sweat starts to gather at the base of my neck. He's right. I played my part. I did nothing to save our mother.

"Mike Gordon, have you heard of him?" I keep my hands raised as I speak carefully.

"Yes, why?" Tom doesn't seem present right now and I need him to be.

"He's aware of what's happening today. He and his men will arrive here shortly to announce they have seized guns, drugs, and stopped the Czech from trafficking women."

"You're lying."

I wasn't, and I needed him to believe me. "If my body is found here today, I've given your name, your rank in the RA, your home address."

He lowers the gun and my uncle seems surprised. "You sneaky little bastard."

"It doesn't have to go down like that, Tom."

Tom has the gun pointed at my head again.

"Don't do this. I've told you what you wanted to know."

"I'll take my chances with Mike Gordon."

I'm surprised at Tom's words. I didn't think he'd have the bottle.

CHAPTER THIRTY-NINE

LIAM

Tom doesn't blink as I stare at him, and I see it in his eyes. He's going to pull the trigger.

The bang of a gun being fired rips through my ears, they ring, as warm liquid splashes across my face. I open my eyes as Tom's dead eyes stare at me before he tumbles to the ground. A clean shot between his eyes has me looking around for the shooter.

"Don't fucking move." Darragh appears holding the gun, while Finn, Shane, and Connor appear out of nowhere. Shane's eyes meet mine. "You okay?" He asks while walking towards us, his eyes darting to the five men.

"Yes." I reach into my suit jacket and remove a handkerchief. Wiping some of the blood off my face, I turn as Connor steps up alongside me.

"Lower them and you can live."

Five men stand against us, but they slowly lower their guns at Connor's foolish words. We couldn't let them live after what they saw. Connor wasn't stupid, he had to know this.

Connor walks in front of them, kicking the guns away. He stops at Matt, who's still tied up on the ground. I don't know what passes through them, but I don't hesitate as I reach down and fire four clean head shots.

"You didn't have to do that." Connor's still standing over Matt, a look of despair on his face.

"Don't be so stupid, of course I did, and he's mine too." I point at Matt as I finish wiping the blood from my face.

Finn is staring at the bodies, his face pale.

"Finn." His eyes immediately snap to mine.

"That's who killed Siobhan." I point at Matt and Finn seems to grow with each step he takes.

Connor steps aside. Of course he does. He knows Finn won't do anything. I meet Connor's eyes and I can see the hate there.

"He shot Siobhan," I say again, daring Connor to try to silence me. Another loose end we could take care of here and now.

"Why?" Finn's shouts have me turning to Darragh who still holds his gun. I give him a nod of thanks and he returns it.

"It wasn't meant to be her." Matt's foreign voice has me looking around us, the ground is scattered with bodies. We had to leave soon.

"Who was it meant for?" I ask, already knowing.

"Shane and Una." Matt's words are mingled with his panic. He keeps looking at Connor like he might save him.

Shane steps forward and I hold up my hand.

"This is Finn's kill," I tell Shane and he stops in his tracks. Connor swings around to face me and I ignore him.

Finn looks up at me, running both his hands through his hair. "You think killing him will bring her back?"

He looks at Shane. "You took Tom's son from him. If anyone is to blame, it's you. Shooting him won't bring Siobhan back to me. Nothing will."

"Please let him live," Connor pleads behind Finn.

I take a step towards my brothers. "Someone has to pay the price. If you want to volunteer..." I trail off as Darragh steps up beside Connor.

"Liam." The warning in Darragh's voice is clear. He will side with Connor. Shane stays firmly beside me.

I smile at Darragh. "It was only a suggestion."

Hate is what I see in my brother's eyes. Darragh looks like he's toying with saying something, so before he does, I speak.

"There is something you all wanted to know about mother. I've kept this hidden from all of you for a reason."

Darragh's jaw tightens as he stares at me. "I'm dying to hear." Darragh's sarcasm fills each word.

"She was having an affair with Tom, and that's where Connor came from." Everyone knew this, but I wanted them to see Connor for what he was.

"So when father found out, he was angry."

"He was hitting her, did you tell them that?" Connor tries to counteract my words with his.

"How can I when you're interrupting me?" I fire back at Connor.

"What?" Innocent Finn looks like his world just shattered.

"He killed her," I say before we get off track. There is a lull and a sense of disbelief among my brothers. I want to leave now. The next question is the one I fear the most.

"How do you know this?" Darragh seems confused. "I was there?" His brows are furrowed as he sludge's through his memories of that night.

"Yes and so was I. I tried to make you forget."

"By drugging me? By making me believe I killed my own mother?"

"This isn't about you right now, Darragh. Right now we need to decide if we let him live."

"Why didn't you stop it?" This was the first time Shane has spoken and I turn to my brother.

I hate the truth, but I give it. "I froze." I froze and watched as he strangled her to death. The only thing that made me move was Darragh, who I glance at now, his sneer is focused on me.

"You're such a fucking liar. You did it."

"I already told you father did."

"You froze?" Shane is still staring at me and as I look around my circle of brothers, I see all of them are.

"We need to leave before the Gardai get here. I've rang this in."

A second wave of disbelief rolls through my brothers. No one asks me if I'm serious, but start to move.

Connor still lingers around Matt. I take out my gun knowing if he didn't move, I would put a bullet in him too.

A gun is fired close to my face, the noise assaulting my ears. Connor curses as Matt's dead body hits the ground. I turn to Shane while touching my ear. He lowers his gun.

"That's for Siobhan," he says.

Finn doesn't thank him or respond as he walks away. Connor follows Darragh and Finn out of the yard, and Shane stays with me. I can't stop touching my ear. I expect the tips of my fingers to come away with blood on them, but they don't. My car with its shattered window screen comes into view. Shane reaches it first and gets into the driver side. I don't argue as I climb into the car.

I try to fix the bandage back over my stab wound that still seeps blood. "We need to get you seen to."

I glance at Shane, who's focused on the road now.

"Go straight to the house."

"Liam, you need to get stitches," Shane growls.

"Your concern is touching Shane, but do as I say." I stare out the window with no clue of how I feel. Everything had gone according to plan. Svetlana was free, our family was free from the RA. There was no hit hanging over Shane's head. With Mike Gordon the new superintendent on our side, the Gardaí couldn't touch us. All my brothers were alive. I had gotten everything I wanted, so why did I not feel a sense of victory.

"You would never freeze." Shane's voice pulls me out of my thoughts. I glance at him only for our eyes to clash, his aren't angry but filled with confusion.

"I did, Shane," I speak softly and I know how hard it is to believe. "She loved us all so much. She made me feel normal." I glance out the window. "With her I wasn't looking through a window, I was in the room."

"What are you talking about?" Shane questions me.

I clear my throat. "Nothing. It's just... I thought he would stop."

Silence fills the car; the drive is long as Shane takes it slow. With only half a window screen left, the wind is strong on us.

I'm glad when Stephen waves us in. I'm surprised to see another car here, but we needed to talk about father.

Shane turns off the ignition but doesn't get out.

"No matter what you decide in here, you have my support."

Shane had always been so loyal; I turn to him now, wanting him to see how grateful I was. Going in here and knowing that I had three brothers that hated me was hard. I couldn't completely close myself off to that no matter how much I wanted to.

"Thank you, Shane."

He nods and gets out.

Connor, Darragh and Finn are in the dining room all seated and waiting. I walk to the top of the table and pull out my father's chair. I'm surprised that Connor is here. A part of me feels tired, but I know that I need to close this chapter on our lives.

Once I'm seated and Shane sits to my right, I look at each brother. "I've made some bad choices," Darragh snorts and I ignore him. "Ones I'm not proud of." I think of John and regret swamps me. "At the time I felt they were the best to keep our family safe." Darragh's shaking his head but he's still listening, still seated.

"I didn't think he would kill her, I thought he would stop. I froze and it's something I will have to live with for the rest of my life." I let the truth sink in to everyone, even myself. I would never forgive myself for the loss of our mother. "She was the best of us all." I have to look away from a table filled with lost boys, who tried to cope with the death of their mother by using pain and more pain. Ultimately, it just led to pain. A full circle that we needed to sever here.

"I wanted to kill him. But, I wasn't going to take our father from us, when we had just buried our mother, so I made up the whole story about the drive by shooting." No one stirs. Finn stares fiercely at me.

"So I told him he had to bury the truth and be a father."

"You think he was a father to us?" Finn's lip trembles and I hate how boyish he looks now.

"Yes, I do."

More silence.

"If any of us had been in Liam's shoes, what would we have done?" Shane asks.

"I would have killed him." Connor speaks bluntly.

"Maybe, or maybe us having no parents would have done far more damage than having one." I glance at Finn. "Even a bad one."

"My wife might be alive." Finn's face is red and I pray he won't start crying.

I don't answer him. His words are false. I froze while watching my father strangle my mother, I wish I hadn't but I had. If I could go back, I would have stopped it. That's all I would have done. But I can't be held responsible for every bad thing that happened in their lives.

"Yes, or maybe Darragh wouldn't drink so much." I fire back and Finn nods.

I smirk. "Or maybe Shane wouldn't have been shot, or father in a coma, or the flowers that died in the vase would still be alive."

Finn snaps his mouth shut and glances away from me. I'm surprised to see a smirk on Darragh's face. He always sees the funny side, no matter the situation.

"You can all fire blame around the table, but don't hold me responsible for every mishap you have suffered." My eyes clash with Darragh's and he holds my stare.

"What do you suggest now?" Shane speaks up, once again I feel so grateful for his presence at the table.

"Now we decide what happens next." In a way, this was a clean slate. All our enemies are gone. All past mistakes aired.

"We take a vote about what to do with father," I add.

Everyone stares at me, no one says anything. Their turmoil is evident on their faces.

"He's healthy. I had him put into a coma."

I let that news settle around them. Finn shakes his head, Darragh looks at me with disbelief while Connor stares at his hands. I glance at Shane, he's watching me like he's not sure who I am, yet I see some amount of pride in his eyes.

"We need to decide if we want him woken up or not."

"You want to kill him?" Finn's pale face and shaky voice has my answer not leaving my lips.

"What do you want?" I ask.

"Kill him."

We all look to Connor who now stares up. I nod. His vote has been cast. I expected him to not care.

"He is my father," Finn barks down at Connor.

"But he's not his, Finn," I answer in Connor's defense. "We all have a say."

"This is sick." Finn leans back in his chair, but he doesn't leave the room.

"Let him live." Darragh casts his vote, and I'm surprised at it. I thought he would want him dead.

I nod.

"Same as Darragh," Finn mumbles. He doesn't want to take part, but his vote is vital.

I nod at him.

I look at Shane. He's playing with his thumb ring. He glances at all his brothers. "He needs to pay for taking her away." He swallows before looking at me.

"Kill him."

That was an even vote. The decision now rested on my shoulders. I got to pick whether he lived or died.

CHAPTER FORTY

SVETLANA (ONE YEAR LATER)

"**O**NE DAY, I'M GOING to be strong enough to do that." I point at Ciara's candy colored hair.

She smiles up at me, her blue eyes sparkling while she twirls a pink curl around her finger. "Your hair is fab and ..." She glances at Liam now, who's deep in conversation with Shane. No doubt plotting and planning. "I don't think Liam would like you with pink hair. Have you seen the way he looks at me?" Ciara grins.

She isn't afraid of Liam like most people, but she had gotten to see the good side of him. When he had helped her off the streets, and given her a job.

But she was right, I could tell that Liam thought her taste in hair colors was a little crazy.

"He's fond of you," I say back, as I take a sip of lemonade. The ice rattles in the glass.

Ciara snorts. "If you had said anyone else was fond of me, I'd take it as an insult. But, it's Liam, so it's a compliment."

I liked Ciara. We had grown closer since Jack arrived. She was becoming my favorite of all the girlfriends. Una and I never patched things up, but I learned to pass myself with her. I had no choice since they were having their wedding at the original O'Reagan home, where I lived. I wasn't exactly happy to have Una prancing in and out of my home, but I bit my tongue for Liam.

The bark of a dog has me smiling now, and I laugh. Finn is on the ground, rolling around with Jan. A frisbee that Jan refuses to release has Finn tugging and pulling at the end. Grass stains are starting to appear on Finn's white t-shirt. I'm tempted to shout at him to just let it go, he could never win against Jan but instead I continue to watch him struggle.

"How's the girls?" Darragh wraps an arm around Ciara's waist while greeting us both.

"Good." Ciara smiles up at Darragh and his own signature smirk slips as he takes some of her hair in his hand. "You look hot," he kisses her and I look away to give them some privacy.

Finn surprises me by getting the Frisbee out of Jan's mouth. He fires it again into the air and Jan races after it. I didn't ever think I would be standing in my back garden watching Jan happily play. I thought I would never see him again.

I glance at Liam again, as he shifts Jack into his other arm, as he speaks to Shane. He was such a good man, and that day when I had finished hanging the airplane mobile above the cot, the door had opened. Jan sat there and I had stood frozen, until Liam had stepped in behind him. He had looked so proud, knowing what he had given me. Jan was my family, he was my friend, he was mine, and Liam had gotten him for me. A lot of tears had fallen until Liam had Jan taken to his bed downstairs as not to overwhelm me.

"Stop it." I glance now at Ciara as she swipes playfully at Darragh, who doesn't move away from her, but takes the push to this chest and over-exaggerates the impact, by falling to the ground.

"You're an idiot." Ciara reaches down to help him up, her cheeks reddening as Darragh rolls away from her hand like a child. She straightens up and rolls her eyes while flicking candy hair across her shoulders. "I'm with a fool," her smile contradicts her words. Darragh gets up and walks back to us, his focus now on me.

"We actually wanted to ask you something."

"No, not we. Darragh wanted to ask you something," Ciara interjects.

Darragh shrugs. "Fine, I wanted to ask you something."

Liam's conversation with Shane has ended and he smiles as he holds a wriggling Jack, walking towards me.

"You know he doesn't like to be held like a baby." I say to Liam the moment he arrives.

"He is a baby." Liam informs me as he glances at Darragh.

Jack was only four months old, but he loved sitting up, watching the world around him, not lying back.

"He's so cute." Ciara leans in and taps his nose. She's oblivious to Liam staring at her. I can see it in his stance, he wants to take Jack away from them, he's too protective. I can't help but smile.

"So what is it you wanted to ask me Darragh?" I say getting everyone's attention.

Darragh diverts his attention away from Jack. He's an amazing uncle and I can see when Jack is older, he will always go to Darragh when we won't give him something. He will be the fun uncle.

"I wanted to take a trip to the Czech."

"No," Liam speaks abruptly.

"You don't even know what he is going to ask."

"I do and the answer is no." Liam is quick to answer and I ignore him.

"What is it Darragh?"

Darragh doesn't sound so enthusiastic now after Liam shot him down. "I was going to take Ciara on a holiday there and thought it would be nice if we could stay at your place."

I can't stop the smile. When I look at Liam, I can see the tightness around his eyes.

"Of course. I would love you guys to see where I grew up." The house and land was all in my name, it always had been, a loophole my uncle could never get out of. But since he had me trapped in the house, the name on the papers didn't matter to him. Now that he was dead, it was all mine. I was waiting for Jack to be a bit older before I brought him over to see where I grew up. I wanted to keep the house for this very reason so we could stay in it, some part of the year.

"You are a gem." Darragh leans in and surprises me with a kiss on the cheek. Liam's face is taunt and Jack has started to wriggle again in his stiff arms.

I hand Darragh my glass of water and he takes it looking somewhat confused.

"Are you coming to mama?" I ask Jack as I take him from Liam's arms. His little smile has my heart swelling. Deep brown eyes stare up at me. He looks so much like his father.

"Roll on the fun times." Darragh's grinning.

"You damage anything." Liam lets the threat hang over Darragh's head.

Darragh isn't grinning anymore but he still looks amused. "I'll go easy on the bed."

"Oh my God." Ciara's face grows red and I hide a smile as Darragh walks away, pulling a red faced Ciara with him.

"You know you don't have to." Liam stands beside me now as we look out on the lawn. More chairs have been added and I wondered when it would end.

"I know that." I glance up at Liam to find him watching me. My stomach flips. "I want to share my home with your family." I add and after a few intense seconds he nods.

He looks back out onto the garden.

"So how many people are coming to this wedding?" There had to be more than four hundred. The numbers just kept growing.

"I don't know. I can tell Shane that's enough."

Jack starts wiggling again. I had him half sitting so he could watch everybody but he was due a feed.

"No. It's their wedding. I better get Jack inside and feed him."

"Maybe one day it will be our wedding here."

My head snaps up to Liam. He's staring at me and there is a vulnerability in his eyes.

"Was that a proposal?" My heart pounds in my chest even as I try to make light of his statement.

"No." His one word had such power and I feel my heart sink. "When I do propose. I will do it right."

I lean in and kiss him softly on the lips. "I love you." I can't stop smiling as I look into his handsome face.

"I love you too." His words are low as he brushes a kiss across my cheek before placing a soft one on Jack's cheek.

Jack starts to wriggle. I give Liam a final kiss on the cheek. "I better get him fed."

I can't help but glance back as I walk back to the house. Liam is watching us and the smile on his face lights up the space around him. I was so lucky to have him and now with Jack in my arms, my life was perfect. I couldn't have asked for any more than what I have right now.

CHAPTER FORTY-ONE

LIAM

I WATCH SVETLANA CARRY Jack back to the house. The swell of pride I feel has me raising my head. From the corner of my eye I can see someone approach me. I turn to meet my father's eyes. He's aged a lot since I last saw him.

I had the final vote and I decided the cruelest sentence would be to let him live, while all his sons knew what he did. Even now I can almost pinpoint where each brother stands as their hate for him radiates.

Justice was sweet. "What are you doing here?" I ask looking out on the lawn. He stands beside me, just like Svetlana had done only moments ago. I'm glad Jack is inside. My father had never seen him and I intended to keep it that way.

"A wedding?" I glance at him now as he places his hands in his pockets.

"I wanted to ask you if I could see my family."

"You sound weak." I say while walking away from him, he follows as I knew he would. "They don't want to see you. I don't keep them away from you. It's their choice." His hand curls around mine stopping me in my tracks. I look at his hand until he removes it.

Shane is moving across the lawn towards us. Each step fueled with anger.

"If you told them to speak to me, they would."

"Maybe they would. But why would I do that?"

My father laughs. "God, I reared an evil little bastard."

"Get out." Shane moves beside me. "You have no right to be here."

"This is my house." He barks at Shane.

I correct him. "When you got stabbed you signed everything over to me, remember."

He shakes his head. "Crafty and manipulative."

"Get out," I said." Shane takes a step closer. I won't allow it to come to blows, but he needs to understand his place now.

"You heard him." Darragh appears behind him and he is the one I need to make sure keeps his anger in check.

Connor and Finn step up behind Darragh. father looks at all his sons before his eyes land on me.

"Why was I allowed in?"

I had informed Stephen to allow him to pass the gates if he ever arrived. "Because I wanted you to see all you lost."

His face falls as he stares at me. He blinks and he tries to reel in his disbelief as he takes a final look at his sons.

"Go." I give the final order and he nods understanding that this is the final time he will see us.

I stand side by stand with my brothers. After all, that's what all this was for. An Chlann. Family.

***

You can sign up to my newsletter so you never miss a new release from me.
HERE

WANT TO READ MORE BOXSETS BY VI CARTER? CHECK THEM OUT HERE.

About The Author

WHEN VI CARTER ISN'T writing contemporary & dark romance books, that feature the mafia, are filled with suspense, and take you on a fast paced ride, you can find her reading her favorite authors, baking, taking photos or watching Netflix.

Married with three children, Vi divides her time between motherhood and all the other hats she wears as an Author.

She has declared herself a coffee & chocolate addict! Do not judge.

Social Media Links for Vi Carter

Website

Facebook Reader Group

Facebook Author Page